Eighteenth-Century Novels by Women

Isobel Grundy, Editor

Advisory Board

The Young Philosopher

Charlotte Smith

~

Elizabeth Kraft, Editor

Of MAN, when warm'd by Reason's purest ray,
No slave of Avarice, no tool of Pride;
When no vain Science led his mind astray,
But NATURE was his law, and God his guide.

THE UNIVERSITY PRESS OF KENTUCKY

Publication of this volume was made possible in part by a grant
from the National Endowment for the Humanities.

Scholarly publisher for the Commonwealth,
serving Bellarmine College, Berea College, Centre
College of Kentucky, Eastern Kentucky University,
The Filson Club Historical Society, Georgetown College,
Kentucky Historical Society, Kentucky State University,
Morehead State University, Murray State University,
Northern Kentucky University, Transylvania University,
University of Kentucky, University of Louisville,
and Western Kentucky University.

Editorial and Sales Offices: The University Press of Kentucky
663 South Limestone Street, Lexington, Kentucky 40508-4008

03 02 01 00 99   5 4 3 2 1

Library of Congress Cataloging-in-Publication Data

Smith, Charlotte Turner, 1749-1806.
    The young philosopher : a novel in four volumes / Charlotte Smith ;
Elizabeth Kraft, editor.
        p.   cm.
    Includes bibliographical references (p.   ) and index.
    ISBN 0-8131-2111-6 (acid-free paper).—ISBN 0-8131-0962-0
(pbk. : acid-free paper)
I. Kraft, Elizabeth.   II. Title.
PR3688.S4Y68   1999
823'.6—dc21   98-32030

CONTENTS

ACKNOWLEDGMENTS

I have incurred many debts preparing this edition, some of which I would like to acknowledge here. The University of Georgia awarded me a Senior Faculty Research Grant in support of this project, and further funds were provided by the College of Arts and Sciences. I am grateful, in particular, to Hugh Ruppersburg, Associate Dean of the College of Arts and Sciences, for his generosity in making funds available for the computer entry of the text. The staffs of the rare book collections at the University of Georgia, the University of North Carolina at Chapel Hill, and the University of Florida were of great assistance at various times during the process of collating and annotating the novel.

The Department of English at the University of Georgia also provided various kinds of support. I was fortunate to have the help of two graduate student assistants, Marlene Allen and (especially) Eric Rochester, who helped with proofreading and with annotations. An enthusiastic and generous undergraduate, Melody Alberson, devoted much time and energy to combing through volumes of poetry for lines that Smith quotes without attribution. She was remarkably successful in her efforts, and her careful attention to detail, her good memory, and her dogged persistence were of immense help early in the process of annotating this novel. I owe a special thanks, as well, to my colleague David Gants, who, before he joined our faculty, kindly took the time to employ the Chadwyck-Healey Index to search for (and find) several quotations. The University of Georgia has since acquired that index, and I was able to continue to find elusive references with its aid, but David's help early on was very encouraging.

For assistance with the Italian citations, I am grateful to T.E.D. Braun, who provided the translations, and to Renata Isabelle Lana, Jonathan Druker, Stefano Mengozzi, and—especially—Janice Aski for refinement and corroboration. My colleagues in the Classics Department of the University of Georgia, T. Keith Dix and Richard LaFleur, helped me with the Latin citations. And I owe a special thanks to Kris Peeters of the University of Antwerp, whom I came to know over the Internet via the eighteenth-century discussion list. He aided me in translating the still largely unattributed French passages, correcting Smith's French and my translations with good nature and forbearance. Thanks also to Adria Bredeman, Catharine Sanders, and Laura Sussman for help with the French.

So many of my friends, colleagues, and acquaintances have answered questions and provided advice that I will probably omit several in the following catalog. Some that I do include may not even remember helping me. But I am grateful to all, including Douglas Anderson, Martine Watson Brownley, Christy Desmet, Roxanne Eberle, Jay Evatt, Miranda Fouts, Bill Free, Coburn Freer, Suzanne Gilbert, Patricia Hamilton, Mike Hendrick, Elissa Henken, Nelson Hilton, Dolan Hubbard, Bill Kretzchmar, Tricia Lootens, George Mosley, Debra Taylor, Frances Teague, Greg Timmons, Anne Williams, and Jennifer Wilson. My thanks too to several people who took the time to answer queries posted on the eighteenth-century list—Harry Duckworth, Vincent Carretta, Nick Sweeney, and especially Tracy Weiner, who provided an important reference that I would never have found on my own.

The other editors in the series have been kind in offering suggestions, encouragement, and advice. At crucial moments in the process I had enlightening conversations with Paula Backscheider, Martha Bowden, and Susan Staves. Paul Hunter's counsel was both verbal and printed; his article "Editing for the Classroom: Texts in Contexts" (*Studies in the Novel* 27 [1995]: 284-94) contains the wisdom distilled from a career partly devoted to preparing such texts. It served as a reminder to me throughout the editing process that this text is, as all classroom editions are, primarily and most importantly an instrument for teaching. I hope it will serve that purpose well.

Smith scholars Loraine Fletcher and Carrol Fry were generous in answering my questions and responding to my speculations about Smith. But I owe my greatest debt to Judith Phillips Stanton and Isobel Grundy. Judith Stanton is, as anyone who works on Charlotte Smith well knows, quite simply the leading authority on this author, her life, and her works. And, to our great benefit, she is open and accessible and generous. She reviewed my introduction at two stages, read the entire manuscript at the final stage, shared letters Smith wrote around the time she was composing *The Young Philosopher,* and spoke with me at length several times about Smith's life. Isobel Grundy, the general editor of this series, has also been of enormous help. Her meticulous attention to every aspect of the manuscript led to many revisions; she patiently corrected mistakes, suggested clarifications, and provided contextual grounding of this novel—especially in the tradition of women's writing. Whatever limitations this edition has are mine; for its strengths I share the credit with my many collaborators—and, of course, with Charlotte Smith herself.

INTRODUCTION

LIFE AND WORKS

When Charlotte Smith emerged on the literary scene in 1784 with the publication of her *Elegiac Sonnets and Other Poems,* she had long cultivated a talent for writing. Anecdotes from her school days tell of her composing at the age of ten a poem on the death of General Wolfe.[1] And, by her own account, she was accustomed to beguiling "melancholy moments . . . by expressing in verse the sensations those moments brought."[2] She had also exercised her skill as a writer of prose in the service of her father-in-law, a director of the East India Company, effectively defending him in print against a libelous charge that threatened to bring scandal upon his family and hers (Dorset, 256; Hilbish, 64). In 1784, however, Charlotte Smith became a professional author—a role she would play for the rest of her life. Given the circumstances that propelled her into print, it is a matter of some wonder just how thoroughly she envisioned her professional identity from the outset. In the preface to the first edition of her *Elegiac Sonnets and Other Poems,* she associates herself with "Sentiment," "sensations," "sensibility of heart," and "simplicity of taste." Her poetry, she says, derives from and expresses this complex of values, and she implies that her life does so as well. She would return to this theme repeatedly throughout the course of her successful twenty-two-year career. And the theme was no small part of that success.

Charlotte Smith was born Charlotte Turner on 4 May 1749 to Nicholas and Anna Towers Turner. She was born into auspicious circumstances. Her father was a "gentleman," a term that in the eighteenth century connoted social superiority, particularly in contrast to men of trade, for gentlemen did not have to "work" for their money. Their wealth was generally inherited and derived from estates that produced rents and other incomes.

Nicholas Turner owned considerable property in Surrey and in Sussex. The latter in particular, the estate of Bignor Park, exercised an important formative influence on his daughter Charlotte. As Florence Hilbish puts it, "the beauty of the South Downs with the Arun meandering among their swells" engendered a love of nature evident in all of Smith's works (26-27). In *The Young Philosopher,* Upwood, the secluded home of George Delmont, is modeled on Bignor Park, as is Willoughby's home, Alvestone, in *Celestina.*

Charlotte was the first child of a family that was increased within three years by the births of Catherine Anne and Nicholas Turner. With Nicholas's arrival, however, came sorrow, for Anna Towers Turner died in childbirth, leaving her three-year-old daughter and her siblings not only without a mother, but for a time without a father as well. To recover from his grief, Nicholas Turner took an extended trip to Europe. He did not return to his family for several years, and the children were left under the guardianship of a maternal aunt who cared for them and supervised their early education. Charlotte first attended school at Chichester, near Bignor Park, where she was a pupil from the age of six to the age of eight, and then in London at Kensington, where she studied until she was twelve. At these schools, as Anna Barbauld put it in her preface to Charlotte Smith's *The Old Manor House,* "she received . . . rather a fashionable than a literary education."[3] Such an education included drawing, music, needlework, French, manners, amateur theatrical performance, and religion.[4] Barbauld points out that there was no serious study of literature, but in spite of that Charlotte "gratif[ied] her taste for books by desultory reading, . . . almost by stealth."[5] Reading was certainly an early and lasting passion, as was drawing, especially the drawing of plants. Both activities would remain constant sources of pleasure for Charlotte Smith throughout her turbulent life.

By the age of twelve, Charlotte Turner had completed all of the formal schooling (such as it was) she would receive. By 1761 she and her sister were living in London with their father, while their brother Nicholas attended school at Westminster. Charlotte and Catherine were taught at home by "the best masters," who continued their training in the subjects they had begun to study at Chichester and Kensington (Hilbish, 22). Charlotte continued to be an avid reader, much to the dismay of her aunt, whose forbidding of the pastime was rendered impotent by the delight of Nicholas Turner, a great reader and sometime poet himself, who encouraged his daughter's taste for literature.

Perhaps most significantly, according to Catherine Dorset's biography of her famous sister, Charlotte was at this age "introduced into society" (254; see also Hilbish, 24-26). Although Florence Hilbish explains that "[t]his entrance into society would seem to mean the appearance at public places of amusement, such as the theatre and opera, rather than a debut into society in the present sense," Charlotte's marriage only four years later, a few months before her sixteenth birthday, suggests that her coming out was meant at least in part to draw attention to her availability as a marriage partner (24). It was a precipitate social introduction; commentators of the time referred to it as early, occurring at an age "when most girls are at school."[6] Nicholas Turner's reasons for varying the usual order of things possibly included both his daughter's precocity and his own expectation that several London seasons would give Charlotte a polish that would help her attract a suitable husband at a suitable time.[7] Nicholas Turner would have wished to see his daughter settled to advantage—hers, of course, but his own as well. His refusal on her behalf of a marriage proposal she received at the age of thirteen or fourteen from a gentleman suggests that, at first, it was primarily Charlotte's happiness that Nicholas Turner pursued. As events played themselves out, however, his pressing needs ultimately prompted a hasty, ill-considered decision that instead of securing his daughter's happiness, purchased for her the trials and tribulations for which she would become famous.

By 1764 Nicholas Turner was in financial straits; four years earlier he had sold one property and mortgaged another (Hilbish, 37). Furthermore, in that year he married again. These two facts are not unrelated, for biographers from Smith's time to ours have assumed that a twenty-thousand-pound fortune was the chief attraction of Turner's new bride. Whatever the case, this marriage spawned another one, for there was some agreement within the family that Charlotte and her new stepmother could not live together peacefully. So, despite her still extreme youth, her family set about finding her a mate, and they settled on Benjamin Smith, the son of Richard Smith, a West Indian merchant who was also a director of the East India Company. The couple were married in February of 1765.

In a sense Charlotte Turner married beneath her, although Richard Smith was certainly wealthy, and his son, a partner in his business, was well positioned too. In terms of financial solvency, in fact, the Smiths outranked the Turners at this time. But of course, in eighteenth-century England, money alone did not determine rank; birth, property, and breeding were vastly more important. Benjamin Smith might have acquired the habits of a gentleman through his father's ability to purchase the accoutrements of such a lifestyle, but Benjamin Smith was not, in the sense the eighteenth century would have understood it, a gentleman. He was the son of a merchant, one of the new moneyed class that was buying its way into the upper ranks of English society, often through marriages of convenience.

The eighteenth century is replete with cautionary tales of mismatched couples. The aristocratic Lovelace and the middle-class Clarissa are one such twosome, though, of course, that pairing is so disastrous that no actual marriage ever takes place. Another ill-paired couple is the Squanderfields of Hogarth's *Marriage a-la-Mode*. The problem, from Richardson's and Hogarth's points of view, is a matter of dissonant values, expectations, and tastes. Charlotte Turner had been brought up to live a life of leisure, in pursuit of social diversion, refinement, beauty. Richard Smith, in contrast, knew the value of hard work and thrift. His son, the beneficiary of Smith's business acumen, had all too eagerly neglected to develop his own sense of middle-class responsibility, because his father's wealth made it possible for him to spend as though he had unlimited financial resources. Eventually, Benjamin's habits of expenditure—his careless squandering of his considerable fortune—would result in imprisonment and degradation.

Benjamin and Charlotte Smith began their married life in an apartment over the office where Benjamin worked. It was here that Charlotte gave birth to her first two children, both boys. Sadly, the first child died a few days after the second was born, and so the young mother very early experienced the grief of burying a child. It was not the only grief she would know. Although this son was the only child Charlotte Smith lost in infancy, she did suffer the deaths of four more of her twelve children. Her second son, Benjamin Berney, died of a fever at the age of ten; another son, Braithwaite, died at the age of sixteen from a similar infection; a third son, Charles Dyer, died of yellow fever in the West Indies in 1801, after suffering a leg amputation eight years before. Most devastatingly, her favorite daughter, Anna Augusta, died in

1795, probably of consumption. There would be lesser griefs as well: a rift with son William Towers that never mended; the ill health of daughter Charlotte Mary; the unhappy marriage of Lucy Elenore; and the medical expenses of Harriet Amelia, who contracted malaria in India.

Although the sorrows associated with her children's sufferings and deaths affected Charlotte Smith deeply, her children were also the meliorating factor in the chief burden of her life: her marriage to Benjamin Smith, which she herself aptly described as an "abyss into which I had unconsciously plunged" (quoted by Dorset, 256). After the death of their first child, the family lived for a while at Southgate just outside London, in a home provided them by Richard Smith. Four years later they moved to Tottenham. In 1774 they moved away from London entirely, to Lys Farm in the Hampshire South Downs, a residence again provided by Richard Smith. This last relocation had in fact been Charlotte's idea. Her father-in-law's acquiescence suggests his recognition that his son was inept at and uninterested in the West Indian business the two of them had nominally comanaged since before Charlotte and Benjamin's marriage. Furthermore, Richard may have been persuaded by his daughter-in-law's argument that a country estate would be better than a London home for her, her children, and even Benjamin, who was all too prone to indulge in the various dissipations available in the city.

Yet, if she had hoped to reform her husband's tastes and habits by a change of residence, Charlotte Smith was disappointed. For it was at Lys Farm that Benjamin's spending became notoriously extravagant and reckless. Although the farm included one hundred acres, Smith purchased more land. He built a mansion, though the dwelling on the farm was both suitable and large enough for his still increasing family. He added to the gardens and outbuildings, increased the staff of servants, and indulged himself in agricultural projects that, because he knew nothing at all about farming, were ruinous. About her husband's expensive projects, Charlotte Smith is said to have quipped, "[F]or Heaven's sake, do not put it into his head to take to Religion, for if he does he'll instantly set about building a cathedral."[8] Yet, in spite of her banter, Charlotte Smith no doubt realized that the situation was dire. It was soon to turn disastrous.

In 1776 Richard Smith died. In his will he had hoped to provide for his grandchildren—his son Benjamin's numerous family and the considerably smaller families of two children who predeceased him. Unfortunately, the will was complicated by codicils the terms of which negated many intentions expressed in the original will; the trustees appointed to administer Richard Smith's property could not or would not interpret the will.[9] Lawyers were employed as advocates for one legatee or the other; the wrangling continued until after the deaths of Benjamin Smith, his wife, and all but six of their children.[10] The effort to procure for her children the settlement intended for them by their grandfather would occupy much of the remainder of Charlotte Smith's life. She came to know the legal profession of her time very well; she despised it, and she rarely let an occasion pass to say so in print. Criticized for her rancor, she responded:

a Novelist . . . makes his drawing to resemble the characters he has had occasion to meet with.—Thus, some have drawn alehouse-keepers and their wives—others, artists and professors—and of late we have seen whole books full of dukes and duchesses, lords and ladies. *I* have "fallen among thieves," and I have occasionally made sketches of them, and I have made only sketches of them, because it is very probable that I may yet be under the necessity of giving the portraits at full length, and of writing under those portraits the names of the *weazles, wolves,* and *vultures* they are meant to describe.[11]

Most galling to Smith was the effect on her children. Assured by the trustees that the terms of the will would be resolved, she brought up her family "as a gentleman's family." Had she known their inheritance would be delayed and depleted by endless legal actions, she says, "I should have been wiser to have descended at once into the inferior walks of life, and have humbled them and myself to our fortunes."[12]

For several years following her father-in-law's death, however, the Smiths did not suffer deprivation. Benjamin continued to increase his debts, encouraged, no doubt, by the belief that he would soon enjoy his own share of his father's fortune. He was even appointed overseer of the poor and later High Sheriff for the county of Hampshire, appointments that speak positively of his standing in the community. In 1783, however, the years of profligacy finally caught up with him. He was imprisoned in the King's Bench in London for debt. Leaving their children with her brother at the Turner estate at Bignor Park, Charlotte accompanied Benjamin to jail, dwelling there with him off and on for the length of his imprisonment, which lasted around seven months.

Charlotte Smith describes her final night within and departure from the King's Bench in terms of a contrast between the horrors of confinement and the soothing pleasures of the natural world:

> It was on the 2d day of July that we commenced our journey. For more than a month I had shared the restraint of my husband, in a prison, amidst scenes of misery, of vice, and even of terror. Two attempts had, since my last residence among them, been made by the prisoners to procure their liberation, by blowing up the walls of the house. Throughout the night appointed for this enterprize, I remained dressed, watching at the window, and expecting every moment to witness contention and bloodshed, or perhaps, be overwhelmed by the projected explosion. After such scenes, and such apprehensions, how deliciously soothing to my wearied spirits was the soft, pure air of the summer's morning, breathing over the dewy grass, as (having slept one night on the road) we passed over the heaths of Surrey![13]

But this sense of relief was not to last long. Within three months of the Smiths' return to Bignor Park, Benjamin Smith was in financial trouble again, and he fled to Normandy, where he was joined by his wife and eight children.[14] Here, in the winter of 1785, in what Hilbish describes as a "cold, dreary, dilapidated chateau, nine miles from the nearest town and market, among turbulent peasants of the crudest manners, in the midst of an almost absolute prohibition of fuel, . . . without proper attention or accommodation," Charlotte Smith gave birth to her last child, a son, George Augustus (113).

In the spring of 1785, Charlotte Smith returned to England with her children to look after her husband's business affairs and to escape the hardships of life in exile. It was also the beginning of her escape from the ill-advised marriage that had been the source of so much mental anguish for her. After two years in England, in 1787, she obtained a legal separation from her husband, freeing herself from the daily exigencies attendant on his financial irresponsibility, his volatile and sometimes violent temper, and his infidelities. Benjamin Smith would remain a part of her life until 1806, the year that both husband and wife died; he would make repeated financial demands and continue to cause her grief and pain.[15] After 1787, however, Charlotte Smith began to define herself as an independent woman and a professional writer. She had to fight for this self-definition—to achieve it and maintain it—and, predictably, she made many enemies doing so. But her impetus—the care and support of her nine living children—was compelling, and her talent, energy, and will were suited to the task. Determined to support her children through her own efforts, Smith was likely given the courage to take this step by the success she had already achieved by 1787 as a poet and translator.

Her first literary achievement had come while her husband was imprisoned in King's Bench. At this time Charlotte decided to gather some of her poetry for a small edition that she hoped would produce some income to offset her husband's debts. She sent these poems to William Hayley, her neighbor (though she did not know him personally at the time), a successful poet and the friend and champion of other poets, including William Cowper and, later, William Blake. With a dedication that spoke of Hayley's "protection for these essays," Charlotte Smith's first publication consisted of fourteen sonnets in a quarto volume entitled *Elegiac Sonnets, and Other Essays by Charlotte Smith of Bignor Park, Sussex,* a title that, in the words of Stuart Curran, "testifies alike to her sorrows and her irreducible self-esteem."[16]

The publication was a success; a second edition appeared within the year. In 1786 Charlotte Smith's publisher, Dodsley in Pall Mall, issued a third edition that included twenty sonnets not printed in the first and second editions. The fourth edition appeared later that year. In 1787 a fifth edition, again enlarged, was published by subscription. Following the fifth edition, a further, two-volume edition was published by subscription in 1797, with less success than the fifth had enjoyed. All together, nine editions of the sonnets were produced during Smith's lifetime. Two additional editions appeared after her death: a tenth edition in 1811 and an eleventh edition, the last, in 1851.

In this initial publication Charlotte Smith presents herself to the reading public as a sufferer. She stakes her claim, in her first sonnet, to pensiveness, melancholy, and sorrow:

> The partial Muse has from my earliest hours
> Smiled on the rugged path I'm doom'd to tread,
> And still with sportive hand has snatch'd wild flowers,

To weave fantastic garlands for my head:
But far, far happier is the lot of those
 Who never learn'd her dear delusive art;
Which, while it decks the head with many a rose,
 Reserves the thorn to fester in the heart.
For still she bids soft Pity's melting eye
 Stream o'er the ills she knows not to remove,
Points every pang, and deepens every sigh
 Of mourning Friendship, or unhappy Love.
Ah! then, how dear the Muse's favours cost,
If those paint sorrow best—who feel it most.[17]

Her own afflictions, she implies, have made her sensitive to the pains of others. Writing about sorrow, she admits, brings some pleasure: the "partial Muse" "weave[s] fantastic garlands," after all, to adorn her hair. Yet this pleasure comes at the expense of pain—her own pain that has taught her to see and to "paint" griefs similar to those she feels. So in this sonnet she attributes her very ability to write to her sufferings. For the most part her career would bear that assessment out. Had she not needed some emotional outlet, she might never have written her pensive poems; had her husband's lack of responsibility not led to her family's deprivation, she almost certainly would not have published as much as she did.

We do not question whether Smith suffered. Unlike the reviewer for the *Gentleman's Magazine* who hopes "the misfortunes she so often hints at, are all imaginary," we know them to have been all too real.[18] Nonetheless, the authenticity of her pain does not obviate the need for authorial strategy. Charlotte Smith's ethos is a deliberate and deliberated self-presentation. She may not have chosen to be a sufferer, but Smith's decision to present herself as a sufferer was calculated and astute.

Sarah Zimmerman has observed that, as Smith's career progressed, she "was sharply aware that her continuing success was generated largely by her readers' sympathetic response to a figure of herself as elegiac poet." This "self-presentation," Zimmerman goes on to say, "helped to make her . . . one of the most popular English writers of the late eighteenth century."[19] To say that Smith was aware of "self-presentation" is not to deny that her sufferings were authentic and unavoidable. Yet such suffering was comprehendible to Smith's readers, and perhaps to Smith herself, at least partly through the mediation of literary tradition. The sufferer—particularly the suffering woman—had been a staple of popular fiction since the 1740s, of popular stage productions before that. Nicholas Rowe and Thomas Otway had depicted the sufferings of Jane Shore, Monimia, and Belvidera in their tragedies, and those heroines were followed by their fictional counterparts Clarissa Harlowe, Amelia Booth, Sidney Biddulph, Emily Woodville, and Maria of Moulines, among others.[20] The spectacle of the suffering woman, it was argued, could effect moral improvement in the onlooker. Clarissa's death reforms the rake Belford; Maria and her sadness affects first Tristram Shandy and then Parson Yorick in a way that each feels to be morally instructive (if erotically stimulating too). In an age when women did not have a wide range of choice for self-fashioning, the suffering woman offered an interesting, and culturally acceptable, persona for the woman who wished to establish herself professionally.

To become a public figure in the late eighteenth century, as at any time, opened one to public scrutiny and public interpretation. Such intense examination would have been daunting particularly for women who lived without the protection and support of a husband or a father in a culture where scandal could mean ruin for oneself and one's children. Charlotte Smith must have contemplated a separation from her husband quite some time before she left him. Her sister remarks that those who knew of the tenor of the marriage "could only regret that the measure had not been adopted years before"—a sentiment that suggests the decision was neither sudden nor unexpected (260). First, however, she had to determine not only her ability to support herself and her family but also her—for want of a better term—survival strategy. To burst into print as a woman newly separated from her husband with the confidence, the self-possession, that was characteristic of Charlotte Smith's personality would have invited detraction, even malice from some quarters. To have been coaxed into print by necessity was another matter. To explain the necessity, to insist that the agents of pain were institutional (the law, especially) as often as personal, to remind her readers of the innocent sufferers—so many children!—all these elements Smith repeated in preface after preface; she alluded to them in her poetry; she embedded them in the plots of her novels. When, as was bound to happen, detractors scolded her for her incessant self-referentiality, she simply continued it. For whatever her reviewers and critics said, Charlotte Smith realized that her status as a victim of lawyers' chicanery, of parental shortsightedness, of marital disharmony and abuse, of financial difficulty, garnered sympathy from her readers. Yet, although Charlotte Smith suffered, she did not suffer meekly and acceptingly. If she emphasized her victimization in the public persona she chose to adopt, it was not because she embraced the role.[21]

In fact, very early in her career as a writer, Charlotte Smith faced a hostile press against which she chose to defend herself. After returning from Normandy to England with her children, she translated into English the popular novel by Abbé Prevost, *Manon L'Escaut*. She published this translation in 1785. Criticized first for the immorality of the tale, Smith then found herself attacked in the *Public Advertiser* for "literary fraud," or plagiarism (Dorset, 258-59; Hilbish, 119). Although there was no truth in the charge, Smith decided, in her words, to "withdraw the book rather than let Cadell [her publisher] suffer." Yet she also defended herself. She complained that the term "fraud" was "rather harsh." She observed quite legitimately, "I really see no fraud in a person endeavouring to make a better translation of a work already translated" (quoted by Dorset, 259; Hilbish, 120). She offered her defense in this case in a private letter; later she would use prefaces or appended advertisements to exonerate her reputation from various charges, ranging from complaints about her subject matter to accusations of dilatoriness.[22]

Charlotte Smith's next project was another translation—this time of a collection of legal case histories, Guyot de Pitaval's *Les Causes Célèbres*. Extraneous detail and impenetrable legal jargon had marred Pitaval's accounts. Smith selected from the large collection the most interesting stories—which include the original story of Martin Guerre, made famous again in our time by Natalie Zemon Davis. Smith translated these tales into what she called *The Romance of Real Life*. This publication was a success—critically and financially. Its popularity continued well into the nineteenth century.[23]

After her separation from Benjamin, Charlotte Smith turned her talents to fictional prose. The decision to do so was financial. Publishing novels was a lucrative business by the 1780s. Frances Burney's recent success with *Evelina* (1776) and particularly *Cecilia* (1782) probably encouraged Smith to try her hand at inventing narratives rather than merely translating them.[24] Like her volume of poetry and her second translation, her first novel was a success.

Emmeline, or the Orphan of the Castle (1788) is the story of a young woman, left orphaned (supposedly), who was brought up in an ancient castle belonging to hostile, but absent, relatives. At the age of fourteen, Emmeline meets and promises to marry her wealthy cousin Delamere, who threatens suicide if she says no. His parents reluctantly agree to the marriage but insist that the couple separate for a time first. During this separation, Delamere hears rumors of Emmeline's unfaithfulness. He confronts her with the charges—a motif that occurs again in *Celestina* and twice in *The Young Philosopher*. In *Celestina* and in *The Young Philosopher*, the women reassure their lovers that the charges are false. In Charlotte Smith's first novel, the young woman angrily breaks with her fiancé, eventually marrying "the generous Godolphin."[25]

Emmeline's spunk may have been conceived in reaction to Frances Burney's *Cecilia*, whose heroine is traumatized by gossip to the point of breakdown. Charlotte Smith, on her first foray into the world of fiction, seems to be responding to the sense of claustrophobia Burney depicted in her second novel—the claustrophobia caused by public attention and scandalous talk. Yet, Smith wishes to suggest that one does not have to be trapped by such gossip. If there are Delameres who believe it, there are Godolphins who do not. Interestingly, she revisits the theme in 1798 with a more pessimistic point of view, much like Burney's in *Cecilia*.

In addition to themes that would preoccupy Smith during her career as a writer of fiction, *Emmeline* also introduced the novel-reader of the late 1780s to stylistic characteristics that she or he would come to expect of any Smith novel. The most significant of these, inasmuch as it was the most innovative, was the use of scenic description. Smith's love of nature is evident in her poetry and in her preference for life in the country to life in London; she was an eloquent and careful observer of the natural world, which was often, as in the following passage from *Emmeline*, made more striking by the ruins of man-made edifices:

> The road lay along the side of what would in England be called a mountain; at it's feet rolled the rapid stream that washed the castle walls, foaming over fragments of rock; and bounded by a wood of oak and pine; among which the ruins of the monastery, once an appendage to the castle, reared it's broken arches; and marked by grey and mouldering walls, and mounds covered with slight vegetation, it was traced to it's connection

with the castle itself, still frowning in gothic magnificence; and stretching over several acres of ground: the citadel, which was totally in ruins and covered with ivy, crowning the whole. [43]

The motif of the contrastive ruin amid natural splendor would appeal to the Romantic sensibilities of writers such as Ann Radcliffe and William Wordsworth, and the elaborated treatment of setting would become a staple of fiction in the nineteenth century. Smith was one of the first and most effective novelists to introduce such scenes.

Like her contemporary Radcliffe, Smith often used landscape to suggest the psychological or emotional state of her characters. As Loraine Fletcher has pointed out, description of the natural world often substitutes in Smith's novels, as in Radcliffe's, for discussion or depiction of natural, healthy sexual passion.[26] And, as for Radcliffe, nature is a healer and a teacher for Smith.

Emmeline, like many of Smith's nine later novels, features some of her poetry. It is even prefaced with a poem entitled "To My Children," in which she portrays herself as "O'erwhelm'd with sorrow" and struggling, though with an "exhausted spirit" to procure for her children "an happier fate." The other poems included in *Emmeline* are less specifically autobiographical, but they too speak of "despair" and "depression" and "remorse" and serve to intensify the gothic and sentimental atmosphere.

Yet, we would be wrong to regard either the nature of Smith's poetry or her inclusion of it in her fiction as evidence of self-indulgence. It does not seem to have been regarded that way in her own time, for early reviews of *Emmeline* praised its poetic passages; reviewers complained that Smith's second novel, *Ethelinde, or the Recluse of the Lake* (1789), did not include poetry; and commentators applauded the inclusion of several sonnets in her third novel, *Celestina* (1791).[27] Readers seem to have responded equally positively to references to the English, French and Italian literature that formed their own shared cultural experience. Smith's inclusion of her own poetry in her fiction and her invocation of other literary works by, among others, Shakespeare, Cowper, Collins, Rousseau, Voltaire, Ariosto, Young, Wollstonecraft, Spenser, Sterne, Johnson, both Fieldings (Sarah and Henry), Richardson, Tasso, Gray, and Thomson, speaks to the centrality of literature to her life, her imagination, and her psychology. Not only did she compose poems as a sort of exercise to overcome or understand despair; she read for instruction, comfort, encouragement, and inspiration as well. Toward the end of her life, in desperate need of money, Smith contemplated selling her library, which by then had grown to one thousand volumes of mainly French and English books.[28] She spoke impatiently of having to complete her novel *Marchmont* while away from her library. Like many writers of her time, she kept a commonplace book.[29]

Literature, for Smith, was like nature—a teacher and a healer. In *Minor Morals,* Mrs. Belmour speaks to these properties of literature, especially its ability to provide a moral education for the young, when she requires her nephew to read Thomson's *Seasons* in order to correct his tendency toward cruelty.[30] The intertextuality of her poetry and her fiction caused some readers of her own time to complain of plagiarism; readers of our time may find the allusions obscure.[31] For Smith, however, the participation in a culture of thought and expression seems to have been one redeeming virtue of a profession that she often found tiresome as well as tiring.[32]

After *Emmeline,* Smith went on to write nine more novels. The two following *Emmeline*—*Ethelinde* and *Celestina*—were written in the same vein; they were sentimental tales with a gothic atmosphere, focused on the trials of a young, unprotected woman who ultimately—after much suffering—finds love with a worthy young man. Neither *Ethelinde* nor *Celestina* was greeted with as much enthusiasm as *Emmeline,* though reviewers liked the descriptive passages and the pathetic heroines of both, and Burney praised *Ethelinde.* After the publication of *Celestina,* a reviewer for *The Critical Review* felt able to offer a general evaluation of Smith's worth in the novel-writing enterprise: "In the modern school of novel-writers, Mrs. Smith holds a very distinguished rank; and, if not the first, she is so near as scarcely to be styled an inferior. Perhaps, with Miss Burney she may be allowed to hold 'a divided sway'; and, though on some occasions below her sister-queen, yet, from the greater number of her works, she seems to possess a more luxuriant imagination, and a more fertile invention."[33] Notwithstanding this sincere if patronizing approval, in her next novel Smith departed from the formula that had won her such praise.

Around 1791 Charlotte Smith began to spend a good deal of time in Brighthelmstone (i.e., Brighton), where she met writers and intellectuals sympathetic to the French Revolution. Smith's life experiences had taught her to oppose arbitrary power; her Brighton acquaintances encouraged her to think more broadly and politically about authority—its uses and its abuses (Dorset 260).

Desmond fuses the issues of domestic tyranny and despotic political power. At the center of the story is Geraldine Verney, who is married to a dissipated, abusive man by whom she has three children. She is also loved—though chastely loved—by Desmond. To escape the tortures of his impossible love, Desmond travels to revolutionary France with the hapless brother of his beloved Geraldine. He has occasion to comment on the politics of revolution and the advantages of democracy with regard to both France and America. He offers his observations in a series of letters to a friend in England who is less sympathetic to the cause than Desmond is and who is also privy to the secret of Desmond's love for Geraldine, about which he also has reservations. Ultimately, Geraldine finds herself in France. Desmond saves her from a corrupt French aristocrat to whom her husband has sold her. Her husband dies a well-deserved and painful death, and Geraldine marries Desmond, accepting into her family with admirable aplomb an illegitimate child he fathered while in France.

Desmond was "greatly condemned, not only on account of its politics, but its immoral tendency" (Dorset 260). Her sister reports that the novel "lost" Charlotte "some friends and furnished others with an excuse for withholding their interest in favour of her family" (260). Yet Smith continued to enjoy personal and professional relationships important to her, particularly with William Hayley, at whose home in Eartham she wrote parts of *The Old Manor House* (1793). Although by 1794 the two were estranged, for reasons that Smith herself seems not to have understood, during the summer of 1792 they enjoyed the camaraderie of literary society, along with William Cowper and the painter George Romney.[34] All part of a sort of artists' colony established by Hayley at Eartham, they would gather in the evenings to listen to Smith read aloud from her day's work on what would be considered her best novel (Hilbish 156-57). Cowper's image of "poor Mrs. Smith . . . [c]hain'd to her desk like a slave to his oar, . . . with a broken constitution, unequal to the severe labour enjoin'd by her necessity" paints a less positive picture of this summer of intellectual and artistic exchange; nevertheless the time she spent at Hayley's home seems to have been, for her, pleasant and productive.[35]

Yet Cowper's observation spoke to one truth: from the midnineties on, Smith began to suffer a variety of physical ailments that would culminate in crippling arthritis, constant pain, and a gynecological disorder (probably uterine or ovarian cancer) that ended her life in 1806.[36] Nevertheless, she continued to write. *The Old Manor House* was a success. It returned its readers to the worlds of *Emmeline, Ethelinde,* and *Celestina,* evoking the Gothic atmosphere by its setting in an old and decaying house and by its central concern with a young woman made vulnerable by the absence of parents or protectors and the love of a worthy young man whose family opposes the union. By setting the tale some twenty years in the past, Smith avoids the temptation to expound on the revolution in France, though Orlando, the worthy young lover of the orphaned Monimia, does fight in the American Revolution. This setting allows her to make political observations that were indirectly applicable to the French situation.

Smith returned to the French Revolution in *The Banished Man* and *The Young Philosopher* and in her long poem *The Emigrants.* She was criticized for insinuating "the strain of her politics" into her works of fiction,[37] but she defends her right to do so in the preface to *Desmond:*

> women it is said have no business with politics—Why not?—Have they no interest in the scenes that are acting around them, in which they have fathers, brothers, husbands, sons, or friends engaged?—Even in the commonest course of female education, they are expected to acquire some knowledge of history; and yet, if they are to have no opinion of what *is* passing, it avails little that they should be informed of what *has passed,* in a world where they are subject to such mental degradation; where they are censured as affecting masculine knowledge if they happen to have any understanding; or despised as insignificant triflers if they have none.[38]

Charlotte Smith often chafed at the restrictions of her life, restrictions imposed by law, by custom, and by words, printed and spoken. Herself a target for detraction because of her political views, she was sensitive to the human cost of gossip and idle talk. She was acutely aware of opinion as a coercive agent of what she terms the "mental degradation" that characterized women's lives.[39]

Catherine Dorset speaks of the "malignity" of the *"literary ladies"* whose responses to *Desmond* were particularly vitriolic, inspired (according to Dorset) by "envy" (260). Anna Seward, we know, was a prominent and influential professional enemy.[40] Smith, however, did not succumb quietly to opinion she felt was biased or malicious. She objected to the *Critical Review*'s treatment of her work, taking to task "the gentlemen—or ladies—(for I believe novels are often left to the latter,)" for their tendency to "transfer their remarks from the books they undertake to criticise, to the private history of the authors."[41]

In the preface to *The Young Philosopher*, Smith excoriates the evils of malicious, idle talk. The literary world of the late 1790s was to some degree dominated by women, but they were not a monolithic group. They existed in a competitive domain, and they—like many professionals during many human eras—fought for dominance and control. Smith, like Mary Wollstonecraft, whom she admired, claimed for herself the right to speak her mind about whatever subject she chose. Her politics were not as consistently radical as some of her day, but she shared with the Jacobin novelists the set of values that Gary Kelly has described as characteristic of this group: "They opposed tyranny and oppression, be it domestic, national or international, spiritual or temporal; they were against all distinctions between men which were not based on moral qualities, or virtue; and they were utterly opposed to persecution of individuals, communities, or nations for their beliefs on any subject."[42] These values alone would have engendered calumny during the 1780s and 1790s; Smith's success as an author and the envy that always attends success intensified criticism as her career advanced.

In 1793 Smith's third son was injured at Dunkirk and lost his leg by amputation. In 1795 her favorite daughter, Anna Augusta, who had married the French émigré upon whom *The Banished Man* was based, died.[43] This tragedy, coming so quickly upon the maiming of her son, was almost too much for the long-suffering Charlotte Smith to bear. By her own and her sister's account, she was tremendously afflicted.[44] She began to change her place of habitation more frequently, becoming, in Catherine Dorset's words, "more than ever unsettled, moving from place to place in search of that tranquillity she was never destined to enjoy" (260). Her pain at the death of this beloved child infuses the works she published after 1795. In *Marchmont* and *The Young Philosopher* in particular Smith transfigures her grief into poignant scenes of loss.

Marchmont (1796) begins with a scene of separation. The young Althea is separated from the beloved aunt who has reared her, first by travel and then by death. The scene in which Althea attends her dying aunt is clearly informed by the death of Smith's own daughter. Here, in what must have been a heartfelt desire, Smith reverses the situation: the "mother" dies, while the "daughter" lives to find love, happiness, and, most significantly, a favorable legal settlement to a vexed inheritance issue. Smith blamed her daughter's death and her sons' sufferings on the fact that they were denied their rightful inheritance. The fortune left them by their grandfather, Smith felt, could have procured for Anna Augusta appropriate, life-saving medical attention and in the case of at least one of her sons, supported a career in the church. *The Young Philosopher* (1798) refigures the scene of separation when Medora is abducted while she and her mother are in London seeking legal advice about an inheritance. The frantic search and ultimate breakdown of the mother are informed by Smith's anguish over her personal loss.

The Young Philosopher was followed by one other fictional narrative, *Letters of a Solitary Wanderer* (1799, 1802), a series of loosely related stories told by a melancholic traveler. Smith's last years were painful, yet she continued to write.[45] Catherine Dorset portrays her "in great bodily pain," lying on a sofa, "with two or three lively grandchildren playing about her," writing and "conversing with great cheerfulness and pleasantry" (260). That is a fitting image of the end of this writer's life, in which love of family and dedication to literary career were so inextricably bound.

Charlotte Smith died on 28 October 1806. In addition to the novels and poetry for which she remains famous, she also published several works for children, a journalistic account of a shipwreck, and a play (see below, p. xxxiv-xxxv). During a twenty-two-year career she wrote more than sixty volumes, or twenty-six works. As Judith Phillips Stanton has shown, Smith supported herself and her children largely by her literary earnings. Moreover, by her writing she managed to compensate for the loss of the social standing to which she had been born. Stanton comments, "For Charlotte Smith, who never forgot that she was the daughter of a gentleman and much fallen in the world, her writing came to represent a certain social standing. She took as much pride in what she earned for her sons by reputation as by income."[46]

Charlotte Smith's literary ethos, the suffering woman, served her well. Despite the detractions and complaints of critics and competitors, the reading public responded to the fusion of life and art, seemingly agreeing with the author that she who has suffered greatly will depict the sufferings of others with an authenticity not to be achieved by one who has not. The persona so dominated the public perception of Smith in her own time that Catherine Dorset felt compelled to close her memoir of her sister with a description that counters the popular view:

> Cheerfulness and gaiety were the natural characteristics of her mind; and though circumstances of the most depressing nature at times weighed down her spirit to the earth, yet such was its buoyancy that it quickly returned to its level. Even in the darkest periods of her life, she possessed the power of abstracting herself from her cares, and, giving play to the sportiveness of her imagination, could make even the difficulties she was labouring under subjects of merriment, placing both persons and things in such ridiculous points of view, and throwing out such sallies of pleasantry that it was impossible not to be delighted with her wit, even while deploring the circumstances that excited it. [261]

To invoke a cliché, Charlotte Smith was a force to be reckoned with. She had drive, will, talent, and intelligence that, when called upon to exercise them, she used to the maximum. Her novels were acclaimed in her own lifetime; and later novelists, Sir Walter Scott, Jane Austen, and Charles Dickens, in particular, bear witness to her popularity and skill.[47] Scott, speaking as a critic, praises her powers of description and her ingenuity, though he regrets her tone of melancholy and the necessary haste with which she composed her works. As a reader, he acknowledges the "many pleasant hours derived from the perusal of Mrs. Smith's works."[48] Austen and Dickens pay what is perhaps a more profound tribute in the echoes of Smith's novels to be found in their narratives. Born of the suffering to which she was consigned for much of her life and reflecting that suffering in tone and subject matter, Charlotte Smith's works are nevertheless infused by the intelligence, wit, and courage that, by all accounts, characterized the author herself.

THE YOUNG PHILOSOPHER

In her preface to *The Young Philosopher,* Charlotte Smith admits that the title of her novel may be "a misnomer," for in many instances "my Hero forgets his pretensions, and has no claim to the character of a Philosopher." Yet "the book itself will be no worse," she concludes coyly. For given the involvement of the narrative with the ideologies and ideals associated with the French and American Revolutions, the title seems a deliberate irony, a commentary on the degree to which a personal philosophy can provide sustenance and solace in a corrupt society. *The Young Philosopher* is an indictment of Britain that traces capricious oppression from its roots in provincial customs to the legal system that codifies and maintains the injustice it should preclude.

Smith began work on *The Young Philosopher* as she usually began work on a novel—in the midst of anxious wrangling with lawyers over her children's legacy. In a letter to booksellers Thomas Cadell Jr. and William Davies, Smith speaks of her latest disappointment: "I have seen Mr Graham (King's Councel), a Man of the first eminence and fairness in his profession, & having shewn him the case, he is clearly of opinion that considering the conduct of the people I have to do with, there is nothing to be hoped for but from Chancery Which, while it is depending, will entirely prevent my receiving for the support of my family, one shilling, for their Grandfathers estate." The purpose of her self-revelation here is financial: she asks Cadell and Davies for an advance on a novel of which she has written one hundred pages and which, she projects, will eventually fill three volumes—perhaps more, as "you know I am very apt to have a great deal to say just at the last, so that it might exceed that number & swell to four."[49]

From the beginning, Smith intended *The Young Philosopher* to be a serious and substantial work. She conceived of it as "a composition of some novelty & more solidity than the usual croud of Novels," one that would "require books and leisure" to complete. Although her preface states that her "original plan differed materially from what I have executed," the difference seems to be a matter of incident—plot—not tone or theme. In particular, she changed details to avoid a charge of plagiarism, such as the one that marred her early career. Still, there is one detail that she retained, despite its affinity to an episode in Mary Wollstonecraft's *The Wrongs of Woman, or Maria:* "the incident of the confinement in a mad house of one of my characters was designed before I saw the fragment . . . by a Writer whose talents I greatly honoured, and whose untimely death I deeply regret; from her I should not blush to borrow, and if I had done so I would have acknowledged it." This comment represents a significant claim to kinship with Wollstonecraft and the position she had staked out philosophically in her *Vindication of the Rights of Woman* and demonstrated in *The Wrongs of Woman.* In a sense, Smith's *The Young Philosopher* is, like *The Wrongs of Woman,* a narrative rendition of the *Vindication,* a narrative that examines the cultural constraints under which women of the eighteenth century had to live their lives and the social proclivities and mental habits that made it so hard to free themselves from those constraints.

For *The Young Philosopher*, despite its name, centers not on George Delmont, the Rousseauesque character to whom the title refers, but on two female characters—Laura Glenmorris and her daughter Medora. This focus is not immediately apparent, as we do not even hear of these characters until the sixth chapter of volume 1. We do not meet Medora until chapter 9; Mrs. Glenmorris does not appear until chapter 11. In fact, the novel begins as a comedy of manners centered on the ridiculous Winslows—the pompous, pious reverend, his vaporish wife, and their phlegmatic, self-conscious son, Middleton. Social satire pervades the first volume of *The Young Philosopher*, though it yields in the second volume to the familiar hybrid characteristic of so many 1790s novels that portray characters of sensibility in gothic settings ruminating on subjects of political urgency. The beginning of the novel establishes the frivolity and emptiness of most social life, with its characteristic preoccupations: money, marriage, class. Against this vapid world is set another—the world of George Delmont, the young philosopher, and his friends, Mr. Armitage and Laura and Medora Glenmorris, who enjoy "the delightful and calm pleasures of a society where confidence and mutual affection" prevail.

As Katharine M. Rogers has noted, from the middle of the eighteenth century novels had viewed "sensitivity . . . [as] an essential attribute of superior people, . . . [which] alienated them from the obtuse society around them."[50] Eleanor Ty agrees; her term for George Delmont and his friends is "ex-centric." These characters, because of their alienation, are "able to look at the patriarchal society with a critical eye."[51] From the beginning, the narrator's ironic voice encourages the reader's alienation from the Winslows and Mrs. Crewkherne and the narrow conventionality that they represent. The events of the novel emanate from this conventionality; the grave consequences suffered by Laura and Medora Glenmorris are a thorough indictment of "existing circumstances," a resounding call to repudiation of the status quo. Smith's narrative strategy accentuates the charges against conventionality most effectively by presenting long first-person narratives in which Laura and Medora recount their sufferings. These "digressions" have been discussed by critics as a weakness of the novel.[52] Yet these narratives, as well as other examples of what J. Paul Hunter has called "stories within,"[53] are important in that they provide occasion for the reader's intimate identification with the suffering victims of society, in particular women. These profoundly personal stories, told with sincerity, serve as a counterpoint to the ironic voice of the omniscient narrator, intensifying our sense of the gulf that separates the mercenary Winslows, Crewkhernes, Grinsteds and Darnells of the novel from the young philosopher and his friends.

In her preface Charlotte Smith speaks of a dual moral aim. First, she says, she wishes to "expose the ill consequences of detraction," as she does in suggesting that the casual, mean-spirited gossip of Mrs. Crewkherne and Mrs. Grinsted can influence the decisions made and actions taken by men in power. Her second stated purpose is "to shew the sad effects of parental resentment, and the triumph of fortitude in the daughter, while too acute sensibility, too hastily indulged, is the source of much unhappiness to the mother." Again, however, she points to men in power—particularly men with legal power—as the cause of distress. Although Smith asserts that her novel recommends fortitude (sense) over sensibility, her narrative scarcely bears her out.[54] Even Smith herself blames Laura's distresses less on her "over-indulgence" than on "such men, as in the present state of society stand in place of the giants, and necromancers, and ogers of ancient romance, men whose profession empowers them to perpetrate, and whose inclination generally prompts them to the perpetration of wickedness."

In fact, Laura does not hastily indulge acute sensibility as much as she suffers from a certain powerlessness attendant on her gender. Like Mary Wollstonecraft, Smith sees a danger in the overdependence on men that women were encouraged, indeed required, to have during the eighteenth century. *The Young Philosopher*'s double invocation of the theme of sexual jealousy (experienced and expressed first by Glenmorris and later by Delmont) brings into sharp focus the double bind that characterizes the lives of both Laura and Medora. When Glenmorris returns to Scotland after his abduction by pirates, he finds his wife linked by gossip to Lord Macarden and Lord Macarden himself suffering from wounds received in a duel with the laird of Kilbrodie: Glenmorris asks Laura, angrily, "Why should the wife or the widow of Glenmorris so conduct herself as to be the occasion of a duel between his nearest relation and Lord Macarden?" Smith repeats this motif in the episode wherein Delmont discovers the abducted Medora safe. She is with an older man upon whose lap she sits, "his arm round her waist, and her head declined on his shoulder." The man is, of course, her father, but Delmont assumes him to be Medora's would-be seducer, Sir Harry Richmond; he suspects Medora's ruin and fears Medora's complicity in it. Both Laura and Medora exhibit extraordinary strength and courage during their trials, yet each is confronted at the moment of rescue not by praise for her strength but by unfounded suspicions born of sexual jealousy. Both women reassure their lovers, not only by explaining the truth of the situation, but also by surrendering themselves once again to their lovers' guidance and control. On the one hand, Smith seems to be suggesting that only through such submissiveness can these women retain the love and protection of men, without which they will be subject to dangers such as those they have already endured. On the other hand, she seems aware that the troubles of her heroines stem directly from their dependence on men who are—invariably in *The Young Philosopher*—somewhere else when trouble occurs. As Laura Glenmorris finds herself more and more frustrated by lawyers, she quite naturally blames the men on whom she has been taught to rely: "The absence of Delmont, though she believed it unavoidable, was so ill timed that it affected her almost like an intentional omission.—That of Armitage too, now travelling with his sick friend in the North, was so unfortunate that it sunk her spirits in despite of every effort of her courage."

Like Wollstonecraft, Smith illustrates the need for feminine strength and character independent of men; and like Wollstonecraft, she sees that the circumstances into which women are born and the culture in which they are reared militate on every side against female independence of spirit and self-sufficiency. Even in lives blessed with the support of loving and generous men—lives such as Laura and Medora lead—the inability to stand alone can be dangerous. Laura's madness and the clear implication that she will not fully recover stand as a silent warning to her daughter as Medora is reunited with Delmont after her own trials. The strength with which Medora withstood the machinations of Darnell, like the strength with which her mother withstood the laird of Kilbrodie, is admirable. It is, however, no guarantee that Medora will not later suffer, as her mother did, the enervation of spirit that attends the overreliance upon men encouraged, indeed demanded, by the culture in which they live.

Although *The Young Philosopher* centers on the experiences of Laura and Medora Glenmorris, they are not the only victims of British society in this novel. Delmont himself is a younger brother whose finances are subject to periodic plunder by the irresponsible, rakish Adolphus. Throughout the novel we receive glimpses of other victims of society: the poor family with whom Medora accepts a ride on her flight from Darnell, the ruined victims of Sir Harry Richmond's ruthless sexual predation, the pathetic suicide of Elizabeth Lisburne. The novel takes us from Brighton in Sussex to northern Scotland, to London, Wales, York, and Ireland. Everywhere the characters encounter the abuses inherent in the class system, the injustices imposed by national institutions. Piety encouraged by the church produces narrow-minded gossips whose social prominence lends authority to the most idle of their speculations. Greed drives both the institution of marriage and that of law, where the collusion of lawyers and moneyed clients make justice unobtainable for the powerless, such as Laura and Medora Glenmorris. As one alternative to this corruption, Smith offers Mary Cardonnel, who, as Ty has noted, enacts justice by simply giving Medora the share of their grandfather's fortune that should be hers by right and that is Mary's by law (154).

Such a solution to the myriad and deep-seated problems *The Young Philosopher* chronicles, however, finally will not serve. At the end of the novel, Laura, Glenmorris, Medora, and Delmont prepare for another alternative—life in America, where, according to Medora, "we never had these hateful perplexities." In her father's more philosophic words, the difference between America and England exists in the possibility for active human involvement as opposed to powerlessness in the face of wrong: "'I do not love to live,'" Glenmorris tells Armitage, "'where I see a frightful contrast between luxury and wretchedness; where I must daily witness injustice I cannot repress, and misery I cannot relieve.'" Although the ideals and ideas of the French Revolution inform this novel, by 1798 those ideals had become tainted by the excesses of the Reign of Terror. Smith, like most liberals of her time, did not repudiate the revolution as such, but the optimism generated by the storming of the Bastille and the Tennis Court Oath had given way to the horror of the guillotine. As Ty puts it, "whereas at the dawn of the French Revolution . . . [Smith's] novels seemed to hold a strong belief in the possibilities of social change, here a break with the patriarchal civilization of England seems to be the only solution" (154).

And what of those who, like Smith herself, cannot leave to begin life anew in an untainted and untried America? The answer offered by *The Young Philosopher* is Nature. In her preface, Smith refers to the botanical observations that punctuate her work as "ornaments" similar to the poetic passages she includes. Yet in a letter to James Edward Smith, the famous botanist, she attributes greater significance to the inclusion of natural history in her novel. She writes from London on 15 March 1798:

Though after a long and successless struggle I am compelled to leave the country, my passion for plants rather increases as the power of gratification diminishes; and though I must henceforth, or at least till peace, or something equally conclusive, dismisses me to the continent, (whither I will go if I have strength whenever it is practicable,) botanize on annuals in garden pots out at a window, it will be a considerable consolation to have an opportunity of being known to the principal of the delightful and soothing study; and who is, as well in science as in benevolence and cultivation of mind, an acquaintance so greatly to be desired.

I have not forgotten (being still compelled to write, that my family may live) your hint of introducing botany into a novel. The present rage for gigantic and impossible horrors, which I cannot but consider as a symptom of morbid and vitiated taste, makes me almost doubt whether the simple pleasures afforded by natural objects will not appear vapid to the admirers of spectre novels and cavern adventures. However I have ventured a little of it, and have at least a hope that it will not displease those whose approbation I most covet.[55]

This letter echoes the preface to *The Young Philosopher,* in which Smith criticizes the prevailing taste for "the wild, the terrible, and the supernatural," as opposed to what she offers, that is, "scenes of modern life and *possible* events." Although Laura's Scottish adventures and Medora's abduction are the stuff of gothic narrative, we must admit that Smith eschews even the imputation of supernatural forces. She grounds her novel in reality as she saw it—what is or what might be.

Much of the reality documented by *The Young Philosopher* is distressing—madness, hard-heartedness, cruelty, poverty, grief. Yet the chronicle of difficulty endured by this novel's characters is balanced by an abiding interest in the natural world. Smith explains elsewhere the value of such an interest specifically in terms of the aftermath of the cataclysmic events in France. Mrs. Woodfield of Smith's *Rural Walks* explains to her niece and her daughter that "a taste for rural beauty" will be "a constant source of amusement and delight; and . . . it may hereafter be a resource against the inconveniences of adversity." She continues:

Reflect, my child, how many persons, who were born in a higher rank of life than you were, even in the first classes of the nobility of France, are now reduced to the necessity of labouring for their daily bread in a strange land; how many derive their support from the little ornamental acquirements of their more fortunate days. Nor is this confined to the natives of a country where the overthrow of its ancient government has overwhelmed the nobility in its ruins. Even in this prosperous land, how often do we see such sad vicissitudes of fortune. How often does the luxury, the folly, or the misfortunes of parents leave destitute and helpless young women exposed to insult, too often to infamy; for those who cannot bear poverty will escape from it, however ruinous the means by which they escape.[56]

The young philosopher, George Delmont, projects a life apart from the forms and conventions of society—a life, as his experiences demonstrate to him, that no one can attain. Neither is it possible to meet all of the exigencies of life with the stoical acceptance that is implied by the word *philosophy*. Yet we do have a recourse in nature, a nature seen as particularly helpful to women in that it makes it easier to bear the deprivations that are attendant on their powerlessness.[57]

Lest this attitude, this consolation seem a meager, almost ludicrous answer to the problems Smith exposes in *The Young Philosopher,* we should remember that botanical study at the end of the eighteenth century was itself viewed as a radical activity, especially when undertaken by women. The activity of "botanizing" was seen as lascivious and presumptuous by such antifeminist writers as Richard Polwhele and Samuel Rogers.[58] Rousseau advises botanical study for women in his *Letters on the Elements of Botany,* but he recommends a casual rather than a scientific approach, a position that Judith Pascoe contrasts with Priscilla Wakefield's meticulous and serious instructions for such study to the women she addresses in *An Introduction to Botany* (198-99).[59] Yet, although Rousseau's dismissiveness toward the intellectual aspirations of women may rankle today, his love of botanical study—and the way he talked about that love— may have held more important implications for his eighteenth-century female reader. In his *Confessions,* Rousseau eulogizes botanical study as "the way to pass eternity without the possibility of a moment's boredom," an antidote to "the wildness of the imagination."[60] Though in itself this study is neither radical nor revolutionary, it does have radical, revolutionary implications, not the least of which is that happiness is and should be attainable by all, even the poorest of society, even the women. Indeed, as Ann Shteir has pointed out, Charlotte Smith "used the theme of women and botany to explore ways of being female in her world" (68). Botany, to Smith, provides an alternative to the conventional ingredients of the eighteenth-century woman's life: gossip and meaningless social activity. The study of nature, Smith asserts in her verse, her children's works, and in *The Young Philosopher,* can strengthen a woman physically, mentally, and spiritually (see Shteir 68-73).

Ultimately, however, *The Young Philosopher* denies that happiness can be found completely within ourselves—in philosophy—or completely outside ourselves—in nature. Society's corruptions and evils have left Laura Glenmorris permanently scarred, the happiness of those who love her permanently attenuated. Nature, though it ameliorates Laura's mental distress, falls short of effecting a complete cure. *The Young Philosopher* shares the notion with another work published in 1798—Wordsworth's *Tintern Abbey*—that "Nature never did betray / The heart that loved her" (ll. 122-23). "Not betraying" does not, for Smith, amount to the possibility of transcendence that Wordsworth found in the natural world.[61] For her, Nature is, rather, a compensation for the evil that mars much of life. In England, that is all it can be. Yet *The Young Philosopher* ends with a vision of a new kind of world, the America that has throughout provided a pastoral counterpoint to the corruptions of British life. Having left that world, Laura Glenmorris may never recover from the traumas induced by British law and customs, just as England may never shake off the corruptions that render evil such a powerful force. Still, there is hope for the human race, *The Young*

Philosopher maintains: that hope lies in America, where life is founded on democratic principles and characterized by close association with the land.

NOTES

1. Her sister Catherine Dorset reports that Smith's school poems "were shown and praised among the friends of the family as proofs of early genius." She is the one who remembers, though it is "an imperfect recollection," that Wolfe was the subject of one of the early poems; she surmises that Smith would have been ten at the date of its composition—"though she speaks in one of her works of earlier compositions." "Charlotte Smith," in *Biographical Memoirs,* in *The Prose Works of Sir Walter Scott,* vol. 8 (Paris: A. and W. Galignani, 1834), p. 253. See also Florence May Anna Hilbish, "Charlotte Smith: Poet and Novelist (1749-1806)," Ph.D. diss., Univ. of Pennsylvania, 1941, pp. 19-20. Further references to these works will be made parenthetically in the text.

2. Preface to the first and second editions of her *Elegiac Sonnets and Other Poems,* in Smith, *Poems,* ed. Stuart Curran (Oxford: Oxford Univ. Press, 1993), p. 3.

3. "Mrs. Charlotte Smith," preface to *The Old Manor House,* in Barbauld's fifty-volume edition *The British Novelists: With an Essay; and Prefaces, Biographical and Critical* (London: F.C. and J. Rivington, 1810), xxxvi.i.

4. Roy Porter, *English Society in the Eighteenth Century* (London: Penguin, 1982), pp. 180-81.

5. Barbauld, p. i. See also Dorset, p. 254, and Hilbish, pp. 22-24.

6. *Public Characters of 1800-1801* (London: Richard Phillips, 1807), 3:46.

7. Dorset writes of her sister's precocity, "her appearance and manners were . . . much beyond her years" (254).

8. Hilbish, p. 83, quotes this anecdote from a footnote to one of Andrew Caldwell's letters to Bishop Percy printed in John Boyer Nichols, *Illustrations of the Literary History of the Eighteenth Century* (London: J.B. Nichols and Sons, 1817-58), 8:35.

9. Hilbish maintains that although the will is "a voluminous document, verbose, complicated, and obscure; . . . it is not incomprehensible" (72), an observation substantiated by the will itself (including the four codicils added by Richard Smith), which she includes in an appendix to her biography of Smith (565-80). The legal wrangling—so much to the profit of the lawyers involved—was *made possible* rather than necessitated by the will's intricacy.

10. In 1798 lawyers and trustees reached a preliminary settlement of Richard Smith's property on Charlotte Smith's children. A second settlement was made in 1807 (Hilbish, 198). Final settlements were not completed until 1813.

11. Preface to *The Banished Man: A Novel.* 4 vols. (London: T. Cadell, Jun., and William Davies, 1794), 1:ix.

12. Preface to *The Banished Man,* 1:vi.

13. Quoted in *Public Characters,* 3:56-57, and by Hilbish, p. 87.

14. In fact, Charlotte Smith accompanied her husband to Dieppe on the first day of his exile, spent the day with him, established him in his new dwelling, and returned the same day to England and her children. Later that month, Smith and her children sailed to Normandy to join Benjamin in the chateau he had purchased. See Hilbish, p. 112-13; Dorset, p. 257.

15. The vexed relationship between the Smiths is chronicled in her letters. A collection of the complete letters, edited by Judith Phillips Stanton, is forthcoming from Indiana University Press. An as-yet-unpublished article by Stanton, "Charlotte Smith and Mr. Monstroso: A Marriage in Life and Fiction," also examines this ongoing, abusive relationship.

16. Stuart Curran, introduction to Smith, *Poems,* p. xxii.

17. Smith, *Poems,* p. 13. The italicized line is adapted from the end of Pope's *Eloisa to Abelard,* l. 366.

18. Review of *Elegiac Sonnets and Other Poems*, *Gentleman's Magazine* 56 (1786): 333.

19. Sarah Zimmerman, "Charlotte Smith's Letters and the Practice of Self-Presentation," *Princeton University Library Chronicle* 53 (1991): 50.

20. In novels by Samuel Richardson, Henry Fielding, Frances Sheridan, Elizabeth Griffith (*The Delicate Distress*), and Laurence Sterne, respectively.

21. Seemingly skillful in terms of self-presentation, Smith had, as Judith Phillips Stanton has noted, "a limited understanding of the literary marketplace," allowing the publishers ("booksellers" to the eighteenth century) "to set the prices of her works" and manage the financial end of things for her, though later in her career, Smith became more astute about the worth of her work and the publication of new editions of her early works. Stanton, "Charlotte Smith's 'Literary Business': Income, Patronage, and Indigence," *The Age of Johnson: A Scholarly Annual*, ed. Paul J. Korshin, 1 (1987): 385, 388.

22. For example, at the end of *Marchmont* Smith offers the following explanation to the subscribers to her poems for the delay in the appearance of the second volume:

Mrs. Smith takes this Occasion of informing the Subscribers to the Second Volume of Poems, with a Portrait and Engravings, that her domestic Misfortunes, and personal ill Health, together with Difficulties that arose in procuring a Likeness, have unavoidably delayed the Publication of the Work greatly beyond the Time when it was intended to appear; but it is now in such Forwardness, and the Ornamental Parts are in such Hands, that she hopes in a very short Time to fulfil her Engagements with the Public. [*Marchmont* (1796), introduction by Mary Anne Schofield (Delmar, N.Y.: Scholars' Facsimiles and Reprints, 1989) 4:(444)]

23. Hilbish records (p. 122) that the last edition was published in 1847.

24. Smith earned during the course of her career a total of £4,190 for her poetry, children's books, and novels. The novels account for well over half of this total figure. Stanton, "'Literary Business,'" table 2, p. 394.

25. *Emmeline: The Orphan of the Castle* (1788), introduction by Zoë Fairbairns (London: Pandora, 1988), p. 552. Further references will be cited parenthetically in the text.

26. See Loraine Fletcher, *Charlotte Smith: A Critical Biography* (London: Macmillan, 1998), pp. 266-83.

27. For praise of *Emmeline*'s poetry, see the *Monthly Review* 79 (1788): 243-44; Hilbish (pp. 139-41) reviews other critical commentary.

28. Rufus Paul Turner, "Charlotte Smith (1749-1806): New Light on Her Life and Literary Career," Ph.D. diss., Univ. of Southern California, 1966, p. 71. She actually did sell five hundred of these volumes in 1803. Stanton, "'Literary Business,'" p. 377.

29. She makes both comments in her preface to *Marchmont*, 1:xi.

30. "Dialogue VI," in *Minor Morals, Interspersed with Sketches of Natural History, Historical Anecdotes, and Original Stories*, 2 vols. (London: Minerva Press for A.K. Newman and Co., 1817), pp. 122-60.

31. Anna Seward, in particular, leveled repeated charges of plagiarism against Smith. For a summary of Seward's various comments, generally concerned with Smith's poetry, see Hilbish, pp. 238-46.

32. For some of Smith's literary trials, see Stanton, "'Literary Business.'" Smith's letters to publishers Thomas Cadell Jr. and William Davies, written during the time she was composing *The Young Philosopher*, speak of her frustration with aspects of her trade.

33. *Critical Review* (September 1791): 318; Hilbish quotes, p. 139.

34. This "estrangement" seems to have been less decisive than Smith represents it in some of her letters. Hayley, after all, served as her "corrector" for volumes 1, 2, and part of 3 for *The Young Philosopher*, breaking off because of his son's illness, not pique with Smith. Cf. letter to Thomas Cadell Jr. and William Davies, 26 Feb. 1798, Beinecke Rare Book and Manuscript Library, Yale Univ.

35. Cowper to Hayley, 29 Jan. 1793, *The Letters and Prose Writings of William Cowper,* vol. 4, *Letters 1792-1799,* ed. James King and Charles Ryskamp (Oxford: Clarendon, 1984), p. 281. This time of literary community was rare in Smith's life, for as Alan Dugald McKillop has noted, "she lived and worked in comparative isolation" (247). See McKillop, "Charlotte Smith's Letters," *Huntington Library Quarterly* 15 (1952): 237-55.

36. Turner, pp. 77-86. Turner refers to an "abdominal tumor" (86); Stanton, phone conversation, 18 June 1996.

37. The phrase is from Barbauld, p. vii.

38. *Desmond: A Novel* (1792), 3 vols., introduction by Gina Luria (New York: Garland, 1974), 1:iii-iv.

39. Gossip and calumny were, according to Edmund Burke, the means by which the *philosophes* fueled the revolution in France: "What was not to be done towards their great end by any direct or immediate act, might be wrought by a longer process through the medium of opinion." *Reflections on the Revolution in France,* Everyman edition, ed. Ernest Rhys (London: J.M. Dent, 1910), pp. 107-8. Smith sees gossip as an equally powerful agent of oppression. Yet her success as a writer largely depended on gossip in the sense that her career was fashioned around public interest in her private woes. The paradox of gossip—its power and potential as a means of social bonding and as a destructive social force—has been thoroughly explored by Patricia Meyer Spacks in *Gossip* (New York: Alfred A. Knopf, 1985).

40. Her many remarks on Smith, uniformly negative, are scattered throughout the first three volumes of her letters. *Letters of Anna Seward written between the years 1784 and 1807,* 6 vols. (London: Longman, Hurst, Rees, 1811). Stanton believes that this enmity was heightened by Seward's jealous friendship with Hayley. Stanton, personal communication, 21 Oct. 1996.

41. Preface to volumes 4 and 5 of Smith, *The Solitary Wanderer* (1802), quoted by Hilbish, p. 207.

42. Gary Kelly, *The English Jacobin Novel* (Oxford: Clarendon, 1970), p. 7.

43. In her preface to this novel, Smith both confirms and denies the identification: "[M]y hero resembles in nothing but in merit, the emigrant gentleman who now makes part of my family." *The Banished Man: A Novel,* 4 vols. (London: T. Cadell, 1794), p. xi.

44. And, as Turner notes, her grief did not lessen with the passing of years. He quotes letters from 1800, 1804, and 1806 in which Smith is still expressing anguish at "'the loss of my loveliest and most deserving child.'" "'[M]y misery,'" she says in 1806, "'has never yet abated'" (39). Quoted from letters to Joseph Cooper Walker, 18 May 1800, and to Sarah Rose, 26 April 1806.

45. There were only three years from 1787 to 1806 that Smith lived "without literary earnings—1801, 1803, and 1805." Stanton, "'Literary Business,'" p. 393.

46. Stanton, "'Literary Business,'" p. 393.

47. See William H. Magee, "The Happy Marriage: The Influence of Charlotte Smith on Jane Austen," *Studies in the Novel* 7 (1976): 120-32; Eleanor Ty, "Ridding Unwanted Suitors: Jane Austen's *Mansfield Park* and Charlotte Smith's *Emmeline,*" *Tulsa Studies in Women's Literature* (1986): 327-28; and Joseph F. Bartolomeo, "Charlotte to Charles: *The Old Manor House* as a Source for *Great Expectations,*" *Dickens Quarterly* 8 (1991): 112-20.

48. Scott's critical remarks are appended to Dorset's biographical account. See Dorset, p. 264.

49. Letter to Thomas Cadell Jr. and William Davies, 22 June 1797, Beinecke Rare Book and Manuscript Library, Yale University.

50. Katharine M. Rogers, "Romantic Aspirations, Restricted Possibilities: The Novels of Charlotte Smith," in *Re-Visioning Romanticism: British Women Writers, 1776-1837,* ed. Carol Shiner Wilson and Joel Haefner (Philadelphia: Univ. of Pennsylvania Press, 1994), p. 72. Further references are cited parenthetically in the text.

51. Eleanor Ty, *Unsex'd Revolutionaries: Five Women Novelists of the 1790s* (Toronto: Univ. of Toronto Press, 1993), p. 144. Further references are cited parenthetically in the text.

52. Hilbish is of that opinion (p. 195), as was one early reviewer for *The Critical Review*, 24 (1798): 77-84. In fact, a general criticism of Smith's novels is that her plots are, in Walter Scott's words, "hastily *run up*" (Dorset 263). He also complains of "want of connexion." For a defense of the inset stories as not only relevant but profoundly effective, see Ty, *Unsex'd Revolutionaries*, pp. 143-54.

53. J. Paul Hunter, *Before Novels: The Cultural Contexts of Eighteenth-Century Fiction* (New York: W.W. Norton, 1990), p. 47. Hunter's discussion of stories-within and other interruptive features of the novel is an important one for understanding the nature of eighteenth-century fiction in general, which does not lend itself to "simplistic notions of unity and organicism that sponsor most discussions of structure" (48). See esp. pp. 47-54.

54. Fletcher, pp. 187-97.

55. Letter to Dr. James Edward Smith, 15 March 1798, *Memoir and Correspondence of the Late Sir James Edward Smith, M.D.*, ed. Lady Smith (London: Longman, et al., 1832), 2:75-76.

56. *Rural Walks: In Dialogues Intended for the Use of Young Persons*, 2 vols. in 1 (Philadelphia: Thomas Stephens, 1795), p. 45. For Smith's identification with the French émigrés, see her poem *The Emigrants*. In this poem the abundance of Nature suggests to the poet the presence of "omniscient goodness," even as she experiences and witnesses "the variety of woes that Man / For Man creates." *The Emigrants*, 2:405, 413-14. Smith, *Poems*, pp. 162-63.

57. Smith says as much in *Minor Morals* through the character of Aunt Belmour: "a taste for the culture of flowers, or for copying the beauties our situation may not admit us to raise ourselves to, is particularly adapted to women; is soothing to their minds, and refines their taste, while it prevents them from suffering from that want of motive to go into the air, and from yielding to that torpid ignorance which hurts alike the body and the mind" (1:42).

58. See Judith Pascoe, "Female Botanists and the Poetry of Charlotte Smith," in *Re-Visioning Romanticism*, pp. 200-201, and Ann B. Shteir, *Cultivating Women, Cultivating Science* (Baltimore: Johns Hopkins Univ. Press, 1996), pp. 27-32. Further references are cited parenthetically in the text.

59. *An Introduction to Botany, in a Series of Familiar Letters* (London: 1796).

60. *The Confessions of Jean-Jacques Rousseau*, trans. J.M. Cohen (1953; reprint, New York: Penguin, 1979), p. 592. Mrs. Belmour calls Rousseau "an author, who, amid many fanciful and some erroneous strictures on the subject of education, has undoubtedly many excellent thoughts." She refers specifically to his thoughts on botanical drawing. *Minor Morals*, 1:40.

61. Katharine Rogers makes the distinction between the Romantic poets, who see in Nature an unfailing resource of strength and transcendence, and Smith, whose "repeated conclusion . . . is that Nature cannot cure human misery" (74).

CHRONOLOGY OF EVENTS IN THE LIFE AND TIMES OF CHARLOTTE SMITH

1749	Born on 4 May in London to Nicholas Turner and Anna Towers Turner
c. 1752	Anna Towers Turner dies; Charlotte and sister Catherine Anne and brother Nicholas Turner placed in care of maternal aunt
c. 1755	Attends school at Chichester
c. 1757	Attends school at Kensington
c. 1761	Living in London with father; introduced into society at the age of twelve
1764	Nicholas Turner marries a Miss Meriton of Chelsea
1765	On 23 February Charlotte marries Benjamin Smith, son of West Indies merchant and East India Company director; lives in London
1766, spring	First child born, a son
1767, spring	Benjamin Berney Smith born (christened in April); first son dies a few days later; Smiths move to Southgate, near London, into a house provided by Richard Smith
1768	William Towers Smith born
1769	Charlotte Mary Smith born 10 April (christened 2 May)
1770	Braithwaite Smith born
1771	Moves to Tottenham; sister Catherine Anne marries Michael Dorset, captain in army; Nicholas Hankey Smith born (christened 4 November)
1773	Charles Dyer Smith born
1774	Anna Augusta Smith born; Charlotte vindicates character of father-in-law against a libel; father-in-law increasingly employs Charlotte to write for him; Richard Smith purchases Lys Farm for son and daughter-in-law; in America, First Continental Congress meets
1775	Second Continental Congress; American Revolution begins
1776	Lucy Elenore Smith born; Richard Smith dies, leaving a problematic will that results in decades of legal litigation and financial suffering; Benjamin Smith appointed overseer of poor; American Declaration of Independence

1797	*Elegiac Sonnets,* volume 2; Napoleon arrives in Paris for French invasion of England; John Adams inaugurated president of United States; Edmund Burke dies
1798	*Minor Morals; The Young Philosopher;* initial settlement of Richard Smith's will relieves Smith of burden of wrangling with lawyers; French forces land in Ireland but do not invade; Irish rebellion
1799	*What Is She? Letters of a Solitary Wanderer* (vols. 4-5, 1802)
1801	Charles Dyer Smith dies in Barbados of yellow fever; widowed daughter, Lucy Elenore, comes to live with Smith, bringing her two children and pregnant with a third
1802	Thomas Jefferson inaugurated president of the United States
1804	*Conversations Introducing Poetry;* Napoleon crowned emperor
1806	*History of England, from the Earliest Records to the Peace of Amiens;* Benjamin Smith dies (in spring); 28 October Charlotte Smith dies
1807	*Beachy Head, with Other Poems; The Natural History of Birds, intended Chiefly for Young Persons*
1813	Richard Smith's will finally resolved

[handwritten annotation: →1798 — year of LB]

NOTE ON THE TEXT

The copy-text for this edition is the first edition, published in London in 1798 by T. Cadell Jr. and W. Davies. It seems to have been the practice of Charlotte Smith to send the advance sheets that she received from her London printer to her publisher in Dublin, John Rice. She did so with *The Old Manor House;* her correspondence (and the existence of a 1798 Dublin edition of *The Young Philosopher*) suggests that the practice was usual with her. I have collated this text with the Dublin edition and noted the significant differences in the list of variants, though whether these represent Smith's corrections or printers' revisions, misreadings, or mistakes is not clear. I have silently corrected obvious printer's errors, reduced ligatures in English words to one letter, and regularized the use of double and single quotation marks. Otherwise, all accidentals (including accent marks in foreign language passages) follow the first edition.

The Young Philosopher

VOLUME 1

Preface

It is, I believe, in a work written by Mrs. Sarah Fielding, and now out of print, called "*The Art of Tormenting*," that I have read the following fable:

"A society of animals were once disputing on various modes of suffering, and of death; many offered their opinions, but it was at length agreed that the sheep, as the most frequent victim, could give the best account of the agonies inflicted by the teeth and claws of beasts of prey."[1]

If a Writer can best describe who has suffered, I believe that all the evils arising from oppression, from fraud and chicane, I am above almost any person qualified to delineate.[2]

I am not so sure that I have made a just picture of a man so calm, as to be injured by fraud and offended by folly, and who shall yet preserve his equality of temper. I suspect that in many instances my Hero forgets his pretensions, and has no claim to the character of a Philosopher; that, however, will prove only that the title of my book is a misnomer, the book itself will be no worse.

My original plan differed materially from that I have executed; why I changed it is not now material; but as I once before heard the charge of *plagiarism* (which however is sometimes passed over to a wonderful degree by the Critics) and as a general accusation of that sort is perhaps sometimes made, because it saves more discriminating criticism, I may just mention, that the incident of the confinement in a mad house of one of my characters was designed before I saw the fragment of "The Wrongs of Woman," by a Writer whose talents I greatly honoured, and whose untimely death I deeply regret; from her I should not blush to borrow, and if I had done so I would have acknowledged it.[3]

I had intended to add a few words on the taste that seems at present to prevail in regard to works of this kind, and of my doubts whether a Novel representing only scenes of modern life and *possible* events may not be accounted of the old school, and create less interest than the wild, the terrible, and the supernatural; but as I have for some time meditated a more considerable examination of the subject than can be included in a Preface,[4] I will now content myself with declaring against the injustice of inferences, frequently drawn by the Reader, in regard to the Author of such books as these; I mean their appropriating to him or her as individuals, sentiments and opinions given to any of the characters intended to be described as amiable. There may be many traits, many ideas, and even many prejudices, which may be necessary to support or render these characters natural, that are by no means those of the composer of the book; I declare therefore against the conclusion, that *I* think either like Glenmorris or Armitage, or any other of my personages.

To those who are of opinion that some moral is necessary to a Novel,[5] I may say, that my intention in this has been to expose the ill consequences of detraction; to shew the sad effects of parental resentment, and the triumph of fortitude in the daughter, while too acute sensibility, too hastily indulged, is the source of much unhappiness to the mother. But as no distresses can be created without such men, as in the present state of society stand in place of the giants, and necromancers,[6] and ogers of ancient romance, men whose profession empowers them to perpetrate, and whose inclination generally prompts them to the perpetration of wickedness, I have made these drawings a *little* like people of that sort whom I *have seen*, certain that nothing I could *imagine* would be so correct, when legal collusion and professional oppression were to be represented. If altogether the story is not uninteresting, and is relieved with such ornaments as a very slight knowledge of natural history, and a minor talent for short pieces of poetry, have enabled me to give it, I trust this latest attempt, and one that has not cost me the *least* pains among my various labours, will not be less favourably received than the greater part of those which have preceded it.

CHARLOTTE SMITH
London, June 6th, 1798.

CHAP. I.

Of moving accidents by flood or field.[7]

A few years have passed, since it happened that Dr. Winslow, a dignified clergyman, who, besides an affluent private fortune, possessed very considerable church preferment, together with his wife, the co-heiress of a rich citizen, their only son, now in his twentieth year, and Mrs. Winslow's niece, Miss Goldthorp, the only daughter of a deceased banker, and possessing above fifty thousand pounds, were induced to pass part of the autumn at a public place of great resort, about sixty miles from London.[8] Mrs. Winslow was extremely *nervous*, and nothing was so good for that complaint as sea air; the Doctor indeed had three excellent houses, in three different counties, but they all happened to be very far inland, and the present state of his lady's nerves demanded the benefit of marine breezes.

Her nerves had received some benefit after a residence of near a month on the coast. It was not certain whether this desirable end had been obtained by gentle airings on the salubrious hills around her present residence, or by another specific, occasionally applied to by ladies of a certain age in such cases, that of passing more than half the night at cards. Something was probably due to the latter cause, as Mrs. Winslow had been unusually successful; she had besides augmented her acquaintance among people of fashion, which was always an object of her ambition—having added five titled friends to her visiting list for the ensuing winter.

His wife now being in a state to bear the journey, the Doctor ventured to propose her accompanying him on a visit he had long meditated, and for which he had received a recent and very pressing invitation. Mrs. Winslow, who was occasionally all sweetness, especially when desired to do any thing she did not dislike, assented readily;— Young Winslow had just purchased a pair of very fine horses of a man of fashion (whose stable-keeper had hinted, in no very respectful terms, the necessity of his selling them) and their present master was glad of this opportunity "to try their bottom."[9]—It was settled that he should conduct his fair cousin in his curricle, while the Doctor and Mrs. Winslow, with her own maid on a seat before, were to proceed in a postchaise.[10] The great object of Mrs. Winslow's life had been to be accounted a woman of most elegant taste, and the word elegant was incessantly uttered on all the opinions she held, and in all the decisions she gave.—It would now have been much more *elegant* to have had four horses, an equipage with which they generally moved when at any of the Doctor's livings, where he had grass and corn of his own; but as he never lost sight of economy, he had now prudently contented himself with a pair; and though he would not have been sorry to have had them on the present occasion, to make an handsome figure at the house of his old friend, he peevishly resisted his wife's remonstrances, who thought post-horses would be more *elegant*; and he asserted, that no body but herself would say such a thing—He only desired, that as their journey was to be four and twenty miles, and the days were so much shortened, she would be ready to set out before noon.

To make any exertion, however, was quite out of her way; had she risen an hour before her time, she would have been nervous the whole day. Instead of noon, therefore, it was near two o'clock before Mrs. Dibbins, her woman, who was as nervous and as *elegant* as her mistress, had collected and arranged all the elegancies they both thought it necessary to provide; then, just as they were preparing to depart, the lady's amiable new friends, Lady Stockbury, and her most elegant daughter Lady Theresa, arrived to pay her a morning visit; they had a great deal to tell her of an elopement in high life, of which they had learned the particulars, and to relate all that passed the preceding evening at an assembly they were at, where several persons of the highest rank were collected. Mrs. Winslow delighted to listen to such conversation, which to relate at the place she was going to would give her the air of frequenting the most *elegant* society, quite forgot that the morning was wearing away, and that the poor Doctor was in one of his most restless fits of fretting, waiting for her in another room.

The clock had told three some time before they departed; and they had advanced two or three miles on their road before the Doctor had vented his pshaws, and his pooh poohs—he then gradually murmured himself to rest, and fell asleep in reflecting, that though they should dine on the road, instead of reaching the house of his reverend friend, yet that they should arrive to an excellent supper, and that the next day being the first of October, he should have the pleasure of a day's pheasant shooting, for which the part of the country they were going to was famous, and the worthy divine, though too corpulent for the more fatiguing field sports, could still knock down a pheasant.[11] The young people had gone on before, and young Winslow had the precaution to bespeak at the inn, where they were under the necessity of stopping, the best dinner that could in such a place be provided; but when after half an hour's waiting it appeared, the cutlets were tough, and the fowls badly dressed; the tart was not eatable, and the wine not drinkable.—Again the Doctor lamented his unfortunate destiny as pathetically as if a bad dinner had been one of the insupportable misfortunes of life; and again his fretting occasioned its usual effect of making Mrs. Winslow "*excessive nervous*."—At length they once more sat forth, though it was already late, considering that they had eleven miles to travel over downs, and through a country they none of them were acquainted with. The people of the inn however assured them, it was impossible they could miss the way—They were to keep strait up over Mayham Down, till they got to Watchet's Corner, and then turn to the right over Ringsted Brow, till they came to the Dip, and then they were to turn again to the right, and then they would see a direction post————and then————

The Dean, impatient to be gone, and testy still on account of his bad dinner, would not stay to have these directions repeated, but peevishly bade his son, who had undertaken to lead the way, go on————.

The young man, glad to get away from his father's murmurs, hastened to obey;

the curricle was presently out of sight—for the new horses went very well, and their master fell into an eulogium on them, which lasted till suddenly the road became so bad that they could keep their admirable pace no longer; he then stopped, and began to recollect what had been told him of the way—and after a short debate persuaded himself he was right.—His cousin, to whom he appealed, answered indolently, that she never attended to the directions—"but never mind," added she, "go on. We shall get to the top of this rising ground presently, and then we shall see our way, and easily discover the high road to the town."

The horses again were urged to exertion, but the hill seemed to become higher the more they advanced, and to stretch in mountainous elevation above them, in proportion as they attempted to reach its summit; partial fogs hung about its sides, and they could no longer discern the country behind them toward the sea, or could they hear or see the chaise that was following them. Mr. Winslow now called a short council with his groom, whom he ordered to ride forward, to see if he could discover a more beaten road or a direction post. He did not return so soon as his master expected, who impatiently drove on in despite of the ruts, and the uncertainty whither the road led. There was not indeed much time to hesitate; for besides the gathering shades of night, heavy black clouds were accumulated in the south-west, and volumes of mist surrounded the travellers, and then for a moment dispersed, discovering to them an extensive vale, on the brink of which they seemed to be wandering; then the fog so entirely obscured it, that all before them appeared like an ocean of vapour, and their way again became so doubtful that Winslow acknowledged it was necessary to stop.

In the mean time the carriage behind had proceeded more slowly, yet not doubting but that they were right. They had by chance taken nearly the same road, but were not advanced so far by a mile, when the Doctor, who had given himself and his hearers a little respite, again began to deplore his ill fortune—"You see," cried he, "it is just as I told you; I knew how it would be!—Such short days; to set out so late was madness; absolutely madness." Before Mrs. Winslow had time to reply, Jerry stopped, and said, "Sir, if you please, this road is very baddish for my chai.—There's no quarter; one mid as well drive on the ridge of an house——and its a most dark—I doubt if we be right."[12]

"Had you not better enquire, Jerry?" said the lady. "Do, good Jeremy, stop at some house, and enquire." "Enquire!" exclaimed the Doctor; "enquire at an house! Why, where do you think, Mrs. Winslow, he will find one? But that's always your way, madam—you always fancy yourself on a turnpike road about London—but let what will happen, you may thank yourself—I never went out with you in my life but my patience was worn down with waiting—and the tiresome custom you have got of never being ready is always occasioning some accident; I remember enough of them; yet you do just the same, as if they had never happened.—Don't you recollect how we were robbed on the Walthamstow road, and lost fifteen guineas[13] between us, and two gold watches worth seventy more, because you would stay for another rubber at Doctor Twaddie's? and had not you warning enough when we were overturned once between Guildford and Godalming, because it was dark? and don't you remember that in the deep snow you——?"[14] "O my God!" exclaimed the lady—"Dr. Winslow! is it not cruel, when you see the nervous way I am in? Oh! pray, instead of all this, tell Jerry

[margin, handwritten]] night-fall

— Storm —

which way he is to go." "I tell him! how should I tell him? There's my son too, he must needs drive on to leave us here to have our necks broke!"

A violent shriek from the lady put an end to this useless contest for the present; her *nervousness* now amounted to a fit, and while Mrs. Dibbins her woman chafed her hands, held a smelling bottle to her nose, and used such other remedies as she was provided with, the Doctor, whose apprehensions were become very serious, got out of the chaise, and directing his servant on horseback to dismount and follow him, they went forward in the hope of discovering a better way. The Doctor was fat and asthmatic, and the hill was steep; his fears made it seem of an Alpine height; and as he looked towards the country he had crossed, to see how far it would be more advisable to return to the inn they had left (even though he should sup as badly as he had dined) he had the additional mortification of seeing a very heavy storm approaching; the thunder already muttered at a distance; large drops of rain fell, and gusts of wind blew with such violence, that after having wasted half an hour, and finding no road more promising than that they were in, he returned to take shelter against the storm in the chaise——very comfortless however was his situation. His wife was come out of her fit; but his renewed reproaches, real terror for her son and herself, and the lightning that flashed vividly around them, threw her back into the same situation.—She had never encountered any real difficulty.—The temporary inconvenience in which she found herself she had no fortitude to bear, and it was therefore rendered tenfold worse to those around her. The Doctor now proposed that the horses heads should be turned towards the inn they had quitted, and determined to try to regain it; but in that direction the tempest beat against them with such fury, that neither of them could be induced to stir, and the Doctor fumed and lamented himself in vain; Mrs. Winslow screamed and sobbed; and her maid deplored her own hard fate, her mistress's, and that of all her best clothes, which were tied on in a large caravan behind the chaise, and having "no *ile* skin o' top of them, would," she said, "be entirely spoiled."[15] The Doctor, had he been a layman, would probably have sent her and her caravan to the devil, with the many exclamations and apostrophes usual on such occasions; but as he never suffered his choler to betray him into any expressions derogatory to the dignity of his order, he contented himself with muttering against the folly of those who travelled with foolish fid fad[16] women, called himself the most unfortunate man in the world, and pronounced it for a certainty, that they were to stay on the Downs all night, if indeed the lightning did not destroy them all before morning.

Here, however, they staid a considerable time without feeling any other inconvenience than from the rain (which came down in torrents) and the fits of poor Mrs. Winslow, who when she saw the lightning flash, or heard the Doctor complain, shrieked a-new, and relapsed. In the mean time, the curricle travellers were even worse off than these. Miss Goldthorp, who affected great strength of mind, and to despise all feminine fear as puerile and even vulgar, was not entirely free from terror when she found herself exposed in such a situation to the double-danger of the storm and the restiveness of the horses, young, pampered, hardly broken, which, though jaded with their journey, shewed symptoms of impatience and fear that it was easy to see alarmed their driver, who knew not how to manage them, or whither to direct them with safety. The rain, driving in cataracts, would have deprived Winslow of the power of distinguishing his way, even if in the intervals of the lightning the sky had been less obscured. His groom was a lad without knowledge or presence of mind, and Winslow found himself called upon to act for the safety of others, while his fears for his personal security (a matter to which he was in habits of giving very great attention) almost annihilated the slender faculties he at any time possessed.

Self-preservation, which has been called the first law of nature,[17] began to operate very forcibly on his mind, and he proposed to his cousin, that the horses should be taken off, as relieving them at least from one danger, and that they should sit in the carriage till the tempest abated, and they could find their way on foot to some habitation, or till the postchaise, in which were his father and mother, should overtake them.

Fear had by this time rendered Miss Goldthorp passive; she had sometimes rallied her cousin on his effeminacy, and asserted that he was designed for a woman, but she now too sincerely participated in his apprehensions to ridicule it—Winslow, therefore, giving her the reins, which he conjured her to hold quietly and steadily, descended gently, and with his servant, who had dismounted, began to take the horses from the carriage. Hardly, however, had they unbuckled one part of the harness before a tremendous burst of thunder broke immediately above them—the foundation of the hill seemed shaken, and the lightning that rapidly followed was like a sheet of fire over their heads—the horses instantly reared, by the suddenness of the plunge disengaged themselves from the feeble efforts of Winslow and his servant to hold them, and ran with the curricle along the worn chalk way in which they had been standing.— The terrified young woman was instantly deprived of all sense and recollection; nor did she return to a consciousness of her existence till she found herself on a bank of turf, suffering extreme pain, and supported by a stranger, who seeing her restored to sense, spoke soothingly to her; and to leave nothing to conjecture at such a moment, told her, that he had been fortunate enough to stop the horses at the moment when another step would have plunged them and the carriage into a chalk pit; that finding them ungovernable he had, with the help of his servant, cut the traces, and taken her out, he was afraid a good deal hurt, but he hoped not dangerously, as she had not fallen, the curricle not having been overturned, though it had struck with violence against the sides of the hollow road.—He added, that he had sent his servant to his house, which was not far off, for assistance; that it would soon arrive; and he conjured her in the meantime to try to recal and compose her spirits, since he hoped she had no limbs broken, and that the danger was now at an end. The voice and expressions were such as, amid the terror, confusion, and pain, felt by the unfortunate traveller, prevented any fears of having fallen into peril as great as that she had escaped; she was, however, unable to speak; she sighed deeply, and seemed again sinking into temporary insensibility.

In some moments a man with a lanthorn, attended by two others, and a woman, appeared; the men bore a mattress on a sort of frame between them, on which the stranger, who acted as their master, assisted the woman to place Miss Goldthorp with great care; but the change of posture, however tenderly attempted, put her to extreme torture.—She shrieked on moving her arm, and that it was broken could not be

doubted.—This discovery, however, made her immediate removal only more necessary.—Again the stranger spoke to her, exhorting her to courage and patience, and she
was at length placed on the mattress, which two of the men lifted gently, and began to
descend the hill, while the woman walked on one side, attentive to the ease of the poor
sufferer, and the humane stranger on the other. Their progress however was slow, for
the descent was very steep, and the rain, which still fell, though the thunder had rolled
away to a distance, made the short turf on which they sometimes trod, or the chalky
road they followed at another, so slippery, that it was not without great care they
avoided falling with their suffering burthen.—At last they reached an house at the
foot of the hill, but to whom it belonged, or what was the condition of life of its
inhabitants, Miss Goldthorp was then in no state to remark.—She was attended to a
chamber, and put to bed by several women, some of whom were young, and seemed
deeply affected at her situation.—She recovered just enough recollection to ask what
was become of her cousin? and whether he was killed? The stranger, whom she had
first seen, informed of this question, came to her bed-side, and entreated her to give
him what intelligence she could relative to the person for whom she expressed apprehension.—He said, that when he met her, she was alone in the curricle, and that he
had neither seen or heard any other person, while he remained on the spot where he
snatched her from the carriage.

A few faltering words from the poor sufferer served to inform her friendly protector of what he so generously desired to know, and he hastened away with his assistants to the scene he had left. In the mean time a surgeon arrived from the neighbouring
town; the arm of the patient was set, and one of the younger ladies, whose compassionate attention was the most sedulously exerted, sat by her.—She was already sunk
into a more quiet state than the operator had expected, when her repose was likely to
be interrupted by the arrival of the rest of the party—for by this time Doctor and Mrs.
Winslow, and their son, had been respectively relieved from their perilous wanderings, and brought to the same hospitable house by the same active humanity as had
rescued the unfortunate young lady from death. The Doctor, almost as nervous as his
wife, was so eager to express his thanks, that there was something almost abject in his
gratitude—he repeated the same thing twenty times in a breath, then habitually began
to complain of Mrs. Winslow as the cause of his misfortune, while the poor woman,
weeping and half senseless, exclaimed, "Oh Doctor, pray let us only be thankful to
this gentleman, and to the great Director of Events, who has given him an opportunity of shewing such exquisite benevolence."—"I am, madam, I am duly thankful to
both; and I hope, let me add, it will serve as a warning to you, never to let that
procrastinating way that you have got put us into such a predicament again—Your
niece, you see, has broken her arm; she may die for what you know, and my son has
had his new curricle torn to pieces, and one of his horses, if not both, entirely ruined;
and all this owing to what? because you never are ready—never—never,—and whatever comes of this unfortunate day, nobody but you will be to blame."—Mrs. Dibbins
now interposed.—One of the females of the family entered to say, the bed prepared
for Mrs. Winslow was ready.—She was led away in a fit of extreme nervousness, and
one of the young ladies of the house brought her a composing cordial, ordered for her

by the medical man attending, who endeavored to quiet her alarms for her niece.—
She at length became more calm, and looked round the room with complacency,
observing, that she had never seen any place fitted up "in *the cottage style" half so
elegant*.[18]

CHAP. II.

The determination of mind, in consequence of which a child
contracts some of his earliest propensities, which call out his
curiosity, industry, and ambition, or, on the other hand, leave
him unobserving, indolent, and phlegmatic, is produced by
circumstances so minute and subtle, as in few instances to have
been made the subject of history.[19]

[handwritten marginalia: development of mind]

Fear and fatigue had not so entirely subdued the spirits of Doctor Winslow, as to
prevent his enquiring of the servant who attended him to his room, the name and
condition of the family from which he had received so hospitable a reception, as well
as that of the young man who had rescued his niece from the imminent peril she had
been in; and his sense of the obligation seemed to be immeasurably enlarged, when he
learned that the house he was in had been the residence of Colonel Delmont, only
brother of the late Earl of Castledanes. The Colonel died in the West Indies, and the
present master of the house was his youngest son, Mr. Delmont, who was a student at
Oxford, but since the death of his father had resided almost entirely at this place,
which was called Upwood with his two sisters and an elderly female relation, reputed
to be very rich, who had the care of the young ladies.

[handwritten marginalia: Delmont]

The Doctor descended the next morning, full fraught with gratitude towards
his hosts, and with admiration of themselves and their house, which he declared to be
the most beautiful, and at the same time the most singular, place he had ever seen.

Mrs. Winslow joined him in thanks and praises; she had never seen such *amiable* people, never beheld so *elegant* a place! If she had to regret the painful accident
that had befallen her dear Martha (Miss Goldthorp) she, on the other hand, felt all the
providential good fortune of having made so interesting an acquaintance, which she
hoped the agreeable and worthy family would permit her the honour of cultivating.

The unfortunate Mr. Winslow heard all this without the power to join in it.—
The loss of his curricle and his horses, one of which was entirely spoiled, and the other
injured so much as not to be worth ten pounds, was a misfortune which, as he was no
philosopher, took from him all inclination to talk, and still more to admit that the
acquisition of any acquaintance could make him amends for such a calamity.—He
stared with two light unmeaning eyes on George Delmont, who, though a man not
much older than himself, seemed to be a being of another species, and not more
unlike in person than in ideas.—Delmont was above the height of six feet, and apparently united the qualities of activity and strength in a very uncommon degree.—From

being constantly exposed to the air he was tanned so much that it was only by the glow on his cheek and the whiteness of his forehead that his complexion could be pronounced fair; and his brown hair was cut like that of the farmer or peasant,[20] while his dress was plain even to rusticity. Winslow, who was quite the "Master Marmoset"[21] of a very weak mother, shrunk before his new acquaintance with a sense of inferiority for which he could not account, for he was a great deal the best dressed man of the two; was pantalooned and waistcoated[22] after the very newest fashion, and except that he did not belong to nobility, of which advantage Delmont seemed to make no account, Winslow imagined that he was in most other respects superior, particularly in the material article of fortune.

Though they were both of the university, Delmont's studies, friends, and pleasures, were found to have been so different from those of Winslow, that they had no notions in common—and after a short trial of his young acquaintance, Delmont turned to the elder of his visitors, whose conversation might, he thought, be rather more interesting than that of Middleton Winslow, who indulged himself in continual lamentations over his recent distress.—"If Goldfinch," he said, "*did* recover, it would be impossible to match him as he was matched with Wildair—he did not believe, nay he was sure, there was not a third horse like them in all England."—The extreme concern which seemed to oppress him as he thus spoke surprised Delmont, who, though he had seen as much of the world as any man of his age, had, since he became his own master, lived very much out of it, and according to the dictates of his own reason rather than according to its fashions; he wondered, therefore, at the consequence young Winslow attached to trifles, which *he* thought unworthy of giving any deep concern to a man of sense; he loved a fine horse, and understood his properties, but had no idea of considering the loss of an animal in such a light as it appeared to Winslow, who spoke in terms, and with an appearance of despair, such as Delmont thought could reasonably be excited only by a great family misfortune, while of the injury sustained by Miss Goldthorp he seemed not to think at all.

Delmont was afraid he should soon be weary of his guests; but the generous hospitality of his nature induced him to shew them every mark of civility and attention—Young Winslow therefore proposing to visit his disarranged cavalry (to which he had by this time summoned every farrier, whose skill was celebrated, within ten miles) Delmont offered to walk with him, and Mrs. Crewkherne, the aunt of the family, was left alone with Dr. Winslow, Mrs. Winslow being in too *nervous* a state to remain with them, and affecting, or perhaps feeling, extreme solicitude about her "dear Martha."

The Doctor, whose curiosity had till this time been with difficulty restrained, now began to ask such questions as he thought would lead to the explanation of the family history.—It seemed strange that Mr. Delmont, who apparently was not of age, or not *more* than one and twenty, should be master of the house, and, though a younger brother, not studying for one of the learned professions, or destined to the army, like second branches of other noble families.

"Has Mr. Delmont left Oxford?" enquired the Doctor. "Yes, indeed, I am afraid so," replied Mrs. Crewkherne, "for he has kept only one term since we lost the Colonel.—It was his *family's* wish that he should study either for the church or the bar; but alas! my good Sir, I don't know how it is——times are strangely altered since my father, Dr. Crewkherne, and my brother, Mr. Serjeant Crewkherne, lived, and were honours to those professions. My father, the reverend Dr. Crewkherne," . . . . "He was a Dean, Madam, if I recollect right—A name so respectable cannot but have made an impression on me—He was Dean, I think, of—of—"

"Yes, Sir," replied the lady, who had a very commodious way of never hearing more than she chose—"Yes, he was a man of the most profound learning, and, I believe, makes no inconsiderable figure on the shelves of the studious in theological controversy to this day. He was, Sir, as undoubtedly you recollect, author of four volumes in folio, written, Sir, in Latin——and seven others of high celebrity, called —————"

Dr. Winslow, who had never heard of either in his life, was very willing to acquiesce silently in the praise of these stupendous monuments of controversial learn-ing—his own was by no means profound—and he was not half so deep in the Fathers[23] as in that sort of information which was to be acquired by other methods of study; by learning the value of the most capital livings in the gift of the Crown or the Chancellor, *who* were likely to succeed to them, and the ages of the actual incum-bents.[24] Unwilling, however, that Mrs. Crewkherne should suspect him of any such merely temporal studies, he bowed profoundly, muttered something that she was will-ing enough to suppose was praise of her venerable ancestor; and the lady proceeded—"*That* Dr. Crewkherne, then, Sir, was *my* father, of course one of the ancestors of this young man; and my brother was, as I observed, a serjeant at law—and had it pleased the Lord to have blessed this country with a longer loan of his great abilities, there can be no doubt but that he would have been a judge, or probably chancellor."[25]

Again Dr. Winslow bowed, and again Mrs. Crewkherne went on; but she seemed entirely to have forgotten that the enquiry of the Doctor was about George Delmont.—At length she brought the praise of the dignitary and the "learned brother" to a con-clusion, by remarking of their descendant, "That when he was a child he *seemed* to have a very great capacity—There was nothing, Sir," said she, "that struck the child, that he did not immediately ask questions about it—questions indeed very extraordi-nary for his age; and he would never be content without some answer that appeared to him reasonable.—I own I thought from this desire of enquiry that he would be a very learned and great man."

The Doctor was not quite sure that an acute enquirer was the likeliest to make a very great man, in Mrs. Crewkherne's acceptation of the word.—It was not an ob-jection, however, that he was disposed to make—and he continued to listen with great attention.—

"And for my own part," she went on to say; "for my own part, I had the highest hopes of him, till his mother, when he was about five years old, and ought to have gone to a grammar school, took it into her head to keep him at home and instruct him herself—Then I foresaw that he would be ruined—for instead of the usual way of bringing up children, she had the most unaccountable notions of her own!—and it was so uneasy to her to have her eldest son, now Captain Delmont, sent to a school to prepare him for Eton, that the late Lord Castledanes and her husband Colonel Delmont, who neither of them ever contradicted her, suffered her to keep this boy till he was eleven years old with her—and so, I know not by what sort of reading indeed, for I never was consulted, she made him a *Philosopher*, it seems, in baby clothes! and my little master had a set of opinions of his own, which he never was flogged out of, as he ought to have been, at Eton—So instead of now proceeding to make his fortune by following a profession, you see the consequence!—Here he is, at twenty-one, calling himself a farmer, and determined to be nothing more. This little bit of an estate—a paltry scrap of earth of not an hundred acres, is to confine his ambition, because, forsooth, he is a Philosopher!—Grant me patience!—to think, Dr. Winslow, that a young man who might be any thing should so throw himself away!—A farmer indeed! which any of our clowns can be!—He!—a young man of his family, of his connections, who might be any thing—but indeed my good Sir, if it were not that I well know every one predestined to their lot, and that all is ordered for the best, I should have many an hour of concern for this family—They are to be sure very unfortunate people."

She then related (repeating that she *always* foresaw it) that the late Lord Castledanes had married, at an early period of his life, a lady of immense fortune, by whom he had no children, and who becoming decidedly a lunatic, was, ten years after her marriage with him, confined as such at a remote seat of his, under the care of proper people, superintended by one of her own relations.—"The children of his brother," said Mrs. Crewkherne, "were of course considered as his heirs, and he seemed to have as much affection for them as if they had been his own, and they were educated at his expence.—But we are blind mortals, Dr. Winslow, very blind mortals!—Mrs. Delmont, who with her children lived more at Lord Castledane's house than at her own, had two sisters, the daughters of her father, a gay extravagant man, by his second wife—these girls became orphans about five years ago—the eldest was seventeen, and the other two years younger—both beauties forsooth!—and they had been brought up in all sorts of idle stuff that is called accomplishments, and danced and sung much too well for modest women—These young Misses then were taken into the care of Mrs. Delmont, and lived as she did, very much at the house of my nephew, the late lord Castledanes.—Nobody was ever supposed to know any thing so well as Mrs. Delmont, and so nobody objected to these girls making a part of the family—They were to teach the Delmont girls, and supply the places of masters when they were in the country—I was afraid from the very beginning that no good would come of it—and to be sure it has turned out so as to bring to an end all the prospects that were before supposed certain; for when Lady Castledanes was dead, my Lord, who had been very partial to Mrs. Delmont, his brother's wife, and regretted her extremely, took it into his head to marry the eldest of those two girls, though she was young enough to be his daughter.—You may suppose, good Sir, that Colonel Delmont was not very well pleased to see himself deprived as it were of his birth-right in this manner—All the family resented it indeed as they ought, except this ill advised strange young man, who being a philosopher by profession, took upon him to defend his uncle's conduct, and to discover that he was well justified in pleasing himself—Fine doctrine indeed!—He chose, in despite of his father's orders, to reconcile himself to

Mrs. Crewkherne believes in predestination.

Lord Castledanes before he died, and with all his philosophy, perhaps, thought to have made some advantage of it; but if he did he was mistaken; for my Lord made no alteration in his will; only left a relation of his young wife's guardian to his children instead of his own family—and here's this young man, his brother Captain Delmont, and two sisters, very slenderly provided for."

"I am grieved, sincerely grieved indeed, to hear it," cried Dr. Winslow (whose respect and admiration towards his young host was now considerably abated)—"But, dear Madam, allow me to observe, that all this makes the measure I took the liberty of hinting at only the more requisite.—I would by all means in the world advise that your young kinsman forthwith proceeds to qualify himself for the church—he must have great patronage—young men of family never fail to rise—he has talents too, doubtless, which it is a thousand pities have not been properly directed—but, no doubt, all that may be recovered—he may yet be an ornament to the profession—and he may emulate the sweet savour left, Madam, by your highly respectable and truly orthodox ancestor of happy memory."

This was touching a string to which the feelings of Mrs. Crewkherne strongly vibrated—her family pride, particularly that which she felt from being the daughter of Dr. Crewkherne, who had wrote ten folio volumes of theological controversy, was one of the few sensations left her, from which she sometimes derived pleasure—her sharp face relaxed into something like a smile; yet soon screwing it up to its former asperity, she cried, "Ah! Doctor! Doctor! all that might very possibly be, if this ill fated, and, as I said before, ill advised youth, was not guided absolutely by others—but unfortunately he has connected himself with those, of whom it is not uncharitable to say, Better had it been for them they had never been born."[26]——"Indeed!—Alas! dear Madam, how unfortunate!—But pray give me leave to ask, Who are these? and how have they obtained this unfortunate influence?"

"One," replied Mrs. Crewkherne, "is, I am afraid, but too well known, Doctor—the poor wretch's name is Armitage—a person whom I understand writes books—very bad books, I am afraid, from what some good friends of mine, and very good judges too, have told me—a person, Sir, who affirms, that by works alone we are safe,[27] and—but I cannot sully my lips with his detestable maxims, which, however, are too many of them adapted to the shallow understandings of modern days—for to be sure, Doctor, you and I are fallen upon evil times!—A strange spirit is got about, and methinks the power of the wicked one is, for the sins of this generation, suffered to predominate.—My ever venerable and truly respectable father, the reverend Doctor Josiah Crewkherne, was accustomed to say, that the people in his time had not the true grace among them: and that their being suffered to read pamphlets and newspapers was a bad thing; for that they, being *ordained* only to work, and to live by the sweat of their brows, it was not fitting and right for them to look at matters above their sphere, and to comment on laws and on government. I remember it was a favourite maxim of his, and highly I honoured him, who lately repeated it, 'the people have nothing to do with the laws but to obey them'[28]—and a very bad symptom it is, as my most venerable father used to say, when any debates and questions are impertinently stated thereon.—Who then, Doctor, can help speaking with indignation of such men

Old lady: people should keep to their spheres

as this Armitage, who would dissolve all the chains of due subordination and obedience, and set the mechanic and the labourer a thinking when they ought to be
working for their superiors; and who avail themselves of the foolish inexperience of
wrong-headed youth, to teach them not to follow in the paths that have led up their
progenitors to honours, and titles, and preferments, and fortune, but to find something they call reasons against the most eligible objects of human pursuit—such a
man, Doctor Winslow, ought to be hunted out of society; yet such is the perversion of
understanding among all ranks, that they tell me this man is almost adored by the half
savage multitude—I do not wonder at *that*—we all know how a little drink, or a little
pretence of doing them good, wins their *sordid* souls; but that men of a *family* such as
ours should be misled by him, or by any such men. Oh! Doctor, Doctor! it must be
owned that such a dereliction of family principle, of the regard due to family rank, to
family principle! I protest I lose myself in indignation when I think of it—and what
with the false notions imbibed from his education, and what with the ascendancy this
man has got over him, he is in my opinion a cast away, a lost man!"

"Come, come, let us hope not," cried the Doctor. "Dear Madam, your young
kinsman cannot possibly fail to pay due deference to wisdom like your's!"—The worthy Doctor, who had always been a prosperous man, had found that two modes of
proceeding had greatly promoted his success in the world—abject flattery, and pretence of great attachment to whoever could promote his interest; with the appearance
of great orthodoxy and strictness: By these he had contrived to marry a woman of
fortune while he was only a curate at eighty pounds a year; and by these, aided by that
fortune, he was now possessed of benefices and emoluments which made him look up
to lawn sleeves[29] as of no very distant or difficult attainment.

Though he was so peevish in his own family, that he would not bear the slightest contradiction, he took peculiar pleasure in offering his advice to others, notwithstanding it was sometimes heard with indifference, sometimes with resentment, and
hardly ever followed. He was, however, so little discouraged by the frequent failure of
success, that his zeal for enlightning his neighbours on their conduct, seemed to increase
in proportion as its inefficacy was evident; and he now, by the consent and even exhor-
tation of Mrs. Crewkherne, set about directing the future conduct of George Delmont.

Mrs. Winslow, in the meantime, had been listening to the lamentations of her
son, and had engaged to obtain his father's permission to his going immediately to
London. He had convinced his mother he ought to do so, by observing, that he could
be of no use to his cousin; and that if he had any chance of matching Wildair, it would
be now, when a great many gentlemen returned to town after their summer tours, and
sold their horses; he thought too he could pick up a curricle almost as neat as his
own—and these reasons were sufficient with his mother; indeed, he seldom produced
any that were not. The Doctor, however, was more difficult to convince, and pshaw'd
and pooh'd for some time before he could agree to his son's departure. Quick-sighted
in every thing else, the worthy divine was totally blind to the feebleness of his son's
mind. As to his person, the folly of his father exceeded even that of his mother, and
they both imagined that he was the epitome of elegance and beauty. The Doctor,
however, considered that his presence now was not necessary to the promotion of

Winslow a "good son" vs Delmont, who disregards
family "duties"

their design on Miss Goldthorp—and he was at length induced to consent to his absence. His mother furnished him with all the money she could command; and he set forward to repair the loss he lamented, leaving his father delighted even with his failings, and thanking heaven that he had given him so proper an education, and that he was not likely ever to commit such errors as had been by Mrs. Crewkherne imputed to George Delmont.

CHAP. III.

Concourse, and noise, and toil he ever fled,
Nor cared to mingle in the clamorous fray
Of squabbling imps; but to the forest sped,
Or roam'd at large the lonely mountain head;
Or where the maze of some bewilder'd stream
To deep untrodden groves his footsteps led,
There would he wander wild.[30]

Not to leave the picture to be finished by the hard and cold pencil of Mrs. Crewkherne, George Delmont ought to be represented such as he was at Eton, where his uncle, Lord Castledanes, had placed, at an early age, both his nephews, whom he looked upon as his heirs.

Always taught from his first recollection to consider himself as such, Adolphus, the eldest of these boys, had never felt a wish that he did not imagine he had a right to gratify. During the early part of his life, the excellent sense of his mother had not been able to counteract the impressions given him, as well by his uncle, who was extremely fond of him, as by his tutor, who attended him to Eton, and the servants and dependants, who seldom fail to make their court to the heir of a noble house. The masters of a great school are apt to shew that pupils connected with title and fortune have a more than ordinary share of their regard; yet among boys of the same age there is always established a certain degree of equality, and to this Adolphus Delmont submitted with reluctance. As he was placed with only his brother, in a private house, attended by a servant, and under the immediate direction of a tutor, who had a large stipend for his trouble, he by no means liked to be confounded in the mass of those so well described by Gray, "as dirty boys playing at cricket"[31]—He was mortified at the little consideration shewn him by his inferiors; the continual consciousness of his rank, to which they paid no manner of respect, kept him aloof from them; and his superiors he liked still less, because they seemed to demand from him the deference he was refused by others——Thus driven to the society of his tutor, whose favourite he was, he obtained the character of a sullen cold-blooded fellow, and a sap,[32] though his passing much of his time, when out of school, with Mr. Jeans, his preceptor, had in reality nothing to do with any attention to books, with which he fatigued himself as little as possible.

Nothing could be more unlike him than his brother George—He had never been made of so much consequence by the people about him; and his mother, though more fondly attached to him than she had ever suffered to appear, had carefully guarded against his falling into the same error as his brother, and had taught him that the feelings of others were to be consulted as well as his own; he had never, therefore, supposed that the whole world ought to pause in silent concern if his illustrious head ached, and every one about him obey his caprice and deprecate his ill-humour. George was sometimes silent without being grave or sullen—careless of the opinion of those he did not like, and scorning to use the least dissimulation, even when he felt himself wrong, to palliate his errors—Often indolent and neglectful, he had at other times fits of study, from which, however, it was not difficult for his friends to rouse him, and engage him in those violent exercises, in which, from the strength and agility of his frame, he particularly excelled.—He was frequently involved in scrapes for harmless frolics and trespasses out of bounds; but from the wildest excesses which the indulgence of these animal spirits led him into, he was recalled by a single word from any one he loved, though the harsh voice of authority wantonly exerted never failed to give something like obstinacy to his resistance, His intelligent countenance, and the acquisition of general information, above what is usually collected at his age, were evidences that his abilities were uncommon; yet such was his indolence, or dislike to the rules with which he was to begin his studies at school, that he fell into continual disgrace with the masters, and was left at the bottom of his class, while many a heavy lad, without the fiftieth part of his talents, looked down upon him with scorn. These violations of rules were frequent, and punishment had no effect to reclaim him; yet, unlike other boys, his eccentricities did not consist of parties on horseback to dine at a tavern, or sailing schemes on the water: he was sometimes indeed concerned in these frolics, but oftener sat out alone on a ramble he knew not whither, and yielding to the pleasure of temporary liberty, quite forgot the restraint imposed upon him, and threw himself down under a tree with some favourite book, then fell into a reverie as he listened to the wind among the branches, or the dashing of the water against the banks, where, among the reeds and willows crowding over the Thames, he not unfrequently delighted to conceal himself from the mirth of his comrades, that gave him no pleasure, and from that needless rigour of enquiry which he felt to be an intolerable persecution. He never could understand that half the restraints imposed upon him did not originate rather in the wantonness of tyranny, that induces men to exercise power merely because they have it, than because it was really their duty to check the eccentricities of the boys whose education they undertook; and therefore, when Mr. Jeans, his private tutor, hunted him with acrimonious reproach from his beloved solitudes, and attempted to compel him to pass hours, which he considered as his own, in listening to uninteresting lectures, or parading details of his learning, George seldom attended with patience and obedience; yet while he was most eagerly bent to indulge himself in one of his favourite rambles, a single word from his brother, whom he loved, though they so little resembled each other; any thing like a reason why he should not indulge himself, from one of the few school friends to whom he was attached, were at any time sufficient to turn him from his purpose; and other accidents often brought him home early from his intended rambles.

The allowance made by their uncle to both the brothers for pocket money was *turns into vagrants: W—ian*

very liberal; it was well known to be so, and known also that George Delmont could never refuse a request, even when he had no regard, or hardly any acquaintance with the boy who made it. These borrowers very rarely remembered their promises of repayment, and George, who was very careless about money, never could prevail upon himself to remind them of it. Thus, when he had shaken off the officious Mr. Jeans, and was springing forth on one of those rambles which were his principal enjoyment, *beggars* he was often stopped on the way by some piteous story of hunger, of houseless poverty, of disasters from fire or flood, from sickness or shipwreck—a wounded soldier shewed him his mutilated limb—a sightless sailor recounted how he had lost his eyes by lightning from heaven, or by an explosion of powder—an old man, bent to the earth by years or calamity, related that he had been driven from his home by the magistrates or officers, who, when the son who used to support him had been forced to go for a soldier, would compel the decrepid father to return to a remote parish, whither his feeble limbs refused to convey him—a woman pale and emaciated presented herself, one infant hung on her breast, two others following her; she was the widow of an Irish soldier, he was dead in the West Indies; she was refused relief in any parish here; she was begging her way to Ireland.[33]—Such, and an infinite number of other objects, in all the sad "variety of wretchedness,"[34] were before the eyes of George Delmont whithersoever he turned—He had not learned, he would never listen to the cold and cruel policy that Mr. Jeans endeavoured most sedulously to inculcate—He would not believe that all these were impostors, as Jeans declared them to be; he would hardly allow that any of them ever deceived him, while his heart swelled with indignation against those whom these real or apparent sufferers described as having been the cause of their wretchedness, and against the systems through which only they could be inflicted. From detestation against individuals, such as justices and overseers, he began to reflect on the laws that put it in their power thus to drive forth to nakedness and famine the wretched beings they were empowered to protect; and he was led to enquire if the complicated misery he every day saw (a very very small part of so wide an evil) could be the fruits of the very best laws that could be framed in a state of society said to be the most perfect among what are called the civilized nations of the world. Whenever any of these unhappy wanderers presented themselves in his walks, he forgot every project he had formed for the amusement of the day; he lost every desire but to relieve a fellow creature in distress, and as, from his thoughtless liberality to his school fellows, he was not unfrequently without a shilling, in such an evil hour he took the claimant on his pity to his dame's, and solicited his brother, or even Mr. Jeans himself, to supply him with the means of relieving the poor object.—Adolphus, sometimes influenced by the pride of giving, at others too indolent to resist importunity, generally gave him what he asked; but Mr. Jeans never wanted an excuse for denial, and instead of assisting the benevolent purpose of his pupil, teased him with remonstrance, or drove him away with reproof, while Mrs. Kempthwaite, the notable gentlewoman of the house, never failed, if she heard the debate, to become a party in it. Her reasons, however, for disliking paupers of every description were entirely on the surface; "she hated them," she said, "for they were nasty dirty creatures; the fellows and wenches were all thieves; she once lost a salt spoon by one of them whom Master

George thought proper to bring to her door for cold victuals; it was true, indeed, he had bought her four very handsome spoons of the same sort, or perhaps a little heavier, but that, though it was very pretty of him, was nothing to the purpose; she could not away with having such tramps lurking round her door for ever; 'twas a disgrace to the house, and she hoped, if Master George would not think better of it, that Mr. Jeans would speak to my Lord."

Her interest, however, with Mr. Jeans was in the mean time powerful enough to engage him to impede as much as he could this inconvenient philanthropy. His unfeeling apathy and systematic callousness on this point gradually gave to his youngest pupil such a distaste to his society, and scorn of his doctrine, that in proportion as he thought more of the duties of mankind towards each other, and read more of those books, whose first recommendation had been Jeans's endeavours to prevent his reading them, he held his tutor more and more in abhorrence. While, however, Mr. Jeans knew himself to be a favourite with the elder brother, he had no apprehensions of being displaced by the dislike of the younger, and at once to gratify his own pique towards him, and effect a conscientious discharge of the duty entrusted to him, Mr. Jeans took every occasion to insinuate to Lord Castledanes and Mrs. Delmont the eccentric, and, as he feared, unfortunate disposition of the young man. Lord Castledanes, who really loved George better than any of his brother's children, gave very little attention to the malevolent hints of Jeans, whom he considered as a pedant without any but college ideas; while Mrs. Delmont, though she heard him with patience, found nothing in his complaints, when they were investigated, but a confirmation of those excellent qualities which had endeared this boy to her even more than his brother. George, on his part, knew that Jeans, amidst all his pretences, was given to sensual indulgences altogether disgraceful to him, and particularly inconsistent with his pretended sanctity; yet such was the generosity of his nature, that he disdained to retaliate against the Tartuffe[35] he despised, and was eager to join with his brother in petitioning their uncle to bestow on Jeans a piece of preferment in his gift, though it did not remove him from his tutorship, but, as George had foreseen, made him more dogmatical, overbearing, and insufferable. This acquisition, however, had not increased to George Delmont the inconveniences of his government many months, before Lord Castledanes and Colonel Delmont agreed, that the time was come when it would be proper for Adolphus, then considered as the heir of the family, to make the tour of Europe.—Neither of them were very partial to Mr. Jeans, but they considered that he had, from long habit, acquired great influence over the mind of his pupil. His deficiency of knowledge in the languages of the people he was going among, a foreigner hired for the purpose, something between a servant and a secretary, was to supply, and with this arrangement Adolphus Delmont had left Eton about six months before his brother was seized with the epidemic distemper, which had in the event been so fatal to the interest as well as the happiness of his family.—At the period of his elder brother's departure, George had just completed his sixteenth year; the interval between that time and his being seized with this dangerous illness was that in which he had acquired more knowledge than during all his former studies pursued under the immediate direction of Mr. Jeans for about five years—He now understood perfectly what had

George's education is casual

before been so indistinctly communicated, or so distastefully enforced, that his attention had involuntarily recoiled. He was at the head of the school, and by his example imparted to such of his associates as had a turn for literature an ardent delight in its pursuits; he no longer wanted friends to whom he could communicate his pleasures, and who animated his enthusiasm by participation.—At liberty to chuse his own reading at his hours of private study, he had made a collection of his favourite poets and essayists. Some modern works, which Mr. Jeans had forbidden him ever to open at all, were purchased and read with attention, greater perhaps than he would have given them had they never been prohibited.—While Adolphus was travelling through France with the idea only of availing himself of such pleasures as were yet to be enjoyed amidst the fermentation of the great and awful changes that were approaching, George was anticipating and tracing their progress in the writings of those who have been supposed to have contributed to their production.

While Adolphus was looking with common eyes on the scene where Tell had resisted the petty tyrant of his country, and Rousseau destroyed the hydra of false opinion and fettering prejudice, George was envying his brother the delights that he was incapable of tasting, sighing with boyish enthusiasm for the scenes of simple hospitality in the Pais de Vaud, and languishing to wander among Alpine rocks and torrents, and to gaze on an imaginary Clarens from the rocks of Meillerie.[36]—Such was the disposition of his mind when he was overtaken by a disease that threatened his life, and so much affected his intellects, that he knew nobody but his mother; her image was the last impressed on his recollection when he sunk into total insensibility, and the first that returned to his memory when from that stupor he recovered to fall into something resembling rather the understanding of a child of four or five years old than his own, in which state he remained for some days, till with his bodily strength his faculties were slowly repaired: he then looked round him in vain for the dear, the tender friend, whom he remembered had never left his bed, and who would, he thought, be the first to watch with maternal pleasure his return to life and reason—he asked for her, but received only evasive answers from the attendants—his sisters did not appear; what was become of them? and why did he not see them since his fever was gone, and there was no longer any reason to dread infection?—His father, he knew, was absent on military business in a distant part of England, but why did he not see his uncle, who used to be so anxious whenever any of the children, whom he considered as his own, were threatened with illness?—As these enquiries pressed upon his mind, he became more and more impatient and uneasy, and questioned his attendants with such eagerness of anxiety, that it was no longer possible for them to evade answering, if not by words, by the confusion and grief they could not conceal. The unhappy boy discovered that he had lost his beloved mother, and that neither his sisters or his uncle were sufficiently recovered from so dreadful a stroke to trust themselves with the sight of his anguish.—This shock, the first he had ever felt of sorrow, fell more heavily upon him; it was bitterly aggravated by the conviction that her tenderness for him had cost the life of this dear mother, a loss so irreparable to her family; and a thousand times he wished he had died, rather than have felt the agonies this cruel reflection brought with it. His despair, at first silent, sullen, and gloomy, was melted into tears when his

George sick

Mother attends him, dies (as in F-stein)

weeping sisters sat by him, or when his uncle conjured him, if he insisted on believing that his mother's death was occasioned by her attendance on him, not to throw away a life which had cost them all so dear. It was to save from more acute anguish, these fond friends, and to prepare to meet his father with some degree of calmness, that George Delmont, making an effort to stifle pain he could not conceal, learnt the first hard lesson of fortitude—His mind, strong and clear, found the practice of this virtue less difficult than he had supposed it when its exertion was necessary to the peace of those he loved—He meditated on the lessons he had received from his mother, and determined that they should not be thrown away—"I will live," said he, "to be the protector of your daughters, my adored mother; I will live to assist them in consoling my father and my uncle."—A deep yet soft melancholy succeeded the transports of grief he had at first indulged. Gradually he returned to the society of his mourning family; but except the silent walks he took with his younger sister, which were directed to every spot that had been the favourite walks of their mother, and particularly those parts of the park and plantation which she had adorned by her taste, he seemed to covet nothing so much as solitude. Hiding himself in the deepest recesses of the woods that bounded the park, and shadowed the feet of the hills near it, he passed whole days alone, or was roused from the indulgence of this melancholy by the entreaties of his father. His father, however, was soon under the necessity of returning to his regiment; Mrs. Crewkherne was sent for to superintend the house, where his mother's sisters, the two Miss Lorimer's, were alike entreated by the master of it, and his brother the Colonel to remain with the two Miss Delmonts (the eldest of whom, Caroline, was now only fifteen) and these their relations, one three, the other two years older.— George Delmont could not see without extreme pain the formal bigot, Mrs. Crewkherne, now directing a family where his mother had presided, the charm of every eye, the delight of every heart.—The cold austere manners, virulent prejudices, and malevolent temper of his ancient relation would have disgusted him, had he not continually had an image so different before his eyes. As he was more remarkable for a careless sincerity than for prudence, he took very little pains to conceal from any one his distaste for the old lady's precepts and conversation, and fled more continually than before to his beloved seclusion. While he there acquired a peculiar taste for the beauty of nature, and fell into a course of thinking which gave a colour to the rest of his life, his uncle, deprived of the society which had made his own house once so delightful to him (even amidst his former incurable domestic misfortune) now found no other resource so consoling as listening to a voice, in that of Miss Lorimer, resembling that of his deceased sister's, and in gazing on a countenance where he could sometimes trace a family resemblance to that charming woman so universally regretted. This, it is true, became every day a more dangerous indulgence; yet of all those who might have ventured to have spoken of it, none seemed to have remarked its progress till the attachment to which it gave rise was become incurable.

Lord Castledanes, hitherto destined by his situation to look forward to no other views than the succession of his brother's family, now found himself at liberty to marry again, of which perhaps he would not have thought while his home had contin- ued pleasant to him by the residence of his brother, his brother's wife, and their fam-

Lord Castledanes — George's
uncle — remarries

ily, or if, in losing them, a less seducing object than Miss Lorimer had been continually present in it; but her ascendancy, though without any appearance of artful management on her side, soon became such as conquered every uneasy reflection on the disappointment of his brother; and he imagined that he could so soften it, that their friendship would not be broken by his marriage.

Mrs. Crewkherne, who ventured to mutter obliquely on what she saw going on, was so accustomed to give indulgence, whenever she could venture, to her petulant malignity, and she thought so ill of every body, and so much delighted to misrepresent the most innocent actions, that none of the young people listened to her malicious and half-uttered sarcasms. The two Miss Delmonts considered their mother's sisters, who were so little superior to them in age, as no more likely to be objects of any thing but fatherly friendship from their uncle than they were themselves; and as to their brother George, who would probably have been more clear sighted, he insensibly absented himself more and more from the house, and as autumn came on shut himself up almost entirely at the Upwood Cottage, which was always called his own, under pretence of the greater convenience with which he could from thence follow field sports, in the pursuit of which, however, it was remarked, he was never seen; very little, therefore, was known of the intentions of Lord Castledanes till he was actually the husband of the fair Mariana.—A few weeks before, the lady and her sister went to London, to pass some time with the only female relation they had—Lord Castledanes followed them very soon afterwards to attend parliament, and the first certain intelligence of this great change in the family was received by Colonel Delmont, then under orders for the West Indies.[37] Thunderstruck with an event which annihilated for ever his flattering prospects, and smarting under the disappointment which his habits of life and manner of thinking had a peculiar tendency to embitter, he wrote, in the first moment of passion, an angry and reproachful letter to his brother, directed that his daughters and his youngest son should immediately remove from their uncle's house, and go to Upwood Cottage, till he should consider how to dispose of them, forbidding their having any communication either with their uncle or the new Lady Castledanes. He wrote also angrily to Mrs. Crewkherne, declaiming against her blindness, either wilful or foolish, which had prevented her giving him notice of the mischief which had happened, and then embarked for a climate already at that period so fatal to Europeans.[38] George Delmont no sooner knew the purport of his father's letters, which so painfully marked the state of his mind, than he hurried to Falmouth[39] with the utmost expedition, hoping to see him, and soothe his irritated spirits before his departure; but on his arrival he found that the fleet had sailed eight-and-forty hours before with a fair wind, and he could procure no vessel that would engage to overtake it.

He then returned as expeditiously as possible, though with an heavy heart, to obey his father's injunctions as to the removal of his sisters. On reaching the house, he found Mrs. Crewkherne had not waited for his interposition, but as full of indignation as if she alone had been the injured person, had taken the eldest of the young ladies, who was her peculiar favourite, to town with her, and had left the youngest at Upwood. This house having been always called George's, and indeed his uncle having given it to him with the little estate round it while he was yet a boy, Colonel Delmont, as well as Mrs. Delmont, who lived very much there, had always affected to consider themselves as his visitors. Mrs. Crewkherne did not love George, and would not become resident in his house without a formal invitation; but as she as little loved her younger niece, she did not wish for her as an addition to her family when she resumed her former manner of living at her house in town. Again she assembled round her her friends, advocates for faith without works; and as an instance of the supererogation by which she recommended herself to their admiration, she introduced her niece, and told the lamentable story of her relation's change of fortune by the most imprudent and ill-advised marriage of Lord Castledane's, whose future infelicity she prognosticated as a matter past all dispute from the nature of his new connection. Miss Delmont, who was one of those of the Colonel's children who suffered most acutely from the alteration in the circumstances of her family, was a young woman whose character, or rather rudiments of character, had yet had no opportunity of appearing. She had an extremely pretty face, and a light and beautiful form; she had learned, and better than is generally learned, all that is taught in the modern system of education under the name of accomplishments, excelled only by her sometimes tutoress (now doubly her aunt) the beautiful syren, Lady Castledane's. The adulation which Miss Delmont had been used to hear, the pleasure with which she had hitherto found herself listened to, either by friends extremely partial, or visitors who imagined they could not be too lavish of their praises to a niece of Lord Castledanes, all, all, were at an end, or exchanged for cold compliments from the sectaries who composed Mrs. Crewkherne's coteries, who very soon began to tell her, that a too sedulous cultivation of such talents was sinful, unless they were dedicated wholly to pious purposes; that so fine a voice was lent her for better ends than to give advantage to seductive and ill-meaning songs; and that nothing became the mouth of a young woman but such pieces of poetry as were to be found in the books they recommended to her, or were to be studied in her excellent relation, Mrs. Crewkherne's repository. These the mortified girl sometimes sung to oblige her aunt; but in spite of her being little accustomed to reflect on the purport of what she uttered, she could not help being disgusted with the strange cant many of them contained, which even appeared to her profane. Indifferent, however, to please in such society as she was now condemned to, she sunk into languor, or was roused from it only by considering how she might remove into a manner of life more to her taste; for nothing could be so irksome to a young woman of her age, who had been so much admired, as to be confined to the company of itinerant preachers, or ladies of a certain age, who divided their time between the chapel and the card table; and it was to obtain some change at least, if not alteration for the better, that Miss Delmont had now for two summers prevailed on Mrs. Crewkherne to pass at least some weeks at Upwood, which she was the more easily disposed to do, because her friends at this period were generally dispersed at places of public resort, where there were established assemblies of their brethren. It was in some sort derogatory to her ideas of gentility, which were supported in the midst of her affected humility, to remain in London, when all people of a certain rank had left it, and as Lord Castledanes for the last two years never visited for above a day or two Belton Tower, the objection she would have had to residing in his neighbourhood was obviated, and she was prevailed upon to indulge her niece with a visit to her brother and sister, a visit which, for the sake of both his sisters, George, unused as he was to it, and awkward at dissimulation, affected to desire, while in truth there was no sound that could reach his ears half so unpleasant to them as the voice of Mrs. Crewkherne; nor did the fortune she possessed, which was entirely at her own disposal, ever influence him for a moment to practise any of those arts, or bend to any of those concessions, by which the favour of women of her description is generally courted, and frequently secured—He wished his sisters might possess this fortune, which was reckoned to be about eighteen thousand pounds, and for their sakes submitted to the residence of Mrs. Crewkherne at his house, however disagreeable to himself.

CHAP. IV.

Why should a man put on fetters, though of silver? wherefore
should he love chains,
though of wrought gold?[40]

When the second marriage of his uncle so unexpectedly took place, George Delmont had been some time entered at Oxford, and was then keeping a term there.

In consequence of the letter and orders he received from his father, he hastened to Belton Tower, where he found only Louisa, his youngest sister, under the care of the old Swiss governess, who had been for many years in the family. Mrs. Crewkherne had some days before, and almost immediately after having been apprized of the marriage, set forth for London with her eldest niece, for whom she had affected to feel some partiality, while Louisa, whose only offence was her great resemblance to her mother, was thus, in addition to her other losses, suddenly deprived of the society of her sister, from whom she had never been separated till her former journey with her aunt. The first care of George was to soothe with the tenderest attention the dejected and deserted girl, now dearer to him than ever, because she seemed to have no protection or reliance on earth but him. Having removed her to the house at Upwood, of which he was henceforth to be considered as the master, and restored in some degree the cheerfulness of which so many deprivations had robbed the innocent Louisa; it was then that the young man began to look forward towards his own future prospects, in which, as well as in those of the rest of his family, the recent event was likely to occasion a very great change.

The destiny of Adolphus, his eldest brother, had been so far fixed, that he already held a lieutenancy in the guards,[41] in which it was, when he took it, very improbable that he should be exposed to more personal danger than his friends would have chosen for the heir of the Earl of Castledanes; but the Colonel, in the first effervescence of resentful passion, purchased for him a captaincy of infantry, and wrote to him to return from Florence, where he then was, and enter on immediate service.

"You have no longer an uncle, Delmont," said the Colonel in this letter, "and I cannot support you in the way you have had hitherto so good a right to expect. I have determined, though I might still have evaded it, to join my regiment in the West Indies; for I am now a mere soldier of fortune,[42] and you must hereafter make your way—the captain of a company of foot.[43] Your future establishment shall not depend for a month, for a week, on the infatuated man who was once my brother, now the slave of that worthless little sorceress, whom your mother nourished in her bosom, little knowing that she would sting to death the children of her sister and benefactress.—Dismiss all the persons you have about you, but your own servant—I can no longer afford to pay Mr. Jeans the salary allotted to him, and he will do well to find some young English traveller, to whom his care on the journey back, or on a longer tour, may be acceptable. The considerable benefices he has received from the family may repay him for past services. For yourself, you will on your return to England make a short visit to your brother and sisters, and then join your regiment wheresoever it happens to be; but I charge you on your duty to me, and your respect for yourself, to suffer no consideration whatever to induce you to meet Lord Castledanes."

Colonel Delmont, before he sailed from Falmouth, had forwarded a copy of this letter to his youngest son, enjoining him at the same time, with even more strictness and severity, to avoid any communication with his uncle; injunctions which were extremely painful to George Delmont, and of which (while he determined as far as he could to obey them) he could not help feeling the injustice.

No pleasure now remained for Delmont in places where he had once tasted so much unadulterated delight. If he rode out, he passed near, or saw from distant heights, the trees that surrounded the house, or were grouped in the park of his uncle, and he imagined that second parent looking with some regret for the figures that once peopled the scene.

Lord Castledanes, however, came very seldom to Belton Tower; when he did, it was alone, and only for a few days, to settle such business as might occasionally require his attention. The old servants, for hardly one of them had been removed, imagined they saw their Lord, when he thus visited the place of his former (almost constant) residence, less cheerful than he used to be when the family of his brother was around him; but by the servants who accompanied him from London they heard of the gaiety of his town-house, the splendor of the new equipages, and the taste of "*my Lady.*" No body was so richly and finely dressed at court as "*my Lady;*" and the compliments she had received were repeated, as the footmen and grooms heard them from the maids, who heard them from Mrs. Gingham, who probably heard them from "my Lady's" sister, if not from "my Lady" herself; and very magnificent accounts were given of sundry sayings, wise and witty, of persons of the most elevated rank, who had been supping at "my Lady's." My Lord, seemed already sunk into a secondary figure; and Delmont, as he listened pensively, and not without an uneasy sensation, to the narratives thus given by his own servants, who had long lived with him, and whom he had indulged in habits of talking to him, could not refrain from asking himself, whether the friend, the uncle he loved so much, was happy in this new mode of life? and when his own taste and turn of mind compelled him to answer in the negative, or at least with doubt and hesitation, he found himself affected by these doubts, and drove them from him as useless and injurious to his own peace: it was more to the purpose to consider, since he was almost entirely left to himself, how he should decide as to the pursuit or profession that was to be chosen for the rest of his life.

His father, wholly engaged by the sudden and mortifying change which had happened in his own views, and in those of his eldest son, seemed to have had no time or consideration left for the regulation of those of the younger.

Though George Delmont had gone to Oxford after his recovery, it was because he was of an age to go thither, rather than return to Eton,[44] that he was sent; and because he already had learned all that a great school teaches as to books, and had miraculously escaped, from the singularity of his temper, all those early *tendencies* to vice which such a school is by some supposed to encourage; it was partly too to remove himself from a scene where every object around him, every face he saw, reminded him of his irretrievable loss, that he eagerly embraced his uncle's offer of sending him to the university. The time he had passed there he by no means repented; yet now his circumstances were so changed, that he saw not how he was to support the expence; nor, if he could, how it would be worth while so to bestow it, unless he determined to devote himself to one of the learned professions.

From law, where the most honest must in a great degree thrive on the perplexities, quarrels, and distresses of others, he was utterly averse. Medicine, that noble profession, which is never enough respected, but which, when attentively studied and conscientiously followed, is the most beneficial of any to the human race, required a course of application and habits of life for which he knew himself to be altogether unfit. The church alone remained, and to provide for him in it had probably been the intention of Lord Castledanes; but of this Delmont thought with reluctance. No man could more highly venerate the character of "a good priest"[45]—a man dedicated in heart and spirit to the edification and instruction of the world—but he felt himself too ignorant on all theological subjects, to believe he should ever be in that line what he felt he ought to be, if ever he undertook it; and he doubted whether the enquiries that would perhaps satisfy himself, might qualify him to convey, in sincerity of heart, such doctrine to those who might be entrusted to him, as the oaths he should take would make a part of his duty.—That it was done without reflection every day he knew—-but though many who did it were, for aught he knew, very good sort of people, he felt it impossible for him to follow their steps.

The vague plans that had arisen and disappeared in his family, while he was yet a boy, for his future destination in life, were now no longer remembered; and that they had never been pursued, he could not prevail with himself to be sorry.

When his high health and unchecked spirits had (yet at a very early period) given him the character of wild fellow, a Pickle,[46] his father and his uncle had apparently destined him to a military life: they sometimes saw another Wolfe[47] in his daring yet calm courage, or fancied, in the then sturdy and spirited navigator of a boat on the lake of the park, a future admiral destined to extend the conquests or avenge the quarrels of "the cabinet of St. James's."[48]—But Mrs. Delmont, though she never violently opposed these speculations, which might fail of themselves, had the art to regulate, without crushing, the ardent spirit that occasionally gave rise to them; she seemed to have in her hands the heart of her son, to be able to mould it as she pleased, and the use she made of her power was to teach him to reason on every thing he learned, instead of seeing all objects, as they are represented, through the dazzling and false medium of prejudice, communicated from one generation to another; while nobody, or at least very few, dare to ask, "if *I* try to do as *those* men have done, shall I really acquire glory; and shall I run *no* risque of being a curse rather than a benefit to the world?"

Mrs. Delmont ventured to strip from the gaudy pictures that are daubed with vermilion and leaf gold, to excite emulative ambition in childhood, their paint and their gilding, and she had reason, long before death snatched her from this dearest object of her maternal love, to hope that her youngest son might be one day something better than either a general or an admiral—the benefactor instead of the successful destroyer of his fellow men.

Delmont had at a very early age acquired[49] a more general and correct knowledge of history than is usually obtained; and his mother had accustomed him, when he read the lives, to give a summary account of his idea of the characters of those who figure in the annals of nations, decorated with crowns[50] and sceptres, or who have otherwise been the curses or the blessings of the people over whom they usurped power, or *by* whom they were entrusted with it.

Much (alas how much) of this retrospection was painful to the generous feelings of his heart; and often had he been tempted to ask, wherefore heaven gave a portion of its delegated authority to such hateful or contemptible beings as had insulted its creatures, and deformed its works, under the title of "the lords anointed," or some other imposing appellation through which the wretched people submitted to be trod to dust?

Mrs. Delmont had sometimes found it necessary to check the indignation of her infant politician; who, after he was nine or ten years old, never voluntarily sat down to read pages that seemed almost exclusively the annals of fraud and murder, of selfish ambition, or wicked policy, involving millions in misery for the gratification of a few.

But there were characters in more remote history, which he contemplated with very different sensations—He read of the elder Brutus avenging the injured honour of a Roman matron on the insolent and cruel family of Tarquin, and cementing the structure of the infant republic, of which he thus laid the foundation, with blood dearer than that which circulated in his own veins.[51] He read of the Gracchi[52] dying in the noblest conflict, contending for the rights of humanity against the selfish usurpations of the rich—He contemplated the younger Brutus deploring the friend, while he devoted to death the tyrant that would have enslaved his country[53]—He saw Cato dying by his own hand, rather than survive its freedom[54]—These and some other such characters seemed to electrify the young student; his eyes flashed fire, his heart beat, and the glorious examples of virtuous patriotism appeared to raise his species in his estimation, which he had sometimes thought so degraded by its endurance of oppression, that he felt ashamed of belonging to it.

The impressions made thus early on the mind are never likely to be erased or enfeebled, if reason is suffered to stifle all those paltry passions by which men coming into life are induced to follow blindly where their interest leads them, and to become the mere creatures of convenience and convention.—Delmont, early taught to have on every point an opinion of his own, now looked at the paths that lay open before him without prejudice, and having done so he determined to yield his freedom to none of those motives which the love of power or of wealth might hold out to him, but to live on his little farm unfettered by the rules he must submit to if he entered into any profession. "I am aware," said he, as he argued this matter with himself, "that I shall incur the ridicule of some and the blame of others. 'What! a young man of *your* family,' cries one, 'to bury himself in solitude, to cultivate turnips, and let his talk be of bullocks.'[55] 'What!' cries another, 'have you no more regard for the honour of your family, than to degrade yourself to the condition of one of their tenants? you, who might be a judge or a bishop! a general or an admiral!—will you sink into a yeoman?'—Yes, my good friends, I shall answer,—I *will* do so indeed; my talk may occasionally be of bullocks, but I trust I shall be able to converse also of other things. If my family are ashamed of me, they have only to leave me out of their genealogical table, as an unworthy branch of the tree, bent towards its native earth, and no longer contributing to their splendid insignificance. If my friends blush for me, let them leave me with a sigh of compassion, though assured that I shall not feel a single emotion of envy when I see one on the bench of Themis condemning wretches legally to die on the gallows, or on the bench of bishops, lending their weight to laws that send forth myriads to slaughter in the field;[56] nor shall I once regret, that I do not with a truncheon in my hand preside myself at those human sacrifices, either by land or sea, where men are collected together by hundreds and by thousands; are ordered to destroy each other, they know not, they dare not enquire, why?"——

The resolution thus taken by Delmont gained strength almost every hour, as the tranquil utility of the life he had chosen acquired greater value in his eyes. He then, for the first time since he became its master, saw the spot he was so devoted to adorned with all the beauty of summer, and his grief for his mother, mellowed and softened by time, was not wholly unmixed with melancholy delight, while he sedulously attended to the plantations she had projected, and was daily carrying into execution other schemes for the improvement of the grounds which she had pointed out, while even the first year of his farming succeeded so well, that he had no reason to believe he should repent, even in pecuniary considerations, the election he had made.

Deprived of one sister, he applied himself to improve the mind of her who was left to him. Louisa had great sweetness of temper, and loved her brother better than any other being now on earth. Whatever he named to her as worth acquiring, she immediately applied to, and was soon qualified to speak with propriety on most subjects of general knowledge; but Delmont, amid her attentions to please him, and her improvement in every study that tended to make her a rational companion, saw, and saw with tender apprehension for her future happiness, a sort of pliability of intellect, which made him fear that her character would not be formed on reason and conviction, but on the sentiments and conduct of those among whom she might be thrown. She was now the simple yet well-informed child of nature; but from the ductility of her spirit, he apprehended, that if she should be elevated into what is called high life, she would as easily glide into the mere flutterer of a few seasons of fashionable dissipation, or the artificial puppet of a drawing-room. George thought the daughter of his mother ought to be of an higher order of beings; it was enough, that to this insignificant class of raree-shew[57] figures, the elder of those daughters was already destined; and he incessantly laboured to rescue the younger from the uninteresting group of those who have "*no character at all.*"[58]

Mrs. Delmont had built in the southward aspect of the small but pleasant house her youngest son and daughters now inhabited, a little conservatory, into which some of its windows, both of the ground floor and the first floor, opened; it was——

A fortress where Flora retreats
From the cruel assaults of the clime;[59]

and every plant, every flower, which were now uncommonly beautiful and flourishing, seemed to George Delmont to speak to him of his mother.—It was there he read, or meditated, or taught Louisa to draw scientifically the blossoms which perfumed the air, or the uncultivated flowers which every hedge and bank supplied them with;[60] and it was there he was sitting with her, when Captain Delmont, whom his father's letters had at length brought home, though he had been expected much sooner, broke in upon them—They had never seen him since the death of their mother, the marriage of their uncle, and the consequent dispersion of the family.

CHAP. V.

Oh! coz, coz, coz, my pretty little coz, that thou didst *but* know
how many fathom deep I am in love![61]

If in the younger part of their lives the disposition of the two brothers had always appeared essentially different, the contrast was now more striking. George, with all the courage and fortitude that reflection and integrity give to a superior mind, had yet so much softness of heart, that when he saw Adolphus, and remembered all that had happened since they last parted, he yielded to momentary tears: his elder brother appeared to notice such weakness only to express his contempt of it. Of all the changes which had taken place in his family, he regretted nothing so much as the loss of those expectations which he had been educated to suppose must infallibly be realized on the deaths of his father and uncle; and he did not affect to conceal his indignation at the disappointment, nor to signify to his brother George, who attempted to appease and soften the malignity and resentment with which he spoke of Lord Castledanes, that *he* was only less disturbed because he had lost less. "It may be a matter of indifference to *you*," said he, "for you, as my younger brother, could only more remotely suffer from the folly of this dotard; but to *me*, Mr. George Delmont, I assure you, it is not a thing to be slightly passed over—it is something to *me*, whether I possess the estate and rank of my ancestors or not."

But though every other plan of life, and every other object seemed sometimes beneath his regard, yet at other times the elder Delmont was as eagerly anxious about every pecuniary advantage as if he had never looked beyond the patrimony he was now likely to inherit. He knew that of his father's and mother's fortune, which together had never been large, ten thousand pounds were settled on him, and ten upon younger children, which gave to his brother George and his two sisters something more than three thousand pounds each; but unequal as *they* might well have thought this division, it yet appeared to him to secure to them too much; for he knew that whenever his father died he should in fact have less than they would, for he had already disposed of his own share, except about fifteen hundred pounds, in that accommodating way called post obit:[62] he now therefore felt, and could hardly refrain from expressing his discontent, that his brother should have landed property, though the house and farm at Upwood were not worth above three thousand pounds. "Hard indeed," he said, "that *he*, who was the eldest brother, was to turn out like a necessitous cadet,[63] while you," added he, sneeringly, "are in time, I suppose, to represent the landed interest of the Delmont family; and as you know what you are about well enough to keep in favour of the foolish old peer, may be brought in as one of his county members."[64]

"If I were," replied George, "I do not see that there would be any thing wrong in it; but assure yourself, neither that or any other advantage would engage me to commit any meanness to obtain the suffrage either of Lord Castledanes or any other man. As to keeping in favour with the old peer, if you mean by that, that I have sought to be received by my uncle, though forbidden to do so by my father, I tell you that you have been misinformed."

"Well, be not angry, my young Agricola,"[65] replied Adolphus Delmont; "I only repeat what I have heard, that old nunky looks upon you as still belonging to him, and sings forth your praises, a *gorge deployé*,[66] while he deigns not to name my father or me. Hang him, an old fool, if I could get him to let me have money, I should take leave of him for ever without a single thought of him, but when I happened to think how he has cheated me of my birth-right."

Such conversation (and for the few days he staid Adolphus seldom held any other) was extremely painful to his brother, who could not help seeing how selfish, arrogant, and unfeeling he was. His opinion of public affairs fluctuated too as interest or caprice directed, and to-day he ridiculed and vilified the people whose favour he tomorrow determined to court by any means however degrading. Of principle of any kind he seemed entirely devoid, even on points where most men, however free in their opinions, have some degree of delicacy and sensibility. Thus he praised the prudence of Caroline, his eldest sister, "who has done wisely," said he, "in attaching herself to that witch of Endor[67] Mrs. Crewkherne, she'll get the old hag's money, and with that she may perhaps marry, as a niece of Lord Castledanes ought to do, some man of fashion. But what is to become of *you*, Louisa?" said he, one day when they were alone. "George, I suppose, when he has rooted himself here a little longer, will be much about as polished and as much of a gentleman as those cropped greasy-headed joskins's[68] that used to dine twice a year in the hall at Belton Tower; fellows who call themselves yeomen, or gentlemen farmers—he begins to look like one already, and as if he was always ready to ask—'*How a score of good wethers?*'[69] The next thing to his entire metamorphose will be his marrying Miss Nanny Peasely, or Miss Jenny Bacon, or the widow Hogtrow, or, perhaps, if none of these happen to charm him, his own dairy maid, Betsy Butterbur,[70] may enchant him by her skill in churning and raising poultry; and let me ask *you*, Louisa Delmont, what is to become of *you?*" Poor Louisa could answer only by her tears. Her elder brother, totally unmoved by them, changed his voice and look, and added sternly—"Though by your father's absence and mine, Louisa, you must be left for the present under George's care, yet I charge you, child, in my father's name and my own, not to suffer any degrading and ungentlemanlike notions of equality, and such cursed stuff, to influence you. I speak as I know your father would speak, when I say, that if you ever presume to think of any body under your own rank, you will be no longer considered as a daughter of his, or as a sister of mine; and it were better for you to go hide yourself in a convent in Italy or Spain, than to fix a disgrace upon us which we should never overlook. I know how girls, and particularly how girls of your temper, are influenced by people they live among; and I tell you my mind, that you may not affect ignorance. We are humbled enough, I think, without sinking into the rank of plebeians, roturiers,[71] fellows who live by digging.—I had rather see a sister of mine mistress to a prince than wife to the richest peasant." With such sentiments, though he did not quite so grossly declare them to George, it is not likely that either of them found much pleasure in the society of the other; and Adolphus, having borrowed two hundred pounds of his brother, returned to London, passed about a month among his old friends in and about St. James's-street, and then, rather from necessity than choice, joined the regiment, in which his father had purchased him a company, at Gibraltar.[72]

Not long after his departure, information was received of the death of Colonel Delmont. His brother Lord Castledanes survived him only seven months, leaving a son about a year old, and his young widow near lying in of a second child; it was born two months after his death, and was also a son, so that the probability of the Colonel's family succeeding to the estate and title was more remote than ever.

Lord Castledanes, notwithstanding the declared enmity of his brother since his marriage, had not changed a will he had made some time before, but had executed with some additions to it a little before his death.—He gave in a codicil two thousand pounds to each of his nephews, and one thousand to each of his nieces, to be paid in six months after his decease. A maternal uncle of his second wife, Sir Appulby Gorges, he named as his executor.

George Delmont, conquering his aversion from Mrs. Crewkherne, that his sisters might not be divided, had invited her with Caroline to pass at Upwood the summer after these events, and the family were in their last mourning for Colonel Delmont and Lord Castledanes, when chance brought the Winslow family to their acquaintance.

When, from what they could collect from Mrs. Crewkherne and the servants, the curiosity of the Doctor and Mrs. Winslow was in a great degree satisfied, wonder succeeded.—The Doctor was astonished that such a young man was *suffered* so to throw himself away; and blamed the improvidence of those who had superintended his education, "for, madam," said he to Mrs. Crewkherne, strutting round the room with an air of sententious consequence, "it is an axiom as old as Solomon, 'Bring up a child in the way he should go, and when he is old he will not depart therefrom.'[73]—Now it is plain that the good lady, your kinsman's mother, took another method, and I grieve that the fruits thereof may be the loss of a valuable member of our ever excellent establishment.—I do indeed wonder, as you say she was accounted a woman of sense, what could so mislead her?"

Mrs. Crewkherne then seized the opportunity, as was usual with her, to declaim against what she called new fangled and pernicious modes of thinking and acting, and while she was so engaged Mrs. Winslow wondered at her warmth, which sometimes led her into terms which were any thing rather than *elegant*.—She was surprised that possessing so handsome a fortune, and being so highly connected, Mrs. Crewkherne should pass so much time in this lonely residence, *elegant* as it was, and not be more frequently at some of the neighbouring places of public resort—and already wearied in a place where there was little more to hear, and where a rubber was with difficulty made up, she understood with concern from the surgeon who attended Miss Goldthorp, that it would yet be some time before his patient could with safety be moved.

Miss Goldthorp was not at all disposed to hasten the period. She had already seen and thanked her gallant preserver, and the interview had been, to use her own expression, "destructive to her repose."—As she had always been taught to consider *herself* as a person of very great consequence in the scale of beings, she felt proportionably obliged to him who had been the cause that the world still possessed so amiable a personage;—but when she had seen him, she was tempted to imagine that heaven had performed a miracle in her favour, and sent an hero to her rescue, such as fables feign when they tell of demigods and knights endowed with supernatural powers.—Soft was her voice, and modulated to the tenderest notes of grateful sensibility, while she thanked him in chosen and studied words for his interposition—She sat up in a easy chair, in an elegant dishabille, and cast on him, from among the laced plaits of an elegant close cap, eyes of the most languishing gratitude. All this had been settled before she discovered that the young man to whom she was so much obliged was one of the handsomest men in England. During the few moments he staid with her she became distractedly in love with him, and before he had quitted her half an hour, it was determined in the secret council she held with herself, that George Delmont should be the fortunate possessor of herself and her fifty thousand pounds. If the hopes she had allowed to her guardian and her aunt, that she would bestow on their son these invaluable blessings, crossed her mind in the midst of this new and rapturous project, she drove the recollection from her with disdain, and thought only how she might convey to the dear youth, with a proper regard to her own delicacy, information of her favourable disposition, and engage him to make those advances which she doubted not a moment of his making with rapture the moment he knew they would be favourably received.

Miss Goldthorp was a young lady naturally of a very tender and susceptible nature, and who, notwithstanding her aunt boasted of the care she had taken to prevent it, was very deeply read in romance and novels, by some one or other of the heroines of which she occasionally "set her mind," so that with a great versatility of character she rarely appeared in her own.—As she hardly remembered an hour since she was ten years old, when she had not heard of a lover from her friends or her maid, she could never divest herself of a sort of restless coquetry, which, when no other object was at hand, condescended to amuse itself with the mawkish attempts of Middleton Winslow to express the passion his father and mother had insisted on his feeling for her. She sometimes affected to encourage, but oftener laughed at him; and when only in parties of young people, and unobserved by the Doctor or his wife, she took a malicious pleasure in turning his lackadaisical-love-making into ridicule before some other pretender to her favour, and then having made him as angry as he dared to be, entreated him to go weeping to papa and mama—"for you know, Middy," would she cry, "that we shall both suffer for it; papa will preach to the naughty girl, and mama will pout, and they'll both plague me, and then I shall revenge myself on you."—Middleton, therefore, when she had treated him the worst, dared not complain; and as in reality he cared as little for her as she did for him, he never gave himself the trouble to undeceive the good folks, who supposed that Miss Goldthorp, however she might trifle and coquet with other men, must see this son of their's with eyes as partial as their own.

The hour was now come when they were to enjoy this agreeable delusion no more.—The longer the fair invalid reflected on the delight of making the fortune of the man she loved, the more charming the project appeared; but when she heard again and again Delmont enquiring after the progress of her recovery, with what she imagined the tenderest solicitude; when she found that he continued to assist his sisters in amusing the tedious hours of her confinement, brought her books, sent for others to a friend's library, which she expressed a wish to see, sometimes relieved the Miss Delmonts in reading aloud to her, and sometimes brought collections of prints, drawings, and books of natural history, to give variety to these long sedentary evenings; but above all, when she beheld his very handsome person, which she thought improved at every interview, her heart was irrecoverably gone, and she thought, she dreamed, of nothing but to inspire the fortunate Delmont with a passion as fervent as she believed her own to be.

For this purpose, while she took care not to make so rapid a progress in her recovery as to hasten their departure, she endeavoured always to be well enough to admit of visits, from which, under pretence of fearing noise and heat, she contrived as often as possible to exclude the card table of Mrs. Crewkherne; and as one of the Miss Delmonts was often compelled to make a fourth in that most formidable party, she frequently succeeded in having the brother and the other sister alone.

On these occasions all the artillery of looks and sighs, and half expressions, was called forth. Sometimes she was in pain from the broken bone, and then her complaints were stifled with the most interesting fortitude, because she would not give a moment's concern to her beloved friend Louisa—for they were already prodigious friends. Her eyes, which were large, and grey, and rolling (though she had always been assured, and was convinced they were blue) those eyes which so many ensigns and lieutenants, cornets and curates, nay even counsellors, had accused of high crimes and misdemeanors, now exerted all their power of soft seduction. They were fixed in gentle languor on the face of "the dear youth," whenever his were turned another way; but the moment he looked towards her, they were cast down with bewitching consciousness, and no pains were spared to add to their expression by a blush; but it was not always to be had; however a broken sigh was no bad substitute. The sisters, young and inexperienced as they were, soon understood all this—but after the third or fourth essay, the tender fair one began to doubt whether her battery was effective, and to dread lest the citadel was already in possession of another.

Chap. VI.

A busy officious body; one that lives at folks houses
as half spy over the servants, half friend to the master
—a tale-bearer, a gossip.[74]

Though by no means endowed with any extraordinary degree of penetration, yet was Mrs. Winslow right in her conjecture, that whatever growing partiality Miss Goldthorp might feel for her gallant deliverer, *he* was hitherto insensible of any particular partiality towards *her*. In the conjecture that the rest of the house were equally eager for so opulent a marriage she was also right. Mrs. Crewkherne indeed took pains to conceal how much she wished it, because she was aware of the intentions of the reverend Doctor and his lady on behalf of their son; but the earnestness of the artless Louisa, solicitous above all other things for her brother's advantage, and the ill concealed stratagems of Miss Delmont, who felt the use that the prosperity of one branch of a family was to the rest, could not be overlooked; they promoted, by a thousand accidents apparently trifling and inconsequent, the meetings of their invalid visitor with their brother; and he frequently joined in their endeavours to amuse her, while the Doctor, Mrs. Winslow, Mrs. Crewkherne, the curate of the parish, and his wife, made up a party at whist; but it was difficult for even the sisters not to perceive that Delmont, though civil and good naturedly ready to follow the dictates of politeness and hospitality, was often absent and silent; and that it was not without considerable effort he thus sacrificed time he had rather have passed in some other place.

He had taken, almost from the commencement of his free agency, the resolution of dropping all that sort of acquaintance which usually passes in the country as good neighbourhood, where, after toiling under the burning sun of July or August, there is collected round a table (to furnish which the mistress of the house has tortured her own and her housekeeper's head for a week) a set of very worthy people, no doubt, but such as had so few ideas in common with Delmont, that their society was the greatest punishment he could undergo. Two or three clergymen, who talked about moduses and compositions, related the events of divers controversies in the exchequer court, complained of the resistance of their parishioners to the payment of certain dues, and recited arguments they had held in favour of tests, or repeated some dogmatical pieces of eloquence uttered at the last visitation;[75] and if, losing his patience in listening to arrogant egotism from men who profess meekness and disinterested piety, Delmont turned to another group, it was of the lawyer of the next town, who, though bound to observe the most sacred silence, was by innuendos and half sentences telling the apothecary his opinion of the state of a client's fortune; on the other hand, the master of the house was disputing with an esquire of lesser fortune a point about the game laws, on which, as they could not agree, both talked very loud, and probably both together; while a young man, who called himself a man of fashion, accidentally down on a visit, having stared at all the women of the party, and finding none of them worth his attention, had taken out his pocket glass, with which he was examining if he had picked his teeth with the scrupulous delicacy which seemed to be one great end of his life. Such, or with very slight variations, were the societies he had for some time mixed with, merely because they lived within twelve miles; but having long discovered, that to continue in them was a very great waste of his time, as well as a needless trial of his civility, he no sooner found himself his own master than he ventured to enquire why he might not recover the portion of his days thus unnecessarily given to persons whom he could not discover were at all the better, while he felt himself a great deal worse, for his irretrievable loss; and though he foresaw that he should make some enemies, and be stigmatized as proud, or insolent, or conceited, he hazarded the experiment; and as he never desired to be chairman at a quarter session,[76] or foreman of a grand jury, to which his family might have entitled him, he quietly submitted to invidious remarks he did not hear, and heartily forgave both his male and female neighbours, if after awhile he was only remembered by them when they had occasion to give an instance of the haughtiness of aristocracy, which, however, accorded very ill with another accusation they had against him, that of being tainted with principles of so contrary a tendency, that both his uncle and his father had therefore disinherited him.

But though he had now for some months established his own liberty, so far as to shake off adherence to these forms, with which, under the name of politeness, men have agreed to fetter each other, he wished his sisters and Mrs. Crewkherne, while she was with them, to keep up any connection among their female neighbours that might give them any satisfaction, making it the rule of his life, as well in trivial as on material occasions, never to trench upon the liberty of others, while he guarded against being cheated out of his own; but Mrs.Crewkherne was too proud to visit the wives of men in business of the neighbouring town, and of those of men of the next rank, many resented that there was no intercourse between their husbands with Mr. Delmont, and others, who had daughters, were glad that the exclusion of the Miss Delmonts from their societies precluded all rivalry; and as they had no hopes of attaching the brother, who was now indeed no object in point of fortune to young women, they willingly relinquished the company of the sisters, to whom they were indifferent, and still more willingly that of the aunt, who was universally hated.

The female frequenters of the house, therefore, were very few. The curate's wife was one, who made tolerable amends to Mrs. Crewkherne for the deficiency of the gossip in which she really delighted above all other things, and her sister, the widow of an attorney in the next provincial town, was so able, that very little passed within the circuit of twenty miles which was not known, by either a complete or incomplete narration, at the tea table of Mrs. Crewkherne within at least the next fortnight after the events had taken place.

Dr. and Mrs. Winslow had now been near a fortnight at Upwood Cottage; poor Miss Goldthorp was gone half an age in love, and trembled at every mention (and such mention now frequently occurred) of leaving the dear, the hospitable roof.— The alarms of Dr. Winslow and his lady increased, and the two Miss Delmonts saw with disquiet, that their fair guest and her fifty thousand pounds made not the least visible impression on their unaccountable brother, when it happened that their evening parties were enlivened by the addition at the vicarage of the notable and intelligent widow—Mrs. Nixon's visits were more welcome than ever to Mrs. Crewkherne, who invited her to bring her work[77] and set of a morning, while her sister was busied in the affairs of her family. It happened that Dr. Winslow had rode out one day with an intention to prevail upon the surgeon to allow of his patient's removal, for which he was become intolerably anxious, his lady was writing letters to her son, and the two Miss Delmonts engaged with their young friend, when Mrs. Nixon, accepting this invitation, began to unfold several entertaining anecdotes, while, to return her confidence, Mrs. Crewkherne, with an air of consequential mystery, told of the hopes she had entertained that Mr. George Delmont might be so lucky as to obtain this rich heiress, "which," said Mrs. Crewkherne, "to be sure, my good madam, will be the making of him and his sisters; for I am assured, and from good authority, that she has not a shilling less than fifty thousand pounds."

"I have heard it called more," answered her companion, "and I have no reason, I am sure, to disbelieve it; but to be sure you have heard that the young lady has been engaged from her infancy to Dr. Winslow's son."

"Yes, I certainly have heard it; and indeed the Doctor and his lady have taken care to repeat it; but I have very little skill in guessing, or the girl herself is of a very different mind. Who can tell what an effect such an accident as she has met with may have upon a person?—I know she thinks young Winslow left her in danger, and saved himself, and she seems to hold him mighty cheap; besides, my dear Mrs. Nixon, I hope one may say without ostentation, that there is not *much* comparison either between the persons or the families of these two gentlemen, and certainly Mr. Delmont's *fortune*, though very far indeed from what it ought to be now, may not always be so much unequal; for my part, even as it is, I think there are few women, even those of the greatest fortunes in England, that either George Delmont, or his brother the major, might not pretend to without much presumption."

"I am quite of your mind, certainly," said the intelligent widow; "and I am sure, from my long regard for the family, there is nobody who would rejoice more sincerely than I should do at such a rich match, and I heartily hope nothing will prevent it."

"Prevent it!" cried Mrs. Crewkherne eagerly for she hated to have any scheme she was fond of doubted; "and pray what should prevent it? I hope you don't suppose me likely to be mistaken about the young woman. No, no, I have observed her, and am sure she likes my kinsman. Dr. Winslow's designs are nothing to us; and surely you cannot suffer yourself to imagine that Mr. Delmont would be so wanting to himself and to his family as to let such an opportunity of establishing his fortune escape him."

The widow answered only with an "hem!" given in a tone sufficiently expressive of incredulity. Mrs. Crewkherne alarmed, then entreated her to say if she knew any particular relative to George Delmont's conduct, which made her believe he would be reluctantly engaged in a pursuit so advantageous, and after some questions artfully evaded, Mrs. Nixon said, "Pray has not Mr. Delmont been more with his friend Mr. Armitage than he used to be?"

"He has been often out, certainly, and generally, since this family have been with us, goes out early in a morning and returns to breakfast, or soon afterwards, that he may not be deficient in politeness to his guest." "His servant, then," said Mrs. Nixon, "can tell you whither he goes."

"He never takes a servant with him, and oftener goes on foot than on horseback; but I know that all his morning absences are not on visits, for he often goes about business relative to his farms, and into the cottages, on I don't know what schemes that he has got in his head about the poor."

A smile of peculiar meaning was added to Mrs. Nixon's answers, who said, "About the *poor* are his mornings occupied? Oh! yes, I have always been told that he is a remarkably *considerate* young man, and he will be able to do wonders in regulating the *poor* no doubt."

Being again earnestly pressed to explain herself, Mrs. Nixon repeated her question about Delmont's increased intimacy with Mr. Armitage, and then said, "What then, my dear madam, is it possible that you should not have heard of the strangers who have now for some time been what I might indeed call your neighbours?"

"It certainly is possible," rejoined Mrs. Crewkherne, "since I have made no enquiry, not knowing that any connection of mine was interested."

"I don't mean," cried the other, "to say what they are, only I will leave you to judge. I do not exactly know how long ago it is since a person said to be a lady, whose husband was abroad, and who was herself an American, was by means of a friend of Mr. Armitage (for he did not like to interfere openly himself, I suppose) received at Denbury farm, which of course you know. It is a little out of the high road, among the woods on the other side the hill, and is, I believe, about a mile or a mile and an half from Mr. Armitage's own house, and about two from hence."

"I know the place well," exclaimed Mrs. Crewkherne, who now with breathless impatience waited for the sequel.

"After the agreement was made for a bed chamber, and a light closet, and a sitting room in the farm house, for which it seems the farmer was at some expence, a considerable time ensued before the arrival of the lodgers, and then, one night, a post chaise arrived quite late from ********** with these females in it—A lady, who is described as a tall genteel figure, who speaks always very obligingly in English, but never willingly enters into conversation with any one on her affairs. Of the two with her, one was a girl apparently about fifteen, or hardly so much, fair and rather pretty, with loose hair of a golden brown hanging wild about her ears, and quite simple, and even childish, in her dress and manners; the lady it seems is her mother, or passes for such, though she looks almost too young; and the third is a French woman of three or four and forty, who cannot speak any English, and who affects to understand so little of it, that she answers only by signs. They live, it seems, very frugally, but after a sort of French way, according to the account of the good woman of the house, who says the French woman has taught their Hannah to make strange dishes for them of stews and soups. They pay very regularly once a fortnight for every thing, and the lady herself seems reserved, and seldom goes out, and nobody ever comes to see them but Mr. Armitage, who does not very often go, and your nephew sometimes with Mr. Armitage, but of late very much alone. Now you know Mr. Armitage's character, which to be sure is a very strange one. You know, after he parted from his wife, that he went to America, and people *do* say that this mysterious lady is a woman who left her husband on his account, and that this young girl is a daughter of his; and there *are* those who have a most sincere regard for your family, who are very much afraid, knowing what an artful man Mr. Armitage is, and the *amazing* influence he has obtained over Mr. George Delmont, that these persons have been brought hither with the wicked view, for indeed I cannot call it any other, of drawing him into a marriage."

"Impossible!" cried Mrs. Crewkherne, half shrieking with ill stifled passion— "'tis impossible any one should dare to think of such a connection for a nephew, for a grandson of the Earls of Castledanes; nor, unguarded, and misled, and degraded as he is in too many instances, would he himself ever think of such a thing—Marry an American girl, who may be a stroller[78] for aught he can tell!—Here in the very face of his family, and next door almost to *me* and to his sisters! Here, on the very spot where his family, inferior to none in England, have been the very first people since the conquest?"

Fear least[79] what she urged as impossible should nevertheless be true (and a thousand recollections crowded on her mind to increase it while she spoke) now stopped for a moment the sharp-noted eloquence of Mrs. Crewkherne, and her companion, who secretly enjoying the sight of the pain her intelligence had inflicted, obtained time to say in a subdued voice, and with great appearance of concern, "Nothing can be more just, dear Mrs. Crewkherne, than all you say. To be sure, such a thing would be not only very affecting indeed to Mr. Delmont's family, but, as one may say, a sort of national concern for nothing can be worse than for great families to demean themselves by low alliances, and especially with folks not properly born according to the laws of England—and then an American too!—a race that for my part seem to me not to belong to Christian society somehow, and who, I understand, are no better than atheists; for I am told there are no clergy in America, as our's are, established by law, to oblige and compel people to think right; but that all runs wild, and there are no tithes, nor ways of maintaining that holy order, as we have, but every body prays their own way, if indeed such free-thinkers ever pray at all, which I dare say they do not.—But I am assured that they are excessive bad people, and that it is a dangerous thing to have any communication with them, which certainly redoubles one's concern, *if* it be true that Mr. Delmont, who might, we all know, do so much better, should be so misguided, as so to connect himself."

"If!" cried Mrs. Crewkherne, who had been recalling numberless circumstances that confirmed her in it—"if!—I tell you Mrs. Nixon, the thing is quite impossible, and I must beg of you to contradict it wherever you hear it; for my part I am resolved to put an end to any such report; for I'll tell Mr. Delmont of it, and represent to him how injurious . . . . . ."

"Give me leave, dear madam," interrupted Mrs. Nixon, "to ask, if it would not spare you some uneasiness, and perhaps some painful altercation with your nephew, if you were yourself to ascertain whether these people are at all like what they are represented to be?—Perhaps, after all, it may not be so; they may merely be some of Mr. Armitage's London acquaintance, and Mr. Delmont may only accidentally have seen them. Suppose, as you have gone out for airings with Mrs. Winslow, you were to make an excuse to go thither, and see Mrs. Jemmatt, at Denbury, yourself; she is a very good kind of woman, and you may make any pretence you please to call at her farm."

"Not with Mrs. Winslow," replied Mrs. Crewkherne, "in the first place, she has such a terror of the roads, that I should never persuade her to go up the hills; and in the next place, if she should once get a notion of such an absurd, ridiculous, wicked, and insufferable inclination, *she* would make her use of it, and mar at once all we are trying to bring about, and in which, if George should not determine to ruin himself by his own folly, we shall succeed."

"Well then, if you think so," said Mrs. Nixon, "suppose you borrow the carriage, as the Doctor's horses *are now* hired ones; and as I shall return tomorrow to——, which is but three miles farther, you may set me down."

To this Mrs. Crewkherne agreed, and promising to say nothing of what had passed, the *gossips* parted; Mrs. Crewkherne, agitated by fear, pride, indignation, and impatience—the other delighted to be disburthened of a secret that had long been very troublesome to her, and obtained her conveyance home without hiring a post chaise, as she would otherwise have been obliged to do; and these circumstances, besides the importance she had acquired by being the first to divulge this news, were extremely grateful to her.

Chap. VII.

Entre nous, dites moi, si jamais un philosophe a causé le moindre
trouble dans la societé? Ne sont ils pas pour la plus part des
solitaires? ne sont ils pas pauvres?
sans protection, sans apui?[80]

Left an orphan at six years old, and educated at a boarding school, without any particular attention save what she had received from Mrs. Winslow during the two vacations of the year, Miss Goldthorp had now attained the age of twenty-one, and had been a few months in possession of her fortune. Her having arrived at her majority had hitherto made no other difference in her mode of life, than that of her assuming somewhat more consequence, and dressing rather more expensively. She seemed to meditate on her power of greater indulgence, and to be for a while passive, never troubling herself to contradict the frequent hints thrown out of the expectations of her uncle and aunt in regard to their son, nor ever saying what might be interpreted into a promise; and till she became of age they had forborne to press a conclusion of the marriage, because, had she died before that period, her fortune would have gone to some distant relations of her father's. Miss Goldthorp was one of those young women, of whom it is common to say, that they are "highly accomplished;" that is, she had made some little progress in the various branches of female education, which usually pass under the name of elegant accomplishments. Conscious of knowing something, she assumed credit for a great deal; and in consideration of her fortune, credit was given her for all she pretended to. On the piano forté she was said to possess wonderful execution; and certain it is, that both on that and on the harp she made a very loud noise, and rattled away with the most perfect conviction that her auditors were amazed at her facility. She spoke French with the same undoubting confidence, and therefore spoke it fluently if not with extreme correctness; besides which, she occasionally interlarded her conversation with words or short sentences in Italian, and had thence acquired the reputation of a very elegant Italian scholar. She often made her friends presents of most beautiful pieces of her own painting and embroidery, and they would have been equally wanting in taste and in gratitude had they questioned whether these productions, which Mrs. Winslow pronounced to be *supremely elegant*, were really the works of her own hands, or whether she had been assisted in them by her masters, or certain indigent young women who sometimes attended her with fashionable works.

As to her mind, she had, with a great idea of her own importance, many other faults of an heiress. She loved and hated with equal suddenness and violence. Her love was seldom bestowed on any but those who flattered her. The least slight, whether real or imaginary, ensured to the person who was guilty of it her inveterate hatred; yet she could occasionally dissemble, and had a way of affecting gentleness and affection towards those whom she would take the first occasion to ridicule or vilify. A coquet from disposition, she liked to be surrounded with admirers, and to persuade herself they followed her not for her fortune, but for her personal perfections. Some of these her adorers, who had become acquainted with her in her late excursion to the sea side, had discovered this foible, and were preparing to avail themselves of the discovery, when her accompanying the Doctor on his visit, and the accident that followed, removed their prey from their immediate pursuit, and threw her into the way of Delmont, whom she had only seen twice, before she fancied she must acknowledge him as the predestined master of her heart.

Dr. Winslow, ever alive to his interest, and piquing himself on his sagacity, was soon alarmed at the symptoms which he thought he perceived of this growing partiality, and he became impatient to put an end to its farther progress, by removing his niece from a scene where she was not only reminded of the obligation she owed, but had a constant opportunity of remarking the many perfections, which, it was not to be denied, were possessed by him to whom she was obliged; but on application to the medical man who had set the limb, he declared, that it would be a singular instance of good fortune, if in a fortnight his patient was in a condition to be safely removed.

All that could be done, therefore, was, to counteract as much as he could the impressions which the good Doctor so greatly apprehended; and as his wife was the only person to whom he could communicate his fears, or on whom he could vent his ill humour, he took the first occasion, when they were alone together, to remonstrate with her on the encouragement she frequently gave to Miss Goldthorp's evident admiration of Delmont. His natural peevishness of temper seized on every trifle. "Why," said he, "why will you always, in your flattering fulsome way, be praising this young man before her? A fine business it will be indeed, if your folly helps to ruin your son's prospects; but there is nothing, no, nothing that is foolish, that would be surprising from you. I stand amazed that you have not sense to perceive, that all the family are trying to bring the match about; and you! you, in mere weakness, mere inanity, and for the pleasure of hearing yourself talk, seem to me to be doing all you can to assist them."

The poor woman began in mild terms to defend herself. The preacher of patience and humility continued to reproach her, till he had nothing more to say, and till she had promised to be more guarded in future, and neither to praise the *elegant* taste of Delmont in his grounds, or ask Louisa for his verses, or remark on his fine person. "And let me tell you, Mrs. Winslow," said the Doctor, "that you are too apt, a great deal too apt to fall into these fits of admiration. As to this young man, I have studied him, and I assure you, that if our dear Middleton was out of the question, I should be sorry to see Martha the wife of such a one. Why, is he not the most singularly obstinate man as to opinions, and blind to his own interest to an incredible degree? Will he take advice? No, not even from those who are best qualified to give it. A very opinionated self-sufficient young man indeed! but he is a philosopher it seems, and it does not become a philosopher to follow any of the most respectable walks of life. Have a care, Mrs. Winslow, have a care, for you will otherwise find that fifty thousand pounds is a sum of which this pretended philosopher understands the value, and he'd no more scruple taking advantage of your folly, and the girl's romantic nonsense, to possess himself of it, than his brother philosophers have done to overrun Europe;[81] for my part, I profess I lose my patience at the idea! and stand amazed at the daily progress of these pernicious principles!"

Mrs. Winslow, declaring that her nerves were so shattered that she must call her maid for her drops, the Doctor finished his reproachful lecture; but the fretfulness it had excited was not easily appeased; and entering the study, he unfortunately found Delmont busied in unpacking and arranging books he had just received from London, among which were some of those works which the Doctor held in the greatest abhorrence from report only, for he had never read a line in them; but encouraged by the good nature and candour with which Delmont had on former occasions listened to him, he began a bitter invective against what he termed innovations in political, moral, and religious concerns.

"Yet, my dear Sir," said Delmont with great mildness, "you will allow, that if no innovations had ever been made, we should still have been what you certainly have learned to think of with a due degree of dislike; we should still have been under the papal tyranny; the fires of Smithfield might yet have blazed,[82] and we should have been denied the milder effulgence struck out from better principles by such worthy and well informed divines as yourself, my dear Doctor."

"Perhaps so, perhaps so," cried the Doctor; "but what has all that to do with government?"

"It might have had nothing to do indeed," replied Delmont, "if the religious and civil government had not been so interwoven, that whoever dissents from the first, as established by arbitrary laws, is immediately considered as the enemy of the other. Church and king, you know, are coupled for ever. If any particular mode of thinking or of education forbids a man's implicit obedience to the first, he becomes disqualified, by I know not what unjust and oppressive regulations, from serving the second."[83]

"And let me tell you, Sir," rejoined the Doctor, "very properly restrained; for he who does not acknowledge the infallibility of one, will hardly own the divine right of the other."

"Softly, softly, good Doctor; your infallibility and divine right there is no contending with. So many quarrels, and so much bloodshed and misery have already happened on account of those two very *sensible* and reasonable words, that we will not suffer them to raise even an argument between us; but give me leave to ask you, my dear Sir, what crimes, in a moral sense, you impute to these unlucky philosophers, against whom your wrath is kindled? Suffer me to ask you, in the words of one of them, 'Avez vous jamais vûe des philosophes aporter dans un païs la guerre, la famine, ou la peste? Bayle, par example, a t'il jamais voulu crever les digues de la Hollande, pour noyer les habitans, comme le vouloit, dit on un grand ministre, qui n'etoit pas philosophe.'"[84]

"Who but those who call themselves philosophers," exclaimed the Doctor, with increased impatience, "who else have occasioned all the bloodshed and misery we have unhappily lived to see in our time, in a neighbouring kingdom?"

"Pardon me, Sir; I believe it to be exactly the reverse; if the persons, whom you call philosophers, sought and imagined they had found truth; if so believing they endeavoured to emancipate the people from the fetters which galled and crushed them, to restore to them the rights of human nature so long withheld by superstition and tyranny; and if, in *trying* to do this, to benefit and enlighten the world, those who had an interest in oppressing and keeping it in darkness have some of them suffered; nay, if the innovators, or those whom they attempted to relieve, have many of them fallen in the shock, it is not just to say, that the persons who would have ameliorated the general condition of mankind have occasioned even this partial destruction. The truth is, that the gloomy and absurd structures, raised on the basis of prejudice and superstition, have toppled down headlong; many are crushed in their fall; even some of those Sampsons, who themselves shook the pillars, have been overwhelmed; but the bastilles of falsehood, in which men's minds were imprisoned, are levelled with the earth, never, never to rise again!"[85]

The enthusiasm which Delmont felt at this moment glowed on his countenance and animated his gesture. Doctor Winslow, who had never in his life been conscious of such a sentiment, and who cared nothing for the state of the world, so long as its arrangements permitted him to enjoy the gratifications he had learned to consider as necessary, knew not what to oppose. However, though confused for a moment, he was not either convinced or passive; but was collecting, as silently he sat swelling, all the common-place sayings he could remember, which, surcharged with anger, and zeal, and personal resentment, might have overcome, perhaps for a moment, the benevolent and hospitable temper of Delmont, had not the latter, who had finished placing his books, and recollected some orders he had to give about his farm, walked away, and left the Doctor to have once more recourse to his wife.

To her then he returned, and recommenced his complaints. Mrs. Winslow, roused by a repetition of ill-humour, then attempted to divert it, by assuring him, that if there was any such partiality on the part of Miss Goldthorp, it was not noticed by Delmont. "Dear Doctor," said she, "how strangely you are prepossessed. I am sure Mr. Delmont is totally indifferent to Martha. We women are often more quick-sighted than men in such matters; and I have besides reason to believe from Mrs. Crewkherne, that the family are very uneasy about some imprudent connection or engagement he has made; and as to Patty, I'm sure he hardly ever looks at her, or takes the least notice of her, more than just common civility requires; and of an evening, when we play at cards, or converse in her room to amuse her, he addresses himself much oftener to me than to her."

This the Doctor pronounced to be art; again gave his wife strict injunctions against expressing any admiration of any part of the Delmont family before Miss Goldthorp; and then repeating his concern and impatience at being so long detained where he thought his favourite scheme was in so much hazard of being overturned, he was relapsing into more than his former ill humour, when he was fortunately diverted from it by intelligence, that a person whom Delmont had employed to procure game for the Doctor to send to some friends in London waited to receive his commands for the disposal of three brace of pheasants and a leash of hares.

His fears and his resentment were for a while suspended, and he hastened to give directions for dividing them between one of his dignified friends and a man who had interest with a certain great bestower of benefices.

CHAP. VIII.

Les travers, et l'insignifiance de ces personnages aux quels
ressemblaient sans doute beaucoup des gens du monde, me
faisaient réfléchir sur le vuide des sociétés, et sur l'avantage de
n'etre point tenu à les fréquenter.[86]

No circumstance of personal inconvenience could make Delmont repent an interference, which had even mitigated the commonest evils to the humblest of beings; nothing therefore could make him regret, even when he was most teased and interrupted by its consequences, the fortunate accident which had put it in his power to rescue from destruction a young, and, as far as hitherto had appeared, an amiable woman, though any thing more tormenting to him than the perplexities that had been brought on by the sequel of this accident could hardly have been imagined by the mischievous malice of the most capricious of those powers which are fabled to preside over the destiny of mortals.

The acquaintance with which it had entangled him were wholly disagreeable to him. The pert pomposity of Doctor Winslow, only restrained by that sense of superiority which inferior minds always feel, though they place it to the account of any cause but the true one, was utterly disgusting to Delmont. The Doctor, ready every moment to offer his advice, and even enforce it by that air of authority which his apron of silk[87] and his wig of stupenduous curl seemed to authorize, shrunk, he knew not why, from the open countenance, the generous glow, the plain but energetic reasoning of a boy, who had hardly numbered twenty years. As the Doctor had not the remotest idea of any other reason than that which had taught him, when only four or five years older, to secure a coheiress with an handsome fortune, and not long after some excellent pieces of preferment (escaping with great adroitness from that very puzzling and disagreeable personage, Simon Magus,[88] who is somewhat like the John Doe and Richard Roe[89] of our admirable and clear forensic practice) the Doctor, when he felt himself subdued and abashed by the strait forward arguments of a stripling, who had never completed a course of logic, could only imagine that there was something irresistibly imposing in illustrious blood—He looked with a look of deference on the fine figure, the animated countenance of the unfeed and untaught pleader who stood before him, while he urged the rights of plain reason and common sense, and never suspecting that it was the omnipotence of that plain reason and common sense with which he was contending, while he had no other weapons than the wretched ones furnished by that inveterate prejudice and selfish interest which hood-winked all enquiry, Doctor Winslow (rubbing his smooth shining forehead, and passing his two fore fingers politely and cautiously under the foretop of his well dressed wig, as if to air a little his brain, which felt heated and confused in the contest) Doctor Winslow concluded with himself, that he was thus abashed merely by the powers of hereditary intellect, and that in argument with a plebeian adversary he could be at no such loss. He said—"this young man's great grandfather was the celebrated Henry Delmont, who so ably (though to be sure he was wrong) declared for certain doctrines in 1688.[90] His grandfather was a man celebrated for the brilliance of his wit, took another line in politics, and (though I am afraid he had rather loose principles as to certain points) and notwithstanding I never heard that his father was remarkably gifted with talents, yet, no doubt, the abilities of his remoter ancestry are renewed in this youth. Yes, yes, certainly strong parts are hereditary; I am convinced of it, and that makes it the more mortifying, when one reflects that this young man, who now suffers his talents to evaporate in wild chimeras, in theories taken from vile, very vile books, might, if he would only hear *reason*, be a judge, perhaps a chancellor, or what is in every sense a character more extensively beneficial to our species, a bishop, if not an archbishop."

Delmont had acquired, whether from hereditary prescription or not, a way of looking at whatever proposition was presented to him, not as Dr. Winslow had been used to do, exactly as it was shewn, but in every light it would bear. The Doctor had never thought of any object but exactly as his predecessors, his masters, had told him to think. He had done so well for himself by this method, that he could not for the life of him imagine how a man of only common sense could throw his bread upon the waters[91] by attempting any other.

For all sort of prejudices the Doctor had the profoundest respect, "because they were prejudices." He loved "ancient opinions;" they saved him the trouble of forming any new ones, and were the only opinions to live by. Why then should he cast them away? why suffer the slightest doubt to rest on his mind? Yet, unless he had suspected that the want of general reverence might in time undermine these "salutary prepossessions," and diminish or do away the emoluments which the regular professors of them enjoyed, he might never have felt that excess of zeal which induced him to try all his rhetoric on this young, and, as he hoped, yet unformed scyon of a noble house, who could not but do him so much honour as a disciple, or fail to prove so beautiful and polished an acanthus leaf in the Corinthian pillar of polished society.[92]

This ardour of friendly instruction, however, did not last many days. There was nothing to be got in the way of preferment at present from the family, and Mrs. Crewkherne, by whose representation his zeal had received its first impulse, not only thought in many points quite out of the pale, but looked, he thought, very coolly on him, and he began at the end of the first week to fear, that the accidental introduction of Miss Goldthorp into the family had opened views much more tempting to the ambition of a young man, than what could ever arise from his most successful exertions to obtain ecclesiastical honours and emoluments; but he was compelled to endure seven days longer these tormenting fears, which the observation of every day increased, and at the end of that time the surgeon seemed still unwilling to pronounce, that in the course of the next week his patient might with very great precaution be removed, and by journies of ten or twelve miles a day return to London. When Dr. Winslow reported this to Mr. Delmont, watching anxiously his countenance, and at the same time making a laboured apology for the trouble he and his family had so long given, he could not perceive any marks of concern on the features of Delmont; nothing that indicated the passions of love or interest. He said in return to his compliment all that civility and hospitality dictated, but with an indifference that made the anxious Doctor a little easier as to the heiress; he began to hope he had been mistaken.

But the female part of Delmont's family, who became every hour more solicitous for the success of their views, were not idle. In a long tête-a-tête between Miss Delmont and Miss Goldthorp, the latter disclosed to her her resolution to break the chains of guardianship, since she was now become of age. She said, that it was true Dr. Winslow and her aunt had been kind to her, and she had nothing to complain of as to their treatment of herself; but she could not help saying they were the most disagreeable people on earth to live with. "Yet, ah! my sweet Caroline," added she, sighing, "it was only since my acquaintance with this family that I knew, by all that contrast can impress, *how* irksome they were. My uncle is the most peevish man in the world, and frets and teases about such trifles, that there is never any repose in the house. He is a great epicure you must know, and piques himself upon understanding a table better than any housekeeper or clerk of the kitchen. In London it is his business to waddle out early in the morning to the two nearest markets to pick up nice things at reasonable prices. He returns to breakfast, to recount with great satisfaction what he has done in this way, which always turns me sick! one so hates to hear of dinner at breakfast-time! Then in due season, before dinner, he goes down to his duty in the kitchen, and directs how it should all be. It is not easy for my poor good aunt always to find cooks who will bear this, and we change about once a month; for notwithstanding all the dear Doctor's codling,[93] it happens continually that the fish is boiled to pieces, or the soup tasteless, or the ragout too salt, or too high, or too something or other; and then the little round man does so lament himself! especially if there is company, that he lives in a perpetual Jeremiad.[94] My aunt used to pluck up spirits, and scold again formerly, and then we had such dialogues of tart repartee that it was sometimes laughable enough; but lately, poor woman, she has fallen into what she calls her nervous ways, and instead of retorting she performs a fit; and really it is piteous to see her; though luckily her fits are of a sort that are miraculously cured by cards and company, when assafetida,[95] and all the horrible drugs she poisons herself with, seem to do no good at all. Then there's dear Middleton, my coz, the son and heir of this worthy couple, who is, they both declare, the first and foremost of created beings, and who may be so for aught I know. I have known, ever since I was eleven years old, that I was intended for the happy wife of this paragon; and I assure you I was not much older when I determined to be no such thing. I let them alone indeed, and do not positively contradict them; and poor Middletony does not put me to much trouble to repulse him, for he is a most chilly and inanimate lover, and had a great deal rather contemplate his ponies than his mistress; and though I know the notion of our being engaged keeps, as it is called, people off, yet, as I do not mean to marry till after I have been some time my own mistress, and never," continued she, sighing, "wished to attract any body, I never took the pains to contradict what I was told of, to be sure, often enough, but was rather amused to see the men, an hundred coxcombs or adventurers, who cared for nothing but my money, laying all sort of plots and schemes to supplant poor Mid, and going slyly to work to find out my opinion of him, and whether this supposed engagement was of my own choice, or I had been teased or compelled into it by the old folks. You cannot imagine how many ridiculous adventures of that sort I have had since I have lived with them. For the first two years after I left school, I resided with my father's mother, who did not much love the Winslow's; and the fortune *she* left me, which is very considerable, the Doctor and my aunt have no power over at all; whereas, of that which was my mother's only, I am not to have the principal till I am five and twenty, unless I marry with their consent, which I shall certainly never do if I do not agree to take their marvellous marmoset. However, I do not much trouble myself, my dear Caroline, about that clause; for the income I shall have will be enough, I hope, for the wishes of any reasonable man; and I can wait for the power to dispose of the five and thirty thousand till I am five and twenty."

Caroline Delmont had never heard her friend so communicative before, nor had she any idea, large as she knew her fortune to be, that it was to the amount she now seemed to hint, for Mrs. Winslow had, for obvious reasons, rather diminished than enlarged, when she spoke of it; Caroline therefore, when she paused after having thus spoken, ventured to ask her how much her income would be, when she was possessed of it all?

"Not quite three thousand a year, my sweet friend," answered she, "which, though it is not a very great fortune, gives me at least a right to please myself, which I assure you I intend to do; not merely in the article of marrying, but, though I am sorry, poor good folks, to disappoint them, in the article of having an house of my own, and living my own way. I know well enough what I shall have to contend with: the Doctor will fret and fume till it will half melt my tender heart; but then it will be hardened again by his *advice*, which I dread more than all his other boring powers. I shall turn a deaf ear, and go my own way, as I often do now (though, since I've been sick I have not been able to shew you a specimen of my managing him). But then my aunt will come with her tendernesses, and her tears, and twiddle twaddle ways of dear niecing and sweet girling me, and a thousand fal lal's about my mother, and how she hoped to have been, not in the fondness of her feelings only, but from the happiness of *her dear Middleton*, another mother to me as well as aunt, and the most affectionate of all grandmama's to my sweet babes, if ever I happen to have any, for the good lady always has a provident eye to posterity. If all this seducing rhetoric should fail, as fail peradventure it will, she will fall into a fit, which I shall be extremely sorry for, I assure you, because I love my aunt very well; but I cannot give up my freedom because of her aptitude to exhibit these pathetic scenes, knowing full well that the attack would be as sharp, if at one of her great routs in the winter the three most boasted of her fine friends should fail to shew their faces—if the counsellor's wife in the square had col-lected more people of fashion than she could do, or any other woeful mortification of the same sort. So I shall certainly oblige myself where myself is so much more in question than any one else; and time, you know, will get the better of the mama's lamentation and the son's love."

"Not so easily the last as the first," said Miss Delmont. "Poor young man! he may be a sad sufferer."

"Not he, indeed! I tell you my dear Caroline, he cares not a straw for me, nor for any woman; between ourselves, poor Middy is very weak, and the fuss the old folks make about him, which is perfectly ridiculous, shews his feebleness more, though he is such a mere cub yet, that his being such a ninny is not generally suspected; but I know very well that he is a mighty poor creature, one of those animals that any one may lead as they will, and who never venture to think for themselves. He never comes from college without having a new horse and a new friend, and it generally turns out that one recommended or sold him the other, so that he discovers at last that they are both good for nothing. Then poor Middleton has another quality; he cannot bear any one should be preferred to himself; for though he has not courage enough to assert it, he really does believe that he is all that his papa and mama declare him to be, so that when any other young fellow is talked of as being clever, or handsome, or dashing, or fashionable, little Mid looks as if an injury was done to himself."

"I remember now," said Caroline, "that during the very few days he staid after your accident, he seemed mightily cold towards George, and not to *take* to him, or indeed to any of us much—yet George is not tonnish,[96] nor dashing, nor fashionable."

"Not fashionable!" exclaimed Miss Goldthorp. "My dear, dear Caroline! you see with the eyes of a sister to be sure; but even those I suppose will not deceive you, or misrepresent such an uncommon figure as Mr. George Delmont's—To such height, such grace, such a form, as strikes you at once with an idea of manly beauty, who ever saw united such a face? the finest complexion in the world, for a man perhaps *too* fine, he would certainly have, if it was not for that *sunniness* which more than compensates for its change. You see by his forehead that he is fair, but it is only because that profusion of fine brown hair is now cut away for that odious crop fashion.[97] Then tell me, Caroline, if ever there were in an human head such eyes as your brother's! How commanding they are, yet how sweet. If they speak such ineffable things in his own family, or among those to whom he is indifferent, think, oh! no, I dare not trust myself to think, what they would be if animated by love."

Caroline, who never heard a declamation of this sort from a young woman before, and never suspected from the soft languid manners of Miss Goldthorp, that she was likely to make such a one, stared with amazement so visible that her friend could not help remarking it. "You seem astonished," said she, "my dear friend, at what I have ventured to say about your brother. It is not many people indeed I should praise so warmly; but as to all squeamish prudery in not speaking what one thinks, I've no notion of it, though I am so teased and so lectured by the old folks that I sit mimpetty mimp[98] before them merely for peace sake; but I don't see why one may not admire an handsome man as well as an handsome statue, or an handsome animal, or any thing else that is beautiful. I am very honest my dear Caroline, though I am forced to be a little of an hypocrite now and then, to save myself from being lectured to death; but there is no reason why, when you and I are alone, that I should not say as I think. Oh! when the blessed time comes that I shall have had courage to exert myself, and be my own mistress, I intend to shake off all this restraint, I assure you. I shall take an house in some pleasant street near the Parks, and it shall be at the command of my beloved Caroline, if she will deign to accept it, exactly the same as at my own. We may be sisters at least in our hearts, Caroline!" (a deep sigh again gave pathos to the sentence.) "We may be sisters in our hearts, if my inexorable destiny should deny me the happy title I aspire to."

Here the enthusiasm, the sanguine spirit, which had a moment before animated the manner, if not the countenance of the love-sick fair, sunk at once. Tears filled her eyes, she sobbed audibly, and hid her face (though not her blushes) in the bosom of her friend. Caroline Delmont, new to all this style of behaviour, was extremely struck with it; she not only felt the tenderest pity for her friend, but found herself materially involved in the success of her passion.

The artful manner in which Miss Goldthorp had thus contrived to address her, was exactly calculated to secure her wishes for success, had she not before felt them. All the ridicule thrown on the Doctor and his wife, as well as the romantic rhodomontade that followed it, and the concluding tender appeal to her pity, were calculated to amuse and interest a very young person, who, since she left her governess and her nursery, had been confined to such society as were to be found at the house of Mrs. Crewkherne, among whom a smile was almost accounted a crime; where no book of amusement was ever suffered to come, and where nothing was ever discussed but religious topics, which received the most gloomy hue from the manner wherein they were represented. Caroline had often been compelled to listen to these saturnine pictures of sins and sorrows, till she had shuddered to find herself in a world so full of calamities, from which it seemed impossible to escape.

CHAP. IX.

Behold the sage Aurelia stand,
Disgrace and fame at her command,
As if heaven's delegate design'd
Sole arbiter of all her kind![99]

While the romantic Miss Goldthorp was thus securing her interest with one part of
the family, the active curiosity of Mrs. Crewkherne, raised by the report of Mrs. Nixon,
was busied in tracing, if possible, the causes that might impede the success of a project,
which seemed to be as near her heart as it was to that of her niece. But other motives
than those which had excited the zeal of the younger, stimulated that of the elder lady.
It was indeed difficult to say, whether ambition to restore to that branch of the family
she was related to the wealth and consequence they had lost, had more influence than
two other wishes that arose in her bosom; one was to mortify the young dowager Lady
Castledanes, whom she detested with the most inveterate malignity, and the other, to
detect the artifices by which she imagined Mr. Armitage had obtained such an influence over the moral and political opinions of George Delmont.

Mrs. Crewkherne did, indeed, abhor Mr. Armitage, with a degree of animosity
that seemed hardly natural, when it was considered that this object of her hatred,
knew her not even by sight, having never seen her above once by accident, and in a
crowd of other company, where such a figure and face as her's, were very unlikely to
make the slightest impression on the memory of a man who was, by habits of retirement, become indifferent to general society, and selected his own among persons of a
very different description. But Mr. Armitage was an author, who had ventured, though
with great candour and liberality, to speculate on certain points which Mrs. Crewkherne
could not bear should ever be discussed at all, and by which he had acquired the
reputation of a free-thinker.[100] In most of the charities of life he was exemplary; the
best master, and the best friend; his humanity to the poor, and his benevolence to all
the world, were bounded only by his circumstances, which were not affluent; but he
dared, in many respects, to live for himself; and, conscious of the equity and integrity
of his own heart, served God less according to the rules prescribed in the country in
which he resided, than according to certain ideas of his own. He had married early in
life; but his wife, who brought him a very large fortune, and who had chosen him in a
fit of romantic enthusiasm she hardly knew why, was not long in discovering that his
notions and her's could by no forbearance on his part, be made so to accord as to
produce any degree of harmony. She hated literary society, was wretched where she
could not be the first figure, and disgusted by the plain truths told her by many of his
friends, from whom she expected adulation. The single tie between them being broken by the early death of the only child they ever had, she assumed the privilege her
fortune gave her (for the greatest part of it she had reserved to her own use) and passed
every summer at some place of public resort; every winter in London; where, had Mr.
Armitage enquired narrowly into her conduct, he might perhaps have found causes
that would have justified his applying to the laws of his country to have dissolved this

ill-assorted connection. But he could not prevail upon himself to expose, in a court of law, a woman whom he had once loved, and who had been the mother of a child he had been passionately fond of. He wished not to try his fate again in a lottery, where he thought the chances so much against him; and it was at length agreed, that this ill-paired couple should separate for ever, Mrs. Armitage taking almost all her own fortune, with which, tired of her own country, she soon after went to France, and on being alarmed by the public troubles of that country, had since established herself at Florence; while Mr. Armitage had yielded to the inclination he had always felt for travelling; and being thus free from every domestic tie, had wandered for near two years over Europe, from whence he had lately passed a second time to America; and only twelve months had elapsed, since he had once more sat down, in literary and philosophical retirement, at Ashley Combe, the seat of his ancestors, not far from Upwood cottage.

Mrs. Crewkherne, in every part of this history, found something to nourish her hatred. She could not speak with patience of a man who had parted with his wife, though it was her own wish. She hated a man who affected to revere, and had written in favour of the Americans; nay, who had aided and abetted, as far as in him lay, the atrocious French revolution; for he had been present at Paris at the taking the Bastille, and had applauded the speech of Mirabeau, in the Jeu-de-Paumes;[101] and, on his return, had ventured to write a pamphlet, in which, while he exhorted the French people not to suffer themselves to be led by the first effervescence of liberty, into such licentiousness as would risk the loss of it, he hazarded a few opinions on the rights of nations, and the purposes of government, which though they had been written and spoken, and printed a thousand times under different forms, and were besides modified by the nicest attention to the existing circumstances of his own country, and softened by a mildness and amenity of language, which was thought very considerably to weaken their effect, yet these high crimes and misdemeanors had estranged from him two or three old friends who held places, and several others who expected them.

One of these, a nobleman of Mrs. Crewkherne's acquaintance, had very gravely told her, that whoever was not a declared enemy of this dangerous Mr. Armitage, must be so to all order, all good government, and to our ever blessed constitution; so she abhorred him not only from the impulse of her own mind, but from that communicated to her by this worthy friend of her's, who was a man of rank, and of course infallible. Her excessive zeal on the other side was, indeed, without bounds, humanity, or reason; and she scrupled not to declare, how greatly she was delighted with the project that had been formed, for exterminating by famine twenty-eight million of people;[102] nor did she hesitate to express how much satisfaction it would give her, were it possible to realize the indignant supposition of Mr. Burke;[103] and that France, republican France, could, by a single blow, be struck from among the nations of the earth.

All this political vehemence, much of which was very opposite to the tenets of her spiritual directors, was compounded from many ingredients which had accumulated in the mind of Mrs. Crewkherne, where, as in the magic cauldron of Hecate,[104] they had fermented, till such a spirit was produced by them as really gave the poor gentlewoman, in the paroxysms of its operation, the air of a priestess of Cybele,[105] in all the horrors of inspiration. Her little red eyes seemed too much inflamed to stay in their sockets: she stretched her cheeks, gasped for breath, and trembled with ire, so that it was, if not dangerous, at least so disagreeable to encounter her in these phrenetic fits, that George Delmont, who did not love to see her expose herself, first, because she was a woman, and next, because she was his grandmother's sister, used to wave the subject himself, and draw off from it any of his friends, who might unwarily be engaged to try with her the friendly controversy of conversation.

If, however, it unfortunately happened, that some luckless wight unwittingly touched on any topic, in a way which she thought indicated the least partiality, or even mercy, towards that great magazine of fuel for her rage, the French revolution, the tygress, robbed of her young, was gentler. In proportion as her prejudices were violent, her arguments were weak. She hated every body born on the other side of the water, because they were not Englishmen; and when it was humbly represented to her, that such a circumstance was rather their misfortune than their fault, since every man and woman would undoubtedly be born in England if they could, she then hated the French in particular, because they were our *natural enemies*, and papists; but on its being gently observed to her, that of that last error they had, as far as they could, cured themselves, she then discovered that she abhorred them ten times more for that very reason.[106]

To all these wide and well-founded causes of her detestation, which she had learned when a girl, and fancied was a part of a sort of second creed, were added her fears, not only for her money, the greatest part of which was in the stocks, but, if the barbarians should invade us, she had terrible forbodings of what might occur to her personal safety, in case of such an event. In this last article, she really had apprehensions of the most distressing nature imaginable, insomuch that Upwood, being only about seven or eight-and-twenty miles from the coast, had been with her one reason for refusing to remain there the two first winters after Miss Delmont became her charge, which, notwithstanding her horror of solitude, she would otherwise gladly have done, to save what she loved extremely, her money.

Then, in addition to all this, she felt an immense accumulation both of consequence and wrath, from the remembrance of having once dined in company with the great and commanding writer and orator, who had enacted Peter the Hermit, and (so fortunately for Great Britain) preached a crusade against "the Gallic savages."[107] Sir Appulby Gorges had invited her to hear and see him. She had been amazed, petrified, enchanted, carried to the seventh heaven by his eloquence; and nobody, unless Whitfield himself was to return to earth,[108] could ever again so affect and convince her. Ever since that blessed epocha, therefore, she silenced every one who ventured to enter the lists with—"Sir, I have heard from that most wonderful man."—"Sir, I assure you, on the authority of the first orator of the age, which I had from himself"—or, "Sir, it was a remark of my friend, the most admirable Mr. B——." The discomfited adversary, whom she thus put down, was often compelled to fly in dismay, having nothing he ventured to oppose to such authority.

Now Mr. Armitage was believed to have written, besides the mild and gentle pamphlet he avowed, a very cutting argumentative book against one of the productions of Mrs. Crewkherne's idol; and when to such offences was added, the terrible suspicion he had lately been open to, of having produced some unknown creature a candidate for the affections of George Delmont, at a time when he had an opportunity of marrying an heiress; the fury which agitated the breast of Mrs. Crewkherne, when she set forth to make discoveries against him, is not to be described. As they went along, it formed the sole topic of her conversation; and Mrs. Nixon, for reasons of her own, artfully fomented her indignation.

It happened that the postillion who was employed to drive them, knew nothing of the way across fields, and through a large tract of woodland, which led to the farmhouse, whither there was not on any side any other way than that made by waggons. The man missed the gate by which he could, through enclosures, have reached the house, and got into a lane leading to the woods, where the soil being deep, the ruts made by the carriage of heavy timber from the wood to the nearest navigable river, rendered the way almost impassable for a post-chaise; so that after a little stumbling on the part of the horses, and grumbling on that of the man, Mrs. Crewkherne's fears for her limbs, got the better of those she entertained for her muslin *sultane*,[109] or her blue shoes, and she determined to walk on to the house, the postillion assuring her that he knew the path, to which he pointed on an high bank, led to it through a copse.[110] He assisted the ladies to gain this path, and then told them he must draw "the chai out backord, by fastening the horses behind un, up athwart the doun, and then he know'd how, by gwine a mile about or there a way, to get un round zafe enough to the fairm," where he promised to be almost as soon as they should reach it themselves.

The path they followed was high and dry for some time. It then led them into a copse, where, as autumn was now very far advanced, the fallen leaves, loaded with moisture, augured but ill to the shoes of Mrs. Crewkherne, while the briars and underwood every moment committed hostilities on her nice gown and elegant cloak, for she had dressed herself very superbly for a morning visit, in order to awe and impose on those she expected to find, by the dignity of her appearance; and with all her humility and contempt for the vanities of this wicked world, she loved as well to be thought *very fashionable*, as Mrs. Winslow did to be *very elegant*.

Busied, therefore, in guarding against the inconvenience of this rude walk, the eloquence of Mrs. Crewkherne for a while was suspended, and her companion, equally silent from the same careful attention to her garments, followed her, when suddenly the path turned short into a somewhat wider way; and Mrs. Crewkherne hearing voices, looked up to enquire if she was right, when she saw before her a young woman certainly not a peasant; her straw hat, filled with nuts, lay on the ground beside her, and her gown was held out to receive more, which were showering from the hazle trees above her, among the boughs of which appeared George Delmont, who, little guessing who was the spectatress of his activity, was making his way among the branches, now shaking their fruit from them, and now crushing down some of the most flexible, that his fair companion might herself gather the nuts.

To be convinced that all she had heard, that even more than she had heard, was true, and that all her projects for securing Miss Goldthorp's fortune, were at an end for ever, were but the ideas of a second in the mind of Mrs. Crewkherne. If she had dared to have followed the first impulse of her rage, she would perhaps have seized and have strangled, if she could, the object that thus excited it; forgetting however all forms, she stepped close to the young person, and drawing herself up, said in a sharp and imperious tone, "Pray who are you?"—"Who am I?" replied a soft and musical voice, which however trembled with fear—"Who am I ?" Delmont, who had from his leafy lodge beheld the questioner, and heard the question, was instantly on his feet, and perceived at once that his visits to the farm had been discovered by the restless curiosity of his aunt, who was determined to know to whom they were made.

Nothing remained but to avow openly an acquaintance, which he had no other reason for concealing, than his knowledge of that invidious suspicion with which his aunt regarded every one in obscurity, or not immediately recommended to her by rank, fortune, or connections.

The independent and self-relying spirit, which had made him shake off the yoke imposed upon him by opinion and prejudice, would not permit him to submit for a moment to any restraint, attempted by one for whose understanding he had a thorough contempt, and of whose heart he had so ill an opinion. He, therefore, without disguising his displeasure, said, "By what right, madam, do you question this young lady? If you have any business in this part of the country, it certainly is not with her."

"Oh, Mr. Delmont, Mr. George Delmont," cried the angry aunt, her voice trembling with rage;—"and is it come to this? I thought indeed what would be the consequence of your intimacy at Ashley Combe. I find my intelligence was but too true. Oh! what times are these!—when such a man as Mr. Armitage pretends to be, is not ashamed of encouraging such vile doings, and of lending his assistance to seduce young men of family from the paths of honour and right. But I am determined," added she, passing by him, "to know the very foundation of all this." She was only a few paces from the termination of the wood. It opened by an hunting gate, into an orchard adjoining the farm-house. Mrs. Crewkherne and her companion stepped hastily on, while Delmont, hardly able to repress the indignation which this impertinent intrusion excited, was employed in reassuring the young person, who, trembling and terrified at the fierce looks and menacing tone of the old lady, though she hardly comprehended the purport of what she uttered, was obliged to lean for a moment against a tree. Then, recovered by the argument of Delmont, she said, "What can this lady have heard against me? Oh! Mr. Delmont, if she should address herself in the same rude and unfeeling manner to my mother!"

"She shall not, by heaven," exclaimed he; "will you remain here, or accompany me while I go to check this insolent intrusion?"

"Let me remain," answered the trembling girl—"I will go round the other way to the house.—I have not courage to encounter those women again.—Save my mother, if possible, from being affronted by them."

Delmont now sprang forward, and overtook the two ladies at the moment they entered the door of the house. He passed them without speaking, and hastened to the room where the lodgers usually sat—the person he sought was not there. He returned hastily to the kitchen, but stopped in the passage—the door was open, and he saw the enquirers were already seated in conference with the farmer's wife, who, amazed at their appearance, and somewhat awed by the air of authority Mrs. Crewkherne assumed, had already told them almost all she knew, which did not, however, much enlarge their knowledge, since it amounted to no more, than that the ladies she believed came from foreign parts, "though I don't justly," said she, "know where—they have a very good sort of body for their maid, although she is a French woman, and can't speak no English at all; but the ladies themselves, they talk English well enough, as far as I see, though to be sure I'm no great judge; for the mother does not speak much to me, being always a writing and such like; and for the young thing, 'tis quite a child as 'twere."

"They are mother and daughter, then?" enquired Mrs. Nixon. "Yes, ma'am, so they say" replied the woman; "and to be sure, the elder gentlewoman is so despert fond of Miss, that she is her mother I dares for to say—she worships the very ground she treads upon, and I don't much wonder at it, for Miss is a sweet pretty creature to my thinkings—so gay and good natured, and affable!—our folks quite takes to her."

"And how came these ladies your lodgers, Mrs. Jemmatt?" said Mrs. Nixon— "you are not accustomed to take lodgers?"

"Why no, ma'am, not since Dr. Greams' lady used to come here for change of air, and to drink asses milk, as you may be pleased to remember. My husband fitted up them there rooms, as we did'nt want, for she; and so when squire Armitage came to ask us to take this lady and her daughter, why to be sure we could not be agin it."

"It *was* Mr. Armitage, then," said Mrs. Crewkherne, "who engaged you to take them?"

"Yes, ma'am 'twas the squire to be sure, and very handsome he have kept his word with us about every thing he agreed for, and very good ladies to be sure they are, and gives no trouble though they pay so genteel. But, howsomever, if it 'twant as good a bargain I'm sure, as my husband says, we are so much obliged to squire Armitage, that we oft for to do any thing he requires to sarve and obligate any friend of his—for if it had not been for him, our Harry would have gone off for a horse soldier, that there time he was so misguided as to list[111] at fair—and if he had, he would have been just as poor Tom Wilson and Philip Houseman are, fine lads, neighbours sons of ours, who would be obstinate and go, and are both dead—dead and gone—and if the same sort had befell our Harry, I'm sure neither his father nor I should have much cared what came afterwards. But squire Armitage, ladies, never rested night nor day till he got Harry released, and persuaded him into the right way again, to mind his farm, as his father did before him, and to be sure what all we in this here country say of the squire is true enough—that he is the very best man, and the kindest hearted that ever lived."

This effusion of gratitude was gall and wormwood[112] to Mrs. Crewkherne.

"Kind hearted," she repeated sneeringly—"kind hearted indeed!—I'm sorry truly, truly sorry for the profligacy of the times.—I see—ah! I see it is too true, *that* profligacy pervades the country, and a man, calling himself a gentleman, forsooth! is not ashamed to corrupt the manners of good plain country people, nor to turn their houses into brothels!"

Delmont, disdaining to listen to the conversation, had departed through the orchard to seek the person on whose account only he was alarmed at it; he did not therefore hear this illiberal sentence; the good woman to whom it was addressed only partly understood it, yet comprehending that it was injurious to the character of her lodgers, she with difficulty refrained from resenting it.

"I don't know, indeed, ma'am," said Mrs. Jemmatt, "what you are pleased to mean about corrupt; but there is no lady more honourable than our lodger, let the next be who she will; and I wish for my part half our gentry was as good."

"Good," repeated Mrs. Crewkherne, contemptuously—"alas, dame, you know not what you say!—what, woman! don't you know the character of that Armitage?— a vile man!—and you pretend not to know that this person is one of his——God forgive me for naming the creature—one of the wicked women who have been the cause of his using his lawful wife so barbarously—and will you tell me, Dame Jemmatt, that this girl is not one of his base-born children, that he has brought here to mislead a young man of honourable family to his undoing!"

The woman stood as if thunderstruck. Amazed at the charge, and the vehemence with which it was delivered, and half-frightened at the grim visage, distorted with passion, of the accuser, she remained in silent dismay, till Mrs. Nixon, who saw that this violence was more likely to baffle their enquiry than to procure the information they desired, said, "Come, come, dear madam, don't make yourself so uneasy; perhaps matters may not be so bad as your anxiety for your nephew makes you fear; perhaps, good Mrs. Jemmatt, you do not know this lady."

"Yes, I have seen the lady," replied the farmer's wife.

"Then I need not tell you, Mrs. Jemmatt, that this lady is nearly related to Lord Castledane's family, and people of that high station, you know, are naturally desirous that the young folks belonging to them may not make connections beneath them, and disgrace their families; so Mrs. Crewkherne having heard that this lodger of your's was a person of rather a slight character, and, to be sure, we did hear that the elder of the persons was Mr. Armitage's mistress, why it was natural, you know, for a lady careful of the honour of a great family to make some enquiry—and if it really turns out as it is to be feared——"

The honest zeal of Mrs. Jemmatt could not bear these imputations on the characters of her lodgers any longer with patience; but interrupting Mrs. Nixon, she struck the iron she held, and with which she had been continuing her work, against the board, and said, "If there was a son of twenty lords, or dukes either, that had a mind to Miss Glenmorris, I am sure she deserves him, and better too than a great many on 'em be; but it's no such thing. As to young Squire Delmont, which is him that I suppose this gentlewoman is in such a hoe about,[113] he have never a bin a nighst the place without Mr. Armitage till this morning, and for any one for to go for to pretend that Squire Armitage is more than a friend to her mother, it's as big a lie, and I don't care who hears me say so, as ever was told. The Lady, as I be told, and verily believes, is the wife of one of his friends, who upon some account or another is beyond sea, and she have business as oblig'd her to come with her daughter to England; and Mr. Armitage, who does good to all that want it, whether gentle or simple, have took her under his protection, because she is a lone woman and a stranger; and I'm sure there's no harm in their acquaintance."

"You sure!" exclaimed Mrs. Crewkherne. "Good woman, learn to confine your assertions to things more within your own narrow sphere of life. How should *you* be a judge! what can such folks as *you* know! Come, Mrs. Nixon, I shall return for this day to Mr. Delmont's on account of my nieces.—Poor girls!—But as to being longer an inmate in the house of that misled boy, who will disgrace his family, I will *not*. You need not give yourself the trouble to say a word more, dame what d'ye call it? (for Mrs. Jemmatt seemed eager again to be heard)—give yourself no more trouble—I am quite convinced—Call my carriage, you maid there."

Mrs. Crewkherne then stalked away to the chaise, her officious friend following, in their way to whose home the latter endeavoured to mitigate the mischief she had made, by intimating, that however appearances were against these women, it was *possible* they might be innocent. Mrs. Crewkherne had heard enough, and having taken leave of her informer, returned to Upwood, resolute to take an eternal leave of her nephew, and vindicate, as far as depended upon her, the honour of her family.

CHAP. X.

Alas! master Doctor! what so wayward
as the will of a woman?[114]

In returning to Upwood, after having set down her very officious friend, Mrs. Crewkherne had time to consider, that by the violent measures she had at first proposed to take, she should inevitably and at once occasion the loss of the opportunity to seize a fortune which seemed to be thrown so providentially in the way of her nephew; whereas, by moderating her wrath, and endeavouring to reason with him, there might be yet a chance of awaking him to a sense of his own interest. That he had some improper connection with the young woman she had seen she did not doubt; but if he was not frantic enough to marry her, the good lady hoped the evil might cure itself; for though, to be sure, Mr. Armitage was a most wicked wretch to have caused such a deviation from propriety, yet the sin, she trusted, would lay at his door; and if Delmont did but raise his fortune, means enough might be found to stifle the whole business; so much difference was there in her opinion between the crimes of the rich and the poor.

Having appeased the violent ebullitions of her choler by these prudent considerations, she arrived at home to dinner, and found that Miss Goldthorp was permitted by the surgeon to dine below on that day for the first time.

It was now that the attentions of Delmont would have been particularly gratifying, and should, according to the laws of hospitality and politeness, have awaited her; but Delmont did not appear. Mrs. Crewkherne had again need of all her prudent forbearance to prevent her displeasure from breaking out. Miss Goldthorp said she was languid and fatigued only from so slight an exertion, and retired almost as soon as the table-cloth was removed, while her uncle and aunt, who thought they saw, in almost all she said or looked, proofs of her increasing partiality for Delmont, were grown so eager to hasten her away, that she became at length impatient of their repeated importunities, and took occasion afterwards, in the course of the evening, when alone with the Doctor, to signify to him in very plain terms, that she should not be at all sorry, since their departure was of so urgent necessity, if they went away without her.

"*I am* not obliged to go to town on a particular day, sir, if you and my aunt are. I do not wish, certainly, to put you to the smallest inconvenience on my account; but surely there is no occasion for me to risk my health. I am very well placed here, and with people of fashion, who are so good as to have taken a friendship for me, and I have my own maid to attend me—I really, dear uncle, will not be hurried."

"You will not! Patty! *will* not! my dear girl! God forbid I should wish to hurry you, however I suffer in my affairs, and those of our dear Middleton, from this unlucky delay."

"It was your dear Middleton's own fault, sir. I am sure I have the most reason to murmur, who have suffered so much pain, and been in danger of losing my arm, if not my life."

"Ah! Patty, Patty!" cried the Doctor, in a moving tone, "there was a time when you would not have spoken so unkindly of Middleton Winslow; a young man of the very first promise; a young man whose affection for you is such, as I should have thought, my dear Martha, might have induced you to have expressed a *leetle* kindness for him."

"Lord, sir!" peevishly interrupted the lady, "I do feel not a *leetle*, but a great deal of kindness for cousin Middy; but one cannot really always be playing at puss in the corner[115] with one's cousin—I wish, sir, you and my aunt would recollect, that I am not a child; that I am now my own mistress; and that it is almost time I should leave off some of my leading strings,[116] least, if I am relieved from them all at once, I should feel such a sudden alteration from my freedom, that I should not know how to comport myself."

"I stand amazed!" exclaimed the Doctor—"Surely, Miss Goldthorp, you never thought proper to address yourself to me or your aunt in this way before."

"Yes I have, sir," replied she laughing; "But it's a great deal of trouble to be always differing with one's friends, and I am naturally lazy. However, I am sorry you stand amazed, for I don't wish to make you or Mrs. Winslow uneasy; but really one must consider oneself a little sometimes. You know I hated vastly to be dragged from the pleasant acquaintance I had just made at a public place, to pay that visit you proposed to your old friend the Dean, who is a very worthy man no doubt, but did not promise *me*, I think, much amusement: you ought to remember, uncle, how good naturedly I consented, and that I never have scolded your Middleton once for breaking my arm; so don't be in violent wrath if I just beg to stay where I am till it is quite well again. In short, my dear uncle, I am not well enough to contest the matter, but my resolution is taken. You may go whenever you like it; and indeed I think it would on some accounts be proper, for it is rather a long visit to make for so many of us; but as to myself, I certainly shall stay till Mr. Cleyton, my surgeon, says I can travel without any hazard."

This peremptory decision, which was delivered in a way Miss Goldthorp had never attempted before, conquered at once the patience which the politics of the Doctor had enjoined; his passion and peevishness broke through every restraint; and again declaring that he "stood amazed!" which was with him a favourite expression, he intimated in very unguarded terms, that her desire to remain where she was did not arise from any apprehension she entertained for her health, but because she had conceived a partiality for the master of the house.

"Well, sir," retorted the spirited damsel, who now saw an opportunity of shaking off, at least in part, a yoke that she had for some time found very uneasy. "Well, sir, admitting it to be so, I think one may have a much worse taste. You must allow that Delmont is a young man of family; and certainly one of the handsomest men in the world."

"You are lost, Miss Goldthorp; I see you are lost. I don't mean to say a word against the family of Mr. Delmont—I respect it—I highly respect it—but for himself . . . ."

"Well, sir, for himself!"

"He is, I am grieved to my immortal soul to say it (and the discreet Doctor lowered his voice) he is, I fear, a young man, abandoned, quite abandoned to his own imaginations."

"Most young men are, sir," interrupted the niece; "but I don't know that they are the worse for it. Whose imaginations would you have them take to?"

"You know my meaning well enough, Martha Goldthorp," cried the Doctor; "you only affect to misunderstand me. Oh! my inward soul is grieved to think what your good, your pious, your honoured parents would have said, had they lived to see this day, when, without any advance on his side, you, a young woman so well, so strictly, so properly and prudently brought up, should fix her mind on a youth without principle, without piety. Why! what! can there be a greater proof of it? Will he take orders? No! though his own relation has told me that all his family have been upon their knees to him as 'twere!—And why?"

"Dear sir, because he is a vast deal too handsome for a parson. 'Twould be shocking to see so charming a figure in an odious black coat; and who could think without screaming of that beautiful hair of his being cut off—and that his face, which is so remarkably fine, should be disfigured in a frightful wig?"[117]

"A wig!—thou art absolutely become an infant again, Miss Goldthorp. Oh! the puerility, the folly of modern young women!—and so you do *not* deny but that you are in love with this young man.—In love!—I stand amazed!—Well may the times and manners be subjects of sincere regret to all serious people!—A young woman so far forgets herself as to say, to profess, to declare, she is in love!"

"Nay, sir, I neither declared nor professed any such thing. *You* were pleased to say it; and certainly there are many things in which your great sagacity and immense penetration might lead you to a less natural conclusion."

"The young gentleman has the character of being misled by evil counsellors."

"Oh! I should soon get him out of *their* hands, and counsel him myself."

"As to fortune, he has nothing, or next to nothing."

"My dear uncle, I have enough for both."

"Then he has the wildest, the most eccentric ideas."

"They must be infinitely amusing, for I understand he has a wonderful deal of genius; and really one is quite bored by being obliged to listen for ever to the same set of notions. I have been tired of such John Trott[118] sort of prosing ever since I was ten years old, and should doat excessively upon a dear creature who could amuse one by starting something new."

"I am afraid, Miss Goldthorp," cried the Doctor, whose wrath was now kindling beyond all restraint; "I am afraid you will repent all this when it will be too late. However, I have done, madam; I have done; I stand amazed at your conduct; and if you have forgotten what you owe to your own dignity and consequence, I must at least take care, as far as I can of you, for the sake of your honourable and respectable parents; and as to the fortune, of which you are not to possess the principal till you are five-and-twenty, I shall put it before the Lord High Chancellor of England,[119] and he, Miss Goldthorp, he shall judge whether a young woman of fifty thousand pounds fortune and upwards shall throw herself away in this manner—on a man!—of good family indeed, but for aught I can learn, with little or no fortune—a man too without a profession, and who takes upon him to cavil and comment—and—and—and—I wish I had died, I say, Miss Goldthorp, before I had lived to see this day."

"Well! but now, uncle, since you have lived to see it, do, there's a good man, be a little calm and reasonable for once. Why, what *is* all this fuss about? Suppose it were true that I should be such a naughty girl as to like Mr. Delmont rather than my own pretty little coz, what then? What has the Lord High Chancellor of England, or five hundred be-wigged and be-robed old fellows, all as ugly and disagreeable, to do with me, beseech you? You threaten to put the fortune I am not to have the principal of till I am five-and-twenty into his power. I don't care whether you do or no. He cannot, now that I am of age, hinder me from marrying—he can only keep that principal, and put me to some expence. My dear uncle, I am not to be so frightened. I know perfectly what I can do."

"Oh! yes," cried the Doctor, now absolutely foaming with rage. "Oh! yes, you have gathered knowledge enough, no doubt, since you have been in this family!"

"There again, dear Doctor, you are in an error. A certain colonel of horse let me into that secret many months since; and now, uncle, since you have forced me to say so much, I will tell you plainly once for all, that *I will not* be controuled in the most important concern of my life; I will not be wheedled or threatened into marrying your son, which is what you aim at; and if I am to be watched, and checked, and teased, as if I was still a baby in leading-strings, I must resolve, though very sorry to give my aunt concern, to leave her, and establish myself in an house of my own."

Doctor Winslow now found he had gone too far, and was beginning to say something which was meant to soften and appease, when a violent shrieking and sobbing in the next room put an end to the conversation; it was Mrs. Winslow, who having overheard great part of this conversation, and unable any longer to restrain expressions of the pain and displeasure she felt from it, was, as her woman Mrs. Dibbins expressed it, "in such a way!!"

The good Doctor was now under the necessity of quieting his own agitated spirits, least the distress of his lady should be increased, till the subject of their solicitude became known in the house, which he desired above all things to avoid. The party in the house, however, were themselves employed in investigating the same concern, as it affected themselves.

Delmont not being returned, Mrs. Crewkherne had closetted his two sisters, and unable any longer to keep to herself the discovery she had made in the morning, related it with several additions, which her own *candid* imagination failed not to invent; and then putting in the very worst light the future prospects of the family, she lamented the probability there was, that this occasion of securing to it so handsome a fortune as Miss Goldthorp's should be so senselessly lost.

"I have always foreseen," said she, "always from the very first, how it would be; but every body, forsooth, was wiser than me. Did I not often tell your mother, that she used to let you all have your own way a thousand times too much, and particularly this ill-fated young man; but she, poor woman! had heard so much praise of her own understanding, that she thought she had found out a new way of educating children, and chose to follow in a great many respects the nonsensical schemes of some wicked atheistical French or German writer[120]—You may know perhaps who I mean—I don't say all this now your mother is dead, by way of reflecting on her memory; but I am sure, if your brother George had been educated and restrained properly like other young men, he would have known his own interest better."

"Do other young men, then," said Louisa (the youngest of the two sisters) "those who have been under the restraint you mention, *always* do what is prudent? I think, madam, that I recollect your saying sometimes quite the reverse, and that you have found great fault with the present race of young people in general, most of whom have, to be sure, escaped the misfortunes of poor George, in having a mother who desired to accustom him to an early use of his reason, instead of compelling him always to act from custom, or according to the humour of others, and never suffering him to reason at all." "Reason!" exclaimed Mrs. Crewkherne (evading to answer the first part of this remark) "reason! I should be glad to know what *reason* children can have. Yes! it is from such sort of wicked and accursed doctrine that all the mischief we have seen, and a great deal more that we *shall* see, originates.—Reason! what is our reason?—poor weak creatures, as even the *wisest* of us are, without grace. If your brother, Miss Louy, *had reason*, which includes *grace*, to know good from evil, he would eschew the one and embrace the other."

"That is, madam," said Louisa, who never heard her brother blamed without pain, "he would find reason contained in fifty thousand pounds, and folly only in poverty."

"To be sure," said Mrs. Crewkherne.

"So then, madam," ventured Louisa to reply, "all that I have heard you say as to poverty, and humility, and self-denial, goes for nothing, or is only a way of talking that means nothing. I am sure I have in my memory a great many sentences which you have directed me to write out at times, in order to impress them more deeply on my memory, which recommend poverty, and are calculated to humble the pride of the rich; therefore it does not seem that grace, which means, as you put it, the power given us to distinguish between good and evil, should only tell us to make ourselves affluent whenever we can, without any consideration of other circumstances, or any attention to our consciences."

"Conscience!—Grant me patience to hear a silly girl prate in such a provoking way!—What would this foolish boy have done against his conscience if he married Miss Goldthorp."

"A great deal, perhaps, if he preferred another to her, and married her only for her money."

Mrs. Crewkherne, internally conscious that simple truth, even timidly as it was brought forward by Louisa, had the advantage; that her hypocritical cant in praise of poverty and self-denial might be converted into a weapon against herself, had now recourse to invective, and what she thought ridicule, which however was in her hands so disgusting, that she presently drove her two young relations from her. Caroline was extremely vexed to see that this angry persecution of her brother would in all probability produce an effect exactly contrary to its intention; and Louisa, though she had hitherto wished that the marriage with Miss Goldthorp might take place, was much more anxious that her brother might be happy, and still more solicitous to know how much of the tale Mrs. Crewkherne had heard was true, and who the persons were whose mysterious residence in the country had at least given her ground for the invention. The good lady had long been eminent for a most fertile imagination, and had very frequently fabricated marvellous histories relative to people in the neighbourhood on the slightest foundations, or without any; there would therefore have been nothing surprising, if the whole she had been telling had been unfounded; but Louisa reflecting on her brother's behaviour for some weeks, and on several trifling circumstances that had occurred, felt a sort of internal evidence that some part of it at least was true.

Certain that Delmont would resent any thing that appeared like impertinent curiosity, she resolved not to betray any part of the anxiety she felt. Her caution, however was useless, for that night, as contrary to his general custom, George Delmont did not appear at supper, and the displeasure of Mrs. Crewkherne was terribly augmented, when she learned the next morning that he had not passed the night in his own *house*.

Chap. XI.

Beware of that relentless train
Who forms adore—whom forms maintain.[121]

Delmont had been betrayed by the sudden appearance and rude remonstrance of Mrs. Crewkherne, into a degree of unguarded warmth, which on a moment's reflection he repented. "Why," said he, "should I suffer the intrusion of those foolish women to discompose me, or why should I convey any of the displeasure they may give me to Mrs. Glenmorris? have I ever desired to keep my visits here secret? or have I ever made them clandestinely? Certainly not. I ought then to have been collected enough to have answered Mrs. Crewkherne's question, instead of appearing angry, as if I was detected in company with one of whose society I was ashamed. Lovely innocent Medora,[122] is it purity and sweetness like thine that I blush to be seen with? and with thy admirable mother, can I feel any other sensation than that of conscious inferiority? What can be meaner and more unworthy of the character I aspire to, 'to dare to think for myself, and to act what I think,' than such pusillanimity as I have just been guilty of, in shrinking from the enquiry of two gossipping women, who will probably, from my weak attempt to avoid them, relate some legend, produced by their own malice; whereas, had I simply described the persons I was with, I should have deprived them of the power they now have to imagine and report evil."

In consequence, then, of having made these reflections, Delmont, instead of seeking Mrs. Glenmorris, to engage her to avoid the inquisitors, whom he had left in full quest in the farmer's kitchen, returned rather in the hope of finding Medora, and prevailing on her not to distress her mother, by repeating the strange appearance and abrupt question of Mrs. Crewkherne, than to guard that revered mother against these intruders. It was however too late for the former of these purposes; for Medora had met her mother, who was coming to join her in the coppice, and had related the extraordinary circumstance of the two ladies so suddenly appearing; the rude question one of them had put to her, and the angry manner in which the same old lady had addressed Mr. Delmont.

Mrs. Glenmorris, unconscious of evil, was indifferent as to concealment; desiring only to avoid visits such as are often made in the country for the mere indulgence of idle curiosity. From these, the sequestered situation of the house where she resided, her being introduced there by Mr. Armitage, a man who was known in the country as a very odd and singular character, and her own retired temper and pursuits, had hitherto exempted her, and she hoped that she should never have been under the painful necessity of declining civilities she could not return, or resenting the impertinence of arrogant intrusion. To the last of these only she could refer the appearance of the two persons described to her by Medora, at least as far as could be judged by the words the elder of them had uttered, which however imperfectly heard, were evidently those of reproach and anger. It now for the first time occurred to Mrs. Glenmorris, that the family of Mr. Delmont might impute his visits, should they happen to know they were made, to motives very different from those on which she had received them, and though she knew nothing of the plan so warmly adopted by Mrs. Crewkherne, to marry him to a woman so rich as Miss Goldthorp, it was natural enough to believe that this antiquated aunt might be alarmed at the idea of his attaching himself to a young woman who was a stranger, and, from every appearance, totally destitute of fortune. As she resolved at once to put any uneasy feelings on this matter out of the question, by speaking frankly to Delmont, she no sooner saw him approaching through the meadow in which they were walking, than she bade her daughter go to the house, and finish the letter she had begun to her father; then advancing towards Delmont (whose face no longer bore any impression of the anger he had just felt) Mrs. Glenmorris enquired what Medora had seen during their walk that had so dismayed her. "Who is this old lady that came to scold?" said she. "Why, did Medora," answered he, laughing in his turn, "tell you she scolded?" "Something very like it; and I guessed directly that it was Mrs. Crewkherne." "You were not mistaken," replied Delmont; "the good lady was not in one of her very amiable humours I believe, but when she is, by the asperity of her appearance, and the sharpness of her tones, she may well impress those not accustomed to her with the idea of her being in a fit of ill humour."

"But seriously, it has never till this moment struck me, Mr. Delmont, that your family may be made uneasy by your visits to me on account of Medora, who they know no otherwise than as a young and indigent wanderer, for such no doubt she is represented. Now, though I have great pleasure in seeing you, and have owed to you some of the most agreeable hours I have passed in this seclusion, let me entreat of you to forbear a continuance of the acquaintance, if you feel or foresee the slightest inconvenience from it. I have no wish that Medora should marry while she is so very young, and I am convinced no such idea ever occurred to you." (Delmont did not look as if he perfectly acquiesced.) "Her father," continued Mrs. Glenmorris, "in a distant country, her future prospects fluctuating between a considerable property, which it is possible she may one day possess, and a provision which in England will set her but little above indigence; I have, I ought to have, no views for her at present, but so to instruct her as that she may bear with an equal mind either of these extremes of fortune. Equivocal as my character and situation may at present appear to the few who may be induced by curiosity, or any stronger motive, to remark on it, I heartily forgive *them*, if they form unjust conclusions, but I should *not* forgive myself, if your visits here became a source of uneasiness between you and your family."

"My family," repeated Delmont gravely; "my dear madam, to what part of my family do you imagine me to be responsible for any part of my conduct? You cannot have higher ideas of the tie, that even after the age when the laws of this country give a man freedom,[123] ought to bind a son to the observance of duty towards a father or a mother, at least such a mother as *I* once had, but as I have her no longer, as I have no father, I feel myself very little disposed to submit any of my actions to the controul, or even the opinion of any other of my relations. Do not think me arrogant or self-sufficient, madam, if I say, that as where submission is voluntary, it should be given only to such as have better sense or judgment, than a man is himself conscious of possessing, I have no scruples in denying it to the female part of my family, well as I love my sisters."

"But Mrs. Crewkherne?" said the lady.

"Mrs. Crewkherne has not, nor ever will have the least influence on my conduct. Good Heaven! have you, can you have had even for one moment, so ill an opinion of me, as to suppose that I should humble myself before her, because she has money?—I *did* hope, short as our acquaintance has been, that you might have seen enough of me to prevent your suggesting such a possibility."

"Be not angry," answered Mrs. Glenmorris, "I am, you know, very slightly acquainted with the circumstances of your family; for besides my thinking such inquiries impertinent, I should make them to very little purpose to Mr. Armitage; and you know he is my only visitor in this country. But forgive me, if I thought of you in this instance, only as I do of the generality of the world. I know how nineteen young men out of twenty would act, when there was a rich old relation in question; and I could not tell that you were an exception, and are in no instance a man of an ordinary mind."

"Believe me, madam," rejoined Delmont, "a man would have in every thing else, not only a *very* ordinary, but a very sordid mind, who would give up the freedom of that mind to the miserable hope of a legacy from a capricious old woman, and I should scorn myself, were I capable of doing it even in indigence; but as *I am*, though I am far enough from great affluence, and though I disclaim many of the ways by which affluence is acquired, I should be indeed a poor and contemptible wretch, if I wore such a yoke. My God!" added he with enthusiasm, "that any man ever *can* so submit, who has the power of earning his bread by the sweat of his brow."

Mrs. Glenmorris looked at him with pleasure, but it was pleasure not unmingled with concern. She sighed, and after a moment's silence said, "I wish you were acquainted with Glenmorris—how well you would in most of your sentiments agree!"

"*I may be* so fortunate," said Delmont, "some time or other."

"Yet," resumed Mrs. Glenmorris, "I hardly know whether I ought to wish it, for the world would say, perhaps, that after having shewn by his own example, how to throw away all which *that* world is accustomed to call desirable, he would renew his instructions to you, till you had done the same."

"And so, my dear madam, we are always to be the slaves of the world; the world, of which after all the sacrifices we make, so few obtain the suffrage,[124] and that suffrage when obtained, is not only so fragile, that the least reverse of fortune deprives us of it; but while we fancy we possess it, it cannot make us happy one single hour. What is this world of which every one talks, and to which every one is instructed, that he must make all sorts of offerings, of his taste, his time, his inclinations. Let us look steadily at it. It is a little atmosphere which every man supposes round the spot whereon he moves. The merchant's world consists of men in commercial life, and his wife's of the wives of these good men, till her spouse gets money enough to remove her world to Bloomsbury or Bedford Square,[125] or occasionally to some fashionable bathing-place. We know the lawyer's world exists in Lincoln's-inn-fields, and the inns of court, with some enlargement, if he happens to be very high in the profession, and in parliament, or with any chance of a seat on the woolsack.[126] The world of a country curate is in the next market-town; that of his employer, the opinion of a few dignitaries of the church. The soldier's world is in his regiment, or in the favour of those who order the most people *out* of the *world* in general: but to me, who neither am or ever intend to be a merchant, a lawyer, a churchman, or a military man, why should I raise around me, by dint of prescriptive prejudice, this imaginary atmosphere, through the medium of which only I can look at every object? No, my dear madam, whatever the world may say of Mr. Glenmorris, or of me, I do believe that we should on almost every subject agree. I am sure we should in our contempt of all such prejudices as enslave the mind, and restrain man's best prerogatives, that of thinking, saying what he thinks, and, where he can, acting up to his thoughts."

"But there are instances," said Mrs. Glenmorris, "wherein, to use a phrase of the day, *existing circumstances*, to which submission is compelled, will not allow this entire freedom of action. For example, look at Glenmorris's conduct about his daughter. No man is so little affected by pecuniary considerations as he is—None have sacrificed more to obtain a perfect freedom of speaking, writing, and acting; for that he has become an alien from his country, and has sought in another hemisphere the liberty which he could not exercise in his native island. Accustomed to the elegancies and luxuries of life, he has relinquished them all, and is become a citizen of an infant republic, though little more than the plain requisites of life are to be obtained even there with the very small fortune he now possesses. For himself he would be content, and I do not believe any consideration would induce him to return to England or Scotland; yet, when his daughter's interest is in question, you see he gives up both that daughter on whom he doats with the most extravagant fondness; he gives up for a time her mother, and sends them to pursue the fortune which he thinks his child has a right to. This is submitting not only to the greatest deprivation that can befal him, for a purpose which, considering the glorious uncertainty of the law, and all we have against us, may never be answered; but it is submitting to present pain for a purpose, which, were himself only concerned, he would despise.—He reasoned however thus, 'my child has an undoubted right, on behalf of her mother, to a very considerable fortune; it may probably be obtained by my inflicting on myself the pain of parting with her. It is true, I have brought her up to share with cheerfulness the lot which is now mine, but may she always be so content with it, as never to feel a sentiment of reproach towards me, if I should neglect, when it is in my power, to obtain for her a better? *The world* esteems riches to be a good; and very certainly, in the present order of things, poverty is a very great evil. Such it may hereafter prove to my Medora, who suffering under it may say, "Why did not my father obtain for me the fortune which ought to have been mine?"' I mention all this," added Mrs. Glenmorris, "to prove to you, that there is hardly any case wherein it is possible for a man, however determined he may be, to shake off the fetters which are for the most part wantonly imposed, so entirely to emancipate himself, as not to be dragged back in some instance to the forms of society. It is Rochefaucauld, I believe, who says;

L'on ne peut se passer de ce même monde que l'on n'aime point, et dont on se moque.[127]

"If any one but you had quoted a maxim," cried Delmont, half impatiently, "I should have asked, almost with ill humour, whether we have not too often recourse to old laws, from habit and prejudice, as guides to our actions? What you have just said, however, is unfortunately true, though the period may not be very far off, perhaps, when its truth may be disputed. In the mean time, my dear Mrs. Glenmorris, pray never let me be mortified with such an hint as that with which you opened this conversation, that Mrs. Crewkherne is to be consulted about my acquaintance. I have not till now preserved my independence, at what is perhaps accounted the expence of my fortune, to have it limited in a single thought, by the interposition of Mrs. Crewkherne, or a whole legion of spinsters equally rich in purse or in prosing, and equally prying in disposition. The eleven thousand virgins of whose accumulated sculls some traveller tells,[128] had they all lived to the age and affluence of my grand aunt, and though each came to offer me her advice and her fortune as the price of one hour's freedom, would certainly be sent away without any applause."

"Well, well, I will abstain from any such offence for the future; but what if the anger of the old lady should fall on me? how may she not represent me? what may she not say of me? by your sisters, if I am thought of at all, I should particularly wish to be thought well of, and who knows in what a light Mrs. Crewkherne may represent us."

"None *know* indeed," replied Delmont, "for none can answer for the excesses of folly, malice, and ignorance; but certainly, whoever should *care* for the effusions of Mrs. Crewkherne, would be very much to blame. Now don't silence me by another proverb or maxim. I know you could talk very eloquently from a book, but I desire rather to hear you from the fulness of your own liberal mind. You have told me, that on many occasions, when a terrific image has been set up before you, by that superstition or that prejudice which make scarecrows of every thing or nothing, you have ventured to approach it, to look resolutely at it, and calculating its real power to hurt you, have presently seen it vanish into thin air. Be assured that my venerable sybil of an aunt, though an admirable scarecrow for the misses of ******* need not curtail you and Medora of one walk, whether you botanize with me, or poetise with Armitage, or philosophize with us both. The only way in which this prying curiosity of Mrs. Crewkherne's can be the occasion of my interchanging with her a sentence more than usual, will be by your considering it as a matter of any importance. I am going," added Delmont, "to Ashley Combe, have you any message to Armitage?"

They then went into the house together, Mrs. Glenmorris having some papers on which she desired to consult Mr. Armitage; and while she collected them above, Delmont, with whom Mrs. Jemmatt was in habits of talking familiarly, related to him the questions that had been put to her by the two unwelcome visitors who had just left her. "I wonder," cried she, "what gentlefolks means by coming in that manner, calling one to account, as if one was afore the justices. I'm sure that Mrs. Nixon mid'nt be so curious after other folks affairs. She'd have enough to do to look after her own, if every one did as they ought; but there, if such as *she* once gets among your quality, they thinks themselves as great as if they were quality too, whereas Mrs. Nixon is'nt a bit better born nor bred than I be, for all her husband was a lawyer, and scraped up a sort of a fortune by such tricks as them there lawyers always play; ruining poor folks. But she's got a little money forsooth, and creeps into favour at great houses, and so she takes upon her to use 'good woman,' and 'dame,' and such like sayings to them that be as good as herself."

Delmont, though very much displeased at the impertinence with which Mrs. Jemmatt had been questioned about her lodgers, could not help smiling at the ready transition she made from the affront done to them, to the want of respect shewn to herself. He told her, that as the voyage of Mrs. Glenmorris and her daughter to England, was made in the hope of their recovering a share of a very large fortune, which rich and powerful relations held against them, it was desirable that their residence in England might be as little known as possible, till they had collected evidence, and taken other measures in regard to the suit, which it might be greatly in the power of their adversaries to impede; "for these reasons," said he, "they live thus retired, and Mr. Armitage, who is the friend of Mr. Glenmorris, is engaged in arranging the business for them, which will be brought forward next month in a court of law. After that Mrs. Glenmorris will desire no secrecy to be observed; but, till then, you will oblige her, if you will let her name, or motive for remaining here, be as little spoken of as you can."

Mrs. Jemmatt, with high encomiums on both the lady and her daughter, and many wishes for the success of their cause, promised all that was desired of her; and Delmont, having received the papers, took his leave, and sought his friend Armitage.

Chap. XII.

Oh! she was a most exemplary gentlewoman;
a very icicle on Diana's temple. St. Ursula and St. Bridget were
but as her handmaids.[129]

At Ashley Combe, Delmont was always a most welcome visitor. Mr. Armitage was reading in his garden, in one part of which, by the judicious disposition of ever-greens, he had contrived a sheltered walk, even at a season when the woods and plantations were nearly stripped of their foliage. He advanced to meet Delmont. "You are not," said he, "come to announce yourself the news I have heard this morning? you have not quite methinks the air of a bridegroom, who has just acquired a beautiful wife with fifty thousand pounds in her pocket."

"What is all this?" enquired Delmont.

Mr. Armitage then said, that his servants had that morning informed him, that it was certain Delmont either was married, or to be married in a few days to the lady he had so fortunately rescued from danger, who had fifty thousand pounds, and was a very fine woman. "The report," added he, "came from Mr. Cleyton, who has had the good fortune to attend the lady successfully as her surgeon, and who has it seems been in the secret from the very beginning."

"You know," said Delmont, "as well as any one, my dear Armitage, how very unlikely it is that I should be induced to marry for the sake of twice fifty thousand pounds, any woman to whom I could not have devoted myself from affection, if she had not fifty shillings. Let me assure you, I have no such predilection for Miss Goldthorp, nor am I coxcomb enough to suppose she feels any such preference in my favour, though I know my good aunt, with whom money and grace are ever the predominant ideas, is very desirous that I may have enough of one, to seize this opportunity of obtaining so considerable a portion of the other. And my two sisters, impressed, as is natural enough at their age, with notions of all the tiffany and tinsel[130] that fifty thousand pounds can supply, are eager, for once, in the same cause as the old lady. I have for many days seen, though I have not affected to see their politics; but it is unnecessary to say more about these golden visions, because certainly they will evaporate and come to nothing."

"And *are* you," said Mr. Armitage, "are you really, Delmont, philosopher enough to look without emotion on a splendid fortune annexed to a fine woman?"

"I am mortified, my friend, that you should doubt it; surely I should have profited little either by the few observations I have been able to make by your conversation, or by the books to which you have directed me, if I felt, for one moment only a doubt about this acquisition, supposing, which it were impertinent vanity to do, that it was really within my reach."

"You dislike then the lady?"

"As an acquaintance I neither like or dislike her. They tell me she is what is called a fine woman—It may be so for aught I know. They say too that she is very highly accomplished—That too may very possibly be—but I declare to you, that these acquired graces have so little power over me, that I am afraid, were I not to see Miss Goldthorp after to-morrow, I should totally have forgotten by to-morrow se'nnight[131] that I had ever seen her at all."

"What if I should remark," rejoined Mr. Armitage, "that such total insensibility on the part of a man of your age towards a woman of her's, may be owing less to any want of attractions on one side, or to any constitutional coldness in the other, than to your liking some other woman better."

"And if you should say so?"

"I should not be much mistaken, perhaps."

"You would not; and as I shall particularly want your counsel, I will open my whole heart to you. You introduced me about two months ago to Mrs. Glenmorris— I obtained liberty to see her in her retirement. A similarity of taste, as well as some trifling services I have had the good fortune to render her, have occasioned my visits to be frequent. The more I have seen of her, the more of those visits I have felt myself impelled to make, till at length——"

"My dear George," interrupted Mr. Armitage, laughing, "you are not, I hope, going to make me the confidant of your passion for the wife of my friend?"

"There are many passions, however, infinitely more absurd than that would be," said Delmont.

"True," answered Armitage; "there is nothing absurd in loving merit under whatever form, or at whatever age it is found."

"As to age, Mrs. Glenmorris is not above six-and-thirty."

"I believe not, and you are——"

"I am two-and-twenty."

"Fourteen years is nothing certainly, *as times go*; but what do you say to the small inconvenience of her being married? You know my sentiments, George," continued Mr. Armitage, quitting the tone of raillery he had till then spoken in. "I have very unjustly the reputation of libertinism in regard to women; for I do assure you upon my honour, that with me a woman who belongs to another is sacred. My friend Glenmorris, who is not insensible of the value of the jewel he possesses, knows that such are my sentiments, or, whatever might be his confidence in me in other respects, he would hardly have put his wife and daughter under my protection."

"Cato, then," cried Delmont gaily, "Cato is a proper person to entrust a love-tale with![132] But recollect, my good friend, whether there is not a possibility of my admiring the daughter of this charming woman."

"I thought it improbable; because I know how strenuously you insist upon *mind* and *character* in the woman who should attach you. Now a girl of Medora's age has no mind; it remains to be formed—Her character must be a mere rudiment—One cannot say what it will be. She is very pretty, and has all that bloom, that simplicity of youth, which renders beauty under twenty so seducing an object to many men; but lovely as I own she is as a child, I did not imagine she would have attractions for you."

"It is precisely," replied Delmont, "because she is so entirely the child of nature, that I find she *has* attractions.[133] She will be, probably, what her mother is, with something of the best part of her father's singularities, such as you have sometimes described them to me. He has brought her up exactly as I should wish a woman to be educated for me. Not one idea has she that she blushes to avow; neither prudery or coquetry, neither a desire of conquest for herself, or envy of the advantages possessed by others, make any part of her studies or reflections. Oh! how unlike the artificial things one sees every where—which *I* see, even in my two sisters, who are reckoned so unaffected and ingenuous. Why may I not hope and believe, that Medora, now the most lovely girl in the world, may, when she is formed, become such a woman as her mother? and then, were I to make the tour of that world, where could I find a creature so well calculated to make me happy?"

"So you really are in love with Medora Glenmorris, the little wild Caledonian-American?[134] and it is for her that you disdain the banker's rich heiress."

"If you mean by being *in love* with one and *disdaining* the other, that I think I should be a very happy man with one in any situation, while the highest degree of affluence could not give me happiness with the other, such is certainly my opinion, and on that opinion I mean to act, if you, my friend, know nothing of Glenmorris's views for his daughter, which ought to make me desist from doing so."

Mr. Armitage then related, in a few words, such circumstances of Glenmorris's history as Delmont was unacquainted with.

"You have heard, perhaps, that Glenmorris's marriage with Miss De Verdon was so much against the wishes of her parents, that it was always the declared intention of both, though Glenmorris was nearly related to the family of Lady Mary her mother, to disinherit this their youngest daughter; and it is understood they did so; but on the death of the father, at a great age, which happened a few years ago, some of Glenmorris's friends, who went to look at the will, thought that resentment thus carried to the grave had not all the effect intended, and that by an oversight the child of the daughter they had thus driven from any share of their great property would resume the rights of her mother. Whoever were the zealous friends of Glenmorris, were likely to pursue this inquiry, as well from their affection for him, as from their abhorrence of the tyranny and injustice that had deprived their friend of affluence, and driven him from society he was so well calculated to adorn, to the wilds of America.

"In consequence of this, copies of the will were obtained, and one among the gentlemen who was the best acquainted with the state of the affairs, drew up a case for the consideration of counsel. Of these, four were consulted; of whom two gave their opinion decidedly against, and two as peremptorily in favour of, the right remaining in Medora Glenmorris to a very considerable part of the property of her grandfather.

"These opinions were sent to America, where Glenmorris had resided some years; but it was not till after several other representations from his friends here, that he was at length prevailed upon to suffer his wife and daughter to come to England, whither he could not accompany them, not only because he is deeply in debt, but because the freedom with which he spoke and wrote has made him enemies in this country, who have now so much the power of hurting him, that the persuasions of his few remaining friends against his return to England were added to the reluctance he felt to revisit a country where he had found that fortune alone was the object of esteem; and where he saw, or *fancied* he saw, a daily innovation on those principles, which, though not a native of England itself, he had been taught to admire and venerate. If he is not," continued Mr. Armitage, "greatly changed since I saw him in his American retirement, you are, my dear George, the very man in the world to whom I think he would, if he knew you, delight, in giving his daughter; nor do I believe him capable of adopting for her any of those ambitious views of which he knows the folly and futility, if, contrary to what he expects himself, her fortune should be great; I see nothing, therefore, that should prevent your openly declaring to his wife in person, and by letter to himself, your sentiments in regard to Medora. I am no advocate for very early or very hasty marriages; but it is because they are often made by the tyranny or the avarice of parents. Where two young people have very good sense, as I believe to be the case with you and your fair American; and where there is a probability that you will rather improve in intellectual qualifications, I think your time of life very far from being a cause even for delay. Life indeed is not long enough to allow a reasonable man much hesitation, when once he has found a woman so well calculated as you think Medora is, to confer happiness."

In consequence of this conversation, which endeared Mr. Armitage more than ever to Delmont (as generally happens when the counsellor thinks like him who demands counsel) Delmont was desirous of talking over his future proceedings, and determined to stay all night, while the charitable and delicate imagination of Mrs. Crewkherne led her to such conjectures as to his stay as raised her indignation to the highest pitch, and though, while with the Doctor and Mrs. Winslow, she checked the ebullitions of her wrath, she vented her spleen with ten-fold acrimony when alone with either of the sisters, who vainly attempted to appease her.

To Caroline she declared, that she could not answer it to her conscience to stay under the roof of so profligate a young man. The world, she said, in its present depraved state, should have no reason to say she countenanced such libertine doings; and therefore she bade Caroline prepare to return to London with her. It was in vain the poor girl endeavoured to mitigate her resentment, by alledging that it was possible some accident might have detained her brother, or that he might have staid at Mr. Armitage's. The very name of Armitage increased her indignation, and all that Caroline could obtain was a sort of promise from the inexorable Mrs. Crewkherne, that she would not attack Delmont on the discovery she had made before any of their visitors.

This promise, however, it was not possible for her to abide by. Delmont, resolute never to subject himself to the controul the old lady had so great an inclination to impose on every body around her, appeared the next day at dinner, and slightly excused himself to Doctor Winslow for his absence. The Doctor answered in the common terms, "that he should be sorry to put him under any restraint;" but Mrs. Crewkherne, who probably expected some apology to herself, began to *talk at him* in so rude and virulent a way, as only the calm and dignified consciousness of his own blameless conduct, and manly compassion for her weakness and prejudice, could have enabled him to endure. His endeavours to laugh off her furious and illiberal attack served only to irritate her the more: at length, dinner being ended, he took a glass of wine with the Doctor, and retired to his study, while Mrs. Crewkherne, whose irascible and malignant passions were now inflamed even to a sort of phrensy, forgetting all the reasons she had for secresy, began vehemently to declaim against the licentious conduct of young men in general, and that of Mr. Delmont in particular; asserting, that it was owing to the profligate manners of modern youth, and the general wickedness of the world, that under the best of sovereigns, and an heaven-born minister, and notwithstanding so many orders for fasts, and other acts of pious humiliation, the war, so just and necessary, had been so little successful.[135] "I am sorry," added Mrs. Crewkherne, "grieved to see that a kinsman of mine should add to the number of wretched souls, by whose delinquency the punishment is drawn down on this generation. And as Doctor Dundermass says, 'Woe, woe unto all who shall appertain to these—and behold the beast hath the upper hand—and the voice of wailing is heard.'" In this style the poor woman talked herself out of breath, Doctor Winslow listening with profound attention; not because he either admired the eloquence or participated the zeal of Mrs. Crewkherne, but because he saw that an opportunity offered, which would deliver him, as he hoped, for ever, from all fear of Delmont's supplanting his son in the favour of Miss Goldthorp.

To her he failed not to relate all that had passed at table (for she was yet unable or unwilling to dine below) expressing great concern that a young man, in many respects so worthy, should be so tainted with the vicious opinions and manners of the age, and expressing his sorrow for Mrs. Crewkherne, "who, poor lady," said the Doctor, "has a truly maternal yearning for the backslidings of a youth so well calculated to fight manfully in the good cause."

Miss Goldthorp wanted not sense to see, nor spirit to despise hypocrisy, and perfectly understood the Doctor's motive for retailing the history; she heard it therefore with some impatience, and then, to the great dismay of the narrator, said, "All who know Mrs. Crewkherne know her malice—She is an hateful old cat, and Mr. Delmont is quite in the right to do exactly as he pleases, without consulting such a spiteful witch."

It is unnecessary to repeat the Doctor's answer to the tart reply of his sometime ward, nor to describe the hysteric with which Mrs. Winslow ended the conversation—before it closed, it became so warm that Doctor Winslow protested his resolution to depart immediately, and Miss Goldthorp as resolutely assured him, that if he did, she should remain where she was.

Never before had the preacher of patience to others so much occasion to exercise it himself. Unused to the least contradiction, and unable to endure it, the opposition he now found from a person over whom he was so unwilling to resign his authority, was not to be borne—It seemed to him the most atrocious injury; and at length his irritable temper so far conquered his prudence, that he forgot at once his dignity, and that the passion to which he sacrificed it was wholly impotent, since he had no longer any power to controul the actions of his wife's niece.

While this angry conversation was passing in Miss Goldthorp's apartment, the party below were far from being very tranquil; for Mrs. Crewkherne, throwing off all restraint, was declaring to both her nieces her resolution to quit the house; and to Caroline she even gave directions to prepare for their departure. The poor girls, who saw the destruction of all the projects they had formed for the prosperity of their brother, attempted, but vainly, to soothe her—The greater she found her power of inflicting pain, the more delight she seemed to feel. At length a note was delivered to Caroline, who, half drowned in tears, found the contents to be these:

> My dear girls,
> Think it not unkind in your brother if he absents himself for some time
> from an house, where you will continue to exercise the duties of
> hospitality towards our guests, so long as Miss Goldthorp's situation
> shall continue to make it a convenient abode for her and her friends.
> The concerns of a friend, to whom I am under obligations, and my
> own resolution never to suffer my personal freedom to be encroached
> upon, unite to detain me. I am sorry to do what may be termed rude to
> Dr. Winslow; but the difference of my going or staying is to him
> trifling, while I should, by doing the latter, subject myself to many
> disagreeable hours, which is, you know, what I determine never to do,
> when the sacrifice of myself can be of little or no use to others. I need
> give you no other reasons; and surely I need not to my Caroline and
> my Louisa say, that they will always have a tender and affectionate
> brother in
>
> G.D.
> Direct to me at Armitage's, should you have occasion to write.

It seemed as if the certainty of having driven Delmont from his house had a momentary effect on Mrs. Crewkherne, and though still vehemently reviling him, she consented to let his absence pass, as being occasioned by business, if his sisters wrote to endeavour to recal him before it should be known he withdrew in anger. While Louisa therefore wrote, Caroline went up to the apartment of Miss Goldthorp, who, irritated and wearied by the conversation she had just before had with her uncle and aunt, and dreading the persecution she foresaw on behalf of their son, hesitated no longer either in avowing her decided partiality towards Delmont, or in consenting that it should be made known to him. In this she did not imagine she made any sacrifice of her pride; for she was persuaded Delmont had forborne to address her merely on account of the distance fortune had placed between them; nor her vanity ever suffered her to suppose it possible, that there was in the world a man who could be indifferent to, or refuse such a woman with such a fortune.

Chap. XIII.

O friendly to the best pursuits of man,
Friendly to thought, to virtue, and to peace,
Domestic life in rural quiet pass'd.[136]

Dreading nothing so much as returning to the gloomy society of fanatics and bigots at the London residence of Mrs. Crewkherne, Caroline Delmont assisted her sister, and both exerted all the little finesse they were mistress of to influence their brother; they represented the attachment of the young heiress, whom so many sought, as demanding all his gratitude; spoke highly of her good qualities, and touched on the independence as well as on the power of doing good, which the possession of such a fortune would bestow.

The letter being finished with great care, was dispatched by a messenger on horseback, and with beating heart Caroline and Louisa waited his return, contriving in the meantime how to proceed, if the answer should be unfavourable. The man who had been sent returned much sooner than they had expected with the following answer from Delmont:

Believe, my dearest girls, that I am sensible of all I owe to your fond solicitude, and were there any consideration on earth that could induce me to swerve from the principles by which I have determined to govern my own conduct, it would be the desire I feel to give even temporary happiness to my beloved sisters; but indeed, my dear Caroline and Louisa, it would be only temporary, for you would soon cease to be happy, when you became conscious that your brother was miserable; and miserable it is very certain he would be, if he fraudulently possessed himself of the person of any woman for the sake of the fortune that belonged to it. Such would be my conduct, were I to avail myself of the good opinion of the lady you name to me. I respect and esteem her, and my opinion of her understanding is raised, not by the preference she honours me with, but by that liberality of mind which has induced her to be sincere. If she condescends to hear what my answer is, tell her, Caroline, that I honour and regard her too much to consider her as the means of acquiring superfluous fortune. That if I had an heart unoccupied, her excellencies, rather than her large property, might induce me to offer it; but it is already irrevocably another's. And I have only to assure your fair friend, that my gratitude, while it will end but with my life, shall be wholly confined to my own breast; and that in respectful silence I shall await the intelligence, that one who deserves her, and knows her value, may render her happy; which that she may be in the highest degree is most truly the desire of

GEORGE DELMONT.

The contents of this letter could not be concealed; and when, after some hesitation, the trembling Caroline gave it to Miss Goldthorp to peruse, nothing but mortified pride saved her from exhibiting her indignation and anger: she restrained her tears however, though with painful and evident effort, and entreated of her two friends to conceal most cautiously from Doctor and Mrs. Winslow the avowal on her part, and the refusal on that of Delmont, which would occasion such exultation to them, and to her a degree of mortification it was hardly possible to support.

Delmont's intentional absence, however, it was now no longer easy to disguise. The Doctor, glad of a pretence to hasten their removal, declared he could not think of remaining in an house from which there was reason to believe his presence had driven the master. Mrs. Crewkherne declared that the time she had appropriated to her stay in the country was already expired; and Miss Goldthorp making no longer any opposition to their departure, suddenly discovered that she could travel without inconvenience.

The parting of the two sisters, however, was a painful idea to both; Louisa, though she loved her brother better than any other human being, knew not how far she might possess that share of his affection which he had hitherto bestowed upon her, when he had avowed his attachment to some woman, who it was probably his intention to make the mistress of his house; while Mrs. Crewkherne, without knowing what he had himself acknowledged, laboured to impress on the timid minds of both the sisters, that their brother's purpose was to introduce into his house some person of doubtful, or of bad character, to whom Mr. Armitage had made him known. Louisa was at once hurt by Delmont's want of confidence in her, and fearful of finding herself in the way of any arrangement he had proposed making, she therefore listened to an invitation given by Miss Goldthorp, and seconded by Mrs. Winslow, to pass the winter with them in Sackville-street,[137] Mrs. Winslow being delighted to continue the acquaintance with the sisters, now that her fears were over about the brother.

Louisa, like most girls of her age, was eager for novelty, and yet fearful of quitting her brother, who, when she was alone and deserted, had proved himself so tenderly attached to her, and had since so kindly instructed, or fondly protected her; yet the dread of this new connection, which Mrs. Crewkherne represented as being formed with some mistress, whom he only wished for an opportunity of placing at the head of his family, almost over-balanced every other consideration. She could not bear to be supplanted in her brother's affection; she could not associate with such a person; it was even improper for her to stay in his house, while he visited such a one in the neighbourhood; yet, if her brother should be offended with her; if she should lose his friendship, she must be miserable.

This debate, which lasted a great while, was terminated at length by her resolving to write to her brother, and ask his assent, or rather his opinion of the proposal made to her, which acquired new advantage in her opinion, when she began to recollect the variety and gaiety of a winter passed in the metropolis, opposed to the languor and tediousness of the same season in a lonely house, far even from the melancholy mitigations afforded by the neighbourhood of a country town.

With apprehensive timidity she wrote, and awaited the messenger's return with even more anxiety than she had done the last. The answer from Delmont was as follows:

> When the unhappy events, which I shall ever deplore, deprived my beloved sisters of the best mother that ever blessed grateful and affectionate children, and of a father tenderly anxious for their welfare, and when it became my duty to fill, as well as I could, the dear and sacred character of their guardian and protector, I endeavoured to acquit myself as I thought would be most pleasing to her, whose memory is so dear to my heart. I will always do so, as long as the charge is left to me; but though I am proud of being the guardian, I will never be the governor of my sisters. You are now, my Louisa, in your seventeenth year; you have a very good understanding, which wants nothing but a little more strength, in points that relate to resolution and firmness. If going this journey is agreeable to you, go my dear girl, and learn to rely, in the few instances where decision can be required, on your own judgment to guide your own conduct. It is not good to have always, even in trifles, somebody to lean upon; for as, sooner or later, every body must act for themselves, the earlier an habit is acquired of considering consequences in every point, and being directed by judgment, the sooner an useful character is formed. I do not love the wavering imbecility of temper, which, if long yielded to becomes an habit; and if my Louisa *has* a fault, it is a little tendency to what the French call, "l'inconsequence."
>
> It is, in a trifling degree, visible in your letter. Why would you not write, in your fair hand, fair and simple truth? Then you would have said, "Brother, I should like to pass the winter with Miss Goldthorp, but I am afraid you will not willingly acquiesce. I love you, brother, but, indeed, passing a long long winter at Upwood, will be very melancholy for your poor Louisa, and it will be sad to be again separated by so many miles from Caroline; besides, they tell me that you have some attachment, and perhaps may wish me away; therefore, dear George, I desire to go."

I can see through the pretty little well turned artifices in her letter, that my Louisa meant all this. I will suppose she had been candid enough to have said it; and I thus answer. Go, my dear sister, and amuse yourself. There can be no impropriety under such protection. "Il n'y à jamais du mal dans la bonne compagnie."[138] A winter in the country to a young woman not seventeen, is, I own, but a melancholy sort of speculation to look forward to, and I would never willingly have you and our Caroline long separated, for nothing is so sweet and becoming as sisterly friendship. As to what you have heard of any attachment of mine, let me assure you, I shall never have one to any woman, with whom my sisters ought not to associate; nor any connection that can ever make me wish them away.

But where there is restraint, let no one look for friendship; I never will therefore, my love, restrain you, unless I see you likely to commit some imprudence injurious to yourself, which I think I never shall. As a residence in London requires more of ornamental dress than the country, accept, my Louisa, of the enclosed trifle, in addition to your allowance. Caroline has a rich friend, and therefore I know does not need it; and now, adieu, dear sharers in my love. Write to me very frequently, as I will to you, and whenever your visit ends, the house and heart of your brother are open to you, and not to you only, Louisa, but to my ever dear Caroline, who never will, I hope, suffer herself to be estranged from her and your affectionate friend,

G.D.

The letter enclosed a bank note of thirty pounds. Louisa, though a little hurt that her brother did not believe her sincere, had yet too much pleasure in being assured of going, to reflect very deeply. Preparations were immediately made for the journey, and post-horses ordered for the next day save one, it being settled that the Winslow family and Mrs. Crewkherne should depart at the same time.

This they accordingly did. The Doctor leaving a long formal letter of thanks to Delmont, who, two days after they left it, returned to his own house.

The interval of his enforced absence from it, he had passed at Mr. Armitage's, visiting however the lodging of his new friends every day. During that time, he had disclosed to both the mother and daughter, the affection he had conceived for the latter. Mrs. Glenmorris received his declaration with joy, which she did not attempt to conceal, and Medora acknowledged very frankly, that she did not believe she ever could like any body so well as she liked him. He had now opportunities of admiring the simple sweetness of her character, and every study of her temper, and her unadulterated heart taught him anew the value of the jewel he had found. From Mrs. Glenmorris he learned some singular circumstances that had occurred in her life, and that of the father of Medora.

The rigours of winter, which soon followed the departure of the London party, sometimes made the return of Delmont to Upwood at a late hour of the evening, painful to those he left, though the distance was hardly two miles by the footway. Mrs. Glenmorris was therefore occasionally prevailed upon to pass two or three days at the house of Delmont, and then it was they tasted the felicity of mutual confidence; of that sort of sympathy which unites people who love, and mutually understand each other. Delmont had seized the first occasion that offered to write to Glenmorris, and he looked forward with anxious solicitude to the time when he was to receive an answer, on which the future happiness of his life depended. Mrs. Glenmorris, however, encouraged him to entertain the most sanguine hopes; and Medora assured him, that if he knew her father, he would have no apprehensions as to the success of his application.

The winter fled away but too swiftly; for such happiness as Delmont then enjoyed was not soon to return. The clamour of the country was, in the meantime, loud and vehement against him; and Mrs. Nixon, as well as many old women of all descriptions in the neighbouring towns, as well as some young ones, asserted that Mr. Delmont had turned his aunt, good lady, and his two sisters, poor things! out of doors, to make room for a mistress.

The optimists (however, very numerous among these good folks) soon began to consider this imaginary crime and misdemeanor, as ordered by superior power; and as one of the proofs which they are fond of seizing, that "good always comes out of evil;" "that all is for the best, and could not possibly be better;" for a few weeks only after Caroline's departure with her aunt, she was addressed by a young man of large fortune, whose mother was the intimate friend of the old lady, and who (doubtless without any view to the fortune Caroline was likely to have) had influence enough with her son to direct his choice. Caroline was indeed a young woman who had great personal recommendations, and Mr. Bethune found no difficulty in obeying his mother, when she desired him to prefer a very pretty girl, of a family to which it gratified his pride to be allied, and who had an almost certain prospect of a fortune of between twenty and thirty thousand pounds.

George Delmont was not consulted—his sister indeed paid him the compliment of writing, to inform him of her intended marriage—to which he could only answer, that she had all his wishes for her happiness.

END OF THE FIRST VOLUME.

VOLUME II

CHAP. I.

Se stava all 'ombra, o se del tetto usciva
Avea di, e notte il bel giovine a lato
Mattina, e sera, ov questa, ov quella riva
Cercando andava, o qualche verde prató.[1]

The interest taken by Delmont in every thing that related to Glenmorris and his family, induced him to seize every occasion of hearing the particulars of their history. Mrs. Glenmorris, as solicitous on her part to be thoroughly understood, embraced the earliest opportunity of relating to him the occurrences of her own and her husband's life; an eventful history, which, though told to Delmont in fragments at various times, shall be related here comprised in a single narrative.

"My father," said Mrs. Glenmorris, "though the native of another country, was one of the richest of those merchants who frequent the Exchange of London.[2] It was in London he became acquainted with a family, of which, though few boasted of a more illustrious descent, the principal of it had the mortification to see himself unable to provide for the younger branches; and one of them, the Lady Mary, was not unwilling to unite herself with my father in consideration of the fortune he possessed. Of this marriage were born two daughters, of whom I was the youngest. Every acquirement usually sought for young women was lavished upon us with a profusion of ill-judged expence. My father, having married late in life, doated on us both during our infancy with extravagant fondness, while the tenderness of my mother was almost entirely engrossed by my sister; and as they had no son, she formed the project of giving to her eldest daughter a larger portion of their fortune, on condition that whoever became her husband should take the name of De Verdon.[3] My father, not insensible of the influence of family pride (though his highest boast in his own country was that of being descended from the magistrates of his province)[4] became insensibly occupied by this scheme; and though he had still a great affection for me, he gradually learned to consider his eldest daughter as the object on which his fond ambition was to rely for its gratification.—Whether it was that our minds were differently disposed by nature, or whether the different ideas with which we were educated influenced our opinions, it is certain that, from the time we acquired some degree of power to think of the future, my sister's views and wishes were essentially different from mine. She had at an early age imbibed all the notions of family consequence, for which Lady Mary was remarked (even among the proudest women of equal rank) and nothing under nobility was at all likely to be accepted by the mother, or was ever thought of by the daughter.—I soon understood that I should be the victim of these exalted fancies;

for as the elevation to which Lady Mary desired to raise her eldest daughter was not to be obtained by personal beauty or accomplishments, but by a very large fortune, it was certain that to give *her* such a dowry mine must be proportionably lessened.—To that I was almost indifferent; for I had already learned that a very great fortune does not confer happiness; and I flattered myself, that if I had not enough to purchase a title, I should yet have enough for all the rational enjoyments of life. I loved the country, and was more delighted to fancy myself a wood nymph or a shepherdess, such as I read of in the Aminta and Pastor Fido,[5] than to pursue the dissipated life of which my sister was fond, who, since she had been introduced into society, or as it is termed, 'come out,' lived, and seemed delighted to live, in a continual succession of what is called pleasure; while, as I was not yet judged old enough to undergo this same ceremony of being 'brought out,' I was left under the care of a governess, at a villa of my father's about six miles from London, where masters, who were paid accordingly, continued even at that distance to attend me.—I will own, however, that my enthusiasm for the scenes of nature was not wholly given to the woods, and lawns, and rivulets; the Italian poets had taught me to people the shades with imaginary beings, such as alone could give them interest; and there was soon thrown in my way a young man who might well have passed, at that period, for the most amiable of their heroes personified.

"Glenmorris, for it is of him I speak, had just left one of our public schools, where he had been brought up on the foundation.[6] He was then in his eighteenth year; his person was tall, large, and uncommonly graceful; his complexion fair, yet not effeminate; a profusion of light hair, not yet dressed, flowed wildly round his face; his form was, indeed, at that period, well calculated for an hero of romance; and the generous undesigning and spirited temper, which his countenance expressed, was not less likely to captivate a girl so young as I then was, especially as I soon learned what he was careful to conceal from every body else, that Glenmorris preferred me to every other part of the family.

"Glenmorris was an orphan, who possessed only the last poor remains of a Scottish lairdship, not amounting to six hundred a year.—Being related to my mother, he was at her request received by the mercantile house, in which my father had still a very large concern, in the hope that he might by a lucrative trade restore his comparatively reduced fortune.—Glenmorris at first had thought of this engagement with reluctance; and certainly neither his disposition nor his education were such as were likely to make it successful. The earlier part of his life he had passed on the mountains of his native land with a father, who still considered himself as the head of an ancient and illustrious clan, though it was now reduced in numbers, and shorn of its power. On the death of this his only parent, and almost his only near relation, his guardian and half uncle, my mother's father, got him received as a King's scholar at Westminster, where, if he soon learned to contemn the feudal pride with which his father's prejudices had fed him, he acquired no knowledge likely to fit him for the monotonous drudgery of a compting-house.[7] He was a scholar, a poet, a young man of extraordinary, though somewhat eccentric genius; and on his very first insight into the business of a merchant's assistant, consisting of dry details, of endless accounts, and letters in a sort of bald jargon peculiar to them, he found so little pleasure in the view of being placed from day to day in a kind of railed box, with his legs dangling from a high stool, and his breast pressed against the edge of a desk, while his mind was to be thus chained down, that he would have abandoned the hope of every advantage which he was told might accrue from it, and have determined to content himself on his small patrimony, if the attachment he soon felt for me had not made him dissemble, and endeavour to make himself acquainted with a business which might one day enable him to demand me of my father.

"Love has often been the worker of great miracles, and such was now the patient perseverance of Glenmorris for near six months. During that time, being received as a relation, and a young lad to whose visits no consequence could be attached, he had continual opportunities of seeing me, and our mutual affection had acquired so deep root, that nothing was ever able to eradicate it.

"A match now offered for my sister Guilielmina. The second son of a noble house, very rich as heir to his maternal grand-mother, was accepted with joy by all the parties, the only objection, his want of a title, being removed by the agreement made by his father to purchase one, and my mother, Lady Mary, as it had formerly been in her family, desired this title might be Daventry, which was at first to be a barony for Mr. Cardonnel, then an earldom, and he was to receive his new name as a wedding present from his illustrious parents.[8] The marriage was to be celebrated at the ancient family seat in the north of England, which had belonged to the old Baronet from whom Lord Daventry derived his fortune. For some reason or other my mother determined that I should remain at the house on the banks of the Thames, observing, that I should lose a great deal of time by being so long absent, and become too much dissipated for a person of my age. I well knew that these were not her real reasons; but I was too well pleased with the resolution to be very solicitous about its motive.—My sister and the bridal train, accompanied by my father, mother, and the governess who had been principally entrusted with us, and who would not be separated from her 'dearest young lady,' departed together, and I was left to the superintendance of a younger governess, who was not likely to be a very troublesome monitress. She was glad to make use of the first moment of liberty to visit her friends, and I willingly permitted her absence, happy to be able for once to see Glenmorris for a whole day—to meet him again unquestioned on the river's banks by moon light (for he affected to depart at an early hour) and, as he took up his abode at an obscure lodging in the village, to rejoin him again at the earliest dawn of morning.

"It was mid-summer, and every object around me breathed, methought, the same delicious sensations as animated my breast. I had never been happy before; closely guarded by my mother's formal austerity, I had never till now felt the value of existence, or tasted the delight of an hour's freedom; I seemed to be inspired with a new soul, and nature kindled in my heart the innocent enthusiasm of affection.— Glenmorris, always passionate and tender, now mingled something of a soft melancholy with his acknowledged fear of offending me by trespassing on my indulgence. He never was so interesting, yet he appeared less content than I had often seen him when we were under greater restraint; he declared, however, that he was but too happy—

for we lived almost all day in the plantations and woods, and it was with reluctance I returned to a short meal alone, when I dared not ask him to accompany me. Some management and precaution was necessary in this respect, because there was an old house-keeper in question, fiercer than ten dragons, who, though she knew nothing of what I did with myself at other times, would, I knew, infallibly acquaint Lady Mary if I had seen Glenmorris often at table.

"Having taken therefore such precautions against her remarks as I simply imagined would secure me from them, I feared nothing but that the return of the family would deprive me of my temporary freedom, and send poor Glenmorris back to the dungeon called a compting-house, in a dark lane of the city.⁹ To this period he looked forward with loathing and abhorrence. A thousand times, as we wandered together amidst the beautiful shrubberies of my father's villa, he declared, that so repugnant was that way of life to his taste and temper, that he would not have staid one week in it for the riches of Peru—'But for thee, Laura,' said he, looking tenderly on me, 'what is there I would not endure?'—Once, I remember, he broke out suddenly in lines which he at that moment composed—

> Ah! think'st thou, Laura, then that wealth
> Should make me thus my youth, and health,
> And freedom, and repose resign?
> Ah! no, I toil to gain by stealth
> One look, one tender glance of thine.
>
> Born where huge hills on hills are piled
> In Calydonia's distant wild,
> Unbounded freedom once was mine;
> But thou upon my hopes hast smiled,
> And bade me be a slave of thine.
>
> Think! mid the gloomy haunts of gain
> Reluctant days I pass in pain,
> And all I once desired resign;
> Ah! let me then at length obtain
> One soft, one pitying sigh of thine.
>
> Though far capricious fortune flies,
> Yet love shall bless the sacrifice,
> And all his purer joys combine,
> While I my little world comprise
> In that fair form, and fairer soul of thine.¹⁰

"You, Delmont, are one of the few persons to whom I believe I may relate many of these circumstances without being thought wildly romantic.¹¹—Oh! what romantic stuff! is a common exclamation, if any one ventures to feel or to express themselves out of the style of common and every day life. But why is it romantic? I should be sorry, it is true, that a daughter of mine, suffering her imagination to outrun her reason, should so bewilder herself among ideal beings as to become either useless or ridiculous; but if affection for merit, if admiration of talents, if the attachments of friendship are romantic; if it be romantic to dare to have an opinion of one's own, and not to follow one formal tract,[12] wrong or right, pleasant or irksome, because our grandmothers and aunts have followed it before; if not to be romantic one must go through the world with prudery, carefully settling our blinkers at every step, as a cautious coachman hoodwinks his horses heads; if a woman, because she is a woman, must resign all pretensions to being a *reasoning* being, and dares neither look to the right nor to the left, oh! may my Medora still be the child of nature and simplicity, still venture to express all she feels, even at the risk of being called a strange romantic girl."

Delmont, it may easily be believed, acquiesced in this with his whole heart.

Mrs. Glenmorris went on.

"I had but little idea then, that I was actually passing the happiest days of my life. They fled too rapidly; for my father being taken ill with the gout, of which he had frequently very severe attacks, he and my mother returned some weeks sooner than they originally intended to their villa on the banks of the Thames.

"The awe I had always felt in my mother's presence was now so much increased by the consciousness of my having encouraged Glenmorris's passion, which, though I did not believe she would finally oppose it, she would, I knew, think most presumptuous and indecorous, that in approaching her I trembled, and could hardly answer the question she put to me. She seemed to have returned in very ill humour, and began by finding fault with every thing that had been done in her absence; and as to me, 'I was grown,' she said, 'so blowzy and robust, that she believed I had passed my time in assisting Sharman (the steward) to superintend the hay-makers.' 'This,' said her lady-ship 'comes, child, of your notions of being a shepherdess, and sitting on a bank of daisies.—Why you are tanned!—so tanned that it will be twelve months before you look again like a daughter of mine. I suppose you have got a tame lamb, and have been making garlands for him, and carving true lovers knots on some of the beech trees. Have you not sighed too for a shepherd? or have you imagined one in a green jacket, and with his crook bound with daffodils?' I feared from this strange attack that some-body had already mentioned the frequency of Glenmorris's visits, and I felt that my cheeks were deeply crimsoned by the idea, and that my knees, for I was still standing, were almost unable to support me. My mother however did not immediately remark it, but turning to Miss Hayns, my governess, asked, 'Who has been here?—has Glenmorris called often?'—

"Miss Hayns had been absent great part of the time herself, and feared my mother even more than I did; she blushed, hesitated, and at length said, 'Mr. Glenmorris has called sometimes, and once or twice, or oftener, I believe, dined here.'

"'You have not been playing at shepherd and shepherdess with *him*, I hope,' said Lady Mary; 'he is almost as absurd, and as little likely ever to do himself any good as even you yourself. Pray, miss, when did you see him last?'

"This question, and the sarcasm that preceded it, almost deprived me of the little courage I had left. I stammered out, however, that I had seen him about two days ago, and then, unable to bear the rigorous scrutiny of my mother's eyes, I turned from her, asking leave to attend my father, which she refused, and bade me go to my own apartment.

"There was every reason to fear, that some person had already been busy to inform my mother of the meetings between me and Glenmorris; and I now felt for the first time in my life the pain of conscious duplicity; I felt that I had done wrong; yet the harshness of Lady Mary's conduct towards me, the little affection she had ever shown me, and her having left me so needlessly in solitude and neglect, were, and I was conscious they were, such palliations of my fault, as in a great degree reconciled me to myself: I had, however, dread and apprehension enough to contend with—I knew that it was Glenmorris's determination to explain his views to my father, and I had in vain endeavoured to prevail upon him to wait some time longer, as I forsaw that our extreme youth would be thought a sufficient objection, if the indigence of Glenmorris should be overlooked, in consideration of his being related to Lady Mary; and if, as we sometimes supposed possible, my father had entertained any project of his succeeding to a share of his mercantile concern.

"The reception my mother had given me was so unpromising, that I was now more than ever solicitous to prevail on Glenmorris to delay his proposals. I knew his impetuosity to be such as would make it very difficult for me to persuade him, even if I had an opportunity; but I dreaded his not giving me one; and I dared not now write to him, or take any other measures to obtain a private conference; and I was aware that if once he attempted, and failed to interest my father, there would afterwards be no alternative between a clandestine marriage and our eternal separation.

"I vainly sought how to meet Glenmorris. It was soon too late; and while I meditated on the means of evading a danger, all I apprehended had already happened. On going down to dinner I found Glenmorris at table with two or three other guests. My father was grave and cold, hardly attended to what was said, and, I thought, looked at me and Glenmorris with concern. Lady Mary never took much pains to conceal her ill humour whenever she felt it, and the party now present was not one likely to impose any restraint upon her.—She had often been abrupt and rude to Glenmorris, which passed as a freedom natural to her, and in some measure authorized by her character and her relationship; she now affected the haughtiest reserve, pointedly avoiding to speak to him, and casting on him looks of anger and resentment which I knew too well how to interpret.

"The moment when I might withdraw from this irksome scene at length came; I ran into the gardens that surrounded the house, hardly knowing with what design, unless to breath freer, and escape from the stern and reproachful looks of Lady Mary. The plantations bounding these gardens were very extensive: I fled as far as I could from the house, and found myself at their extremity, where only some high paling and a border of flowering shrubs within divided it from an heath. My tortured imagination was busied with what had passed, and the dread of having lost Glenmorris for ever, when a few paces before me I saw a person spring over the fence, and I remained a moment terror struck, till I heard the voice of Glenmorris, who endeavoured to restore to me the courage which I wanted even to hear what he had to say.

"'I must be brief,' said he, 'for we are every moment liable to be interrupted. I have spoken to your father.'

"'Ah! Glenmorris,' exclaimed I, 'how could you risk it? You have undone us.'

"'That,' answered he impetuously, 'must depend upon you. Cured as I am of family pride, which, as a foolish boy, I indulged to a ridiculous excess, I yet feel as a man who is in nothing but riches inferior to M. De Verdon; and the insolence of high blood, with which Lady Mary insults most other people, is surely very ill placed when addressed to me, whose family was in fact the original stem from which her own derived its consequence. They have already shewn you, Laura, what they intend in regard to you. Your sister is to succeed to their great possessions, while you, if they indeed allow you to marry at all, are to be sacrificed to some old man, who, in consideration of your youth and beauty, will take you without a fortune. Your father, in answer to my application, hinted as much; and when I urged that I would devote myself to business, in the fond expectation of being permitted to *hope*, and that I would be content with whatever fortune he gave you, he answered me without anger indeed, but coldly, that he could shew no encouragement whatever to such a proposal; that such chimeras were the mere visions of inexperience; and he was sure Lady Mary, to whom he must at all events refer himself, had very different views. We were then interrupted by a summons to dinner. Soon after you left the room your father left it also, and Lady Mary sent by her own footman this note.'

"Glenmorris then produced a paper, on which was written,—

Mr. Glenmorris,
You seem so little to understand yourself, and have so strangely
presumed upon my kindness to you as my distant relation, that I can
no longer in justice, or in prudence to my family, countenance your
visits here, you will therefore think of these doors as shut to you for the
future.

M. De V.

"Imagine," continued Mrs. Glenmorris, "with what mingled emotions of terror and anguish I read this! I saw my lover torn from me, and that I should be exposed to the ill-treatment of my mother, enraged against us both; I could not articulate a word. It would indeed have been cruel to have reproached Glenmorris for his rashness. I trembled and listened in silence, therefore, while he thus proceeded—

"'The great fortune your father has amassed makes him look on mine as a contemptible nothing; and it is true that in this country it would not enable me to live as well as his maitre d'hotel.[13]—But, Laura, we are not confined to this country! Where his forefathers lived Glenmorris can live also. If Laura really loves him, as she has sometimes deigned to own, if she wishes to save him from these impetuous passions that threaten, if he is left to himself, to plunge him into intemperance, perhaps disgrace; if for him she does not fear to quit the luxuries she is surrounded with!'—'Oh! stop, Glenmorris,' cried I, 'and do not drive me distracted.—*If* I would do this—and can you *doubt* it?—But surely I ought not to determine upon it till I have at least tried what humbling myself before my father may obtain for us. I ought not, for *your* sake, to throw myself thus hastily out of the probability of obtaining what is justly due to me, a share at least of my father's fortune. Do not think I am of so abject a spirit as to fear the loss of luxuries and refinements that never have given me any pleasure.—What your forefathers have lived upon, it is true, may suffice us—I am sure it will content me—But why would Glenmorris refuse to his Laura the power of restoring him to such ease, as well as to such pecuniary rank, as we each of us have enjoyed in our country? Let me try my father—he loves me, and I have hopes.'

"'They will be vain,' interrupted Glenmorris.—'You will be intimidated by ideas of undutifulness; you will yield to the violence of your mother; I shall give way to my despair, and become, perhaps, a very wretch; for you know not, Laura, from how many errors my love has saved me—the hope I have cherished once crushed—Ah! take care, my dear girl, least you destroy him you profess to love. When you are lost to me, why should I care what I do, or what becomes of me?'

"I was about to answer, when I saw, at the other end of the walk, my mother and Miss Hayns approaching. Fear conquered for a moment every other sensation.—'Oh! fly,' cried I to Glenmorris; 'for pity's sake do not let us be found together.'

"'No, Laura,' answered he steadily, 'the guilty may fly; I have done nothing that I ought to blush at, and I will not escape like a thief. I saw you, and came the shortest way to meet you, but I shall leap no fences either to seek or to avoid the presence of Lady Mary.'

"Glenmorris then walked towards her, but I was so foolishly, so childishly timid, that I dared not go on with him to the interview that I now saw must inevitably take place between him and my mother; but with trembling feet made my way to the house, stopping at intervals to listen for my mother's voice, which I expected would be very loud; and I fancied I heard her reproaching Glenmorris, and tormenting him with threats of the confinement and punishment she meditated for me. I would have sought my father, but he either slept, as was his usual custom, or had ordered his servant to say he did, to avoid my importunity."

CHAP. II.

I am no pilot; yet wert thou as far
As that vast shore wash'd with the farthest sea,
I would adventure for such merchandise.[14]

Mrs. Glenmorris thus continued to relate the circumstances of her life.

"Imagine all that an angry and malicious woman is capable of uttering to those she has been accustomed to consider as in her power, when her authority has been, she believes, insulted and her projects disarranged—All that you can imagine would probably fall short of what Glenmorris heard with contempt, and answered with firmness, but which, when it was repeated to me, I was far from being in a condition to answer at all.

"My father, when he was allowed to see me, seemed, I thought, to look upon me with pity; but he had no voice. My mother's original ascendency was now confirmed by her violence and arrogance, and more implicitly submitted to on account of his daily increasing infirmities; and he could do but little more than express his compassion by his looks; yet that compassion never seemed to amount to a wish to make any effort to save me. He was absorbed in the care of his own health, and in contemplating the honours done to the new Lord and Lady Daventry, at a town for which he had been a member during the short interval between his being twenty (for he waited not his majority)[15] and his accession to a seat among the hereditary legislators of his country. These sort of details gave my poor father great delight, and he was fed with them incessantly; while I, amidst the mournful solitude I was condemned to, was so far from envying my sister these ceremonies and festivities, that I would not have exchanged lots with her, though half the world had been thrown into her scale. I was, notwithstanding, very miserable, and every day my wretchedness encreased. I had now an older governess put over me, for Miss Hayns had been dismissed immediately after my mother's conversation with Glenmorris. From him I never heard, though I had every reason to think he had attempted to convey letters to me; and my father being recovered of his indisposition, we set out at a very short notice for an estate he had purchased in Lancashire, where, I suppose, they imagined Glenmorris would not follow me, and where, as it was an insulated house, far from a post town,[16] the Lady Mary probably thought I could not easily find the means of corresponding with him.

"Lady Mary had prevailed on my father to purchase this place, because it had, above two hundred years ago, been the principal seat of her family. It had at that period been a fortress, and still retained many marks of its former strength. The country it stood in was wild and gloomy, and from its gothic windows there was a view of the Irish Channel, and an immense extent of sand, covered only at times by the tide, which took off the bold grandeur of a sea view, and left only ideas of sterility, danger, and desolation, in its place.

"No stronger proof could be given of the influence of Lady Mary over her husband, than the purchase of this place; for my father, bred in a Dutch compting-house, and having passed all his life in great cities, immersed in commercial pursuits, had no idea of any pleasure resulting from landed possessions and rural improvements; still less could he share the delight Lady Mary expressed at being possessed of Sandthwaite Castle, which he thought the most gloomy and comfortless abode that ever the caprice of a wife compelled a poor husband to inhabit. He confined himself wholly to one apartment, which was indeed rendered luxuriously habitable by modern improvements, imagined by Lady Mary, and executed at an expence which the worthy old merchant shrunk at internally, without daring openly to complain. The walls, which were in no part of the edifice less than seven feet thick, were made to yield to the slight and elegant introduction of modern windows with brass frames, enclosing the largest crown glass;[17] and these were double; one sash opening door-wise within the room, the other at the other extremity of the wall's thickness, and in the interval there were placed pots of exotic flowers and shrubs. The old wainscotting was removed, and its place supplied by French damask in pannels with gilt frames. The sophas and low chairs, stuffed with down, were covered with the same, and the most expensive Brussels carpet covered the floor. A chimney piece of statuary marble, enclosing a register stove, and all the lesser inventions of modern luxury, entirely obliterated in these rooms, and in those appropriated to Lady Mary, which were still more splendidly furnished, all ideas of antiquity—and in his easy chair my poor old father sat like the statue of a gothic king, brought from some other part of the house, and new clad and modernised to represent the passive master of this. The ill humour, however, which he felt at being compelled to pass two months, and those two autumnal months, at Sandthwaite, he could not vent on his wife; it consequently fell on me; and I found him so peevish and ill humoured that I dared not attempt the project to soften him in my favour. My days, therefore, passed in a sort of hopeless languor. I heard not from Glenmorris—and sometimes fancied that with the sudden fluctuation to which tempers so ardent as his are often liable, he had determined to forget me. My heart shrunk from the idea. I recalled all he had said—every look, every sentence was present to me, and then I felt myself re-assured, and once more ventured to hope we were destined for each other.

"Lady Mary, occupied by giving directions for improvements round the house, and for renewing by new plantations those of the last year, in which most of the trees had absolutely refused to grow, troubled herself very little about me. She was sure I could hold no correspondence with Glenmorris. My old governess was very vigilant, and followed me in all my walks; no servant dared take a letter from me under pain of instant dismission without a character;[18] and contented with having made me unhappy, and with the power of keeping me so, Lady Mary rarely persecuted me with her presence. Hopes were given my father, that Lord and Lady Daventry would cross the country, and stay a fortnight with him at his new-old castle; and Lady Mary was, after receiving that intelligence, doubly active in preparing another set of apartments for them, and giving the best appearance possible to a place of which they were to be the future possessors.

"In consequence of these new arrangements, I was directed to remove from the rooms I and my duenna inhabited, and *which were now wanted*, to a part of the building where no other *improvement* than what sufficed to keep out the weather had, I believe, been made since the place was a fortress in the wars between the Yorkists and Lancastrians.[19] My own bed, however, was removed thither, and my ancient governess was most unwillingly compelled to follow with her's, which was placed in a recess of the thick wall, not very unlike a cavern in a mine. The only entrance to both the rooms was opposite the foot of her bed, where a narrow door of oak, with iron nails, opened to a something between a passage and gallery, so high that the rafters could hardly be seen, and so long that the eye failed to distinguish through the gloom any object that appeared at the other end. Two doors, besides that which gave entrance into my room, opened into this forlorn avenue—that nearest to us had been nailed up for ages, the very cause of which was now forgotten; the legend had faded away with the ancient inhabitants, and the farmer, whom the last possessor of the estate had put into the house, had never opened the room, merely because he did not want it; the next he had made a repository for his wool, and for lumber, which had lain about the house—old rusty breast plates and gyves;[20] a gauntlet[21] which was bruised, and, as it seemed, was encrusted with the blood of the hand which it had once guarded; the heads of lances; an iron cap, a barred helmet, and a shield intended to guard against arrows, which was made of slight bars of iron covered with leathern thongs, once thickly interwoven, but of which nothing now remained but a few shreds, explaining what it had been. You wonder, perhaps, that among the piles of lumber, scraps of moth-eaten furniture, and old banners, together with the packing cases accumulated by the arrival of Lady Mary's London furniture, and the rubbish left from generation to generation in this repository, I should be able to recollect these relics of ancient chivalry. My retentive memory about things apparently so little interesting will hereafter be explained.

"Lady Mary had taken it into her head, from I know not what dream of her grandmother's, that her illustrious blood was derived from Geoffry Plantagenet, the second son of the second Henry, not indeed by the unfortunate Constance, but by a French lady of family in Armagnac.[22] Nothing was said of this in the records of the race; it was therein supposed to be derived from quite another source, but of less antiquity, and less nearly allied to royalty. But Lady Mary was so much better satisfied with this illegitimate descent from so illustrious a stem, that she would have christened her son, had she been happy enough to have produced one, by the name of Geoffry; and it was a great effort of complaisance when she yielded to call both her daughters by names which belonged to the family of her husband, and forbore to insist on calling one of us Elinor, after the mother of her great progenitor.

"Why any one should find delight in fancying that some of the most hateful characters in history were their ancestors I never could imagine. If any man calls another the son of a woman of loose character, he would run the risk of being knocked down; yet these worthy folks find all that is not endurable to day so mitigated and softened by the medium of one hundred or two hundred years, that the fame of being the descendant of some elevated ruffian, by a damsel of doubtful reputation, who lived at that period, is sought for as an honour, as if the simple offspring of the humblest cottager was not a thousand times more respectable. Of this honour, however, the head of my poor mother became so full, in consequence of some old parchments which she pretended to have found at Sandthwaite, that she talked of nothing but Plantagenets, and the bough of broom was worked, painted, and flourished on all her furniture. Every body that had any sense laughed at her; my father, who was no great laugher naturally, could not forbear to smile, till he found that Geoffry Plantagenet was likely to occasion him more expence than all the living relations of Lady Mary, yet they had by no means been a cheap connection.

"Lady Mary had heard of, or perhaps seen, the sword of Sir Bevis, who was one of the seven champions of christendom; she had gazed on the helmet of Hotspur, and looked with respect on the ribs of the dun cow, victim to the prowess of the Earl of Warwick.[23] In rummaging therefore over Sandthwaite Castle, these pieces of armour had been discovered, which only their being worth nothing, even as old iron, had probably preserved so long; and on an old sword, with a cross of iron by way of guard, she seized, as the weapon undoubtedly used by Geoffry Plantagenet himself; this therefore was hung up in the entrance hall in great state—and her ladyship meditated forming a trophy of what remained to decorate the lodge which she was building as an entrance to the park, meaning to have them, as she observed, 'tastefully disposed in a sort of festoon, and painted white.'—Till they could undergo this operation, and be dedicated to the memory of Geoffry Plantagenet by a Latin inscription, they were suffered to remain in the lumber room, where the servants now began to imagine some nocturnal mysteries were celebrated by this Geoffry Plantagenet, of whom they heard so much, and his associates. The upper housemaid was of opinion that there was money hid there, and told a very true story, how her mother's great uncle had found, in one of his fields, a sort of an house under ground, where there was a pavement of comical[24] shaped bricks, all blue, and yellow, and red, making the figures of snakes and birds, and a pot full of money, with some heathen gods upon it, which he sold to a silversmith at Liverpool, and which was supposed to be hid by the fairies, 'or such like *spiritous creturs.*'

"'As to fairies,' cried my father's man, (a person of erudition and consequence from London) 'the stories of them there sort of *inwisabel* beings, and such, appearing, is all nonsense and stuff, and nobody believes such things now a days; as to this Geffry somebody, that my lady makes such a talk about, I wonder what *he* was?—some Lord or Duke I warrant, or she would not claim a cousinship to him—I suppose such another as Duke Humphry,[25]—but for my part I should like to see one of them grim goblins rise up out of a church yard now, or under the great hollow yew tree by the old chapel wall, with saucer eyes, and spitting wild fire out of his nostrils—Egad, nothing would divert me more.'

"'How *can* you talk so, Mr. Malloch,' said my Lady Mary's own woman, a person of infinite delicacy and superior feelings, who only occasionally condescended to hold converse with the rest.—'I'm surprised you have so little notion of propriety. I assure you, people of consequence *do* believe in spirits, and if you would but read some sweet books I met with just before I came from town, which I got from the circulating library, I'm sure you would never be such an infidel. You can't think how frightful the stories are—all about tapestry waving in the wind, a bloody dagger, and voices calling at midnight, howlings in the air, and dark passages, and coffins full of bones, and poor young ladies got among these alarming objects; quite shocking, I'll assure you.'

"'Cursed fee fa fum nonsense,'[26] cried Malloch, 'I heard a very good judge of them there things say so.—But I cannot stay prating about them now, I must go up to old Hogen Nogen[27]—he is the most frightful thing in *this* house' (this was the name his servants gave my father, from their idea that he was a Dutchman) 'and I wish this Jeffry Plantaget, or Jeffry Belzebub, would fly away with him and his damned old place together; and if they took Lady Mary into the bargain so much the better.'

"I give this specimen of the conversation of her ladyship's domestics, which by an odd chance I overheard, to shew what the sort of arrangement really was on which Lady Mary prided herself, being accustomed to say, there was not any house of equal fashion half so well regulated as her's.

"This resuscitation of Geoffry Plantagenet continued to make part of the conversation of the house, till folly begot folly, and all the stories of spectres and sprights that were remembered by any of the servants, or could be collected in the neighbourhood, were at length related with exaggerations every night at the second table, growing more terrific as they reached the servants hall, and in proportion as the evenings grew dark and long, till at length there was hardly a maid who would go to turn down the beds, or a stable boy who would venture to attend his horses alone.— The infection did not stop there—it reached my old governess, Mrs. Margyson. This prim gentlewoman was near sixty, very upright, very precise, and very weak. She had possessed a small fortune left her by her mother, who kept a boarding-house at a public place, but having entrusted it to the management of an attorney who was her relation, he had contrived to rob her, *secundum artem*,[28] of so much of it, that she was glad to accept the offer of a woman of some fashion, who had lodged in the house, to live with her, in a sort of indefinite capacity between a lady's woman and a governess.—As she knew nothing, she could teach nothing; but she was careful of the children's health, and scolded the other servants so much to the satisfaction of her employer, that on her dismission she received an handsome present beside the yearly stipend, which she had saved almost entirely, and she only wished for a little addition to enable her to return to her native place, and live in part of a small house of her own, play a six-penny rubber or pool every night, and attend chapel three times a week, as well drest in her way as Mrs. Simmings, Miss Buttterworth, and other persons with whom she associated in her younger days, and to emulate whose present manner of life was the object of her actual ambition.

"Being recommended to my mother on the dismission of Miss Hayns, as a person who might be confided in, Mrs. Margyson accepted the offer, as likely in the event to answer her purpose, by compleating the little competency she coveted.— To me it was indifferent who was set over me, for I had determined never to tempt them to forget their fidelity.—Mrs. Margyson was very formal, very tedious, and very disagreeable, but not so ill-tempered as she was wearisome, by a sort of fid fad ceremony about trifles, which often tried my patience to the utmost—it had been dreadfully irksome to me while we were near London, but now as the apprehensions about Glenmorris gradually faded away, and there appeared no possibility of my seeing him, the poor woman was not sorry to relax in her vigilance, and the more readily suffered me to walk out alone, because the evenings were very cold, and the sharp air and cold house had already given her the rheumatism, of which she most piteously complained to the few who would hear her complaints.

"We had now been above a month at Sandthwaite, and the name of Glenmorris had hardly been mentioned—One evening, however, at dinner, Lady Mary took occasion to relate many articles of news, which she had learned by a letter from one of her relations—and at length she added, casting a significant glance at me, and addressing herself to my father—'It is very lucky indeed, Mr. De Verdon, that you dismissed my unhappy relation, that poor ill-starred Scotch boy Glenmorris, from all connection with yourself or your house; for Lady Bab assures me he is in a most dreadful way indeed—and in the short space of time since he has been his own master, has quite entirely ruined himself by gaming—and that not like a gentleman neither, and in an handsome way, but by frequenting all the lowest gaming houses and most blackguard societies in town.'

"My father, who, though he dared not own it, had always a sort of good-natured partiality towards Glenmorris, answered drily, 'If it is so, I am sorry for it.'

"How I looked I know not, but my mother seemed to enjoy my confusion; and that I might gratify her as little as possible, and breathe freer, for I felt choaked; I rose from table, and hastened into the garden.——

"It was a mild evening—the wind blowing from the sea, brought with it the hollow murmur of the waves with the rising tide; they broke shallow and ripling on the broad bed of sand, on which, where it was not dry, and on the surf as it whitened beyond, the trembling lustre of an early moon was reflected.—The very circumstance of being alone, and at liberty for a few moments, was a species of enjoyment, and I soon recovered recollection enough to consider, that what Lady Mary had said was probably unfounded; that it was unlikely that the person with whom she corresponded, an old woman of quality, who associated with beings so very unlike Glenmorris, should know any thing of him. My spirits were quieted by these reflections, and recalling to my mind every reason I had to rely on the affections of Glenmorris, I had once more felt myself capable of enduring with calmness my present situation however comfortless.

"I knew, that not to forfeit by indiscretion the privilege I had obtained from poor Margyson's illness, that of walking alone, I must not be long absent; I forbore therefore to lengthen my walk beyond the end of a terras, or embankment, which was carried on before the house, at the distance of four or five hundred paces, rather as a guard against the sea, which in high tides overflowed the place, that if grass would have grown in it might have been with more justice called a lawn, than as affording any ornament. On reaching its termination towards a sort of salt marsh, I stopped a moment to observe some sea birds, whose white wings catching the moon beams, seemed like transient meteors floating from the sea, which was now covering the sand, where at low water they sought their food. Every thing was so still that I could hear the whispering of their wings, when my attention was suddenly and forcibly arrested by a low yet strong voice, which, issuing from beneath the place where I stood, sang an air, of which Glenmorris had written the words, and it had been set to music by one of his friends; once before I had heard it; now, without waiting for its conclusion, I called, hardly knowing what I did, on Glenmorris, and in a moment he was before me.

"I was at first unable to speak, but conscious that we were in view of most of the windows of the house, fear mingled itself with surprize and pleasure. I explained to Glenmorris, in a few words, the danger we were in. He asked me if I had courage to venture down from the terrace, which would then afford us a shelter, to the sands below it; and when I assured him I had, he sprang down before me, and assisted me to follow him. I still dreaded the enquiry of Mrs. Margyson, and therefore listened trembling.

"'Laura,' said he, 'we have now been separated four months—how have you borne it? and do you still love me?—Ah! Laura, I will tell you the cruel effect this enforced absence has had on me—It drove me at first to attempt dissipation as a cure for despair. When it seemed so uncertain whether we should ever meet again, when I thought you might be induced to forget me, I became careless of every thing. My friends, who love me best, were absent—I found a poor substitute for them in acquaintance—and I will tell you, Laura, the whole of my folly—You may yet save me, unless you believe him, who solicits you to snatch him from perdition, already unworthy of your regard, and then I have nothing left but to complete my undoing.'

"I interrupted him, entreating him to explain himself.

"'You know,' said he, 'the heart which is wholly yours, and you have lamented its extravagant and ungovernable temper; you alone can mould it as you will. When I am no longer under your influence, I am under that of those violent passions which I feel I have not reason enough to govern—and—alas! Laura, I have been the prey of men with whom I ought never to have associated—I wandered about the town, forlorn and wretched—my feet involuntary took the way to that part of it where I had been used to see you—but you were gone!—and nothing remained but the cruel remembrance that we might never meet again.

"'Thrown from your father as unworthy of his countenance, and detesting the occupation which I had attempted to follow, when every chance was removed that you would be the final reward of the sacrifice I should have made of my taste and my time, I seemed to be burthensome even to myself, and an outcast from the world.

"'There were moments in which I felt a dreadful temptation to quit it—But you were in it, and amid the wild tumult of my mind, hope did not wholly forsake me—yet, to quiet by momentary forgetfulness the misery that preyed upon me, I rushed into company. The mere conversation of men, whose ideas and pursuits were altogether unlike mine, irritated rather than appeased the agitation of my mind; I wanted something that could animate me, could induce me to take some interest in what was passing; I went to a gaming table, and my purpose was for the moment answered.

"'Again and again I repeated the dangerous experiment—I won, and fancied I understood what I was about; I even imagined, fool that I was, that fortune might favour me to such a degree as to renew all my hopes of engaging your father's favour. My gains, however, were merely the result of the finesse of my companions. I soon lost to three times their amount, and found it to be impossible, for me to continue long in the same line—but I sought tables of an inferior description, and often, instead of trying by rational means to sooth and reduce my fevered spirits to reason, I have rambled all night from one of these receptacles of desperation to another.'

"Glenmorris, who held my hands within his while he spoke, felt that I trembled, and had no courage to interrupt him.

"'Yes, Laura,'—he went on to say,—'I have wasted in this senseless and destructive vice some of the little property I possessed, and lessened, in the phrenzy of my despair, the little hope I had of happiness—if it vanishes quite I will no longer resist ruin, I will rather court it. Consider then, my first, my only love, if you can resolve to share my destiny, inferior as it is, to what you ought to expect, or whether you more prudently, as the world would think, determine to abandon me to my fate.—I know I am unworthy of you, every way unworthy, save in possessing an heart which knows your value, and adores you. I have yet a property left in the highlands—there lived my ancestors—why should I, falsely refined, suppose that I cannot also live there? With you, Laura, the wildest mountain of my rugged country would be to me an Eden.'

"You may imagine what was my answer to this proposal. I not only passionately loved Glenmorris, but had no pleasure in that way of life which my parents wished to force me to continue in. The assurance that my sister would be with them obviated all objection to my leaving them, and appeased the concern I should otherwise have felt for my father. The idea of saving Glenmorris from the errors, the ruin, which his impetuous temper was hurrying him into, suspended in my mind every other consideration. 'I will follow you, Glenmorris,' said I, 'as your wife, as your friend, whithersoever you will, at any hazard—I dread nothing but your forgetting me.'"

CHAP. III.

> With love's light wings did I o'er perch these walls,
> For stony limits cannot love hold out:
> And what love *can* do, that dares love attempt.[29]

"A moment only remained," said Mrs. Glenmorris, continuing her narrative, "to consult on the means of our escape. The impossibility of my passing through the bed-chamber of Mrs. Margyson, whose bed exactly fronted the door, was our greatest impediment, and such as for the moment appeared insurmountable. She herself locked the door every night, and usually sat up later than I did—To obviate such a difficulty was not the contrivance of a moment, and lights being now seen, and voices calling me from the house being heard, Glenmorris, hurrying to assist me to regain the terras,[30] had only time to entreat me to see him again the following evening.—'I' said he, 'will in the mean time walk round the fortress, and as you have given me an idea of your chamber, I think I shall find some means to settle our plan by to-morrow night.' I implored him to take care, which he promised, and in his turn entreating me to have courage, and not betray myself by the appearance of fear, we parted. Glenmorris disappeared, and I walked towards the persons whom I observed coming from the house in search of me. Mrs. Margyson, though quite a cripple with the rheumatism, came towards me as nimbly as she could, and enquired why I walked so late? I answered with apparent unconcern; and as she saw me safe her fears and her displeasure vanished together. I went in to supper, not without dread of hearing a more severe remonstrance from Lady Mary; but I found that during my absence she had heard by an avant courier[31] of Lord and Lady Daventry's proposed arrival the next day save one, and had been too busy in giving orders, and settling every thing that was to be done the next day, to think about me. Indeed she hardly seemed to recollect that I existed.

"I hastened most willingly to my chamber, and waited impatiently till Mrs. Margyson should be asleep, as I then hoped to see Glenmorris reconnoitring as soon as the servants should be retired; but the windows, if they might be called windows, of the room I inhabited, were so far from the ground that I could not reach them, or if I had I could not have opened them, I was therefore compelled to restrain my impatience till the following evening, when every body being busied in preparations for the great event of the ensuing day, I was suffered to take my walk unnoticed; I even told Mrs. Margyson, who was busied as the rest, that I should go for a long ramble on the sands, to which she made no objection.

"I soon met Glenmorris, and we got as quickly as we could out of the way of observation.

"He then told me, that as soon as the lights were extinguished he had gone round the house; and 'there is,' said he, 'very near the room which I know to be your's, an high heap of ruins, or rather rubbish, which has been piled up, I imagine, at different times, in that recess, as alterations have been made in the building; I am sure that if I mounted on these ruins I could either get into the room myself, or take you from the window safely. What is in that room? Does any person sleep there?'

"I informed him that the room, as has been so frequently the case in such houses, had been nailed up nobody now knew why; that I had never been in it, and believed that no person now in the castle had ever ventured to explore it.

"Glenmorris declared that nothing could be better for our purpose.—'I am sure,' said he, 'by the appearance of the window, that I can force it open. If any noise is heard while I do it, it will be imputed to the evil spirits who have doubtless held their vigils there from time immemorial—Expect me, therefore, as soon as every thing is quiet round the castle—When I am once within side I have no doubt of finding the means to conduct you safely without.'

"I recollected at that moment, and mentioned the remains of the armour of Geoffry Plantagenet, which was deposited in the lumber-room, from whence it occurred to me that there was a door opening from that he proposed to enter, though it was half hid by boxes, packing cases, pieces of worm-eaten furniture, and immense frames of old pictures, which, for aught I knew, might heretofore have furnished the apartments of Geoffry Plantagenet himself. Glenmorris smiled at my description, and replied, that if the inside of those rooms answered to their appearance without, he had no doubt of being able to force any door with little difficulty or noise. He desired that, as I had access to the first room, I would take some safe occasion to remove as much as I could of the obstructions near the door that opened to the other; then pausing a moment, he said, 'What if to secure our flight I were to enact your mother's illustrious ancestor, and stalk in the armour of Geoffry himself? Yet,' added he, his natural generosity prevailing, 'yet I should not like to owe my success to a stratagem which might terrify fatally your poor old governess. There is something so pitiable in the situation of a little unprotected old being, who is forced to eat the bitter bread of dependence under a woman like Lady Mary, that I feel it almost unmanly to inflict on such an one any additional dread.'[32]

"The idea, however, was too happy a one to be given up. 'We may have to encounter,' said he, 'persons against whom I shall have no scruple to use any means that may fall in my way; endeavor, therefore, my Laura, to have the armour ready; take such other precautions as occur to you; prepare a little packet of linen, and if possible make your appearance resemble that of a peasant girl.'

"The part Mrs. Margyson voluntarily took in the bustle my mother chose to make about my sister's reception had greatly fatigued the poor woman, who was also very much indisposed by one of those rheumatic affections which occasions particular suffering as soon as the patient is warm in bed. To save herself from this pain Mrs. Margyson was accustomed to take an opiate, and she had on this night, I believe, doubled the dose, for she was, contrary to her custom, soon in a fast sleep.[33] I never heard any sound more delightful than that which convinced me the good woman was in a state of forgetfulness; I listened to the shutting the doors in remote parts of the house, and at length heard the clock tell twelve; but there were still distant murmurs about the building; I could not hear any thing distinctly, but I imagined the house-keeper, and the servants under her, were kept by their confectionary and pastry from their beds till a later hour than usual. My heart beat so violently during all this suspence, that I was almost unable to breathe. I had dressed myself, as soon as I was sure Mrs. Margyson slept, as nearly as I could in the manner Glenmorris had directed, and lay down in my clothes. When one o'clock sounded sullen from the entrance tower through the building, I arose, and in still more breathless expectation listened, while a thousand fears assailed me. I figured to myself that the pile on which Glenmorris proposed to mount might be hollow; that, light and active as he was, it might give way with his weight, and that not only discovery but danger to himself might follow; I dreaded too, least if he reached the window and attempted to force it, the stone work, which was very much disjointed, might crush him; and in truth I believe, though he afterwards made light of it, that mounting a breach would not have been a much more dangerous exploit than that he thus engaged in. The walls, however, on that side, were so thick, and his precautions such, that attentively as I listened I heard nothing, till a sudden crash very near me announced that Glenmorris had made his way into the adjoining room. My anxious terror was now insupportable, for I thought it impossible that so loud a noise should not awake my duenna. She still was fast asleep; I had previously had the precaution to unlock the door which was near her bed, and now, after waiting a moment, I crept softly to it, opened it, and shut it after me as gently as possible, and then almost sinking to the ground from the violence and variety of the fears that assailed me, I entered the lumber room. Glenmorris had already forced away the rotten door, and was waiting for me with a light he had struck by means of one of those little tapers prepared with phosphorus. 'We have not a moment to lose,' said he;— 'arm yourself with courage, for our escape is more difficult than I had reckoned upon.— I doubt whether the men in the stables are not up; they are preparing to go forth before daylight to meet the bride and bridegroom with your father's horses—I am sure of it, as well from the conversation I have heard as from the light that yet remains in the stables and hall, from one of which to the other men are passing backward and forward.—This would not signify if I saw any other means of your getting out of the house than going through a passage immediately near them.'

"I enquired eagerly why I could not descend, as he had got up, by the ruined pile? Glenmorris replied, that I might assure myself it was impossible; that he could not suffer me to hazard it; but would sooner relinquish all hope of taking me with him, dear as that hope was to his heart.—'Have you then courage,' continued he, 'to venture through the house?—To hesitate is to ruin every thing.—We can now pass over the sands in safety, while in two hours our flight that way will be rendered impossible, and by any other we shall be exposed to the probability of meeting the persons we most wish to avoid.'

"Eager and anxious as his manner was, and trembling as I did least Mrs. Margyson should awake and miss me, I consented to whatever he proposed, while my dread of our failure, and the anticipation of what I should inevitably suffer if we were detected, were so terrible to my imagination, that with difficulty I could follow Glenmorris, who pushed open the heavy door that closed the passage leading down a staircase which communicated with an unfrequented passage below, that might rather be called a stone gallery.—He stept softly on before me, provided with a small dark lanthorn, into which he had put his taper; but on descending the last step he saw a servant whom my father had long kept, rather on account of his imbecile simplicity than because he was of much use.—Old Amos, desirous that every thing might be in great order for his fine young lady, and not finding elsewhere sufficient employment for his officious zeal, was mighty busy in cleaning a sort of marble cistern fixed in this place, and which served to save the servants the trouble of going farther for water to supply this side of the house.—Glenmorris stopped, concealed his light, and by a motion of his hand pointed him out to me as he stood with his back towards us engaged in this needless work. To pass him as we were was impossible; but it occurred instantly to Glenmorris, that here the armour of Geoffry Plantagenet might most effectually befriend us. We saw beyond the foolish old man a door most conveniently open to the moonlight, and knew that from thence we could gain a path among Lady Mary's paled[34] plantations, which would soon lead us out of sight of the house to the sands. Glenmorris, as soon as we had re-ascended the staircase, communicated his idea to me. I knew that old Amos was the butt of all the servants on account of his cowardice and superstition, and I silently acquiesced, while I helped to equip Glenmorris in the armour of the heroes of the red rose.[35]—But little of it was necessary to make him a most formidable figure, and he would not encumber himself with any thing that might impede our speedy march across the grounds. The clock struck two as for the second time we descended the stairs, and found Amos still busy, though apparently near the end of his labours—He was arranging some fire buckets, of which this place was a receptacle,[36] and talking to himself, as he usually did when he thought he had performed some notable service for which he suspected nobody else would applaud him.

"Glenmorris advanced on tip toe close to him, struck the candle down that stood on a chair, and then throwing the light of the lanthorn directly on his own figure, pronounced in an hollow voice—'Amos! Amos! Amos!' There was no occasion for the repetition, for the very moment Amos heard himself so called, and caught a glimpse of the frightful figure from whom the summons came, he uttered something between a shout and a groan, and fell on his face on the floor, invoking most piously the assistance of all the powers of Heaven. We left him to his ejaculations,[37] and fled through the open door, which let us out to a place used for drying linen, and communicating one way to the stable yard, though by another we could pass out to the nurseries and shrubberies.—Thither we were hastening with quick and light steps, when the gate from the stable yard opened, and we saw an under groom appear, probably with the intention of calling Amos, as their work in the stable was done, to go to bed.—This was a country lad about seventeen, who had never been five miles from the foot of the fell[38] where he was born, and whose head was full of such stories as have been the terror and delight of the Lancashire clowns for ages.—Glenmorris putting me behind him faced the affrighted boy, who had he ran back the way he came would probably have alarmed the rest of the men; but following the first impulse of terror he rushed forward to the door of the place where we had left poor Amos, when not being able to open it, and on looking back seeing the spectre again, he stood apparently petrified with fear, his hands upon his eyes, and supporting himself against the door case, while we, fortunately finding the little wicker gate open, passed with all speed through it, and never stopped till we gained the sands. There Glenmorris disengaged himself from his armour, and fondly clasping me to his heart, whispered, that with a very little more exertion we should be safe. I was, however, so breathless between the haste and terror of our flight, that he insisted on my stopping a moment to recover myself. I did not long indulge this weakness; but fancying I heard voices from the house I implored Glenmorris to hasten on.—He took from me the small packet of linen I had provided myself with, and putting my arm within his, we proceeded silently, yet as fast as we could well walk, along the sands.

"The moon now lent us her latest light; we saw her sinking in the sea, and Glenmorris, while we stopped to listen if any noise came from the Castle threatening pursuit, was alarmed by the murmur of the tide, which seemed to be nearer covering the sands than he had calculated. Without communicating to me the extent of his fears, I observed him very anxious that we might quicken our pace—I ran rather than walked; but notwithstanding our utmost exertions the tide gained so fast upon us, that Glenmorris became soon terrified, even to agony, especially as he found that it would hardly be possible for me to continue much longer the haste I now exerted myself to make.

"His ardent and rapid imagination represented me as perishing among the rising waves, while unable to save me he was to stand an helpless spectator of my death.— With an emotion that communicated quite a convulsion to his whole frame, he grasped my arm within his, and I heard him murmur, 'I can always, however, escape the misery of surviving her.'—Finding by my shortening breath and feeble step that it was impossible to proceed so fast much farther, he stopped, and looked towards the water, which was now very near us, with an eye of despair—and much as we had before dreaded to hear any sound approach us from the quarter we had left, I believe Glenmorris now felt a sort of relief when the silence was broken by something else beside the hollow ripling of the approaching waves. We heard an horse that seemed to be coming fast to the place where we were.—We listened; the sound of his feet on the sand came nearer and nearer, and now they splashed the water which we felt rising over our's.—The light was yet sufficient to enable us to discern a man on horseback, now almost close to us, and to conceal ourselves from him was impossible. Glenmorris hallowed to him to stop, though we neither of us doubted but that it was somebody dispatched from the castle in pursuit of us.—Rudely and surlily the man answered

Glenmorris's enquiry of who he was? and whither he was going?—He was going, he said, to the village of Kenthwaite, if he could get there before the tide overtook him, and he had no mind to be drowned by staying to give an account of himself to us—so saying, he was urging his horse by us, when Glenmorris stepped on, and seized the bridle.—The man lifted a great stick and aimed it at him, but he caught it, and then said in a loud and authoritative manner, 'Whoever you are you *shall* hear me—I am overtaken by the tide with this young woman—our lives are at stake—I am well armed, and I will not suffer you to leave us in this situation; but if you will take her up upon your horse and land her safe at *Kenthwaite*, I will make it the best night's work you have done in your life.'—The man, at once awed by the peremptory manner and tempted by the promises of Glenmorris, agreed; but I positively refused to mount the horse unless he also was admitted to the same conveyance.—There was no time for debate—Glenmorris enlarged his promises, and at the same time contrived to make a pair of pistols and a cutlass visible. The man, who was a smuggler employed in conveying contraband goods inland from the coast opposite Ireland,[39] at length suffered Glenmorris to place me behind him, while Glenmorris himself took a third place on the horse, and straining me in his arms conjured me to have courage, and trust to his protection.—We then proceeded more rapidly than could have been expected, especially as the water gained upon us every moment, and the overloaded horse must soon have sunk with his burthen, if we had not, just as the water was almost obliging him to swim, arrived at the end of our perilous journey. Nor should we ever have reached it in safety if the man, whose hazardous trade thus threw him in our way, had not been one of those employed during the day in conducting passengers across these dangerous sands, and who therefore knew, even when covered with water, the places which were to be avoided.

"Glenmorris was anxious that I should stop at the first village we came to; but fatigued and half drowned as I was, I had such a dread of being betrayed by the accidental guide, who seemed to be a ruffian capable of committing any baseness for money, that I assured him I had a thousand times rather remove to a greater distance than risk his informing the inhabitants of Sandthwaite Castle which way we had taken.—My entreaties were so earnest that Glenmorris at length consented.—We crossed the river Ribble, and the next morning reached, on hired horses, the village of Charley.[40]—I know not with what story Glenmorris amused the people at the little ale-house where we took shelter, but I found every accommodation such a place afforded, and consented to remain there a day, Glenmorris assuring me there was no longer any thing to fear from the information of the smuggler; and that it was far more probable Lady Mary, if she thought proper to pursue us, should send northward, as imagining we were gone towards Scotland, whither it was now Glenmorris's intention to hasten by cross roads,[41] and along the eastern coast.

"I pass over a journey which had nothing in it remarkable. At the first great town we came to, Glenmorris furnished me with clothes, and on our arrival in the country where the laws do not oppose the marriage of minors, our fates were united for ever."[42]

CHAP. IV.

Length of years seemed to be the lot of my love, yet few and
fleeting were his days of joy; he was strong as the tree of the vale,
but untimely he fell; the morning sun saw thee flourish as the
rose before the noontide heat;
low thou droopest like a withered plant.———[43]

"During our subsequent journey," continued Mrs. Glenmorris, "my husband endeavoured to prepare me for the new scene I was going to, and the new manner of life I was
to lead in it.—I was indifferent to every thing so long as he was to be my companion,
and my girlish imagination delighted itself with the prospect of the wild romantic
solitude which love only was to embellish.

"The paternal house, or rather castled tower, of Glenmorris was in Sutherland,
and not far from the part of the county joining Caithness, the most northern extremity of the island.

"It was a stone fortress, built on an almost perpendicular rock, its base beaten
by the waves of the German ocean.[44] To the West arose mountains, whose summits
crowned with eternal snow, were often concealed by, and seemed to mingle with the
clouds. Nearer the house these pointed acclivities were less towering, and a few spots
near the bottom were shaded with birch and hazle. From between two rocks of fantastic form started a mountain torrent, which at the season I first saw it was swelled by
the autumnal rains, and appeared like a river precipitating itself from an immense
height, its foaming water looking bright and pellucid amidst the brown and purple
hues of the projecting eminence, covered with faded heath and other scanty vegetation. This stream, raising a perpetual cloud of mist where it fell, dashed away among
huge fragments of stone, till it was received, at the distance of half a mile, by the Loch,
that winding through the valley of Glenmorris, was at length lost among the mountains, which in many places beetled over it, and in others receding, left a small tract of
cultivated or pasture land, which with their fishery served to support the simple natives, whose circular huts doubly wattled,[45] and the interval filled with sods and roofed
with turf or heather, were thinly scattered along the glen—the whole of the inhabitants amounting then to about three hundred persons.

"The house, if house it might be called, had never been inhabited since the
father of Glenmorris, having lost a wife he adored when his son was about eleven years
old, took him in his hand, and set forth to wander round Europe, often on foot, and
at other times by such accidental conveyances as offered.

"He died of a fever in Spain about five years afterwards, having in that time
traversed the continent of Europe twice, and visited many of the islands of the Archi-
pelago;[46] it was then that Glenmorris, an orphan, and supposed to be even more
indigent than he really was, having found his way back to England, was patronised
after her manner by Lady Mary as a relation of her own—for while the acknowledged
antiquity of his family prevented her from disowning him, she felt a degree of exulta-

tion in having it said, that she rescued from poverty the last heir of his ancient house.

"Glenmorris, during his minority, had derived more pride than profit from being possessor of a large tract of land thinly inhabited and poorly cultivated; and since it had been in his power, he had unfortunately managed so ill as to be under the necessity of selling two of his farms; but sanguine in his disposition, and ardent in the pursuit of any project that struck him, he now returned to his native mountains with the expectation of improving his small inheritance by the knowledge he had acquired in other countries, and he supposed he could enforce the practice of what he knew by the most benevolently directed use of his power as feudal chief and the head of his clan.[47] With such hopes he soon shook off the gloom which the recollection of his parents, now both dead, and of the many changes of his fortune since, unavoidably brought with it.—He was delighted to see that I did not affect or feel any of the fastidious delicacy which might be disconcerted at the sight of the rude and remote habitation he had brought me to.—His affection for me and his country was equally flattered, when he saw the honest highlanders of his clan crowding round me, and felicitating each other on the happiness of their young laird, whom they appeared to consider as a tutelary divinity: they could never enough admire his fine and manly figure, which brought to their minds the heroes celebrated in their traditional songs;[48] while the women, unpolished as they seemed themselves, knew how to admire the grace and beauty of the laird of Glenmorris.

"The interior of our house, though far enough from being cheerful or convenient, was better rather than worse than my imagination had figured it. The extreme thickness of the walls made it warm—The furniture, though old, was clean, and many conveniencies but little known in the highlands had been conveyed thither during the residence of Glenmorris's mother.—Our beds and couvrelits were of eiderdown, the produce of one species among that myriad of sea-fowl that almost darkened the air amid the rocks under my window.—I did not dislike the smell of the turf fires,[49] and I procured a female servant who had been used to wear stockings and shoes, which removed the uncouth and uncomfortable appearance of having a woman gliding around me with naked feet.

"Our little arrangements completely employed us for some weeks, and by that time winter was set in, but not with that severity of cold that I had expected in a situation so far north.—The storm, however, of November and December was loud and heavy on our elevated roof, and the huge waves of the eastern ocean broke incessantly at its base; but within I had the countenance of the husband I loved to cheer me—I heard his voice repeat that he was happy, and bless me for constituting his happiness—I saw him, though almost despotic, the beloved monarch of a group of people, to increase whose comforts was his study—He found in that benevolent task, and in the cultivation of his little farm, sufficient employment during the day—At night, as we had a few books, and sometimes got a supply from Edinburgh, he read to me, while I was occupied in preparing clothes for the infant, whose birth we looked forward to as the completion of our felicity.

"During these months—ah! months too swiftly fled! it seemed as if our happiness was too great to admit of permanence; and sometimes when Glenmorris, enjoying the present and looking forward to the future, would dwell on the superiority, in his estimation, of the rational course of life he now passed, compared with the tumultuous and feverish existence he had experienced during his short career of dissipation, when despair had driven him from the haunts of luxurious idleness to the frenzy of the gaming house, I heard him with I knew not what emotions of apprehensive tenderness, and though I had no distinct idea of what so affected me, my eyes were frequently swimming in tears.

"Glenmorris, imputing these transient fits of despondence to my situation, sought only to soothe and tranquillize my mind. He had always designed to take an house at Edinburgh for three months before my expected confinement, that I might not be subjected to the inconvenience of a journey through the Highlands immediately near it. It was now the beginning of March, and as he fancied, though he forbore to notice[50] it, that my dejection increased, he one evening mentioned his intention of writing to a friend he had at Edinburgh to secure us this house immediately. I opposed his proposal as an unnecessary increase of expence, and assured him that I was perfectly well, and had not a single wish to desert our romantic home while he was happy in it. Glenmorris, who thought that some regret at having left my parents might at this time prey on my mind, then turned the discourse on them. I understood why he did so, and confessed to him, that though I often thought with tenderness and concern of my father, yet I was so well convinced that the presence and prosperous fortune of my sister consoled him for the loss of me, that I knew I inflicted no unhappiness on him, or unhappiness so transient that he had long since forgotten it. 'And as to Lady Mary,' added I, 'I believe my absence is so far from having given *her* pain, that she is happy in having found so good an excuse for throwing off for ever a daughter, for whom she seemed not to have room enough in her heart. I should, however, like to hear of my father. I should, I own, feel satisfaction in knowing that he has not withdrawn entirely from me that little share of affection which I used sometimes to think he *wished* to express more than his desire of domestic quiet would give him leave to do.'

"Glenmorris, fondly embracing me, promised, that if I would make myself easy he would find means within a very short time to procure for me intelligence of my father, and even to let him know that, though withdrawn from his immediate protection, I still felt for him the affection of a daughter, and whenever he commanded it would hasten into his presence. Such was the watchful tenderness of Glenmorris to prevent my very wishes, and such the consoling ideas I carried with me to my pillow; so that whatever presentiments I might before have felt or fancied, I had none of the hideous calamity at that moment impending, and threatening to crush me for ever.

"The evening had been cold and tempestuous, with a strong breeze from the east. As we sat at supper in the tower, of which the windows looked eastward, Glenmorris remarked that he heard two guns off at sea, and the weather was turbulent enough to make him fear they might be signals of distress. As nothing was so habitual to him as acts of humanity, he called his people, and bade them look out, as well as put out lights to mark the rocks and breakers, should any vessel, ignorant of the coast, be driving near it with this strong wind.

"He went down himself to the path cut in the rock, just wide enough to suffer one person to walk round on that side of the castle, and looked anxiously out, seaward, for the lights of the vessel which he fancied might need assistance; but the sky was so darkened by great rolling clouds driven impetuously by the wind, that he could distinguish nothing but the white surf thrown up with violence, and breaking against the rocks, of which three were sharp, and rising like huge ruins out of the sea about an hundred yards from the foot of the castle-cliff.

"Believing therefore he had been deceived, or that, if not, the guns might not have signified the peril of any vessel, but that they were perhaps fired by two ships that they might not part company during the darkness and storm, Glenmorris ordered his people to retire at the usual hour, and the whole family, which consisted, besides ourselves, of four female and five male servants, were buried in sleep. It was three hours after midnight when I suddenly was startled from an uneasy dream by a loud and unusual noise which seemed very near me.—Glenmorris, instantly awakened by my starting and exclamation, had hardly time to attempt re-assuring me, before the noise, yet nearer, was repeated, and in half a second four fierce and terrible looking men, armed with pistols and cutlasses, were in the room.—Glenmorris snatched a broad sword that hung by the side of the bed, and protesting he would perish a thousand times rather than suffer one of them to approach me, he kept them for a moment at bay, while he demanded what they were, and what they wanted? It was soon understood that they were the crew of an American privateer, and that their business was plunder.[51]—Glenmorris, who had at first conceived still more frightful ideas of them, made light of his property when put in competition with my safety, or even with my fears; and to draw them from the room where I was, he desired them, with great presence of mind, to give him time to put on his clothes, and said, that he would then shew them himself where the few valuable things he possessed were deposited. This the men refused. They knew that the alarm would soon be given to the clan, and that, overpowered by numbers, they should be compelled to relinquish their booty if they did not immediately secure it; they therefore demanded of Glenmorris to give up his broad sword, and to suffer himself to be bound. He staid not to hear the conclusion of a proposal so infamous, but rushing forward struck the ruffian who made it a blow which felled him to the earth. Two pistols were then fired; I saw Glenmorris fall. I saw no more; the shades of death encompassed me. I shrieked in frantic agony to Glenmorris, and my eyes closed in the stupefaction of anguish and despair.

"When my recollection returned, I found myself on the bed, with my maid and several highland women weeping over me, and endeavouring to recal me to life. I raised myself, and looking wildly around me, enquired for Glenmorris. The lamentations of the women were redoubled, and all that had passed flashed horribly on my fevered brain. Again I heard the pistol, which had, I concluded, destroyed Glenmorris— again I saw him stagger and fall—I started from my bed, and beheld the floor covered with blood.—The ignorant and affrighted women who surrounded me knew not how to soothe the first agonies of desperation; their ignorance and their own terrors served only to irritate the phrenzy that seized me; but my misery was so severe that I have now no distinct remembrance of what I said or did. I heard from them that Glenmorris was carried away, they knew not whether dead or alive, by the pirates; that two of his faithful servants had been desperately wounded in attempting to rescue him; that before the free-booters retired, the inhabitants of the glen being alarmed, had come down to the shore, and that it was with difficulty, and not till several shot had been fired on both sides, that they had escaped to their vessel with their prisoner, or their murdered victim, together with the booty they had gathered in the castle, which was almost every thing portable that it contained.

"I was incapable of hearing this narrative but by snatches and intervals. The horror of what I had seen, the dreadful uncertainty I was left in as to the fate of the only friend I had on earth, my lover, my husband, my protector, was such as to deprive me at intervals of my senses; I gave myself up to despair; I desired to die; nor would any thing have prevented my seeking death during those dreadful paroxysms, but the wish I was still conscious of to preserve the infant of my murdered Glenmorris—whenever that occurred to me I consented to take nourishment;—I tried to calm my agonized spirits, and then I sometimes sunk from this enforced resignation into a state of morbid tranquillity, and placing myself at that window of the tower which commanded the greatest horizon, I watched from morning till night the boundless extent of ocean, and half stupefied, half delirious, fancied I saw a distant sail, and that it might belong to the vessel where was the bleeding corse[52] of Glenmorris.

"This horrible image was ever present to me, and hourly gained upon my mind, whether I raved or was composed; whether I was awake, or yielded through mere fatigue to unquiet and feverish sleep. Of every personal inconvenience or personal fear I was totally insensible, but it was not so with the women about me, or the servants of the house. Their dread was least the pirates might return; and with lamentations for their dear master, and their unfortunate companions (one of whom had by this time died of his wounds) these poor people mingled fears for their own safety and mine.— It was in vain, however, that they entreated me to quit the castle, and remove farther up the country. When I was capable of understanding them, I refused with anger and indignation to hear any mention of quitting it; but at other times I sat totally un-moved, and neither spoke nor gave any sign of comprehending them.

"There was not a superstitious notion, with which this poor and ignorant race of people are taught to torment themselves, that did not receive its confirmation from the miserable catastrophe thus overwhelming me. The shrieks of spirits, portending future evil, were nightly heard, either from the sea or among the rocks. This idea was repeated till it reached me; but *I* feared no future evils; *mine* were inevitable and incurable, and I felt something not unlike an horrible kind of pleasure in prognostics,[53] which, if they might be depended upon, announced to me the end of my insupport-able sufferings; at other times I wished to live only to give birth to my child—yet when I had reason enough to consider how unprotected and desolated a little wretch it would be, I desired rather that we might die together before it saw the light.

"I gradually learned to check the violent expressions of my despair, observing that the giving utterance to them occasioned me to be more closely watched and restrained by the people about me, and nothing was now so grateful to me as being left quite alone, where I might hear only the hollow breaking of the waves against the cliffs, or the cries of the innumerable sea fowl, which now covered every rock within my sight and often appeared like living clouds floating above me."

CHAP. V.

Whom shall I now call my friend? or from whom
shall I hear the voice of joy?[54]

"The only relation Glenmorris had in Scotland was the widow of the laird of Kilbrodie, who was the sister of his grandfather, and whose son, the present laird, was heir to what was left of the Glenmorris estate, if Glenmorris died without children.

"There had been a family feud between this old lady and her brother, which she had suffered to transmit itself to her son and her brother's grandson. She was a Roman Catholic, bigotted to her religion, and one of the few remaining adherents of the unhappy race of Stuart.[55] Excluded by her prejudices and her remote situation from the knowledge of modern improvement, her notions were those of an hundred years ago, and to them were added the strange and wild dreams of local superstition.—Her pride and her poverty had made her avaricious; not for herself, for she seemed to support her withered form on the mere air that surrounded her, but in the hope of aggrandizing her two sons, the eldest of whom was major of an highland regiment; the younger had been sent, when he was almost a child, to the East Indies;[56] and so little had been heard of him since, that the Ladie of Kilbrodie, who had no more notion what he was doing there than of the occupations of the inhabitant of another world, imagined that some time or other he might return loaden with gold and diamonds, and that in the interval the most interesting point to her, was, to scrape together every thing she could amass for his brother, now a man near fifty.

"The supposed death of Glenmorris, and the probability there was that his child, if born alive, might not long survive, were circumstances not to be overlooked by Ladie Kilbrodie. The good humoured generosity of Glenmorris, who had visited his old relation, (saying he could not keep up a family quarrel about nothing with a poor old woman) had opened an occasion which she otherwise would not have had to come to the house, where now, alas! there was no Glenmorris to protect from her folly or her malice his wretched and heart-broken wife.

"Lady Kilbrodie then, whose gloomy habitation, (being one end of a ruined monastery) was near six miles from Glenmorris, made her appearance one morning, about five weeks after the cruel event I deplored, and with very little ceremony informed the servants about me, that as I was oout of my moind, she was coom as my nixt of kin to tak the care of the cheel, and should tak me too her ain hoose. The people around me had no authority to interpose, but when I was made to understand her intention, I resolutely resisted it. I had seen her but once, and had conceived a dislike to her bordering on aversion; and when now she proposed to make me a resident in her house, and to take me from that where only I could weep over the misery of my destiny unmolested, I positively refused to accompany her; and as it was no time for ceremonious insincerity, I very plainly told her, that I had no inducement whatever to visit her abode, while the only consolation I could taste was, being allowed to remain uninterrupted, even by intended kindness, in my own. This ingenuous declaration irritated my assailant, but by no means turned her from her purpose; and, notwithstanding my tears and entreaties, I was placed on one of the little horses of the country,[57] and led away, guarded by two of the Ladie Kilbrodie's highlanders, while those more immediately belonging to Glenmorris, and even the servants who still remained in the house, dared not oppose what they believed the Ladie Kilbrodie had a right to do, as Glenmorris's nearest relation. My own maid only was permitted to attend me, and even that was refused till my tears, and the importunate entreaties of the poor girl, prevailed on the old lady to grant it, though with evident reluctance.

"Figure to yourself, my dear Delmont, if it be possible for imagination to reach it, the place and the people I was now among.

"The abbey of Kilbrodie had formerly been a very large building, and great masses of ruins were scattered, for some acres, beyond that part of it which served as an habitation for its present Lairds. Above it, on a rising ground, now overgrown with scanty brushwood and furze, were still seen part of a single tower, the largest relick of the castle, from whence they had in other times looked down upon, and guarded the pious monks of St. Cuthbert.[58] The feuds that levelled the fortress had spared the religious house, till Knox and his reformers had destroyed that also;[59] but to the walls of the kitchen, refectory and dormitory, still left standing, roofs had been restored within the last fifty years, and an habitation, large, cold, and dreary, made up; an habitation, which served at once to evince the former consequence and present penury of the Lairds of Kilbrodie. This forlorn abode was situated, like many other religious houses, in the bosom of a deep glen, and on the banks of a small river, whose sullen waters, making their way through a deeply worn channel, were rather heard than seen, and gave an additional gloom, instead of any degree of chearfulness, to the scene. A few scattered yew and stunted elder-trees, grew among the ruins; and all that part of them which was either known, or supposed to have been consecrated as the body of the abbey, or as its cemetery, was left unclosed for fear of profanation; so that nothing like a spot cultivated for domestic use, mitigated the dark horrors of the "*half ruined aisles and intermingled graves.*"[60]—Among them, hardly sheltered from the weather, the old lady had contrived to repair a small chapel, which she had furnished with crosses and relicts; around it were interred all those of the clan who died in the Catholic persuasion, and the demon of superstition himself could no where have chosen a spot more congenial to his rites.

"The country beyond was in unison with the horrors of the cell I have described, mountainous and barren; scarce would the hardiest plant that tapestries the rude bosom of the north, lend its reluctant vegetation here.—No glittering stream fell from the chaotic and misshapen masses of rock about it; though some were, indeed, heard roaring at a distance, and the murmurs of the ocean were sometimes brought by the wind; but its view, often chearful and always sublime, was shut out by the intervention of a chain of hills, or what would in any other country have been called mountains. To the north-east, arose Carmor,[61] one of the highest in that part of Scotland, which, rearing its enormous crest over the sea, seemed to be set as a mark, visible even on the coast of Norway—On a scarred crag near its summit, inaccessible even to the adventurous highland fowler, a pair of eagles had for ages made their eirie and their screams at this season, when they were continually in search of food for their young, were almost the only sounds that broke the mournful stillness of this frightful solitude.

"Such was the outward appearance of the place I was compelled to remove to— within it was still worse.

"The Ladie of Kilbrodie was fortunate not to have lived a century and an half earlier, for she would most undoubtedly have been in danger of being tormented, or killed as a female warlock.[62] Imagine a shrivelled and distorted countenance, disfigured rather by evil passions tracing their lines upon it, than by the lapse of above seventy years;—a long and sharp nose, the point depending lower than the nostrils— little fierce grey eyes, round which a red and raw border had succeeded the fire-coloured lashes they might once have had—a mouth falling in, so that two withered lips were seldom visible but in speaking, and a thin sharp chin, with dewlaps depending beneath it. Such were the features of the Lady of Kilbrodie; but to the expression of these features it would be difficult for any description to do justice.

"The usual dress of this ill-favoured head, was the piece of strait cloth pinned across the forehead, peculiar to the highland women; but by an economist, like Lady Kilbrodie, the cleanness of this ornament was but little considered. The rest of her dress was usually confined, by the same economical considerations, to a gown of black stuff, very rusty[63] from time—and in some places rather injured by the quantity of Scotch snuff, which had for a series of years fallen about it. A cotton handkerchief, black and grey, covered her neck—and on Sundays, yielded precedence to an old ermine tippet which had been long in the family, while her rusty stuff gown was exchanged for one of silk of the same shades, or rather of a more varied appearance.

"When I tell you that the domestics were exactly suited in the style of uncouthness to their mistress, you will have some idea of the inhabitants of the abbey of Kilbrodie.

"During the first days of my enforced abode among them, I sunk into such dejection, that I hoped and believed my wretchedness was nearly at an end; but my faithful Menie, the servant who was suffered to follow me, exerted herself to support my failing courage, and by degrees succeeded. Her principal arguments were founded on the preservation of my unborn infant; and on the hope that Glenmorris, though wounded and a prisoner, might yet survive, and hereafter return to bless me and his child. The natural love of life at my age, and the natural strength of my constitution insensibly conquered even the additional discomforts of my present abode. I once more suffered Menie to lead me out; I saw once more the light of the sun shining on the distant mountains, for his beams were yet too remote to be felt or seen in the dark and inhospitable vale of Kilbrodie.

"But it was very soon visible that my recovery, my health, and the birth of my child, were circumstances which were not desired by my hostess. In proportion as I

seemed to resist the bitterness of my destiny, and likely to emerge from the gloom that
overwhelmed me, the countenance of the old gentlewoman became darker towards
me. She perpetually annoyed me with her irksome presence, and talked to me of the
judgments of heaven, which she said always pursued, and sooner or later overtook,
undutiful children. She deplored the condition of her kinsman's soul, who doubtless,
she said, had died in a state of reprobation; adding, that she had caused prayers to be
put up for his poor sinful spirit in her chapel, and hoped I should repent me of the
great wickedness of having left my affectionate parents to run off with him. I had
listened to such cant before; and though it shocked me to hear Glenmorris thus named,
I despised the folly of the old hypocrite as much as I detested her cruelty. But she soon
opened other batteries upon me, which she thought must answer her inhuman purpose. As the time of my lying-in approached, she caused the superstitions of the country to be brought forward, to alarm me with ideas of danger and dread of death.

"Sometimes portentous sounds were heard in the air; and at others the corpse
candle[64] was seen to go from my chamber to the burial ground of the abbey. The cry
of an English bogie or sprite[65] was heard, intimating the death of a person of that
nation—but that was rather a miscalculation on the part of those who directed this
machinery, for I was not only *not* a native of England, having been born at Florence,
but I had never been naturalized. This, however, the *graunie*[66] did not know; though
it helped me to repress such fears as might have arisen from the "cry of an English
ghaist!"[67]

"The old highlander, who had the care of the boats by which the Lady Kilbrodie
supplied her house with fish, never went down to the sea but he returned with a tale of
kelpies of the maist eldritch kind, which skreeked around him[68]—and these stories were
sometimes repeated in my presence as if by accident, and sometimes told to me with
great appearance of concern, by the old witchlike-looking woman, who was, I found,
engaged by the lady to attend me. This frightful creature boasted of possessing the gift
of second sight, or at least a degree of prescience nearly approaching to it; and I soon
was given to understand that she foresaw some great calamity was about to befal me.

"These presentiments of evil are often the causes that evil really arrives, especially to persons in my circumstances, even when surrounded with every convenience,
and assured of every assistance. On me, however, the cruel impressions thus endeavoured to be made would have had little effect, had I not known that the persons who
prophecied, had the means of assuring the truth of their predictions. I now too clearly
understood the reason of Lady Kilbrodie's officious zeal, which I had at first but imperfectly comprehended. I remembered an history I had read of the cruel machinations used to deprive a Countess de Guiche[69] of her child; and I saw in Lady Kilbrodie
the same motive as influenced the perpetrators of that crime, with more easy means of
effecting it.

"The horror which seized on my mind is not to be described. Sometimes I so
yielded to the influence of this dread, as hardly to have any other consciousness of my
existence than that which fear impressed—and I refused to quit my bed to see the
light, or to take any nourishment but what Menie gave me, first tasting it herself; then,
roused by the still active principle of self-preservation, I tried to assume some degree of

apparent chearfulness, and went out with Menie, meditating on the possibility of escaping. But, alas! whither could I go? From the castle of Glenmorris could I have taken shelter there, the same pretence, and the same usurped power, might again have compelled me. I had neither money to procure the means of removal, by any carriage which could be obtained in that remote country, or strength to seek on foot a place where such might be hired. I now thought of writing to my father, and imploring his pity and forgiveness; now of throwing myself on the mercy of Lady Mary, and then of trying to interest my sister, and her lord, in my deplorable fate. But I doubted whether any letter of mine would ever reach my father, and even the mercy of my mother I thought of with terror. My sister might perhaps scorn and neglect me; and to her husband I was almost a stranger. And far from assisting me, they might fear my restoration to my father's favour as likely to be injurious to themselves. It was in vain I consulted with Menie. She was a Scotch girl, who had never left the highlands, and was totally ignorant of any mode of life beyond them. All she could do was to weep with me, and to promise that nothing should induce her or force her to leave me.

"Every observation I made, every word that fell from Lady Kilbrodie, now served to confirm my apprehensions. To secure to her son the succession of Glenmorris, it was necessary my child should perish; for that reason only, had it appeared to Lady Kilbrodie worth her while to take me from my own house; that we should die together, was probably a yet greater object, and that we might indeed do so was the next wish I formed, after those that perpetually tempted me to try to escape were evidently fruitless.

"To a young mind, to one yet uninformed by sad experience, of how much wickedness avarice may render a human being guilty, it is hard to believe that such atrocity could exist, as I now imputed to this old woman. But her whole conduct, as well as that observed by her people by her orders, the dark hints and mysterious phrases of old Meggy Macgregor, the howdie[70] who was to attend me; the continual endeavours, that were evident, impress my mind with ideas of impending danger; and the anger Lady Kilbrodie expressed, if any mention was made of the possibility that Glenmorris might survive; the satisfaction which lightened in her eyes when she saw me sinking, and crushed beneath the weight of my miseries; all these, and many other circumstances, left not a doubt remaining, either of what her expectations were, or of her being equal to any detestable action that might render those expectations not ineffectual.

"No dreary description, drawn from imagination of tombs and caverns haunted by evil spirits, could equal the gloomy horrors of the place, where I was doomed to linger out the few and wretched days of my remaining existence. The long, narrow, and only partially glazed windows of my cell, looked upon the fragments and half fallen arches of the ruined convent.—Caverns yawned in many places beneath them; among which echoed only the howling of the hunting dogs, that were kept, (or rather half starved) by the Lady Kilbrodie, to procure her game from the mountains and muirs,[71] which they perhaps pursued more successfully, as the entrails of what was taken, was almost the only food they ever got, unless the sea, to which they frequently resorted, afforded them a repast of dead fish.

"Often has the little rest I could obtain, been broken by the cries and yells of these wretched animals—

And loud and long the dog of midnight howl'd.[72]

"On such occasions Meggy Macgregor, the howdie, never failed to assure me, that—'quhan the collies gan scrachin and makin croon, dule wad befa.'"[73]

CHAP. VI.

One only boy, her last sweet hope, she warms,
Hush'd on her bosom, circled in her arms,
Daughter of woe! ere morn, in vain caress'd,
Clung the cold babe upon thy milkless breast;
With feeble cries thy last sad aid requir'd,
Stretch'd its stiff limbs, and on thy lap expir'd.[74]

"Such," proceeded Mrs. Glenmorris, "was my situation, and I had yet two months to look forward, with anguish, to the dreadful moment that must in some way change it. It was now the month of May, every where save in the place I was confined to; but hardly any additional verdure, or even a reluctant flower, marked to *me* the progress of summer—cold and joyless was all around to me—cold and hopeless as my own sad heart!

"At this time the major, Laird of Kilbrodie, and, alas! as his mother almost ventured to call him already, of Glenmorris, arrived from America, where he had been some years with his regiment.

"His mother had, probably, in their first interview, explained to him the likelihood there was that he would succeed to the estate of his nephew, Glenmorris, for when the day after I was introduced to him, a ceremony I would most willingly have avoided, he eyed me with looks, where I thought the exultation of successful avarice, was mingled with other odious passions, which, though I could not define them, terrified and alarmed me. The major was a very tall, bony man, above fifty. His red hair, and his bushy eyebrows, which had been of the same colour, were now mingled with grey—and between the latter and his high cheek bones, his eyes would hardly have been distinguished, had they been less wild and fierce; a sort of light flashing occasionally from them, like flames of sulphur—his complexion, by being exposed to the air of various climates, was nearly the colour of logwood in chips, assuming towards the nose and lower part of his cheeks a dull purple hue; on one cheek was a scar, which seemed to have been a continuation of his immense mouth, where appeared a tremendous row of great teeth, still white and strong, but which, from their size and their colour being so strongly contrasted with that of his skin, were far from being an advantage to him.—He wore the phillibeg and bonnet,[75] with a long coat, which made a strange uncouth dress; and there was in his whole appearance a degree of ferocity, which took off all those ideas we are willing to admit on the sight of a brave man, whose life has been dedicated to what we have been taught to call the service of his country.

"His mother took the earliest occasion to introduce the subject of American prisoners, and the major had certainly received his lesson, for, without seeming to advert to the particular situation of Glenmorris, he entered into a circumstantial account of the treatment of such British subjects as had fallen into the power of 'the rebels,'—He began by relating the death of some who had been hanged, or suffered to die in dungeons in the most squalid wretchedness and want; then, as if the picture was not sufficiently terrific, he added that others, particularly those who had been seized by privateers, and who were not therefore considered as being in the slightest degree protected by the laws of nations, had been given up to the natives of the country, to be tormented by every hideous invention of cruelty, till fainting nature could endure no more. The barbarous wretch, seeing by the changes of my countenance, how unable I was to sustain the recital, proceeded to relate these scenes, so disgraceful to humanity, more minutely, as having been described to him by an officer who had witnessed them. The terms he used, the wild contortions of his countenance, and the terrible idea, that, to the reality of what I could not bear to hear, Glenmorris might have been exposed, at length so far overcame me, that I could suffer no more.—A cold dew covered my face—I felt the room turn round with me, and fell totally insensible on the floor.

"When I recovered myself I was on my bed—Menie weeping over me, and applying such remedies as were in her power.—I was unable to speak; a faintness, like the approach of death, hung upon me—cold shiverings succeeded—and such were my general sensations, that I believed and was glad to believe myself dying.—My dread, however, of the howdie Meggy Macgregor, was so great, that I entreated Menie to conceal that I was otherwise affected than is usual after a fainting fit.—By means of one of the servants, she procured me something to swallow; put me to bed, and told the people I was gone to sleep.—But to forget myself for one moment, was I well knew impossible. The terror the major had raised pursued me; I saw Glenmorris expiring in tortures, writhing beneath the bloody hands of murderers, or rather fiends.—And I soon found that the effects of this horrible recital, would be of other consequence than merely subjecting me to terror.—I was seized with violent pains, and could not long doubt of what nature they were.—Once assured that my hour was at hand, I determined to bear my sufferings, if possible, in silence, so great was my dread of the old woman, in whom I had long accustomed myself to see my murderess and my child's.—I know not now how, in the reduced state I was in, I had resolution enough to persevere in the concealment of my pangs; but I did so; and having only my faithful and tender Menie with me, was at two in the morning delivered of a boy.

"Born at seven months, he was small and feeble; yet when I heard his weak cries, and beheld him, my desire of life returned; I wished to preserve him, and to live for him, with an ardour amounting even to agony.—But though he had thus escaped the destruction intended him, how could I believe I could continue long to preserve him—Lady Kilbrodie and her creatures could easily take him from me, or destroy him even before my eyes, without my having the power to prevent it—I could neither conceal nor protect him in their house; but it came into my mind, that if I could hide him a few days, I might escape with him to the clan of Glenmorris, and call upon the adherents and vassals of his family to save this last remains of the blood of their ancient lords.—Menie, willing to hazard every thing to assist me in flying from the detested power of Lady Kilbrodie, entered into my scheme with such zeal, that before day-break we had made all our arrangements.—It was settled that I should complain of being so tormented with the head-ache that I could neither speak nor bear the least noise, and that at an early hour of the morning, and before there was any danger of a visit, either from the old lady or her agent Macgregor, she should engage one of the servants, who was her friend, to bring her all she wanted to the door of my chamber, under pretence that she could not leave me a moment. Lady Kilbrodie, who hoped her expence on my account would now be ended by my death, was easily kept away; but it was more difficult to divert the officious and gossipping howdie from her enquiries.—In this, however, for three days, we succeeded, and longer was unnecessary.—Towards the close of the third I observed a visible change in my infant; but I knew that if I called for assistance his danger would only be accelerated.—Soon I found that the best assistance could not save him—he fell into convulsions, and died upon my bosom.

"Once convinced he was lost to me, I had no longer any measures to keep.—The frantic shrieks which despair drew from me soon brought the two old women into the room, and an immediate explanation ensued. Though I believe the crone, Lady Kilbrodie, was glad to be thus spared the commission of one crime which she had meditated, she yet seemed willing enough to commit another, by hastening the death that her cruelty had, she hoped, made inevitable.—Instead of manifesting the least pity for the agonies which she saw the loss of my child inflicted on me, she bitterly reproached me for my wickedness in concealing its birth, and suffering it to die unbaptized, by which, she said, I had given it over to eternal punishment. Her revilings I was unable to answer; but prejudices so barbarously enforced at such a moment, my long established ideas of the goodness of Omnipotence suffered me not to heed.

"To have preserved this lovely and innocent memorial of my murdered husband I would have encountered with pleasure the lowest degree of human wretchedness; but of its fate in another state of being my trust in the justice of God would never allow me to doubt; and the arrow which this unfeminine, this inhuman woman, thought she had barbed to pierce my heart with the most incurable wound, fell harmless—I know not whether it did not help more than any thing to rouse me from the torpor of despair.

"As among other consequences of my child's dying without the ceremonies she so strongly urged, was, that his poor remains were not to be received in consecrated ground, I determined, with the steady resolution of hopeless grief, to bury him myself—and I so vehemently protested they should not take him from me, that I was at length left to indulge my sorrows with no other witness than Menie.—With her assistance, at an hour when the rest of the house were asleep, I wrapt up my poor dead baby in the best linen I had, and Menie having procured me what answered the purpose of a coffin, I deposited him in it without shedding a tear—I could not shed tears—but with apparent calmness, though I felt it to be at the risk of my life, stole out with my maid, and having made in the most obscure part of the ruined abbey as deep a grave as we could, I placed in it the little lifeless object of so many months of fond solicitude—that object which I had so tenderly considered as the dearest bond of union between me and my adored, my lamented, Glenmorris; I then, with trembling and feeble hands, assisted the weeping Menie to pile on the spot some fragments of the ruins, as well to preserve it from violation as to mark the place, and having done so in speechless anguish, which I now shudder to recal, I cast a last look on the grave, and suffered myself to be led back to my room, returning to my bed conscious of no other sensation than the hope that I should rise from it no more!

"Certain that her son was now secure of the possessions of Glenmorris, and knowing that I had no settlement, and of course no claim on any part of it, the purpose of Lady Kilbrodie was, to be relieved as soon as she could from the burthen of my stay, and whether this was to be done by my voluntary departure or by death was no otherwise an object to her, than as she thought the latter gave her the most certain assurance of never hearing of me again.

"Her neglect, however, was so far from being injurious to me, that the entire freedom I enjoyed from her hateful presence helped more than any other circumstance my slow and undesired recovery. I heard no voice but that of Menie, always soothing, and, as far as her knowledge went, sensible; I saw nothing for some time, but from my window the spot where I had interred my infant—and as, even of a night, I could distinguish it by the pieces of pale marble piled upon it, which had once been part of a monument, I accustomed myself to sit for whole hours with my eyes fixed on that last deposit of all my earthly hopes, relieved when the stubbornness of my grief was subdued enough by tender recollections to allow me to shed tears.

"Youth, even when deprived of all visible support—

—When even the flatterer hope is no where found—

makes a long and often a successful stand against calamity. I was not yet eighteen, and my constitution, naturally very strong, had never before been shaken by any of those sorrows that undermine the principles of life; gradually therefore, though heaven knows how little I at that time wished it, I regained some degree of strength, and when I was able to think, my mind incessantly ran on the means of my escape; yet still the same unanswerable question occurred, whither could I go? who would receive me? where in the whole universe had I a friend to whom I could apply for protection?

"It was in vain I revolved this in my mind; no prospect offered itself of any resource, save in servitude, and that I determined upon; but before even such a situation of life could be embraced, it was necessary for me to get to England, and how to do that, was a difficulty which appeared nearly insurmountable.

"Though Lady Kilbrodie was evidently embarrassed by my presence, she knew not how to relieve herself; and though I never saw her but to renew my misery, and avoided her by every means in my power, yet she sometimes seemed to take a malignant pleasure in tormenting the victim she held; and I was shewn to the very few accidental visitors whom kindred brought, though very rarely, to this gloomy habitation, as an object who, notwithstanding my delinquency, sullenness, and ingratitude, her charity induced her to shelter.

"It was hard to conceive how such a condition as I was now reduced to could admit of any aggravation—yet a severe aggravation overtook me.

"In despite of the deep dejection which I had so much reason to indulge, I had in a few weeks regained a portion of that beauty which had first attracted the eyes of Glenmorris. At this distance of time I may be allowed, with little imputation of egotism or vanity, to speak of myself as I then was—A very fair skin, with dark eyes, and eye-brows a shade darker than the profusion of light brown hair, too luxuriant to dress, which flowed round my face, would have rendered very indifferent features shewy and attractive at the age I then was; but you, Delmont, may perhaps form a better opinion of those advantages which have now so entirely vanished, if I tell you that Medora very much resembles my then appearance, except that she has her father's blue eyes, and something the turn of his countenance. Suffice it, however, without dwelling longer on the description of myself, to say, that such as I was, I had the misfortune to captivate the laird, and when nothing was less, either in my thoughts or wishes, he took occasion to follow me in one of my solitary walks, and very abruptly to tell me that he loved me, and expected I should make him such a return as the honour conferred upon me deserved.

"I had so little understood the meaning of the grimaces intended for soft looks, by which he had attempted to recommend himself whenever we had lately met, that this declaration equally amazed and grieved me; hardly could I recover myself enough to tell him, that from *him* to *me* such a speech as he had just made could be considered only as an insult; that I had *no* return to make him, nor any favour to ask of him and his mother, but that, from the advantages accruing to them by my cruel losses, they would afford me as much as might enable me to return to England—'and this sir,' said I, 'I demand rather as a right than as a favour.'

"I was, perhaps, rash in thus irritating a man in whose power I was, and who had already shewn himself incapable of any honourable or humane feeling; but my indignation conquered my prudence; I could not speak with patience to him who enjoyed the spoils of my lamented Glenmorris, and who now attempted to seduce his wretched widow from her affection to his memory. The arrogance with which he dared to insinuate that I was honoured by his preference was insupportable, and though immediate death had been the consequence, I could not have commanded myself to have spoken more temperately; indeed death was what would least have deterred me from this plain dealing.

"Kilbrodie, however, could not bear it. The ferocious brutality of his nature broke out at once. He gave me to understand, that he knew I was wholly in his power; that it was impossible for me to escape him; and that if after two days I still preferred weeping over my widowhood to the honourable station he could offer me, I must take the consequence; he then rudely attempted to kiss me, but by a sudden exertion of strength almost supernatural I flung from him and fled away, I knew not, I heeded not whither; the only idea that, on the instant, occurred to me, was to reach the summit of the highest cliff I had strength to mount, and from thence, by precipitating myself into the sea, end at once my insupportable miseries.

"Whether the air of desperation with which I repulsed him, or the swiftness of my flight, prevented Kilbrodie from following me, I know not; but he did not attempt it, and I soon found myself on the borders of the sea, at a place where the mountainous cliffs that guarded the greater part of this wild coast sunk suddenly in a sort of chasm, through which the fishermen and fowlers had made a path down to the shore.

"I followed this path, careless whither it led, so long as I might hide myself for ever from the eyes of the wretches I had left behind; but hardly had I reached the margin of the sea when my breath and my strength failed me, and I sunk down insensible.

"I must have remained there some hours, for when I recovered my recollection it was evening; the sea fowl were settling themselves in their nests among the cliffs, and the sun's rays had long since forsaken these eastern waves; I looked one way on a boundless tract of ocean, broken only by some of those fantastic rocks which seem to guard this inhospitable coast, and are the resort of those innumerable flocks of birds, whose feathers form the sole riches of its hardy inhabitants. On each side of me I saw nothing but a chain of cliffs, in some places forming sharp promontories, in others eaten into caverns by the ever restless waters. Here I was determined to remain and perish—for such a death, cruel and lingering as it must be, was far preferable in my opinion to being exposed, even for another moment, to the atrocious insults of Kilbrodie. His menace was re-echoed by my throbbing heart—for two days he would await, and at the end of that time enforce my compliance!—If I should now return, my flight at the end of those two days might be impeded, and the horrors that in such a case presented themselves to my imagination were not to be endured; I resolved then, since I failed of courage to terminate my sufferings by one desperate exertion, to enter one of the excavations where there appeared the greatest probability of concealment, and there to remain till hunger, or the rising waves, finished my deplorable career.

Chap. VII.

Forlorn she sits, "up turns her tearful eyes,
Calls her lost lover, and upbraids the skies."[76]

"It was not without difficulty that I acquired strength to reach what appeared to me the most secure of these caverns, half a mile from the path by which I had come to the shore; there, however, I observed by the sand and shells strewing its floor, that the sea entered in high tides. It was narrow towards the entrance, but within rose into an high irregular arch, and it went so far back, though still more irregular and ragged, with projecting crags and masses of stone, that I dared not venture to explore the deep obscurity; around, near the entrance, were great piles of flat stones, forming almost natural steps and benches; I contrived to seat myself on one of these, where the projection of another concealed me; a third, a little more raised, served as a pillow for my weary head. Here at least, cried I, the detested voice of Kilbrodie will not reach me; here at least I shall cease to breathe the air, infected by those who occasioned the death of Glenmorris's child; and here I shall surely be permitted to die unmolested.

"It was at this time the last week of September; for more than three wretched months had crept along since those sad hours that made me a mother and condemned me to despair. At this season the approach of winter is evidently felt in the north of Scotland; but it happened that the night was unusually mild and still, and the little wind there was blowing from the west, I felt from thence no inconvenience, and my hard resting place was perfectly dry. When Kilbrodie met me, I had gone out in the design to take a long walk after their dinner, which was always at two o'clock; I had therefore a cloak and hat on, and if my wishes and designs had been less gloomy than they were, I should have had no fear of suffering from cold—My only dread was, least as night came on, and I was missed at the abbey-house, Kilbrodie or his servants might search for me, and these caverns of the cliff were as likely as any to strike them as my probable hiding place—I was afraid too that my poor maid, not knowing the reason of my absenting myself, might in the eagerness of her affection promote the search, and even assist in it. These fears, which the longer I thought of them became more formidable, prevented my taking any repose during the beginning of the night—I listened to every noise—but the low still sound of the untroubled waves murmuring on the sand, or eddying round the rocks, was all that reached my ears—Night wore away—I perceived the stars reflected faintly on the waves, for the sky I could not see.—As my dread of pursuit became fainter, my spirits, subdued by fear and fatigue, lost something of the sullen desperation that I had at first felt—I melted into tears, and tears I had of late been so frequently unable to shed, that I felt my head and heart greatly relieved by them—I called upon the dear shades of Glenmorris and his boy— I besought of God, that in his mercy he would permit me speedily to rejoin them— and save me from the terrors that I was threatened with. By insensible degrees the wild tumult of my spirits subsided, and I fell into a slumber, confused and broken indeed, but still such as composed and refreshed me, when before day-break the succeeding morning I was awakened from it by the cries of the gannets, petrels, gulls, and sea snipes[77] without, as well as by the gurgling murmurs of the wild pigeons within my cave.

"Whoever recals to mind the odd sensation a person is often conscious of when, awaking in a strange place, he can hardly recal the circumstances that brought him thither, or remember where he is, will easily conceive the astonishment with which, for a moment, I gazed around me, when these noises dissipated my unquiet slumber—instantly, however, all that had passed recurred to me—I saw myself destitute of every thing, and cast like a shipwrecked wretch on the shore, from whence, if I attempted to return, greater horrors awaited me than those I was sure by staying, to encounter from famine.

"I hesitated not a moment, however, which of these alternatives to prefer; and doubted not but that I should meet death with firmness. Suddenly it occurred to me, that as the tides were now low it was possible I might keep along the coast and reach the castle of Glenmorris, where, if I could not attain the top of the rock, and be received into the fortress, I might hope that some of the clan, who fished almost daily during summer on the rocks beyond it, or went thither for the purpose of gathering feathers, might be induced to compassionate me for the sake of their chief, whom they had all professed to love so much; they might even be persuaded to conceal me in one of their huts till I could escape from the near neighbourhood of my persecutors. After a short consideration of this plan, it appeared still more desirable on some accounts, but less so on others; I remembered, that there was a deep and singular excavation in one of the cliffs not far from that on which our residence was situated; I had heard, that here it was usual for the boat-men of Glenmorris to deposit their cargoes till their wives or comrades came to assist them in carrying them to the glen; and I thought that should Kilbrodie here attempt to force me back, he would be more likely to meet with opposition than at a greater distance from those who had till now been considered almost as my own family; yet I could not conceal from myself, that near Glenmorris it was most likely Kilbrodie would begin his search. The former considerations, however, appearing of the most weight, I resolved to begin my journey, though how far it might be made by the winding of the shore I knew not, nor did I calculate my own powers to undertake a walk which might be from three to seven miles.

"My strength was greater than appeared likely. I continued to walk as near the base of the cliff as I could, as supposing *that* the most secure from the observation of those above, who might be on the watch for me. With fear and trembling I went on, and at length saw the perpendicular and steep rock, on whose summit were the well-known towers of the *castelet*[78] of Glenmorris. My faint heart beat quicker at the sight. 'Ah! wherefore,' cried I, 'is not the dear, dear master there to receive and protect his unhappy Laura!—If he yet lives, where is the power that could so long have detained him from me.—But he exists no longer; I shall never see him more; I am a wretch whom heaven and earth abandons!—Wherefore should I fear to die? For what should I live if I have lost him!'

"Fatigue, despair, and that weariness of life, which it is impossible for the wretched not to feel when their sick spirit bows beneath the weight of accumulated and long inflicted misery, now were united once more to persuade me, that as probably I must, in despite of all my endeavours, fall again into the power of Kilbrodie, I should be justified in escaping from it by suicide. Young as I was I was not ignorant of the arguments that have been used on that and many other questions of importance to human happiness, little thinking, when I read them, that the time would ever come when I should reconsider their force as applicable to myself.[79] I was now reduced to the state of him who, meditating on his dismission from life, is said to

Gaze with eager glance upon the trembling flood,

And where,

Beck'ning the wretch to torments new,

Despair for ever in his view,
    A spectre pale appeared;
While as the shades of evening rose,
And brought the days unwelcome close,
    More horrible and huge her giants shape she reared.[80]

"When the actual pains of faintness from inanition were felt; when I imagined it certain that I must either suffer the lingering horrors of dying by hunger, or become the most degraded, the most miserable of human beings, I asked myself, whether I was not in that situation when—'En me rendent la vie insupportable Dieu m'ordonne de la quitter.'[81]—To die, appeared to me much less offensive to heaven and earth than to live on the terms I must suffer life, if I were again in the power of Kilbrodie.—My endurance of evil, the fortitude I might be able to exert, could not, in this case, be useful as an example to any one; for the wretched people among whom my shameful and polluted life must pass would be insensible alike of my misery or my resolution; and for whom ought I to attempt to brave the existence with which I was menaced?— I had never had a mother, for she who bore me seemed to have thrown me off in my infancy as an impediment to her ambition. To my father should I now return, and solicit my readmission to his protection, I should be only a cause of unhappiness; for if he were disposed, and had courage to receive and befriend me, the continual reproaches and ill-humour it would expose him to from my mother would embitter, and, perhaps, shorten his life if he yet lived; my husband was dead; my child too, for whom I could have endured any thing but disgrace, was snatched from me almost as soon as I had known the new and delightful sensations of maternal love.—For what then should I live?—My life, burthensome to myself, could be useful to nobody—my death would injure no human being—the arguments therefore against a voluntary escape from the evils of existence, however just in general, were not applicable to me; I determined to die, and believed I should have resolution enough to walk into the sea, and remain till the rising tide overwhelmed me.—Near the rocks opposite the fortress of Glenmorris was the spot where I wished to end my life; for it was the sight of that habitation, where I had passed the short period of my felicity, that had irritated the anguish of my mind even to that despairing phrensy which now made the evils I suffered and feared utterly insupportable.

"There was at this period what are called neap tides,[82] the sea had receded much farther than in its accustomed reflux, and, I knew, would be still lower in the evening— to that time I determined to wait; for had I now traversed the sands towards the rocks, I might have been seen from the cliffs—retiring therefore into the deepest of the caverns, I awaited there the return of night, and took my last leave of the sun. I found such a place of temporary rest as had served me the preceding night, and sat down faint and sick, for I had now fasted above twenty hours, and I doubted whether, when the present day was passed, I should have strength to execute my purpose. The wind, which was low during the night, and had blown from the west, had now changed to the east, and while by driving the sea towards this coast it was likely to accelerate the fate I sought, it rendered my present shelter more cold and dreary. I wrapped myself up in my cloak, and bound my handkerchief over my hat, then reclining on a fragment of the rock, a sort of stupor, the effect of inanition, crept upon me—I ceased to feel so acutely the terrors of my condition—I almost ceased to be conscious of my miserable being; and I hoped that my life was ebbing slowly away without any act of my own to hasten its close.

"This state of almost unconscious languor was of all others the most desirable, and yielding to it I had dismissed my fears for a life of which heaven in its mercy seemed about to dispose, and at length sunk to absolute insensibility, when I was suddenly recalled from it by loud talking immediately near me, and then by being roughly seized—I gazed with terror on the person that held me—it was an highlander, who spoke in Erse,[83] and so quick and indistinctly that my knowledge of the language was insufficient to enable me to comprehend his meaning—his gestures and countenance, however, did not strike me as expressing ferocity, but rather wonder and doubt, as he addressed himself to some other men, who having, as I supposed, learned that I was a living being, and not a kelpie,[84] approached—I knew one of them; he was a young man who had formerly been employed by Glenmorris, and who spoke a little of the language of the lowlands; he immediately recognised me; expressing the greatest astonishment and sorrow at the situation in which he saw me. I explained, as well as I was able, the causes that had forced me from the abbey of Kilbrodie, and the resolution I had taken, to die rather than return thither.

"Kilbrodie was now the master of these poor people; a master from whose power they could not appeal, and on whom their daily subsistence depended; yet there was not one of the three, but who, the moment they were acquainted with what had passed, even in the imperfect way in which I was able to explain it, offered to defend me to the last extremity, and spoke of my lost Glenmorris in a manner that drew tears from eyes that I thought could have shed no more. I now acquired strength to entreat of them to take me to some place where I might be concealed from the search that I thought would be made for me, till I could find means to go to England, where I told them I had friends who would amply reward them for their humanity. I had a few hours before deplored the sad certainty that I had not a friend on earth who would receive me, but with the prospect of escaping from Kilbrodie my hopes were reanimated, and I thought I might yet find relief from poverty, if not protection, in the bosom of my own family.

"These honest and faithful mountaineers, however, needed not any such inducement to engage their best services; the name of their lamented chieftain was enough; and they each swore in their rude way to die in defence of his unhappy widow.

"Malcolm, the elder of these men, was the uncle of him to whom I was known, though not of the same clan: he had engaged his nephew Donald, and another whose name was Duncan, to go out with him on a fishing party, when, the wind suddenly changing, they had put into the little creek near Glenmorris, instead of returning to their own cove, which lay almost two leagues farther to the southward, and which they had doubted if they could reach before nightfall, when they apprehended, from the appearance of the weather, an equinoxial storm[85]—but all their apprehensions and doubts were made light of when my safety was in question. Donald proposed immediately putting to sea, and by rowing to reach the cabin of his uncle, where I might be in less danger of discovery than in any place nearer Kilbrodie.—I eagerly listened to the offer, and the old man, as well as the younger boatman, his other companion, who was of the same place, readily assented to it. It was now nearly dark. They got their boat as near as they could to the shore, and carried me to it in their arms. The wind, which continued to rise, augured but ill for the voyage; but my friends were stout and resolute, and my fear of death so much less than of the fate I supposed I was escaping from, that I should not, I think, have been sensible of fear, even if the state of weakness I was reduced to had allowed me to see the peril which I afterwards found I had been in.

"The boatmen struggled the whole night with a very tempestuous sea; but each from time to time, as he was relieved from his oar, came forward to the place where I lay covered with a plaid and a coarse seaman's jacket, and gave me as much as I could be induced to swallow of oatmeal mixed with water, or of a root called cormielle,[86] which they supposed to afford the best substitute for good food in cases of fatigue and exertion—I drank also, at their earnest entreaty, a few small spoonfuls of their whisky, which, perhaps, by occasioning giddiness and stupor, helped to quiet the apprehensions I might otherwise have been under from the tossing of the boat.

"Towards day-break we entered a sort of creek, formed by the disemboguing of a rivulet into the sea; it was, they told me, three miles from thence to Malcolm's cottage. I most willingly exerted myself to go on shore, and, supported on each side by one of these friendly men, I walked without much suffering, except from the weight of my clothes, which, by the quantity of water the boat had taken in, were quite wet.

"The hut of the venerable Malcolm was not at all better than the wigwam of an Indian—a few large stones placed circularly[87] were the basis of its wall, which was afterwards wattled and filled with earth; the top was covered too with sods, with the heather yet growing upon them; it consisted of only one room with the fire place in the midst, but towards the opposite end from the door there was a sort of recess, where, before my arrival, the family, which consisted of Malcolm, his wife, and two daughters, both grown up, slept; it was now entirely appropriated to my use; and several pieces of old plaids being joined together by Jeannie, the elder of the daughters, composed something like a curtain, which at once contributed to conceal me from strangers, and to my repose when there were none.

"Nothing could be more cordial than the reception I had met with from these highland women, and all that their limited power afforded they did for me with such readiness and humanity, as I should not perhaps have found among more civilized people. I was now refreshed by new milk from their goats, my clothes were dried, and I reposed in security. Donald, who seemed to take a more lively interest in my fate than the rest, proposed returning the next day to Kilbrodie, from whence, he told me, he would come back to let me know what effect my disappearance had produced at the Abbey, and what they were doing to recover me. He gave the strictest charge to the auld weif,[88] one of whose daughters he was soon to marry, to watch over me with care, and by no means to suffer any person out of their own family to know that they had a stranger in their house.

"I awaited his return to consult with him on the best means of beginning my journey southward. Alas! when I ventured to think steadily of the great distance there yet was between me and England, my heart once more sunk in despondence. I had but a few shillings in my pocket; the only article of any value I had about me was a gold locket with three diamonds, and a small ruby set at the top, in which was a lock of Glenmorris's hair.—This, as I could have taken out that dear relict, I could in some countries have disposed of; but how in the north of Scotland could I expect to find a purchaser for such a trinket?

"Donald, whose re-appearance I impatiently expected, returned with the dawn of the next morning. As soon as I could see him, I eagerly enquired what he had learned; and he related, that there was the greatest consternation at the Abbey. The laird was in so great a fury, when I could not be found in or near the house, that he had dismissed Menie and some other of the servants and dependants, bidding them never dare to venture back till I was discovered. The castelet of Glenmorris had already been searched, and the vengeance of its present owner threatened to crush any one who should know and conceal my retreat, while, on the other hand, immunities and indulgences were promised to any of the vassals who might give notice of my hiding place. It was evident from this account that I could not long be safe where I was; yet whither go? and what would become of me?—Donald, whose zeal seemed to increase in proportion to my danger, was wholly at a loss, and almost afraid of consulting with any other person. His visible perplexity and indecision aggravated my fears. I was afraid he doubted the fidelity of the gued man of the house. Every noise I heard, my heart beat so that I could not breathe, and suspense and dread, such as I now endured, seemed to be even worse than the hopeless state from which I had been rescued.

"Donald returned to me again in about half an hour, and told me, he recollected a place, where, if I had courage to remain, I might perhaps rest securely till I could write to my friends in England, or find some means of conveyance thither. I eagerly implored him not to lose a moment in conducting me thither. The rest of the people of the cottage were now absent; Jeannie and Donald alone remained, and they agreed that it would be better to seize the opportunity.—I proposed, as a means of disguise, to exchange my outer garments with this young woman, who, after making some difficulties on account of the superior value of mine, consented, and I was directly equipped in Jeannie's best apparel. She took a bottle of milk, half a dozen bannocks,[89] a blanket, and a piece of linen, which had served me for a sheet in the cottage, and we set forth.

"As we went, Donald described the place to which he was conducting me, and which, he said, he had discovered in consequence of having been lost in hunting, and overtaken by a violent storm. The distance from the habitation of Malcolm he reckoned to be four miles, but I thought it nearer ten. At last we reached the summit of an elevated and rocky ridge of land, from whence appeared an almost perpendicular declivity, covered with birch, holly, and thorn, so thickly interwoven that it appeared difficult to pass among them. This was almost the only resemblance to a wood that I had seen in Scotland.[90]

"My guide led the way down a narrow path, or rather stair, which one would have thought only practicable for a highlander or a goat; no alpine road could be steeper; and without his assistance, and that of Jeannie, I could never have reached the spot, where, half way down, the rock was fashioned into the rude semblance of an human habitation.[91]—'This,' said my conductor, 'is a place made, as is supposed, by the laird of a neighbouring castle, now quite demolished, to hide his family, and what he had most precious, from the search of his enemies. Afterwards, as some old men relate, an hermit lived here, but now the very existence of the place is hardly known; and I am sure, if your courage does not fail you during the loneliness and darkness of the night, you will here be in perfect safety.' I entered with Jeannie, and examined the place, while Donald ran again to the brow with the swiftness of a roe buck to collect heather for my bed. Jeannie, soft-hearted and compassionate, could not refrain from shedding tears as she surveyed this dismal abode; but to me the gloominess of its appearance was mitigated by the hope of safety it would afford me, and its privacy promised me that tranquillity which in her father's hut I could not obtain. For the rest, the survey certainly afforded nothing flattering; the place was about twenty feet long, and about ten broad, cut like a shelf in the acclivity, and roofed by I know not what contrivance, which prevented its seeming to be a roof without. There were two apertures, which appeared once to have resembled windows more than they did now; the door was a great flag stone that did not very completely shut the entrance, yet served well enough, except at the top, to keep out the weather. There were now no marks of any human inhabitant, but a cross cut in the rocky wall at the upper end, and a great stone that probably served the hermit for a seat. A bird's nest or two, and the remains of others, hung in the corners and about the crevices. At the farther extremity then of this place Donald made my bed, piling up as much heather as he could bring at twice; and having prepared every thing for my convenience as well as circumstances allowed, they reluctantly departed, Jeannie being, I could observe, extremely solicitous, as well as her lover, to return before a certain hour, and though they did not avow it, I perceived that they wished, and had consulted together, how to conceal from the rest of the family that they were parties to my retreat. I knew not by what story they meant to account for my disappearance, but it was evident they were unwilling that the place of my concealment should be known to any but themselves. They promised that both would come the next day with a supply of provisions, the best they could obtain, if not together, each as opportunity occurred; and that I might not be surprised, we agreed upon a signal by which I was to be assured it was one of them that demanded admittance. I saw them depart with fear and regret, and resigned myself to solitude and tears."

CHAP. VIII.

Her tender heart so thrill'd,
That sudden cold did run through every vein,
And stony horror all her senses fill'd
With dying fit, that down she fell for pain—

The knight her lightly reared up again,
And comforted with courteous kind relief;
They lesser dread can bear, who have endured the chief.[92]

Mrs. Glenmorris thus proceeded to relate her sensations in the new and strange situation she was thrown into.

"I was now left alone to my own sad contemplations. As long as I could hear the steps of Donald and his companion mounting the precipice above me, I listened as if it afforded me satisfaction to listen. The sound became fainter and fainter, and at length totally ceasing, I heard nothing but the *sugh*[93] of the trees around my tomb-like dwelling, bending in the autumnal blast which already began to strip them of their leaves. Low and hollow it murmured among them, bringing at intervals the sound of a cataract which precipitated itself with violence from between a chasm of the woody height half a mile farther. Of the noise of this torrent, heard particularly loud before great rains or storms, Donald had informed me, least it should alarm me if I could not account for it. It now portended such a change of weather as might too probably prevent my friendly purveyors from visiting me the next day, I therefore eat sparingly of the little stock of provisions they had furnished me with, and as I was denied the comfort of light, least any accidental wanderer should be led by it to examine 'the cell' (as the place I was in was called) I laid me down on my bed of heather, which being made after the highland way, with the tender shoots uppermost, and covered with a blanket and a plaid, was far less uncomfortable than might have been supposed.[94] I endeavoured to persuade myself I was for this night at least in security, and fatigue helped me to enjoy a more tranquil slumber than I had tasted since I left the Abbey; for in Malcolm's cottage the noise of the people within so near me, and of poultry and goats in a shed close to the *ben*[95] where I was, together with my dread of discovery and pursuit, had effectually murdered sleep.

"Now, however, in my rude and savage lodging, I had some hours of undisturbed repose, and when I awoke the following morning I found myself refreshed, and my spirits lightened of much of their dread.—I ventured to steal out, and at first looked fearfully around me, but the nature of the place, wild, solitary, far as it seemed from the haunts of men, and almost inaccessible to any but the adventurous sportsman, helped to reassure me. The storm I had apprehended had passed off, and though there was a strong breeze, the sky was perfectly blue, save where the fleecy clouds, separated by the wind, floated lightly before it. I had soon collected courage enough to remark the outward appearance of my rustic house, where the little art that had been used was so connected with nature's masonry, which had laid horizontal strata of rock easily excavated, that without it could hardly be distinguished from the mass it belonged to, especially mantled as it was with such plants as wind over rocks and walls under the shelter of trees.—The holly,[96] whose shining thorny and spiny head so much shadowed the whole eminence, had found amidst the roof place for three or four young plants mingling with the larger growth above them; the common bramble[97] crept over another part of it, and hung in long festoons, half concealing the windows; the net-work of the houseleak[98] clothed another spot; and from others waved the pellitory,[99] the fescue grass, and the poa.[100] The stonecrop[101] had in summer made one place gay with its yellow blossoms, and near it were yet a few lingering flowers of the mountain crane's bill[102]—All these I knew and recognised as once of my acquaintance under warmer suns, and for the most part associated with very different objects.—Within, my hermitage was not wholly destitute of those vegetable ornaments with which nature delights to decorate, or to hide the deformity of her most rugged surfaces.—My walls, which were only partially damp, were tapestried with the rocklichen,[103] the tessellated lichen, and the silver bryum.[104] Through the defects in the roof, some of the plants growing without had insinuated themselves, and dangled over my head with the spleenwort[105] and the wall[106] hawkweed. Amidst the many sad hours I have passed, I have never failed to feel my spirits soothed by the contemplation of vegetable nature, and I have often thought that, wherever I could gaze on the clouds above, and see the earth below me clothed with grass and flowers, I could find some, though a melancholy, pleasure in existence.—My bower was not ornamented like the grotto of Calypso,[107] but nature was not quite torpid within and about it, and I hoped I might find security, and endure life till I could reach England, though still my heart's deep wounds unceasingly bled, and still the image of my lost happiness haunted me.

"I was sorry that the season refused me the company of the birds, the remains of whose nests hung among my rustic cornice. It was uncertain how long I might stay here, and, methought, any inoffensive animated being would have given me comfort.—I now began to look out for my friendly Donald and his interesting Jeannie.— It was already evening, when they both arrived breathless with haste, and bringing with them such provisions as they could obtain. I was not fastidious, and found their oat-cake and butter-milk excellent; they had added some dried fish, which I could not yet learn to eat, and some of the cloud berries,[108] which at this season ripen on the boggy summits of the mountains, and which I thought an admirable desert. I entreated them to tell me, while I eat my simple fare, what effects my absence had produced in the cottage of Malcolm. They appeared rather unwilling to enter into particulars, but at length I learned that some of Kilbrodie's people had actually been at the cottage, and among those of the neighbourhood, offering a reward to whoever should discover me; and the family of Malcolm seemed comforted with the certainty that I was out of the reach of my pursuers, though they affected not to suspect that Jeannie and her lover were accessary to my disappearance. My blood ran cold at this information; I fancied I already heard the voices of my pursuers, already saw the terrific countenance of Kilbrodie, such as I had last beheld it, and supposed myself dragged back to the prison where I had so cruelly suffered from his detested mother.

"The comforts of my repast were not increased by these reflections, nor by the haste in which my friends were to leave me. Jeannie had indeed brought me every thing within her reach, which she thought could contribute to my comfort, and Donald had provided me, with great difficulty, with a pen, ink, and paper, borrowed from a servant at Glenmorris, as he told me, for of such implements the fishers of the coast, or the herdsmen of the hills, knew not the use. With these I had determined to write to my sister, and Donald was the next day to take my letter, which he had an opportunity, he said, to send to Inverness by a friend of his on whom he could depend. Before these simple lovers left me once more to my sad reflections, Donald endeavoured to re-assure me. The emissaries of Kilbrodie, he said, though apparently compelled to obey him, were so far from being zealous or active in his cause, that he was universally detested; and he again protested, that none knew of 'the cells' as being a likely place of concealment, or would think of looking there. With these and other such arguments as he could offer I was obliged to be content; and the tranquillity in which I passed this and several succeeding nights, one or other of my faithful friends visiting me every day, at length subdued the most alarming of my fears. I had now been a fortnight absent from the Abbey, and I began to hope that the search, being wholly useless, would languish, and at length cease, and that my persecutors would suppose I had found the means of transporting myself to England.

"I had still, however, inconveniences enough to encounter. As the autumn advanced, the cold began to make itself felt; and though Donald had contrived to procure me another blanket, and Jeannie every thing else that, without its being missed, she could secrete, I suffered considerably from the severity of the nights; nor was I always during the day free from terror. The wood, which I found much more extensive than I had at first imagined, and terminating in a pine forest, almost the only one within many miles, was infested by wild or martin cats,[109] that not only destroyed the birds, of which I would willingly have made companions, but terrified me by their fierceness: I frequently saw them spring from tree to tree, or traverse the roof of my hermitage; what was worse, they were the cause of hunters frequenting the wood, and climbing, in pursuit of them, even the steepest part of the rocky acclivity; and though I had never seen any of these sportsmen, I had heard them very near, and even the shot rattle among the branches. As the leaves fell I knew my dwelling must inevitably be more exposed, and I doubted whether it were possible for me to remain concealed till I could receive an answer from England.

"Donald, having now married his bonnie Jeannie, was building a cottage near that of her parents; the difficulty of their visiting me was therefore considerably lessened, and they obtained the means of assisting me more easily; and when I expressed to Donald my apprehensions of their injuring themselves by kindness, which it was impossible they could afford, and very uncertain whether I could ever find means to repay, he protested almost with tears in his eyes, that he would not only serve to the last hour of his life the widow of Glenmorris, but sacrifice his life itself, if it was required, in her service. Such a tribute of affection to the memory of my husband affected me more than could any friendship of which I was alone the object.

"With an heavy, cold, desponding, heart I calculated the length of time that might still intervene before I could hear from my sister, if indeed she deigned to answer my letter. Though we had always lived on terms of sisterly affection, I knew not how her change of situation, and the ambitious or avaricious views of her husband and his family, might have changed an heart that never had any great portion of warmth and energy. Of herself, perhaps, she might not be able to send me assistance, and if she meant to do it by application to my father, the interested views of Lady Mary and her husband might unite to prevent her success.

"Amidst such reflections passed my mournful days. Sometimes I gave myself to the darkest despondence, and reproached myself for the meanness and cowardice with which I was content to drag on a life useful to no human being, and to myself intolerable; at other times the lingering love of life, which is so deeply implanted in our nature, that wretches are seen to cling to existence, even when loathsome disease and excruciating pains are added to the horrors of the most squalid poverty; that innate principle of self preservation, which often seems the most predominant where life is the least worth preserving, drew me back to the abject endurance of evil, and my youth, my disposition, naturally sanguine and cheerful, held out occasionally some faint sketches, that though they were not drawn by the hand of hope, (for with hope I seemed to have nothing more to do) were yet of a less gloomy cast; and this happened when the sun was bright and the air pure, and I could breathe freely, and tasted something that gave me an idea of the liberty of a disembodied spirit. I was alone in the universe, I might expatiate at my pleasure on every part of it, and if I interested no one, none had at least the right to controul me. But rare were these aspirations; and when for a moment I indulged them, I was dragged back again to a sense of my wretchedness, by remembering how helpless I was from my sex and age, and that another hour might put me into the power of a tyrant who might destroy me by the most dreadful of all deaths, by degrading me, and making me hateful to myself.

"It happened in the third week of my seclusion in the cell, that, the weather having been for the season unusually mild during two days, I had slept better because less incommoded by the cold, and very early one morning, imagining that no person was likely to be near my remote abode at that hour, I determined to indulge myself in a ramble into the valley which lay beneath this rocky descent; it was a sort of morass formed by the stagnation of two or three small streams, which filtered out of this acclivity, and which, finding no rapid admission into the neighbouring lake, had made the glen, winding among the mountains for about two miles, of little other use than to produce turf for firing, and that species of wild fruit called cranberries,[110] which the children from the most neighbouring cottages had now for a day or two been employed in picking, as Donald informed me, of whom I had enquired from whence came the clamours of infant voices, which I had heard during that time in my solitary cave. I was very fond of this berry; but the mere indulgence of a childish appetite would not have induced me to hazard an alarm; however, believing I should go and return long before the little collectors of the fruit began their morning's toil, I ventured. The descent by steps among the rock, holding by the branches of trees, was rather slow than dangerous, and I soon found myself on the marsh, and began to fill a little basket in which Jeannie sometimes brought my bannocks. Eagerly employed that I might return directly, I heard nothing but the wind buzzing in the plaid with which my head was bound, when suddenly an human figure stood before me. I uttered a faint shriek without having courage to look upon it, and endeavoured to retreat, though instantly feeling the attempt vain; and no other idea than that of Kilbrodie being present to me, I sunk on my knees, and with lifted hands appeared to implore the mercy I had no voice to ask, and no hope of obtaining.

"The person pursued and spoke to me. It was not the voice of Kilbrodie. Oh! then my fainting heart told me it was that of one of his people—but as that afforded me rather more hope, since *they* might perhaps pity me, I ventured to look on the man who had now taken my hand, and in the Erse language asked me why I was terrified?—and why I attempted to run from him?—He was a young man in the dress of an highland hunter,[111] but gentleness and compassion were evident in his voice and countenance, and the moment I asked myself if this *could* be an agent of Kilbrodie's? I was re-assured by the consciousness that it could not. I as instantaneously comprehended that he was merely a sportsman, whose curiosity was raised by my attempt to escape; and who, if I could make him suppose me an highland girl, such as my dress indicated, would think no more about me. This, however, was impossible, whatever presence of mind I endeavoured to exert. Though I understood, I spoke only a few words of the Erse, and it was impossible for me to frame a sentence without betraying myself. However, conscious of this, I attempted it—the effect was exactly what might have been expected. The young man, with apparent amazement, then spoke to me in English as free from the accent of the country we were in as that was in which I answered him.—I told him confusedly, that I was an English woman, whom some singular events had separated from her country, and who having unhappily lost her protector, desired, without knowing how, to return to it. I cannot now relate the exact words in which the stranger offered me not only an immediate asylum in his house, but every assistance I wanted to return to England. It was long since I had heard the words of kindness and humanity—My heart vibrated to the sound, and tears, the first I had shed without bitterness for many months, fell from my eyes.

"Every circumstance concurred to excite the curiosity of the stranger, who entreated me to tell him where I lived? and how he could befriend me? He told me that he had a considerable property in the country, and that that advantage never could otherwise give him so much pleasure as it might do if he could be of use to me.—I knew not how to tell him where my lonely abode was, nor the reasons that had driven me to seek so strange an asylum; still less could I shew it him; but I felt myself unable to continue our conversation where we were. He saw that some terror hung over me, and that I could hardly support myself; he therefore proposed that I should find a seat under shelter of the trees, 'where,' said he, 'if you will allow me to sit by you, I may perhaps learn how you will permit me to serve you—I have two servants somewhere about the hills, within hearing of my gun, which if I fire twice in a particular manner they will attend to, and I can employ them, as well as myself, in the execution of any commands you may honour me with.'

"I suffered him to lead me to a seat formed by projecting rocks, and concealed by a few straggling trees, and then, soothed by the pity his looks and words expressed, I began to relate, as well as I could, the succession of cruel circumstances which had made my hiding myself in a rocky recess of the wood above my only means of safety. I no sooner named Glenmorris than he started up, and in a most affecting manner told me, he had once been his intimate friend, and that on arriving in Scotland for the shooting season, he had heard with grief and astonishment that Glenmorris had been killed in defending his house against the descent of some marauders, calling themselves the crew of an American privateer. The rest of my narrative was more distinctly told, when I recovered from the first burst of anguish recurring to me from the renewal of the cruel images of separation and death, and when I knew that I was speaking to a friend of Glenmorris.—This friend no longer left me any choice in the future disposal of myself, but firing his gun twice, at an interval of two minutes, he told me that, when his servants came, who would soon be with him, he should direct one of them to place me on his horse and walk by me, while the other should fetch such things as I desired to have from my hermitage; 'and I,' said he, 'will be your avant-courier, and give notice at Ardendale of your arrival; I have a sister there with me, who will be happy to receive you, and will unite with me, dear Mrs. Glenmorris, in trying what we can do to mitigate these calamities, the sense of which time only can effectually blunt.' I believe he guessed at the objection I was about to make to this hospitable proposal, for he said, 'you need not fear any attempts from the master of Kilbrodie; he cannot intrude upon *me*, as, if he thought proper to do it, I should soon know how to prevent any molestation from such a quarter.' From thence I understood that a secure asylum, rendered unobjectionable by the presence of his sister, and under the roof of Glenmorris's friend, was offered me. It would have been folly and madness to have refused it—I accepted it therefore with gratitude. His servants arrived at his summons, and received his directions. I begged they might go with me to my friendly cell, as I not only wanted the little linen and other things I had there, but was desirous to account to Donald and Jeannie for my absence. This I did in a few lines, which I left on my stone bench, expressing that I was by a fortunate chance removing to a place of safety, and would write to them in a short time.[112] My few effects being put up, I descended again to the place where the men had left their horses, on one of which they placed me, while they walked carefully by my side—their master was already gone to announce my arrival to his household."

CHAP. IX.

Chi mette il piè su l'amora pania,
Cerchi ritrarlo, e non v'inveschi l'ale,
Chè non è in somma amor se non insania,
A giudicio de' savi universale.[113]

The narrative thus proceeded:

"As I rode along, I could not help reflecting on the singularity of my fate. I was alone in the mountainous wilderness of Scotland, under the conduct of two strangers, going I knew not whither; to an house, the name of whose owner was unknown to me. I failed not, however, to ask the servants, to whom I was about to be obliged for a reception? and one of them, who was an Englishman, told me his master was Lord Macarden, a young Scottish nobleman of large fortune, who resided chiefly at a fine estate he had in England, inherited from his mother, who had been a great heiress; that his house in Scotland was the constant residence of his sister, the Honourable Mrs. Mackirk, who was the daughter of the late Lord Macarden by a former wife, and who having married unfortunately, and been left a widow with a family of children, his lord took care of them all, and had as good as given them his Scotch house, and land enough round it to supply them; 'and it must be own'd,' said the man, 'that there be very few gentlemen or noblemen, either in this here country or any other, as be one tythe as good as my master.'

"I could not fail to have my spirits revived by this account, and I acquired by it courage to sustain me during a much longer journey than I imagined, as we proceeded for six Scottish miles, which I thought more than equal to twice as many English,[114] before we entered the avenue of the great house to which I was to be conducted. This avenue appeared at a distance marked by the old pines that bordered it, and were the only trees visible among the wild and hilly heaths; it was near a mile long; the front of the house, or rather castle, was very extensive, old, heavy, and presenting ideas of gothic splendor and melancholy magnificence. Lord Macarden hastened out to meet me, lifted me from my horse, assured me his sister expected me with impatience; but,' added he, 'after the fatigue of such a journey, and the alarm of the morning, it is possible you may wish to retire for a short time to your own apartment before strangers are introduced to you, I have therefore given orders to have a room ready, where you may be alone, and where I hope you will find every accommodation the time has allowed my sister to procure.'

"I accepted this offer, expressing as well as I could my thanks for his considerate kindness. A female servant immediately appeared, who led the way up an old and wide stair case to a very handsome dressing room with a large bed chamber beyond it; they were richly furnished, and though the furniture was old it was in excellent order—Good fires were in both the rooms—and on a table in one of them was spread a quantity of linen, two morning dresses of muslin, which from their make would fit any one, and every article of female apparel, with a note from Mrs. Mackirk, entreating me to consider them as my own till I could provide myself with such articles as from my late situation I must have wanted.

"I had long been deprived, not only of the decencies, but the necessaries of life, and the comfort of being thus restored to them was not inconsiderable.—To persons of such fortune as my benefactors I had no hesitation in being obliged; and I endeavoured to calm my spirits, and prepare as speedily as I could to shew them that their kindness was not bestowed on an ungrateful being—but my hands trembled, my weakness from scanty food and perpetual fear became more apparent, and it was not without accepting the assistance offered me by a female servant, that I was able to dress myself. She then brought me some refreshment; but still I was so feeble that it was with difficulty I at last collected force to ask permission to thank Mrs. Mackirk.— A message was returned, that she would wait on me in my dressing room, and in a few moments she entered, accompanied by her brother, who led her up to me, and in a manner equally polite and humane, introduced me.

"But in the air, in the countenance of the lady, there was nothing responsive to the open and generous warmth with which Lord Macarden seemed to delight in having rescued me from distress. She saluted me, indeed, and made a civil speech, but there appeared to be an invincible coldness and hardness in her deportment. I thought the glance of her eye, as she surveyed my person, expressed any thing rather than friendly approbation. She seemed haughty, stiff, and formal, and there was about her I knew not what of a repellent quality, from which involuntarily I shrunk. She was fourteen years older than her brother, and appeared yet more. I had seen many plainer women, but never any whose countenance pleased me so little, and this dislike, as in such cases generally happens, was mutual. Mrs. Mackirk liked me as little as I did her; but the common habits of civility, and the necessity she was under to please her brother, were sufficient to induce her to conceal her coldness under such forms of hospitality as the occasion seemed to call for.

"Far different, however, are these from the genuine and interesting expressions of real sympathy and generous affection. I felt, even in the first interview, that Mrs. Mackirk would never be my friend; that I could never communicate to her the emotions which swelled or depressed my heart; and that though she had herself lost an husband, I could not weep to her, and talk of Glenmorris.

"In a few days I had recovered my strength, and with it some degree of that bloom of youth, which, at first, grief, and since, famine and solicitude, had blighted— not that I was now free from anxiety, far otherwise—I waited with the most painful anxiety for the answer I hoped to receive from Lady Daventry. Donald, who now knew where to find me, would, I knew, bring it as soon as he got it; but none came; every hour, therefore, encreased the probability that none might come, and I began to consider what I ought to do to remove myself from the painful necessity of being for any length of time wholly dependant on the bounty of strangers.

"Mrs. Mackirk had six children—The three eldest sons were already provided for[115] by their generous uncle; the youngest, who was a child of six years old, and the two girls, one of nine, the other of eight, were with their mother. These children were supposed to be in a course of some sort of education between their mother and a person who was to act as a kind of governess to them and waiting woman to her; but Mrs. Mackirk herself was not only of a very inert disposition, but had no taste for books, and detested music—She had learned to speak a little French, but so ill, and with so much of the Scotch accent, that she could not even direct their reading it; and as to drawing and fine works she had not single idea of any thing of the kind—Her assistant was still less qualified; for even the slender stock of information obtained as an half boarder[116] in an inferior school in town, she never had patience to communicate, being, I think, the most peevish and irascible being I ever met with—Her look, which might have qualified her to sit for the *pendent* to the caricature before Churchill's poem of The Prophecy of Famine,[117] was so forbidding, and her voice, in which vulgar London phrases were uttered, was so sharp and painful to the ears, that the poor children fled from her as from their torment, and never were compelled to go to their lessons but by threats, and sometimes severe punishment. Insensibly, as I had books from a very good library in the house, the little boy, who was a most interesting child, began to hang about me, and ask me to tell him some of the stories I read, which I had once or twice done to amuse his sisters when we were alone; and I found my own sorrows suspended as these innocent creatures appeared to derive pleasure and a little intelligence from me. Nothing was wanting but to excite their curiosity, and invite them with kindness to gratify it. In a very few days after they had taken a fancy that I should hear them read, their progress was astonishing, and the boy, of whom Lord Macarden was particularly fond, repeated to his uncle some of his new acquisitions with correctness and intelligence, such as he had before no idea of. Lord Macarden was delighted, and said so much about my kindness, that it occurred to me I might perhaps, by making myself useful to the children while *I did stay*, return, though only in a slight degree, some of the many obligations I owed—Flattered by this idea I became almost indefatigable with my voluntary scholars, and their progress was wonderful. The eldest girl had a decided talent for drawing—I gave her a few instructions, and Lord Macarden was never weary of admiring the little sketches she did;—he produced from his library all kinds of materials for drawing, which he had collected for his own amusement, and divided them among the children, saying, 'Now beg Mrs. Glenmorris to continue her favour to you, and shew you, when she is quite at leisure, how to use these things, and then we will send to London for more, the best that can be had.' The boy, who was leaning at that moment on his uncle's knee, looked up in his face, and said, 'Do you know, uncle, that Mrs. Glenmorris understands how to do every thing? Mama has had a great many pretty coloured threads in her drawer a great while, and Mrs. Glenmorris has made a pattern, and painted with these silks or threads, and a needle, such pretty flowers for a skreen for mama, that you would think you might quite smell to them; besides, I know what else she can do.'

"Lord Macarden eagerly asked what? 'Why she can sing, and could play upon the harpsichord in the billiard room if it was but in tune. One afternoon, when she thought I was gone out walking with Jamia and Matilda, I came back to fetch one of my bows, and she sat by herself singing *so* sweetly, and made the harpsichord sound now and then—but when I ran to her, and desired her to play to me, she sighed, and seemed very sorrowful, and shut up the harpsichord; for she said she could not play upon it, it was not in tune. Uncle, send for a man to tune it, will you? We should so like to hear Mrs. Glenmorris play upon it, and so would you, mama, should not you?'

"'No,' answered his mother abruptly, 'I should not; I am not fond of music.'

"I could not be insensible to this rudeness, which, though the lady had often exhibited something of the same sort before, was more marked than usual. Tears, in despite of the effort I made to conquer them, rose in my eyes, and my emotion choked my utterance. 'Madam,' said I, in a voice hardly articulate, 'do not apprehend that I shall intrude upon you with sounds of gaiety or of pleasure—I am too unhappy—too conscious of my unhappiness.' This was the first time I had ever appeared to notice the ill humour of Mrs. Mackirk, or the sullen reluctance with which she rather suffered, than encouraged, the little kindnesses I endeavoured to do her children. Cold in her manner, and struggling, as I soon perceived, to conceal under the common forms of civility the distaste which a narrow mind feels towards those who possess any advantages of education, intellect, or person, I had from the first, found the behaviour of this lady very displeasing. Her brother's manly politeness, while it endeavoured to conceal, had greatly palliated the unpleasantness of such behaviour; but for some days I observed the bitterness of her spirit acquired new force; she could not look at me without giving a malignant turn to her features; she could never speak to me but in the petulant voice of repressed aversion; and I failed not to perceive, that the trifling services I did to her children, on which her brother often descanted, giving them, perhaps, more consequence than they could possibly deserve, were thought of by the lady rather as proofs of superiority which she could not bear, than as instances of voluntary kindness. But while I saw that Lord Macarden was so much delighted with my attempts to instruct them, and while the children themselves were at once improved and happy when they were with me, I seemed to be paying a small part of my debt of gratitude to my benefactor, in devoting my time to their instruction.

"I had now no sooner repelled with something like resentment what I considered as a sarcasm, than I turned my eyes on Lord Macarden, and saw concern so strongly expressed on his countenance, that I repented of my warmth, and unable to subdue the various emotions that assailed me, I arose and left the room, strolling, I knew not why, beyond what is called a policy, into a plantation of firs, pines, and other hardy trees, which were grown to a considerable size, being in a spot open to the south, and defended from the north and north-east by high land, whose base was ornamented by their shade.

"The night resembled exactly that when, twelve months before, I had, after our first separation, met Glenmorris, and agreed to unite my fate with his; except that then an early moon had lit my way, and now it was at the full. The moon in northern countries[118] shines with a more powerful and brilliant light than nearer the tropics; the contrast formed by the dark pines that waved above my head, added to her calm and soothing splendor, affecting the mind, not with the enlivening cheerfulness it receives from the vivifying light of the sun, but with a sort of pensive and melancholy delight which no other object in nature equally inspires. The trouble of my ruffled spirits subsided as I walked gazing on this lovely planet, and listening to the murmur of the wind, which has a peculiar sound among fir woods. I thought of all that had passed since my first quitting Sandthwaite Castle, the short period of happiness I had passed with Glenmorris, the still accumulating bitterness which had marked my days since I lost him, and hardly did I venture to trust myself with the thoughts of what was to come; but when I acquired resolution to consider steadily what it was best for me to do, I soon took a resolution to relieve Mrs. Mackirk from the uneasiness of my presence; I knew that there was no other way of doing this but by applying to Lord Macarden for the means of returning to England; I was indeed very unwilling to increase obligations already so great, but it was better to suffer him to exert his generosity in conveying me where it was possible I should acquire the means of repaying them, than to continue burthensome to him in Scotland, and, what was yet worse, becoming the cause of coldness, if not of disagreement, between him and his sister.

"I resolved then to address myself to him by letter, for I knew I had not courage to speak, and I busied myself in considering what form of words to use, when turning to go towards the house along the broad grass walk I was in, I saw a man close to me, who seeing by my starting back that I was alarmed, stepped forward and spoke—it was Lord Macarden.

"'Forgive me,' said he, 'for the apparent impertinence of thus breaking in on your solitude, but I cannot, indeed I cannot, bear to see you uneasy, and I came to apologize for my sister. She is unhappy, her temper is become irritable, and I am afraid the weakness of hopelessly repining at her destiny grows upon her.—You,' added he, softening his voice, and taking my hand—'You have greatness of mind enough to pity and forgive her petulance. You are too candid, too generous to expect that every woman, that women of inferior minds, can bear adversity and sorrow as you do, with the mild resignation of an angel.'

"Lord Macarden had sometimes made me such speeches as this before, but I had considered them as nothing more than the effect of that sort of unmeaning gallantry which a man of his age accustoms himself to shew towards a woman of mine. His present address, and the time and place he had chosen to make it in, made it more pointed. I wished, however, to pass over it as mere common place, and tried to enter at once on the subject of my departure; he would not, however, give me time to explain myself, but having heard enough to understand what I desired, he stopped me at once by declaring, in terms not to be mistaken or evaded, that he was devoted to me almost from the first moment he had seen me; that his passion had since made an hourly progress, and could now neither be concealed nor controuled. He concluded by offering to make me immediately mistress of his fortune as his wife, or, if I wished to have the sanction of my father and Lady Mary, he would conduct me, he said, to London, and receive from their hands the only blessing the world could give him.

"Though to his love I instantly resolved never to listen, I was affected by his generosity; so much affected that it was with difficulty I found voice to tell him, that my heart was buried in the grave of Glenmorris, and that he deserved better than that any woman should give him her person who had not an heart to bestow. This was, I suppose, such an answer as he had expected, for he seemed but slightly repulsed. He suffered me, however, to return to the house, assured me he would not press me for my answer, but give me whatever time I wished to consider of what he had said; yet he conjured me not to think of leaving him, and again besought me to forgive his sister's peevish weakness. I promised nothing, but hastened to my apartment, where breathless surprise, not unmingled with terror, soon gave way to the certainty that I must immediately depart from his house, yet could no longer solicit his assistance for that purpose; and that the faithful Donald must be again my resource.

"I now comprehended the cause of Mrs. Mackirk's still increasing hatred towards me; she had seen what I was myself unconscious of; and I had understood, though hardly heeding it at the time it was told me, that Mrs. Mackirk was always alarmed at any report of her brother's being likely to marry, and had forborne to ask any young ladies to the house, or to have a young well educated woman as governess to the children. Mrs. Mackirk was no favourite with the servants, and this was the gossip of her who waited in my room, which I had heard once, but discouraged too much ever to have it repeated.

"The recollection of it however, added to some other circumstances that crowded on my mind of the same nature, determined me to lose not a moment in preparing at any hazard to go. Yet how? I had no means of sending to Donald, whom I had seen but once since I left the cell; no means but what might discover where I was to Kilbrodie, and give him an opportunity of intercepting me as soon as I should leave my present asylum. My faithful Menie was not with me—Donald had informed me that she had been driven from Kilbrodie with menaces as privy to my escape, and had called at their cottage, on her way to Inverness, with a young highlander of Glenmorris's clan, to whom she had engaged herself to be married.

"What to do under such circumstances it was hard to decide. I never slept during the night, but the morning found me wretched and perplexed. I mingled with the family, and endeavoured to appear as usual; but I observed the countenance of Mrs. Mackirk darker towards me than ever, and when I saw her brother I thought him uncommonly grave. He did not play with the children after dinner as was his custom, but went early to his study, where the servant told Mrs. Mackirk he was busy with the steward—At the usual hour, however, he appeared at supper, and seemed to exert himself to force something like conversation, but as he was ill seconded the meal was short and melancholy, and as soon as it ended Lord Macarden told his sister he was engaged with a party of sportsmen to shoot on some distant muirs, which he named; that he should set out before it was light; and that she must not expect him home till night, or be surprised if he was detained till the next day from his own house.—He wished us both good night, and retired."

CHAP. X.

And weeping said, ah! my long absent lord,
Where have ye been thus long out of my sight?

Alas! e'er since mine eye your sight did miss,
My cheerful day is turn'd to cheerless night,
And oh! my night of death the shadow is.[119]

Delmont's curiosity was now raised to the highest pitch as Mrs. Glenmorris proceeded.

"The following morning I was sitting with the children in a room which was at the end of the house, looking towards the avenue, when a crowd of people—a crowd for that country, for there were ten or a dozen,—appeared among the trees, while others ran eagerly towards the house—Then I saw some of the servants hurrying to join this group, from whence two or three of them returned with frantic gestures—I listened in the gallery, and then on the top of the stairs—Confused sounds reached me from the distant offices—Trembling, though I knew not why, I suffered the eldest of the girls to go down and enquire what was the matter—Hardly had she reached the end of the gallery before my alarm was encreased by a loud shriek; I ran forward and met the child, who told me, though almost in convulsions, that her uncle was dead; that somebody had killed her dear uncle—I no longer knew what I did, yet recommending the children to the care of their maid, who had been at work in another room, I flew down stairs to the drawing room, where I no sooner appeared, than Mrs. Mackirk (around whom two or three female servants were standing, administering drops and chafing her temples) uttered an hideous scream, and in a voice I shall never forget, bade them take that monster from her sight, that monster who had been the cause of her brother's death.

"Amazed, bewildered, terrified, I fled away from the accuser, to learn the reality of the horrors I was accused of causing. The house was deserted—I met nobody to question—I ran out towards the spot where I had seen people assembled, and soon reached that where my eyes were blasted with the sight of Lord Macarden, pale, covered with blood, apparently lifeless, and borne between four or five men. It were vain to attempt describing what I felt at this sight—To see this excellent young man thus destroyed in the flower of his age was of itself dreadful—to suppose that *I* might have been the cause of such a misfortune, though how I could not imagine, aggravated my sufferings, till the stupor of grief seemed to overcome my senses—I stared wildly around, asked incoherent questions that nobody attended to, and followed with unconscious officiousness the bleeding body of my murdered benefactor.

"Some harsh words from one of the attendants, who took and held me rudely by the arm, constraining me to keep back, served by the shock it gave, to restore me to recollection. I sat down in a passage room, and burst into tears—my burning brain was relieved, and I was able once more to follow the people that surrounded their lord—'For the love of God,' cried I, in a shrill and distracted tone, 'send for some help—Tell me where a surgeon can be found, and I will go myself for him—Your lord is not dead—is there nobody who knows where to go for help?'

"The steward, who had been absent in the grounds, now appeared; he had more presence of mind than the inferior servants, and gave me the most satisfaction I could now derive from any one, by telling me Lord Macarden was not dead, and dispatching a servant on horseback for a surgeon, who lived, he said, about four miles off—I could have knelt and blest this man for the consolation he gave me, had he not, on returning from the room whither his master had been carried, poisoned it all by saying, that though it was true he yet breathed, yet it seemed impossible he could long survive.

"Miserable indeed to me was the time that intervened before the arrival of the surgeon—I could not enter the house, dreading not only the cruel reproaches of Mrs. Mackirk, but the intelligence of my benefactor's death; yet I could not go far from it till the person arrived, who had perhaps skill, if he yet lived, to save him. I hid myself like a wretched and guilty creature among the remotest plantations, till I thought the time arrived when the surgeon might appear; I then watched at the gate through which I knew he must pass, still concealing myself as if conscious of all the ill Mrs. Mackirk's phrensy imputed to me. How could I have caused the death of Macarden? Whose hand could I have armed against him? That question brought to my mind the image of the ferocious vindictive Kilbrodie, and I no longer doubted what was in a few moments confirmed to me, that he had sent a challenge to Lord Macarden on his refusing to give me up.—I now detested myself as much as the raving Mrs. Mackirk seemed to detest me, and wished I had died a thousand deaths rather than have occasioned this cruel event.

"The surgeon arrived; I crowded unheeded to the door of Macarden's room among the servants, while he was examining the wounds; trembling, breathless, I hardly dared hear what I was so desirous of knowing. His opinion was, that the wounds were probably mortal, but he had by no means experience enough to pronounce; nor could he venture, he said, to attempt extracting the ball; he recommended that an express should immediately be sent to the house of a nobleman ten miles distant, who had a surgeon resident in his family.

"Mrs. Mackirk, instead of exerting herself for her brother's relief, continued to lament herself, and to rail against me; I therefore wrote what was necessary to procure this gentleman's attendance, and the steward sent my letter off by a man on horse-back—I then sat down in a recess formed by a window which had been closed up in the anti-room to the poor sufferer's bed chamber—His groans, which however he seemed still struggling to stifle, pierced my heart; yet dreadful as they were, they gave me assurance that he lived, and I hoped he might recover—This hope mitigated the tortures I endured, and totally careless of myself, I did not feel that I had hardly eaten during the day, and that great part of the night was passed, and I was still awake to anguish, which none seemed to heed. Towards three o'clock in the morning the second surgeon arrived—On his opinion seemed the destiny of the house to hang—But I, who had waited for it with such extreme anxiety, was now unable to stay to hear it. I fled to my own room, again passing through the deserted house, and throwing my-self on my bed in my clothes, endeavoured in darkness and in silence to collect resolu-tion enough to enquire what fate would do with me. The death of lord Macarden, his death occasioned by me, however innocently, seemed such an addition to the weight of calamity I already endured, that to sustain it and live I believed altogether impos-sible.

"But I have sometimes thought, when oppressed with sorrow, that there is too much truth in the lines of I know not what writer, who says:

Yet venture not to say, ah! wretch accurst,
Thy miserable days are at the worst!

For evil seems sometimes so enchained with evil, that the sufferer loses one sensation of misery only by the petrifying stroke of some greater misfortune. After I had been alone near an hour, endeavouring to recollect all the instances I had ever heard, of those who, wounded, survived, and had collected all the hope I could from recapitu-lating the chances in Macarden's favour, from his youth, his apparently good constitu-tion, and his manly and calm temper, I thought I could venture to listen in the nearer rooms, sure that where ever any of the servants were I should hear something of their master's situation, as pronounced upon by the surgeon.—I opened my door therefore, and was proceeding along the gallery, at one end of which was my dressing room, at the other a stair-case.—The moon was in its wane, and already so near the horizon, that it afforded but little light, and that little was still obscured by the sort of windows that admitted it—stepping softly along I looked before me not without dread, and that dread was increased when I thought I perceived through the gloom some object moving at the extremity of the gallery—I stopped and listened with a throbbing heart—I no longer distinguished any thing, but I fancied I heard some person breathe, yet as if they wished not to be heard—In a moment, however, the noise ceased, and I went forward a step or two, half ashamed of fears I could not conquer; but instantly the door from the stair-case opened softly, and I perceived a light, which, however, vanished before I could see who held it, and all was almost totally dark.—Terror of various kinds now assailed me; among others, the superstition I had always despised obtruded itself, and I was weak enough to dread least this mysterious something was the spirit of Macarden, who dying under the operation he had gone through, came to reproach me with having caused his death—I might at the same time have recollected, that if it were so the spectre could follow me to my own room, whither I hastily retreated, and that, the door I shut would be no defence against it—without considering that I attempted to lock the door, but it was in vain; my feeble and tremulous hands could not force the old and clumsy bolt of the lock to obey a key that had long rusted in its ward, and as I continued still to try, I felt the door pushed open, and I rudely was seized by two persons, whose strength immediately put all resistance on my part out of the question—one of them, without speaking, confined my arms, and as I earnestly, and with shrieks and cries implored their mercy, and intreated I might know what they would do with me, the other whispered, that all questions and prayers were vain, and that to prevent them he must bind an handkerchief over my face—my shrieks, my struggles were fruitless—a plaid was bound strongly across the lower part of my face, hardly admitting me to breathe, and I was lifted up between the two men, and conveyed to a sort of covered cart, such as are used in the highlands by persons rather above the poor peasantry—A woman sat in it to receive me, whom I easily distinguished to be Meggy Macgregor, the old woman of whom I had conceived such an ill opinion before the birth of my child—I could no longer doubt whither I was going, or the dreadful destiny that awaited me!

"The woman had perhaps directions to soothe me; but there was so little humanity in her nature, that her malice got the better of every precaution, and she reviled me in the bitterest terms for my flight from Kilbrodie Abbey, and all the mischief it had occasioned.—I should have suffered her to proceed, even if I had possessed the power of interrupting her—My consternation, the sickness of my soul was too great— The tears ceased to flow from my eyes—my heart seemed frozen—faintness occasioned by fasting and want of rest—sorrow for the death of Macarden, which the cruel monster told me was pronounced to be inevitable, and the horror of being again in the power of Kilbrodie, was altogether an accumulation of wretchedness that might have overwhelmed a stronger mind and stronger frame than mine.—I heard, however, among the enumerations this beldam made of the mischief I had occasioned, that the master of Kilbrodie was himself wounded in the hand so severely that there were doubts whether he must not suffer amputation.

"I know not how long we were on the road, for I was become senseless before I was removed from the cart, and knew nothing that passed till I found myself on the bed I had formerly slept on at Kilbrodie, and a woman, whom I did not know, attempting to make me swallow something out of a cup she held.—I positively refused to receive any nourishment whatever, and once more I thought I should have courage to die.

"I persevered in the resolution to swallow neither food nor medicine, till Lady Kilbrodie herself appeared, and with the most unwomanly menaces of force, compelled me to take what she offered.—Having done so, and heartily hoping it might be poison, I threw myself on my bed, where a stupor fell upon me, which I hailed as the forerunner of the death I coveted.—It was only a short remission gained by the medicine I had taken operating on my exhausted frame.

"I awoke from forgetfulness, which could hardly be called sleep, about the same time as that on which I had been seized by the ruffians on the preceding night, and all the transactions of the last six and thirty hours rushed on my mind. The bleeding corse of my unfortunate defender again seemed to rise before my bewildered sight; I put aside the curtain, and actually fancied I saw him beckoning me to the window; agitated certainly by some degree of delirium, I threw myself from my bed, I flew, I knew not why, to the window, which looked into the ruined cloister of the abbey—indeed the room I inhabited was once a part of the dormitory which let into those cloisters—Within the room, the shadow that my fevered imagination had embodied was no longer painted to me as present; but the many miserable hours I had passed in the spot where I now stood, the dear dear infant who had seen the light only to suffer and to perish, and whose little grave I again beheld, that grave where had fallen the bitter tears of a wretched mother over her last her only hope!—all these sad objects reminding me of calamities passed, while I felt myself again fettered, imprisoned, tormented by the same inhuman monsters as had inflicted them on me, was more than my senses could sustain—I suddenly took the resolution to force myself out of the window, less with an idea of escape than meaning to dash myself against the ground and end my tortures.—This was impossible, for the window, of itself narrow, was divided in the middle by a stone pillar, and each casement again divided by a strong iron bar, through which hardly a slender arm could pass—I was, however, incapable of calculation, and stood up on the low seat beneath this gothic casement, which I opened; but the freshness of the air, and the abortive attempts I made, both helped to restore me to my senses; I leaned against the stone-work, and like a child who cannot obtain some object out of its reach, I began to weep—my throbbing temples ceased to beat so violently; the dreadful pain that, since I awoke, I felt in the back of my head, abated, and I breathed less laboriously.

"Tears continued to fill my eyes as they were fixed on the pile of white stones I had collected to mark the burial place of my poor baby. The night was bright, calm, and starlight, though the moon was gone, and I could plainly distinguish the spot. Suddenly I thought that from a dark recess behind it, shaded with holly and elder that grew straggling among the ruins, I saw a form slowly emerge—It was an human creature, or the semblance of one, and seemed clad in a light colour.—I tried to recollect myself; I wiped my misty eyes, and had sense enough to ask myself, if this was not again 'an air drawn vision?'[120] I looked steadily, and at that moment without fear—The shape was still there, still stood and seemed to gaze as in sorrow on the very spot where so long and so often my heart breaking sighs had been directed; it then with slow and measured pace crossed the ruin, and came nearer to the place where I was, and where the ruins were partly removed, so that there was more light.—I was afraid of moving, of breathing; my faculties were suspended in wonder and dread—my eyes, however, still followed the figure, which seemed—Gracious God!—it seemed to be Glenmorris!

"It *was* then his spirit!—The injuries of his wretched wife had called his shade from its distant grave; for he had now been lost to me eight miserable months, and I had long since ceased to flatter myself with an hope of seeing him again.

"Yet he now actually seemed to be separated from me only by a single bar of iron, and the distance of about sixteen feet, for it was no more from the window to the ground. It was still the semblance of Glenmorris!—I looked more earnestly; his height, his manner of walking, appeared more striking while I gazed; and as I saw the figure more immediately opposite to me I felt the trouble of my spirits so great, that I was afraid my senses would forsake me, and without power to weigh any consequences which might follow should I speak to a stranger, or to any of Kilbrodie's people, I put forth my arms towards him through the bars, and half shrieking uttered the name of Glenmorris!—The figure stopped, looked towards the window, and uttering an exclamation of surprise, added, in an hollow and mournful voice, 'Laura!—is it, indeed, Laura! *my* Laura!'—I should find it difficult to recount the words we each of us uttered.—My only remaining idea is a confused sensation of overwhelming joy and astonishment, with a sort of agonizing dread least I could not escape to him, and least all I saw, or believed I saw, was the dream of feverish delusion.—I uttered something of this wild variety of emotions, for Glenmorris seemed to understand that I was confined, and enquired what it meant—'They told me,' said he, still speaking in the same mournful tone, 'they told me you were *not* here. How is it that you are now here a prisoner?' I entreated him to come to me that I might explain it, but I dared not ask him to attempt the door, or go to that of my room to see if it could be opened; of nothing had I so great a dread as of losing sight of him even for a moment—for I had a disturbed notion still, that all this was illusive, and that if I once quitted the window it would vanish.

"Glenmorris seemed to pause a moment, and then, as if he had suddenly fallen on an expedient, walked hastily away, while I, heedless of the hazard of being overheard, called after him, 'Glenmorris, Oh! do not, for God sake, leave me.'—In less than a moment he returned, bringing a ladder with him, on which he was instantly at the window; I seized his hands, held them to my eyes, to my temples, and bathed them with my tears. 'Take me from hence, Glenmorris,' said I. 'Oh! never again let your poor Laura endure what she has suffered from these people.' He answered, 'that some strange mystery, which the present was not a moment to explain, hung over us; but whatever it may prove, Laura, you shall go with me.'—The question then was, how? 'Why not,' said he, 'force this bar, and you could descend from the window.' He tried; the iron was so rusty and decayed that it broke in his hand, and he forced out the lower part, together with some of the stones it was inserted in, which fell with a noise that made me tremble least it should be heard in the house.—I was already wrapped in a cloak, and without waiting for any other accommodation I got through the window, not without difficulty, Glenmorris receiving me in his arms, and conducting me down the ladder. I felt that I was likely to faint on reaching the ground, but the strength with which I found myself fortified, when I remembered the necessity of immediate flight, convinced me that by resisting this sort of failure of the animal spirits it may sometimes be conquered; for I now conjured Glenmorris to hasten away at least from the sight of the abbey windows, and I even ran for a quarter of a mile, when arriving among the ruins of the old castle of Kilbrodie, which afforded a temporary conceal-ment, I threw myself into Glenmorris's arms, and declared to him that I could go no further. His words were such as, amid all the confusion of my mind, made a deep impression. As he embraced and held me to his bosom he said—'Is it, indeed, my Laura, my heart's own Laura, that my arms enfold?—And is she the same dear and tender girl that she was before our separation?' I was affected both by the words and the manner they were spoken in; but I was no longer in a condition to reply. He saw I was not, and added, 'We must not talk now, however, but when you are a little recovered, endeavour to reach a place of greater safety before the morning light over-takes us.' Glenmorris then remained silent, and I continued, as I leant on his shoulder, to look round me, questioning still if I was not in a dream—yet I saw the stars, and felt the air blow on my face. I knew the pieces of wall and broken ruins around me were the same as I had before been shewn as those of Kilbrodie castle; but to be restored to my husband, to be delivered from the power of my persecutors, was happiness so great, so incredible, that hardly dared I ask if it was real, least even as I did so it should dissolve.

"When I seemed to have recovered my breath, Glenmorris asked if I thought it was possible for me to reach the cottage of the Dorna Dune, one of those situated in the most remote part of the glen, near a remarkable hill, by which it was distinguished;[121] 'it is there,' said he, 'and not at my own house, that I have found shelter since yesternight, and there, Laura, we must decide on what we are to do.'

"I assured him, that since I was once more with him, saw him restored to me from the grave, there was no fatigue, no exertion, that I did not think myself equal to. We pursued our way then, which was still above four miles, Glenmorris sometimes bearing me in his arms over the most difficult parts of the road, and sometimes en-couraging me to perseverance, by assuring me that the remaining distance was short. At last we arrived; there was a light in the small house that received us, and the people, who were Glenmorris's faithful adherents, had expected him; for me the woman in-stantly hastened to procure some refreshment and a bed, on which I threw myself, though certain that to sleep was impossible. Glenmorris told me he should sit up the little remainder of the night in the other division of the house, consulting with his host on the steps to be taken the next morning. I made him most solemnly promise he would not leave the cottage, and on that condition only agreed to attempt sleeping.

"The next day I had an opportunity of observing the great change that had taken place in the appearance of Glenmorris; he was thin and pale, and his counte-nance expressed solicitude and even pain of mind. Amidst the wildest and most inco-herent of those expressions with which I endeavoured to convey to him some idea of the extravagance of my joy at meeting him again, he seemed, methought, as if his delight was blasted by some evil either felt or feared.

"However, after a short previous conversation, as if to prepare me, he began to relate, that Kilbrodie was in possession of his house, from whence all the furniture left by the buccaniers had been removed, 'so that I have not, Laura,' said he, 'a shed to receive you in—I shall recover all that; Kilbrodie must give up what he has usurped;

but,' added he, fixing his eyes on me with a look half stern, half tender, 'but if I have lost my peace, if I have lost my honour, tell me, Laura, who can restore *them*? where shall I find my peace, my honour again?'

"'Your peace, Glenmorris!—If we live together, though condemned to the severest labour, shall not peace, nay, shall not happiness be ours?—And for your honour, my dear love, who shall blemish it, is it not in your own keeping?'

"'Not always,' answered he; 'the honour of an husband is sometimes in the custody of a wife.'—He hesitated, and looked at me with eyes expressive of anguish, and yet as if he doubted whether I had strength to bear what he had to say. 'Is it because of *your* wife then, Glenmorris, that you fear for the safety of your honour?' said I.—'Good God Almighty!—what can you mean?'

"'Laura,' replied he, 'you know the openness, perhaps I should say the impetuosity of my temper—I cannot for a moment disguise my feelings—How I have loved you, Laura, I need not surely repeat—Love is, indeed, too poor a word—I have worshipped, I have idolized you, and if I am to lose you, Laura—'

"'Explain yourself, and quickly, Glenmorris,' exclaimed I, 'least I should die with terror before I know your meaning.'

"'Do the innocent feel terror, Laura?—But I will be calm, and ask you, why you were so ready to throw yourself under the protection of Lord Macarden? why, not knowing that I existed no longer, did you suffer *him* to be your champion, and to defend you as one whose fate was united with his?——Why should the wife or the widow of Glenmorris so conduct herself as to be the occasion of a duel between his nearest relation and Lord Macarden? I have endeavoured in vain to obtain an explanation of all this elsewhere; it is from you, Laura, I now ask it.'"

CHAP. XI.

It gives me wonder, great as my content,
To see you here before me.—O! my soul's joy,
May after every tempest come such calms![122]

"A moment's consideration," continued Mrs. Glenmorris, "a moment's consideration opened to me the consequence of this request. He had been deceived, though I knew not by whom, as to the motives of my having quitted the abbey, and had heard of the wound Macarden had received, though from what quarter these misrepresentations came I had no means of guessing. It was easy to foresee the probable consequences of revealing the iniquity of Kilbrodie and his mother; yet I was well aware that Glenmorris had so great an abhorrence of falsehood, which he always disdained to use in the most apparently inconsequential matters, even such as related to the mere forms of the world; I knew myself so awkward at any dissimulation, and indeed had so little reason to palliate the conduct of either the mother or the son, that I should not have hesitated a moment, but for the fear I had that the impetuous spirit of Glenmorris might urge him to endanger his personal safety, by calling Kilbrodie to an account; this, however, must be remote; I might find means to detach him from any such indulgence of his vengeance—and it was better to hazard nothing in an affair on which the sole happiness of my future life depended, for it was now evident to me that doubts of my conduct had empoisoned the delight with which my beloved husband, after so long and cruel a separation, had found me once more restored to him; yet that he *could* doubt was, I own, a most bitter conviction; *so* bitter, that, added to the cruel remembrance of all I had suffered, the death of my child, undoubtedly produced by terror I was purposely exposed to, and the sad event of which I had been the occasion in the person of Marcarden, I seemed deprived for a time of the power of relating all that had befallen me, so heavy was the crowd of cruel recollections pressing at once upon me.

"At length, however, I regained strength of voice and intellect to relate all I had feared or felt from the moment, when recovering my senses after he was torn from me to the circumstances that preceded the death of my poor baby.—Glenmorris's attention was only interrupted by marks of extreme impatience and resentment; but when I spoke of the loss of my child, my voice failed—that cruel remembrance, added to the effect it had on Glenmorris, was in my present state too much for me, and it was some hours before I could resume my narrative.

"This, however, I at last got through, and brought down my story to the moment when Lord Macarden was brought home wounded. I had not disguised his conversation with me of the preceding evening.

"But the indignation of Glenmorris against Kilbrodie was so great as to swallow up every other sentiment, and I could see that he stifled his resolutions of vengeance not to alarm me, whom he now only thought of soothing and consoling with the tenderest love—A thousand and a thousand times he besought me to forgive him for having dared to harbour a suspicion of my purity and affection—He would have knelt to me for my forgiveness; but I loved him too passionately not to have forgotten already that these suspicions had hurt me, and sweet, oh! how sweet to my heart would have been this moment when Glenmorris was restored to me, as it were, from the grave, if we had not both remembered, and wept together in bitterness of heart, over the first pledge of our affection, lost, and so cruelly lost, to us for ever.

"When the various emotions excited by the recital I had made had subsided, I could not repress my curiosity to know by what miracle it was that *he* was returned, whom I thought I had seen covered with wounds, and dragged from me a bleeding corse, and how it happened that, instead of re-appearing as its master in the castle of Glenmorris, he was, as it seemed, concealed, and unwilling to be known?

"He thus related what had happened:

"'The men who plundered our house,' said he, 'were the crew of an American privateer, or rather of a large vessel fitted out at Morlaix,[123] under the American colours, but commanded by an English outlaw, and manned by English, Americans, Scotch, Irish, Portuguese, and even three or four Genoese sailors; they were literally a party of buccaniers, holding themselves accountable to no government, and ready to use their arms against all. The excursion in which they made a landing at Glenmorris was their second successful descent on the eastern coast, and as they had before met with no resistance, they were provoked by the attempt which, naked and unarmed as I was, I had made to repel their insult; and supposing they might extort money for my ransom, they dragged me half dead to their vessel. Ah! Laura, judge of my despair, when, unable to defend or even avenge you, I was not yet so much deprived of my reason by loss of blood, but that I heard a project for taking you also, and one of the wretches had the audacity to speak of your youth and beauty in terms which seemed to conclude for me the mischief their weapons had begun; for unable to punish them, unable indeed to speak, I thought the stifled fury of my soul would have destroyed me. Fortunately, before they could return to execute this infamous project, the clan was alarmed, and came down upon them so quickly that they were glad to retreat to their boat, and depart with the booty they had already got and their prisoners.

"'They soon gave up the idea of my being immediately ransomed, for the distant sight of two English frigates, which they believed were in pursuit of them, obliged them to steer for the coast of Holland, whence they kept close to the land till they took shelter at Dunkirk.

"'As the expectation of my obtaining money for my ransom was the chief reason of my detention, it was not the interest of my captors to let me die. There had been a man on board who had done what his little knowledge dictated to my wounds; on landing in France I was consigned to the care of a more able surgeon, and my situation was greatly meliorated in regard to bodily sufferings; yet my recovery was slow, and with a less strong and sound constitution might never have been effected at all. As it was, the anguish of my mind continually impeded the healing of my wounds; I never could for a moment divest myself of the cruel idea of your agonies and despair, which, in the state you were in, I dreaded as being of the most fatal consequence. Sometimes I felt as if I dared not, had I liberty and strength, return to enquire what had been the event; at another time I was ready to beat my head against the walls of my prison, walls which detained me from flying to know the extent of my misery. In more rational moments I thought steadily of the means of procuring my freedom, and conversed with my French jailer on the subject, till I fancied I discovered in him some disposition to serve me; and had I had money I am persuaded I should have found no difficulty in effecting my escape; but being destitute of that resource, I seemed to have no chance but of engaging some officer to procure my release, and at length found means to convey a letter written in French, to the commandant of the town, representing my situation, and entreating him by the honour of a soldier and a gentleman to interest himself on my behalf.

"'This gentleman had not only the feelings I imputed to him, but had them in a superior degree; yet nothing could be more unfortunate than my application. He, whose prisoner I was, was an Englishman only in the deep-rooted and inveterate aversion he bore to every thing French, and as soon as he found the commandant anxious for my release, he signified to him in the rudest terms his resolution not to be dictated to in the disposal of his own prisoner; and piqued that the commandant offered to advance the money, which he seemed to expect as the price of my liberty, and afterwards enraged by something that fell in their conversation from the military man, who expressed himself as if he considered the commander of such a ship as no better than a pirate; my captor, indignant and enraged, determined to shew me that the good offices I had sought should have exactly the contrary effect from that which I had hoped for, and instead of releasing me, I was hoisted like a bale of goods into the vessel, and after an imprisonment of five weeks at Dunkirk, began, under these wretched and inauspicious circumstances, a voyage to America. My complaints would have been vain, but I disdained complaint; yet there were times when I could hardly sustain myself. It was not personal hardship, the pain of my wounds, or the confinement on board a small vessel, that overwhelmed me; it was the uncertainty I was under what was become of my Laura and of our infant; it was the cruel doubt continually recurring, whether the existence I yet struggled to preserve was worth the pain, the misery I went through to preserve it—for if you were gone, was I not prolonging life only to taste of the most cureless and hopeless wretchedness.

"'Hope, however, was not quite extinct in my heart, and that alone preserved me. Our passage was tedious, lasting near two months, and it was only by an extraordinary exertion of skill and good fortune that the captain escaped the English frigates, of which many were stationed on the coast. *I* as eagerly desired this as *he* sought to avoid it. The success was his, and his booty and his prisoner were landed at Boston.

"'I was now among a new race of people—a people who with manners, customs, and general habits of thinking quite unlike my own, had one great and predominant feature in their character which I loved and honoured—they were determined to be *free*, and were now making the noblest exertions to resist what they deemed oppression. I found that with a few of them the inveterate hatred generated by the unnatural war they had been driven into, extended to me, merely because I was an Englishman, or, what was the same thing to them, a Scotsman; but in others the noble flame of liberty seemed to have purified their minds from every narrow and unmanly prejudice, and when they found that my heart beat in unison with theirs, when they heard me declare that, Englishman as I was, I would never have drawn my sword against men struggling in that glorious cause for which *Hampden bled in the field and Sydney on the scaffold*;[124] they forgot that I was born a Briton, a North Briton too,[125] and belonging to those whose legions were then carrying fire and sword through their country, and they embraced me as a brother.

"'When I had met with such friends my chains were first lightened, and then entirely removed. My captor still insisted on being paid a sum of money, which my new friends could by no means presently supply me with, and for which I could not bear they should risk distressing themselves, by making any engagement to the freebooting savage who had taken advantages so unjust; yet such was my impatience to return to England, that I would have sacrificed even my life to have obtained only time enough to ask if my Laura lived? If she did not—Oh! heaven and earth, how dared I trust myself with a thought so horrid—I could *not* often, but hurried my mind from the question which terror so continually suggested, "Glenmorris! what will you do in England if Laura has fallen the victim to her affection for you?"

"'Tedious is the progress of time to the unhappy; to me, who now passed some weeks in the cruel vicissitudes of hope and despair, it seemed to be indeed endless. During this time I felt much of that attendance and dependence which is truly described as being so bitter to a liberal spirit; for I made applications to two or three officers serving in the British army; but my case was singular, and they thought, I believe, mysterious; so that after some letters had passed between us, I found myself still a neglected prisoner, and at last my American friends accepted the best security I could give them, for a sum of money which they paid to my ferocious captor, who, in the present state of things, was under no authority (not being a native of the United States) which could compel him to desist from the unjust demand he made as the price of my liberty.

"'Stripped and almost pennyless, for I would not accept of what my American friends, though they liberally offered it, could ill spare, I embarked on board a small vessel, which was going with contraband articles of trade to Jamaica, where I was put on shore, and was to find my way afterwards to England as well as I could.

"'Once more I seemed like one dropped from the clouds, for I knew, as I believed, no soul upon the island. Ill furnished as my purse was, I was afraid of entering a tavern at so expensive a place as Kingston, and had not yet discovered any receptacle that seemed more suitable to the low ebb of my fortune; I walked therefore through the streets undecided, and thinking rather how I should get from thence, than how I should live while I was there, when a gentleman passed me, who seemed to look at me with an air of curiosity and doubt. I looked back, he also looked back, and, turning, made a step or two towards me, yet still irresolutely; at length approaching me, he asked if my name was not Glenmorris, and hearing that it was, he embraced me as an old and beloved friend, and I rejoiced to acknowledge Edward Wallingford, whom I had known intimately while I was trying to learn to be a merchant under your father, and he was placed with the same view among the clerks of a great Jamaica house, from which the death of his elder brother, and his consequently succeeding to a very great estate, had removed him, soon after I had forsaken the desk.

"'He listened with the most lively interest to the account I now gave of myself, and seemed to participate in the eager anxiety to return to England, which on your account devoured me. He checked however the desire I testified to sail in the first ship that was going to England or Ireland, whatever it might be, and bade me consider, whether being again a prisoner, a thing so likely to happen, would forward my wishes. With difficulty he prevailed upon me to remain with him at one of his estates, till the convoy, appointed in about three weeks, should sail. He introduced me to his wife, a very lovely young woman, whom he had married in England, and I saw his two beautiful children, one of them yet in the cradle. While I rejoiced at his felicity, I enquired of myself in the anguish of my heart; "have *I* a wife? have *I* a child? or am I wretch without attachment, without connection, without hope?"

"'A month passed away—the sailing of the convoy was still delayed—I became half distracted with impatience—continually I saw you, Laura, in my restless sleep— I saw you sometimes pale, languid, a beautiful corpse, bearing in your feeble arms the infant which I was destined never otherwise to behold; at other times I thought you present, arrayed as I was used to see you, in youth, and health, and beauty—

I stretch'd my empty arms, you fled away!——[126]

What I endured is not to be described, nor will I dwell upon it. At last the moment came when I was to depart—I left Jamaica deeply impressed with the sense of Wallingford's kindness and friendship, and once more endeavoured to hope, that my misfortunes and your's might end; but at sea I never was prosperous—just as we believed ourselves off the Scilly Islands,[127] the fleet was dispersed in a storm, and the vessel that I was in, ran for shelter to an Irish port. As soon as I got on shore I went to Dublin, meaning from thence to have crossed to Scotland, if I could have found a vessel ready, but not doing so, I hastened to Carrickfergus, from whence I hoped to pass to Port Patrick;[128] but at Carrickfergus I was taken ill of a malignant fever—many died around me—however, after being three weeks on the brink of the grave, I once more set out to cross the sea, and afterwards my native country; but the winter was now advanced, and my frame was not yet strong enough to second my extreme impatience.

"'The last miles to Glenmorris I undertook, however, to travel on foot, and when I was about three miles from it I was overtaken by an highlander of my clan, whom I knew, though he did not recollect me, so greatly was I changed during my seven months absence—hardly able to command myself, and breathless with apprehension, I entered into conversation with him, and my consternation need not be described; it can only be imagined, when he told me that the Lady of Kilbrodie, on the certainty of my death, had taken possession of every thing for the laird her son, and had invited you to her house, from whence, soon after you had lain in of a dead child, you had disappeared, and was, at the time we were conversing, living with Lord Macarden. As the man related all this as matters of indifference, and seemed to know it merely as the general report of the country, I put a force on the violence of my emotions, and determined not to discover myself till I could be fully informed of the truth. On reaching my native glen, on coming within sight of my native house, that house so lately the scene of my felicity, oh! God, what were my sensations!—I entered a cottage, the master of which, I knew to be sincerely attached to me—fortunately his family was absent, and I revealed myself to him, beseeching him to tell me all he knew of you. When he had recovered from his first astonishment, he repeated nearly the same story as I had heard before, and at that moment, had I not been restrained by this faithful retainer, I should have rushed out, and have taken vengeance on you, on Macarden, and on myself.

"'But this honest fellow not only attempted to soothe me by such arguments as are usually offered on these occasions, but he said that there was a probability that all reports might not be true; that Menie, the maid who had lived with you, had spoken to the few she conversed with before she left the country in a very different manner; and that, though fear of the Kilbrodies had made her cautious, she had described the usage you received among them as very harsh and cruel—He implored me therefore to remain concealed, till I could myself be convinced of the truth.

"'With this advice I was at last prevailed upon to comply, and last night, which was only the second after my arrival, I set forth, attended by my faithful James, who undertook to shew me the place where he knew my infant had been buried, and which Menie had shewn to his wife as the spot that enclosed the last remains of the head of the Glenmorris family. Dreary and sad were indeed my contemplations!—but I was calm and cool, and therefore my guide more willingly obeyed my peremptory orders to leave me. I had passed above an hour alone among the ruined part of the abbey, not with any expectation of finding you in the inhabited part, but merely to indulge my own mournful reflections, while I considered what I should do to discover your real situation, when having left it to walk round towards the habitation of the family, which I had determined to enter in the morning to demand you, I saw you—I heard you speak—my living Laura was present to me—I held her once more in my arms.

"'And now, my dear dear love,' continued Glenmorris, 'no question remains but for the laird of Glenmorris to be restored to his property; vengeance must be for hereafter; for this wretched man, this Kilbrodie, has, as James has learned to-day, lost his hand by amputation, in consequence of its being shattered to pieces by Macarden's pistol.'

"'And Macarden himself,' enquired I? 'I know my Glenmorris is too generous not to feel interested for that noble minded gentleman.'

"My husband promised to enquire after him the next day, and then began to talk of what must be done to regain possession of Glenmorris castle, and the furniture and effects spared by the freebooters, which had all been removed to Kilbrodie; and for the first time of my life I listened to Glenmorris without pleasure—he soon perceived it, and I told him with my usual frankness, that though with him I could be content any where, yet that it would be long before, if ever, I should recover the terror that I had undergone; that it would be on many accounts a comfortless abode to me; and that I certainly should be happier any where else.

"Glenmorris then communicated an idea that occurred to him of settling in America, a country to which he owned himself extremely attached. 'But I will not,' said he, 'carry you, my Laura, to the seat of war, nor will I myself ever take any part in it. We will settle our affairs here, and go to Switzerland till peace shall enable me to realize our projects in America.' I need not say that I was happy to agree to this; and Glenmorris seeing how uneasy I was at the idea of his pursuing Kilbrodie, yielded to my tears and intreaties, and contented himself with the restitution which the Kilbrodies, overwhelmed with shame and confusion, were glad to make. The wretched woman who, instigated by avarice, had been the original occasion of all my sufferings, now repented, as much as she was capable of repenting, her cruelty and injustice; but Mrs. Mackirk, whose dread least her brother should attach himself to me, had betrayed me a second time into the power of Kilbrodie, had still a severer punishment for her unfeminine and malicious conduct; her brother, to whom the part she had taken became known, refused afterwards to admit her to his bed-side, or ever again to hold converse with her, while slowly and with much personal suffering he recovered as much strength as enabled him by easy journeys to reach London, where great medical skill at length restored him to health. Before he quitted Scotland, Lord Macarden sent for Glenmorris, and in the most noble and ingenuous manner begged his pardon for his conduct towards me, 'which nothing,' said he, 'but my ignorance of your being yet alive could possibly excuse.' Glenmorris, who knew the generosity of his nature, and who considered him as my deliverer, renewed with eagerness their former friendship, and then, as soon as we could regulate our affairs, and had raised what money we could, without oppressing the people who depended on the estate, we set out for

Switzerland. At Lausanne,[129] where we resided near two years, Medora was born, and is thus, like her mother, a foreigner in this country. Now my dear Delmont, having perhaps tired you with my somewhat eventful history, you shall not at this time hear of my continental adventures, which were less remarkable, and I will leave it to Glenmorris himself to relate his reasons for resorting to America, and the progress of his metamorphose from a Scottish chieftain to an American farmer."

CHAP. XII.

If Heaven a draught of heavenly pleasure spare,
One cordial in this melancholy vale,
'Tis when a youthful, faithful, modest pair
In simple guise breath out the tender tale
Beneath the milk-white thorn that scents the vernal gale.[130]

While in the delightful and calm pleasures of a society where confidence and mutual affection presided, the days of Delmont passed on, and while every one, as it passed, increased his ardent love for Medora, his admiration of her mother, and his friendship and esteem for Mr. Armitage, who was very frequently with them, spring gradually approached; and would have been greeted by Delmont with more than usual pleasure, had he not feared as much as he loved. The early notices of vernal delight, the copses, where a tender and pale yellow already preceded the opening leaves, from the tasseled katkins[131] of the sallow, the willow, and the hazle; the bright tufts of the spurge, and the hollow folds of the arum, the white violets, and half blown primroses lurking under the southern hedges, reminded him that April would soon arrive, and in April the future destiny of his life might be decided, for then letters from Glenmorris would probably arrive.—His courage to look forward often failed when he represented to himself how many difficulties might arise to prevent his union with Medora. "How often," said he, as he considered this matter with himself, "how often have I had occasion to observe, that men are frequently quite unlike the representation made of them. The world agrees to call Glenmorris a very singular character; but frequently are traits obliterated by time and change of circumstances, which the world has called singular. Traits of disinterestedness and high-minded generosity are those that to the greater part of mankind appear the strangest, because such they are incapable of imitating or comprehending—But whatever of these noble qualities Glenmorris might, in the earlier part of his life, possess, who shall say that in more mature age, when the character so often changes, he will be exempt from feeling the influence of other considerations, and as he has contended himself with many of the evils of a narrow fortune, how am I secure, that if his daughter is found to be heiress to a considerable property, he may be willing to give her to so poor a man as I may then appear to him?—Is it possible then, nay, even probable, that I may lose her? What will then become of me? Of what value will my life be without her? and where is the philosophy of having suffered myself thus to depend for the happiness of that life on the events of so many contingencies, and on the will of a man I do not know?"

Delmont, while he continually became absent and uneasy as these speculations forced themselves upon him, was careful to conceal the subject of them from Mrs. Glenmorris; and it soon appeared that his fears of losing the object of his love by her acquisition of fortune would not be immediately realized; for the time now being come when the adverse party were to put in their answer to the bill filed by Mrs. Glenmorris, they demanded time, and by a letter she received from her solicitor, it was evident, not only that these persons were determined to leave nothing undone to protract as well as to perplex the proceedings, but that the solicitor's zeal was very much abated, and his assurances of success sunk into doubt if not despondence.—

About the same time it was that Mrs. Glenmorris, having occasion for a small sum of money for her's and her daughter's current expences, had drawn for it, and given notice to the merchants entrusted with Glenmorris's affairs, that she had done so, when a few days afterwards she had the mortification of receiving the following letter—

London, Feb. 28, 17—
Mrs. Glenmorris,

Madam,
We are favoured with your's of the 20th current, and by desire of our J.P. are to inform you, that your draft for £25 to Robert Buckly, shall be duly honoured—Same time are sorry to remark that it must be the last which we can so take up, having been disappointed in not receiving remittances as expected, and promised, from Mr. Glenmorris, per last Halifax packet,[132] and it not being in our power to make farther advances of any kind, unless assured (and with security) of speedy repayment of same.—Wishing you health, we are for our J.P. Madam, Your very humble servants,

PETRIFY and Co.

Mrs. Glenmorris, to whom the want of money had never been familiar since her residence in America, now recollected, and with pain recollected, the mortifications she had once been exposed to in Scotland, when pennyless and dependent, and the dread of suffering again with Medora all the anxiety, and submitting to all that humiliation which attends on the unhappy suppliant for pecuniary aid, oppressed her so much, though she took great pains to conceal it from her daughter; but Medora, who listened to her sighs (as they slept in the same room), and knew that she passed many hours of the night in wakeful uneasiness, soon found that some additional cause of solicitude was added to those her mother acknowledged.—She named to Delmont, when they were alone, what she suspected; that her mother had lately heard something which added to her disquiet.—He imputed it to the delay threatened by the adverse party in the suit. "Oh! dear," exclaimed Medora, "the very name of that suit already puts me out of patience.—Why did my father ever suffer himself to be persuaded to send us to England to engage in it?—We never had these hateful perplexities in America.—My mother never lost her spirits there, and sunk into dejection as she does here!—Of what use will this money be to me if ever I should get it, if my mother loses her health and cheerfulness to obtain it? Oh! that we had never left America."

"Do you really wish so, Medora?" said Delmont, mournfully—"You wish then that you had never been acquainted with *me*, Medora?"

"No indeed; but to tell you the truth, my dear friend, were it not for you England would be utterly intolerable to me.—I never recollect a moment's uneasiness till I came to England, and since I have been here I am sure I have felt a great deal, and a great deal more than I have owned, for my mother suffers so much more if she believes me unhappy, that I keep it as much as I can to myself—but I know not how it is, the pleasure of our country rambles here, or the more agreeable hours of study, which would have charms as great as I used to find in the same occupations in America, are now always dashed by something which embitters our delight—Politics, and lawsuits, and old ladies finding out that we are people of bad character, and gossips repeating the malignant nonsense of other gossips—Oh! my dear Delmont, if ever I should belong to you, take me, take me to America!"

"I will, Medora, if I have not then the power of shielding you from every evil, every inconvenience in this country—for what other purpose shall *I* have in any country but that of making you happy?"

In consequence of this and some other conversation of the same sort, Delmont took the first opportunity that offered of speaking to Mrs. Glenmorris, who, determined as she was never to owe him a pecuniary obligation after the sarcasms thrown out by Mrs. Crewkherne, avoided any mention of the letter she had received, and imputed the dejection that Medora had noticed to the painful uncertainty she was likely long to be kept in, and her uneasiness at being so long absent from Glenmorris.— "Indeed Delmont," said she, "I should most heartily repent me of having yielded to the remonstrances of my friends, were it not that I believe *your* attachment to my poor girl, your affection for her, may make her happy, when all this vision of fortune is vanished for ever.—When I think how destitute she would be of friends if her father and I should die, and how young, how ingenuous, how lovely she is, I would see her, whether in affluence in England, or the simple American peasant, inheriting nothing but a farm, still secure of the protection of a man of honour, who loves her and knows her value."

Delmont forbore to press farther an enquiry, from which he fancied Mrs. Glenmorris shrunk, and on the other hand he endeavoured to quiet the apprehensions that still haunted Medora, and which she was not enough versed in dissimulation to conceal from him; yet these attacked her only now and then, and her natural chearfulness sometimes revived in all its seducing sportiveness and gaiety.—The perfection she attained, in delineating some of the earliest plants which the fields, as well as the garden and conservatory produced, was a source of the most delightful amusement to her, while her mother sat by her gazing on her with looks that expressed how dear she was—and Delmont, often "hanging over her enamoured,"[133] found in all she did, in all she said, in all she looked, new charms and attractions.

The weather was so fine that spring had now made a rapid progress.—The leaves of the beech were unfolded in the more sheltered spot; and thorns, willows, and hazles, were in the state which throws over the woodland scene, that light tint of verdure so soothing to the imagination, while the tender grass on every bank was strewn with primroses; the woods spangled with anemonies, and every little humid dell and grassy recess at their extremities gay with the harebell and lychnis dioica. Medora was not unwilling to own that spring in England, at least in such a situation as that in which she now beheld its progress, was certainly not inferior to the rapid vegetation of the western continent; and more true enjoyment it would have afforded to none, than to the little party at Upwood, if solicitude for the future had not embittered to them all the tranquil pleasures of the present moment.

The time, however, was arrived, when letters might hourly be expected from Glenmorris, and the anxiety of Delmont, as well as that of Mrs. Glenmorris, had an avowed object, which might well conceal the other painful apprehensions that preyed on the latter.—The messenger was dispatched every day to the post-town, and every day his return was waited for by them all with throbbing hearts.

Mrs. Glenmorris, who did not always accompany them in their walks, desired one morning to be left at home, while Delmont and Medora strolled out to a favourite wood, where, under the sheltering brow of the highest down, it spread itself on a declivity, and the green or glossy stems of the beech-trees formed the happiest foreground to the views of the country, with the sea beyond it, which met the eye to the south—the woods thickening behind, and in some places darkened with holly and thorn, gave these brilliant parts of the landscape all advantages of contrast.

It was in one of these nooks that Delmont, while yet a boy, had contrived a grotesque seat of the roots and boles[134] of two old beech-trees, that by some accident had been made pollards,[135] and had assumed phantastic forms, which, with a very little assistance, became somewhat like a low sopha. Nature had covered them with her greenest moss, and in some of the deepest crevices, formed by the twisting stems, she had planted tufts of wood sorrel.[136] Delmont and Medora here sat down. He gathered one of those beautiful plants, and was admiring its crimson stalk; its leaves of the brightest verdure, falling into folds like pendant hearts, and the delicate veins of vivid purple so elegantly penciled on its silver petals—when their remarks were suspended to listen to the nightingale, now first heard very near, and in full melody.

Every object around him conveyed to the heart of Delmont images of delight. Medora seemed as little disposed as he was, to break the silence of that delicious reverie they had both insensibly fallen into. But to Delmont it was not long a dream of unmixed delight. The very consciousness of present happiness, brought with it a dread that he might soon lose it. In vain he endeavoured to reason himself out of the weakness he was sensible of, as he looked at Medora.—"Am I never then," said he, "to enjoy one moment of delight lest it should not last? What feebleness of mind is this, and how ridiculous it would appear to me in another?"

But had he suffered an accidental circumstance to impress his mind with the notion, that impending evil is announced by some pre-disposition to sorrow and despondency in him who is to suffer, the present moment might have confirmed it; for hardly had they left their seat, when the servant who usually went for letters approached them.—

Delmont sprang forward to meet him—and took from him, not the answer he expected from America, but one of which this was the purport:

> Dear George,
> I have been in England about a fortnight, and should have informed
> you of it, but that one disagreeable thing or other has crossed me—and
> I did not imagine, from what I have heard of your *arrangements*, that
> you would be very willing to put yourself out of the way. However,
> things are just now in a situation that I must call upon you to give me
> the assistance, which neither your brotherly regard, or your respect for
> the name of Delmont, will permit you to refuse.—I can make nothing
> of Sir Appulby Gorges. He alledges, as a reason for not paying me the
> two-penny legacy left me by the man I once called uncle, that you have
> made no claim to yours, nor on behalf of the Miss Delmont's, which he
> seems to imagine a very sufficient excuse for with-holding the whole.
> Paltry as the thing is, it will be of use to me at this moment, and I must
> have it. You will therefore let me see you as speedily after you get this as
> possible, as well to set about this business, which I wonder you have let
> go by so long, as to lend me your name to get through another damn'd
> affair or two; and what money you have you must bring with you. Your
> philosophy and your farm has, undoubtedly, kept you in cash,
> notwithstanding your pretty Columbian,[137] whom I cordially salute,
> and shall expect to be introduced to her, when I have got out of the
> hands of these scoundrels.—I must find myself cursedly ill off, you may
> suppose, when it induces me to write so long a letter as this.
>
> Your's, till we meet,
> ADOLPHUS DELMONT
> You will find me at the old place in St. James's Street, April 28th, 17———

Surprise was instantly overcome by vexation, when Delmont (who hardly comprehended the meaning of what he ran over the first time) read this letter more attentively, and saw too evidently that his brother was returned to England extremely involved,[138] and called upon him to disengage him in the same spirit of arrogant selfishness, which had always, in their boyish days, been the character of Adolphus, who never could divest himself of the idea he had imbibed so early, that if not the whole world, at least all his own family, were to sacrifice every thing to any want or wish of his, as a matter of course. From the style of expence in which he had lived, even since he had been master of his actions, it was probable that all George possessed in the world, including his little property at Upwood, might be insufficient for his brother's purposes. From the time he had suffered to elapse, before his application, or even letting him know he was in England, it was most likely Adolphus had addressed himself to his former friends without success. The sum, therefore, which was to be raised was certainly considerable, and such as would perhaps reduce him to a state of indigence, which he could not think of suffering Medora to share. Nor was the pain these reflections gave him all.—The invidious hints that related to her, stung Delmont to the soul. Where could his brother have learned any thing that related to her?—and who was likely so to misrepresent her?—The contending passions that agitated his bosom were visible in his countenance, as he slowly walked on towards the house, almost unconscious whither his steps tended.

Medora, who saw the change which the letter instantly produced, enquired simply if it was from America, and hearing it was not, she cast a mournful look at Delmont, and hastened to rejoin her mother, unwilling to appear inquisitive after more information on his affairs than he seemed ready to communicate.—She saw her mother looking out for her from the door, and in her hand was a large packet of letters.—Dreading she knew not what, Medora hastened to meet her, and breathlessly asked, if there were accounts from America?—if all was well?—"All well, my dear girl," replied Mrs. Glenmorris, fondly embracing her—"Your father is happy, beyond expression happy, in your prospects; our beloved Delmont will be satisfied, will be delighted with all he says.—Come and read the letters together.—It is very long, Medora, since any thing has afforded such pleasure to your mother."—Medora could only answer by throwing herself into the arms of her mother, where she burst into tears—they might well pass, as at first they did, for tears of joy; but when Delmont appeared, and Mrs. Glenmorris, disengaging herself from her still weeping Medora, hastened to communicate to him the contents of these welcome letters, she was so struck with his look, that she retreated into the next room, and waited in a state of breathless suspence, while he read that she had given him.

To be relieved at once, and in a manner so flattering, from all the fears he had entertained of a refusal from Glenmorris, would have been, half an hour before, the circumstance on earth most delightful to him—but the cruel letter he had just read from his brother, had blighted all the prospect now so fairly opening before him—and might perhaps close it upon him for ever.

While he followed Medora slowly to the house, he had resolved not to speak of that unwelcome letter, at least not to relate all its painful contents, and to set out the same evening for London, and at least know what was expected of him, and what he could do, before he communicated any part of his uneasiness to Mrs. Glenmorris; but now, as it was impossible for him to dissemble without raising doubts of the ardency of his affection, he took the first moment he was alone with the mother, to tell her that he had received a summons from his elder brother to meet him in London, he was afraid on some very unpleasant pecuniary embarrassments; from which, though he knew not that he could relieve him, he could not let him remain in them, without making some effort for his service.

Mrs. Glenmorris no sooner understood this, than she pressed him to lose no time in setting out.—She saw, for it was not in his power to conceal it, how reluctantly he acquiesced in the necessity of his doing so; and that it might not be all bitterness, she began to speak of the services he could now do for her and her daughter; authorised by his approaching alliance, and even engaged by Glenmorris's own wishes, to assist them with his countenance and council. Now too she ventured to entrust to him the vexation she had lately suffered, from the cold refusal of the merchants to advance her money, which the bills Glenmorris had inclosed to her, would, she hoped, obviate.— These Mrs. Glenmorris gave Delmont to negociate for her; and having explained to Medora the necessity of his short absence, he at last thought of it himself with more resolution—yet when the mother and daughter were about to take leave, and return to their own cottage at an early hour, that he might immediately begin the few preparations necessary, Delmont found it impossible to suffer them to depart.—A thousand times he attempted to bid them farewel, with that firmness which he on most occasions piqued himself on maintaining—as often the words died away on his lips— he returned to repeat them, and again faltered and hesitated, till at length he discovered, that it would be much better if he saw them to their home, while his servant packed up a small portmanteau of linen, and that no time would be lost by this arrangement.—Mrs. Glenmorris saw how cruelly his mind was agitated, and she was at once softened and alarmed.—Something of more heavy import than what he had communicated, seemed to press upon his spirits; and while he forced himself away from Medora, who did not affect to conceal her sorrow at his departure, his eyes were filled with tears—the infection became general. The mother and daughter both sat at the window as long as Delmont was in sight; but when he arrived at the gate at the end of the field, and after turning his horse and looking steadily towards them a few moments, hastily disappeared, Medora, drowned in tears, retired to her own room, and her mother found it necessary to recal to her mind, so many instances of more real and lasting affliction, which she had borne with resolution, before she could acquire the composure which her own reason, and her tenderness for her daughter, equally directed her to assume at the present moment.

END OF THE SECOND VOLUME

VOLUME III

Chap. 1.

A man of *business* may *talk* of philosophy—
A man who has no business may practise it.[1]

Slowly and unwillingly as Delmont left the spot, where all his hopes of happiness were centered, he no sooner found himself a few miles from thence, than he proceeded with as much haste as if he expected to find happiness where he was going.

Nothing was to him so intolerable as suspence. He thought, though he had not yet known many, that when an evil presented itself positively before him, he should find resolution to combat or to endure it; but as it has often been remarked, that an English soldier immediately loses a great portion of his natural courage if he does not see his enemy, Delmont found his fortitude shaken by the apprehension of he knew not what unpleasant and embarrassing circumstances, which his brother had undoubtedly prepared for him; and he was impatient to know what he was expected to do, and how much of the future tranquillity of his life he was called upon to sacrifice to the splendor of extravagant dissipation, which, he supposed, must have occasioned the demand.

He arrived in London, where he had not been for four or five years, more fatigued than he had ever before felt himself, and leaving his horse at a livery stable, walked to a coffee house near the Hay-market, from whence he wrote a short note to his brother; but the messenger immediately returned, to inform him that Major Delmont was gone to dinner at Windsor with a large party, and was not expected to return to the house (which he had named as that he usually frequented) till the next day.

Delmont now repented of his haste. "This brother of mine," said he, "is as a fine man just what he was as an Eaton boy; now making every thing that relates to him of the mightiest import, and demanding the attention of all the world; then in half an hour forgetting this important matter, and flying after any casual amusement with as light an heart as if he had never felt a moment's concern."

Every object that now surrounded George Delmont was almost as new as it was displeasing to him. He felt himself no longer an inhabitant of the world he saw about him, yet had no ambition to renew his existence in it; and smiled when he saw one or two of his old school-fellows, now officers in the guards, come into the coffee-room, and stare at him a moment as a stranger, while probably some slight idea recurred of their having somewhere seen such a face; but then, as if the enquiry was not worth their trouble, they turned on their heels, and addressed themselves to those whom they were sure were men of the world. Nothing, except the alteration a few years had made in his person, was really changed in Delmont; but the more material change in *their* opinion would be, he knew, *that* which had happened in consequence of his uncle's marriage; and he could not forbear to wish that Adolphus had submitted to retreat from witnessing the consequences of such an alteration, rather than by again emulating the expences of his former associates, have become *really* an object of compassion, and to George many of these appeared to be fitter to excite pity than envy.

As he knew that there was no probability of meeting his brother before five or six o'clock, he contented himself with sending a note to let him know he was in London; and he then determined to give up the morning to execute the commission Mrs. Glenmorris had given him, which was, to procure acceptance and money for the bills from America.[2] He set out therefore for the house of the merchants on whom they were drawn, at the extremity of the city. He found the house, but waited a considerable time at the door, and was at length informed by a person, who had the appearance of a clerk, and who came out from the next door, that Messrs.————and————were bankrupts; that their effects had been seized about a fortnight before; and that their names were in the Gazette[3] of the last week.

Delmont's countenance expressed what he felt at the intelligence—He was but little acquainted with business of this nature, and knew not whether there were any means of retrieving a loss so considerable. The man still stood at the door, and Delmont enquired if he could inform him where any of the partners could be found, or how he could proceed to get the bills honoured?

"Oh! as to that," replied the man, "it is quite out of the question; the house is utterly ruined; ruined by the war—It was first shook by the bad turn of affairs in Holland, and some late losses and failures have done it quite up.[4] As to the bills, sir, they are waste paper. You may see the second partner, poor man; for he is safe enough at lodgings provided for him in St. George's-fields;[5] but as for the other, I suppose you wont think of seeking him, for he has settled *his* accounts for ever another way." Perceiving Delmont looked extremely shocked, the clerk added, "Why ay, sir, we were all very sorry I assure you; it was a terrible affair to be sure, and the more so as the poor gentlemen were in no wise to blame—'Twas entirely the times that did the job, and unlucky and perverse accidents falling out; and there are two fine young families quite undone, and turned out to shift in the world; but such things are common, I think, of late, and we shall have more on't no doubt if the war lasts; however, one gets used to every thing in time." Delmont then informed himself of the name of the attorney concerned for the bankrupts, and he set forth with an heavy heart towards his lodgings, meditating on the best means of softening, of rather wholly concealing this painful circumstance from Mrs. Glenmorris; and after some consideration nothing seemed feasible but to send her down the amount of at least one of the bills, without noticing the failure of those on whom they were drawn (who were not the same persons as those who had refused her any farther supply)[6] and he hoped to obtain time to try if nothing could be done to save her from losing the whole.

His brother was too impatient under his present embarrassments to wait for him;—at an earlier hour of the afternoon than he expected to see him, Adolphus appeared—The meeting was on his part conducted with the composure which ought never to forsake a man of fashion. "I have got into a disagreeable affair as to money, George," said he, "and I sent for you to be security for me, rather than commit myself *farther* to people that it is not altogether pleasant to be obliged to."

That what he asked of his brother might ruin him seemed either not to be considered, or thought of as only a secondary consideration, when to accommodate himself was in question. Ideas of his own consequence were so habitual to him, that he lost sight of every other consequence; nor did he ever stay to enquire, when any gratification or satisfaction was to be obtained for himself, how it would affect those whose services he required to procure it for him.

The sum for which he now desired his brother George to be security, was within five hundred pounds of all he possessed in the world, except Upwood.—George Delmont saw no way whatever by which it could ever be repaid, for his brother's fortune, though originally much more than his own, had been so far from profiting by the profession to which he had devoted himself, that it was, if not all gone, engaged beyond redemption; yet did the Major, (for he was now preferred to that rank,) require his brother's unconditional acquiescence in what he demanded of him, and seemed determined not to observe, what George could not help shewing, the reluctance with which he should make himself responsible for so large a sum.

"Why what use," said Adolphus, "hast thou, my honest George, for money? Thou art a philosopher, and bore with admirable composure to see the family title and family estate made over, by the act of a dotard, to a couple of brats that, I'll answer for it, have no more *claim* to them by blood than the children of my coachman. You could philosophize *then*, I remember, and represented, in the mightiness of your wisdom, to my father and to me, that we had no right to complain. Besides, you are a practical farmer, you know, and great in the first best *metier* of man, agriculture. While 'God speeds the plough,' you can never want money, and I dare say you have already got a drawer full of canvass bags stuffed with guineas; I am persuaded of this; because, had it not been so, you would have taken to some profession that might have given you an income, or you would have married. Why, I hear you refused a devilish fine woman with fifty thousand pounds? Prythee, if it is not too late, George, make her over to me. I always think, so far, your fine highflying notions of liberty are right enough; that I would have every man live as he will, and with whom he will, whether he mutters over a few musty words, or dares to appropriate some fair one to himself without them, all's right, and your ideas of freedom don't go beyond mine; but when a foolish fellow refuses to mumble over these said nonsensical words for fear he should lose his liberty I laugh at him. What a bourgeoise[7] idea! Tell me, George, faith now, was it such a notion that made thee coy to the fifty thousand pounder? Was thy morality—*Morality*, I recollect, is thy cant; was it *that* which told thee, that if thou marriedst the heiress, thou must give up thy little American, thy fascinating yankee?"[8]

Well as George Delmont had formerly known his brother's manner, he had been so long unused to it, and this attack on such an occasion was so extraordinary, that he knew not immediately how to parry it. At length collecting himself, and remembering that it was the son of a mother he had adored, his brother, who thus insulted him, he answered—That as to money, his *not* having entered into any profession, for which he thought himself not obliged to account to any one, was the very reason why he was likely to want money. "Farming, Major Delmont," said he, "never attracted me by the lucrative prospects it offered, but because I hoped to keep myself independent by it; and if it was in my nature to retort upon you, I should say, that I have done better to engage the little I had in any honest way of making its interest, than to lose it, as I am afraid you have done, among sharpers."

"Oh! no," replied the Major with astonishing sang froid, "devil take me if I have lost a guinea among the Greeks,[9] as you suppose; it has been all among ourselves; honest fellows who never do any thing but fight, or play, or love, or drink, and who are as poor as church mice; for example, I have taken up fifteen hundred pounds, for which I expect you to join me in security, to pay Jemmy Winsly, as honest a lad as ever lived. The whole regiment knows that he won it fairly. As for the other two thousand, it is dispersed round the world, and will find its way back to me some day or other; and you know that when I touch the pitiful legacy of that old dupe, our late uncle, which I shall make Gorges pay me before I leave London, this may be paid. But, George, you don't answer, methinks, about these *bonnes fortunes* of your's? If you have really resigned the banker's golden daughter, is your philosophyship disinterested enough to give a letter of recommendation to your elder brother? Eh, George?—On that condition I will not insist on going to Upwood, and being introduced to thy little humming bird from Massachusets. Nay, never look so gloomy and grave, Geordy, but answer."

"I have determined to keep my temper, Major Delmont," answered the younger brother.

"There you are right," interrupted the elder.

"And to do you all the service in my power," added he.

"Right again," exclaimed the Major.

"And you shall not find that to this paltry raillery you sacrifice the brotherly offices, which if, *as* a brother, I owe you, I would *more* readily pay you as a friend."

"It is all the same why you do them, if you do but do them speedily," said the Major, coldly; "so let me know at what hour this evening we shall meet; for I have promised to bring my surety in the course of the day, and am to have the fifteen hundred to-morrow.—So you wont make over your heiress to me?—Why, you blockhead, if I can get her you will be made whole again, and I'll do something handsome to help the next festivity of thy harvest supper, or for the gossips at the christening of my little Anglo-American nephew or niece.—Come, come, don't monopolize—You have made your election for the new world—put me, my dear boy, in a way to enjoy the old one."

"I do not know what folly you have in your head," said George Delmont; "but you ought to think me the most senseless of all coxcombs if I even named a lady, who was supposed to honour me with any partiality; I know of none such, nor can I guess where you picked up so foolish a story."

"Not guess! Why from whence is one sure of drawing all such delectable histories? our own aunt Crewk."

"Mrs. Crewkherne!—You have not seen her, or my sister, then?"

"Neither; but on my arrival, hearing of Caroline's marriage, and that the venerable old grimalkin[10] had taken Louisa with her, and accompanied the married folks into Suffolk, I wrote to her, hoping she would forget our old quarrels, and for the honour of her family send me a supply of cash.—Not a bit on't.—Instead of money the withered sybil writes me a letter to tell tales of you, as if that would do *me* any good! Oh! she has made a precious story of a Miss—Miss—faith I have already forgot the name, who *would* almost have you perforce whether you would or no; and then all about your taking into keeping—Oh! naughty master Geordy!—a sad little vagabond girl from the rebel Americans, whose father was . . . . . . let me see—I have destroyed the letter, I believe—but faith, I think she says he was transported for some grievous misdemeanour or other, and ran away with some woman of fortune, or who would have had a fortune if she had not been disinherited, and afterwards her husband, (for she is still handsome it seems,) sold her,[11] by way of bringing himself home, to your neighbour the philosophical, philanthropical, poetical Mr. Armitage, who contrived to introduce you to her daughter."

"And is this really," said George Delmont, "the story Mrs. Crewkherne has written?"

"Yes—or at least very like it—I cannot be very exact, for I read it over but once, and I don't know what I did with the infernal scrawl afterwards—if I did not burn it you may see it if you will."

Delmont then, as he walked with his brother, entered very gravely into a detail of all that had really happened; explained who Medora was, and the reason why she came with her mother to England.—The Major listened with a sort of half sneer on his countenance; and when Delmont concluded what he had to say, observed, that there were two ways of representing every thing; "and it must be owned," said he, "that our delectable aunt has made a most terrible and terrific history of this, while your's is just fitted for the amiable young heroine of a romance.—You know, George, I hold in utter abhorrence all interference in love affairs; so it will never be by me that an inquisition shall be set on foot, as to who has made the truest resemblance—but as your discarded nymph is probably one of those tender yet mutable dear creatures, whose affections are not absolutely so adhesive as not be transferable from one handsome young fellow to another not at all his inferior, I shall try to make an acquaintance with her. Prythee, George, where does she live?"

"Still with Dr. Winslow, I suppose; but I know not on what pretence you can introduce yourself, and I have no means of introducing you."

The Major then smiling, for he was never seen to laugh, declared he should be at no loss for an introduction as soon as he had determined to give himself that trouble; adding, however, with haughty bitterness, "it was once probable that I should have had the choice of all the girls of great prospects in England, instead of looking out, like a needy adventurer, for one of only moderate fortune like this."

The truth was, that whenever the recollection occurred, as it perpetually did, of the disappointment occasioned by his uncle's second marriage, the elder Delmont lost all that apathy, which, as a man of fashion, as well as from the pride and sullenness of his nature, he usually appeared to possess; and though he had conquered that unguarded and intemperate heat in which he had at first indulged himself, he could never think or speak with patience of an event that had deprived him of the fortune and titles of his ancestors.

The splendor and expence he now saw around him, among young men of family, his former school associates; their studied emulation of every form of profusion and luxury, and the sums which he nightly saw won and lost among them, with apparently the most perfect ease, were circumstances that corroded the heart of the Major, who made continual comparisons between what he was and what he might have been, if now, in the heigh-day of youth and health, he had possessed the income and the power of an Earl of Castledanes; an income which, he thought, all the gratifications he meditated could hardly affect, or, if they did, the power annexed to his parliamentary interest would, he knew, very easily repair any losses that, "in the course of a man's living," (that is playing and betting every night) might occur.

George Delmont, on the contrary, saw the scene into which he was thus, for a passing moment, initiated, with very different eyes.

Even while yet a schoolboy he had occasionally witnessed, though never experienced in his own person, the tumultuous vicissitudes that agitate the mind of the gamester, for at a public school this vice at least precedes, though for less objects, the more serious hazards of the adult—He had then fled from societies where it was pursued, because he felt no delight in the amusement, and knew that a great deal of mischief, and many hours of bitter repentance, follow its indulgence—He now saw some few of the same set, with whom he was at school, who yet held their places in the higher circles; but others had disappeared for ever—more than one by suicide, and some by degradation from the life they had attempted—while of those who yet remained, many were become profest gamesters; some were supported, as was alledged, by the sale of a beautiful wife, more by the sale of themselves.

Enough became known to him during the short time he now passed in attendance upon his brother, to convince him that all he had seen, all he had read, heard, or imagined, of the life of a gamester, fell short of the various modes of misery which, having chosen, that pursuit inflicted on men, many of whom were born to be the legislators, and all of whom might have been honours and supports to their country.

Yet once infected with this fatal passion, it seemed to be impossible ever to obtain a cure—and while George Delmont waited to execute deeds on behalf of Adolphus, deeds which made his own present fortune (almost all he was ever likely to possess) liable to demands incurred by this wretched infatuation, he saw with extreme concern that it was growing on his brother like a rapid disease; having discovered, that after he had been, by his persuasions, drawn away from tables where some thousands were staked, he shook off this brother who had embarrassed himself to serve him, as a troublesome monitor, and (under pretence of going to rest,) afterwards went forth to those nocturnal societies where hundreds only are hazarded, from whence he returned not till morning, and from whence, if he once brought any gain, he three times lost to double the amount.—"What am I doing," enquired George Delmont, when convinced of this; "am I really serving this unfortunate brother of mine, while I am thus impoverishing myself? Would it not be better, were I to reserve the small property I possess, to afford him an home when he shall have totally undone himself?—when he shall have been compelled, perhaps, to sell his commission,[12] and when he shall be convinced of the futility of those hopes with which he now solaces himself; while he reckons, that because he is a soldier, and of an illustrious family, he shall never vainly seek a resource in the favours of government?"

Delmont, however, had gone too far to recede; in the first slight explanation his brother had made of his difficulties, he had yielded too readily to his projects for their removal, and the hour was now fixed when he was to complete the sacrifice.—Besides the money lent, he had agreed to give a mortgage on Upwood for fifteen hundred pounds, which was nearly half its value; and as farther and very pressing claims against Adolphus were still to be provided for, he had personally bound himself with his brother to answer them in six weeks, by which time Adolphus had persuaded himself that the attorney, whom he had, on the recommendation of some of his gambling friends, entrusted, would have obtained from Sir Appulby Gorges the legacy of two thousand pounds left him by his uncle Castledanes.—This attorney, brisk, busy, and plausible, with great assurance and great volubility, became now necessarily introduced to George Delmont, who after hearing him parade and prate for an hour, in terms of which he understood very little, was prevailed upon to entrust him with the recovery of the demand he also had on his uncle's estate for the same sum.

These ill-omened affairs being adjusted for the present, much more to the satisfaction of the elder than of the younger Delmont, the latter prepared to return to Upwood.—He first paid an unsuccessful visit to the persons who transacted the business of the merchant, on whom Mrs. Glenmorris's bills were drawn, and had the mortification to find they were certainly worth nothing.

On taking leave of his brother, George thought it incumbent upon him to speak with more plainness than he had yet done, of the danger of that sort of life he seemed to be engaged in. "You have often, Adolphus," said he, "turned into ridicule the singularity of my mode of living—I will not ridicule yours, for it is too serious a subject. Let me entreat you to consider how little your fortune, aided by your profession, is equal to answer frequent and great losses at play; and do not be angry if I add, that the assistance I have now given you I cannot repeat."

Adolphus, without hearing more, replied in a supercilious tone, that if, from the trifling kindness he had done him, he assumed a right to criticise his conduct, it were well if he had sooner known the condition with which his friendship was to be clogged. "Go, dear George," added he, sneering, "return to thy native fields like a sabine hero of old,[13] and cultivate cauliflowers—but do not pretend to tell thy elder brother how he is to live, or with whom. Thy views and mine, George, were always and will always be wider than the antipodes, as to our general modes of life. Take no care for me—I shall live as it seemeth good unto me—probably stay in London while any society that one can live with is visible—and perhaps may, towards the dog-days,[14] stroll down to thy hermitage, though I had rather meet the devil, than have a distant view of Belton Tower; but I must see thy Columbina. Eh? George—you would not be jealous I suppose?—She who has been brought up among the strait-haired, lop-eared[15] puritans of the United States, will look with no predilection on a being like me."

Delmont, though he had no doubts of the opinion of Medora, was very far from wishing for the visit he was thus menaced with. The brothers parted with civility, but with a mutual diminution of kindness. Adolphus did not love George the more for being so deeply obliged to him, and George was shocked and concerned to see how little all he had done to serve him, was likely to be permanently useful.

CHAP. II.

Medora idola mia fra queste frondi
Fra quest' erbe novelle, e questi fiori
Odi come susarra,
Dolci scherzando, una leggera auretta
Che all' odorate piante,
Lieve fuggendo, i più bei spirti invola
E nel confuso errore,
Forma da mille odori, un solo odore.[16]

From a scene that had so painfully agitated him in London, and so baffled his philosophy, Delmont returned with eagerness to Upwood, where, in his own beloved hermitage, as he often called it, Medora, he hoped, waited to receive him with those smiles of tenderness and affection that have power to soothe every uneasy feeling, and restore to the heart the sweet sensations of hope and love; while in the understanding of her mother, and the steady and useful friendship of Mr. Armitage, he thought himself secure of finding counsel and relief against that dread of pecuniary distress, he now felt for the first time in his life; and which the conduct of his brother having created, was but too likely to perpetuate.

Medora was indeed ready to meet him with all the attractions of youthful hope, and with the most artless and bewitching tenderness; and while he saw her eyes beaming with the pleasure his return gave her, while leaning on his arm she led him through the garden, and seemed enchanted with every plant expanded, since his absence, to its early summer perfection, and seeming like her to greet him with beauty and freshness; when she then returned with him to the house, and with even infantine simplicity and gaiety, yet chastened by the sweet retiring sense of her own dignity, shewed him her drawings of some of his favourite plants and flowers, to which she had incessantly applied herself during his journey, Delmont, intoxicated with pleasure, forgot for the time that he had been unhappy. But the next day, when at their own habitation, he sought a private conversation with Mrs. Glenmorris, and related to her what had passed in town, and the engagements he had entered into with his brother, he saw, that however she endeavoured to conceal it, she suffered great pain from the recital, and once more he dreaded lest these embarrassments, however justifiably and even honourably incurred, should be the cause of his having Medora torn from him for ever.

In the friendly counsel and strong reason of Armitage, he had not now his usual resource, for this valuable friend was gone to a remote part of England, to attend on an old friend suffering under recent and most severe affliction; Delmont, therefore, who failed not to perceive the dejection which frequently stole over the countenance and manner of Mrs. Glenmorris, checked on his own part every expression of fruitless regret; and when they met, which was a least once in the course of every day, he seemed to have resumed his usual tranquillity.

The very effort to conceal and stifle uneasiness, arising from such causes as had lately perplexed him, half operated his cure. Every object around him served to restore him to peace; and he became ashamed of suffering the dread of pecuniary distress, which might never arrive, to disturb him. "Am I not," said he, "young and healthy— am I not a man?—and shall the mere luxuries and indulgencies of that artificial state of life, in which I have been brought up, have so much enervated my mind, as that the fear of losing them shall render me unhappy?" It was, however, the apprehension of being deprived of Medora, that had alone weighed on his heart. Habituated now to her society; more acquainted with her temper, and more apprised of what would one day be the perfections of her mind, he was no longer able to sustain for a moment the idea of losing her—and very vain was his youthful philosophy, when opposed to the remotest probability of such a calamity.

This apprehension, other letters from her father soon served greatly to remove. Glenmorris expressed in them even more than his former satisfaction at the prospect of his daughter's marriage; and gave his wife unlimited power to retard or hasten it as she saw fit. Whatever change of fortune Medora might experience, from the accession to a moiety of her grandfather's property, should, he declared, make no difference; he only requested that, either immediately before or immediately after their marriage, Delmont would accompany Mrs. Glenmorris and her daughter to America, and re-main with him three or four months.

"Of an ordinary character," said he, in a letter to his wife, "of one of those men who cannot exist without the accommodations, the luxuries, the frivolous amuse-ments of London or Paris, I know this would be asking a great sacrifice: but it is not to the fastidious fine man of the day I give my child; it is to a citizen of the world;[17] to one divested not only of local prejudice, but I hope of all prejudices; to him, who can live wherever his fellow men can live; to him who can enjoy the spectacle of a new conti-nent rising into a great state by its cultivators—*fair cities, substantial villages, extensive fields, an immense country filled with decent houses, good roads, orchards, meadows, bridges; where an hundred years ago, all was wild, woody, and uncultivated.*[18]—Such a man, I know from his letters, and from your account of him, Delmont is; on such a man I bestow the second blessing I have on earth; and ask only in return, that I may person-ally be acquainted with him, whom, on report, on correspondence only, I have agreed to entrust with the happiness of my life."

Delmont, who now saw in the universe only Medora, hesitated not a moment to promise Mrs. Glenmorris, that the will of Glenmorris and her's should be his; and that whether in America or in Europe, wherever that will should direct his steps, his most ardent wish would be to consult the happiness of the lovely creature they were to give him, and to shew how grateful he was for the gift. But now as the moment, when he was to call her his, evidently depended on her mother, Delmont made the most earnest and ardent supplications that it might not be procrastinated. He found, however, that Mrs. Glenmorris, contrary to her usual candid and unreserved manner, declined assigning any reason for the delay which she told him he must submit to. Her delicacy alone was the cause of this reluctant concealment. The truth was, that the law expences she had been drawn into, and the disappointment she had experienced (to which Glenmorris, being still ignorant of it, had applied no remedy in his last letters), were likely together to expose her to the severest distress for want of money; and under such circumstances, she shrunk from the idea of engaging Delmont in a connection, which would encrease the embarrassment that his brother's demands upon him had already brought on. It was painful to her to affect any mystery with him; yet this circumstance she felt herself compelled to conceal, assuming however a cheerful tone, and assuring him that whatever, besides the extreme youth of her daughter, were her reasons for desiring that the marriage might be postponed, those reasons could exist but a few months, and might even be removed sooner. Delmont vainly endeavoured to obtain an explanation; and as vainly pleaded that months were to him ages. She contrived to evade giving a positive answer, and endeavoured to soothe his mind, and direct it to such pursuits as she knew would have most power to lighten the hours of uneasy suspence now, and embellish those, which, when such happiness attained, might, without resources, be liable to satiety hereafter.

Nothing, however, of all he knew or was still in habits of studying, gave him any pleasure, but those branches of science in which he could instruct Medora. To cultivate that mind, on which his own must hereafter rely for the encrease of its pleasures, and the mitigation of the evils of life, was so delightful an occupation, that while he was engaged in it, he seemed to enjoy an heaven of his own creation.—Of many of the acquisitions which are deemed necessary in polished society, and pass under the name of accomplishments, Medora knew little in the way commonly known; she had a soft and particularly sweet voice, and sang most correctly by ear, but hardly knew a note of the gamut[19]—she had never learned to dance—there were no dancing masters established in America; but Medora, when divested of a little of that *gaucherie*, which diffidence gave, and which lent her as many charms as it deprived her of, was all grace and ease; her form was perfect, and every air and attitude, when unrestrained by a certain degree of retiring shyness, was exactly what art would have taught her, could art teach how to be truly lovely. With such an ear for musick, and a form so finely proportioned, her dancing wild and without rule, was like what fancy would give to the fabled nymphs of the woods;[20] with other arts, however, she was more scientifically acquainted; she wrote remarkably well—her style though simple was elegant, and her orthography faultless. Having learned to lisp her first accents in Switzerland, the French was in some degree her native tongue; and the servant who had brought her up, and had attended Glenmorris and his wife to America, being of that country, and still remaining with them; the French language as being most familiar to the whole house, was that in which their domestic conversations were always carried on.—There were few Englishmen so well acquainted with the Italian as Glenmorris, and he had taken great pains to teach it to Medora; while her mother, who was passionately fond of plants, had instructed her in describing them with the pencil, and she had profited so much, especially since they had resided in England, that she rivalled not only her mother, but some of the first artists in that branch of natural history. But something better than all this, was the good sense which every look and action of Medora expressed.

An ingenious, though somewhat fanciful writer has said, that he could distinguish a person of good understanding from one who had none, merely by their manner of walking;[21] and it is certainly true, that sense may be discovered by the air, the look, and the tone of the voice, even in asking or answering the frivolous questions of common introduction.

Medora, though yet in early youth, and with all that playful vivacity which in early youth only is so very enchanting, was always, amidst her half infantine gaiety, a person on whose understanding there was no one would hesitate to pronounce.—Her sensibility was not the exotic production of those forced and unnatural descriptions of tenderness, that are exhibited by the imaginary heroine of impossible adventures; it was the consequence of right and genuine feelings.—She loved, she adored her mother, and fondly fancied there was in the world no other such woman; nor was she less affectionately attached to her father; while that intuitive sense, by which she knew how to put herself, in imagination, in the place of another, and to feel for all who were unhappy, made her active in doing all the good that her age and situation admitted. It was impossible to look in her face, though it was far from being regularly handsome, without being sensible of some degree of interest; and whether she smiled archly, or her features expressed a pensive affection, excited by fearing her mother was uneasy, or by some story of distress, there was always a charm in her countenance, not the less attractive for being very versatile.

Delmont, as he looked at her, or listened to the artless yet just sentiments she uttered, when she was induced to talk to him, doubted whether more knowledge of the world, and more of that information which books are supposed to give, would not rather tarnish than heighten the beauty of a mind, that now seemed to resemble one of those lovely spots, where every object that enchants the sight, or delights the imagination, is assembled; but which, if once the hand of art is introduced, loses that *Arcadian* bloom,[22] for which no improvement in clearing its wild rocks, or calling in more extensive prospects, can compensate. Medora, though she had read and heard of such things, knew not how to imagine, that fraud and perfidy, malice and selfishness, were so thickly sown, that the unguarded and innocent were every moment liable to suffer from them in the commonest walks of life.—Medora knew not, and it was impossible for her to understand, from any correspondent feelings in her own breast, that there were people who would detest her for being young and lovely—who would despise and shun her if she was poor—and yet calumniate without knowing her, if she should ever be distinguished either for talents or fortune. She knew not that there are a race of men, who live ostensibly and avowedly on contention and pecuniary disputes.—Others, who exist on the follies and fears of mankind, which they therefore encourage and perpetuate.—That there are persons, who fly from every subject that can give them trouble, or interrupt their epicurean indolence, even if angels were in question; and that there are figures, born of women, and calling themselves men, who have no feeling but for themselves—and can hear the wretched execrate their fate, and see the bitter tears of despair, without one sensation of humanity.—To learn all this was a sad lesson, and Delmont, who hoped to fold this lovely girl to his heart, and shelter her from every evil of life, sometimes enquired of himself why he should pollute her mind by describing the monsters "of the great Babel,"[23] where she might never be; then, as if he had foreseen how different was to be her fate, from that he had fondly projected, he thought that occasions might arise, in which perfect ignorance of the ways of the world would occasion a feebleness of spirit, and a want of that feminine fortitude, which, in many instances, is not the most unnecessary quality in the mind of a woman.

Their reading then, besides poetry, of which the whole party was passionately fond, was extended to history, and to such pictures of human life as authors represent; but Medora, who liked very few of them, continually contrived to exchange the study of the morning, for some of those travels, where descriptions of scenery are exchanged only for accounts of the simple lives of the natives; or for such books as describe the great phenomena of nature, and speak rather of the works of God, than of those by whom his fairest works are too often disfigured.

Engaged as they were every hour in some study or pursuit, equally agreeable to them all, the days passed away but too rapidly, and when Delmont had been returned above a month, it seemed as if he had hardly been a week restored to the manner of life he so much loved.—From the delicious visions of its continuance after his marriage, and return from America, with even an encrease of felicity, he was suddenly roused by two letters.

One was from the man of law, who had procured him on his personal security, jointly with his brother, a part of the money Adolphus Delmont had borrowed; the other was from another person of the same profession, who informed him, that as to that sum for which he had agreed to engage Upwood as a security, and which was to be replaced with the legacies left by Lord Castledanes, and to be furnished by both the brothers, there was no hopes of obtaining it from Sir Appulby Gorges, who seemed resolved to delay the payment by every means in his power; and both these gentlemen agreed, that George Delmont must immediately be in London, to answer as well personally, as by his property, for the engagements he had made; for Major Delmont was gone to Ireland, and the time when this business must be closed was directly at hand. As this was the first intelligence Delmont had received of the departure of his brother for Ireland, he was as much vexed as any thing of such a nature could vex him. He now saw both his person and his little estate deeply pledged, for a man who appeared to have no principle whatever; he saw pecuniary embarrassment overclouding a life, which he fondly thought his having avoided those fettering connections and professions, by which men of family usually make what is called their way in the world, would have permitted him to dedicate to literary leisure and love.

Thus, without any fault of his own, he was compelled to enter into that wretched sort of contention, which lawyers foment and live by. He was to resign the independence he had so earnestly endeavoured to preserve, and could now hardly call his own the house he inhabited. To procrastinate, however, was to encrease the evil—he therefore determined to go to London, and endeavour, by personal application to Sir Appulby Gorges, to procure the legacies, which would in a great degree relieve him.

Without any misrepresentation or insincerity, Delmont accounted to Mrs. Glenmorris for the necessity of this second absence. He simply told her, that his brother's careless improvidence had left some business undone in London, which would become more intricate if he did not immediately attend to it, and that he thought it therefore best to go for a few days. He next endeavoured to prevail upon her and Medora, to take up their abode entirely at Upwood during his absence; this, however, Mrs. Glenmorris declined, but promised to be there every day, and that Medora should go on with a series of wild flowers she had begun, and laughingly added, that they would make a Flora Upwoodiana;[24] for from the great variety of ground around this beautiful spot, which consisted in some places of a rich marly[25] earth, in others of a strong clay, where the soil of one field was a light loam, and adjoining to it a heath, with sand in one spot and peat earth in another, and where a stream starting from the foot of a chalk hill, wound through rocky hollows and woody hangers[26] of beach, there was an assemblage of almost every plant indigenous to England, except those that are the immediate inhabitants of the sea-shore.

With an heart heavier than it had been on his first parting, Delmont mounted his horse; Medora saw that he made every effort to appear cheerful, and therefore resisted, as well as she could, the disposition she felt to weep. Her mother, contrary to her usual custom, was unable to assume the semblance of cheerfulness; but the moment Delmont was gone, told Medora she was going to write in a closet, particularly appropriated to her use, at Upwood; and then, in a walk alone through Delmont's favourite copse, Medora gave way to a weakness, which she felt to be a weakness even while indulging it; but accustomed always to reason with herself, she soon began to enquire whether these useless tears could be agreeable to her lover—"Ah! let me rather," said she, "occupy my time in something that may be pleasing to him." She returned to her drawing table, and went on with the flowers Delmont had himself gathered, and placed there in the morning.

"Sweet pliability of the human spirit," says a favourite author,[27] in speaking of the facility with which books beguile our sorrows; "sweet pliability of man's spirit, that can at once surrender itself to illusions, which cheat expectation and sorrow of their weary moments; and, when the path is too rugged for the feet, enable us to get off it to one, which fancy has strewn with rose-buds of delight."

And thus it is with those who are fondly attached to music[28] or to design; for each have power to charm away many disquiets. There *are*, undoubtedly, sorrows which neither these nor any other occupations can mitigate, which distract the head and unnerve the hand, while every object appears hateful, and most so those that were in happier times the most delightful: but for a young person, yet uncrushed by heavier afflictions, and for a transient vexation, there is nothing more desirable than to urge the mind to one of these occupations. What can more forcibly illustrate the force of such impressions, than that interesting passage of Rousseau. He describes himself walking with Madame De Warens. "En marchant elle vit quelque chose bleu dans la haie, et me dit: voilà de la pervanche encore en fleur. Je n'avois jamais vue de la pervanche, je ne me baissai pas pour l'examiner, et j'ai la vue trop courte pour distinguer à terre les plantes, de ma hauteur, je jetai seulement en passant un coup d'oeil sur celle là, et pres de trente ans se sont passés sans que j'aie revu de la pervanche, ou que j'y aie fait attention. En 1764 étant a Cressier avec mon ami Monsieur du Peyrou, nous montions une petite montagne au sommet de laquelle il a un joli salon, q'uil appelle avec raison, belle vue; je commençois alors d'herboriser un peu; en montant et regardant parmi les buissons, je pousse un cri de joie. Ah! voila de la pervanche! . . . . . Le lecteur peut juger par l'impression d'un si petit objet de celle que m'ont fait tous ceux qui se rapportent à la meme epoque."[29]—Medora, thus occupied, soon felt the pain appeased, which Delmont's departure gave her; she imagined his early return, the pleasure she should have in showing him her improvements, and hearing his criticisms. It was now the middle of June, and the country was in its most luxuriant beauty— Myriads of the sweetest and gayest of those plants that form the chaplet of the English Flora[30] were every where scattered in profusion beneath her feet, and she herself might have sat for a picture of that delicious imaginary deity, as for a day or two after Delmont's departure she returned home from her wood walks loaded with innumerable flowers; but then (and Medora half fancied that his absence had something to do with it) the weather grew so extremely hot, that even her early morning walks, and those of an evening after sun-set, became extremely fatiguing. To this oppressive state of the atmosphere succeeded a day of the most tempestuous weather, thunder and lightning, hail and wind. Another interval of excessive heat lasted almost a fortnight longer, and then storms seemed to clear and cool the air, till they were again succeeded by heat equal to that felt under the torrid zone.

Medora often spoke to her mother of the fatigue Delmont must suffer in London—"a place," said she, "which he hates so much, and which I have heard you say is so disagreeable in hot weather. Oh! would he were returned." Other days however passed on, and Delmont came not: he wrote punctually, and Medora, fortunately less read in the ways of the world than her mother, was satisfied with his letters, because they expressed his ardent and even increasing affection for her; but Mrs. Glenmorris thought she perceived a great deal of effort to hide his uneasiness, and while he merely mentioned that the business was cruelly spun out by the people he was concerned with, she perceived that, impatient as he had reason to be at frivolous and vexatious delays, there was yet some pain yet more serious, though he endeavoured, with his usual pretence to[31] philosophy, to pass slightly over it.

Among other proofs of this, was his continual charges to Medora to pursue her drawing—He sent her down a new set of colours, some fine papers, and every useful article, and added a petition, that he might find on his return his favourite plants, which he was thus deprived of seeing in bloom, described by her pencil.

Mrs. Glenmorris, though less able even than he was to divest herself of her particular anxiety, that now increased but too rapidly, was willing to disguise her solicitude, and in a sort of half playful, half melancholy disposition, answered this request, by the describing the premature approach of Autumn in the following

SONNET:

The fairest flowers are gone!—for tempests fell,
And with wild wing swept some unblown away,
While, on the upland lawn or rocky dell,
More faded in the Day-star's ardent ray;
And scarce the copse or hedge-rows shade beneath,
Or by the runnels[32] grassy course; appear
Some lingering blossoms of the earlier year,
Mingling bright florets, in the yellow wreath
That Autumn with his poppies and his corn
Binds on his tawny temples.—So the schemes
Rais'd by fond HOPE, in life's unclouded morn,
When sanguine youth enjoys delusive dreams,
EXPERIENCE withers! till scarce one remains,
Flattering the languid heart, where only reason reigns![33]

Very different from such ideas as beguiled the house at Upwood were those which Delmont was under the necessity of submitting to; in spite of all his philosophy they disturbed his peace, and threatened to deprive him (if their causes could not be removed) of the independence he had so anxiously cherished, and so fondly flattered himself with enjoying.

It would be painful to follow him to the chambers of Mr. Solicitor Cancer, of Gray's Inn, and from thence to those of a special pleader in the Temple.[34] These were the persons employed by Adolphus, and through whose advice George had engaged himself, both personally and by consenting to pledge his landed property; they now looked very grave on the subject, seemed internally to blame the conduct of the elder brother, yet would not speak out, or direct the younger how to act, so as to escape the very unpleasant consequences that were likely to follow. The counsellor hum'd and haw'd; observed that there had been great, very great errors committed; things were very unlike what he expected; he understood matters to be very different, or should have advised otherwise; and at length ended by contradicting every thing he had said before; and George Delmont found he was himself answerable for all the money Adolphus had borrowed, whose failure in fulfilling the conditions had made him liable to the whole. This, which was confirmed by the conduct and manner of Cancer, was indeed an exercise for his philosophy; yet he would patiently have supported it, had he not dreaded, as the probable consequence, the loss of Medora. Though he never dissembled the truth, he considered it unnecessary to enter into the mortifying detail to Mrs. Glenmorris, till he was sure of the extent of the evil that was to be encountered; his letters, therefore, contained sketches of the persons he saw, most of whom were new to him, and therefore struck him as being strange; for he had never before had occasion to converse with such sort of people as lawyers, or had he ever before seen Sir Appulby Gorges, who, though now a statesman, belonged once himself to the honourable fraternity of attornies. "Sir Appulby," said Delmont in one of

his letters, "is a strange being; he appears to me never to have had any intellects beyond what might qualify him for the same honest calling excercised by his father, who
was, they say, an exciseman, at some little town in the north—This man, who is
celebrated for the effrontery with which he has made his way to fortune, by dint of
accommodating those above him, and who, to the basest humiliation towards them,
adds the most supercilious insolence towards every one who has been incapable of so
rising; whose heart is hardened by undeserved, unexpected prosperity, and whose head
is so confused, that no one can be astonished at the disorder which pervaded the
department he directed when he was in office—this Sir Appulby Gorges received me
with fawning civility, and by way, I suppose, of dazzling my imagination by his magnificence, carried me round his improvements. Lavish and absurd expenditure of money
wrung from the people (for such one must consider the wealth of this ephemeron)
could give me only pain. I affected not satisfaction I could not feel, but hastened to
enter upon the business which alone could have brought me to Sir Appulby Gorges.
He was very reluctantly brought to the point; at length, as I resolutely returned to it
again and again, he began in his odd north country snapping sort of croak, which it is
not easy to describe, to say, 'that in regard to the legacies left to myself and my family
by his late dear friend, Lord Castledanes, [*he* the friend of such a man as my uncle!]
would give orders and directions to his solicitor, Mr. Anthony Cancer, that all might
be *seen about*, ordered, and settled, as should be *right*, *proper*, and *legal* (legal is a
favourite word with Sir Appulby) and he hoped, and believed, and supposed, that the
whole would be arranged, concluded, and finished in a short time, as should be legal
and proper, and proper and legal, according to the different demands, claims, and
expectations of the several persons and parties to be interested in, or benefitted thereby,
according to their said several claims, liens, demands and rights, be the same more or
less, lying and being in the estates, fortunes, assets and effects, sums of money in
government securities, mortgages or bonds, or lands, domains, forests, woods, cop-
pices, parks, warrens, marshes, heaths, orchards, gardens, or paddocks, commons,
rights of common, fee farm and copyholds, service or fines, mansion houses, barns,
stables, granaries, out-houses, mills or granges, rivers, water-courses, fisheries, manors
or reputed manors, or any other property or properties, wheresoever and whatsoever,
of his late dear and honourable friend the Earl of Castledanes, as by his last will and
testament, recourse being had thereto, shall and may, or will more fully appear.' You
smile, dear madam, or perhaps are half angry at my writing all this unintelligible
jargon, but such, I do assure you, is the style by which Sir Appulby hopes to drive
people away, whom he has no inclination to satisfy; and I own I was for a moment so
astonished by his impudence, that though 'nil admirari'[35] is my usual maxim, I remained almost five minutes silent. Sir Appulby taking advantage of it, found it convenient to suppose I was willing to await his reference to his solicitor, Mr. Anthony
Cancer, and putting by me, cried, 'I rejoice, Mr. Delmont, to see you among us—I
hope you are come to lay claim, in a certain line, to some of the place of consequence
which your birth, and rank, and family pretensions entitle you to—I assure you I shall
be glad of it.' I replied with very little attention to this civility, 'If you mean, Sir
Appulby, that I am come among you in a political sense, I answer, that I neither am,

nor ever intend it; nor should I ever have left my name at your door, had you not been executor to my uncle, which I am heartily sorry for, and which is the only part of his will I ever regretted.'

"You may easily suppose how a man, who has never listened to a word of truth, nor spoke one for years, *looked*, on hearing this plain sentence. He can occasionally be extremely deaf, and thought it convenient to have this auricular imperfection at the present moment; for far from resenting what I had said, he affected not even to have heard it, but went on to say how much he had been told of my talents, and of the great and advantageous marriage which he had understood with great pleasure it was in my power to make with that fine young woman, Miss Goldthorp, the daughter of his old friend [all rich men are his friends]. In a word, I found he had his lesson from Mrs. Crewkherne, and was at her instigation, as well as for reasons of his own, disposed to exercise on me those *attractive* qualities which have obtained for him the name of *Old Rhodium*.[36] You, dearest madam, who are so perfectly in possession of my sentiments, will believe, that after this discovery the dialogue did not proceed much farther; I flung from him with disdain and abhorrence; and though I have seen him once since, our conversation was on my side peremptory, on his evasive, and much less civil. I never will pollute another sheet of paper, if I can help it, with his odious name; and have merely told you what this man is, because I foresee delays and difficulties arising from his having the management of my uncle's affairs, that will demand the exercise of more patience and philosophy than I may be able to find, if, besides the extreme unpleasantness of holding any communication with him, it occasions the necessity of longer absence from the place which you and Medora have rendered so dear to G.D."

CHAP. III.

Però ch' ogni altro amaro chi si pone
Tra questa soavissima dolcezza
E un augumento, una perfezione
Ed un condurne Amore a piu finezza.[37]

Delmont had been a fortnight absent, and Mrs. Glenmorris perceived from the style of his letters, that though he forbore to say so, his perplexities increased, and that there was but little probability of his immediately getting through them; yet with the slight mention which he thought necessary to make of business, he mingled so much of literary anecdote and sensible remark, that she hoped the affairs still detaining him were not likely to have any very unpleasant consequences. Though possessing herself an unusual share of fortitude, she did not imagine so young a man as Delmont, with acute feelings and warm passions, could so easily call off his mind from any very embarrassing circumstances, and apply it with so much gaiety to matters of amusement. But all the worth of Delmont Mrs. Glenmorris could not yet know, nor how greatly his constant habit of reflecting on the real value of every object had given his reason the ascendency over all those inferior motives which agitate the greater part of mankind. It is only at a later period of life that most minds, however strong, dare venture to leave the beaten track, and deviate into sense and freedom. Delmont, at an age when the laws of the country had but just emancipated him from tutelage, was already exempt from the dominion of those paltry pleasures and servile prejudices that influence the conduct, or disgrace the understanding, of the generality of young men.

There were, however, vulnerable parts about his heart, and to those a strange fatality seemed to direct its arrows. The first sentiment he had been conscious of was tenderness for his mother. Whatever *she* had loved was dear to him; every sensation she had encouraged had taken deep root in his memory and in his heart; and his affection for his family had formed a part of the system grown up in his mind, which neither the haughty coldness of Adolphus in their early youth, nor the essential difference of their characters, since the character of each were formed, had been powerful enough to destroy—He carried it perhaps to excess. Even while his brother mingled a degree of insult with the demand of service he expected, and while his reason told him how probable it was, that he was, in gratifying Adolphus, undermining the structure he had fondly imagined of his own happiness, he had not courage to refuse engagements that, had no such happiness offered itself, must have embarrassed his affairs, and embittered his life with the interference of lawyers, and perplexities among money lenders, which his temper was ill calculated to sustain.

Of all this he was soon to become perfectly conscious; for he suddenly received information, that his brother, Major Delmont, whose departure for Ireland was already sufficiently embarrassing, had so entangled himself there, and had contrived to collect so many disagreeable circumstances together, that nothing could either extricate *him*, or relieve George himself from the consequences of the engagements he had entered into, but his immediately going to Ireland himself.

Once convinced of this, George Delmont hesitated not a moment. He wrote a short letter to Mrs. Glenmorris, explaining his reasons for the sudden resolution he was thus compelled to take, and departed directly.

Medora, who had hitherto considered his absence as necessary, yet likely to be of short duration, and without future consequence, could not now think of the distance that was to divide them without extreme pain. Her mother was unwilling to encourage any of that languor of spirit, which avails nothing, and of which the indulgence in early life is very likely to enervate the mind, and to render women helpless and burthensome on occasions where to exert resolution may be their duty; she therefore sometimes gravely reasoned with her daughter, representing that Delmont had certainly gone to Ireland merely to accelerate the time when he might return to them freed from all solicitude about these unpleasant affairs relative to his elder brother; and that there was nothing worth being alarmed at. At other times she applied to ridicule; and laughing, besought her daughter not to sigh like a young heroine of a novel for the absence of her shepherd: but, in fact, the heart of Mrs. Glenmorris was very heavy; the gaiety she thought it necessary to assume was forced merely to prevent Medora's perceiving uneasiness that every hour as it passed served only to increase. The events of her past life had taught Mrs. Glenmorris, that by calmness and fortitude alone, remediable evils are to be sustained and conquered, and she endeavoured to resist the pain which the present circumstance unavoidably inflicted on her; but it was not in her power to call her mind from the uneasy recollection that she was almost without money, and that she knew not where to obtain a supply. Her soul revolted from the degradation of soliciting Mr. Petrify, the merchant, who had transacted Glenmorris's business since she arrived in England. To him, however, she had twice written, expressing her distress at the circumstance of the un-honoured bills, and her anxiety to know when she might expect a remedy against the inconvenience she might soon sustain from this circumstance; but instead of any offers of temporary assistance, which the obligations he formerly had owed to Glenmorris might have induced a liberal minded man to give her, she was saluted by such lines as these:

Mrs. Glenmorris,
Madam,
Your's received—am concerned at your having been still disappointed as to the bills drawn on A and B.—but can say nothing thereon.— Hoping for good news remain, Madam, your humble servants,

J. Petrify and Co.
P.S. Should we hear any thing thereof will drop you a line.

Mrs. Glenmorris, while dreading for Medora rather than for herself, the pecuniary distress thus rapidly approaching, had concealed it even from Armitage, to whom she might have written, and whose liberal spirit, greater even than his fortune authorised him prudently to exert, would have relieved every uneasiness, and even have resented that she had for a moment felt them while he had the power to assist her—But it was her knowledge of his generous temper and straitened circumstances that withheld her; and because she also knew that nothing relative to her and Medora would long be concealed from Delmont. Armitage had, in common with his friend, ideas on the subject of money very different indeed from those that influence the generality of the world—They both thought that true friendship consisted in a mutual communication of the good, and a mutual alleviation of the evils of life—They were not like those who profess unbounded regard, yet shrink from any man, whatever may be his merit or their pretended affection for him, the moment there appears any danger of his wanting pecuniary assistance; and Mrs. Glenmorris, well aware of this singularity of character, could not determine, situated as she was now, to reveal her difficulties to either of her friends; yet she doubted whether it was not false pride, and whether it would not subject her to their blame, should it at any time be known.

Now, however, since Delmont was gone, her scruples would have been partly removed.—While Armitage was at Ashley Combe, he had always assisted her in settling with Mr. Petrify, and even in lesser concerns; and had he now been there, and from thence visited her as he used to do, she could hardly have hidden from him the distress that preyed on her mind; she had therefore determined to write to him; yet as the first fleet of American merchant ships were soon expected, and she thought it certain she should hear from Glenmorris, she delayed from one day to another to begin a letter, which it was very unpleasant to her to write at all.

In the mean time Delmont waited some days at Milford Haven[38] for a wind to convey him to Ireland.—The delay might perhaps render this journey, so reluctantly taken, abortive; and he thought with heaviness and uneasiness of a long separation from all he loved, while the business he was thus compelled to engage in included every sort of association that he most hated.

The tedious interval of waiting for a wind he amused by writing to Mrs. Glenmorris and Medora an account of his journey through Wales.—The country was now in its richest summer luxuriance; but the wild and magnificent features of nature; the mountains and cataracts, which on a former tour had so much excited his admiration, he passed by, if not with indifference, at least with very different sensations from those with which he had formerly surveyed them.

Some of these variable sensations he described to Mrs. Glenmorris, in a letter which he wrote to her from the sea-port.

"You can imagine," said he, "nothing more unlike my former self than I am at this moment.—I now enjoy nothing as I did five years since, when I passed two months in wandering over Wales—and yet I am in perfect health—I am unfettered by the restraints which at that period of my life it was fit I should submit to; and I know that in a few weeks I shall return to you and Medora, in a few months belong to you, and that the rest of my life will be dedicated to her.—There is something very childish, and certainly very unphilosophical, in this foolish depression of spirit, and in quarrelling with the wind, which pertinaciously insists on blowing a steady gale exactly from the quarter which makes it impossible for me to put to sea.—I was not, however, at all more reasonable during my journey—Every beautiful scene made me regret that I was alone—I wanted you and our lovely little paintress to share with me, or rather to create for me, the pleasure I now could not find without you.

"The last day of my journey, I sent my servant on before in the chaise, and hoped to fatigue myself by walking the eight miles that remained to the next stage; for since I have left Upwood I have acquired a foolish custom of setting up half the night, yet without being able to sleep the rest of it—I left the road and followed, on a green hill that rose on one side, a path made by the sheep and their shepherd, which, still mounting, brought me among other hills, till I came at once to a point where this mountainous tract sinks suddenly into a narrow valley, bounded by precipices of greater height—a valley which Nature seems to have cleft on purpose to make way for a wide and shallow but noisy stream, clear as the purest crystal that bursts from the caverned bosom of an immense crag, quite unlike the turf clad downs I had been passing, and dashes away over fragments of stone, till by the intervention of other high grounds it is lost to the eye—its banks are green and smiling; copses creep half way up the hills, and tufts of oak and ash aspire above the hedge-rows that part the emerald meadows on either side.—The evening was beautiful, and the last rays of the sun, before the hills shut them out, fell on a little thatched cottage immediately under the path I was in, so that I looked down upon it with its haystack, hop-ground and orchard, all in miniature.—I sketched it for Medora, and the anticipation of the delight I shall have in sitting by her while she completes the composition, was the only pleasurable idea I had felt in the course of the day.

"The labourer returned from his day's work before I left my post above his humble happy dwelling, and at the same moment a boy of about eight years old, mounted on a Welsh poney, who had been sent to the neighbouring town, came with his basket, and the good woman, with one in her arms, and four younger children following her, surrounded them both—I added the group, as they stood, to my landscape.—The picture of domestic felicity is always delightful; I would have descended by the path that led immediately to the cottage, and have asked for a glass of milk, and directions how to proceed on my way, but one of those fits of moodiness which I catch myself in too frequently, and which will degenerate, perhaps, into sullenness and ill-humour, stole, I know not how, over me—and I determined, as I had yet light enough, to recover the road from which I had deviated, without exchanging a word with any human being. Within half a mile I crossed the rivulet by a bridge, and soon regained the way to the post town, where, not desirous of remaining, I ordered horses immediately, and without stopping, except to change again, arrived here at midnight. I bade poor Clement, who was much more disposed to sleep than I was, go to his bed as soon as he had supped, and I wandered out alone to the sea-side. Satiated as I, and as I suppose two-thirds of the reading world have been with sonnets, your's from Upwood has reconciled me to them, and even tempted me, as I traversed the beach, to sonnetize myself—

SONNET.
Huge vapours brood above the clifted shore,
Night o'er the ocean settles, dark and mute,
Save where is heard the repercussive roar
Of drowsy billows, on the rugged foot
Of rocks remote; or still more distant tone
Of seamen, in the anchored bark, that tell
The watch reliev'd; or one deep voice alone
Singing the hour, and bidding "strike the bell."
All is black shadow, but the lucid line
Mark'd by the light surf on the level sand,
Or where afar, the ship-lights faintly shine
Like wandering fairy fires, that oft on land
Mislead the pilgrim; such the dubious ray
The wavering reason lends, in life's long darkling way.[39]

"You will laugh perhaps, as Armitage sometimes does, when he says of me, that

My nobility is wonderful melancholy,
Is it not most gentleman-like to be melancholy?[40]

And when he supposes that I shall be enlisted, if I commence sonnetteer, among the moody minstrels, 'mewling out their imaginary miseries in magazines.'—I murmured myself to sleep however, invoking the presiding powers of every point of the compass to blow favourably, or forbear to blow perversely, so that I might have sailed this morning; but I find it still impossible, and here I must wait, endeavouring to recollect and apply all the wise sentences I have ever heard recommending the virtue of patience; I have no books, and must now wander about till night, or return, after the walk I am going to take, to tell you again the nothing that occurs in my present mode of existence.

"I laid down my pen, and sauntered out along the beach, watching if any of those signs appeared by which the seamen told me change of weather might be foretold on this coast.—But there was nothing that could flatter my hopes for to-morrow. I gathered a few wild plants that grew on the rocks, and among the shingles of the shore, then threw them peevishly away; and went into a cottage about two miles from the town.—The inhabitants, an old fisherman and his son, who are occasionally pilots, were within at their early supper; I entered into conversation with them, and the more cheerfully continued it, because they assured me that there would be a change of weather within twelve hours.—They saw my impatience for it, and the old man, put into good humour by the half-crown I had given him, said; 'Ah! master of mine, you have for certain some fair lady waiting for your honour t'other side the water, for I saw you last night asking about the wind.'

"'There may be other causes for my impatience,' said I, 'besides a fair lady; I may have business you know, for my self or for my country.'—

"'Belike so,' cried the man, 'but methinks your honour is rather of the youngest to take much hoe about all them there botherations of business and politics and the like.—Ah! master, I've seen somewhat of your lovers as they're call'd, and indeed have reason enough to remember um, for what betided about a *misfortunate* young gentlewoman who you must know would needs come and lodge in this here old cottage of mine—and it was the last lodging she ever had occasion for.—I took up her poor body indeed, and because they said she was *felo de se*,[41] I think, they would not let her be buried in our church-yard,—So my wife and I, my wife was living then, it will be two years agone come old Michaelmas,[42] and our Ned, who help'd dig the grave; we buried her in the lee of the great Mavor Crag; I mark'd the place, for I thought some time or other perhaps her friends might make enquiry about her.—But none ever came, and to this hour we don't know who the poor young gentlewoman belong'd to.—She had always paid us very handsome, week by week, and the night before she made an end of herself, she said to my dame, that being sure she should not live long, she desired that if in case she died, we should take her cloaths—every thing but just a sheet to wrap her in, and a sort of a piece of glass that open'd and shut, that was done about with little shining stones, and tied round her neck; and *that* she said must be buried with her; and so it was, for I would not have touch'd it for all the world.—My wife dress'd her in a suit of white linen, for she owed us nothing, and we could not bear to wrong her after she was dead.—So we kept the rest of her cloaths, and a little gold box that she had, for above a year; and we put, as our landlord at the Harp advis'd, an advertisement into the news-papers, to tell any body that belong'd to our lodger where they might come for the things that belong'd to her; but hearing no manner of tidings of nobody, and times going hard with us, while my poor wife lay sick, at last we sold the rest of her cloaths and the box; but there be now some books and papers which mayhap might tell who she was, if any body cared to enquire; but, poor soul, I reckon she had disobliged her friends for this said love; and so they took no reck[43] of her.'—

"You may imagine my curiosity and pity were at once excited; I enquired the name of this unhappy young lady, and how she died?

"'As for her name,' replied my informer, 'she bid us to call her Elizabeth Lisburne; but I do not believe that *was* her name. She used for the month she was here to send our Ned, or else I used to go, every day to the post at Milford for letters directed to that name; but only one came—and after that she grew more and more sad and sorrowful till we lost her.'

"'And how lost her?' enquired I.

"'Why, master, she was wont every night to go wandering about. Indeed she did not do much else all day, and I thought she expected some body from over the water—for *she* was always making enquiry concerning the wind—but one night (she had shut herself up in her room all the day before) one night, she went out, took a small boat, a sort of punt that serves me to go after my lobster pots to the rocks, and pushed it off as we suppose, till she came into deep water, and then threw herself in. When we found she did not come in to go to bed, I said nothing of what I was afeard on to my wife, but I miss'd the punt, and thought how it was. With the next tide her handkerchief came ashore, and the little boat; I went out, and found her body!'

"The old man, whose rugged outside hid a compassionate heart, pass'd his hand across his eyes.

"I asked him if he would let me see the books and papers he mentioned? 'Yes,' he said, 'willingly if your honour desires it, I suppose it can do no harm to the poor deceased; perhaps—but 'twill be of no use at all now; or else they that left such a fine young creature to die, ought to be made to feel for their hard heartedness; but there! *she* would be no better for it. She don't suffer any more pain now. I hope she is in heaven, for all our justice, and the parson together, would not let her be buried in holy ground. I hope God Almighty took pity on her for all that.'

"If I was affected with this conversation, I was much more so on perusing some of the papers, which I purchased, together with five books, of my honest fisherman; bidding him consider what I gave him for them as the last legacy of the unfortunate Elizabeth Lisburne. I told him, that as she had certainly wished to be concealed,-I should not think it right to seek those who might have belonged to her, but that if any accident ever brought them to my knowledge, I should endeavour to obtain for him a farther reward for his humanity to an unhappy stranger.

"I then—for I was disposed to indulge the melancholy thoughts this incident had given rise to—I then bade him lead me to the Mavor Crag, near which this luckless young woman was buried. It was a place fit to meditate in on such a story. Beetling rocks, barren, cold, sullen, hung over a stony cove, and on all sides enclosed it, save when it opened to the sea. One point, towering above the rest in tremendous majesty, threatened to overwhelm, in the first violent storm, the humble grave of the poor suicide, which was now marked by a slight rising in the sand, and by two blocks of lime-stone which the fisherman and his son had placed at the head and feet, imitating, as well as they could, the receptacles of the dead so mark'd in those places, where those who die in the common course of nature are huddled together in consecrated earth! The remote and lonely grave of this poor girl, she would perhaps have preferred, had she chosen one. I sat down on a fragment of rock near it, and when I read the following lines, contained among several copies of verses, I was glad, methought, that she was dead. They seem to have begun as an invocation to the winds, but her mind, overwhelmed with anguish, started from imaginary beings to its real and deeply felt sorrows.

> Ye vagrant winds yon clouds that bear
> Thro' the blue desart of the air,
>   Soft sailing in the summer sky,
> Do e'er your wandering breezes meet
> A wretch in misery so complete,
>   So lost as I?

> And yet where e'er your pinions wave
> O'er some lost friend's, some lover's grave,
>   Surviving sufferers still complain;
> Some parent, of his hopes depriv'd,
> Some wretch who has himself surviv'd,
>   Laments in vain.

> Blow where ye list on this sad earth,
> Some soul-corroding care has birth,
>   And grief in all her accents speaks:
> Here dark Dejection groans; and there
> Wild Phrenzy, daughter of Despair,
>   Unconscious shrieks.

> Ah! were it death had torn apart
> The tie that bound him to my heart;
>   Tho' fatal still the pang would prove;
> Yet had it sooth'd this bleeding breast,
> To know, I had 'till then possest
>   Hillario's love.

> And, where his dear dear ashes slept,
> Long nights and days I then had wept,
>   Till by slow-mining grief oppress'd;
> As memory fail'd, its vital heat
> This wayward heart had lost; and beat
>   Itself to rest.

But still Hillario lives; to prove
To some more happy maid, his love;
   Hillario at her feet I see!
His voice still murmurs fond desire,
Still beam his eyes with lambent fire,
                  But not for me!

   Ah! words, my bosom's peace that stole,
Ah! looks, that won my melting soul,
   Who dares your dear delusion try,
In dreams may all Elysium see,
Then, undeceiv'd, awake like me,
                  Awake and die.

   Like me, who now abandon'd, lost,
Roam wildly on the desart coast,
   With eager eyes the sea explore;
Yet hopeless watch, and vainly rave,
Hillario o'er the western wave
                  Returns no more!

   Yet go forgiven, Hillario, go!
Such anguish may'st thou never know,
   As that which checks my labouring breath;
Pain so severe, not long endures,
And I have still my choice of cures;
                Madness or death.[44]

"The verses are not very good, yet they are surely the language of the heart, and mine aches when I think of what this poor unfortunate must have endured. Who could she be? I will not lift up the veil that her misfortunes have rendered sacred. To us in this world, she is now nothing.

"I have some other pieces that I at this moment think worth transcribing. I will keep them, however, till my feelings give me leave to consult my judgment. The shade of poor Elizabeth, sitting forlorn on her desolate rock, and resolving on suicide, is now too strongly before me. I have something to think for to night, that may make me think less of the distance, alas! the increasing distance between us.

"Adieu! for the present, to my two dear friends.

"G.D.

"Thursday morning.

"The wind has chopped about, as the sailors term it; I do not exclaim, with my favourite Sterne—Oh! the Devil chop it[45]—for I want to be gone. Yet alas! what has it done for me—what will it do for me, but put the sea between me and all I love on earth!

"But they call me!—Once more farewel!"

Chap. IV.

Why dost thou treat me with rebukes, instead
Of kind condoling cares and friendly sorrows?[46]

When a summons, which she reluctantly obeyed, came from her solicitor as well as from Mr. Petrify, to attend in London, the low ebb of Mrs. Glenmorris's fortune was such, as left her hardly twenty pounds in her pocket, and she had some weeks lodging to pay.—She had resolutely declined any assistance either from Delmont, when the affair of the protested notes was necessarily explained to her, or from Armitage, whose fortune was very limited, and whose continual exertions in the service of his friends, left him often in distress himself. The doubts, therefore, of Mrs. Glenmorris whether she should be able to support, even for a short time, the expences of sojourning in London, had made her for a moment entertain the thought of going to the house of a friend of her family's, and once of her's, a Mrs. Grinsted, to whom some time before she had applied, with an hope that this lady, who was an intimate at the house of Lady Mary, might have brought about a reconciliation; but either the attempt was languidly made, or the long rooted antipathy of the dowager to her youngest daughter was become too inveterate, for it proved wholly fruitless.

Mrs. Grinsted was the daughter of a baronet of very ancient family, but who being born at a remote distance from the title, (for there were nine or ten persons to precede him, who all died in the course of a few years) had been taught to shuffle through the world as well as he could, with especial care however not to sully his honourable lineage by the degrading acquisitions of commerce, so that having only one of those places under government, that are created for the convenience of younger brothers of a certain rank, whom the people support (on account, no doubt, of their hereditary virtues) and having no talents to rise above such of these places as are attained by being abject without being useful, Sir Griffith Grinsted succeeded to the baronetcy, without carrying any thing to it in support of the honourable distinction; yet he felt all the dignity of the bloody hand, and would not have yielded a day's precedence after the first year, when James the first created a baronet, for all the wealth of Leadenhall street.[47]

Not that he thought contemptibly of money.—His necessities, and the deprivations he was compelled to submit to, that he might apparently make a figure not altogether unworthy his great descent, had taught him that money was an excellent thing—and his three daughters had imbibed under him and a weak mother, the most confirmed notions that title was the first, and fortune the second requisite for happiness; they were persuaded, that with those who possessed neither one or the other, it was a sort of degradation to them to associate, but that where both these advantages were united, they could not testify too much respect.

In consequence of the operations of such "salutary prejudices"[48] on feeble minds, the elder and the younger of these ladies had given themselves up to be humble and useful friends[49] in great families. The second too had commenced her life in the same line, but had most terribly deviated from the hereditary haughtiness of her race, and cast her eyes on an handsome butler, the son of a neighbouring farmer, who served in the family where she resided as a companion. The man, either dazzled by the honour, or tempted by the thousand pounds which was in the lady's possession, forsook

> Plump Dolly's fresher charms,
> For wither'd, lean, right honourable arms.[50]

and Mrs. Mary Grinsted became the wife of Jonathan Sawkins. Her elder sister, who was by that time possessed of a considerable fortune, left her by the dowager with whom she had lived, was so shocked at this terrible blot in the escutcheon[51] of her house, that it was supposed to hasten her death. She died, however, never having suffered the odious name of Sawkins to pollute her chaste and honourable ears; and left all her property to her youngest sister, Mrs. Judith Grinsted, who now enjoyed it in a very genteel house in a fashionable street, occasionally however passing a few months with her great friends, to whom she was not the less welcome on account of the affluence she now possessed.

She had become, in the course of the last five or six years of her life, acquainted with a set of those well-informed ladies who have acquired the cant name of blue stockings.[52] Among others she was known to Mrs. Crewkherne, but no great intimacy had subsisted between them.—Mrs. Grinsted thought herself of the very first class, and associated chiefly with those who were the most acknowledged patronesses and judges of literature. She was besides always busy in a political circle of her own, and deriving a certain degree of consequence from her independent situation, was become a very useful personage among her friends; and all her friends were people of the very first consideration. Of course all that related to them was matter of the utmost gravity; and Mrs. Grinsted, whether consulted on a suit for court, or a settlement on marriage; whether she was to make a party for the Opera, or bring about a match between two poor young victims who both happened to be rich; the good lady was always of opinion, that she had the most momentous affair in the world on her hands, and that a business of such weight could not be entrusted to any but a person of so much importance as herself.—On Mrs. Glenmorris's arrival in England with her daughter, she had addressed herself to this lady, whose continued intimacy with her mother, might, she thought, have opened between them a means of reconciliation.—Mrs. Grinsted received her overtures with cold civility, till she understood that her business was to try to regain a share of Mr. De Verdon's fortune, and that her principal reliance in England was on the friendship of Mr. Armitage; but as soon as, from the openness of Mrs. Glenmorris's character, these circumstances became known to her, she changed her tone; observing, "that she had a great and almost filial tenderness for the dear venerable Lady Mary, and wished Mrs. Glenmorris very well—had known her, indeed, from a child, as well as her dear and sweet sister the late Lady Daventry; but the present was too delicate an affair for her to interfere in. She had so sincere an affection and respect for all parties, that she felt herself unequal to the arduous task of attempting a *conglomeration* of the unhappy divisions that had arisen between persons so nearly and dearly *approximated*; and whose characters were so full of amenity, and so perfectly *eximious*."[53]—Mrs. Grinsted was a lady of prodigious ratiocination, as well as of profound information: her style, though not always clear, was elevated, and she hardly ordered her footman to bring her tea, without contriving to ornament the sentence with a sesquipedalian word.[54]

It is certain that nothing but doubts whether she should find resources to support herself and her daughter in London, would have induced Mrs. Glenmorris to have thought for a moment of fettering herself by a temporary abode in the house of Mrs. Grinsted. The idea was now soon given up, on her describing her quandom[55] friend to Medora, who besought her mother not to think of it. They drove therefore to an hotel; where, notwithstanding her finances were, by paying her country bills, and leaving money with her old servant, reduced to a very low ebb, Mrs. Glenmorris hoped to be able to remain for the few days she was likely to be in town; and it was probable she would very soon receive letters from America. Her purpose, however, was to introduce her daughter to Mrs. Grinsted, still entertaining, in the fondness of maternal affection, an hope, that if Lady Mary, now above seventy, could through her means see Medora, she would admit her to her heart, and to some share at least of her grandfather's fortune.

Checking, therefore, her dislike, she once more determined to try if Mrs. Grinsted could not be induced to befriend her; but she first went to her interview with Mr. Petrify. While she found that from this man, (whose heart seemed callous to every impression but those made by his own pursuit after money) there was no chance of her obtaining any temporary assistance, she thought that there was something in his manner very strange and mysterious. He was naturally cold and repulsive, especially when he thought it likely he should be asked for money; but now he seemed even more than usual to wrap himself up in reserve. He said, these were times when a man might well be justified in refusing pecuniary help even to his own father; that for his part he never was so hard run for money.—Knew not where to get wherewithal to pay his duties—and stocks—stocks were so low that his hands were tied—absolutely tied; and even if it was not so, he must say, that he should be unwilling to advance any thing for carrying on the suit at law against Lady Mary, for he had it from good authority that it would come to nothing—"Nay, even your own solicitor thinks so madam: And if them there gentlemen are of opinion against their client, why there's but little to expect."—Mrs. Glenmorris at last discovered, that the careful merchant had enquired of her attorney as to the probability of her success; it was evident that the deficiency of money on her part had operated on both these honest gentlemen alike, and that they foresaw, reasoning from analogy, that her's was one of those cases, where

The gilded hand of power would shove by justice.[56]

This unpleasant conference with Petrify ended, by his telling her, that he had closed his account with Mr. Glenmorris, and found that there was a balance in his favour of seven pounds five shillings and nine-pence halfpenny, which, money being at this time particularly scarce, he hoped she might make it convenient to pay. Mrs. Glenmorris now felt how mortifying it is to be under pecuniary obligations to those we despise.—So far from being able to pay Mr. Petrify his seven pounds five shillings and nine-pence halfpenny, she had not seven guineas in her purse, nor did she know where to go for a supply.

With an heart more heavy than she supposed any embarrassment of this kind could have occasioned her, Mrs. Glenmorris returned to the hotel, and went from thence to Mrs. Grinsted, whom she found at home; noticing as little as possible the cool formal manner in which she received her, entered on the subject of her affairs with the candour and openness which was eminently a feature of her character. Mrs. Grinsted at first affected to make light of any right Medora could have to a moiety of her grandfather's fortune.—"It does indeed," said she, "seem to me highly improbable that your poor good father, who was *incontrovertibly* a gentleman to whom no *incogitancy*[57] could rationally be imputed, should in his will, on which he had *indubitally* meditated with due *profundity*, leave any echappatoire,[58] any *evasionary indecisiveness* on which a doubt might apend, as to his meaning and intention; and I am free to confess, that might I offer in great humility my counsel, it should be, my good madam, that you should *apologetically* address yourself to your worthy and venerable mother, Lady Mary, and endeavour to engage her *maternity* to *advigilate*[59] over the interest of your daughter not as a right, but as a favour. Perhaps her ladyship might *amortise* the *interdictory prohibition* that in the early *effervescence* of parental indignation she *fulminated* against you,[60] and that her affections might not be irrecoverable."

If Mrs. Glenmorris listened patiently to this parading affectation of superior talents, it was not because she felt the advice reasonable, or believed it to be sincere, but she wished to procure a quiet hearing for what she desired might be, and knew would be, repeated to Lady Mary; and a quiet hearing she was sure would *not* be obtained but by first lending a certain degree of attention to the *verbosity* with which Mrs. Grinsted *obnubilated*[61] her real meaning.

When an interval at last occurred, Mrs. Glenmorris, without denying the justice or the sublimity of the oratorical and elaborate flourishes she had heard, took out the opinions that had been given as well against as in favour of Medora's claims; and then said, "My daughter has had the good fortune to engage the affections of a man of sense and honour, to whom she will soon be married. Her rights will then devolve upon him, and he will probably pursue them in whatever way the persons whom he has the means of consulting shall direct. In the mean time, it is so much my wish to return to Mr. Glenmorris, and so little my inclination to disturb the tranquillity of Lady Mary, that if Mr. Delmont . . . . . ."

"Mr. Delmont!" exclaimed Mrs. Grinsted, "pray, what Mr. Delmont? it is not *he* I apprehend who has a disposition to espouse your daughter?"—

"There may be many of the name," replied Mrs. Glenmorris, "I do not know which *you* mean—I am acquainted with only one Mr. Delmont. He has, however, a brother."—

"You certainly cannot mean any of Lord Castledane's family?" said Mrs. Grinsted.

"What is there so improbable in it?" enquired Mrs. Glenmorris.

"Oh! I had heard—I understood that Mr. Delmont—I am acquainted with some branches of his family—was to be united to a Miss Goldthorp, a young woman of considerable fortune, and I heard also—but perhaps—yes certainly—I have been misinformed.—So he is engaged to *your* daughter then? and it is of *you*, madam, that some friends of mine really spoke who have been in that neighbourhood?" A series of artful questions followed, and from the candid answers of Mrs. Glenmorris, who had no notion of concealing any thing, Mrs. Grinsted was soon mistress of every particular relative to Delmont, and to her own views. She then desired leave to consider in what way it might be best to open to Lady Mary the present situation of her daughter and grand-daughter, and promising that they should hear from her in a few days, they parted. Mrs. Grinsted seasoning her adieu with rather more kindness than she had received her with.

Mrs. Glenmorris returned to her beloved girl. Her friend hastened to inform Lady Mary, that the pretensions of the innocent Medora, (which she knew the old lady was determined to oppose at any expence, and by any means) were likely to be supported by a man, whose intelligence they could not doubt, and whose perseverance they could not baffle.

Impotent as may appear the malice of an old woman of seventy, Lady Mary was rich enough to point, with the most infallible of all metals, the arrows that she from every quarter aimed against the peace of her own child. Mrs. Crewkherne had been of her council; from Mrs. Crewkherne she had learned the legend of Mr. Armitage's supposed attachment, and of Medora's being brought by him as a bait to George Delmont, with a thousand other stories invented by falsehood, and registered by malignant imbecility.—And Lady Mary had even affected to deplore, as the greatest calamity of her life, that she ever had such a daughter as Mrs. Glenmorris.

Sir Appulby Gorges was also one of those whom Lady Mary was in habits of consulting. Loadsworth and Brownjohn, the council and attorney employed by Major Delmont, had also been occasionally her's; for the old lady was naturally extremely litigious, and had continual quarrels with her tenants and her tradesmen; and now no sooner was a consultation called, in consequence of Mrs. Grinsted's intelligence, than the lawyers, who well knew the solidity of Medora's claims, and that they would be established whenever they were properly pursued, declared to Lady Mary, that unless ways could be found to put off this intended marriage, nothing would prevent Medora's recovering near half her grandfather's fortune. This task, however, was no easy one. The character of Delmont, open, brave, generous, daring to think and act for himself, was well known to them.—And Mrs. Grinsted had assured them, that such was Mrs. Glenmorris's situation, both on account of her want of money and her anxiety about her daughter, that the moment Delmont returned from Ireland, which might every hour be expected, the marriage would take place; and though she had discovered that immediately afterwards the whole party would depart for America, there was but little doubt, but that Delmont would take care the recovery of his wife's fortune should not be neglected.

It was a maxim of Mrs. Grinsted's, that evil might always be done, and in short, that it lost its nature, and was no longer evil, when good was intended to be promoted by its commission.

These accommodating maxims of policy are so convenient, that they are adapted as well to the enlarged views of the statesman, who deluges half the world with blood, and sweeps millions from its bosom, (for what he pleases to term general good, or the balance of power) as to the minor projectors in private life, whose limited operations only allow them to contrive, how to render a few couple of simpletons miserable by tying *them together* (however ill suited they may be) for *their good*, that is, that they may be sure of a certain income, probably six times as much as they can possibly want; and that though each may execrate their being ten times a day, they shall at least do it in a coach of their own, or in a splendid house, surrounded by an handsome establishment.

It was therefore positively with the best *intentions* in the world, that Mrs. Grinsted became the active agent in plans which Sir Appulby Gorges and Loadsworth the coun-sellor, though feed[62] on the other side, together with Brownjohn, with her assistance, contrived, to relieve Lady Mary from all solicitude; to prevent Delmont from commit-ting so great a folly as following the dictates of his heart, or of his jacobinical friend Armitage; and at the same time to compel Mrs. Glenmorris to return to her husband, that Lady Mary might not have her latter days, good Lady! disturbed by her doubts or her convictions as to the conduct of this her rejected daughter. It was sufficiently calamitous that the excellent and venerable person had lost her elder daughter, and seen her fairest hopes levelled with the dust; because Lady Daventry had left no male heir, Lord Daventry had married again, and had another family, so that all the later expectations of the Lady Mary were centered in Miss Cardonnel, her grand-daughter, whom she had taken to live with her; and it would have been a misfortune not to be endured, had this young lady, owing to a mere mistake, a flaw in her grandfather's will, (which however there were some suspicions of his having left on purpose) been heiress to only ninety thousand pounds instead of an hundred and seventy, which she would possess if this unreasonable claim of her obscure cousin could be baffled; and it was the duty of every one of her friends to prevent so great a calamity. Sir Appulby Gorges thought it particularly *his* duty, because he intended one of his grandsons, about the same age, should marry Miss Cardonnel, if her fortune did not suffer this diminution. The duty of Loadsworth it undoubtedly was to prevent his client Delmont, from forming an alliance with a stranger rejected by her family, and the daughter of Glenmorris, whom he hated, because there had formerly been some pique between them, which Glenmorris had long since either had indifference enough to forget, or magnanimity enough to forgive.

Loadsworth however never forgave—and he gloated with infernal delight over an opportunity of revenging himself on Glenmorris. A better instrument for this pur-pose could not be found than Brownjohn. With very little understanding, he had a daringness of conduct, and a fluency of speech which were for a moment imposing. Not supported by the regular practice of his profession, but living by shifts, he con-trived by impudence, and a flourishing way of talking, to pass himself upon those who had not found him out as a man of fortune; and being a most adventurous lier, he was the less frequently detected, because nobody imagined such assertions, so roundly and confidently delivered, could be false. Destitute of every principle, and totally without feeling, he made no scruple of taking money from two adverse parties; and once (per-haps oftener) when he was employed for an imprisoned client, he paid the debt for which he was entrusted with the money, at the very moment when he gave notice to have a detainer for a still larger sum, put in by his client's enemy; and fixed him in prison (he thought) for life.

Either by recommending clients to Loadsworth the special pleader, or from coincidence of disposition, they had long preyed together on the unfortunate. And when such men were employed under the direction of Sir Appulby Gorges, and aided by Cancer, and while the collusion with Mrs. Crewkherne and Mrs. Grinsted as auxiliaries, was supported and set on foot by Lady Mary de Verdon, cemented by her money, and rendered fearless by her interest, the mischief was to be dreaded, but could not be calculated, that might arise from its whole force being directed against the unprotected Mrs. Glenmorris and her innocent Medora.

CHAP. V.

Virtus repulsæ nescia sordidæ,
Intaminatis fulget honoribus;
Nec sumit aut ponit secures,
Arbitrio popularis auræ.[63]

Though Mrs. Glenmorris concealed the event of the conferences she had held, and struggled to hide the pain they had given her, Medora was too intelligent, and had already acquired too much judgment to be deceived. She saw that the cheerfulness her mother assumed, was entirely the effect of effort; and that while she talked of their prospects, and their plans of happiness, her voice betrayed anguish rather than hope, and her looks refused to second what her tongue uttered. Medora could not bear this; her mother had never before concealed any thing from her, and it now seemed, as if she thought her too weak to resist the misfortune, whatever they were, that threatened them, or rather her mother for her sake; unable to endure the sight of her mother's uneasiness, while denied the comfort of sharing it, she determined to speak to her, and if possible to put an end to a state so insupportable.

"I know," said she, "you are very uneasy my mother; and why do you attempt to conceal it from me?—For God's sake let us give up this chace after fortune, and return to my father; Delmont will not be less attached to me—fortune is no object to him—it is none to us, if my father determines to remain in America, where we had always enough for our wishes. We were very happy before this project of going to law, that I might share Miss Cardonnel's fortune, was unfortunately put into our heads. We may be very happy again, if we determine to hasten back to America, and think no more about it; if Delmont loves me as he says he does, he will go with us, and if he does not—[her voice had nearly failed, but she recovered it] if he does not—it would be a misfortune to me to be married to him, whatever situation I may be in, and indeed, my dearest, dearest mother, I can get the better of my attachment to him, should he be found unworthy of it: Oh! easier, much easier than I can bear to see you thus unhappy, and wearing out your health in solicitude for me! What could make me amends for the loss of your cheerfulness, your health—and what could make amends for the loss of such blessings to my father? Nothing, oh! nothing in the world! Let us then bring all this to a conclusion at once—pray let us. Write to Delmont, my dear mama, and if he cannot disengage himself from the business which has called him to Ireland, let us not wait for him, but go, before the winter sets in, back to my father. Delmont, if he loves us better than his family, will follow us, and if he prefers them—Oh! God forbid that I should interfere with his collateral affections."

The last words were uttered in a tone that was almost like sobbing. Mrs. Glenmorris folded her daughter fondly to her bosom—a bosom that throbbed with anguish when she reflected, that so far from being able, had she wished to realize the proposal of her generous girl, and directly begin their voyage back to their natural protector and dearest friend, she was absolutely without money to answer the expences of the day that was passing over them.

The absence of Delmont, though she believed it unavoidable, was so ill timed that it affected her almost like an intentional omission.—That of Armitage too, now travelling with his sick friend in the North, was so unfortunate that it sunk her spirits in despite of every effort of her courage. Yet from neither of these, had they been present, would she have accepted of money; and the cruel calumny which had been disseminated by Mrs. Crewkherne, and which had lost nothing by having passed the medium of Dr. and Mrs. Winslow, their niece, and all the elegant acquaintance of the one, and the sentimental *sweet friends* of the other, would have deterred Mrs. Glenmorris from availing herself of the friendship of Armitage, had he been in London, in a thousand instances wherein he could have been of use to her.

The charming spirit and generous affection of her Medora brought tears into her eyes. She was too much affected to enter at that moment into a farther discussion, and contented herself with endeavouring to re-assure Medora in regard to Delmont, of whose love, his absence, which had now been of near a month, had induced her, naturally enough, to entertain some infant doubts; and then, telling her she would determine in a few days what it would be best to do, she retired to bed; not indeed to sleep, but to suffer unobserved the tortures of reflection, and to form vague plans for the next day.

Nothing, however, occurred to her by which she could get through the present pressing necessity she was in for money, unless it was an application to Mrs. Grinsted, the most painful measure she could be condemned to, though not because she feared a refusal. Another resolution she took was to write to Mr. Armitage, whose advice at least might be obtained, without exposing her to the invidious reflections which Mrs. Grinsted had taken care to tell her had been already made on her intimacy with him. Yet while she sacrificed to this cruel and malicious report the plan she would otherwise have pursued, her heart revolted against the chains which malice and prejudice combined induce her to submit to; and she enquired of herself, who those were, to whose opinion, or rather to whose gossip, she for once consented to give up the real advantages she could derive from the judgment and friendship of Armitage, who, had she not cautiously worded her letter, and if he had understood the real exigencies of her situation, would, she believed, have quitted his friend, at least for some time, to have come to her assistance.

When, conquering with extreme difficulty her repugnance, and taking Mrs. Grinsted apart, she asked for the loan of ten or twenty guineas, she saw a strange expression arise in her face, for which she could not at that moment account. Mrs. Grinsted, however, instead of immediately obliging her, began to say, in the common cant of refusal, that money never was so scarce.—That she really had found her tenants in Northamptonshire so backward, that she was a good deal straitened herself, and was quite at a loss how to go on till she should receive her next dividends. But, however, she had five or six guineas then at her service, and would write to a friend in the city, on whom, if Mrs. Glenmorris would herself call the next day, he would probably supply her with the rest, "at my request, my dear," said the friendly lender; who immediately assuming the privilege lenders usually assume, of giving advice to the borrower; went on thus, "I assure you, dear Laura! Ah! those were delectable days when it was my accustomed manner so to address you—I assure you that whatever may be my exigencies, I have an infinitude of gratification in being able to testify my affectionate wish for the acceleration of your accommodation, and therefore permit me the liberty, in the effervescence of my regard, to advise you—I am some gradations more elevated on the theatre of life than you are: I mean as to our time of abode in this sphere of existence; and I hear and see a considerable deal as to existing circumstances.— How shall I express myself? Alas! the world is censorious! yet perhaps generally justifiable in its conjectural strictures.—Alas! it is a verity, and much to be deplored, that the generality of its observations are founded in experience of the irrationality of its inhabitants; and at the present period of political mania more especially. Let me caution you, dear madam, against any degree of intimacy or confidence with that Mr. Armitage. If you were more known, believe me you could not escape without more severe strictures. As it is, every body by whom you *are* recognised, animadvert upon it. He is a man whose principles are most inimical to all good order. His morals are extremely lax, and the notions he has disseminated extremely dangerous to the regulation of polished society. Let me therefore adjure you, Mrs. Glenmorris, to exonerate[64] yourself from all communication with this man. Indeed, prudential precaution prescribes it, and decorous dignity demands it. I must perforce add, however reluctantly I shall advert to it, that if any thing is expected from my interposition with my venerable and dear friend Lady Mary, this renunciation must be a preliminary condition."

The spirits of Mrs. Glenmorris were so depressed; her heart, which could have proudly resisted any evil threatening only herself, was so heavy when she thought of Medora, that for almost the only time in her life she was unable to repel impertinence as it deserved, and contented herself with saying, "I imagine you really mean this as friendship, and therefore I will not resent it; but if it is with reflections on Glenmorris, and on his and my best friends, that your kindness is to be empoisoned—keep your money, dear Mrs. Grinsted—I had rather be without it; and as for your interposition with Lady Mary, I expect, I desire, nothing from it. If she had any feeling, she would receive her grand-daughter, a creature who would do honour to any family—if she has none"—Some cruel recollections pressed on Mrs. Glenmorris at that moment, and her voice failed her.

Mrs. Grinsted had reasons why she did not wish to lose the hold that necessity had given her over Mrs. Glenmorris, she forbore therefore to press on so jarring a key, and paying some slight compliment to Medora, she repeated, that she was willing to supply her with money on her application in the city the next morning; and then suffered all farther discourse on business to drop.

Mrs. Glenmorris had no courage to renew it. The dread of poverty, of not being able to find support till she could see her beloved child in the protection of her father or of Delmont, was an apprehension at once so new and so painful that her fortitude sunk under it; and when, after she returned to their temporary abode with her daughter, and had dismissed Medora (who watched her every look with distressing solicitude) to her repose, Mrs. Glenmorris retired to her own reflections; the immediate prospect appeared so gloomy and so hopeless, that, instead of urging her mind to meet the difficulties before her, she shrunk from them in fear, and dared not investigate the causes of dread, which was even more than the occasion seemed to call for.

Sleep was a stranger to her eyes till towards morning.—Then she awoke to the recollection of her appointment in a street, at the farthest end of this great town, where she was to meet one of the lawyers employed, and to receive the money (while her very soul recoiled from the weight of the obligation) which Mrs. Grinsted had promised her. Leaving then Medora once more alone in her room, from whence she never stirred during her mother's absence, Mrs. Glenmorris set out about two o'clock to walk to the extremity of the city.[65] The solicitor was not at home, but expected in a short time; she waited above an hour; he came not.—Wearied by delay, her next attempt was to see Mrs. Grinsted's agent.—He too made her wait above half an hour before he appeared; and then he was so slow, so tedious, began such a long relation of the time he had known Mrs. Grinsted; the business he did for her; what her income was; and how well she economised, that more than another hour was wasted: At last, however, bewildered and fatigued, Mrs. Glenmorris returned once more in search of her attorney.—It was late, and he was by this time sitting down to dinner.—With great parade and affectation of respect, he solicited her to dine with him; declared he knew not when he could wait on her, because he was just at this moment overwhelmed, absolutely crushed, and annihilated by business.—But if she would but honour him with her company at dinner, he would immediately afterwards attend her commands with the greatest pleasure.

Mrs. Glenmorris, to whom every absence from Medora was painful, and who felt that it was improper to leave her long alone in a house of public resort,[66] resisted this invitation; till being again told that if she did not now consent to stay and talk over the business, it might be some days or even weeks before she could say what was necessary to Mr. Brownjohn, she at length reluctantly acquiesced, and desiring to have a porter called, one of the servants of the house presented himself, by his master's orders, and undertook to carry to Miss Glenmorris these lines, which her mother wrote hastily with a pencil:

> I am detained, my dearest girl, and cannot, as I intended, return to
> dinner, without risking the necessity of having this disagreeable walk
> again.—It is absolutely necessary for the peace of my mind to decide on

something directly, therefore you will not be uneasy if you do not see me till the evening.

Your most affectionate,
L.G.

Mr. Brownjohn and his *wulgar* wife, (one of the coarsest, weakest, and most illiterate of all pretenders to gentility, was *wastly* the most disagreeable *lady* it ever had been Mrs. Glenmorris's misfortune to meet with) were *purdigious* civil in their way.— At the table were several other persons, whose manners were equally new to her and equally disgusting.—*Gentlemen* they called themselves, and *Esquires*, from dark lanes and narrow alleys in the city, who passed their summers at Brighton, and hunted at Windsor in the winter, and talked very loud and very magnificently of their exploits at both places.[67]—Ladies too, who were so extremely fashionable that they looked with great contempt on Mrs. Glenmorris, and whisperingly enquired who that odd looking woman was, and whether she was not an author? These ladies talked of the croud at the opera, and all the people of fashion they had seen there.—It was *purdigious* crowded; and Miss Fanny Simpkinson, whose papa formerly kept a tavern, complained how Lord Edward Evelyn and Sir Charles Sedley *squeeged* her, and how impertinent they looked at her; and then how frighted she was at coming out, for she *rayally* thought her *carridge* would have been broke to smash. Mrs. Brownjohn also assured her friends that she had been herself quite frighted in the park the preceding Sunday, for her *coatch* was as near broke as any thing—"And then," added she, "Brownjohn would have made a fine noise, and I should not have heard the last of it for one while."— "No, faith," cried the attorney, "that you would not;—not that I mind the coach so much, though it cost me an hundred and sixty guineas without the harness—but I can't bear to have my horses hurt, and women never have any mercy upon horses.— That there pair of horses, by G——, and the third at grass in Hertfordshire, that I bought of Sir Miles Whisker, cost me upwards of three hundred guineas.—But Mrs. Brownjohn thinks no more of 'em than if they were dray-horses.[68]—She is utterly insensible of their value, and minds them there sort of things no more than the pump at Aldgate.[69] Why now Bagshaw, (addressing himself to a tall awkward young man, who looked somewhat like a groom out of place)[70] I'll tell you what; that brown horse, by Spanker, you saw me upon the last time we hunted; don't you remember you said you'd give me a cool sixty for him.—Well, Sir, I offered him and forty guineas to boot, for a bay-gelding, a match for these three, and, by G——, my Lord refused the offer." "Lord who?" said the macquignon[71] in a surly tone, "Lord—why Lord—Lord Maccurragh, *he* as we used to hunt with along o' the Brighton hounds."

"He was a cursed fool," said the grumbling voice, "not to take you at your word."

"I was staying two or three days at his house in Essex," continued Brownjohn, "and he and I——"

"He has no house in Essex," said a pert looking young man, at the other end of the table, "I happen to know, for my uncle Crockham serves his lordship with wine—

and his house is in Surry."—"Aye he *has* an house in Surry," said Brownjohn, "but this is an hunting box[72] where he only goes now and then."

"'Tis in the hundreds[73] then I'll swear," said the *gentleman* groom, "and he goes a hunting of widgeon,[74] for I'll be d——d if he has an house in any other part of Essex."

Brownjohn persisted, and the other contradicted.—One was undaunted in lying, the other obstinate in maintaining an insignificant truth.—They were very noisy and very rude to each other; and would perhaps have quarrelled, if the attorney had not had an interest in keeping his client in general good humour, and if the client had not been deeply indebted to the attorney.

From such conversation, however, Mrs. Glenmorris would at any time have retired in disgust, and now that her heart was heavy with many troubles, in which she expected council and relief, it was altogether insupportable, she therefore rose from table, dinner being now over, and addressing herself to the sporting solicitor said, "that she was sorry to interrupt him, but as she must immediately go, she wished to have the conversation she had requested in the morning."

The man promised to follow her in a few moments, and did so in something more than half an hour, when she found his boasted hospitality had so operated upon himself, while he exerted it to his guests, that he was not capable of uttering three consequent words; the little degree of rationality which he usually shewed had quite forsaken him.—Convinced of this, Mrs. Glenmorris forbore to waste her spirits and time, but desiring to have a coach called, returned home astonished that Mr. Petrify could recommend her to such a man; disgusted by the whole party she had seen, and saying to herself with a sigh!—"Of people like these is made up the bulk of that world, to which prejudice and fear induce us to sacrifice real happiness.—It is this mob, which overbears all retiring and simple virtues, and destroys all simple pleasures.— This affectation of the manners of upper life—how ridiculous!—and how very unlike are these people to those they would copy!"—"Ah! it is not the *swinish multitude*[75]—the 'plebs et infima multitudo,'[76] that disgust one with the species. It is such people as these; people who hold the honest labourer and the industrious mechanic in contempt, yet are indeed poor in intellect and vulgar in all they do or say.—Gross, stupified, and ferocious, yet affecting aristocratic ideas—not knowing even the meaning of the word—and fancy their opinions of importance, and that they belong to a party!"

Mrs. Glenmorris had been above a week in London, and though she had given her whole time to the business that brought her, nothing was done in it.—With a desponding heart she now repented not having referred herself entirely to Mr. Armitage, and accused herself of weakness for having been deterred from taking advantage of his friendship by the malice, which to despise was to render impotent, and to which it was feebleness of mind ever to listen.

CHAP. VI.

——Your looks are pale and wild, and do impart
Some misadventure!——[77]

Before Mrs. Glenmorris could determine, on the following day, what it would be best to do in her present difficult and uneasy situation, a young man was introduced, who said he came to her from Mr. Brownjohn.

Mrs. Glenmorris imagining him a clerk, spoke to him of business.—But he immediately gave her to understand that he was not Mr. Brownjohn's clerk—by no means. He felt his dignity injured by the very supposition. He was a gentleman.—Mr. Brownjohn's brother by the second marriage of his mother. His name was Darnell. He had an independent fortune, and the honour of bearing his Majesty's commission.

Mrs. Glenmorris refraining with difficulty from smiling at the very great importance of this very great man, then desired to know what had procured her the honour of a visit from him, and after another parading speech, he had at last the goodness to inform her, that he came at his brother's request to apologize for the delay which had unavoidably happened, and to say that if on the next evening save one, she would be at the house of a conveyancer[78] in Threadneedle-street,[79] Mr. Brownjohn would attend with the copy he had at last made of her father's will, and that he would appoint a consultation of counsellors to meet her, on whose final advice she might depend. The hour of seven in the evening was that on which Mr. Sergeant Sedative and Mr. Counsellor Clang, gentlemen of the first eminence in the profession, could attend, both being under the most indispensable engagements for the next day.

Mrs. Glenmorris having promised to be there, imagined that Mr. Darnell would relieve her from the necessity of any longer entertaining him; but he seemed now to have recovered from the sort of awe, which those that are elated by the presumption of monied ignorance, involuntarily feel before superior elegance of mind and manners, though they know not what it is that deprives them of their usual forwardness and consequence. As if by proper reflection on his own value, Mr. Darnell had conquered this uneasy sensation, he entered on what he seemed to suppose very entertaining conversation, and gave an account of the fine people he had lately seen at Ascot races,[80] and the money he had won by betting. He then launched into a dissertation on his skill in horseflesh. Informed the ladies, that his curricle horses had been admired by people of the first distinction, his manner of driving them still more; and mistaking passive civility for approbation, he began to be so very pert and familiar, particularly in his looks, and his manner of addressing himself to Medora, that Mrs. Glenmorris at last lost her patience, and giving her daughter an hint to leave the room, she told her unwelcome visitor, that she was obliged to him for having taken the trouble of bringing Mr. Brownjohn's message, but *that* being done, she must beg not to be detained, having no time to give to uninteresting talk about things indifferent to her, and with people who were strangers to her. The countenance of Darnell immediately fell; he looked as if he was on the instant of emerging from Trophonius's cave.[81]—Yet there was an expression of malignity mingled with his visible dismay.—He soon, however, disappeared.

While Mrs. Glenmorris and Medora were thus uneasily passing their time in London, waiting with anxiety for letters from Glenmorris, and doubting how they ought to act, Delmont was not happier at Dublin.

The Major no sooner saw the alacrity with which he had come over, than he ungenerously sought for means to make advantage of it; but George, who could not forget the unhandsome manner in which he had left him answerable for all the engagements contracted in London, resisted his importunity: Coldness and even anger succeeded; but Delmont was steady to his purpose, and Adolphus' conduct was every day such as convinced him that he might utterly ruin himself, yet neither benefit his brother's affairs, or derive, from any sacrifice he could make, either friendship or gratitude. Adolphus, far from feeling any disposition to return to London, and release George from the heavy consequences of the engagements he had entered into, was plunging into deeper play, and under pretence of retrieving his fortune, inevitably involving himself in tenfold ruin.

He persisted, however, in considering George as one born only to promote his views and obey his mandates. Impressed with ideas of primogeniture at a very early age, he could never submit to any mention of equality even among brethren. Nothing, he said, was more infamous than the change made in that respect in France—he thought it scandalous that in any country, the younger branches of a family should be suffered to diminish the property of the elder, and wished he could have said to his sisters—"Au couvent Mesdemoiselles,"[82] that their share of the fortune of his father might have been his; while as to his brother, he wanted only the power to treat him (allowing somewhat for the superior amenity of modern manners) not very much otherwise than Oliver treats his brother Orlando,[83] in one of Shakespeare's most interesting dramas.

As it was, he had no hesitation in calling upon his purse or his services, nothing doubting of his right to command both.—And when he at length found that George was induced merely by his regard for the memory of their common parents to befriend him any farther, he affected in all companies to turn his manner of life, his propensities, his taste, into ridicule, and was not ashamed to do so, even among the strangers to whom he was introduced in Ireland—but the real dignity of Delmont nothing could degrade. Such was the influence he soon obtained wherever he was known, by the manly sweetness of his temper, and by the good sense and just feelings appearing in all he said or did, that the former admirers of his arrogant and selfish brother, immediately discovered how inferior that brother was; and even the arts of insinuation, which the Major well knew how occasionally to use, could never, after George's appearance, restore him to the same degree of favour and fashion that he had enjoyed in the principal Irish families before George's arrival.

Yet the younger brother neither drank with the men or coquetted with the women—He neither played nor romanced, and he had none of the gaiety which usually recommends young men of his age, and particularly in that country; for his heart was not gay, and he could not affect it, and though he neither coldly or rudely repulsed the hospitality of the very hospitable Irish, he pretended not to enjoy society as he might have done under other circumstances, but confessed that he was impatient to return to England.

More than one young woman of rank, and of considerable fortune, found George Delmont so much to their taste, that they scrupled not, with more decisive kindness than even Miss Goldthorp had betrayed, to signify that they were very favourably disposed towards him.—He allowed that they were extremely handsome; but answered all his brother's railleries on the subject by declaring to him, that if Medora (who was, he acknowledged, possessed of all his affections) were out of the question, he would not marry either of these ladies.—"Nor should I like," said he, "to live in Ireland, highly as I respect the inhabitants, and greatly as I honour the talents of the many illustrious men it has produced.[84] I should be miserable where I must daily witness, without having the power materially to alleviate, the miseries of the lower classes of people."—"The people!" exclaimed the Major with a contemptuous smile,—"the people—what the devil hast thou to do with them?—Egad I begin to be almost afraid of associating with thee, George.—Why thou hast certainly picked up this damned cant at some presbyterian meeting-house,[85] or got it by rote at a debating society from some greasy chandler[86] or grim smith.—Oh! pray let us never be bored by such eternal nonsense.—Rights of men!—The people![87]—Rogues who would cut *our* throats, and thine among the rest, George, because thou hast a little better blood in thy veins; but it would be hard indeed wert thou to pay the penalty, who have nothing of nobility about thee but that blood, not even thy ideas.—No haberdasher of small wares[88] has more plebeian notions! Why one would think thy every days had been passed in measuring buckram;[89] and thy Sundays in walking to Islington to eat hot rolls at White Conduit House.[90] It is amazing to me where thou hast picked up such vulgar cares— and by what warp in thy head, it has happened to take this reforming twist."

"It is equally astonishing to me," replied George, "that you are so totally devoid of feeling, or perhaps I ought rather to say of the sense of self-preservation; for very great men to fail in feeling for *others* is not extremely uncommon, but they seldom are deficient in the business of taking care of themselves; and it is not difficult to foresee what will be the end of the system they are now urging. However, it is not with you, Adolphus, I ever desire to hold political controversy. Nothing will ever bring our views into the same line." "No, by G—, I believe not," replied the other; and there the dialogue ended.—Such conversation, however, was often renewed; for the Major, who had the most perfect reliance on his own powers, and the most arrogant contempt for the talents and opinions of his brother, sought every occasion of contest; this intrepidity of insolence George bore with apparent indifference, but it insensibly weaned him from his attachment to Adolphus, and only that strict integrity which prescribed to him to adhere to his engagements, however ungenerously he had been drawn into them, and however injurious they might prove to himself, could have induced him to continue so patiently to arrange the business which had brought him to Ireland; business which his brother was so far from assisting him in, that he gave himself no manner of trouble, and merely signed or did whatever his lawyer told him was necessary, entreating only not be annoyed any more with it.

Delmont had at length accomplished this painful and uneasy task, as far as it could be done till the money could be recovered, which Sir Appulby Gorges seemed determined to retain. And while he regretted the loss of so considerable a part of his property, he with true greatness of mind forbore to reproach his brother, determined to return to England to complete what he had begun (this extrication of Adolphus, as far it depended on him), and then dismissing from his mind the loss and the vexation, resort quietly for the present to his farm, where he hoped to prevail on Mrs. Glenmorris to bestow Medora upon him, and having regulated his few remaining concerns in England, to leave all his troubles behind him, and cross the Atlantic, the happy husband of the woman he adored.

Such were the visions with which he appeased his impatience, and beguiled the time that must necessarily pass before he could return to Upwood, where, or in its immediate neighbourhood, he concluded Mrs. Glenmorris and Medora yet were. The very moment he could disengage himself he took leave of his Irish friends, and resisting the invitation of one of them to see on his way the Giants Causeway,[91] and other remarkable places in the north of Ireland (from whence he might have crossed to Port Patrick) his impatience urged him to take the shortest road to the southern part of his native island.—Adolphus, however, at the same time left Dublin, and took the route by Port Patrick, hating the longer passage, and intending to pass some time with a friend in Yorkshire.

No letter from Mrs. Glenmorris, in which she had named her sudden journey to London, had ever reached George Delmont; had he known she and Medora were there, surrounded by difficulties and destitute of money, thither he would have directed his steps.

But the destiny of Mrs. Glenmorris, and of her daughter, decided otherwise.

Delmont was already on his way, when letters from both reached him.—The mother demanded his advice, whether she should pursue or relinquish the prospects of fortune that had offered to her daughter. It was necessary for her to come to a resolution, however, before she could have his answer. And that resolution was to be taken in the appointment she had now made at the house of one of the lawyers.

Thither then Mrs. Glenmorris repaired alone. Some of the parties who were to assist at the consultation were not yet arrived; others, and Brownjohn among them, had *been dining*. When at length they all assembled, there were no two of them that thought alike—they all talked at the same time, and it seemed to be a contest not of reason or of law, but of assurance and lungs. One quoted a case in point to maintain his opinion; a second supported his, by one which he affirmed was much more to the purpose. A third begged leave to dissent from both, for reasons that he gave at a great length, but to which (all parties being heartily tired) nobody listened. Mr. Counsellor Sedative fell asleep; and Mr. Clang and his friend Brownjohn, having both talked themselves out of breath, could at length agree in nothing but a resolution to adjourn to the dining-room, and consider the matter farther over some excellent Madeira, which the solicitor assured the learned counsel had been to the East Indies,[92] and was a present from a very good client of his.

Mrs. Glenmorris, who saw that nothing was to be done, desired, however, to speak a few words; but the gentlemen giving very little attention to what she said, observed, that things of such moment could not be decided in a day—no, nor in twenty days; that ladies, however great their understanding, were apt to be a little impatient in matters, which to hurry would be to mar; that they could not commit themselves by an hasty determination; begged to think farther of it—and would name an early day, after their respective returns to town, for that purpose: Mrs. Glenmorris thought she plainly perceived what all this meant, and determined to write to Brownjohn (her former aversion from whom now amounted to antipathy) and to withdraw the affairs entirely from him; she was not aware that this was already impossible.

Avoiding, however, every discussion, she desired an hack[93] to be called, and vexed at the loss of time and of money she had thus incurred, resolved, as she was driven toward the hotel, to return the very next day to her country retirement; the money she had borrowed would,[94] she hoped, be sufficient to carry her and her daughter home, and it could not be very long before they should have letters, and probably remittances and orders, from Glenmorris; it could not be very long before she should hear from Armitage, and see Delmont. Having taken this resolution her mind became calm, and she felt a great degree of satisfaction in figuring to herself the pleasure their journey into the country would give her Medora.

Arrived at the hotel, she went up to the room where they usually sat; Medora was not there, but as in her absence she had usually remained in the bed-chamber, as more private, Mrs. Glenmorris sought her above stairs—Medora was not there!

She returned, not without some disquiet, to the lower apartment, and rang the bell. A waiter appearing, she enquired for the young lady. "The young lady, ma'am," said the man, "why she has been gone out above these two hours."

"Gone out! Good God Almighty—with whom—how gone out?"

"Indeed, ma'am," answered the man, "I do not know the gentleman, for I never saw him before; but he came in a coach, and sent in a note writ with a pencil, for I carried it myself to miss, and she read it, and bid me I should tell the gentleman to please to walk in, and she would soon be ready, but he said he would sit in the coach till miss was ready—and presently she came down in her hat and cloak, and got into the coach, and so it drived away."

A deadly sickness stole over the unhappy mother while the man spoke. She knew that Medora had not an acquaintance in the world that was not also hers; that it was uneasy to her to be separated from her for a moment, and extremely improbable she should go any where voluntarily without her knowledge. Where could she be? Into what hands might she not have fallen! Where could she seek her? Distraction seemed to be in the enquiry! Yet to remain in ignorance, to be tortured with uncertainty, with dreadful conjectures, was not to be endured. Hardly able to speak, she enquired of the waiter what kind of a man it was with whom her daughter went. He answered, "that he did not much notice him, but thought him a jollyish, middle-aged man, with a roundish, fresh-coloured face; and that he seemed very complaisant to miss, and got out himself to hand her into the coach; but miss did not seem somehow to know him, and stared at him like as one does at a stranger."

"What coach was it?" enquired Mrs. Glenmorris.

"Why I think, ma'am, it was what we call a glass coach;[95] though it might to be sure be the gentleman's own; howsomdever 'twas not remarkable genteel—and there was ne'er a footman."

It now suddenly occurred to Mrs. Glenmorris, that it was possible some opportunity had offered to Mrs. Grinsted, of introducing Medora to Lady Mary, and that she had seized it without waiting for her return or consent; but then would she not have written to her? Would Medora, who liked her so little, and who had such a dread of her grandmother, have gone unprotected by her mother!

This was, however, the only conjecture between her, and horrors which threatened, if she dwelt upon them, to deprive her of reason. Eagerly, therefore, endeavouring to cherish any hope that afforded a temporary relief, she sent again for an hackney coach, and ordered it to be driven in all haste to Mrs. Grinsted's. Mrs. Grinsted was gone out to supper, at the house of a friend in May Fair,[96] and her woman, to whom Mrs. Glenmorris now spoke, in a state bordering on phrenzy, assured her that Miss Glenmorris had not been there, and she was very sure her lady had not written or sent any person for her.

The woman, seeing the dreadful situation of mind into which the loss of her daughter had thrown Mrs. Glenmorris, had the humanity to ask her to come into the house. She accepted the offer, hardly knowing what she did, and glad to have any body who would listen to her conjectures, and feel an interest in the cruel circumstance overwhelming her with astonishment and terror—Yet hardly had she got into the house, when fancying it possible Medora might return to the hotel, she started up, and without attending to the entreaties of the servant that she would be composed, and putting by the refreshment offered her, Mrs. Glenmorris again hastily entered the coach, and bade the man hurry back to the place where he had taken her up.

As she went, the fears that crowded on her mind were so cruel, she was so destitute of every ray of light that might guide her to the recovery of her lost child, that her head became affected, and when she arrived at the door of the hotel, and heard that nothing was known of Medora, she stared wildly around her, lost all power of immediate recollection, and getting out of the coach, walked quickly away along the street, without any reflection whither, absorbed only by the idea that Medora was gone, Medora lost, Medora in the hands of ruffians, of wretches—she knew not whom! Soon grown incapable of reasoning, she knew not what was said to her, when the coachman followed her to be paid, and the waiter begged her to return to the house. This man, not without sense and humanity, perceived the melancholy condition to which the disappearance of her daughter had reduced the unhappy lady, and half persuading, half leading her, he at length succeeded in getting her back into the house, where he called his mistress and the women servants to her assistance.

They led her, scarce resisting, to the room she had inhabited since their residence at the house; but there she had been used to see her Medora waiting her return; there now lay the gown she had worn that morning—there was her travelling hat on the chair. The sight of these things seemed to give new poignancy to the anguish that tore her bosom; she shrieked aloud, called incessantly on her daughter, walked in a frantic manner round the room, insisted on being allowed to go out in search of her, and when the women remonstrated that it was past twelve o'clock, and that it would be impossible to find her that night, the agony of her mind became so great as to produce all the appearances of actual madness. She raved incoherently, endeavoured to force the door, and threatened punishment to those who should dare to detain her. The mistress of the house, who now foresaw a great deal of trouble and very little profit from her lodger, heartily wished her gone—and repeated—"But let me send for somebody, madam—Let me send to some of your's or misses friends,"—"Yes, yes," cried Mrs. Glenmorris, after having stared wildly at her a moment, without appearing to understand her—"Yes, yes, yes!—send for her father to America—send to Ireland—to Ireland for Delmont, and tell—yes, tell Armitage he has been unkind to abandon his friend's child. They would all have come if they had known it sooner—but it is too late!—And now Lady Mary will not let them; Mrs. Grinsted knows it is in vain; and Glenmorris!—Oh! he ought to have been here—Poor Glenmorris, what will he say!"

The woman, who had no doubt but that the young lady had eloped with a lover, began in the common phrases of consolation to say, "that she hoped all would be for the best, though to be sure it seemed a little hard at first for parents, when young people chuses them as are not altogether agreeable, but after all, when a thing was done there was no use in fretting, and happiness was every thing. Riches did not so much signify—and perhaps the gentleman, ma'am," said she, "may prove more agreeable than at present you seems to think. Pray, good madam, compose yourself—a great many other ladies have had the same thing happen. It was not a fortnight ago, that a young miss, an heiress to above thirty thousand pounds, ran away from her father and mother too, with an officer of dragoons from this here very house; and her parents to be sure, especially the old gentleman, took on very much about it; the young folks, however, got the start of them, and were clear off; and they made it up, and all was settled mighty agreeable after they come back from Scotland."

Totally unconscious of the purport of this harangue, Mrs. Glenmorris heard nothing but the word Scotland, which fell on her ear as a sound to which some affecting remembrances were annexed. "Scotland!" exclaimed she, "who says she is in Scotland? No, no—there is no use now in going to Scotland, no use in going without me, for she will never find the place—but I will go with her—and I insist upon it, madam, that you do not detain me here. Pray," added she, addressing herself to the housemaid who had usually waited in her chamber, "pray, my good girl, get me a coach—here is money for you, (and she took out her purse with six or seven guineas in it) here is money—Go—make haste, get me a coach or a post chaise—I can call upon Mrs. Grinsted and let her know as I go along." She then began to take her cloaths and Medora's in an hasty way out of the drawers, and requested the maid to help her put them into a portmanteau; but her manner and her looks were so wild, and she appeared to be so entirely without any rational plan, that the mistress of the hotel, who thought she might not be paid for the days still due if she suffered her lodger so to depart, refused to let her leave the room; and as she was evidently not fit to be left, directed the maid to stay with her, at least till she was quieter, and consented to go to bed. The provident landlady then counted the money before the maid, and put the purse in her own pocket, after which she fetched up some bread, wine, and water, and endeavoured to prevail on Mrs. Glenmorris to eat, but as she put every thing away by a motion of her hands, and still continued to insist on being allowed to go, the woman, tired of the contention, left her to the care of her servant, and retired.

CHAP. VII.

She talks to me that never had a child![97]

All night—a most dismal night, Mrs. Glenmorris sat up; listening to every carriage that passed in the streets, eagerly attentive to every noise, sometimes even fancying that she heard a coach stop, and Medora's voice on the stairs; and then, starting from the gloomy silence she had sunk into, she insisted upon being suffered to go out of the room, demanded by what right she was detained, and protested she would severely punish those who so barbarously prevented her seeking her child. The servant could only appease, by assuring her that when it was morning she should go whither she would. The morning at last came, but having been without rest or food, and suffering such distracting anxiety for so many hours, she was unfitted for any of the exertions which might really have been of use; and notwithstanding the eagerness with which she insisted on being allowed to do something, she really was not enough in possession of her senses to have decided what were the most probable means of recovering her daughter.

Mrs. Glenmorris had, on all other occasions, shewn great strength of mind, and now, dreadful as the calamity appeared, she would probably have had resolution enough to have acted, had not the miserable uncertainty she was in, quite bewildered and overwhelmed her; the various forms of horror which crowded on her mind as to the fate of Medora, while she dared not look steadily on any of them; and the impossibility of her guessing with whom, why, or whither she was gone, were circumstances unlike any evil either dreaded or known. Had she been assured of what she had to dread, she would have bent her mind to counteract it; or had it been inevitable, the necessity of enduring would have benumbed and steadied her faculties, as it is seen every day to do those of persons suffering under irremediable misfortunes. But her child, her beloved, her adored Medora! The cherished object of her maternal affection; the only hope of her Glenmorris; a creature so eminently lovely, and with such an heart, such a mind! She might now be vainly calling upon her mother to save her from evils to which death would be preferable. She might be shrieking in vain for that father to protect her, who was divided from her by almost half the world; that father who had so reluctantly parted from her, and might now never see her more.

It was these thoughts that drove the unhappy mother to despair. Her senses became more and more bewildered the longer she dwelt upon them; and she had no friend to speak words of comfort, to participate her anguish, or with friendly resolution to set about the search, which she was herself incapable of directing. There was not on earth another calamity which could thus have affected her.

The mistress of the hotel made her appearance about eight o'clock in the morning, and found her miserable lodger had not slept the whole night, and that she had, with hardly any interval of tranquillity, incessantly raved for her daughter, talking incoherently of different people. Her countenance was changed, her eyes haggard and swollen, though she was unable to shed a tear; her hands burnt, and her discourse was more wild and disjointed than before. The first impulse the mistress of the house felt, was to send for medical advice. Some apothecary[98] is usually employed at such an house, and to him accustomed to attend her hotel, she now thought of applying, being certain that the money she had in her custody was more than sufficient to pay her own bill for the four days due, and to satisfy the demand of her physical friend.

It happened that the apothecary was one of the most mercenary and interested of his class. He first acquainted himself with the circumstances of the person he was called upon to attend, and as he thought they promised him but little advantage, and had no doubt but that the girl, as he called her, was gone off with a lover, he advised Mrs. * * * * to have as little trouble, and to get the business off her hands as soon as she possibly could. He represented, that it was extremely improbable a lady of fashion or fortune should travel without a servant of any kind; and that as the person had uttered so many incoherences about a law-suit and lawyers, it was best to secure what money she had about her for payment of what was already due, and send her as soon as possible to her friends.

"I dont know who her friends are," replied Mrs. * * * *, "not I!—Scarce any body have come to see her here, though she have been here going on three weeks, except some odd looking people, as I took for lawyers, and them there sort of gentry;[99] but no gentlemen and ladies of quality in their own coaches. The man that came to carry off miss, which I dare to say was a concerted thing, was in the only coach, except an hack, which has ever been at my door on their account. I believe as you do, indeed Mr. Colocynth,[100] that this Mrs. Glenmorris—the name dont sound somehow like an English one neither—is some poor woman come over from America (for I know they are Americans) about a law-suit which she has lost, and so is not able to find money to return; and miss, seeing how the case was, has very wisely and properly provided for herself."

"Yes, that is the truth of the thing—there's no doubt on't," replied Colocynth; "and I suppose you cannot doubt neither, if it be, what is your best step to take. There is no prudence at all in hesitating about such a matter. As you have enough in hand to pay yourself, make your bill; just for the sake of satisfying, you know, any enquiries that may be made—and let her go—I warrant she's not so mad but what she can tell of some one or other that will take her in, but if not, you know you are not in any way answerable. It cannot be expected that you should be bound to keep all the strangers that may come without money to your house."

Carrying with her a bill for five days board and lodging, Mrs. * * * * proceeded to the chamber of her mourning guest.

She was sitting on the side of the bed, her head resting on her hands; and heeded neither the house-maid, who was exhorting her to patience, nor the entrance of the mistress. The latter, however, roused her by saying, "that as she was so desirous of going to consult her friends about misses' elopement . . . . ."

Mrs. Glenmorris looked up—and in a hollow and tremulous tone of surprise, repeated the word "elopement?"

"Yes, ma'am," said the woman, "to be sure it must be counted so, that's for certain. No doubt the young lady is gone to be married in Scotland."

"In Scotland!" repeated Mrs. Glenmorris, with a deep and broken sigh.

"Why yes, ma'am," cried the woman, "that is the most common way, and most natural, as I was a saying t'other day—and so I think, Mrs. Glenmorris, it would be better for you, ma'am, to make yourself easy about it, and go to your friends till such time as——"

"Friends!" answered the patient, half shrieking, "friends did you say? *I have* no friends."

Mrs. * * * *, whose philanthropy was not at all increased by this declaration, was only the more determined to clear her house of a person in so unfortunate a predicament as soon as possible; and finding her lodger, as she believed, perfectly sensible, was decidedly of opinion that there was no time to lose; she presented therefore her bill, and the purse which she had secured the night before, intimating, in plain and unequivocal terms to her guest, that she must go to her friends. "For besides that, to be sure, ma'am, it will be a great deal more convenient to you," said she, "I assure you it would be quite a thing impossible for me to let this here apartment after tomorrow, for I have had a letter, to inform me that Squire Canterly and his lady, and two misses, and five sarvunts are a coming to-morrow, to stay three weeks, on their way to *Northumbellan*,[101] and to be sure, as the young ladies have always been used to have this here room, and as the fammully are as good customers as any I have, and always comes here when they are in Lonnon, I could not upon no account let it be full when they come."

Mrs. Glenmorris, who heard not a word of all this, understood however the purpose of her hostess was, that she was desired to depart; she motioned therefore to Mrs. * * * * to take the money for her bill—who immediately did so, and returned, of seven guineas, two pounds ten shillings. She then intimated to Mrs. Glenmorris, that it was always usual to distribute money among the servants—and two guineas more were conscionably taken for that purpose. Her cloaths and Medora's were then packed up, save a few trifling articles, such as muslin and cambrick handkerchiefs, and silk stockings, which Mrs. Biddy, the maid, thought the lady would not miss, "bin she was to be sure a little crazed," and that the young lady her daughter would never think it worth while to enquire for; and this honest and humane arrangement being completed, Mrs. Glenmorris was led unresistingly to a coach, and her baggage placed on the opposite seat. The waiter then desired to know whither she would be driven?—and absolutely incapable of answering, she gave him, on his repeating his question, a card, on which was written Mrs. Grinsted's address. He read it to the coachman, returned it, and the coach drove away.

This brutal conduct on the part of Mrs. * * * * was in some degree beneficial to the unhappy mother of Medora; it awakened her for a moment from that torpor of despair into which she had sunk, when her spirits having been so long agitated, she had exhausted every conjecture of where Medora could be, and rejected every vague plan for her recovery that successively arose. She felt not the unjustifiable behaviour of the hostess. She thought not about it. If no intelligence was to be obtained at the hotel, why should she stay; yet when she was for a moment calm and reasonable enough to ask herself whither she should go, her heart sunk again, and a deadly sickness crept over her. It was almost mechanically that she had given the coachman orders to go to Mrs. Grinsted's, the first person whose name occurred; but from her she had no hope of assistance in recovering her lost darling—and but little of sympathy and pity, though she in fact wished not for either, and felt that the pity of most people would irritate rather than soothe the dreadful anguish she laboured under.

Mrs. Glenmorris, however, did not expect—it was not in her nature to suppose it possible, that there could exist in a human form—in the form of a woman—a being, who would feel an horrible and malignant pleasure in aggravating the misery of a mother for the loss of an only child.

Mrs. Grinsted had not left her bed when the poor heart-broken and almost senseless mourner entered her house. Her woman seemed much concerned when she saw her.—"You have not heard of Miss Glenmorris, ma'am, I fear?" said she.—The wretched parent shook her head, but could not speak.—

"Am I to have the trunks taken in, that are in the coach, madam?" enquired the servant.

"I know not," replied Mrs. Glenmorris, in a faint voice. "I have no place to go to; I do not want to go to any place, unless to my poor girl—or to die!"—

Mrs. Grinsted's woman saw how incapable she was of giving any direction, and ventured, though by no means sure her lady would approve of it, to order in the baggage.—Mrs. Glenmorris sat down in a parlour.

She was unconscious how long she waited there, nor had she any fixed purpose in seeing Mrs. Grinsted. Her mind, in its anguish, reverted, yet confusedly, to the past, and she reproached herself for having been so weak as to have been frightened from applying to Armitage. "Had he been here, I should not," said she "have lost Medora.—To what, to whom, have I sacrificed her and her father?—Oh! Glenmorris, you never can forgive me. I never can see you more!"

It was, in fact, towards Mr. Armitage alone her hopes turned, faint as they were: but even were he in town, how could he assist her in a search which she had not the smallest clue to direct? She had, however, resolved to write to him, had rung for a pen and ink; the same servants, she had before spoken to, brought it, and Mrs. Glenmorris took up the pen, attempting to begin, but her hands trembled—her eyes failed her—the room seemed to turn round with her, and she was compelled to rest her head on a table—after having illegibly marked something that she meant should be "dear sir"—and still more illegibly the name of Armitage. Breakfast was now brought in by the footman, and after near an hour Mrs. Grinsted made her appearance.

Mrs. Glenmorris was hardly conscious of her entrance. When she saw her however, half rising from her seat, she held out her hand; but, unable to support herself, sat down.

There was nothing friendly or compassionate in the countenance and manner of the rigid spinster. She did not even spare her unhappy visitor the painful task of relating what had happened, though her maid had informed her of the enquiry of the night before, and now, that the young lady was still missing.

"You have not breakfasted, Mrs. Glenmorris," said she formally—"you will take some tea?"

"You know what has befallen me, Mrs. Grinsted?—you know that I . . . ."

"Yes, I *have* heard.—I am sorry—sorry—but not surprised."—

"Not surprised!—Why then," asked Mrs. Glenmorris, collecting her wild and half frantic thoughts—"why then did you know any thing of it; did you expect it?"

"*I* knew any thing of it," haughtily returned the lady—"*I* be acquainted with the clandestine operations of some nefarious libertine, and an inconsiderate young girl?—No, madam, I have no such irrational confidencies, I assure you.—Would to God, Mrs. Glenmorris, *your* conduct had always been as irreprovable. I am not astonished at the flight of your daughter; for this reason, that I saw her averseness from all society that was castigated by prudential reserve; and I am afraid, pardon me Mrs. Glenmorris, but the propensities of young persons have frequently their first volition given them by parental example. And you must now have severe recollections, indubitably; for you now feel perhaps, solicitude and even consternation, such as eighteen years ago your mother, my admirable and revered friend, Lady Mary, endured, when you unadvisedly, to call it by no harsher name, left the paternal roof, and threw yourself, if I must speak my sentiments, with as little prudence as delicacy, into the arms— upon my word the idea is shocking—of a man of so dissipated a reputation as Mr. Glenmorris."

The distracted spirits of the mother were all collected to repel, as soon as she understood this charge; but she could not express what she felt—she could only say, "Medora! Oh cruel to suppose it, Medora has no lover. Medora is incapable of leaving me. She has no lover."

"I have heard Lady Mary say, that *she* thought *her* daughter incapable of so acting. Besides, madam, give me leave to remark, that you yourself communicated to me that Miss Glenmorris had an admirer—that Mr. Delmont—a disciple, as I have since learned, of *your friend*, the philosophical poet, Mr. Armitage. *I* see nothing impossible in such a personage taking advantage of your predilective[102] imprudency— and matrimonial engagements are now, you know, spoken of with great levity.—Mr. Delmont, perhaps, knowing the predilection of yourself and Mr. Glenmorris for the manners and morality of modern Gallia,[103] may have conjectured that he acted not very injuriously to your principles, in appropriating for a short period your daughter to himself."

"Delmont!" cried Mrs. Glenmorris, roused by so cruel a supposition, "Delmont is incapable of such conduct—My poor Medora! had Delmont been in England, would never have been so lost. No, madam, had Delmont—had Armitage been here."

"Upon my word, Mrs. Glenmorris," said the good and charitable lady, "you oblige me to say harsh things, when I am very unwilling to do it. Why will you persist in attaching yourself with adherency of infatuation to a man so obnoxious. I am not naturally censorious, madam, but as a friend in your days of juvenility, interested for your welfare, on account of your excellent mother, my venerable friend Lady Mary;

and as lately you have been pleased to suppose my interposition might be beneficial, I think there is a degree of incumbency upon me to state to you my unqualified opinion of *that* ferocious character, and to implore you, if it be only for the sake of your own reputation, that you would discard that man from your acquaintance. You know not how very injuriously the fatality of his pretensions to be your confidential friend has already operated; and, indeed, it would be a discovery that would superinduce very little astonishment, if, on investigation, it were discovered that this *friend* was himself an auxiliary, and instrumental in what has befallen your daughter."

Mrs. Glenmorris, heart-struck before, was quite incapable of answering; she sunk back in her chair, and for a moment was again deprived even of the power of calculating the extent of her calamity. Nor did she distinctly hear a long harangue made by this humane and religious lady; yet she comprehended that it was composed of very severe strictures on her conduct, from the hour of her leaving Sandthwaite till the present moment, and reflections on the education and manners of Medora.—"It is now too late," added she—"the evil is no longer admissable of a remedy; but one laments! one laments the denunciation so evidently fulfilled against disobedience—'Behold the fathers have eaten sour grapes, and the teeth of the children are set on edge.'"[104]

Mrs. Glenmorris uttered a broken sigh; but she was still silent. The pious and humane gentlewoman, hoping her eloquence had produced, or was about to produce, penitence, proceeded:

"If you, and the person whom you so indiscreetly elected as the arbiter of your destiny, had in due time been visited with due compunction for your ill-advised dereliction of the very best of parents; and if you had thought proper, at an early period, to have transmitted your daughter to the protective matronage[105] of your truly estimable mother, she would doubtless, with the benignity so particularly inherent in her disposition, have protected, educated, and superintended her—approximated to all that was praise-worthy and estimable among her own relatives, Miss Glenmorris might then have added a ray of illuminosity to the elevated hereditary respectability of her ancestors. As it *is*, however"—a pause ensued, the worthy lady seemed silenced by the shocking contrast she had painted, and to wait till she could recover eloquence enough to pursue her charitable purpose. Her auditor became less and less in a situation to interrupt her; and she again, sipping her tea at intervals, went on.

"Do not think, Mrs. Glenmorris, that I say all this with the intention of communicating any painful retrospections. I speak in the plenitude of amicable solicitude; and I should indeed be very unworthy of the confidential regard of dear Lady Mary, if a misapprehended tenderness with-held me from probing to its foundation the ulceration of principles and connections, inimical to real sobriety of character and conduct; when you seem to expect that I shall be persuaded to an interference with your venerable mother on your behalf."

Lost in the contemplation of her own misery, Mrs. Glenmorris heard nothing of all this parading harangue but its conclusion.

She answered faintly—"It is not of my mother, 'tis of my child, I think."

"Alas," rejoined her persecutor, "If you had originally meditated more effectually on the one, you might not now suffer as you do for the other. But pray inform me, Mrs. Glenmorris, what is it you intend to do?"

"To die," answered the unhappy mother of Medora; whose senses again began to wander—"on this earth I have no business, if my daughter is taken from me."

"There!" cried the pityless Mrs. Grinsted; "that is another shocking proof of your erroneous principles. What!—because consequences have followed the result of your own misconduct, which there was so much reason to expect, you would rush uncalled into the presence of an irritated and vengeful Deity, instead, oh! unhappy infatuation, instead of humbling yourself in the dust, before the angry Omnipotent, and owning, with tears of contrition, and a chastised spirit, that you have deserved the punishment inflicted upon you, and deprecate the wrath to come; so may your sorrows in this world suffice, and you may not be accounted among those, who, following the new modes, have verily 'sacrificed their sons and their daughters unto devils'— Besides—has it escaped your recollection, have you forgotten, that you are forbidden to fix your heart and mind on any sublunary creature—you are not to love any thing over much—but to consider yourself as a sojourner here on earth, and get the mastery over all passions, and affections, and inclinations. I am in good hope this untoward circumstance, may bring you to a due sense of your past indecorous errors, which will contribute to your salvation hereafter; but give me permission to repeat my question,—what do you intend to do at present?"

The heart-broken sufferer, understood no more of these barbarous reproaches than that they were meant to aggravate her sorrows; and that the person to whom she had addressed herself with a vague hope of being assisted in the search after her child, endeavoured to persuade her she deserved the dreadful misfortune of having lost her. Mrs. Glenmorris was by this time totally incapable of answering; she was incapable of forming any resolution, except that she would listen no longer to the inhuman woman, who, abusing the name of religion, could thus pour corrosive poison on the dreadful wounds of her heart, bleeding for the loss of an only child.

If instances did not daily occur, of the use made by hypocrites of the cloak of piety, to gratify with impunity the most odious passions of the human heart, it would be almost incredible that any creature, in the form of a woman, could delight to irritate the anguish of a mother weeping over misfortunes that might be even worse than death; but, besides that the heart of Mrs. Grinsted was naturally malignant, and her temper selfish and arrogant; besides the early prejudices she had acquired, which had taught her that the high-born and affluent only were worth her consideration, or worthy to be ranked in the same class of beings, she had never forgotten that when Glenmorris was a young man, frequenting the house of Lady Mary, where she was occasionally an inmate, she had vainly endeavoured to attract his notice, and that he never shewed either attention to her person, though she was then thought young, (being not much turned of thirty) nor the least deference to her opinions, though every body else allowed her to be "a remarkably sensible woman." She still bore in mind, that he and Laura were once overheard to turn into ridicule her supposed attempts to engage the heart of Mr. Vanhugheynbourg, one of Mr. De Verdon's rich partners—and these recollections were sufficient to add personal hatred to the other motives, which engaged her to assist in delivering from the importunity of her daughter, or claims of her grand-daughter, her dear, venerable friend Lady Mary, from whom she also expected for her services, a very considerable addition to a legacy which she knew that excellent dowager had already bequeathed her. When, however, she said that she believed Medora had eloped with some young fellow, she for once declared what she at that moment believed to be true, though, like Mrs. Crewkherne, she held it to be perfectly justifiable to alter, change, or falsify any thing, if the *existing circumstances* required it—a sophistry, in which she was countenanced by some of the greatest and most successful orators and statesmen of the present enlightened period.

CHAP. VIII.

No—rather I abjure all roofs, and chuse
To wage against the enmity of the air,
To be a comrade with the wolf and owl.[106]

When Mrs. Grinsted had undertaken to assist, in what she called the "pious combination of justifiable deceptions," that were to put Lady Mary de Verdon at ease; and when she therefore engaged not to lose sight of Mrs. Glenmorris, and to accommodate her with a small sum of money, at once to convince her of friendly intentions, and acquire some power over her; Mrs. Grinsted by no means intended to embarrass herself farther, and certainly not to receive her into her house for any time. She hated to be put out of her way; and when she had satiated her malignity, by sharpening and striking deeper the empoisoned arrow which lacerated the bosom of her wretched guest, she shrunk from the fear of having sickness and sorrow near her. Mrs. Grinsted had sometimes little elegant assemblies of literary ladies at her house; where, if any male creature was admitted, it was an author of satire on the opinions of reformers, or the preacher of a court sermon, printed "by particular desire."[107] This party sometimes begun in discussions of poetry and politics, but ended almost always in rubbers and pools.[108] The science of cards being, notwithstanding any affectation of more elevated pursuits, the true alma mater of this respectable community. Her tenderness for a sick friend, would indeed have been almost as good a subject of panegyric to Mrs. Grinsted, as was her liberal contribution to all public charities, where the names of subscribers are registered; but when once it were known, that this inmate was the disobedient daughter of Lady Mary, the wife of Glenmorris, who had been much talked of as a political writer of republican principles, and the avowed friend of Armitage, a man still more obnoxious—and when it was known, that she was supposed to be made over by her profligate husband to this wicked Armitage, and that her daughter, who was trying to deprive sweet, dear, lovely Mary Cardonnel of half her fortune, had been so ill educated, that she had already eloped from her mother and was gone off, none knew with whom—when all this was known, it was impossible that either Mrs. Grinsted's long acquaintance with her family, or her compassion for a stray sheep, or indeed any other consideration, should be allowed, to qualify her reception of this unhappy woman, with the name of "an amiable weakness." Oh! no, such undistinguishing indiscriminate charity, would be said to give encouragement to the too much relaxed morality of modern innovators, and be derogatory to the dignity of her own immaculate reputation. To let Mrs. Glenmorris, in her present affliction, stay in her house, was therefore for this reason impossible. But had not the opinion of her dear friends been in question, there were two other reasons sufficient to determine her not to do it. One was, that she hated any kind of trouble, and the other, that she had a still greater aversion to any kind of expence.

No sooner, therefore, was Mrs. Glenmorris retired to a room above stairs, where she begged leave to remain a few moments alone, than the lady of the house, who was always ready to cry out with the Pharisee—"God, I thank thee that I am not as others are,"[109] began to murmur at Mrs. Battins, her maid, for having invited Mrs. Glenmorris into the house, and taken in her baggage.

It has been said, that "no man is an hero to his valet de chambre."[110]—And it is perhaps equally true, that no saintly gentlewoman has quite, in the opinion of her own woman, so great a share of perfection as she endeavours to exhibit to the rest of the world.

Certain it was, however, that Mrs. Battins appeared, occasionally, to lose towards her mistress that reverence which she desired to extort from more distant spectators. And, whether presuming on the confidence her mistress had in her, or on the opinion that she could not do without her, Mrs. Battins governed her almost as despotically as she did the two servants who executed the business of house-maid and cook.

This woman had probably more feminine feelings than her lady, for she resentfully answered, that whatever her mistress might do, *she* had not the heart to shut the door against a poor lady in such distress.—"I am really quite sorry to see her—It is enough to break any Christian heart; and to be sure it must be a cruel thing for a mother to lose such a sweet daughter, and not know into what bad wicked hands she's fallen."

"And what is that to us?" cried the mistress—"you know I am to have the last party of the year on Friday, and what am *I* to do with her?"—"I thought," said the maid, "that Mrs. Glenmorris had been your friend."

"I wish you would not think for me"—rejoined the lady with more asperity than she generally used—"as to friendship, this is no time to feel much of that; and besides it is Lady Mary, the mother whom this unfortunate person abandoned, that is my friend; and it was for her sake I troubled myself about her at all."

"Then I should think you mid as well interfere for Lady Mary, who is as rich as an old Jew,[111] and goes about with three footmen behind her coach, to have some bowels[112] for her own lawful daughter, and not suffer her to be so unhappy and without money. I'm sure she seems to me to be a worthy lady; and I'm sure—" "*You* are sure!" cried Mrs. Grinsted, "and who gave you authority to be sure? What! she is a worthy lady—that is, she has given you money, I suppose, because she has so much. Such folks are always generous when they will not be just; but I tell you I'll not be incommoded, nor I cannot. Go to Lady Mary with a note I shall write, and see if you can persuade *her* that this unhappy daughter of her's is a worthy lady. For my part it is an unthankful business, and I'll have nothing more to do with it."

"I hate Lady Mary," said Mrs. Battins, sullenly—"and if I must go to her I shan't be afraid to tell her my mind, I assure you—you had much better, ma'am, go yourself."

"You are impertinent, methinks, Mrs. Battins."

"No, ma'am, I'm true and just, and that's what I will be as long as I can. I won't tell a lie to please the king; nor twenty kings and queens too—and I'm free to say I do think Lady Mary a cross and wicked old woman, and let her own daughter want a place to put her head in, when she have three or four houses, and besides rolls in money, and all her servants are always a boasting how well they live, and seem to think no other people are worthy for to wipe their shoes.—'He that providest not for their own,' saith the Scriptures, 'is worse *nor* an infidel.'"[113]

Mrs. Grinsted continued to insist on the former undutifulness of Mrs. Glenmorris; and declared that what had happened looked very like a judgment upon her; and the conversation became so warm, that neither mistress nor maid were any longer guarded either in their tone or their terms.

Mrs. Glenmorris, when alone, had reflected as well as her overwhelmed and distracted mind would allow her to do, on all she recollected of the discourse she had heard from Mrs. Grinsted.—Another night was now approaching—Another night! and Medora lost—Medora suffering, perhaps, every terror, every indignity, and calling in vain on her mother—that mother who had never, since her birth, been one day absent from her. The idea was so dreadful, that to endure it was impossible; yet the very anguish it inflicted nearly annihilated the faculties of the unhappy sufferer, and deprived her of power to consider of the best means for recovering her child; who, notwithstanding the cruel intimations of Mrs. Grinsted, was, she well knew, incapable of having voluntarily left her. Innocent, candid, ingenuous, Medora never had a thought that she desired to conceal from her mother.—Delmont was the only human who had ever spoken to her of love; to Delmont her young heart was attached, with all the tenderness his merit deserved; and to him she had been authorised by the approbation of both her parents to dedicate her life. It was not in nature, therefore, that any other man should have estranged her from him and from her duty, had any one had an opportunity. But no such opportunity had been given—Medora had no acquaintance—she had never been out of her mother's sight save only thrice, when Mrs. Glenmorris had gone among the lawyers, where it would have been unpleasant for her daughter to have accompanied her; and at those times she had remained above the stairs during her mother's absence; and the maid who waited on her there had declared, that till the note was delivered to her from the person with whom she had left the hotel, no one had ever been admitted to speak to her, or ever asked it, or had she received any letter or message whatever. It was then certain, that some stratagem must have been used to decoy her from her mother's protection; but why or by whom? Her sweet and youthful figure, and countenance, though eminently lovely, were less captivating at first, than irresistible after the mind that informed them was understood. Many young women were as handsome—a still greater number more shewy—and it was not likely in these times, when beauty is so common, that in this country any one should carry her off against her consent, merely on account of personal attractions. Medora was poor—and therefore it was equally improbable that any other motive could engage an adventurer or fortune-hunter, in so hazardous an undertaking. Why, therefore, and by whom was she thus torn from the arms of her mother—and where could that wretched mother seek her?

Far from having received any consolation or advice from Mrs. Grinsted, all the anguish of heart which Mrs. Glenmorris sought to assuage by her advice had been redoubled; and finding she had nothing to expect from the compassionate assistance of a woman who knew not how to feel for her, she had endeavoured to collect all her strength, and to take some steps herself. It occurred to her, that by advertising she might gain some information, as well as by enquiring of persons who let out hired coaches, and for this purpose she was descending the stairs when the animated dialogue between the mistress and the maid reached her ears—for the stairs and passages were all carpeted, and the door of Mrs. Grinsted's dressing-room, where they were talking, was half open.

Mrs. Glenmorris then, descending the stairs, heard her name mentioned, and heard too that she was considered as likely, from the state of her mind and her fortune, to be a troublesome inmate; that she should be looked upon as an unworthy acquaintance by the coterie to which Mrs. Grinsted belonged, and was spoken of as the disgrace of her family, and the unhappiness of her mother. There were not many circumstances that could have added to the anguish of mind Mrs. Glenmorris at this moment endured, but the undeserved stain thus thrown on her character; the cruelty of imputing to her, twenty years of whose life had been passed in the most affectionate execution of the duties of a wife and a mother, errors and crimes, the commission of which had never entered her mind; the malignant arrogance with which Mrs. Grinsted decided, that the deepest wound which could lacerate the heart of a parent was inflicted on her by the just vengeance of heaven, were circumstances that (when added to the fatigue, fear, and want of rest for so many hours, during which she had hardly swallowed any nourishment) quite overcame the little fortitude she had been trying to collect, and instead of going again to speak to Mrs. Grinsted, and name to her the means she meant to pursue, Mrs. Glenmorris now walked hastily out of the house, unknowing whither she was going, yet resolute to return to it no more.

In her pocket she had two five pound notes (the remainder of Mrs. Grinsted's loan) and some silver. The idea of advertising for her daughter returned to her mind as soon as it was impressed no longer with the strictures of the cruel-hearted woman she had left; of herself she thought not; her whole soul was again absorbed in the idea of having been deprived of Medora, and in vague and half-formed projects for recovering her.

That with an husband, who idolized both her and her daughter; with such a man as Delmont, so fondly attached to that daughter, and such a friend as Armitage, Mrs. Glenmorris should be so destitute of protection, appeared to be the most strange as well as lamentable of all circumstances; yet her long residence out of England, and her estrangement from the family of her parents, had prevented her from cultivating the acquaintance of the former friends of her house, and those of Glenmorris were, besides Armitage, men who had either been carried to different parts of the world by the extraordinary changes which had happened within the last ten years in Europe,[114] or had retired to their estates at a great distance from London, so that Mrs. Glenmorris could not recollect one person to whom she might, in this cruel exigence, apply for advice and assistance.

Thus forsaken and forlorn, her frame sinking with weakness, and her heart agonized with pain, she continued to walk along the streets towards Charing Cross, where she had some recollection of having seen the office of a news-paper.[115] The hurry in the streets, the noise of carriages, and the busy faces, all eager in some pursuit, and none probably, at least none in her rank of life, who had not an house to receive them, and friends who participated in their disappointment or success, contributed to distract her; so that when she at length found the place she wanted, and entered the office, she was unable to relate the occasion of her coming; and when the person who attended asked her commands, she sat down and had nearly fainted, for tears had not once come to her relief, since the dreadful conviction that Medora was torn from her.

The man in the office, like those in offices of more consequence, was totally void of feeling; he again, and somewhat roughly, demanded to know her business; and with difficulty she explained to him, that she wished to put into the papers an advertisement relative to the disappearance of a young lady; but the moment she had said so much, the cruel necessity of describing her daughter, of making her loss public, and exposing her to the malicious animadversions of the brutal and vicious, struck so forcibly upon her mind, than when the man with an ironical sneer on his countenance asked her for the particulars, informing her at the same time of the price paid by the line at their office, Mrs. Glenmorris found herself utterly incapable of executing her plan; her senses were again forsaking her; she left the place abruptly, and once more found herself in the street.

She then, without any settled resolution, went to the hotel which she had quitted that morning; but the mistress of it was conscious that she had been imposed upon and ill-treated, and apprehended she had either returned to reproach her, or might be again come to take up her abode there, which would be attended with trouble greater than the profit that could be derived from it; and of her madness the hostess doubted not. For these reasons that prudent person disappeared, and ordered her servants to give such answers as might deter her late guest from renewing her enquiries there. Rudeness and denial, when she had so much need of consolation and pity, completed the distraction that was now gaining rapidly upon her, and impressed only with the idea that she was seeking Medora, and that Mrs. Grinsted had driven her from her house with menaces and reproaches, she for some hours wandered about the streets, unconscious whither, and becoming every moment less and less fit for the purpose she fancied she was executing, that of seeking her daughter. Towards evening she found herself in one of the streets near May Fair. Her wild looks, her disordered step, and something that at once demanded respect and excited pity, had been unnoticed while she had rambled through the great avenues of the city; but now several women observed her with curiosity, and servants standing at the doors looked after her. There

was nothing about her that gave rise to ideas of her being a person of doubtful character. She was still very handsome, but such was the dignity of her figure and the expression of her face, that even the vulgar could not mistake her; her derangement of mind,
however, becoming more and more visible, exposed her to the designs of those wretches,
always on the watch for prey, who lurk about the streets of the metropolis, and two of
them were following her, when a woman who observed them, and the object of their
pursuit, went also after her, and as she was turning to go towards Hyde Park, (for a
confused notion had suddenly struck her that Medora was perhaps gone back to
Upwood) the woman, who was one of those good body's that attend the sick, or lying-
in ladies, accosted her with, "Madam, I am afraid you are not well; I am afraid you
have lost your way—It is a late hour rather for a lady like you to walk alone in the
park."

Mrs. Glenmorris looked wildly a moment on the stranger who accosted her,
then answered in a breathless, incoherent way, "That she was going to Upwood—She
thought her daughter might be there—Delmont would assist her, and they should
find her she hoped—Only," added she, "my fear is that Mrs. Crewkherne may have
got there first, and have hid her from us—and Mrs. Grinsted, I am sure, would never
let me know it—It must be some such thing—I am astonished I did not think of it
before."

The woman, who had now an opportunity of observing her more nearly, was
convinced that it might be well worth her while to take care of a lady, whom some
calamity seemed suddenly to have deprived of reason. She had a valuable watch by her
side, and a diamond ring on her finger, while the fine linen and muslin, of which her
dress was composed, and the handsome laced cloak she was wrapped in, left no doubt
in the woman's mind as to her rank of life; and of course she calculated, that any
services done to such a person would be sufficiently advantageous to herself, and perhaps they might also be the means of getting her recommended to some "good families." Mrs. Deacon had just left a lady whom she had attended, and was likely to be for
a fortnight disengaged. Having nothing therefore to intercept her humanity, and imagining it could not fail to be profitable, she persisted in following Mrs. Glenmorris,
who, having once spoken to her, suddenly conceived that she was sent to engage her to
go back to Mrs. Grinsted, and to divert her from the purpose her mind was now bent
upon, that of hastening to Upwood, and to Denbury Farm, at one of which places she
was sure to find Medora.

Impressed with this notion, the unhappy distracted mother started away from
Mrs. Deacon, who would have taken her hands, and ran back along the street from
whence she had just issued. Mrs. Deacon pursued her, but, fat and heavy, was likely
every moment to lose sight of her, if she had not called aloud to the passengers to stop
her. "The lady is mad," cried she, in a voice that echoed through the street; "stop her,
pray stop her, or she will do herself a mischief." Two footmen, who were lounging at
the door of a great house, came forward at the cry, extended their arms to prevent her
passage, and the poor affrighted Mrs. Glenmorris sunk down before them—while she
tried, but had no voice to implore their mercy. Mrs. Deacon, who followed quickly,
found her fallen on her knees on the pavement, her hat had fallen off, and her still fine

hair, flowing over her face, added to the wildness of her countenance, while she grasped the iron bars of the area, and protested that no force should compel her to return to Mrs. Grinsted, who had used her so cruelly; that she would go to Upwood; and that nobody had any right to detain her. The woman now began to expostulate, while a crowd gathered round them, and Mrs. Glenmorris, whose phrenzy encreased by opposition, by heat, and by the strange faces that surrounded her, answered only by repeated shrieks, and by protesting, that she would severely punish any one who attempted to detain her from going to Upwood.

Lady Mary de Verdon was at cards in her front drawing room, with Lady Limpston, Lady Barbara Grieves, (her old friend and correspondent) and Mrs. Bayley, one of those good sort of folks who are so useful in the houses of superannuated dowagers, to make up a rubber, or do any other little service that may be required of them.[116] Miss Cardonnel, the darling grand-daughter of Lady Mary, and a Miss Richmond, one of her young friends, were practicing a new duet in the adjoining dressing room, which, as the house was large, was also in front, when the meditations on the long trump[117] in one room, and the musical harmony in the other, were interrupted by the increasing noise in the street. At length Mrs. Bayley, who was the only one of the elderly party whose ears were very quick, could not refrain from going during a deal, to the window; but as what she could see from thence rather irritated than satisfied her curiosity, she rang the bell to know what was the matter, and the only servant, who was not by this time engaged before the door, attending the summons, was interrogated by Lady Mary, as to the noise in the street. "Oh! my lady," said Michael, "'tis a crazy person, my lady, who have scaped away out of a mad house, my lady, and got to be start staring mad, just here before your ladyship's door; and Missus Dacon, my lady, the nuss tinder,[118] as used to be at Lady Benton's, over-right, is trying, my lady, to make her quiet, and get her back to the mad doctor; but she's despert mischievous, my lady, and Abel and John are a helping to hold her."

Miss Cardonnel, at this moment, ran into the room, and told her grand-mother, that the unfortunate person in the street was certainly a gentlewoman—"It is shocking to see her," said the young lady. "Mrs. Bayley I wish, if my grand-mama has no objection, that you would go down and see what can be done for her." Lady Mary, who understood very little, and cared still less about the distress of a person at her door, never however contradicted a wish of Miss Cardonnel's, even though the rubber must stand still, and Mrs. Bayley, glad to oblige the young heiress, went down.

There was by this time a collection round the door of near three hundred people. Mrs. Bayley, on the first glance at the unhappy object before her, saw she was a person of some consideration, and being shewn the watch and ring which Mrs. Deacon had taken into her care, nothing more proper occurred to her therefore, than to have the poor sufferer brought into the house, in the lower part of which there was no likelihood of her incommoding Lady Mary, who was too infirm ever to come down stairs, (except when carried by her servants to her coach). Miss Cardonnel, who with generous solicitude had by this time ventured to the door, was eager that the unhappy stranger might be brought away from the rude gaze of the multitude. Her will was the law of all the family, and the men servants were now directed to what was very easily performed, for by this time Mrs. Glenmorris was quite exhausted, and, unresisting, suffered herself to be carried into the house, whither Mrs. Deacon followed her by Miss Cardonnel's directions, and the men being dismissed, she was placed on a sopha in a back parlour, appropriated to the use of the house-keeper.

CHAP. IX.

—————The worst
Of evils, and excessive, overturns
All patience![119]

Mrs. Glenmorris was now in the house of her mother, brought thither by accident, after the lapse of near twenty years; but she was totally unconscious where she was, and Lady Mary little knew the inmate whom the compassion of Miss Cardonnel had induced her to receive.

Miss Cardonnel was of an humane and generous disposition; and though her education had been ill directed, and every possible pains had been taken to make her proud, selfish, and insensible, by the foolish admiration and boundless indulgence of her grandmother, and the adulation of the dependents and domestics, she was a rare instance of a young woman possessing an heart which prosperity could not harden, nor bad example vitiate.

The general calamities of poverty and sorrow, which distress those who are not determined to be blind, in every street, and form a shocking contrast to the splendor and luxury of the rich in the metropolis, had always hurt the sensibility of Miss Cardonnel, who had frequently been remonstrated with by her governesses, and laughed at by her young companions, "for collecting," said the elderly ladies, "such crowds of beggars round the coach door, that there was no comfort in their airings," while the gay giddy flutterers of fortune, who threw away their time and money in pursuing all sorts of trifles round the town, thought it vastly absurd that Miss Cardonnel often put aside half a crown or half a guinea, which she was solicited to lay out, saying, she made a conscience of not throwing away in frivolous purchases money which so many unfortunate people wanted to enable them merely to exist.

With this general disposition to benevolence the appearance of Mrs. Glenmorris could not fail to affect her, and probably would have done so, if she had not observed in the haggard countenance, the glazed unconscious eyes, and incoherent ravings of the unhappy stranger, something that appeared familiar to her memory. Who was it the person before her was like? and where had tones exactly similar been present to her?—The form of the face, the figure of the person, and the voice, all bore a most extraordinary resemblance to her mother, who died when she was thirteen, and whom she perfectly recollected. This resemblance was, she thought, merely accidental, but it affected Miss Cardonnel so much, that when after a short interval of silence, the consequence of her being totally exhausted, Mrs. Glenmorris again began to call upon her daughter, to entreat them to let her go to her child, her angel child, and to consider what might be the consequence of her mother's being thus torn from her; when she again shrieked and raved, calling on heaven to witness how barbarously she was treated, Miss Cardonnel could not remain in the room, but recommending her earnestly to the care of the house-keeper and Mrs. Deacon, retired in tears; yet recovering herself as soon as she could, went to give an account to Lady Mary of the situation of the unfortunate lady, and ask permission for her to be put to bed, and taken care of in the house, till her friends, who would undoubtedly miss her, should come to take her into their care.

Lady Mary, who was in no danger of being herself incommoded by this arrangement, willingly consented, but Mrs. Bayley, though with great deference to Miss Cardonnel, raised some objections. She said the poor lady was most undoubtedly raving mad, and, she should have thought, had broke from her confinement in some house destined for the reception of lunatics, yet some appearances contradicted that supposition; her dress, and her remarkable fine long hair; the watch she had by her side, the ring on her finger; therefore to be sure, mad as she was now she had not been long so, "and for myself, I freely confess," said Mrs. Bayley, "that I have my doubts— If the poor lady should be afflicted with a phrenzy fever[120]—It may be infectious; it may be attended with very disagreeable circumstances—I own I have my doubts how dear Lady Mary might like to be put to the inconveniencies it might bring on."

Lady Mary heard not half this, and what she did hear made very little impression upon her—She bade her dear Mary (Miss Cardonnel) do just as she pleased, and then returned again to her rubber with her two venerable friends, who took no part whatever in the conversation, and seemed to have outlived every faculty and every feeling but those which enabled them to deal, shuffle, and calculate their winnings.

But if tranquillity was thus restored above it was by no means the case below, where the house-keeper, who never loved any kind of trouble, and began to apprehend she should have a great deal, was very much out of humour with Mrs. Deacon, with whom she was acquainted, and after many oblique remarks on mercenary officiousness, said, "I hope you will stay yourself, ma'am, and look after this person, if Miss Cardonnel's whim is for her to stay here; for my lady is going out a town in a few days, and for my part I shall have fatigue enough, and cannot have my rest broke in upon by strangers, not I."—She then desired Miss Cardonnel's maid to ask her mistress what room the strange lady was to have, and who was to stay with her—"We shall be waked all night, I suppose," said she, "and mid as well pass it in Bedlam,[121] if once she begins her tantarums.[122] A strange fancy, I think, of Miss Cardonnel's, to bring mad folks into our house; but I hope we shall be quit of the trouble on't tomorrow."

The unhappy subject of these selfish apprehensions was once more sunk into silence. Exhausted and breathless, almost senseless, she suffered them to carry her up stairs, where she was put into bed, and Miss Cardonnel, directing Mrs. Deacon to stay by her, and assuring her she should be satisfied for any trouble she might have, ventured once more to approach, and to take her hand, which now lay lifelessly on the quilt. It was very feverish, and communicated an heat like that which is felt after touching nettles; her pulse could not be counted, and Miss Cardonnel, alarmed for the life of the unhappy stranger, dispatched her own footman for the physician that attended the family.

This gentleman, as humane as he was skilful, highly applauded the generosity of Miss Cardonnel. He told her the lady, who was certainly oppressed with fever, which seemed to him to arise from violent agitation of spirits and excessive fatigue; that of the disarrangement of her intellects he could not judge in her present state, but that he would order what should quiet her, and prevent, if possible, her relapsing into those alarming fits of raving and exclamation that had been described to him. This done, he went away, Lady Mary not knowing of his visit, and the medicine being soon after, though not without difficulty, administered, Mrs. Deacon entered in due form on her office of nurse, valuing herself highly on her sagacity, and thinking with complacency that she was sure of being handsomely paid by Miss Cardonnel, besides the advantage she expected to derive from the friends of the lady whom she had so opportunely met and protected.

It was only by repeated doses of the medicine that the unhappy patient was kept during the night in a sort of unquiet slumber. With the morning a slight degree of consciousness returned, and Mrs. Glenmorris starting up, undrew her curtain, and looking wildly on the woman who sat near the bed, said in a hurrying manner, "Where am I? My child, my Medora, is she here? Has any one had the humanity to restore her? Pray, madam, tell me, where am I?"

Mrs. Deacon, who imagined her patient had a lucid interval, and that she should take advantage of it to find where her friends resided; she therefore began with more exactness than discretion to relate what had passed the evening before, adding, "So you are now, ma'am, in the house of a lady of fashion, who is very willing you should remain, till such time as you are able to be moved to your friends."

Mrs. Glenmorris now endeavoured to recal all that happened the preceding evening till after leaving the news-paper office, she had found fatigue of body and anguish of mind insensibly overwhelm her. She was now become an object of charity to a stranger, and admitted to her house from wandering in the street! But it was the cause of all this that hung with dreadful weight on her heart. However humiliating the consequences, they were nothing, and only the image of her dear lost girl dwelt on the mind of the wretched mother.

In the severe trials she had been exposed to in the early part of her life, Mrs. Glenmorris had shewn no want of fortitude and force of mind. The series of years she had since passed with a man, the strength of whose understanding had subdued the violence of his passions, and who possessed the rare assemblage of genius and reason, had given to a mind naturally of superior rank every advantage which it could derive either from observation or books; but during that time, protected by his tenderness from every inconvenience, she had not felt the evils of life, and was now but ill prepared to resist what had so unexpectedly fallen upon her—the heaviest, the severest of all miseries—the loss of a beloved child.

A partial recovery of that reason, which this great misfortune had shaken, was to her only a renewal of anguish. She had just enough recollection of the general habits and sentiments of her mind, to know, that, instead of giving herself up to despair, she ought to collect all her powers, and exert them to recover her child. With her hands pressed closely over her eyes, as if at once to conceal from her the light of day, which was become odious to her, and to stop the throbbing pulses in her temples, Mrs. Glenmorris endeavoured to acquire calmness enough to act with more effect than she had hitherto done. Two nights, and the greater part of two days, she had been lamenting instead of acting; and perhaps rendered incurable, evils she might have remedied— and duty, affection, every motive now called upon her to practice maxims she had a thousand times recommended. While the nurse continued therefore to talk, Mrs. Glenmorris heeding her not, and, unconscious of what she said, was contriving how she might avail herself of the kindness of the woman of rank in whose house she understood herself to be, to set on foot those enquiries for Medora, which Mrs. Grinsted had been so far from assisting in, that, instead even of words of pity and consolation, she had heard from her only taunts and reproaches.

In pursuance of this plan, Mrs. Glenmorris desired to have her cloaths brought her, and exerted all her strength to rise and dress herself; but having with difficulty done so, she became so faint, and found her head again so confused, that she was under the necessity of lying down on the bed for a few moments, when she told the nurse, she thought she should be a great deal better.

Mrs. Deacon was one of those good women, who are paid for their attendance on others, and apply the advantages derived from their labour to the indulgence of themselves in articles of luxury, which from their own situation in life they could never obtain.[123] She was a jolly dame of fifty-four, with a round red face, an almost gigantic person, and an herculean constitution; so that she could sit up for months together, and eat and drink the whole day, with a perseverance which was, apparently, extremely beneficial to her health. Lady Mary had always been remarkably attentive to the elegance and nicety of her table; and, as she advanced in years, she became more fastidious and luxurious. At two o'clock, every day, a collation was served up in her dressing-room, and as soon as it was over, Mrs. Spicer the house-keeper, and any one among the domestics whom she chose to honour, were admitted to share the same repast in Mrs. Spicer's parlour. The brawny attendant on poor Mrs. Glenmorris was extremely disposed to avail herself of this occasion of indulging her appetite, and of tasting some sweet white wine, with which she knew the guests in the housekeeper's room were occasionally treated.

As Mrs. Glenmorris desired to be left alone, the opportunity was not to be neglected; gliding, therefore, down the back stairs as silently and nimbly as her bulk would permit, the good guardian of the sick, who was received kindly by Mrs. Spicer, was soon so busy with the niceties before her, and the Spanish wine had so powerful an influence, that she forgot the poor lady above, and began to relate history after history of all "the good *families*" she had *tended* in—told "how such a lord behaved to his lady; and how genteel Sir Marmaduke Mandrake was to all the *nusses* and sarvunts, when Lady Mandrake, after being married nine years without arrow[124] child, pursented Sir Marmaduke with as foin a boy as iver the sun shoon upon."

Mrs. Glenmorris, being thus relieved from her impertinent prate, regained once more that degree of recollection, which was necessary to enable her to carry into execution the vague plan that had before occurred to her. She got up, therefore, and having twice rang the bell, in the intention of sending a message to the lady of the house, but no one attending the summons, she determined to go herself. On reaching half way down the stairs, however, the opiate, which had failed of giving her quiet sleep, added to the giddiness and confusion of her head. She had just presence of mind enough to hold by the balustrade, that she might not fall, and slowly and with difficulty arrived at the drawing-room floor, which consisted of two very spacious, and one smaller apartment, splendidly furnished. Passing through the first of these, which was empty, Mrs. Glenmorris advanced through the open door to the second. An old lady was there alone, seated on a damask sofa, and surrounded by silk pillows. Not hearing very distinctly, and imagining it to be one of her attendants, she took no notice of the person approaching her, till Mrs. Glenmorris, at that moment, conscious that she beheld her mother, uttered a loud shriek, and fell at her feet.

Lady Mary, terrified and confused, not directly knowing her daughter, yet having recollection enough of her face and figure to be shocked and amazed, rang violently for the attendants. A man and two female servants flew in alarm to my lady—"My lady! your ladyship!"—they were struck dumb, as well by the prostrate and agonized figure of Mrs. Glenmorris, as by the exclamation of Lady Mary.

"Who it this?" demanded she angrily—"how came she in *my* house; who dared bring her here?"

"It is the lady, ma'am," replied the man—"the lady that was taken mad in the street last night, and that Mrs. Bayley—"

"Mrs. Bayley!" it was she then whose officious impertinence had contrived this interview—for Lady Mary was now certain it was her daughter she saw kneeling before her; that daughter to whom she had been indifferent and severe in her youth, and who now was the object of her dislike and dread.—"Mrs. Bayley!" cried she angrily, her voice trembling with passion—"Let Mrs. Bayley be sent for this moment—how dares she take such liberties—where is my Mary?—where is Miss Cardonnel?"

Mrs. Glenmorris, distracted as she was between the loss of her child, and this sudden and unsought interview with her mother, was hardly able to articulate—"My mother!—have mercy upon me!"—uttered in a tone of anguish, which would have moved any other heart, had no effect on the callous bosom of the Lady Mary.—She moved away from the place where her unhappy daughter knelt, and, assisted by her woman, was carried to her dressing-room, when she again gave peremptory orders that Mrs. Bayley might be sent for; and continued loudly to call for Miss Cardonnel—her dear Mary.

The footman informed her that Miss Cardonnel was gone out in the coach with Miss Richmond. A servant was dispatched for her, and another sent to desire Mrs. Bayley would instantly attend. Lady Mary then began to lament herself, and soon explained to such of the wondering servants as were present, who the lady was, that till then had appeared to be a stranger, introduced into the house by the active compassion of Miss Cardonnel.

Mrs. Bayley being really one of those officious persons, who are generally detested by the servants of a great family, was now without an advocate to remind Lady Mary, that she had, in fact, opposed the admission of the stranger, while Miss Cardonnel had insisted upon it; but, besides that, none of them felt disposed to speak in favour of the busy whisperer, Mrs. Bayley; they were thunderstruck, when they perfectly comprehended that the unhappy person, whose distressful entrance into her house was so offensive to Lady Mary, was her own daughter. No offence that she could possibly have committed eighteen or twenty years before, seemed to be a sufficient reason for this unnatural rejection of her, and however their interest might compel them to follow their lady's orders, there was not one of them who would go with a message to Mrs. Glenmorris to leave the house. They lingered instead of obeying, in hopes that the generosity of Miss Cardonnel might obtain a respite, at least, for the unfortunate lady.

She was herself again unconscious of her miseries—for some moments after her mother so abruptly left her, she remained still kneeling, with her head on her arms, which rested on a chair—and the short though extraordinary scene she had passed, appeared like a wild dream. The delirium which had been gaining on her ever since Medora was missing, returned with accumulated force, and she was seized with a paroxysm more violent than that of the preceding day. Her cries soon brought Mrs. Deacon, and several of the servants into the room, and with great difficulty, assisted by the footmen, they forced her back to the room she had left, where, as it was at a great distance from the apartment of Lady Mary, they imagined she might remain unheard, at least till Miss Cardonnel arrived.

That amiable girl came back in about an hour, and at the same moment arrived Mrs. Bayley. The latter, with difficulty obtained an hearing in vindication of her innocence; the former was shocked and amazed to understand, that the poor wanderer she had been induced to succour from motives of humanity, was so near a relation.—She could not listen, without shuddering, to the severe anathemas which Lady Mary uttered—insisting upon it, that the whole was a plan artfully contrived, to force her to receive an ungrateful and worthless woman, whom she never would consider as her child. Miss Cardonnel had often attempted, but in vain, to soften the resentment that, whenever they were named, her grandmother expressed against the family of Glenmorris. This was the only point wherein she had no influence, and Lady Mary had frequently enjoined her silence in so peremptory a way, that Miss Cardonnel thought she did more harm than good in attempting to plead for them. Since it had been known, that they intended to try how far the will of old de Verdon left an opening to the succession of his youngest daughter's heirs, this hatred on the part of Lady Mary had received an accession of inveterate malignity, and she had never heard the subject named without reproaching Miss Cardonnel for her weakness. "These are the people," cried she, "you would have me be kind to—these very people who are now going to law with you, and would rob you of your birth-right."

Lady Mary, far from being moved to compassion, when the deplorable situation of her daughter was represented to her, persisted in her resolution of having her removed from her house. Miss Cardonnel resolved not to execute so cruel an order, at least till some comfortable situation could be found for her aunt, sent for Mrs. Grinsted, who was, she thought, the likeliest person to assist her with counsel, and to appease the anger of her grandmother.

Mrs. Grinsted arrived at a late hour of the afternoon, and appeared neither much shocked, nor much surprised at what had happened. She explained the cause of

Mrs. Glenmorris's insanity by relating, that having come to London with her daughter on the law business, they had lodged at an hotel, where the young lady had it seems some acquaintance, with whom, in the *inconsiderateness* of her juvenile enthusiasm, the effect probably of an ill-directed education, she had evaded—in a word eloped.

Miss Cardonnel was more affected than before, when she had learned the source of that sorrow, which had crushed to the earth a woman, whom even in her present state of mental imbecility engaged her affection, while she called forth her pity; but Mrs. Grinsted did not encourage this generous sympathy; she appeared very reserved; hinted that there were circumstances in the case, with which it was not desirable that Miss Cardonnel should be acquainted, and represented how very improper it was, that she should interfere in an affair that could only properly be decided by the feelings and judgment of Lady Mary.

Having thus damped, as she imagined, the indiscreet zeal of this young and disinterested advocate, Mrs. Grinsted renewed her private conference with Lady Mary; while Miss Cardonnel, whose affectionate heart was agonized by her aunt's distresses, went up to enquire after her. Mrs. Glenmorris became every hour in a more distressed state. The fever which had seized her brain gained upon her, and whoever had seen her at that period, would not have hesitated to say, as the nurse and people about her now did, that she was absolutely insane. At Miss Cardonnel's request, the physician again attended her in the evening, and she appeared to him to be in a state that would require remedies and discipline, such as could only be obtained in an house appropriated to the reception of patients labouring under the loss of reason. Miss Cardonnel wished to conceal this opinion yet another day from her grandmother and Mrs. Grinsted, in hopes that some alteration for the better might happen, but Dr. * * * * * thought it his duty to announce the truth to Lady Mary—he knew not how nearly the stranger was related to her.

In consequence of this intelligence, which was still farther confirmed in his visit the following morning, it was determined that the name and condition of Mrs. Glenmorris should be kept a secret from every body, and that she should be conveyed, as privately as possible, to one of the most remote houses, within twenty miles of London, where lunatics are received.[125] It was by no means proper, that one so nearly related to Miss Cardonnel, should be known to be in this unhappy condition—And Lady Mary, in agreeing to pay a very handsome salary,[126] tried to persuade herself that she should acquit herself of her duty—She was sure at least of gaining many points of great consequence. Impressed from the reports of Mrs. Crewkherne, with the most invidious idea of her daughter's attachment to Mr. Armitage, she really thought that to conceal her from him, was to save her from future misconduct. She would, by holding Mrs. Glenmorris in her power, put an end to the prosecution of a suit which she could not think of with patience, and acquit herself of her maternal duties in a manner even exemplary, by receiving, though under another name, the daughter who had thrown off her protection, and defied her authority.

Mrs. Grinsted undertook to settle this business for her, assisted by Mrs. Deacon. Lady Mary hastened a few days her intended departure from London, and Miss Cardonnel, no longer suffered to exercise her generous humanity, was compelled to leave the unfortunate mother of Medora, who, sometimes raving for her daughter, sometimes sunk in dejection, was conveyed under the name of Mrs. Tichfield to an house in Hertfordshire, on the borders of Essex.

CHAP. X.

If she is gone—*if* I have lost her! If?
Ah! how endure I now to think it may be—
How, should it prove so, *live?*[127]

When, after a rapid journey, George Delmont arrived at Upwood, his disappointment and consternation are not to be conceived.

By a series of those perverse circumstances, which frequently occasions the delay of letters between England and Ireland, Delmont had never received any of those written to him by Mrs. Glenmorris or Medora, after the first week of his absence, so that now, without the least previous information, he found his house deserted by those, whose love and esteem he had considered as the dearest addition to the comforts of home; and to which he had looked forward as a compensation for all the perplexity and uneasiness of his long absence.

He hastened over to Mrs. Glenmorris's lodging at Dalebury[128]—there it was still worse. He approached the farm-house, on the side where were Mrs. Glenmorris's apartments. Susanne, her Swiss servant, was sitting in the old fashioned projecting window, where, on a sort of shelf that went round it, within, was Medora's little collection of geraniums and myrtles, with some curious roses and mignionet.[129] Susanne was at work, but her mind seemed indeed to have strayed from her fingers, and she seemed as if she was ready to weep over the plants left to her care. Delmont stood looking at her a moment; but when she perceived him, the poor woman flew round to the door, and eagerly enquired for news from her dear ladies? He came to her, he said, for news, for he had only heard at home that they had been gone a fortnight; the countenance of Susanne immediately fell, and it was with difficulty she sufficiently recovered herself to tell him, that she had every day expected her ladies home, because she had not heard of them for above a week, and could no otherwise account for their silence. She had never since she entered on her service, which was when Medora was an infant, been so long separated from her and her mother; and now poor Susanne felt so deserted and forlorn, that she tormented herself with a thousand wild conjectures and apprehensions, which, vague and unfounded as he thought them, failed not to add to the disquiet of Delmont.

Ashamed, however, of being alarmed at what was probably only a common occurrence, he checked the disposition he felt to indulge despondence which might be groundless and childish, and endeavoured to re-assure Susanne; while she continued however to lament herself, and to tell, in her motly language, which had often a ground of French, oddly embroidered with English and German, how dull and sad a life she led. The farmer's wife was a very good woman to be sure, but then she was always busy brewing and baking, and getting the men's dinner, or else out at market, and some-times there was nobody in the house, Susanne said, but herself and *alors elle avoit peur, des Bohemiens, des mandiants, des matelots avec des jambes de bois, qui rodoient autour de la maison;—"et dont il y'en avoit un Monsieur,"* said she, *"qui parceque je lui ai repondu en François, a pesté juré, et m'appellé* FRANCHE BICHE*—avec des* GODE DAMS, *et des jurements effrayant."*[130]

Delmont, to relieve poor Susanne from any such disagreeable rencontres[131] for the future, told her she should remove to Upwood till her lady's return; a proposal the poor woman joyfully accepted, and the same evening Delmont sent one of his men to attend her, in a convenient cart, with Medora's moveable garden, which Susanne de-clared she could not leave to the chance of their being taken care of by the farmer's maid.

Her arrival did not serve to appease the restless anxiety of Delmont. He had now somebody to talk to of it, and his wanderings round his house and grounds no longer yielding him any delight, usually ended in a conference with Susanne—whose solicitude every hour encreased, and after two days she said, *"Il est impossible que madame, ou mademoiselle ne soit pas malade; mon Dieu!—Ah! monsieur, si vous vouliez ecrire!"*[132]

To write had been Delmont's first idea—yet there was something like impro-priety in writing, as if to require Mrs. Glenmorris's return as soon as he himself ar-rived. There were, undoubtedly, letters that had missed him, accounting for her ab-sence; and all that seemed now necessary was for her to know (which he had informed her on the instant of his arrival) that he was once more at Upwood.

He waited her answer, which might have arrived on the second day, with inqui-etude. It was, however, possible that a transient absence, the pressure of business, or many other circumstances, might have prevented her replying exactly by the post's return. Another day, however, came—no letter!—a fourth arrived, and still the comfortless answer that there was no letter at the post for him.—Susanne repeated, *"Ah! si monsieur voudres ecrire un petit mot."*[133] And it occurred to Delmont, that possibly Mrs. Glenmorris might have removed from the hotel, whence her letters to Susanne were dated, and had gone into lodgings, while it was very probable that the people at their first residence had forgotten her address, or neglected to send her letters.

On the fourth day, therefore, after his return, Delmont wrote to the mistress of the hotel, and on the fifth received the following letter from one of her men:

SIR,
With my missus's humbel dutty, this comes to let you no, that Mrs. Glenmurry and miss, has been gone from here about a wick. The young lady went fust, and the older lady stade on night, but no more ater her. Cant pertend to say were there gone two, not havin leef a drickshon.[134] From, sir, your humble servant to command,

CHRISTOPHER CRUET.
* * * *'s Hottel,
Jully 30th, 17——.

Delmont was astonished at the purport of this letter—and when poor Susanne heard it, he was obliged to suppress his own feelings, to appease the grief and fear it inflicted on her. He then walked out to consider what he should do, and after weighing maturely every circumstance that related to Mrs. Glenmorris's situation, he could not help concluding, that it must be some disagreeable event which had compelled her first to go so suddenly to town, and now to take what appeared to him measures to conceal herself.—If she was in the slightest degree embarrassed, he could not too soon be with her; he therefore pacified Susanne as well as he could by assuring her, that if her ladies had occasion to stay much longer, she should be sent for to them; and then mounting his horse, he set out that evening for London, where, merely allowing time for his servant and horses to rest on the road, he arrived at noon the following day.

Delmont hastened immediately to the hotel. His eager looks, and quick manner of questioning the waiter, soon baffled that secrecy which had been recommended to this man.[135] He became confused, and that there was something to hide, could not escape the penetrating eyes of Delmont—reserve in such a case indicated some painful mystery. He therefore put an half-guinea into the waiter's hand, who, after a sort of preamble, informed Delmont that the young lady, after whom he enquired, had gone away one day, unknown to her mother, with a gentleman who came to fetch her in a coach—"Her mother, sir," continued the man, "but Lord, sir, your honour looks very white! shall I fetch you a little something?"

"Go on!" cried Delmont, eagerly.

"Well, sir, as I was a saying—Upon this, that is upon the mother's coming home, she was quite beside herself like, to think as her daughter was missing; and out she sets again to some frind of hern where she thought miss mought be?"

"You distract me," exclaimed Delmont, "pray hasten what you have to say."

"Well, sir, and so, sir as I was a saying, Mrs. Clanmurry, after she comed in, out she goes again to this frind's. But no miss was there, sure enough. Well! so about twelve and one, she comes back."

"Who?" cried Delmont, stamping impatiently.

"Why, sir, the elder lady; the mother; I was a gwine to say the old lady; but to be sure she is not old—only that her daughter is younger."

Delmont's patience wholly failed him—"This is insupportable," cried he—"What, my good fellow, do you mean?"

"Are you the lady's brother, sir?" enquired the man—"If so be, as you are a very near a-kin, why. . . ."

"Why, what then? For God's sake, friend, tell me—Suppose I am her brother?"

"Then, sir, to be sure you must be concerned; for though the young lady's mother could not abide for to think so, I must say, to speak the downright truth, that the lady did certainly elope, as they call it."

"Elope!" repeated Delmont, "impossible, Medora leave her mother?—Medora elope?—with who?"

"Nay, sir, that's more than any of us knows. Why, that's what her mother said; says she, it's no such thing, says she. My daughter Dorer is not capable of no such thing, says she, and, . . . (poor lady, she seem'd quite distracted mad) and so says she . . . "

"Where is the person who keeps this house?" asked Delmont, "I must see her."

The waiter began to give many reasons why it would be of no use for him to see Mrs. * * * *; but Delmont push'd by him, and went into the room where she sat.

Though her account was more formal and more guarded, and though she took care not to say that she had desired Mrs. Glenmorris to quit her house, because she believed her insane, Delmont thought it even less satisfactory than that of her servant. He besought them to recollect the name of the friend to whom Mrs. Glenmorris went, but they both declared they had not the least remembrance of the lady's name. All they could recal was, that she lived in one of the new streets beyond Oxford Road—"Could they remember the number of the coach she went in?"—Neither of them had noticed it.

Delmont then summoning all his presence of mind, insisted upon having every circumstance repeated to him that had happened. But when they mentioned a gentleman in a coach who had fetched Medora away, he found their descriptions differ entirely. And at last the good woman, who chose to draw him as a tall, genteel, handsome young gentleman, owned that she did but just see him through the window, and being very busy just then had not much noticed him.

Delmont, having exhausted every question by which he hoped to gain any information, left the house in a state of mind of which he had before formed no idea. He walked along the street perfectly unconscious whither he was going. Amazed at what he had heard, and bewildering himself in conjecture, he tried to recollect the persons Mrs. Glenmorris had occasionally named as those she had business with in London.— Petrify, the merchant, was the only one he could at that moment think of; he turned, and went towards his house.

On enquiring for Mr. Petrify he was shewn into a compting-house, where one clerk was running over aloud to another the Banker's book. They heeded him not, civility being no part of their character, unless towards those by whom they expected to profit. There was, however, something very imposing in the figure of Delmont, and having at last obtained the notice of a lad who was writing in a corner, he went out to call the master of the house, and Delmont was shewn into the parlour.

Such was the uncontroulable anguish that tore the heart of Delmont, that when a little short-legged Jew-looking man entered and announced himself as Mr. Petrify, he could not find terms to express himself. To mention the words lost, disappeared, eloped, with that of Medora, he found impossible. He therefore, though in visible agitation, enquired whether Mr. Petrify could direct him to the present residence of Mrs. Glenmorris.

The little shuffling man, (with a look much resembling that which a young Israelite turns towards a purchaser for his oranges whom he meditates to cheat,) examined Delmont's countenance while he spoke.—It was agitated by struggling passions; but Petrify knew nothing about them. He would have understood better the sharp etchings made by disappointed avarice; and had Delmont come to enquire after an insurance, or deprecate the attempt to put an end to

that dreadful trade,
Which robs unhappy Afric of her sons,[136]

Petrify would from sympathy have comprehended his sensations. As it was, he neither understood nor liked Delmont. Conscious that his treatment of Mrs. Glenmorris, though all proper and justifiable in the way of business, might be differently considered by such a man as the person before him, he thought it prudent and proper to give such answers as might put an end to all farther enquiries addressed to him. He therefore replied that he knew nothing, nothing at all of Mrs. Glenmorris; had not seen her for some days; imagined she was gone back into the country; and was sorry to say he could give no information whatever.—Delmont urged him to try to recollect the names of some persons with whom she had been acquainted in London; Petrify protested he had not the remotest knowledge of any of her connections; declared that it was merely by chance he was introduced to Mr. Glenmorris's correspondence, from which he had derived so little advantage, that he had determined wholly to decline it.—Delmont asked where the friend, who was the means of introducing him, was to be found? Petrify answered that he had long since returned to America; and Delmont, finding he could obtain no information, left the "little Jew-looking" merchant to return to speculations on profit and loss.

Whither could he now go? The name of Mrs. Grinsted occurred to him; and after a long search, and by enquiring of several tradesmen in the part of the town where he remembered she lived, he found the house; Mrs. Grinsted had left London the day before for the remainder of the summer; and there was nobody but a man and his wife, hired to take care of it, who could not even tell him where to direct to its mistress. They only knew that she went first to the house of *some lord*, a long way out of town; but was to stay there only a few days, and had said she would write to let them know where her letters should be sent after her.

It had been the business of Delmont's life to acquire that firmness of mind which can alone render a man satisfied with himself, or respected by others. This he knew was to be obtained only by shaking off his prejudices, and subduing his feelings—By determining never to be misled by the passions of others, or hurried into dangerous pursuits by the ardour of his own; but in the present instance all his philosophy was useless. He was wretched; and his endeavours to escape from his misery were vain. In attaching himself to Medora, he had followed the purest dictates of reason and nature. He had lost her, and the hideous obscurity that involved the circumstances of his loss, became deeper as he tried to remove it. He would have reasoned with himself; but the pain that distracted him was not to be appeased by sentences, or mitigated by comparisons. It was in vain he recollected the cruel certainty which had at an early period flashed on his mind, that man is born but to suffer and to die—and equally vain were the examples that occurred to him; examples of the power of reason to raise the soul above the transient sufferings of humanity. There are still some instances where the greatest vigour of intellect had failed under the pressure of human misery;[137] and the fortitude of a philosopher of twenty-three might well desert him, when evils were felt that had subdued the stoicism of the most illustrious characters.—Delmont tried (and for the first time in his life, since the loss of his mother, when he was too young to have that command over himself which he had since obtained, fruitlessly tried) to argue away the anguish that now overwhelmed him.

While his calmness thus deserted him, he could find no comfort in exertion, no relief from local circumstances—even the certainty of Medora's death, though his spirits seemed to fail him at the very idea of it, appeared to him now as an evil less horrible than the dread that oppressed him. It was not possible for him to imagine that Medora had voluntarily left her mother. Simplicity might be misled, and innocence betrayed; but when simplicity and innocence were united with such good sense and *integrity*[138] of understanding, as Medora possessed, he believed it impossible that the arts of a libertine (for men under that description are generally the most shallow and contemptible of their species) could in a short period change her heart by vitiating her judgment. Her mother, he knew, was as attentive as tender. Over this dear and deserving object of her fondest affections Mrs. Glenmorris watched with unremitting vigilance; and it was to him incomprehensible that any man should have an opportunity of executing so daring a scheme, (even supposing such had been formed) as to snatch Medora from the vigilant care of such a guardian.

And this dear, this venerated and beloved mother, where was she? Why could he not participate with her the anguish this cruel event had inflicted on them both?—"Oh! dearest and fondest of mothers," cried he, "had you been less influenced by scruples, and by false delicacy, unworthy a mind like your's; had you confided your lovely daughter to me, we should now have tasted altogether, almost unexampled happiness. Instead of which, we are condemned to such wretchedness that I dare not trust myself steadily to look upon it."

Chap. XI.

Multo putans, sortemque animo miseratus iniquam.[139]

At the approach of night, Delmont found it impossible to attempt taking any repose—Yet whither could he go, or what could he do to relieve himself from the misery of suspence?—Had he ever cultivated any acquaintance in London, it was not now that society could relieve him—Armitage was the only man to whom he wished to speak; *his* voice the only one that he thought he could endure to hear. Fortune, as if to teize him with trifles, than which nothing is more difficult to bear with temper, while any heavy sorrow presses on the mind, contrived to throw him into the way of Dr. Winslow, who was waddling along the Hay Market,[140] and whom he did not see, till he was so near that it was impossible to escape him.

The doctor, who had long since lost all fears about his neice, and all resentment for what had happened at Upwood, and who was proud of such an acquaintance as Delmont, advanced to him, expressed great pleasure at seeing him, and began to inform him, as if it was a matter of great import to all the world, that he and his family were in London only for a fortnight, having come from his house in Wiltshire, to furnish themselves with a few articles for a tour to Scarborough, which had been settled for the rest of the summer. Before the doctor had half finished what he had to say, Delmont had totally forgotten that he was speaking at all; the doctor however ended some sentence, to which his companion had given no attention, by saying, "I am sure Mr. Delmont you must be of the same opinion?"

Delmont,

Answering neglectingly he knew not what,[141]

but which the doctor took for an assent to his proposition, he cried, rubbing his hands, "Ah! now that's right, my dear sir—*I thought so*—I *thought* good sense like your's would at last induce you to hear reason—Indeed I often stood amazed it could ever be otherwise. I was afraid you were carried too far among the enemy, but I rejoice, and with exceeding great joy, to find that I am deceived. No no, the enemy must have nothing to do with persons of eminent merit, and I hope . . . . . ."

"What enemy, doctor?—who are you talking of?" cried Delmont, "but I beg your pardon—I am in haste; good evening to you—my compliments to the ladies." Delmont would then have hastened away, but the doctor said he was merely going to take a turn in the park for a little air, after the fatigue of his day's shopping, and would walk with him. He began a long history about his son; (Delmont walked on in silence, hoping every moment the hum of the doctor's monotonous prose would cease); he then detailed the history of a trial he had had with the farmers of one of his parishes, about setting aside a modus—quoted precedents temp. Eliz.[142] to justify his demand; made a short philippic[143] against the unreasonableness of farmers; from thence glided into an episode, which described the dinner given by a nobleman to the judges on the circuit; retailed a bon-mot of Dr. Squably's; and was entering, with the most persevering desire of being heard, on a second history relative to Mr. Middleton Winslow, when Delmont, unable to preserve the forms of politeness, turned from him, and quickening his pace, was soon at the end of Bond Street, the coffee-house he had usually frequented being in that neighbourhood; when suddenly he saw before him a figure which seemed to be that of Armitage. Delmont hastened to look in his face—it was Armitage himself.

Hardly were they able to express their joy at meeting, before Delmont eagerly enquired if he had seen Mrs. Glenmorris or Medora? "No," replied he, "but I was now going to Mrs. Grinsted's to obtain a direction to them—for I cannot tell why, but the people at the hotel gave me evasive answers, and denied knowing any thing about them."

Delmont now found that his friend was ignorant of the strange and most distressing intelligence relative to Medora. The street was not a place in which to communicate it, but entering a coffee-house together, Delmont there related all that had passed—and if any thing could equal the pain he felt in telling, it was that with which Armitage heard him. The latter then told Delmont that Mrs. Glenmorris had written to him, "and though," said he, "I could see by her manner of expressing herself that her heart was ill at ease on other subjects, she touched very gently on her pecuniary embarrassments, which I am afraid have been more perplexing than either of us were aware of, and it is impossible to tell how far those embarrassments might have been the cause of the extraordinary and most distracting catastrophe of her disappearance. I lose all patience when I reflect that nothing of all this could have happened, had Mrs. Glenmorris possessed resolution enough to have despised the paltry gossip of I know not what foolish women—and if with every other virtue under Heaven she had but possessed that decided character which, self balanced from conscious rectitude and superiority, is above being put out of its course by every whif of malice or folly. Mrs. Crewkherne, and some other contemptible cats, chose to suppose, in the purity and delicacy of their vestal imaginations, that I could not have an affection for my friend's wife without desiring to supplant my friend; and here has this dear woman, as she almost acknowledges herself, been deterred from applying to me by this infernal crew. I cannot speak of them with patience—and who can now tell what may have been the consequence to her daughter, to herself, and to my poor friend Glenmorris, who would not, I am convinced, survive, or at least not possess his reason, if he should be deprived of those two creatures so justly dear to him!"

He who is in desperate circumstances, catches at every hope however feeble. Delmont had a vague expectation of receiving some consolation from Armitage— Armitage had none to give him. Their mutual doubts and conjectures served only to augment their mutual disquiet, and they agreed to separate at an early hour, that each during the night might consider what could be most effectually done the next day to discover their lost friends.

By day-break Delmont was again on foot, and Armitage did not long suffer him to wait. Yet when they once more reconsidered the projects of the preceding night, they neither of them saw any light to direct their search. The morning passed in fruitless efforts on both sides, and they met again at five o'clock, only to relate their vain enquiries, and to aggravate the apprehensions with which they were both tortured.

A note was brought to Delmont while he sat at table, (not while he dined, for he had neither eat nor slept since his first knowledge of Medora's being missing); he opened it eagerly, for all his thoughts being on that subject he concluded it could relate to nothing else. At any other time it would have given him pleasure, for he was fondly attached to both his sisters, but particularly to Louisa; but now he was incapable of joy, and every thing like happiness seemed an insult on his misery. Louisa wrote thus:

My dearest George,
    I came to London last night with my aunt Crewkherne, and Mr. and Mrs. Bethune. The latter are going into Wales to attend on Mr. B—'s mother, who is much indisposed. Mrs. Crewkherne, who is very civil to me, though you know I am no great favourite, gives me my choice whether to accompany her to Ramsgate; accept an invitation I have had from Miss Goldthorp to accompany her, with Dr. and Mrs. Winslow, to Scarborough, or return to you. You have taught me, where I am alone concerned, to act from the impulse of my own heart; and you will surely guess that its fondest wishes are, to be once more in that beloved spot, and under that dear protection, which I prefer to every

other. This may not be politic in regard to Mrs. Crewkherne, but it is pleasant, and I cannot sacrifice my affection for you, to the hope of sharing her fortune with Caroline. But, my dear brother, if you have any reasons that make this inconvenient, say so at once to your Louisa—I am sure however that you will, for you are candour and sincerity itself. I am almost ashamed of the doubt this enquiry seems to imply; but you know not the legends I have been compelled to listen to on the subject of persons who must I am sure be deserving, since they are dear to you.

Mrs. Crewkherne having room in her house only for my sister and Mr. Bethune, with their servants, I have taken advantage of Miss Goldthorp's obliging invitation, and fortunately heard from Dr. Winslow that he had met you in the street, and remembered your address. I wait impatiently to see you, my dear George—and I hope nothing that passed at Upwood will make it unpleasant to you to see at this house

your ever affectionate
LOUISA DELMONT.

At any other time Delmont would have flown with impatience to Louisa for her own sake; he now hastened to Dr. Winslow's, glad indeed to embrace her whom he had not seen for some months; but now the tender interest he took in his sisters was overborn, by his agonizing solicitude for Medora and her mother, while a confused idea forced itself upon his mind, that Louisa, who evidently alluded to them in her letter, might have heard something of them. He thought not of the awkwardness of meeting Miss Goldthorp; but hastened to Dr. Winslow's, and regardless of forms, sent for Louisa into a parlour. Louisa, enchanted with his kindness, ran down to him immediately, and throwing herself into his arms, wept for joy. The sight of her called forth anew all those affections which his sisters particularly inherited in right of their mother; but when his mind recurred with new force to the lost object of his love, to his innocent lovely Medora, exposed to insults which his soul shuddered to think of, he betrayed symptoms of grief and despair which could not escape the observation of Louisa. "For God's sake, my dear George," cried she "what is the matter?—You look very ill!—you seem very uneasy?"

"And do you know nothing, Louisa, that is likely to make me so?"

"I know that Adolphus has embarrassed himself and you; and that your journey to Ireland was on his account, and has distressed you; but I was in hopes. . . ."

"And does Louisa know me so little as to suppose that mere money matters, however perplexing, could inflict such a degree of uneasiness as would empoison my meeting her, and not admit of palliation or concealment at such a moment? Oh! no, Louisa; I have learned, should it be necessary, to be content with a little; Adolphus has not acted towards me quite as I think I should have done towards him; but it is over, and I give my paltry troubles on that score to the winds. Ah! my Louisa, there are sorrows for which there is no cure—which no philosophy can combat, no resignation endure."

Louisa, more alarmed by his look than even by his expressions, exclaimed, "Good heaven! my dear George, what do you mean?—for pity's sake keep me not in suspense, but tell me—what is the misfortune you deplore?—Is the young lady dead, to whom you were attached?"

A deep groan preceded Delmont's answer—"Louisa, there *are* misfortunes worse than death."

"You torture me," cried she, "pray explain yourself."—Delmont then related, as coherently as he could, the history of the growth and progress of his love for Medora; and ended with the extraordinary recital of her being missing from an hotel; of her mother's leaving it the next day in a state of dejection—for he had extorted as much from the servant at the hotel—and the more strange circumstance of their both disappearing, though certainly *not together*—which distracted him—yet in some way so unaccountable, that he had not been able to discover the least trace of either.

Louisa listened to him with amazement and concern—"My dear George," cried she, "how my heart bleeds for you, and for this unfortunate young woman. You hoped, you say, that *I* could give you some intelligence!—Would to God I could; but I have never heard her name, or that of her mother mentioned, since Mrs. Crewkherne was so extremely angry with me for taking her part, that I thought I should have been sent back to you in disgrace; and so I certainly should have been, if Caroline and her husband had not good naturedly interposed. My aunt Crewkherne's abhorrence of poor Mrs. Glenmorris is to me unaccountable; I should think there was some great personal animosity between them, if I did not know that Mrs. Crewkherne never saw her.—My aunt, to be sure, seldom spares any body; but her violent aversion to these friends of your's exceeds in virulence and ill humour all I ever saw before—and she does not scruple to say such things. . . .!"

"What does she say?"—asked Delmont, eagerly.

"There is no use in repeating what she has said," replied his sister. "I am convinced of its untruth, and was so even before I heard the particulars you have now related; for I was persuaded in my own mind, that such persons as she described could never interest or attach my brother George."

"Surely," said Delmont, meditating a moment—"Surely this malicious old woman cannot have imagined and executed any plot to carry off Medora?—There is nothing of which I do not believe her capable; but I do not see that she could, in this case, have the power to execute so detestable a purpose. She undoubtedly knew, Louisa, who Mrs. Glenmorris was?"

"Oh! yes, perfectly.—She learned it very soon, I believe, and she mentioned, in the way of pitying Lady Mary de Verdon, how much she had said to that lady about her daughter's misconduct—her connection with Mr. Armitage and . . . ."

"Do not repeat her infamous, her infernal malice, Louisa; I cannot bear it. I will not see her; for to keep my temper with her would be impossible. When did she see Lady Mary?"

"After she left Upwood, I believe; I was not then with her; but she delighted to relate, I know not what, stories of Mrs. Glenmorris's youth, and to tell how she ran away from her mother. And because she saw that it teized me, she was pleased to dwell on every circumstance (many of which she invented I am sure) that could throw any reflection on Mrs. Glenmorris, or her daughter."

"Where does Lady Mary de Verdon live?" said Delmont, still musing.—Louisa had never heard, or had forgotten. He knew, however, it would be easy to learn at any of the shops about St. James's—and telling his sister he would see her again in an hour, he left her.

Delmont hastened to the house where he learned Lady Mary de Verdon resided. There was only the porter and his wife. The former a very surly fellow, who gave short and reluctant answers, holding the door in his hand. The woman who had at first opened it, seemed more disposed to be communicative; but when her husband heard the questions that Delmont was asking, he came hastily forward, and bade her leave the door.

Delmont, as well by persuasions as by the offer of money, endeavoured to prevail on this man to give him the intelligence, which it seemed in his power to do, of Mrs. Glenmorris. The more eagerly he appeared to desire this, the more sullenly and rudely the old pampered domestic repulsed him, till Delmont finding it difficult to keep his temper, left him to consult Armitage, and returning for a few moments to Louisa, then sought his friend.

Armitage had not had better success; but, as well as Delmont, had been met every where with oblique insinuations of the improper nature of the friendship he professed for Mrs. Glenmorris, sneers on the motives of his anxious enquiry; and the reports which had given rise to all this, he traced in more than one instance to Mrs. Crewkherne.

To what he had thus learned himself, were added the intimations Delmont had received from Louisa, which he now repeated, and Armitage heard, with more emotion than either of them were accustomed to shew.

Armitage, pausing a moment, said; "I have made it an invariable rule to despise slander where it affected only myself, and have always found that to notice it served only to feather the *elf-bolts*[144] which otherwise fell harmless, and were forgotten; but in this instance, where the character of a blameless, an amiable woman, is traduced—where my affection for my friend, and my consequent protection of his family, is converted by the diabolical malice of an old woman, impotent in every mischief but this, into the means of blasting the fair fame of the wife and child of my friend, and has perhaps been the cause to them of most irreparable evils, I must endeavour to stop it. Have you any objection, George, to my going to Mrs. Crewkherne?"

"No, indeed.—Let us both go to her instantly."

"Not so, Delmont. She is your relation, and may think that gives her a right to talk to you in a way which she will hardly venture to me, or which I shall know how to answer if she does. When I reflect on the weakness and violence of her conduct, ever since she first discovered your attachment to our poor Medora, I cannot help fancying (though I own I know not how it should be) she has something to do in the witchcraft that has occasioned the disappearance of that dear child and her mother; for that either of them have been to blame, I cannot allow myself to suppose for a single moment."

It was now late. Armitage, however, who disdained all forms, when good was to be done or evil prevented, set out for the house of Mrs. Crewkherne, and Delmont, who intended to re-commence his search with the dawn of the next day, took the only occasion he thought he should have, to press the demands of his family against his uncle's estate on his executor, Sir Appulby Gorges.—No business, no consideration whatever, had power to call off his mind a moment from the mysterious and cruel circumstance that had blighted, perhaps for ever, all the prospects of happiness he had imagined; but as money was absolutely necessary, whether he was to seek, or to avenge Medora; and if he regained her, such as his fond hopes sometimes suggested (the same lovely, innocent, and blameless creature he left) necessary to secure her future safety and comfort; it was therefore forwarding the sole purpose for which he now lived, if he could obtain any satisfaction from Sir Appulby Gorges.

It happened, contrary to his usual custom at this season of the year, that Sir Appulby was in town. Sir Appulby was *negotiating*; and as the party was not one whom he could, with any effect, invite to witness the advantages of mercenary politics at his splendid villa of *Wicket Hall*, he had taken up his own abode in town, to wait the favourable moment of closing, on behalf of his employers, with his young proselyte, who, from some unfortunate events that had befallen him at certain houses near St. James's,[145] found it unexpectedly requisite either to sell himself or his estates; and prudently preferred the former; but chaffered[146] about the price, in hopes of making a better bargain.

His *ultimatum* was to be given by a friend that evening; and it happened that George Delmont, who, in height and general appearance, resembled that friend, was as such admitted by the porter, and without question shewn up stairs, where Sir Appulby, who expected a very different person, was very far from being glad to see him.

"I came to you, Sir Appulby," said Delmont, "on the affairs of Lord Castledanes.—It is some months since you assured me that you would hasten the payment of money which has been unaccountably delayed.—Give me leave to tell you, that this sort of conduct in an executor has the worst appearance imaginable."

"My dear Sir!" replied Sir Appulby, in visible confusion, his fat gills quivering, and his swollen eye-lids twinkling—"my dear Sir! have I not already and before told you, and informed you, and desired Mr. Cancer to signify to you, and let you know and acquaint you, that the moment it could be done legally and properly, and in due course, these matters should be settled, paid, and discharged? Have I not said, and repeated and declared so? and . . . ."

"Yes, Sir Appulby, you certainly have said and repeated all this; and because you *have* repeated it so often, and because of your general character for prevarication—or you must forgive me, Sir Appulby, if I call it by a shorter name, and say, that because you have so declared and so shuffled, I do not believe you."

"Sir," cried Sir Appulby, "I assure you I am not used or accustomed. . . ."

"I know nothing of what you are accustomed to.—I come not hither to enquire into, or to conform to your customs; it is mine always to speak plainly, Sir Appulby, and you must permit me to tell you, that you have behaved very ill in this affair already, and that it must be my business to prevent your behaving still worse. You are not, perhaps, used to such plain language; but it is time for me to use it, at least as far as relates to my family's affairs, which, after what I know of you, I really should wish out of your hands, even if we did not want the money you so needlessly keep back."

There is no being so meanly fearful, as he who having dared to do wrong, *because he dared*, dreads every moment the detection which sooner or later overtakes villanous actions. Sir Appulby, from his earliest practice as an attorney in the north, till the acme of his political consequence, had been in habits of taking advantage of every body who by any chance fell in his power; and had for the most part done it with impunity. Some were afraid of what he could do through the influence of his patron, who was what is called a man in power (one who, with an overgrown fortune, has neither feeling nor principle); others were held in awe by the supposition that Sir Appulby might himself be a great man hereafter, and *then* have the means of serving them; and others dreaded him in the united qualities of a lawyer and a retainer to the insolent profligacy of exorbitant wealth, whither they dared not lift their eyes.

Sir Appulby had long been one "whom every body knew to be what nobody chose to call him." He had robbed, and helped to rob his own relations, and since had as successfully robbed the public; till, as success always ensures a certain degree of impunity, he had long been too rich to mind what *those* said, who were so little people of the world as to look through *his purple* and *fine linen* with scrutinizing contempt, and pretend to see in this *Dives* an object of greater scorn and abhorrence than the Lazar at his gate, who demanding in vain the crumbs that fell from the *rich man's table*, is repulsed by his high fed and insolent domestics.[147]

Sir Appulby Gorges, had it not been that his luxury subjected him to the palsy and the gout, might have forgotten that he was mortal. In his own family a furious and gloomy tyrant, his poor wife was less considered than his servants, and neither one or the other ever presumed to contend with him. He saw none but clerks in office, or men who either were or wished to get into place; and his pursy[148] existence was passed in administering adulation, or in receiving it. As unaccustomed, therefore, to hear truth as to tell it, he shrunk from the manly, plain dealing of Delmont as an affront; yet an affront which he feared to resent, because he knew how well he deserved that it should be repeated.

"After what you have heard of me, Mr. Delmont? I must remark, Sir, that language and expressions—such as that . . . . . ."

"Are not, as you observe, Sir Appulby, what you have been used to—I know it—but be assured *I* shall never take the trouble to give you many lessons in it. They will come, perhaps, from those whose contempt for the weakness of an old man will not mitigate the effects of their indignation against a wicked man. *I have* heard things of you, Sir Appulby, which I know to be true, that sink you, in my opinion, to the lowest rank of human degradation."

Sir Appulby, half choked with passion, and half trembling with fear, asked what?

"Enquire of your own conscience, Sir Appulby—Or if that is callous, look in the records you have in the form of letters from two families, whom I know you have ruined. Do you remember nothing of a young woman, your near relation, whose money you took from her, under pretence of being her guardian, and then refused to refund so small a sum as even ten pounds, and bade her go to service? Has your flinty soul retained no impression of the fearful catastrophe, your cruelty and injustice (in suffering their whole property to be kept from them) occasioned in another part of that family?—Have you *no* remembrance of the ruin of innocent children?—None of the sufferings of their mother?—But you go to church, Sir Appulby Gorges, and put shillings in the plate at the door, and you talk of religion, and are desirous of being called a pious man!"

Sir Appulby now crawled like a wounded beetle about the room, puffing and gasping—"As to my conduct, Sir," said he, "you do me great injustice—you mistake the thing altogether—as to that family of the South—why-a-a-a-Mr. Delmont, upon my honour, Sir, you—you—wholly misunderstand the thing.—I have done a great deal for them, Sir, a very great deal—and . . . . ."

"There is a way, Sir Appulby, of enacting the fable of Penelope;[149] undoing at one time what you have done at another, and I believe your counteraction has quite annihilated the good effects, if there ever were any, of your *benefits*. These boasted benefits, of which, even admitting they were all you state them to have been, these poor people may say:

To John I ow'd some obligation,
But then friend John thought fit,
To publish it to all the nation;
So John and I are quit."[150]

"I thought—I thought—Mr. Delmont," cried Sir Appulby, who now looked like a bad picture one has seen of a strangled malefactor—"I thought, Sir, you came here on the business of my friend, Lud Castledanes, and not on this sort of extraneous . . . . ."

"I loved my uncle," answered Delmont, coolly, "don't call him *your* friend, sir Appulby Gorges, *before me.*"

"My Lud Castledanes, Mr. Delmont, was . . . . . ."

"I knew perfectly *what* he was, Sir, and cannot but regret that he was so mistaken as to entrust the executorship to a person so totally unlike him. Pray, Sir Appulby, do you happen to know any thing of a Mrs. Glenmorris, the daughter of Lady Mary de Verdon."

Sir Appulby was not prepared for this sudden question—his face, from a dirty *tile* colour,[151] became purple. "How should *I* know any thing of that person? I must beg to be understood, Mr. Delmont, that——"

"Oh! Sir, you *are* generally understood, believe me. I wish, however, to have an answer. You are acquainted, I believe, with Mrs. Crewkherne?"

"I have seen Mrs. Crewkherne—I respected her on account of her piety and virtue, and of her alliance with my Lud Castledanes."

"Oh! mockery of terms!" cried Delmont, hardly restraining his indignation "——

Oh! revolting hypocrisy—come, Sir Appulby, try to speak truth for once.—Its rarity from you will give it double value.—Do you happen to know where Mrs. Glenmorris is now? or where her daughter is?"

"I know, Sir!—I assure you, Mr. Delmont, that I have no connection with those persons—I know nothing of them, Sir.—I repeat, Sir, that you have totally mistaken my conduct—and . . . . ."

A servant here announced "Lord Robert Rangely." Sir Appulby seemed relieved, yet doubting whether his present guest would not continue his unwelcome visit, he therefore said, "I must beg your pardon, Mr. Delmont; my Lud Robart has some business with me, on which his ludship is come on purpose—and in regard to the affairs of my Lud Castledanes, if you will be so good as to go and apply to my solicitor, Mr. Anthony Cancer, of Gray's Inn, there is no doubt but that you will find all *is in a fair train to see light*, in such a manner as council shall advise, as legal and proper, and proper and legal." So saying Sir Appulby, without waiting for Delmont's answer, puffed and waddled away into the next room, where, in the obsequious civility of Lud Robart, he endeavoured to lose the painful sensation that had been inflicted by the rough and unwelcome truisms of the unbending Delmont.

END OF THE THIRD VOLUME

VOLUME IV

CHAP. I.

Pour moi je n'ai point de systeme à soutenir, moi,
homme simple et vrai, que la fureur d'aucun partie n'entraine.[1]

Mr. Armitage, sending up a message that he was a stranger, who waited upon her about business, was admitted to Mrs. Crewkherne. Had he given his name to the servant, she would certainly have refused him an audience; she expressed herself very much surprised when he announced himself; for notwithstanding the virulence of her animosity against him, she did not know him even by sight.

The good lady was in her dressing-room, and with her was one of those men who seem to have taken in some houses the place formerly occupied by the director and confessor. Mr. Armitage, from his countenance and appearance, immediately guessed what he was; but as he wished the whole world, had it been possible, might witness what he had to say, he hesitated not to address himself immediately to Mrs. Crewkherne on the subject of his visit.

"I came to you, Madam," said he, "to remonstrate with you. It will not be easily possible for me to forget that there is a certain degree of respect due to your age and your sex; but as a human being, as a person who has, without any provocation, done me the greatest injury in your power, I mean not to dissemble my sentiments."

"I, Sir!" interrupted the lady, her voice trembling, and her complection assuming a deep orange hue; "I injured you! Sir, what do you mean? I never saw you that I know of, I am sure, in my life before."

"Had the malice with which, notwithstanding you never saw me before, you have incessantly pursued me," said Armitage coolly, "been levelled against me as an individual, I should never have taken the trouble to have spoken to you; but your unprovoked assaults may have been of serious consequence to an innocent and excellent woman; to a young and lovely girl her daughter. These ladies you never saw, or at least obtained a sight of them only by impertinent and unjustifiable intrusion on their solitude."

Mrs. Crewkherne, whose wrath had began to conquer her fears at the words *age* and *sex*, now found it rising to a degree not easy to be restrained.

"Upon my word, Sir, you take great liberties," cried she. "Very extraordinary indeed, that *I* am to be insulted in this manner."

"I mean not to insult you, Madam—I only intend to put an end to the unwarrantable conduct by which you have injured others. Why, Madam, did you assume it as a fact, that Mrs. Glenmorris and her daughter were people of doubtful character?"

"Since you oblige me to speak, *I will* then. I said so, Mr. Armitage, because I was told so; and because . . . because . . . why because that nobody could suppose that a woman of any fashion, of any character and reputation, would conceal herself clandestinely in a . . . a sort of an obscure, mean place, as if she had some bad design in view—and I suppose you wont *prosecute* me—as I am free to say what all the world says—as free, I hope, as another—I suppose it is no scandal to say, that every body knows your name is not very good, and that it was not very likely any person who was very nice about their reputation would put themselves into the care of a person of your character."

"Since *my* character then," replied Armitage, "thus becomes the means of injury to my friends, it is worth my while to ask you, my good lady, what parts of it have the misfortune to be so displeasing to you?"

"All, Sir, let me tell you, all. I am assured that you are an atheist, a deist, a freethinker, an illuminy; I don't know what, not I; a jacobin, and a republican."[2]

The grave personage that sat by turned up his eyes, lifted up his hands, and uttered a deep groan.

Armitage smiled.—"Really, Madam," said he, "these charges are so numerous, and so heavy, that I hardly know where to begin my defence. I fear too," turning a little towards Mr. Habbukkuk Cramp, (the man who sat by) "that my audience are not very favourably disposed towards me. First, however, I must beg leave to remark, that I cannot be both an atheist and a deist."

"I don't see why not—I am sure there are people that go the length of being every thing that's bad and abominable."

"I don't imagine you expect that I should make to you, or this gentleman, a confession of my faith; but I beg leave to assure you, that I am not only not an atheist myself, but that I do not believe any man exists who will sincerely assert himself to be one. I speak not of fools or coxcombs, who may fancy some daring deviation from common sense, or some wild system, of which they understand nothing, gives them a sort of consequence with the ignorant and superficial; I speak of men of solid understanding and sober reflexion; I beg leave therefore to assure you I am not of that description of men called atheists. If you will give me leave to quote a play, which was written by one of the best and most pious men of the last age, I would say in his words:

If there's a power above us,
(And that there is all nature cries aloud
Through all her works) he must delight in virtue.[3]

And the question what that virtue is, in which a benevolent and omnipotent being must delight, seems to me as clear as the indisputable fact of his existence. I imagine that our way to please God is, to do all the good that is in our power to his creatures; never wilfully or wantonly to hurt or injure one of them; never, that we may gratify ourselves as individuals, violate that immutable law which he has given to every man—a sense of rectitude we have agreed to call conscience—Conscience, which till it is stifled, and at length destroyed by sophistry and falsehood, is implanted in the breast of every human being who has common sense."

Mrs. Crewkherne here testified marks of extreme impatience, and Mr.

Habbukkuk Cramp seemed very uneasy in his chair; but Armitage not appearing to notice their inquietude, proceeded.

"Now, Madam, I have really spoken more on this subject than I should have thought worth my while, if this declaration of my opinion did not lead to an inference in regard to the person on whose account I came hither. These being my sentiments, and these the maxims by which I govern myself, I am the last man in the world who would rob another of his honour or his peace; I should most certainly consider it as a great crime to deprive a stranger of the affection of the woman he loved, but to injure my *friend*, the *friend* who trusted me, who made me the temporary guardian of those who constituted the sole happiness of his life! to become the basest of all traitors, to violate the sacred charge he has given me! There *have been*, I believe, hypocrites, and even men professing unusual piety, who have committed such crimes. They are said to have ways of appeasing this conscience, this internal monitor, and that sometimes the loud declamation of the pulpit, or the prescriptive clamour of the bar, are engaged to bribe it to silence—but *I* find nothing proceding from either, that would be capable of reconciling *me* to myself, if I broke through the fundamental rule of all religion and all morality—Do unto others as thou would'st they should do unto thee."[4]

"Humph!" cried Mrs. Crewkherne, "I see the wolf *can* put on sheep's clothing—I speak my mind, Sir. *You* can quote scripture as well as plays. I am sure it's a shame, if you don't follow it more, that you know it at all."

"I not only know it, Madam, but have studied it, as well as my time and means have permitted, and I dare venture to recommend sundry excellent maxims to you, particularly all that relates to lying and slandering; to taking away the fair name of innocent and blameless persons, and that merely to gratify a paltry desire of lowering them, which, if your pride was not so remarkable a feature in your character, one might suppose to be, because you *felt* their superiority."

"There is no bearing this insolence!" exclaimed Mrs. Crewkherne, hardly able to restrain tears of malevolent rage, which might well have become the iron cheeks of Alecto.[5]—"Mr. Cramp, I am at a loss to understand how you can sit silent, and see me so affronted."

"Indeed, Mr. Archimage," snuffled the preacher of the tabernacle—[6] "Indeed, Sir, this is very odd behaviour—to a lady, so respectable and worthy a lady, in her own apartment and *ous!*—I don't, Sir—I say, Sir, I don't, Sir, I can't, Sir, understand why you pertend for to persume on any such like freedom; and I begs leave . . . ."

"I have nothing to do with you, Doctor. Pray do not interpose. What I have to say to this lady is for her good—you know that humility and charity are among the virtues it is your practice to enforce.—Mrs. Crewkherne is not yet too old to listen to lectures on any of the cardinal virtues,[7] and she will now be so good as to hear me, remembering that she has been the aggressor.—Besides, Sir, the lady, as I recollect, has not heard my vindication of the other charges she brought against me, and it is an equitable maxim, which you have undoubtedly been taught at school, to hear before you give judgment. I think, Madam, that besides the names I have disclaimed, you were pleased to say I was a freethinker, an illuminé—a something else which I had not the honour to understand, a jacobin and a republican—and first of the first.

"If you mean by a freethinker, that I venture to think on every topic of human enquiry, and most on those which seem most to involve the happiness or misery of my species, I must plead guilty to the charge; but I hope and believe there is no turpitude annexed to the use of that faculty with which God has distinguished man above the rest of his creatures. I claim the boundless use of this power of thinking, of this power of enquiry; but I by no means am offended at those who find more convenience and ease in letting their own faculties in this way lie dormant, and commission others to think for them; they may be very good sort of people, and fit for five hundred excellent purposes. Not a sentence shall I ever utter, not a line shall I ever write to disturb their quiescent tranquillity, and all I ask of them is, that if I do not perplex them by putting it into *their heads* to exercise this troublesome quality, *they* would generously permit *me* to make what use I please of my own, which certainly in that case (if it is a bad thing to do) can hurt nobody but myself. Having allowed then, that if to be a free-thinker is not to think always as I am bid by those who perhaps know no more than myself, I must submit to that appellation. The third count is, I believe, that I am an illuminé. I have read one nonsensical book on that subject, and tried to read another, but it was so childish and foolish, and I so little comprehended what the author means to establish, that I could not get through it. If you, Madam, or if you, Sir, who doubt-less are better informed, will have the goodness to acquaint me what an illuminé means, I will tell you whether I belong to the sect or no; but at present I know not how I can be a member of a party whose maxims I am so far from understanding, that I doubt the very existence of the society itself. It seems to me to be a chimera raised to terrify the credulous with apprehensions of plots and machinations imagined by they know not whom, they know not where; and whatever is involved in mystery and obscurity always impresses a sort of dread which no specified and distinct object of alarm could effect.[8] The next charge against me (but really they are so grave and numerous that I ought to have taken notes); the next charges against me are, that I am a democrate and a jacobin. An explanation of each most alarming term is almost as necessary to me as an explanation of the former. I remember, when I was a boy, hearing in every society a vast deal about whigs and tories, though the names were then becoming more obsolete than they had been some years before—I read even more than I heard about them, and Fielding and Smollet introduced the mention of parties so distinguished into novels, while every pamphlet of fifty years ago, which I read in a collection of my father's, vented the virulence of one of these parties against the other.[9] After an interregnum, during which nobody seemed to care about either, have succeeded the names of aristocrate and democrate, which I wish people, who use them as terms of reproach on either side, would first understand. We more immedi-ately borrowed the name from France; but like many other imported words, we apply them in senses wholly foreign to their real meaning.[10] I believe, however, you, Madam, understand a democrate and a jacobin to mean nearly the same thing."

"To be sure I do," answered Mrs. Crewkherne, indignantly—"And I wish, with all my heart, they were all destroyed."

"Doubtless you do," resumed Armitage, "the charity which you so loudly pro-fess would induce you to order them all to fire and faggot; but even the power of executing so benevolent a purpose would not gratify your humane intention towards *me*; since in your sense of the words I am neither. You *apprehend* that these democrats have a prodigious and unquenchable hatred against all established governments, and have an horror of kings and of nobility. Now I have nothing of all this. I respect the established government of my country, and never disturb it. If I could not live contented under it, I would go to another. I venerate, I honour, I would die, were it necessary, for a good king—for a king shewing himself worthy of the sacred charge, by devoting himself to the real happiness and prosperity of the people; and so far from having any detestation of nobility, I think the common objections made against their order, puerile and inconsequent. I do not believe the order inimical to the community, and I hold all the wild schemes of universal equality as utterly impracticable, and altogether absurd; so impracticable, that if it could be established to-morrow, inequalities more unjust and more shocking would exist in six weeks; if, therefore, you annex this system to the word democrats, I am none.

"Lastly, as to my being a jacobin, which, I take it for granted, includes every thing that you can imagine horrible, and to be a sort of a constellation of terrible charges; I have only to say, that if you mean, among other heavy misdemeanors included under it, that I either approve, or ever did approve of the violence, cruelty, and perfidy, with which the French have polluted the cause of freedom, you are greatly mistaken;[11] far from thinking that such measures are likely to establish liberty, and the general rights of mankind, I hold them to be exactly the means that will delay the period when rational freedom, and all that its enjoyment can give to humanity, shall be established in the world. I deny many of their maxims, and I abhor almost the whole of their conduct. I never do believe that axiom of politicians, which says, that evil may be done to produce good. In the present case I know the evil to be certain and immediate; I am not arrogant enough to pretend to calculate the amount of the good, which may never be produced at all; or if it is, may not be considered as such by those who shall then live; but you must allow me to remark, that if the folly and wickedness, by which mankind have, in every age of the world, endeavoured to establish tenets, either of religion or government, were to prove the falsity of those tenets, there is no one system which would not be liable to the same objections as have been made to the revolution of France; that it has been the source of misery, of bloodshed, of crimes, from which reason and humanity recoil with terror and detestation.—I believe I have now told you why I deserve none of the epithets with which you have chosen to load me, and in return for this plain dealing you will tell me, whether you know the present residence of Mrs. Glenmorris and her daughter."

There is nothing half so irritating to determined malice as the consciousness that it is impotent.—Mrs. Crewkherne found that, repelled by integrity and truth, the shafts she had delighted to throw against Armitage would fail of every effect she intended. She was one of those worthy personages who are never in the wrong in their own opinion; and she had too much money to have heard the possibility hinted as being the opinion of others; but she felt, however unwilling to acknowledge it, all the power of truth; yet detested more than ever him who had brought home to her the humiliating conviction of that black malevolence which lurked in her heart.

Malignant satisfaction therefore flashed on her mind, when she understood by Mr. Armitage's manner of asking, that he knew not what was become of Mrs. Glenmorris and her daughter; that they had both been removed from the residence where they had occasioned her so much concern, she knew; and believed a circumstance so fortunate had been occasioned by the information she had given to Lady Mary, who had taken measures to prevent their disturbing Miss Cardonnel in the rightful possession of her grandfather's estates; and though the scheme, so warmly adopted by Mrs. Crewkherne, was now no longer in question, though Miss Goldthorp's fortune had probably escaped her family for ever, she was overjoyed to believe that Delmont had lost sight of Medora, who was the occasion of his overlooking his own advantage, and despising her advice, she

Grinn'd horribly a ghastly smile;[12]

therefore while she answered—"*I* know the present residence of those people! No, indeed! *I* have no acquaintance with them—it is not likely I should! What, don't *you* know where they are? Perhaps your friend *Delmont*," added she with a particular emphasis and toss of the head, "may be able to inform you. I dare say the person you call Mrs. Glenmorris understood her own interest too well to lose sight of *him*."

Though Armitage imagined, that by watching the countenance of any one, he generally discovered their real sentiments, he could make nothing of the expression, compounded of ill-natured triumph and gratified malice, that predominated on the hard features of Mrs. Crewkherne. His remonstrance, far from having made any impression on her, appeared to have added to the horrid delight with which she seemed determined to hunt down by defamation his injured friends; but he doubted, whether she knew how strangely they had disappeared, and feared to afford her a new subject of triumph if he discovered it. Instead therefore of pursuing the enquiry, he said, he should probably be able to obtain a direction to Mrs. Glenmorris from some of her acquaintance in town, and then added,

"Look ye, Madam—I came to you to represent to you the injustice and cruelty of the attacks you have made on the reputation, and, for ought you know, on the peace of two persons, who are not only innocent, but eminently superior to *you*; because they are as incapable, not only of the crimes you have so industriously attempted to brand them with, as of that inhuman spirit, which generates in your breast the passions of envy and malice, and, one may truly say, all uncharitableness.[13] So good, so blameless, do I know them to be, that if I could for a moment believe in the doctrine of eternal punishment, I might be tempted to parody what the brother, whose feelings were outraged by a cruel bigot, is made to say by Shakespeare:

I tell thee, damned priest,
A ministering angel shall my sister be
Whilst thou liest howling.[14]

But *I* who have not always maxims of charity in my mouth, have yet so much in my heart, that it would give me pain to suppose that even such crimes as you are guilty of should be so chastised. Nevertheless, as neither your age, your sex, nor your fortune, ought to give you the privilege you have hitherto taken, I desire to tell you before this gentleman, your friend, that if I hear that you continue to pursue with inveterate malignity these inoffensive and deserving ladies, I shall be compelled to notice it in a very different manner." Armitage then, without waiting for the answer, which was retained by rage, and trembled on the lips of Mrs. Crewkherne, opened the door, and departed, while she, breathless between anger and awe, could not for some time re-cover herself, or find sufficient voice to utter the virulent abuse with which she, how-ever, at last loaded him, her obsequious confessor listening with something like terror, while he saw her distorted countenance, and her mouth foaming with fury. Instead of speaking to her of patience and calmness, he acquiesced in the heavy accusations she continued to insist upon against Armitage, exclaiming—"Oh! madam, madam, my worthy lady!—what times do we live in, when such sentiments as we have just heard are not only entertained, but avowed and gloried in! Verily the dragon, and the winged serpent, and the griffin, and the hippopotamus are assembled, and the nations of the earth shall be subdued."[15]

There was, however, an assemblage just then announced to be on the table of Mrs. Crewkherne, which Mr. Habbukkuk Cramp contemplated with more pleasure— A small turbot, an excellent neck of venison from Mr. Bethune's park, a fricasee of chicken, and a marrow pudding. So the dragon and Co. and even Mr. Armitage him-self, and all his shocking opinions, were for the time forgotten.

Chap. II.

L'argent fait tout; va, c'est chose tres sûre
Hâtons nous donc, sur ce pied de conclure.[16]

Baffled in his hopes of obtaining any information from Mrs. Crewkherne, Armitage returned in increased uneasiness to find Delmont.—Delmont, on his side, disappointed in every scheme he had formed to trace either the mother or the daughter, had set out post for Upwood, leaving a short note to inform Armitage, that he thought it possible, by the means of Susanne, who he intended to bring to London with him, to find some person who might give them information.—He would return, he said, immediately. Armitage did not foresee much advantage from this plan, but conscious that he had nothing better to propose, he continued to occupy himself in the same fruitless search.— His pain and solicitude increasing in proportion as time wore away, and deeper mys-tery involved the objects of his anxiety.

A fleet from North America, which had been detained by the necessity of wait-ing for convoy, and since by contrary winds, now arrived at the port of London. Armitage hastened to the compting-house of Petrify; he found there several letters to Mrs. Glenmorris from her husband, one to Delmont, and one to himself also from

Glenmorris. Petrify, careful only about the postage, which Armitage willingly paid,[17] delivered him the letters, and he retired, eager to read that which was addressed to himself.

But the pleasure with which the husband and the father spoke of the return of his wife and child; the satisfaction he expressed at the approaching marriage of his Medora with a man so esteemed as Delmont, and his lively expressions of gratitude towards Armitage, gave extreme pain to him they were addressed to.—"How often," said he, "have I reflected on the different lots which have fallen to Glenmorris and to me; rejoicing, indeed, in the happiness *he* possessed in such a charming wife, in so sweet a daughter, yet regretting the cold and comfortless life to which *I*, who have neither, should be condemned, did I not animate my otherwise joyless existence by the interest I take in the friends I love—But now I have only to share by anticipation in the pain this once happy husband, this once fortunate father, must endure, when he knows these objects of his affections are—what are they?—Alas! I know not; and this fearful uncertainty seems to me more hideous, and will surely appear to him (should I be compelled to the wretched task of relating it) more distracting than if I were to tell him that they were no more."

To reflect, to argue, and to content himself with moralising instead of acting was never any part of Armitage's character, when the service of his friends, or of the distressed, of whatever description, was in question; yet he had now absolutely exhausted every plan which conjecture had pointed out, and he knew not whither to go next.—His affection for every body that was related to Delmont, rather than any hope of hearing of Mrs. Glenmorris, led him to the house where he understood was the temporary abode of Louisa.—He enquired for her, heard she was at home, and not remembering at the moment that he wished to see her alone, found himself in the midst of a circle, which he soon understood to be composed of Dr. and Mrs. Winslow, their son, Miss Goldthorp, and four or five of the Doctor's friends.

Louisa, blushing and trembling, was hardly restrained by the presence of so many witnesses from questioning Armitage about Mrs. Glenmorris and Medora. The sudden departure of her brother George, in such excessive anxiety and distress of mind, had cruelly affected her; and incapable of giving much attention to any thing else, she endeavoured to discover if Armitage had brought any favourable news; but his countenance soon declared that nothing satisfactory had been heard. Miss Goldthorp, however, who knew but little, and cared still less about the real cause of the uneasiness she could not but observe in Louisa, was herself very desirous of attracting the notice of Armitage; first, because she heard he was an author, and a man of uncommon taste and erudition; and secondly, because of the ascendancy he was supposed to have over Delmont, for whom, though her pride had assisted her to conquer every apparent symptom of it, her heart still entertained a decided preference, and to whom, had he even now offered humbly to put on the chains he had before rejected, she would most willingly have resigned herself and her fortune.

To obtain the suffrage of Armitage would, she knew, be no small advantage; she therefore threw out her lure by saying, "Oh! Mr. Armitage! if you knew how much you gratify me by being so good as to call here."

Armitage, though he had by no means her gratification in contemplation, answered in the common words used on such occasions—"You do me great honour, Madam."

"You must know," rejoined the lady, "that no creature alive is so enthusiastically fond of poetry as I am. When I had the ill fortune, or, perhaps, I ought to say, the good fortune to be confined in consequence of my cousin's skill in driving a curricle," (poor Middleton, on whom she cast a look half malicious half contemptuous, shrunk back) "by which you know, perhaps, I had a broken arm, at the hospitable house of Mr. George Delmont, he used frequently to read to me passages from your charming works; I have purchased them all since, and read them over and over with such delight!"

Armitage, who had really all the modesty of real merit, was distressed and disgusted; he was too sincere to affect what he did not feel, and was besides too anxious and unhappy at this moment to be amused by this foolish affectation of admiration and literary taste; he answered, however, civilly, and soon sickened by such sort of society as he was now among, was enquiring of Louisa at what hour the next morning he could see her alone for a few moments, when the door opened, and a servant loudly announced—"Mr. Delmont." Louisa started forward out of the circle; Miss Goldthorp was violently fluttered, and adjusted her hair and her handkerchief. A tall, handsome, fashionable man entered. It was not George Delmont; but Louisa, running to embrace him, acknowledged her elder brother, the Major.

He saluted her rather politely than affectionately, and apologizing for his intrusion, told her he had occasion for her introduction to enable him to make his excuses properly to her friends. Mrs. Winslow, delighted with every thing that was tonish and *elegant,* was soon pleased with her guest; but Dr. Winslow fancied this gallant and martial looking soldier might be a much more formidable competitor for the favour of Miss Goldthorp than his brother, and dreading every body likely to impede his favourite project, which he hoped to conclude in a few months, he expressed himself but coldly towards the Major, while Miss Goldthorp, immediately penetrating his motives, was at once desirous of teasing this mercenary monitor, and of attracting the notice of the elder Delmont, who in his figure so much resembled one, whose image had taken possession of her mind as the perfection of masculine beauty.

It was not difficult either to alarm the divine or attract the soldier; and one was the immediate consequence of the other. Mr. Armitage, who saw that the literary enthusiasm of the fair lady was now forgotten, most willingly relinquished her notice, and telling Louisa he would see her the next morning, retired; while the Major, who had not without design sought his sister at Dr. Winslow's, found himself favourably received by the only person to whose reception of him he annexed any consequence. His natural vanity and self opinion, which seldom suffered him to doubt of his own power of pleasing, gave his conversation so much animation, threw so much agreeable assurance, mingled with an affectation of admiration and sentiment, into his air and manner, that he had not conversed half an hour with Miss Goldthorp before she thought him infinitely more agreeable than his brother, and if there was any difference, rather handsomer; much superior to him as a man of the world, and beyond comparison better informed, more elegant, more polished, with a certain gallantry and scavoir vivre[18] that ranked him in the very first class of irresistibles!

Adolphus Delmont saw all his advantages, and pursued them. It was in vain the Doctor, who was very restless, endeavoured to engage for a moment the attention of his visitor. Adolphus seemed hardly to recollect that he was in the room. Mrs. Winslow as fruitlessly talked of fashionable people and *elegant* houses, and all the charming things that occupied her imagination. The Major stared at her a moment, totally careless of answering, and then recommenced his attack on the heart of Miss Goldthorp, to besiege which, he now determined to proceed in form. Her person was better than he had imagined it; but had she been only four feet high,

> Lame, swart, prodigious,
> Full of foul blots and ugly blemishes,[19]

he would have been nearly as content, and as much pleased by her evident and sudden partiality; for not only the circumstances that had obliged him to call on his brother for money, but others yet more recent, had made a present, and a great acquisition of fortune, an affair of the first necessity.

Miss Goldthorp, throwing herself carelessly back in her chair, while her new admirer seemed disposed to prostrate himself at her feet, beckoned to Louisa to sit by them, and understanding that she wished to have some conversation with her brother, invited him to stay supper.—Dr. Winslow, who was neither prepared for his entertainment, or desirous of his company, could hardly refrain from expressing the displeasure he felt, while he took occasion to lament that he had no servants in town—no cook—only a kitchen maid—quite an ignorant creature—and it therefore was not in his power to entertain his friends. Adolphus would not understand him; but assuring Miss Goldthorp that no mortal was ever more indifferent to the pleasures of the table, said in a whisper, "If *you* continue to invite me, I shall stay, notwithstanding the Doctor's repulsive attacks." Then, turning suddenly to Middleton Winslow, who had sidled up to the part of the room where they sat, he said, "You are in the army, I think, Sir?"

"No, Sir, no," replied Middleton, who felt the superiority of this man of war, and seemed to shrink into nothing—"No, Sir, I never was in the army."

"I beg your pardon, Sir; I judged only by your appearance," cried the Major, as he proudly surveyed him.

"Why, as you observe, Major," said Mrs. Winslow, "Mr. Middleton Winslow has an air, an appearance, that has given people very often the same idea. I have had it remarked to me frequently—he has the air of a . . . .!"

"Of an haberdasher's apprentice," whispered the Major to Louisa, loud enough for Miss Goldthorp to hear, "or a spruce pastry-cook, in his Sunday's suit."

Miss Goldthorp could not resist her desire to laugh. Middleton, who, like all weak people, suspected himself to be the subject of mirth, assumed all his courage, and stepping up to his cousin, endeavoured to say, in what his mother used to call his *elegant sprightly* way, "Pray, dear Matty, what's the joke?"

"You are," replied she.

"I am! am *I* indeed! I'm sure I'm very glad you are amused, though—I don't know, though, how I've contrived to be so entertaining just now."

"Oh! you are always infinitely agreeable—the most useful, good, little pocket cousin in the world."

"Pocket cousin! Lord, Miss Goldthorp, that is somehow such an odd expression; pocket cousin!"

"Yes, for you know you are always creeping so close to one as if you were ready to nestle into one's pocket like a squirrel; and really, if one had a conveyance of that sort made a little bigger than ordinary, one might pop you into it if one was weary of you, and just give a signal for you to come out in any public place, you know, or at any time when a creature in the shape of a man was necessary to one's protection."

"Upon my word!" sobbed Middleton, stifling his vexation under an ill-disguised laugh—"Really, Cousin Matty, you are very kind!"

"Nothing can be a greater instance, I think, of kindness," cried the Major; "would I had any pretensions to so happy a *gite*!"[20]

"You!" exclaimed the Lady—"Heavens! what a pocket companion would you be!"

"Try me," whispered the Major, "and you will find me, though a sort of a folio compared to your little duodecimo[21] of a cousin, as *correct* as he can be, and then I shall look as well *bound*."

"Bless me, Mr. Delmont, what do you mean!" replied Miss Goldthorp in the same tone.

"Shall I give you an explanation? Will you have a catalogue raisonée[22] of my good qualities?—First, then, I am in love to distraction."

"Now, for goodness sake, do not talk such excessive nonsense—one would really think you mad."

"Then I am in the next place the most sincere, the most faithful, the most attached of human beings."

"My dear Louisa," said Miss Goldthorp aloud, "do speak to your brother—He really has so singular a way of talking . . . .!"

"No, no, Louisa, do you entertain Mr. Winslow. Sir, I assure you, if you do not happen to know it already, my little sister Louy here is one of the most agreeable and accomplished young ladies of the age. She can write an admirable riddle, guess at the most intricate charade, and develope a conundrum like a little sphinx. She has written at least two eastern tales, and had it not been that the market was overstocked, would already have had a novel, 'by a young lady,' in the press. She has, moreover, very considerable talents for poetry, *though I say it that should not say it*, and has frequently figured in the Ladies Magazine, under the name of Parnassia—and, to say nothing of her odes, her sonnets are exquisite, and, I assure you, strictly legitimate."[23]

"Good heavens! brother!" cried Louisa, "what do you mean?"

"I told you," exclaimed Miss Goldthorp, laughing excessively, "that your brother had really lost his senses."—

"Dear Adolphus," said Louisa, "what do you intend by all this rattle."—"Nothing in the world," replied the Major, applying still more gayly to Miss Goldthorp, "but like a good brother to display the extraordinary qualities of my pretty Louisa here, which her excessive modesty would conceal. I dare say now, Sir," (addressing himself to Middleton Winslow, who stood half petrified before the group) "I dare say you have never discovered half her accomplishments." Winslow understood nothing of this style of raillery, but took literally whatever was said; and his grave professions of admiration towards Louisa, which he thought the Major expected of him, redoubled the bursts of laughter that Miss Goldthorp either could not, or did not wish to restrain.

The Doctor, in the mean time, cast many an anxious look towards that side of the room, hardly heeding what the Reverend Mr. Kittiwake and Mrs. Kittiwake, his lady, were talking of, though Mr. Kittiwake was a popular preacher, and his lady one of Mrs. Winslow's most *elegant* friends, who knew all the latest fashions, and retailed all the most recent little histories in *the upper circles*, and told the most interesting anecdotes in the world of some of the greatest people in it, who possessed the greatest number of virtues, and were the greatest wits as well as the greatest politicians upon its surface. Not even such delectable conversation, nor Mr. Kittiwake's account of a person who had seen the apparition of Algernon Sidney[24] without an head, (raised by the magic powers of one of the illuminati, who was supposed to have sold himself to the devil on condition of being able to raise the spirits of traitors, either with heads or without, at his pleasure); no, not even an anecdote so strange, so well authenticated, and so much to the Doctor's taste, could win his attention from what was passing at the opposite end of the room—He caught now and then a word; he understood his son to be the object of ridicule; and he thought that he and his wife should be as little spared, if Miss Goldthorp once got into her violent spirits; and the figure, the manner of the Major, who was handsome, tall above the common size, conscious of his own perfections, and knowing how to display them, distracted him; he could not bear it, but approaching the young people, who were still laughing immoderately, he cried, "Upon my word, good folks, you are very merry!"—"And that is very delightful, Sir," said his niece. "It happens so seldom that it is quite a novelty to—to me."

"Cannot I be permitted to participate in your mirth?" enquired the Doctor.

"Oh! most undoubtedly, Sir," replied Adolphus; "and if you will only give us the subject we will be as merry over it as possible. My brother, you know, was a grave, sententious, prosing fellow; his philosophy was of the sober kind; now mine is a light, gay, airy system—a vast deal more amusing—I can laugh either with my friends . . . ."

"Or at them," said Miss Goldthorp.

"Yes, if they deserve it—why not you know?—but faith I seldom take the trouble—for if the honest fellows are vastly absurd, I am so apprehensive of laughing in their faces, that I generally cut[25]—So *now*, Louisa, if you have any thing to say, I am ready to go down stairs with you—Doctor, I have your permission." The Doctor, whom the stroke in the last speech did not escape, and whose jealousy and apprehension were now raised to an higher pitch than they had ever been at Upwood, was willing to understand that this formidable visitor was taking his leave; he therefore said, "I wish you a very good night, Major Delmont—Sorry we cannot ask the honour of your company to supper—Hope we shall be more fortunate another time."

"Lord, uncle," cried Miss Goldthorp, "Major Delmont means to sup here. Louisa, my love, bring your brother back. I am surprised, Sir," continued she, as soon as the drawing-room door was shut, "that you can be so rude to a man of Major Delmont's family and fashion—a family too that we are so much obliged to."

"And *I* am surprised," replied the Doctor; "I stand amazed at you, Niece Goldthorp; I must say, that when one is so unprepared, and here at one's townhouse, at this season of the year too, it is not at all a pleasant or desirable thing to have strangers, and I know not who, invited without any notice to sup with one; I say, Niece Martha, I stand amazed."

"Well, Sir, do sit down then, and get rid of your amazement. *I* have the most reason, I think, to be surprised; for you know when I consented, foolishly enough, I think, to give up to my aunt's entreaties, my darling scheme of having an house and establishment of my own, you assured me I should have the liberty of inviting to your's any person I pleased, and . . . ."

"Yes, child, yes, my dear Martha, yes; that to be sure is true, and it is very proper and right, in general; but then consider, dear child! consider a little what is consistent, and *decorous* you know, and right. A young lady's reputation, my dear niece—a young lady's reputation is like . . . like a sheet of the finest white paper—it must not have the least, the minutest blot or stain—it has been justly compared to . . . to . . . to . . . "

"To a fiddlestick," cried the impatient heiress; "for God's sake, my dear Doctor Winslow, keep all this common place stuff for your parishioners at Gandersfield Green; it may do well enough for May-day girls and love sick dairy maids, and may keep them from the *false arts of parjury lovyers*, who woo them with a Sunday posey all set round with sweet marjorum, and win them by half a pound of gingerbread and a cherry coloured top knot[26] from the fair; but do not, beseech you, my nunky now, do not lecture *me*, just for all the world as Squire Alworthy preaches to Jenny Jones in the Foundling."[27]

Miss Goldthorp then, half sportively, and half indignantly, courtesyed, and went up to her own apartment to consult her glass, and adjust her looks against the hour of supper, leaving Dr. Winslow standing more amazed than ever, Mrs. Winslow ready to go into a fit, and their son but little recovered from the shock his vanity and self love had received from the striking superiority of Delmont, and the arrogant manner in which he had been treated by him.

In the mean time Adolphus Delmont no sooner saw himself alone with Louisa, than he said—"Well, Louy, shall I have her or no?"

"Have who, my dear brother?"

"Why, Miss Goldthorp, the fifty thousand pounder. Hah! how lies the ground? George has not renewed his addresses there, has he?"

"George! no, not renewed them, certainly; for he never made any."

"But . . . prythee tell me, Louisa; has nothing happened lately in regard to that girl, that American, that, what was she? with whom he carried on some ridiculous, romantic connection; has nothing happened which may have restored him to his senses, and have brought him back to your heiress here?"

"How long have you been in London, Adolphus?"

"I came last night; but that is a strange way, methinks, of answering my question."

"I would know," said Louisa, "what you have heard, and from whom?"

"Never mind what I have heard, nor when, nor where—Tell me briefly what is become of George's American girl?"

"American girl! what a way of speaking of her, brother!"

"Nay, nay, call her what you will—where is she?"

"Indeed I do not know, Adolphus; but by your manner of enquiring, perhaps you do?"

Major Delmont, smiling significantly, said—"And how should *I* know, Louisa? Do you think our philosophical farmer would not keep this phenomenon out of *my* way, of whose libertinism his philosophyship has such terrible ideas?"

"Now this is merely cruel, Adolphus; where is Miss Glenmorris?"

"Aye, where is she? that is exactly what I ask you."

"We know not where she is—poor George has been distracted on her account. Surely *you* have had nothing to do with her disappearance?"

"How is it possible I should, Louisa; you know I am but just come from Dublin. By what magic dost think, my poor little Louy, that I could win this Anglo-columbian, or whatever she is, from that exemplary young man, so sober, so good, our own brother George! you know I never saw her in my life . . . but, Louy, pray tell me——you were in their secrets—of what nature was Delmont's connection with this girl?"

"Of what nature?" said Louisa, confusedly.

"Aye, child—of what nature? come, come, no prudery. He kept her, I suppose, as a mistress—Eh! He did not pretend, whatever the girl may do, that it was what you call honourable love?"

"Good God, Adolphus! what have you got in your head? From all I ever heard, I believe Miss Glenmorris is a young woman of the most unblemished character, such a one as George was well authorized to consider as his future wife, and to whom he would have, by this time, have been married, if . . . . . . "

"If she had not eloped while he was in Ireland, with somebody else! Poor George! I am really sorry for him; his coup d'essai[28] in sentimental, honourable love, has succeeded miserably to be sure."

"Let me beseech you, dear Adolphus," said Louisa, "let me entreat you, if you know any thing of this unfortunate young woman, or of her mother, to tell me; you know not the consequence of your concealing any thing."

"Tell *me*," answered the Major, "whether you are quite sure, that of whatever nature might be George's engagements with this girl, he has no design to make his addresses to Miss Goldthorp."

"I am very sure he has no such intention."

"And you believe I may succeed with her?"

"I don't see why you should not, unless her engagements, so long talked of, with her cousin, should . . . . . ."

"Her cousin! What, that little milk-faced splacknuc?[29] Pooh! she is a girl of too much sense and spirit to waste a thought on such a thing as that. Louisa! what are the odds she is not Mrs. Delmont in six weeks?—Oh! I'll tell you what I have had time to hear—That the brat produced by our fair Jezabel of an aunt, and who now is called Earl of Castledanes, has never been well since he had the measles, and the mother, who by the bye is going to be married again, is carrying the little wretch about for the air. He'll die, I hope, and I shall be a little nearer the place from whence the damned folly of a dotard and the art of a coquet have thrown me."

"There is still another little boy, however."

"Oh! but he was a posthumous child you know, and mama's grief for the loss of papa of course renders that little squab unhealthy—so you must *say*, however, to Miss Goldthorp, Louisa, for I intend to make the most of all my advantages, and to put the poor Doctor's mind at ease as soon as I can."

"And would you really, brother, marry so precipitately?"

"To be sure I would; why not? there are no doubts, I suppose, about her fortune?"

"But you cannot be acquainted with her temper, with her disposition?"

"I shall know enough of them afterwards, never fear—more, egad! than I wish to know."

"But if you should not be happy together?"

"Why then we must be happy as other folks are, apart."

"And are those your notions of marriage, my dear Adolphus?"

"Yes, and very good notions too, Louisa. I cannot conceive how a man of fashion can ever have any other. Thine, I suppose, are sweet, pretty ideas of connubial felicity, taken from novels, where the hero and heroine are so vastly happy at last, as never was the like, and have a sweet babe every year, the very picture of their amiable parents—Oh! delectable! Well, Louisa, if I should meet with a dear, gentle youth, likely to suit you, I'll recommend you as a very beautiful and accomplished young lady, adorned with every excellence likely to render the marriage state completely happy; and do you, my good girl, in your turn, do your best for *me* with your fair friend, for to tell you the truth, that is an affair which will not conveniently admit of any delay, and I intend that it shall be settled forthwith."

The Major was then about to return to the company, but his sister stopping him, entreated him to tell her what he knew of the Glenmorris's. He smiled in a way peculiar to him, and said, "Why, what would you think of a young lady, vastly modest, and inexorably virtuous, and so forth, who should run up to a man in the court of an inn, throw her arms about him, and call him by the sweetest names!"

"Who has done this? what can you possibly mean? who has acted in this manner?"

"Oh! it may be the American mode perhaps—the Transatlantic way for young ladies—or the hint may have been taken from our Gallic neighbours. Don't you think aunt Crewky would be immeasurably delighted with a niece who should so comport herself?"

He then hastened away, leaving Louisa in astonishment, and without any clue by which she could guess at more, than that he knew something of Medora, and that it was greatly to her disadvantage.

The vexation and distress of her brother George, which would, she knew, be extreme, and the uncertainty how she ought to act in revealing or concealing such imperfect intelligence, hung upon her spirits the rest of the evening; but Adolphus, gay, presumptuous, and not doubting of his ultimate success, made so great a progress in the heart of Miss Goldthorp, that she consented to an appointment with him the next day at the house of a friend, where he was to explain himself fully; and he no sooner took leave at a late hour, than the impatient reproaches of Dr. Winslow provoked her to declare she had now met with the man of her heart, and was determined to give him her hand. It was in vain the Doctor implored, soothed, threatened, and lamented; in vain that Middleton produced tears, and his mother an hysteric; the cruel and resolute fair one went very calmly to her room, and poor Louisa, who found she was considered as having been the cause of all this, was impatient to see Mr. Armitage in the morning, to whom she meant to disclose what she had heard from Adolphus, and to ask his protection to Upwood, if George Delmont was not likely immediately to return, for at the house of Doctor Winslow she was certainly now a most unwelcome visitor.

Chap. III.

A ray, half seen, from hope at length appears![30]

While the elder brother pursued his project of re-establishing his fortune by marriage, the younger passed two days at Upwood in a state of mind such as he had never before experienced, and had not imagined possible. The scenes which he had hitherto considered as the most soothing to his taste and his imagination presented nothing now but images of his lost happiness. The charm which the presence of a beloved object had lent to them was vanished, and he no longer possessed that tranquillity which, before he had seen her among them, he had found in this lovely solitude.

He now wandered about restless and wretched, unable to endure the thoughts that crowded on his mind in regard to Medora, yet incapable for a moment to think of any thing else. From Susanne he obtained no information; the faculties of the poor creature seemed annihilated; she wept incessantly, and was comforted by nothing but Delmont's assurances that she should go to London, and assist him in the search which he was resolved unremittingly to make till he could obtain some information.

From every pursuit that used either to occupy or delight him he now recoiled with a kind of dread. His books he feared to open; he had read them to Medora; her sweet intelligent countenance would beam upon him no more, when he remarked on some favourite passage; he should no more see her lovely eyes filling with tears of native sensibility, at a description of human misery, or gaze enraptured on the smile irradiating like an emanation from Heaven her soft face. As little could he endure to visit his garden, and when at night he passed through the conservatory to go into the house, the scent of the plants, the recess where Medora had often sat at work or drawing, seemed so forcibly to recall his past happiness, so forcibly to contrast it with present misery, that he fled as if for refuge into his study; yet there he again found that Medora pursued him; and no alleviation of his torments offered itself, but what he could find in forming new projects to unveil the unaccountable mystery that the loss he had sustained was involved in. . .

Some papers that he had brought from Ireland lay on his writing table; the sight of them renewed in his recollection all the vexation he had endured in an ill-fated journey, owing to which his present insupportable misfortune had befallen him, and he took them up to throw them into a drawer, that he might see them no more, when among them he remembered a small packet of the sketches of poetry left by the unfortunate young woman, Elizabeth Lisburne; *they* at least were likely to be in unison with his present feelings. The following lines, though descriptive of a later season of the year, were highly congenial to the comfortless and desolate sensations of the present moment.

SONNET; written in October 179—.

The blasts of Autumn, as they scatter round
The faded foliage of another year,
And muttering many a sad and solemn sound,
Drive the pale fragments o'er the stubble sere,
Are well attuned to my dejected mood;
Ah! better far than airs that breathe of Spring
While the high rooks that hoarsely clamouring
Seek in black phalanx the half-leafless wood
I rather hear, than that enraptur'd lay
Harmonious, and of love and pleasure born,
Which from the golden furze or flowering thorn
Awakes the shepherd in the ides of May;
Nature delights *me* most, when most she mourns,
For never more to me the Spring of Hope returns.[31]

Delmont shuddered—If the sad close of this little melancholy effusion should be prophetic of his own destiny! Another, however, presented itself; a few slight and simple lines, which appeared to be almost an impromptu.

TO VESPER.[32]

Thou! who behold'st with dewy eye
The sleeping leaves and folded flowers,[33]
And hear'st the night wind lingering sigh
Thro' shadowy woods and twilight bowers;
Thou wast the signal once that seem'd to say,
Hillario's beating heart reprov'd my long delay.

I see thy emerald lustre stream
O'er these rude cliffs and cavern'd shore;
But here, orisons to thy beam
The woodland chauntress pours no more,
Nor I, as once, thy lamp propitious hail,
Seen indistinct thro' tears, confus'd, and dim, and pale!

Soon shall thy arrowy radiance shine
On the broad ocean's azure wave,
Where this poor cold-swoln form of mine
Shall shelter in its billowy grave,
Safe from the scorn the world's sad out-casts prove,
Unconscious of the pain of ill-requited love.

Images like these, where despair seemed to have taken entire possession of the mind that assembled them, were but ill calculated to relieve the excessive depression of Delmont; he reproached himself for yielding to it; there was indeed but little wisdom or philosophy in lamenting evils that were not yet irremediable. He started up to shake off this enfeebling temper, and once more meant to put away the packet, the melancholy memorial of an unhappy attachment; a paper folded like a letter dropped out from it; he stooped to replace it, when casting his eyes on the words written on it, he saw they were a direction to himself—and in the hand of Medora.

His heart beat violently; yet he immediately recollected that it must be some note written before he left Upwood. On examining it, however, he found it had never been opened. He eagerly unsealed it, and to his astonishment read these words:

I know not the day of the month—I have lost some days by the terror
and fear they have passed in.—Oh! Delmont, Oh! my mother, where
are you both! what have I suffered, what have I dreaded for you!—I
write, not knowing whether you will ever get my letter.—I know not
where to direct; but surely Delmont will be at Upwood.—My dear,
dear mother, I dare not trust myself to think on the state of mind you
may have been thrown into.—I am watched—I am confined—Hardly
dare I hope ever to see you more—and I know not where I am, but it is
far to the northward of London.—I hear footsteps, and dread least the
only opportunity that occurs may be lost.—If . . . . The house is, I have
just heard, in Yorkshire—the name of the woman, Dartnell, or
something like it. God preserve my mother; and you, my friend
Delmont! my dear friend, do not forsake her.

M.G.

Delmont, hardly crediting his senses, ran over the paper a second time. The writing was indistinct, and had evidently been done by snatches. How long had it been written, and from whence came it? There was only the London post mark, and he decyphered with difficulty the date of that mark, which ascertained that the letter had left London about eight days before, and that it had lain at Upwood when he arrived there, before he went to London. Trembling and agitated more than certainly became his philosophy, he now summoned his servants, to enquire wherefore this letter had not been given him among others at his arrival, and at length the house maid, who had newly supplied the place of one who had married out of the family, acknowledged that she had been absent on a visit to her friends for some days before her master's return, and had engaged the cook to receive in her place a sister of her's, a girl of thirteen, who, having been employed to dust the library, had probably received this letter, and put it there, and afterwards bundled it up, not knowing its consequence, among the other papers which Clement had taken out of his master's portmanteau.

With this account Delmont was compelled to be satisfied; but his impatience to return to London, and recommence his search, now that he had some clue to guide him, was beyond all he had ever felt before—Hardly giving poor Susanne time to arrange her little packet, he hurried with her into a postchaise as soon as it could be obtained, and travelling all night, reached London at day-break; then scarce allowing himself time to take the necessary refreshment, he hastened to Armitage, for whom, being an early riser, he did not long wait.

A short consultation followed, when Armitage related what he had heard from Louisa, by which they thought it certain that Major Delmont knew something of Medora. Conjectures were vain and useless. George Delmont flew to the lodgings of his brother, who, as soon as he knew he was waiting for him, arose, and came to him.

"What, George!" cried the Major, in his usual tone; "what has my young Cincinnatus[34] again quitted his plough? Well, however, I'm glad to see thee—But you are not come, I hope, to renew your pretensions in a certain quarter, because, if you are, we shall have something to say to each other in the way of Castalio and Polidore,[35] and I shall wave my droit d'ainesse[36] and enact the younger brother."

"I am not lucky enough to understand you," said Delmont; "speak plainly and immediately, for it is a subject on which I cannot bear raillery."

"Nor I neither; of what would you have me speak plainer than I do?"

George Delmont thought only of Medora; for though Louisa had hinted to Armitage what she supposed was likely to happen as to her elder brother's successful address to Miss Goldthorp, he had been so entirely occupied by his anxiety for his friend's child to have omitted naming it in his short conference with the younger.

"You have seen, I understand, a young lady, for whom, you know, I am very deeply interested."

"Oh! yes, certainly, she is a fine girl, but a devilish coquet."

"A coquet! what can you possibly mean?"

"Call it what you will; if the word coquet offends you, she is fond of admiration, and cares not much what advances she makes to obtain it. However they are all alike, and I have nothing to object on that score. I hope you are not going to try your fortune with her again."

"To try my fortune *again*, with Medora, with Miss Glenmorris!"

The Major could not, or at least did not try to check a sort of triumphant smile, which would have amounted to a laugh, but that he never laughed.

"You have then been very successful already," said he, "have you?"

"It is impossible for me to comprehend you, Major Delmont," answered his brother. "This may become much more serious than you seem to imagine."

"What, my philosopher thrown quite out of his steady course, and ready to cut his own brother's throat about a woman!—Oh! fye, fye!—What would all the cynics, and stoics, and other sage fellows, both ancient and modern, say to such a violation of their magnanimous rules and orders.[37] You will never be niched with . . . . . . faith I have forgotten their names . . . . ."

"I must insist," said George Delmont, with still more gravity, "that you end this ill timed railing, and tell me where, when, and by what chance you saw this young lady?"

"First then I answer, that as to the place *where*, it was at the house of Dr. Winslow; the time *when*, was the evening before yesterday, and again yesterday evening; and as to by what chance, chance had nothing to do with it, it was altogether design. I went to see her, and I saw her, and perhaps too I might say with Caesar, *Veni, vidi, vici.*[38]

"Saw Miss Glenmorris at Dr. Winslow's! went on purpose to see her! impossible! there must be some mistake in all this—Of whom are you talking?"

"Of the lady *my brother* (having less pretensions to be sure than *I* have) is said to have *scorned* and *rejected*—of Miss Goldthorp."

"Miss Goldthorp!—I imagined you were speaking of Medora Glenmorris; I understood you had seen her?"

"And suppose I have! What the devil, is no one to see pretty women but yourself, I wonder!"

"Tell me, I conjure you, Adolphus; it is more serious to me than you seem to suppose. *Have* you seen Medora Glenmorris?"

"What, if I should answer that I *have* seen her; that I . . . (I suppose, though, you will not believe me, if I were to tell you) that I . . . have had her pretty arms, potelè et blanc,[39] encircling my neck . . . and . . . ."

"Damnation," exclaimed George Delmont, totally losing his temper, "'tis impossible."

"I will not take in offence the lie you so unequivocally give me, George—but I tell you, on the honour of a gentleman and a soldier, and if it still has credit enough in your eyes to enforce the truth, on the honour of a Delmont, a name that till lately was never stained either by the falsehood or folly of those who bore it; I *do* tell you, Sir, that all this happened, and a great deal more."

Never till that moment had Delmont felt such acute pain; there seemed no motive for a falsehood so cruel and so useless; but to believe Medora a guilty, an abandoned wanton!—Delmont was unequal to sustain the hideous idea a moment; his faculties seemed for a while crushed and annihilated, and he could only utter in a mournful tone.

"I am prepared, Major Delmont, to hear all you have to say—Only relate plain matter of fact, and keep me not needlessly in suspense and anguish."

"I thought you worthy gents, who profess philosophy, and so forth, disbanded all this paltry sort of anguish—Look upon women as only necessary machines in the eternal dance of atoms, and with true Mahometan sang froid do not consider them as having souls of consequence enough to recall by their misconduct *your* elevated minds from the haut volée of abstract studies on matter and space, materialism, immaterialism, and all the incomprehensibility of metaphysics."[40]

"This is inhuman trifling, Major Delmont," said George.

"Upon my soul, considering what you profess, George, you do most terribly betray the cause of philosophy; however I'll humour your frailty, and relate briefly my adventure with your Transatlantic nymph, assuring you, however, that if it had not another catastrophe,[41] it was no fault of mine."

"Where is she now?" cried Delmont, impatiently.

"Across the Atlantic again for what I know; but listen to me like a disciple of the stoic philosophers, and then—

I will a round unvarnished tale deliver
Of my short day of love; what sighs, what oaths,
What protestation, and what charm of flattery
(If such proceeding I am charged withal)
I would have won her with."[42]

"I am in the wrong, Sir," cried George Delmont, "to expect from you any thing but unfeeling ridicule and misplaced buffoonery."

"Poor George! jilted by a baby! crossed in love by a coquet in leading strings. This comes of your horror of women, 'in a certain style of fashion.' Oh! forsooth, you had the trembling abhorrence of a country curate towards women of the world. They were dissipated, they were vain, unfeeling, insatiable in avarice for money to stake at the gaming table;

They lisped, and they ambled, and nick-nam'd God's creatures.[43]

You would have a creature fresh from the hands of nature; a beautiful piece of unadulterate clay, which you might mould as you would.

But the first 'lawyer' she saw, she changed her love."

"A lawyer!" cried Delmont with increased passion and impatience.

"Yes, yes, let me recollect. Upon my soul I have forgotten now whether it was the lawyer himself, or the lawyer's clerk, or only his brother, or cousin, or some relation; however there was a lawyer in question, who decoyed her, poor pretty maiden, from her Mama."

"Decoyed her! Curses light on . . . "

"Why now there it is again. I am trying to recollect all about it, and you wont have patience to hear me. I should get through my story as well again if you would not

disturb my naturally clear and methodical manner of narration by bouncing and flying round the room like a mad cat."

George saw that his solicitude really defeated its own purpose, and therefore
made an effort to stifle the expression of the cruel emotions he felt. His brother went
on——

"I was travelling, as you know, from my friend Willesly's in Yorkshire. My way
was on the great north road. I stopped at Skipton[44] to change horses. It was evening,
I ordered coffee, and while it was preparing, sauntered in an idle sort of way into the
inn-yard. The people were tedious. I went up to the bar, and asked some inconsequential questions of the bar-maid. The wench was pretty and saucy, and I remained talking a country-quarter kind of nonsense to her, till I was suddenly, faith I may call it
embraced, by two very sweet white arms, and called upon by the name of 'Delmont,
dear Delmont,' to which of course I answered like a preux chevalier,[45] and the more
readily when I saw those very kind words were uttered by the pretty mouth, and
assisted by two bright yet soft eyes of a very lovely girl."—He paused.

"Go on," said George Delmont—"Go on, I beseech you."

"But however flattering this was, it did not proceed quite so delectably; for the
dear little flutterer no sooner saw my face, and heard me speak, than she gave a scream,
and fled away like a lapwing."

George now thought he comprehended, that Medora had mistaken his brother
for him, since in their height and size they very nearly resemble each other. He became
more impatient than ever when the Major added, "However, I could not let the charmer
escape me, so I pursued her."

"You did not dare to insult her?"

"The most unpardonable insult to a fine girl would surely be to seem insensible of her charms, and especially, you know, after such an attractive salutation as
that. So I made the best of my way to apologise to her, and at the end of a long
passage, up stairs, overtook her, and returned with interest the *accolade*[46] she had
favoured me with."

"Medora! my Medora!" cried George, "Good God, to be so treated."

"How should I know she was your Medora? She seemed to me to be every
body's Medora. But she made, to do her justice, a very tolerable story of it; but take
notice, I did not know it was your little Yanky till . . . ."

"Till when?"

"Why, not till—till I had made violent love to her, and proposed her making
the same journey with me, that she had intended with the foolish fellow she set out
with—Not that I meant to have carried on the joke even as far as the blacksmith's[47]—
I thought there would be no great difficulty in persuading such a pretty chitterface[48] as
that long before we reached the confines of Scotland, that she had made an excellent
exchange. However, instead of listening to me a l'aimable, as the little dears generally
do, she made a prodigious to do about her mammy, moaning like a stray lambkin, and
at last told me she belonged to you."

"And had *that* declaration," said George Delmont, sternly, "no power to restrain your licentious conduct towards her?"

"How do you know," replied his brother, "that my conduct *was* licentious, as you call it. But have patience, and I'll go on. The mention of your name of course brought on an explanation. The dear little girl made it out very prettily, though not very probably, that she was carried away by a stratagem from the hotel where she lodged, and taken great part of the way into Scotland; but the adventurous cavalier, who was, as far as I could understand, a lawyer's clerk,

Some clerk foredoom'd his master's soul to cross,
Who sought adventures while he should engross;[49]

this knight of the quill, unused to any such refractory damsels as was this young squaw from the wilds of America, was so much alarmed by her threats, or awed (if you like that better) by her *virtue*, that instead of carrying her any farther, and marrying her whether she would or no, he *took* her to his mother's, and as the mother was not likely to prevail where the son's gallantry had failed, they kept her pretty much confined, for poor Quill began to be frightened at what he had done. However, there was no restraining a nymph who had been reared on the broad basis of continental freedom, and off she went out of the window to get *from* a lover, who, for aught I knew, she had sprung out of another to get at; but the fellow was certainly a fool, and knew not how to manage what he had undertaken, and the girl was of course sick of him."

"What was the name of this accursed rascal? and where may I find him?"

"His name I am not clear in—Never mind his name—Let me go on with my story—So not liking, I tell you, her confinement, your fair Columbian, *un belle soirée*,[50] the moon being at full (which in such cases is always requisite) sat forth alone, and walked with supernatural powers, as your heroines always do, till she overtook a cart with a woman and her children in it, who were removing on some parish complaint to Skipton—They were a sad sick crew, and dying of an infectious fever . . . ."

George Delmont started in horror, clasped his hands eagerly together, and seemed almost unable to endure this additional shock.

"Fever!" cried he, "an infectious fever! and my Medora!"

"Your Medora, as the woman at the inn told me, nursed the children, and gave money to the mother; all she had about her, and bought them wine; and so they all got to a small hedge ale-house together, from whence that carter, who had driven them, shewed her the way to a better inn—and there she put herself into the protection of the man and his wife, who had agreed to put her into one of the night coaches for London, when from a window on the other side of the inn-yard she saw me, and, as many other beautiful young ladies have done, threw herself into my arms."

"You cannot misunderstand *that*, I think, Major Delmont, it was on *my* protection she meant to throw herself. You must immediately, nay you did immediately, understand it so. And *had* you then so little honour, so little principle, as to abuse this confidence? Tell me, Sir, where is she now?"

"Really, George, this sort of treatment I do not understand, though I have borne it for some time."

"Nay, Major Delmont, it is I who have had to endure the contumely, which not only now, but on all occasions, you think proper to treat me with; but which, on any other occasion, I could much better forgive. To end discourse which is insupportable, tell me where Miss Glenmorris now is?"

"Upon my soul I do not know."

"That answer, Major Delmont, will not satisfy me."

"It must, Farmer Delmont, for I have no other to give you."

"Where did you leave her, Sir?"

"I did not leave her at all—the little ungrateful baggage left me."

"And would she have done so? would she have fled from protection which, from so near a relation of mine, she would have thought she had a right to claim, had you not, instead of befriending her as a brother, insulted her as a libertine? I know Medora well, and know that no false prudery would have driven her away alone and destitute. You rudely, you cruelly took advantage of her helpless situation."

"Upon my soul I only told her she was a bewitching girl; and would you, who are a professed lover of truth, quarrel with me for that?"

"It was unworthy of you as a gentleman and as a man."

"I represented to her, that if she was disposed to continue her journey northward, I was very much at her service; or if she would honour me with her company in my postchaise to London, she would make me the happiest of beings, and so forth."

"And if you had made such an offer as a man of humanity, of honour, ought to have made it, would she not joyfully have accepted it?"

"I assure you I intended she should have accepted it; and upon my soul she was frightened at nothing; or she might repent, for ought I know, and wish to return to Goosequill. Yet, hang it, the dear rogue looks too intelligent for that; she can never have so bad a taste. I declare, George; nay, now I am serious, that I began playing the fool, that is, only making fine speeches; for I did not touch the end of her imperious little finger; I began, I say, playing the fool—only because the witch was devilish handsome, and I had no very exalted opinion of her sublime virtue from what I had learned one way or other about her; but when I saw I could make nothing of her for myself, and had been convinced she was a true turtle dove to thee, why I should have quietly made the best of it, and brought her back as properly and soberly as a cardinal or a judge. The monkey, I tell you, took fright at nothing. A girl, who had seen only one winter in London or Dublin, would never have thought of such skittish nonsense; but your rice bird,[51] forsooth, would not trust me, a little deceitful toad, but was off again in the morning—I could not find where or for what."

"And have you no means of telling me, Major Delmont," said George, shewing him the letter he had found at Upwood, "whether this letter was written before or after you met Miss Glenmorris."

"Before, I think most likely," said Adolphus, after he had perused it. "Well!— and so now. What do you intend to do?"

"I know not. I am distracted! Oh! Adolphus, would *I* have acted towards the woman you loved, as you have done towards this dear, innocent, injured girl!"

George Delmont then, without waiting for an answer, went again to consult Armitage, meaning to set out instantly for the north. His brother, forgetting in five minutes all that had passed, dressed himself to ride in the park, where Miss Goldthorp had promised to meet him, and where the plan was finally arranged. Miss Goldthorp, in a week afterwards, became Mrs. Delmont. Dr. Winslow stood amazed at her cruelty, and lost his appetite in consequence of this bitter disappointment. Mrs. Winslow's fits were so serious, that she was hastened to the sea; and poor Middleton determined to escape from the raillery of his acquaintance, the amazement of his father, and the nervousness of his mother, by driving his curricle on a tour to the Lakes, about which he cared nothing.

The Major and his bride sat out in great splendor for Southampton, in the neighbourhood of which his regiment was quartered.

Chap. IV.

Helas!—où trouver des traits et des couleurs,
Qui puissent retracer l'exces de ses douleurs?[52]

Ten miserable days had passed since Mrs. Glenmorris had been confined and treated as a mad woman. Reduced to the last stage of weakness by a devouring fever, she recovered her reason only to know that she had lost every thing else. Why she was where she found herself she knew not, nor by whose authority she had been placed there. Her extreme languor and feebleness permitted her not to remonstrate; it hardly suffered her mildly and plaintively to entreat of the persons she saw around her information as to the cause and duration of her confinement, and implore them to tell her if Medora, her dear child, had been heard of, and would be restored to her.

Those whose business it was to attend the invalids in the house treated her now with gentleness and humanity; but they told her that all questions were useless, and that she must forbear to make them. Very fain would she have known if the idea, that confusedly floated in her mind, of having seen her mother, had any foundation, or was merely the dream of delirium. It was in vain the unfortunate mother of Medora endeavoured to recal distinctly the succession of images which seemed to have passed through her mind, before they were totally lost in the overwhelming misery of her loss; a loss which, though it had not at first wholly annihilated her faculties, had from its very commencement so shaken them as to be absolutely insupportable when her endeavours to recover that loss were evidently vain; and even now, when she thought of what the present state of her daughter might be, she became sick and giddy. The earnest, the agonizing desire to set forth once more in search of Medora, and the cruel certainty that she was herself a prisoner, continually overcame the little strength she had acquired, and she was compelled to throw herself on her bed, and shut out the light—the light that seemed to reproach her for beholding it, when the only object she delighted to gaze upon was no where to be seen.

The woman, who was chiefly her attendant, endeavoured sometimes to reason with her and sometimes to amuse her; but in such a state of mind the most profound reasoning would have failed; and such as a coarse and uneducated woman could offer, served only to tease and irritate her; yet as she could never prevail on the woman to leave her alone any where but in her own room, she often declined what the woman told her was directed by her physicians, to walk in a large garden that belonged to the house. It was surrounded by an high wall, and terminated by a group of old limes, to which there had formerly been a walk of cut holly, but it had long been suffered to grow as a shade and screen for the unhappy patients, of which there were never less than six or eight in this large and melancholy abode, which had formerly been a nobleman's villa, and fifty years ago had frequently received the statesman at his hours of retirement, and the courtier in his moments of relaxation; but sold on the extinction of the male branch of the family, it had been now for many years a receptacle for lunatics, whose friends could afford to give very high prices for their accommodation.

Like all those, who with even morbid sensibility, have encountered singular calamities, Mrs. Glenmorris found nothing, that during her convalescence, was so soothing to her as the air—There, it seemed as if, shaking off the weight that impelled her to the earth, she could expatiate in boundless space, and again meet that angelic creature, who, she feared, was for ever lost to her in this world of woe and disappointment. In the air she breathed more freely; her heart, though it unceasingly vibrated to anguish, was less choked (if such an expression is allowable) in the air than when in a room, and with the poor equivocal maniac, who was for a while the object of (*talked of*) charity, and then heard of no more, the unhappy mother of Medora often said, while deep drawn sighs seemed at once to rend and to relieve her heart, that *there was nothing good but liberty and fresh air.*[53]

This indulgence, however, was now for some days positively refused her, unless her guard accompanied her, whose prate was distracting to her, and who, by way of reconciling the poor languid patient to the loss of reason, real or supposed, thought it very proper to tell her how many ladies she had attended in the same disorder, some of whom had been released after two or three years, while others had died in the deplorable condition of lunatics. Mrs. Glenmorris had no heart now to attend to the sorrows of others; her senses, her feelings were all absorbed in her own. Hardly conscious that the world had contained any other than her husband and her child, she was awake to little else than the consciousness that from Glenmorris she was divided by the great Atlantic Ocean; and that the wretchedness that had overturned her reason, and was hurrying her fast to the grave, would, as soon as Glenmorris should know it, deprive him of reason, and probably of life.—Hourly feeling it more and more impossible to survive the loss of Medora, she was conscious that Glenmorris could as ill outlive the certainty either of her death or her disgrace—the disgrace of his adored child would be to him more insupportable than death.

Images of what might have been came incessantly to her mind, aggravating by contrast that which was.——If at any time she could prevail on her talkative attendant to be silent, as she sat on a bench in the small grove of limes, she closed her eyes, and wrapping the green sarcenet[54] round them, with which her bonnet was enveloped, felt the air blow softly on her face, and listened to the sighing of the wind among the trembling leaves, such were the sensations, such the sounds she felt and heard in the beginning of summer, when Delmont and Medora were with her, or when she looked towards the woodwalk, certain of seeing them return with collections of wild flowers, Medora, perhaps, singing to Delmont one of those simple airs she had learned in America, or Delmont repeating to her some favourite passage in one of those poets in whose works he delighted. The breath of Heaven was still fresh and pleasant, diffusing the musky scents of summer declining into autumn; but fancy could not long delude her; she opened her eyes after it had embodied awhile the figures she used to see; she looked around her, but how different were the objects from those so dear to her heart—a woman set over to control her, from the idea that she had lost her reason, and was no longer capable of self-government, and every inanimate object strange and foreign to her; she neither knew the gloomy place where she was, by whose means she was conveyed thither, or who supported her—to die unknown here would have been her only wish, had she been sure that she should never again have seen Medora.— Medora happy as the wife of Delmont, or in the protecting arms of her father.

As from mere inability to resist, the unfortunate Mrs. Glenmorris had sunk into passive silence, and did or submitted to whatever she was desired to do, the persons about her, and the medical man who attended her, took it for granted that she was gradually settling into melancholy madness, a transition very frequent from raving delirium; they therefore by degrees contented themselves with keeping from her every instrument by which she could injure herself, and insensibly relaxed in that vigilance which had at the beginning of her recovery so distressed her. Her guard at first trusted her to walk within her sight at some distance; then satisfied herself with looking after her now and then, and at length suffered her to walk or sit whole hours alone among the lime trees. The attending apothecary (for the physician only came in cases of emergency) perceiving that his interesting patient became calmer in proportion as she was subjected to less restraint, ordered all appearance of suspicion to be as much withdrawn as was consistent with her safety; and nothing contributed so much as this release from officious persecution to restore to the poor mourner the power of thinking, which the irritability of her nerves had so long taken from her.

By degrees then Mrs. Glenmorris recalled, though it was still confusedly, the circumstances that had preceded her total loss of reason. She had no traces of any thing afterwards, but some faint yet terrific idea of Lady Mary de Verdon. If it could once be ascertained that she had really been in the presence of her mother, it would give her an insight into the causes of Medora's disappearance, for she well knew that the Lady Mary was capable of taking any means, however unjustifiable, to prevent what she so greatly dreaded, the success of a competitor for Miss Cardonnel's fortune. There was so much ease in the hope that Lady Mary had conveyed away her grandchild, that the mother delighted to cherish it; for though, only a few weeks before, she would have considered such a deprivation as the most cruel outrage, yet as Lady Mary would merely prevent the appearance of Medora to claim the estate, and she would suffer no other injury than confinement remote from her mother, the contemplation of this sort of robbery now was relief and satisfaction, compared to those fearful apprehensions that had driven that mother to distraction.

This hope, which hourly became stronger, served more than any thing to relieve the mind of Mrs. Glenmorris, and restore it to its former tone. She assumed a more tranquil air, flattering herself that she should by that means induce the people she saw, and particularly the apothecary, to trust her with the secret they had hitherto so guardedly kept, viz. *who* had engaged their care of her, and by whom they were paid? But the man, on whom she principally relied for information, though very attentive to her, and appearing unusually interested for her health and ease, was so cautious in his answers, and so artfully evaded the oblique interrogatories of his patient, that, though she could find nothing to contradict her hopes, nothing escaped from him that confirmed them.

Mr. Seton (which was the apothecary's name) was one day sitting with her, when she commanded herself so much as to converse on indifferent matters, which she had never done before, and even with some degree of cheerfulness. On a sudden she said, "Mr. Seton, whatever may have been the state of my mental or bodily health when first I came under your care, I think you must now for some time have been satisfied that my confinement is wholly unnecessary; it becomes therefore so unjust, that I am convinced you, who are an honest and a good man, will never be accessary to its continuance. You cannot deny but that I am perfectly in my senses. Who has a right to make me a prisoner? By whose orders am I detained here?"

Seton appeared very much confused. "I own, Madam" answered he, reddening, and in great agitation; "I own that your cure has very happily advanced within these last few days; I shall undoubtedly make my report accordingly; but you must be sensible, dear Madam, *that* is all I can do. I am not a principal in this concern—I am merely employed to follow the orders of Sir John St. Dennis, the physician, and beyond the directions Sir John has given, you must be sensible I can do nothing."

"Yes," said Mrs. Glenmorris, taking a letter out of her pocket, which she had prepared, "you can oblige me in an instance with which Sir John St. Dennis has nothing to do; you can convey this letter for me to the post."

Mr. Seton looked at the address; it was to Armitage; he shrunk back, and again his countenance, which Mrs. Glenmorris narrowly watched, expressed something extraordinary.

"No, no indeed," said he, "I cannot; 'tis utterly impossible—I must not—I am particularly *ordered* not to take any letter to *that* . . . . . any letter at all, I mean, from any of the patients in this house."

"And particularly not from me to *that* gentleman," said Mrs. Glenmorris— "Oh! I understand—you received that prohibition from Lady Mary de Verdon, or from Mrs. Grinsted."

"No indeed, Madam; I never saw Lady Mary, never in my life."

"Nor Mrs. Grinsted?"

"I protest, dear Madam, that I am not acquainted with Mrs. Grinsted."

"You may as well tell me; for that sort of evasion by which a man of natural integrity shrinks from the falsehood he is ashamed of, while he yet cannot determine to tell the truth, is so easily understood, that I need no other than the sentence you have just uttered to convince me, that my being here, as well as the cause which gave an excuse for hurrying me hither, is owing to the machinations of Mrs. Grinsted (whom I trusted) under the directions of my mother, Lady Mary de Verdon. Nay," continued Mrs. Glenmorris, "do not look so much alarmed at my having discovered this; it is so far from being unwelcome to me, that nothing will so greatly relieve my mind as a confirmation that I am right in my supposition. My mother alas! must I call *her* mother who would rob me of my child! My mother, who expelled me from her affections long before I could have done any thing to forfeit them, had first the cruelty to take from me my only delight, the sole pleasure and comfort of my life, by which she knew I should be driven to despair, and then took advantage of the anguish she inflicted, to affix on me the charge of lunacy, and to confine me, *she* hopes, for life. And why has she done all this? To prevent the just claims of my child, and my own, from being established, while for the daughter of my sister she is accumulating more than any one person ought to possess, with the hope of marrying her to some man of equal fortune, as if such exorbitant wealth had the power of bestowing happiness. Gracious God!" exclaimed Mrs. Glenmorris, eagerly clasping her hands, and *looking* the appeal she made to heaven—"Gracious God! what is there in this redundancy of fortune that can secure one hour of superior enjoyment! I, who have possessed so little of the great riches of my father, have never been unhappy on that account. Medora has learned to do without any superfluities; her pleasures are all such as are easily obtained; her wishes moderate; the sweet simplicity of her character has formed her taste." (Mrs. Glenmorris could with difficulty proceed to speak of her daughter.) "Medora has a thousand times implored me to relinquish the attempt we were per-suaded to make for the acquisition of fortune, which she desired not. Oh! would to God we had done so! I should not now in bitterness of heart have missed my lovely girl without knowing what has been her fate.

"But," added she, after a momentary pause, during which she endeavoured to conquer these painful emotions, and to speak with firmness. "But if Lady Mary has deprived me of my daughter, I know that deprivation can be only temporary; and let me, Sir, implore you to bear to this mother, who has outlived her feelings, my message relative to my child and me. Oh! tell her, Mr. Seton; go to her instantly, and tell her that I will sign any paper she shall send me, resigning every claim I can possibly have, either for myself or my posterity, on the estate of Gabriel Anthonio de Verdon, my father. Tell her, if she will restore Medora to me, we will most sol-emnly engage ourselves to go immediately to America; and indeed I will neither resent the inhumanity of her conduct towards me, or ever again let her hear my name or my child's."

Mr. Seton, in fact, understood nothing of the latent cause of Mrs. Glenmorris's confinement; he only knew that she really was, at the time she was brought to the house he attended, in a state fit only for confinement; and that Mrs. Grinsted, in the name of Lady Mary de Verdon, had given directions for her reception, and under-taken the payment. All that the interesting patient said, therefore, appeared so prob-able, and her earnest, her affecting manner influenced him so much, that hardly had the sense of his own interest weight enough to induce him to refuse her first request of conveying a letter; yet he had been strictly enjoined not to take any letter, and had heard orders given against suffering her to see or to hear from a person of the name of Armitage.

Mrs. Glenmorris, though now appearing so clear and reasonable, might be only in a lucid interval, and he should commit himself both professionally and otherwise if he yielded to her importunity. All he would do, therefore, was to assure her, that though he could not charge himself with a letter, since it was contrary to a general promise he had given, which ought to have the force of an oath, yet he would make such enquiries as might help to tranquillise her mind about her daughter, and give such a report as should, he hoped and believed, hasten her own release from confinement.

Having said this, Mr. Seton, afraid of hearing again the voice, and listening again to the entreaties he had no power to resist, hastened away, and left Mrs. Glenmorris more and more convinced that her conjectures were well founded, and that Medora had merely fallen into the power of her grandmother; and while her heart revolted from the cruelty of such a proceeding, it was yet soothed by the hope that Medora had suffered no outrages from the profligate, no personal distresses, either from poverty or insult.—"No," said she, "Lady Mary will content herself with taking from us the power of sharing her fortune with Miss Cardonnel, and *that* we are ready to resign— She will give me again my Medora, innocent and lovely as she was when I lost her. Delmont will not love her less because these visionary projects of fortune, on which he never bestowed a thought, are faded for ever. We shall be reunited, and rejoin Glenmorris before his heart can be wounded by the intelligence of this mysterious, this cruel separation."

This way of accounting for all that had befallen her was so salutary, so soothing to the sick heart of Mrs. Glenmorris, that it considerably accelerated the return of her strength, for she now slept, and still awoke in the hope of terminating her confinement and being restored to her daughter. Three days thus passed, and in their progress she endeavoured to amuse her mind by a recurrence to such of those studies as used to delight her, and were still within her reach; but when she contemplated a flower, or gazed of an evening on the immense volume of magnificence and radiance above her, all the precious hours she had passed with her daughter, instructing her in botany or astronomy, returned to her recollection, and the question, shall our morning our evening studies ever be again so enjoyed? came to her mind so embittered with doubt and apprehension, that it was impossible to proceed, and she threw away the jasmine which she gathered, as it half embowered the window, being the growth of half a century against the wall of the house, or closed the shutter, rather than behold the stars or the moon, whose brilliance or whose progress had so often been the subject of their evening conversations.

CHAP. V.

Spes addita suscitas iras.[55]

Delmont, after a short conference with Armitage, set out in hopes to obtain on the road, where the cruel behaviour of his brother had driven her from the protection she sought, some intelligence of Medora.

He hastened to Skipton, cautiously at every place on the way making such enquiry as he thought might lead to the discovery of the person he sought. Arrived at the town, and at the inn, he asked with a beating heart after the young person who at such a time (of which he had taken care correctly to inform himself) came from a remote part of the county with a family of paupers, and afterwards was conducted to this inn.—It was of the landlady he made this enquiry, who seemed extremely unwilling to answer.

"Oh! Madam," said Delmont, who could no longer conceal the deep interest he took in her relative to whom he asked information, "if it were possible for you to understand all the anxiety the absence of this young lady creates, I cannot but believe that I should interest your kindness to assist me in discovering her."

"I know nothing of her now, Sir, I assure you," was the answer.

"But, Madam, she disappeared from hence?"

"Yes, Sir."

"And without your knowing whither?"

"I assure you again, Sir, that at present I know nothing at all of her.—I wish I did; for she seemed to be a mighty pretty sort of a young body, and I am afraid is too handsome not to have fallen into some bad hands."

"If you had such favourable thoughts of her, Madam, how very unfortunate it was that she was under the necessity of quitting the protection you were so kindly disposed to give her."

"Yes, indeed; but perhaps you know more of all that than another, for the gentleman who drove her away by his bad behaviour was so like you, that if it is not himself I am talking to, which I should really almost fancy, only that he was a little lustier than you, and somewhat darker; I say, that if it was not for those differences, I am sure I should think it was the same person."

"It was my brother," said Delmont.

"I am sure then, if I knew where Miss was, I should not be over fond, Sir, of letting you into the secret."

"Surely you would, if you were assured that I have long been engaged to marry her with the approbation of her parents and her own, and that her having been stolen, I know not how or by whom, has made her mother as well as myself most wretched."

There was in the air and manner of Delmont so much candour and openness, that it was impossible, looking at his countenance and hearing him speak, to suspect him of any deceit. Mrs. Tarbat, however, still recollecting that the Major, who so much resembled him, had behaved very unlike what he professed to be his intentions, could not entirely divest herself of doubt; but Delmont continuing to speak to her, she became at length convinced of his sincerity, and declared she would relate all she knew relative to the young lady.

"I cannot exactly recollect," said she, "how long it is ago, since a young gentleman in a postchaise and four, and this pretty looking creature with him, came here late one evening, and as you know we see such parties our way very often,[56] our folks thought, to be sure, they would take four horses to go on; but instead of that, the man that went into the room to carry a glass of negus[57] said, the gentleman seemed in a great deal of trouble, and tried to make the lady alter some resolution she had taken, yet did not like to have her speak before the waiter, and kept saying, 'Pray, my dear madam, let us talk of this when we are alone.' 'No, Sir,' said the young lady; 'No, Sir, I will not be alone with you; you have infamously trepanned me from my friends, and I insist upon being carried back to my mother, or rather left here, for with you I will not travel.'—Upon this, Sir, as my waiter told me, the gentleman was in a most terrible passion, yet was somehow afraid, as it were, of shewing it to the young lady, seeing her so resolute—and he kept saying, 'After your conduct towards me, my dear Miss . . . .' calling her by some christian name that my man forgot—'after you had favoured me so far as to come hither, this sure is very strange.'—'It is false,' said the young woman—'as false as Heaven is true; you know I never did give you any encouragement, never, never; you know you brought me hither by a base and shameful artifice; you know I detest, despise, abhor you.'—'Go out of the room you fellow,' said the gentleman to my servant (who could not help stopping, for you know, Sir, it was natural enough to wish to hear the end of such a long conversation,) 'Go out of the room,' said he.

"'No, stay, I beg of you,' cried the young lady, 'or if you do go out of the room, let it be only to call other witnesses to what I declare, that I did not voluntarily leave my friends with this man, whom I do not even know; and that I absolutely will not proceed with him.'—Upon this, Sir, the waiter comes out and tells me what was passing, and I went in.—The young lady immediately spoke to me, and with great spirit, and told me just the same as she had said before, only said besides, that the young man, who I thought looked very foolish and sheepish, had declared to her that he would carry her back at every stage, instead of that, when he had persuaded her to get into the chaise, the postillions had always had secret orders to drive forward, and that she would be so imposed upon no longer.—I own I was quite taken with the spirit and beauty of the young gentlewoman, and the man I thought, somehow, seemed undeserving of her."

"What sort of a man did he appear to be?" said Delmont impatiently.

"A middling sized man, rather thick made, pale, rather large featured and with a strutting sort of a way with him, somehow as if he thought a great deal of himself—I thought him a very ordinary man to be sure."

"Pray proceed, Madam," said Delmont.

"So, Sir, I said that I hoped there was nobody as would think of carrying a young lady to Scotland to be married against her will; that I could not think of suffering any person to go with such a design from *my* house, nor would not. The man had the assurance to say it was only a lover's quarrel, and that the young lady had promised over and over again to be his wife; but she denied it in the most positive way, and seemed so hurt and provoked, that she burst into tears. Well, Sir, after a great deal had been argued, she continuing to insist on returning to her mother, and the gentleman trying to persuade her against it, she would not give up, but declared that she put herself under my protection and my husband's.—I told her I had no husband, having been a widow above five years, but that I thanked God I had spirit enough to hinder any body from such a monstrous proceeding as to marry a young creature whether she would or no. So Miss, said I, if you are in earnest in wishing to quit that gentleman, I'll take care that neither he nor nobody shall molest you."

"A thousand blessings on you, my dear woman," cried Delmont. "But how, after that, did you lose her? Satisfy my impatience, I intreat you."

"The young lady, Sir, after that, would never suffer me to leave her. She desired me to let her have a bed in my room, which I did, happening to have a good bed in a closet[58] within it, where my daughter Nancy sleeps when she is at home for the holidays. Well, Sir, all the next day she staid with me, nor would she see the gentleman, the Captain, as he called himself, upon no account. He was in a great fuss, and wrote several letters; some he sent by the post, and he wrote the young lady one or two, for she would not see him.

"In this way passed another day. Miss wrote a letter also, but I have since had reason to think he contrived to stop it.

"I talked to him a great deal, and told him how sad a thing it was, and what trouble he would get into; and I thought he seemed to repent of what he had done, and to wish himself out of the scrape, which I don't believe he would have undertaken himself, only it was put into his head. He always, however, maintained, that Miss came away with him of her own accord.

"At last, on the evening of the second day, he sent for me and said, that since it was so that the young lady had altered her mind, he was come to a resolution not to restrain her will, and so he would take her back, and deliver her up safe to her friends, if so be as she would trust his honour; and he swore abundance of oaths, and said, that by all that was sacred he would not offer her the least rudeness, and bade me ask her if he had attempted the smallest ill behaviour all the time they had been travelling together. So, Sir, he begged so hard, that I went with this message to the poor young lady, who, though she began to recover a little from her fatigue was yet very ill, I thought, and did nothing but fret about her mother, who would be distracted, she said, to think what would become of her. I did not know very well what to advise, but as the man seemed to promise so faithfully, I thought perhaps it might be best upon the whole for her to determine to go back with him. I thought, as he would have our post-horses, we should know how he went on the first stage from here to London, and that he seemed to have had enough of it, and would give the attempt up. The young lady was very unwilling to be persuaded, but at last did agree; and he took an oath before me, that he would carry her back, and beg pardon of her friends.

"Accordingly the next day, though when the time came the young lady was not very willing to trust him, they set out in a postchaise and pair, for the gentleman said he was in no such haste to go back as he had been to come, and so that he should not hurry so much. I thought that did not look very well, I must own. However away they went, and my postillion, a boy that drove them, came back at the usual time, and said that they were going on; and I was in hopes the Captain, though I cannot say I ever quite liked the looks of him much, had repented him of this rash attempt."

"Oh! why," exclaimed Delmont, passionately, "why did you suffer her to put herself in his power again?"

"Why, Sir, what could *I* do? it is difficult interfering in these matters. The gentleman, though to be sure he looked at every shilling he paid as if a drop of blood came from his heart, did pay, however, very handsome; and you know I did not know what might be the young Miss's means. Indeed I knew that as to herself, at the time, she had not much above a guinea in her pocket, for she told me so."

Delmont was so shocked to think that Medora might finally be lost from the operation of these mercenary politics, that he had hardly patience to suffer Mrs. Tarbat to go on. He checked himself, however, and she proceeded——

"Well, Sir, I have not much more to tell you. Some days passed on, it may be eight or nine, and I thought no more of the matter, when all of a sudden one night, as I was sitting in the bar, in comes the same young lady, and falling into quite a passion of tears as it were, entreated me to protect her. I promised to do my best, for I am sure I was very sorry for her—and so after she recovered herself a little she told me, that instead of carrying her back to her friends as he had promised, the false base fellow had had the monstrous audaciousness to take her across the country about sixteen miles, to an house which belonged to his mother, where it seems he had confined her ever since, till she got out of a window, and partly by walking, partly by getting into a cart with some sick people that were sent away by the parish, she got back here, and knowing by the name of the place that it was the same as she had staid at two days, she came away to me.

"The next day we consulted how she might be sent safe to London; and to be sure the stage coach was a great deal the best conveyance. So she gave me her direction where to send for the money, and I agreed to let her have enough to pay her expenses up to London; but that evening an officer, a fine handsome comely man to be sure he was, came on his way from Ireland, as we understood, having been stopping on the road somewhere to visit some friend of *his'n*, and for my part I am free to say I was quite astounded, as it were, and did not know what to think of my young gentlewoman, when the moment she spied him, away she flew, and almost embraced him as she would her father or her brother. To be sure when she saw his face she was, or seemed as if she was, frighted; but I thought it a vastly odd thing that she should behave so, and was afraid I had been deceived in her. The gentleman seemed mightily familiar with her, and assured me she was one of his acquaintance, and in short, when she declared it was no such thing, and began to desire to explain, I looked as if I doubted the truth; and to speak plainly, I did then begin to believe that she was some poor young creature quite lost, that one might get into trouble about, and lose one's custom, and could not do much good neither; I hope I am not uncharitable, but what could one think—and then when a man, that seemed to be quite a man of high rank, and that his servants said was related to great lords, and would one day or other be a lord himself, I say, Sir, when such a gentleman seemed to speak of, and treat this young lady like one of slight character, what you know *could* I suppose. However my doing any thing one way or t'other was soon out of the question; for that night the young body disappeared. She left a piece of paper, here it is, with these gold bracelets in it, and this smelling bottle set in gold." Delmont took them trembling, and read these words:

Madam,
Having expended the little money I had about me, I have no other means of securing you the repayment of the expence you may have incurred on my account, than by leaving the only things of any value that I have here. If you will send them to Mrs. Glenmorris, as Dalebury Farm near * * * * *, she will thankfully redeem them, and pay you whatever may be farther your due from,

Madam, your humble servant,
M. GLENMORRIS.

Delmont was ready to weep over and to worship this proof of independent and courageous spirit; but fearing that if he appeared too deeply interested, he might not prevail on the landlady to tell him what might betray her own mercenary conduct, he only desired she would proceed to inform him of what else she knew.

"Why but little more," said Mrs. Tarbat; "next to nothing indeed, for I never heard of the young lady afterwards, only a few days ago I discovered that she had changed all her clothes with one of my chamber maids."

"Her clothes!"

"Yes, and to be sure she did it that she might not be known. She gave Sally Watts her fine laced cloak for a common handkerchief shawl, and her hat, and her beautiful sprigged muslin gown for a common cotton gown, an oldish black bonnet, and some articles of clean coarse linen of Sally's. I was very angry with the wench when I knew it, for I should have been glad to have given Miss much better things in change for her's, myself."

Delmont, who found his indignation was not likely to subside while he continued to hear the narrow minded and illiberal views with which all this woman's professions of zeal for Medora ended, was now desirous of closing the conversation. He reimbursed every charge she made, as well for what Medora had had during her stay as the earnest the woman pretended she had paid to the coach, in which she was to have proceeded to London. He kissed the trinkets he redeemed, as precious proofs of that strength of conduct to which he still looked forward as being what was to constitute the future happiness of his life, and then sending for the servant girl, who had exchanged clothes with Medora, he procured from her a description of the gown, and every thing else that might assist him to trace the disguised wanderer, for whom his heart bled even while he suffered not himself to doubt but that he should, from the information he had received, recover her.

Two circumstances still appeared very unaccountable to Delmont; one was, who the man could be that had hazarded a measure at once so infamous and so dangerous; the other, by what arts Medora had been betrayed to take another route instead of going on towards London. As the postillion who drove the chaise was the only person who could on that last point give him any information, he spoke to him, but though he gave him a crown, and promised him that no harm should befal him if he spoke the truth, the boy persisted in saying, that he set the lady and gentleman down at the White Lion at————, and knew nothing more about them. Delmont did not think it true, but finding every attempt vain to extort any thing else from the boy, he hastened back to that town, where he hoped to recover traces of his fair fugitive.

CHAP. VI.

Passo di pene in pene,
Questa succede a quella;
Ma l'ultima chi viene,
E sempre la peggior.[59]

As Delmont proceeded along the road he had before passed, meditating on the most probable way of obtaining some farther intelligence of Medora, all the inconveniencies, distresses, and terrors that she must have undergone occurred to him. Exposed, in the disguise she had assumed, to the familiarity of the inferior ranks of people, whose grossness must shock her, whose licentious freedoms terrify her, he thought with apprehension of all she might have endured, and with still greater of the uncertainty whether he should discover and protect her; her mother too, in anguish and despair, was perpetually before him, and his mind turned with disgust from the reflections he was compelled to make on his brother's conduct, so ungenerous, so little like what he felt he should have done if they could have changed places; for it was evident that the last disappearance of Medora was entirely owing to the alarm she had felt from the behaviour of one, towards whom, from his relationship to her betrothed lover, she had probably looked in the hope of protection.

It would not be easy therefore to find a man (whose misfortunes were not *certainly* irremediable) more miserable than Delmont was at this moment. His imagination full of Medora under the appearances of a servant, he rode slowly along, looking earnestly at every group of country people, or every peasant girl he saw, and occasionally consulting Clement, his old and faithful servant, from whom he concealed nothing.

Clement was of opinion that Miss Glenmorris would certainly endeavour to return to London, and most likely would procure a conveyance in some waggon or return chaise. The idea of Medora exposed to hear the conversation, and being liable to be treated as a person of their own rank, by waggoners and hackney chaise drivers, again conjured up all Delmont's fears; he allowed, however, that it was extremely probable she had been reduced to some such expedient, and began himself, while he commissioned Clement to do the same, to enter into conversation with such men of those descriptions as they met on the road.

Clement for this purpose sometimes preceded and sometimes followed his master. On the second day of their journey, Delmont having gone on without him, waited for him at a little cottage on a heath, where a sign was hung out. It was now the last week of August, the weather was intensely hot, and Delmont, afraid of proceeding, since every step he took might lead him farther from the object of his solicitude, remained for some hours stationary, in that sort of hopeless languor which is the usual consequence of a man's not knowing whether the means he is pursuing are not rather inimical than advantageous to his views.

As he sauntered in this way in a sort of garden reclaimed from the heath, and divided from it by a slight fence of earth and thorns, he perceived Clement at a considerable distance, galloping through the deep sandy road with a degree of speed that made it certain he had something important to tell. Delmont sprang over the fence, and they met. Clement, half breathless, between eagerness and haste, replied to his master's earnest question—"Oh! Sir, I do think I've got news of Miss Glenmorris!"

"You have not found her then?—you have not seen her?"

"No, Sir—Oh no! not so lucky as that neither; but, Sir, we're on the wrong road; there are four different roads, and I'll venture my life we are not right."

Clement then, dismounting, began, amidst much puffing and gasping, to relate the reason he had for hoping he had discovered some traces of Medora.

"I overtook," said he, "a waggon that goes twice a week from Skipton to a town, I forget the name on't, eleven miles t'other side Harrowgate. It comes as far this way as a place you might have noted, Sir, as you came along, where three roads meet, and then turns off to the left; so seeing the waggoner riding along after his carriage, I began to talk with him, and from one thing and another led the discourse to the matter of my wishing to know if he had had among any passengers that he might have carried across the country, ever a pretty looking young woman, quite young, that was dressed so and so, as you had told me, Sir; for, says I, I have a niece, as I am afeard, has fallen into bad hands; for her friends have not heard of her since she came this way for to go to a service. The man, who had children grown of his own, as he told me, began to consider with himself, and after a little, says he, 'I do think, mon, now I cooms to remember, that I *did* give such a young body a lift in my waggon.' Then, Sir, he asked me how long agone it was, and when I told him, 'Gollys,' says he, 'I do believe 'twas the very same, and,' says he, 'I'll tell you how it was,' says he."

"Prythee, my good fellow," cried Delmont, "make thy story as short as thou canst; I am upon the rack."[60]

"I will Sir—I'll not make more words than I can help—so Sir, says the waggoner, whose name is Thomas Smithson."

"Never mind his name."

"Well, Sir, so said Thomas Smithson to me, 'It was much about the toime, friend, (for he is a north-countryman, and talks broad Yorkshire, with a burr[61] like in his throat) it was much about that toime you speaak on.'"

"Don't make thy narrative more tedious by imitating his dialect; what signifies *how* he spoke, tell me only what he spoke."

"I am going on, Sir; 'about the time,' said he, 'as you name, that a little beyond, it may be a mile or so beyond this place where we are now, but out of the high road, that there is a sharp hill called Cobthorn Top, and plaguey sandy for the poor beasts. So a woman body as I had in my waggon, who was a going to live at one of Sir Harry Richmond's farms; (I knew her, she came from Boroughbridge, a middle aged woman, who was hired for the dairy by Mrs. Crowling, Sir Harry's steward's wife, who manages all them there things)' I put down the names Sir, upon this here paper," added Clement, "for fear I should forget them."

"You did well," answered Delmont, "but if you explain yourself no faster you will drive me mad."

"Well Sir, so says the waggoner. 'This dairy woman was feign to get out to walk up this pull,[62] and I drived on, when presently on the side of the road, and out in a sort of green patch among the bushes, I sees a young girl sitting on a piece of stump of an old tree, and leaning her head against a pollard that was there, and she looked so pale and faint, and seemed such a pretty young thing, that I could not help asking her what she sat there for? and if she was by herself? She seemed ready to cry, and told me she was a stranger in this country, and was walking towards London, when she became so tired that she could go no farther. And to be sure well she might be tired. So I asked her if she would get up into my waggon a bit; but she seemed *timmersome* and to be afeard, though I spoke to her as 'twere to one of my own children. At last the other woman overtook us, and then seeing a good decent looking sort of a person to keep her company, and finding there was no body but she and I and the boy, she was persuaded, and went with us as far as Bardsley Cross, which is just as you turns to go to the lodge at Sir Harry's; and there they both got out; the other woman body having persuaded the young gentlewoman, for to my thinking she looked more like a lady than a poor man's child, to go along with her.' This Sir," continued Clement, "was the most part of what Thomas Smithson said, but I'm almost as sure as if I had seen her myself, that it is Miss Glenmorris, and nobody else that this man has seen; and as I knew you would like to speak to him yourself, I made haste after you, because though he is five or six miles on before, upon the cross road, I am partly certain we shall overtake him if we make haste, and he can shew us the very spot where he set Miss down."

Delmont, aware of the advantage thus gained in a point which was so near his heart, lost not a moment to hasten, according to the direction shewn him; and with less consideration for his horse than it was his custom to shew, overtook the man about two miles from the place, where, from all the circumstances Delmont could gather, it seemed certain that Medora had indeed been left in company with a woman with whom she had become acquainted on the way.

Informing himself then of every particular which could assist him; Delmont dismissed his guide with an handsome present, and leaving his servant and tired horses at the nearest public house on the road, he determined to reconnoitre on foot the house of Sir Harry Richmond, which he was shewn at a distance, among old woods, and extensive plantations creeping above them, half way up hills which were naturally rude and barren, and appeared grotesque and wild, and once to have been covered, as the colour of their summits still denoted, with heath. The place called Bardsley Cross was where the road turned that led to the avenues and ridings cut through the woods with which this fine old seat was every way surrounded. A lodge, where lived the widow of an huntsman and her children, gave entrance to this forest-like domain, and Delmont, giving the woman half a crown (which she received with thankfulness that denoted a necessity not very creditable to the humanity of the master she served) he accepted her invitation to rest himself a moment in "the poor place," as she termed it, where she lived.

There were great remains of beauty in the features of this woman, who, though yet young, appeared to be the victim of sorrow and of poverty. In her face, though marked by the hard lines that adversity engraves, there was a softness of dejection extremely interesting, and far removed from that harsh feeling of the injuries and injustice of the world, that too often gives even to the female countenance, in inferior and laborious life, an expression which excites a sentiment compounded of disgust and compassion. Mrs. Billson seemed quite resigned to a destiny that Delmont wondered should be so wretched, since she was, he supposed, still considered as a servant to Sir Harry Richmond, a man who with one of the largest fortunes in the county had only a son and a daughter, both grown up, and both possessing, in right of their mother and maternal grandmother, independent and even affluent fortunes.

Delmont now engaged Mrs. Billson in conversation, hoping he might gather something from her that related to the object of his solicitude, and among other things he said, "I would not be inquisitive, but it seems to me that your master is, for so affluent a man, not so kind as he might be to his servants; perhaps he may be unacquainted with your distress?"

"Ah! no, Sir," replied Mrs. Billson, "his honour, Sir Harry, knows it well enough," (and sighed deeply) "he cannot well help knowing it indeed; but great gentlefolks don't consider always what poor folks suffers; Sir Harry, you know, Sir, has always been a rich and prosperous gentleman, and besides (she hesitated) there be ways that such as we know nothing of, that great gentlemen *must* lay out their money in."

"He keeps a great deal of company, I suppose?"

"No, Sir, very little indeed now. The gentlemen and ladies of the country round seldom comes unless Miss Richmond is here."

"Sir Harry then is not fond of company?"

"Not of set dinners, Sir—and there ben't much offal victuals[63] now to give away, as I have heard say there was in my lady's time."

"Sir Harry is a great sportsman, perhaps. Pray has he a large family of servants?"

"About twenty, Sir, besides those in the gardens and stables."

"And who directs the economy of his house?"

The poor woman annexed but one idea to the word economy, and seemed tempted to smile.

"There's not much economy," said she, "in the case. I believe, indeed, that . . . ."

but, however, to be sure it's no business of mine. Poor folks must have nothing to say about such gentlemen as his honour, Sir Harry."

"What I meant to ask was," added Delmont, "whether there is not some house-keeper, or the wife of his steward, I think I heard, who hires the servants, and directs the domestic concerns of the house?"

"Oh! yes, Sir, to be *sure* there is."—This, said with a peculiar expression, made Delmont believe there was some mystery.

"The steward's wife, I think?"

"Yes, Sir—Steward he is *now*—he *was* only an attorney's clerk but t'other day; unluckily for all Sir Harry's servants, his good old steward died lately, and so this man is in his place."

"And his wife?"

"His wife . . . . is Sir Harry's *friend*, Sir—and directs his family . . . Sir Harry, you know, Sir, has been—nay, I suppose may be so still, a very wild gay gentleman."

Delmont now thought he comprehended what Mrs. Billson would say. About the character and arrangements of Sir Harry Richmond he had not the slightest curiosity, but he believed it highly probable that as the woman Medora had met with in her way, and whom she seemed to consider as a sort of protection, was hired in this family, Medora, being without money, and above two hundred miles distant from London, might have sought an asylum under the same roof till she could find the means of returning to her mother, which, destitute as she appeared to be, was almost impossible without assistance.

"Do you know if Mrs. Crowling has hired any new servant, lately?" enquired Delmont.

"She is seldom long without three or four new ones, as I hear, and they are always beauties, forsooth! Sir Harry," added Mrs. Billson, with a significant half smile, "is so fond of pretty people, that he don't like to have even his cows milked, or his work at the dairy farm done, but by the best looking girls that Mrs. Crowling can find out for him."

"Indeed!" cried Delmont, as much alarmed as if he had been sure Medora was already in the power of this profligate man.

"Yes, it is very true, I assure you, Sir; but I hope you'll not speak of it as coming from me, for . . . . . I must not disoblige Sir Harry, though, God knows, if every body as have suffered dared to *speak*; but then, indeed, what would be the good of speaking; he is a rich and powerful gentleman, and can do just as he likes, and for such people as *we* to complain is just nonsense."

"How far off is the dairy farm," said Delmont.

"You'll hardly get there and back tonight, Sir," said Mrs. Billson; "for it's a pretty long way, and besides 'twill be dark long enough before you get through the Netherwood, so that you would see nothing at all of the *curosities* of the place."

"Curiosities! and pray what are they?"

"Dear, Sir, all sorts of fine improvements that Sir Harry has made. There is places all lined with marble and china, that his honour calls challets,[64] or challots, or some such name, and he've carried a stream of water through them from the lower cascade; and there's rooms fitted up very grand indeed, with sattin and silk and *chinchs'*[65] for *curtins* and settees, and such like, and sweet smelling flowers in pots, and oranges and *gereenums*—fine large looking-glasses, shells, china, and a heap of beautiful things that there's no telling; and there is beside an ice-house to make vittels into ice,[66] and a cold bath, and an hot bath, with water that is let into a place with a copper to heat it. The cold bath is the most beautifullest thing; all lined with moss and shells, and clear streams of water, that comes as 'twere out of a rock where there's a white image of a lady, that they say is a roman catholic goddess, brought from the pope of Rome." At any other time Delmont would hardly have forborne a smile at this description of luxuries collected by a determined voluptuary.[67]

Of Sir Harry Richmond, Delmont now remembered to have heard. He had been brought up in the sea-service, being the youngest of four brothers, but in consequence of the death of the three others, he had quitted the navy, retaining nothing of the best part of a seaman's character, and only having learned to refine on that grossness with which he had practiced the worst. He was a tyrant both from nature and habit; and hardly took the pains to attempt concealing that determined preference of himself, which made him as careless of the feelings, as indifferent to the opinion, of others. Having married young, he was yet only entering on middle age; and though he began to feel the effects of his intemperate life, his person was still handsome; and when he had any point to carry, his manners very pleasing. That Medora might be even an unwilling resident in the house of such a man, was a suspicion so very uneasy to him, that he could no longer bear to be unsatisfied; he, therefore, giving half a guinea in addition to his former present to the poor woman, asked her whether, if he should return late, she would let him sit up by her fire all night, unless she could accommodate him with a bed, for he was determined to visit the dairy farm that evening.

Mrs. Billson wondered, but forbore to comment. She told him that he should be welcome either to stay by her fire, or to sleep, if he chose it, on some clean fern and straw in a little room at the back of her small habitation, which she told him was dry, and over which she would spread a blanket and clean sheets, and it was in fact a better bed than she had for herself and her children. This arrangement being made in case he returned, Delmont departed, taking the way she directed him through an avenue of the woods, which would carry him, she said, near two miles before he would come to the broad avenue that led, at a quarter of a mile farther on, to the great house, which he must leave on the left, and make through the fir plantations towards the lake, on the banks of which, where it was fed by waterfalls from the heights beyond, were the chalets, concealed by thick woods from the dairy farm which stood in the center of the meadows. Delmont thought himself well enough instructed in the way not to miss it, and having made a note of the name of the woman with whom Medora had travelled, he hastened with impatience to gain some intelligence that might relieve the fears for her safety, now again tormenting him to a degree altogether insupportable.

Before he had passed through the first wood, which was composed of fine timber and underwood of considerable growth, it was nearly dark; but arriving where the copse was cut away on high ground, he beheld the moon, now at full, rising red, yet clear, glowing, and seen to infinite advantage through the dark boughs which surrounded him. The idea that occurred to him was one that is common with those who love—"Beautiful planet! are the eyes of Medora fixed on thee at this moment? Does she now in peace and safety, though in humble life, gaze on thy orb, and recollect that blessed, that short period of our lives, when we together watched thy appearance over the eastern hill, and delighted in thy beams as they danced on the collected waters of Upwood brooks, or as they chequered the path where lay our evening walk among the beech trees. Oh, fleeting period of felicity! how little did I know how to value it, for I was not then content; and yet now, perhaps, I shall never be restored to such enjoyment again!"

Indulging such reveries, Delmont came to the second barrier of the woods, where two pillars, surmounted by the crest of the family (an eagle in white marble) marked the gate which enclosed what was called the inner park; but still covered with a magnificent growth of ancient wood, it seemed rather a continuation of a forest; the trees, however, became more regular, and at length stretched in linear grandeur into a long and overarched avenue of Spanish chesnut, of which there were four rows, rich in the most luxurious foliage; on each side of them several rows of old beech, feathered down to the ground, so as to form on the largest scale a complete berceau,[68] hardly pervious any where but in the center (through which lay the coach-road) to the rays of the moon.

Delmont kept his way on the side, where was a path made by foot passengers towards the house; he moved slowly, and hardly discerning his own way could not be perceived by any one who should pass along the other vistas. The dews fell heavily, as is usual after an hot day, but hardly did the slightest noise break the stillness of the air, save at intervals the call of the partridge, or the shrill cry of the mole cricket.[69] When these night sounds of departing summer ceased, all was so perfectly in repose, that nature seemed for a while to have forgotten her progress, and to slumber in voluptuous tranquillity.

Delmont, looking down the middle avenue to see if he could yet discern the front of the house, perceived, as the moonbeams through the trees chequered the raised causeway, two figures in white, walking slowly, and, as it seemed, arm in arm in the road. Afraid of alarming them, as he concluded they were ladies belonging to the house, he stepped yet more cautiously on, and as he had as little desire to disturb them as to be observed himself, he stopped, concealed by one of the large trees, till they passed.

But great was his agitation when he thought that the voice of one of them was that of Medora, he paused—he gazed earnestly, and listened in breathless anxiety.—The figure indistinctly seen, seemed to be her's; the voice, though he only now and then caught its sound, strongly resembled that always so delightful to his ears; yet he might be mistaken; he might intrude upon and terrify some young person to whom he was a stranger. Again he listened—the two persons approached, and were within a few yards of the place where he stood.—He distinguished great part of what one of them said—the voice so like that of Medora answered.—The words he heard from the first were; "To seem to arraign the conduct of a parent . . . . . distressing to me.—Already he seems to wish . . . . would I knew how to act . . . ."

The second answered in short, and, as it seemed, consolatory sentences; but though the words fell indistinctly on the ear of Delmont, he listened with more and more eagerness and solicitude, convinced it could be no other than the voice of Medora.

Yet a slight gust of air, momentarily swaying away the boughs which impeded the moon-light, it suddenly fell on the figure towards which Delmont had actually determined to advance; he saw the face and form of the young person more distinctly.— Was it the face and form of Medora he beheld?—The resemblance must be strong, when seeing it as clearly as he now did, he yet hesitated a moment; but no!—it was not Medora.—Medora was rather taller, and certainly the face had not her features; yet there was something in the air of the whole person, and a likeness of tone in the sweet and plaintive voice, that had together so strongly impressed on his mind the hope of his having found what he sought, that the conviction of his being mistaken threw him off his guard, and by a sudden motion he was perceived by the two ladies, who observing so near them a person they might well suspect of some sinister purpose, since he evidently sought to conceal himself, they both betrayed signs of fear, and hastily retreated towards the house.

Delmont, conscious that he had already acted improperly, and at once anxious to apologize and to relieve them from their apprehensions, gave himself very little time to reflect before he hurried after them, and soon overtaking them, though fear quickened their pace, he besought their pardon in a voice and manner that soon quieted their alarms, while it excited their curiosity.

These two young women were Miss Richmond, the only daughter of Sir Harry, and Miss Cardonnel; who had obtained permission of Lady Mary (as she was herself in unusual health, and had Mrs. Grinsted with her), to pass three weeks with her favourite friend, at the magnificent seat of Sir Harry, where, not entirely to set at defiance the opinion and the censures of the world, he had his daughter as his inmate during two or three summer months.

As soon as the apprehensions of these two lovely women had subsided, by the conviction that it was a gentleman who spoke to them, Delmont, with the frankness natural to him, told them his name, and added—"I came into this country, and even into this neighbourhood, in search of a person whose disappearance has caused the greatest misery.—I dread lest my enquiries may be as fruitless here as they have already been in other places, but I will take care at least that my nocturnal rambles shall not again be the cause of any alarm to you Miss Richmond, while I hardly know how to ask, whether, in consideration of our families being well acquainted, you will give me leave to pay my respects to you at a less improper hour, than that in which I so inadvertently broke in on your evening retirement."

Miss Richmond, who was extremely well bred, answered, that she was sure, were her father at home, he would be extremely glad to see any one of the name of Delmont; and that even in his absence, though she had not the same powers of entertaining his visitors, she believed she might say that none who bore that name could fail of a welcome.

Delmont, enquiring how long Sir Harry would be absent, and hearing it was uncertain, desired permission to wait on Miss Richmond the next morning, and on its being granted, he conducted them to the house whither they were returning, not, as they assured him, in consequence of the alarm he had given them, but of the dews falling so profusely as to have wetted their thin summer clothes, nearly as much as would have happened had they been exposed to rain. At the hall-door he took leave, his mind hardly diverted a moment, by this accidental rencontre, from the object which occupied all his thoughts, and continued the way he had been directed towards the Chalets.

To his new acquaintance, however, this accidental meeting was not a matter of such indifference. There was something romantic in it that had the air of an adventure, and Miss Cardonnel, possessed of a naturally excellent, as well as highly cultivated understanding, was not without a considerable share of that sort of imagination, which produces what is termed a romantic turn of mind.

As her grandmother, Lady Mary, never thought any one who had yet offered, (though among the offers she had had were men of the first consequence and fortune) equal to the merits and pretensions of her dear Mary, they had all been declined almost as soon as heard; and the heart of Miss Cardonnel, now in her twentieth year, was absolutely free from any impression.

Never, perhaps, did a man possess more requisites than had Delmont to win the affections of a young woman. His person was uncommonly handsome, his manner easy without familiarity, and polite without formality, was remarkably attractive, and his sentiments, every one of which carried with them the conviction, that they were the result of a reflecting mind on a good and generous nature, were so much in unison with the feelings of Miss Cardonnel, that though she had passed hardly three quarters of an hour in his company, she felt an extraordinary interest in his favour. "This Mr. Delmont," said she to Miss Richmond, as soon as he had left them, "is a very agreeable man—surely he is wonderfully interesting." "Indeed I think him so," answered her friend, "I cannot imagine of whom it is he is in search?"

"And where is he searching for this lost friend?" rejoined Miss Cardonnel, "or wherefore should he suppose this friend among your woods, my dear Annabelle?"

"I cannot even guess.—And from whence can he come or whither be going? It is inexplicable when one comes to reflect on it."

"It is indeed—I wish we had asked him—however, you will have an opportunity of enquiring to-morrow, you know," said Miss Cardonnel.—

"Oh! perhaps not—it is not certain you know that he will come."—

"Not certain!—why should he not?"

"Nay, say rather why *should* he?—He is already certain we cannot give him the information he wants.—And when a man of his sort has any scheme that occupies his imagination, he does not care much for any thing else."—

"What do you mean, my dear Annabelle, by a man of *his* sort?"

"A young man, gay and *etourdi*,[70] and in the pursuit, as I suppose him to be, of some woman."

Miss Cardonnel felt at this speech a sensation to which she had been hitherto a stranger.—"A woman," cried she, with quickness, "why should you think so—Surely, my friend, such a supposition is inconsistent with your natural charity and candour.— Why should you suppose Mr. Delmont is pursuing some intrigue?"

"My dear Mary, how can you ask *why* I should suppose it?—It is true I have lived in the world but some eighteen or twenty months longer than you have, but I must have made but very little use of my eyes, if I did not see that some such project, some scheme of self-gratification, occupies every individual; and that nobody cares for those who cannot in some way or other contribute to their pleasure or their profit."

"Nobody?—Ah! my friend, do you then make *no* exceptions?" "Oh! certainly— it were illiberal not to make *some*," said Miss Richmond, sighing, "and you know I have at least one exception; but when my dear Mary has lived to observe the men of the world, such as *I* have been used to see, she will know how rare those exceptions are, and how rarely they can safely be made in favour of a stranger, a young man such as we have just seen.—Mr. Delmont will call to-morrow, perhaps, if he thinks he can pro- cure any intelligence of this *friend* of his from us, but I dare say he will otherwise forget that he has seen us at all."

Miss Cardonnel, who felt pain without knowing why, was not sorry to let the conversation drop, and the fair friends soon after parted. Miss Cardonnel, in spite of herself, continuing to recall the looks, the manner, the sentiments of Delmont; while Miss Richmond was compelled to entertain very unpleasant speculations, as to the actual situation of the person he had come into that neighbourhood to seek.

Chap. VII.

These are thy triumphs, thy exploits, O Cæsar![71]

While all that was pleasant and interesting in the voice and manner of Miss Cardonnel, affected Delmont from the general resemblance she bore to Miss Glenmorris, he could not but compare their destinies; and his heart bled afresh to reflect on what might at this moment be the situation of the wandering, unprotected, Medora.—If mere scen- ery had possessed the power to suspend, for a moment, the anguish of the heart, he might have found a transient relief in the uncommon beauty of the place he visited. A lake, reflecting the moon-beams on its broad and clear surface, was fed at its extremity by three waterfalls dashing, in different directions, down rocks which were shadowed by trees, in some places hiding, in others receding from the silver torrents—round the edge of the lake the shade became darker, and the wood seemed to mingle with the reeds that crowded into the water. A narrow path, however, serpentined on the bank, and Delmont pursuing it as he had been directed, it led him along the margin of a sequestered branch of the lake, which was indeed the river that carried its still accumu- lating water to other parts of the estate. Here its channel was deep, but not wide: the weeping willows, planted on either bank, mingling their flexile boughs together in streaming arches over it. He came to an almost circular recess of turf; it was screened by immense oaks and ash, whose old fantastic arms started out as if to embrace the two rustic buildings that now appeared. They were white without, thatched with reeds, and partly mantled by odorous shrubs that crept round windows shaded by green lattices. A stream was heard to murmur through them; which then fell down a small dark declivity (along which the path still led), and supplied a rustic bath; where, though simplicity was its character without, there was within such contrivances as a luxurious Roman would have chosen for his accommodation. But of these Delmont was content with the description Mrs. Billson had given him; and pursuing his way still through a narrow and somewhat declining path, winding through the woods, he found himself in a quarter of an hour at their extremity on this side, where a long tract of meadows was spread between high lands on each side, richly clad with trees. The streams from the lake, which here fertilized the grazing land, glittered in various currents. Its principal branch directed his eyes to a group of buildings, which Delmont imagined to be the farm-house, where he might, with great probability of finding her, seek for Medora.

By the time he reached the house, for the way was longer than it appeared, the moon, hitherto friendly to him, was so low that it lent him but little light around the dwelling, and the extensive farm-yard adjoining to it—all was hushed, save at intervals the noises of domestic poultry, which seemed to answer the cry of the wild-ducks and other water-foul from the river and lake, whose keen sense of smell[72] informed them that a stranger had intruded among their reedy recesses and willowed haunts.

Delmont, prepossessed with the idea that he should see Medora, was so agitated that he stopped at the gate, leading into a sort of court before the house, to recover breath and recollection. He surveyed the windows. There was a light in one of the rooms.—"She is there," whispered the heart of Delmont;—as if it could be inhabited by no other than Medora. Approaching, and earnestly fixing his eyes on the sashes, he fancied he saw the shadow on the opposite wall of some one who sat not far from the window. The figure rose, took up the candle, and moved along the room till the light disappeared. Delmont was convinced it was a woman, and became more and more persuaded it was her whom he sought.

After a short interval light was again visible in a room on the ground-floor; and Delmont passing as softly as he could, through the gate towards the window, approached so near that he could distinguish a young person whose figure, as she sat stooping over a table, resembled that of Medora, but her back was towards him, and she seemed occupied in some kind of work which lay before her. Her whole appearance was very unlike that of an inmate of a farm-house; and if it was not, as on a steadier examination he believed, her whom he so anxiously sought, the presence of such a person in such a place confirmed his idea of the arrangements of Sir Harry Richmond. The young woman rose and crossed the room—opened a piano forte, which stood on the opposite end, and touched it with a grace and precision which, as well as a side-view of her face that he now obtained, convinced Delmont it was not Medora. But was it not possible he might obtain some information of her? Yet how hazard alarming a young person by the abrupt appearance of a stranger, at such an hour, in such a place?

After a short prelude she sang—Delmont listened to a plaintive Italian air: the words were from Metastasio,[73] and the manner of executing them shewed that they were felt by the songstress;—while there could be no doubt from her manner of singing, as well as from the deep sigh with which she concluded, that she was too sensible of her own situation to be accessary to the enforced confinement of another under the same circumstances. After what he had heard from Mrs. Billson, there was little doubt but that this young woman was one of the residents in Sir Harry's house whom she had described. Delmont, however unwilling to alarm her, could not resist his desire of speaking to her.

He opened the sash slowly; the young person, who was arranging her music books, started, and turned towards the window, and perceiving Delmont, was hastening in terror out of the room, when he said, "One moment, I beseech you, Madam, I would not terrify . . . . . . I would not intrude upon you, but give me leave merely to ask you a question."

His manner was certainly not that of a robber. And though she could not prevail upon herself to leave the door, the unknown songstress, not perhaps altogether unused to attract by her music, stopped near it, and desired him to explain himself.

"Will you, Madam," said he, "condescend to tell me whether a young person who came hither dressed as a servant . . . . . a young woman of family and respectability, whom a strange and alarming circumstance compelled to have recourse to that disguise . . . . . will you tell me if she is still here?"

"No," replied the lady, "she is not. I will not deceive you. Such a person undoubtedly was here; not, however, brought here by Sir Harry Richmond, who is, as I suppose you know, the master of this house, but by mere accident. It is not, however, a place where such a young person could remain. Means were found to acquaint Miss Richmond of her situation, and she was removed to London, but there is reason to believe Sir Harry has followed her thither. If you are her brother, Sir, or one greatly interested for her safety, I advise you to hasten after her, or it will be too late. I dare not stay, but believe that I heartily wish you success."

"Oh yet a single moment," cried Delmont. His informant was already gone. And a woman of a very different appearance, fat, red faced, and over-dressed, entered the room. Delmont retired from the window; she came forward and shut it. In a few moments all the shutters were closed, as if those within had taken some alarm. Delmont gazed on them a while, as if in hopes that he might again see her who seemed so humanely to take an interest in his distress; but no one appearing, he slowly and reluctantly trod back his steps to the lodge—repeating to himself, "Miss Richmond found means to release her, but there is great reason to think Sir Harry has followed her to London. I will go," said he, "to Miss Richmond; yet how relate what I have heard? how question her on such a subject, when it is of her father's infamy I must complain?" It then occurred to him, that the indistinct conversation he had heard in the avenue between her and Miss Cardonnel, related to this very circumstance, and a new field of enquiry was thus opened. "Did Miss Cardonnel know it was her cousin? Had Medora, in the concealment she had been obliged to have recourse to, changed her name?" These, and many other cruel solicitudes, prevented Delmont from sleep, when he laid down on the humble bed which his hostess at the lodge had provided for him. With the dawn of the following day he was on foot; and in a short conference with the unhappy woman, to whom he gave a sum greater than she had long been mistress of, in return for the little hospitality she had been able to shew him, he learned, that she was a servant in Sir Harry Richmond's house, to whom unhappily he took a fancy. A conquest over a poor country girl of seventeen was not difficult; she was soon obliged to quit the house, and he had two children by her, one of which was the elder of those whose apparent poverty had excited the compassion of Delmont. The other was dead.

Sir Harry then insisted on the poor girl's marrying one of his huntsmen, who being a man of a fierce and brutal disposition, continually reproached, and not unfrequently beat her during the five miserable years she lived with him. He then luckily broke his neck, and his widow and his children, as well as that which was known to be his master's, had since lingered on in poverty at the lodge; where the poor woman acknowledged she must often have wanted the common necessaries, which even such an existence demanded, but for Miss Richmond, who was, she said, quite an angel. "Yet," said Mrs. Billson, "for all Sir Harry indulges himself so in every thing though ever so wrong, he crosses poor Miss Richmond in her love, though for one of the worthiest, honestest, and most generous gentlemen in this country, and he will give no reason for it, except that he does not chuse it because of an old grudge about game between their families, but every body hopes that when Miss is of age, she will have spirit enough to marry Mr. Archdale; though she is so soft tempered, and so afraid of disobliging her father, that people are afraid she won't have courage."

"These are indeed," thought Delmont, as he walked towards the great house— "these are indeed among the wrongs of woman."[74]

It was yet early when he arrived at the splendid old mansion of the ancient family of the Richmonds. Miss Richmond, however, was breakfasting in a summer parlour that opened to the park, with her fair friend, whom Delmont no sooner saw than he was again struck with the resemblance she bore to Medora.

He apologized for so early a visit, as well as for his appearance, accepting however their invitation to breakfast, and endeavouring to force his mind for a moment to converse on common topics; but it was easy to see that the effort was painful to him, and he relapsed into that evidently anxious state which he could not disguise. He felt it equally awkward to desire a private conference with Miss Richmond, or to speak before her friend on such a subject. After their breakfast was ended, however, Miss Cardonnel, as if she guessed that he wished to be alone with the Lady of the house, left the room on some slight pretence; and Delmont, though his faltering voice, and the blood mantling in his cheeks, gave testimony how painful was the subject, entered upon it at once.

"I will not apologize," said he, "for the liberty I am about to take in asking Miss Richmond some questions, which in any other case would be extremely impertinent. But the happiness of my life is at stake—the peace, the preservation of a young person, lovely and innocent as yourself, or your charming friend, to whom indeed she is nearly related. Need I then make any other claims to the indulgence, the pity of Miss Richmond? My heart, and her own amiable and generous character, assure me I need not."

Miss Richmond, though prepared by what had passed the preceding evening for some enquiry from Delmont, was surprised at that part of his speech which related to Miss Cardonnel. She answered, however, "It is enough, Sir, to know I can give you any information relative to a person for whom you are interested; and if a relation of my dear Mary is concerned, it will add to my satisfaction if I can render her any service."

"Give me leave then to ask," said Delmont, "if a young person appearing in the character of a servant, who was driven by some extraordinary circumstances to an house of Sir Harry Richmond's, was not supposed by you, madam, to be so circumstanced as to make her removal necessary, and if you did not generously contrive that removal?"

"I did," replied Miss Richmond, deeply blushing, and appearing for a moment as if unable to proceed. She then, in a faint voice, and with downcast eyes, went on. "To Mr. Delmont I may say that the errors of a parent ought to be sacred with his child, but when those errors go to the injury of the innocent and unhappy, a duty superior even to that due to a father demands our interference. I will briefly relate what has passed, and willingly dismiss a subject so painful to me, indeed, that nothing but my wish to relieve your solicitude, and what I owe to truth, could induce me to speak upon it. To wave every account of preceding transactions which gave rise to any enquiry from me, I learned that a young person, whose appearance and manners rendered it certain that she could not belong to the class which her dress indicated, was brought, my informer knew not by what contrivance, to the house, which, though it is inhabited by the steward, and a wretch he calls his wife, is a place where it is by no means fit a young woman of any character should reside. My pity has always been excited towards those who, from whatever inducements, are its inmates, but for them nothing is in my power. I had soon the mortification of learning, that Sir Harry was pursuing, in regard to this very young girl, the same line of conduct as has already given me so much pain on other occasions. I contrived, though at the risk of incurring his heaviest displeasure, to see her. Without telling me her name, she related her history, and the reasons which had driven her to seek a temporary asylum with a woman who was hired as a dairy servant for one of Sir Harry's farms. Falsehood never looked or spoke as she did. I was immediately convinced that her narrative, though singular, was true, and I took measures to deliver from the imminent peril she was in, a young creature for whose fate I felt the liveliest interest. I succeeded, three days since, so far as to send her safely to London, recommended (as she doubted whether her mother was still there to receive her) to the wife of a very respectable tradesman, whom I engaged to secrete her from the enquiry I was much afraid Sir Harry Richmond would make after her. He was then absent, but returned the evening after her departure, and I have too much reason to believe he suspected that I had been a party in her evasion. I am very sorry to say, that Sir Harry Richmond immediately set out, as I fear, in pursuit of her, for unfortunately he usually perseveres in any project of this sort, which once seizes his imagination; and I now wait, with extreme solicitude, to hear from the person in London, to whose care I recommended her, whether she was conducted safely to the place of her destination."

Miss Richmond then interrupting the just eulogium that Delmont warmly began on her virtuous and generous conduct towards an unprotected stranger, gave him the address to the person to whose care Medora had been consigned. He was ready to fall at her feet, and could with difficulty restrain himself from imprinting on the fair hand that presented to him this paper, a kiss of gratitude and respect, but the emotions which he could not wholly suppress were painful to Miss Richmond; Delmont perceived they were, and in the narrative it was his turn to give, he endeavoured to confine himself to the simplest detail: when it was concluded, not without having made a very sensible impression on his auditor, Miss Richmond asked if she had his permission to inform Miss Cardonnel how greatly her near and almost only relation was implicated in the history of the till then nameless young woman, who had excited their mutual compassion.

Delmont, hastily running over in his mind the circumstances of the family, had no difficulty in deciding that it was better to let this remain a secret. He saw not that any disadvantage could arise from suffering their near relationship remain unknown; and it seemed as if Medora desired her name to be as little called in question as possible. Delmont indeed recollected how much she and her mother had already suffered from the misrepresentations of malice; and though the two amiable women he had now met were undoubtedly of a very different description from Mrs. Crewkherne and her satellites, he thought it would be more agreeable to Glenmorris and her mother, and felt it to be so to the delicacy of his own affection, not to suffer her name to be more known than it already was, while she was under circumstances which were doubtful, and might be represented as discreditable.

Miss Richmond assured Delmont that she would observe the most inviolable secrecy. "I should make," said she, "a point of conscience of not deceiving my friend in any thing she had an interest in knowing; but as this particular circumstance can only give her pain, and cannot in any way be useful, I have no hesitation in assuring you, that from me it shall never be communicated."

Miss Richmond seemed then very solicitous to close the conversation, and rang the bell for her cloak and parasol, directing at the same time that Miss Cardonnel might be desired to join them. "I know," said she, to Delmont, "you are justly impatient to begin your journey; but recollect, you will lose no time in eating a sandwich here, since you must take refreshment some where on the road; and as you say your servant and horses are waiting for you at the Richmond Arms, which is above two miles from this place; you shall regain the time you would otherwise lose by having an horse from hence, and therefore while they prepare you a slight repast, you cannot refuse to walk with us round the home grounds, which are," added she, sighing, "what are called worth seeing."

Delmont could not refuse an invitation at once so good natured and so accommodating; Miss Cardonnel joined them, and they made the tour of some part of the beautiful plantations that were near the house, Delmont forcing himself to remark, as a matter of complaisance, what at any other time would have given him real pleasure, for the place, in a superior degree, united magnificence with beauty, and modern cheerfulness with the nobler features of gothic grandeur, yet without any thing incongruous in their union.

Delmont's conversation, though to those who had seen him under happier circumstances it would have appeared evidently forced, yet seemed to his two fair companions, who had never seen him in happier days, so very attractive, that they agreed they had never met with so agreeable a man. Miss Richmond saw, not without pain, that the favourable impression he had on their first interview made on Miss Cardonnel was now confirmed; instead therefore of rallying her friend, she endeavoured to check the growth of this infant partiality, by intimating, that Mr. Delmont had an attachment, without repeating any part of their conversation, which might betray more than he wished to have known.

Delmont, had he not indeed borne a charmed heart, would have parted with the fair friends with great regret; but his eagerness to overtake and protect Medora against the machinations he had so much reason to dread, conquered and absorbed every other thought, and accepting the offer of an horse, he hastened to rejoin his servant, and without allowing himself any time to rest, proceeded towards London.

CHAP. VIII.

It is well observed (says Lord Bacon) that to be in love,
and to be wise, is scarce possible even to a god.[75]

Arrived in London, Delmont hurried to the house of Mr. Meyrick, a linen draper in the Strand,[76] whither Miss Richmond had directed him, and eagerly enquired at what time the young person, recommended by her to the care of Mr. Meyrick, had reached his house, and when she had left it?

Mr. Meyrick answered, that the next day after her arrival in town, he had at her own desire conducted her to the stage, going thrice a week to . . . . Had recommended her most earnestly to the care of the coachman, whom he had paid, and from whom he had received assurances that the greatest attention should be shewn to the young lady; that he had himself furnished her with money to pay her postchaise to Dalebury Farm, whither she said he should instantly go; and Mr. Meyrick added, that he had no doubt but that she was now safe in the protection of her friends.

Delmont, satisfactory as this account appeared, was not content with it. A thousand questions, which he had no means of having resolved, occurred to him. Had Medora then found her mother? Was she assured of protection at Dalebury? Yet certainly going thither was the most prudent step she could take whether Mrs. Glenmorris was there or not. He now repented having brought Susanne away, and determined to set out with her that night for Upwood, where he trusted he should now once more behold Medora. Yet doubts and fears hung heavy on his heart. He sought Armitage, in the hope of relieving his apprehensions, and above all in the hope that he had discovered Mrs. Glenmorris, a research in which he knew he would be indefatigable. On enquiring, however, at his lodgings, he found he went suddenly out of town the day before, but whether intending to go to his own house, or any other place, the people where he had lodged did not know.

On more mature reflection, Delmont determined to send Susanne away immediately, and to stay one day in town, as well to inform himself of Armitage's success in the search he had made, which he thought he should hear, as to see the coachman, to whose care Medora had been committed on her journey, and who was to be at the inn where the coach put up the following morning. Having then dispatched Susanne, he slept not till he had seen this man; but what was his distress and consternation at hearing the following account.

"Sir," said the coachman, "the young gentlewoman was put into my coach by Mr. Meyrick, whom I know very well. I had no passenger but a very elderly woman going down to live with her grand-daughter, deaf and almost blind; and I'm sure, to see the good nature that the young miss shewed to the poor old woman quite did my heart good. We set out, you know, early, because the . . . . . coach meets mine to go sixteen miles bad road; and at this time of year the mornings are getting dark. Well, Sir, at the turnpike at Vauxhall, I was hailed by the landlord of the Queen's Head, with 'What, Ralph, any inside place?'[77]—I said yes, and asked how far. 'Why all the way to . . . .' says he. So presently out comes a fine jolly handsome middle-aged gentleman" (the heart of Delmont sunk with apprehension, while it swelled with indignation); "and he said he had only a little parcel in a cloak-bag, and a black servant, who was to go outside. So I opened the coach door, you know, as to be sure I could do no other, and I saw Miss was not much pleased to have another passenger, for she wrapt the silk and gauze-like what d'ye call it, that the women folks wear, over her pretty face,[78] and sat snug up in the corner by the side of the old gentlewoman. So, Sir, on we went for five miles, when all of a sudden the gentleman (whose name I could not find out, for the black man would not say a word) all of a sudden, as we came by the French Horn Inn, where, you know, there is postchaises to let, the gentleman calls to me to stop—got out, helped Miss out, who had been crying till her eyes were all red, and seemed hardly able to stand, and so giving me his fare and his servant's, and half a guinea to boot (and Miss's he would have given me, only I told him I had been paid before) he went away with her and his servant into the French Horn Tavern."

"And did the young lady say nothing," cried Delmont, impatiently, "did she not resist being thus stopped on her journey?"

"No, Sir," replied the coachman, "cannot say she did, only she seemed despert molloncholly, I thought, and I am sure she had been crying. I made bold, as Mr. Meyrick had given me such a charge, to say to the gentleman, that I hoped he was one as had a good right to take the care of the young gentlewoman, otherwise I should be answerable for her to her friends; and he answered, 'Be in no pain on that account, honest Ralph; I am one of her best friends, and have the best right to protect her.'— So then to be sure, as Miss did not contradict him, why what could I do?—So there I left them, and as I came by the French Horn this morning, I stopped to enquire about them a bit, and John Newton the landlord said how they staid about an hour or so, and that Miss was in a sort of a fit, and forced to have hartshorn[79] and water, and such like; and when she seem'd for to be a little better, the gentleman ordered a postchai, and a saddle-horse for the neger,[80] and they went off back to London."

Delmont, as patiently as he could, listened to this relation, and then asked every question which he thought might enable him to trace and to punish the man who seemed now to have finally closed upon him all the prospects he had indulged of recovering Medora and happiness. That this man was Sir Harry Richmond not a doubt remained; yet it was impossible to guess by what stratagem he could have prevailed on Medora to abandon her intention of going to Dalebury, and to put herself under the protection of one, of whose nefarious designs there could be little doubts, when she was hurried by his daughter from Ardly Forest (his Yorkshire place). The longer Delmont reflected on all the circumstances he had heard the more incomprehensible appeared the conduct of Medora, and for the first time, amidst all the uneasiness he had undergone, he suffered himself to doubt whether she merited the excessive, and even agonising, solicitude which he still continued to feel—yet hardly had he suffered such thoughts to gain upon his mind, before the image of her he loved returned to it as if to reproach him, in all the candour and sweetness of youthful innocence, unsuspecting, because unknowing of evil, and he asked himself, whether there were not too many ways by which such a man as Sir Harry Richmond might take advantage of the simplicity of a girl hardly seventeen, and so new to the world as was Medora?—The instances of courage and propriety of conduct which he had admired when they were only slightly related to him by Mrs. Tarbat, served only to increase his wonder and embitter his regret. And what was now to be done? Whither could he go? He thought of and rejected many plans, and at length determined to go down to the inn the coachman had described, which was on a heath about six miles from London, on the Surry road, and endeavour to see the postillion who had conducted them from thence to London, imagining that by knowing where they had been set down he might trace them.

Losing therefore not a moment, he got into a chaise at the first livery stable, and was driven to the French Horn—There Delmont soon found the lad he enquired for, and learned that with the middle aged gentleman, the handsome young lady, and the black servant, he had gone as far as the stand of coaches at Charing Cross, where the two former had got into a coach, and the latter mounted behind, and he, being himself discharged, had immediately turned his horses heads towards their stable, and knew not which way the hackney coach had been ordered to drive, nor what was its number. Here then again all traces of Medora seemed to be lost.

The people of the inn gave him the same account as he had already had from the stage coachman; and in renewed despair, instead of the information he had hoped for, Delmont returned to London.

He had absolutely forgotten, till reminded of it by unusual faintness, that he had hardly eaten, and that he had not slept for six and thirty hours. The increased agitation of his mind, together with excessive fatigue, now made him sensible of personal uneasiness; he felt his blood inflamed, and his head giddy, while, though he was not himself conscious of it, his looks were wild, his eyes bloodshot, and his whole appearance—(an appearance altogether strange to him) such as a man falls into who has passed nights and days at the gaming table and the tavern.

He began, however, to suspect, that if he did not allow himself a few hours repose, he should be reduced to a state in which it might not be in his power to seek Medora or her mother; he was therefore returning to his lodgings, when in crossing towards Picadilly from the Haymarket, he saw in an hackney coach (which was for a moment in an embarrassment between some coal carts) Medora sitting in conversation, and, as it appeared, unreluctant conversation, with the well looking middle aged gentleman. He even saw that she smiled, yet it was a faint and melancholy smile, while he hung upon her every word with an expression of the fondest delight. This was not to be endured—Regardless, indeed not thinking of consequences, Delmont rushed forward; but at that moment the impediment being withdrawn, the coachman whipped his horses on, and as if to recover the time he had lost, drove with unusual speed up Swallow Street.

Delmont, in all the haste *he* could make, followed it—But it was now hidden from him by other coaches, and he was now impeded by a cart unloaded on the pavement. The people who saw him imagined he was either some unfortunate young man pursued by a bailiff, or one who had just escaped from the keepers of a madhouse. Delmont heeded not what they thought; he did not even see them, but with eyes eagerly straining after the coach, he crossed in pursuit of it Oxford Street, and at last saw it stop at the door of a private house in Portland Street. He waited in breathless agitation a moment. He beheld Sir Harry Richmond get out and assist Medora, and they went into the house together—The black servant took a parcel that was in the coach, paid the coachman, and was going to shut the door, when Delmont, without asking or answering any questions, pushed by him, and as, by the door of the parlour being open, he saw that those he sought were not there, he rushed up stairs, and threw open the drawing room door—He saw what completed his astonishment, indignation—Medora sitting on the knee of her companion, his arm round her waist, and her head declined on his shoulder.

"Monster! villain! seducer!" exclaimed Delmont, who stepped on, as if he meant to wreck his vengeance in another manner—when Medora started from her seat, and threw herself almost speechless into his arms, faintly attempting to utter some words which he could not hear.

The stranger in the mean time, after a very short pause, seemed to guess who Delmont was, and advanced towards him. "Mr. Delmont," said he, holding out his hand towards him—"Is it not Mr. Delmont?"

"Dare you ask?" exclaimed the enraged Delmont. "Oh! God!" cried Medora— "what do you mean, my dear friend! it is my father!"

"Your father!"

"Oh! yes, my own dear father."

Delmont felt the revulsion of his blood to be so violent, that he was compelled to sit down, still holding Medora's hand—"Your father!" repeated he—"Oh! Sir, what have I not endured of agony within these few moments—but Medora is safe, safe in your protection."

"And shall never leave it, Delmont," cried Glenmorris, embracing them both with great emotion, "but for yours—Yes, my dear friend, Medora is restored to us, the same innocent, the same lovely and admirable creature; but her mother!"

"What of her?" asked Delmont, eagerly, "what of Mrs. Glenmorris?"

"Alas, we know nothing," said Medora, sobbing—"We have not yet been able to trace her, my father . . . ."

She paused, not having the power to proceed—"Delmont," cried Glenmorris, his voice trembling; "where can she be? By what unaccountable accident have I lost my wife? Think what I have suffered even in so unexpectedly regaining my daughter, to know that of her mother nothing has been heard since their separation. Before I sat out for the country I had learned that no one in London knew where she was; all they were certain of being, that she and her daughter were separated, and nothing known of either of them."

Delmont put up his hand to his head—He was giddy and confused—The images he saw before him of Medora and her father seemed hardly real. He doubted whether he was not in the illusion of a dream. Yet, attempting to soothe the anguish which he saw overcame Medora, he could only inarticulately express himself; and after some words, attempting to comfort, though they only added to her disquiet (since she thought he knew more than he would tell) he stopped merely from inability to speak on any subject with clearness at that moment.

"My dear friend," said Medora, taking his hand, "I believe you are very ill!"

"No, not ill; only a little fatigued; but that is nothing. Why should the soldier only be capable of long marches? Are not we farmers as hardy a race?—Come, dear Sir," added he, summoning his usual cheerful manner, "let us not bring disgrace on our profession. Send me, I beseech you, in search of Mrs. Glenmorris, and I shall forget that I have been fatigued at all."

"Let us go, my dear Delmont," replied Glenmorris, who was already as well acquainted with him as if they had known each other for years. "Yet whither go?"

"You must not go, Sir; we must not leave Medora unprotected. I cannot now relate all the reasons why I intreat you not to lose sight of her; but let *me*, I implore you, go instantly any where that is likely to yield us an hope of finding my excellent, my admirable friend; then may I once more see Medora happy, and be so myself, beyond all that I have hitherto believed possible—happy in proportion as I have lately been miserable."

In despite of the effort Delmont made, it required less sagacity than Glenmorris possessed, to discover that he was extremely ill; and at length he was induced to own that he had not been in bed for several nights, and that he *did* feel himself somewhat disordered; "Nevertheless," said he, "I assure you, that were any thing less pressing in question than an inquiry after her mother, it is Medora's account of what has befallen her since we last met, that would the soonest assuage this foolish sensation of fatigue which I have about me."

Glenmorris, however, would not suffer him either to begin his enquiry after the mother, or to listen to the daughter, but insisted upon his going to his lodgings, and endeavouring to obtain some repose. "To begin our united search after my poor Laura," said he, "with effect, we must not set out as invalids, liable to be affected by personal illness; go, therefore, my dear Delmont, take the rest which is, I am sure, necessary for you, and return to us when you are better able to hear, than you are now, what my daughter has to relate, and then we will consult together what can be done to relieve us all from so cruel a suspence. I have written," added he, "to Armitage, who will, I hope, be in London to-morrow."

Delmont saw that Medora was extremely solicitous he should follow her father's directions; he therefore consented, though with reluctance, to go for a few hours to his lodgings, where, having changed his clothes, he threw himself upon the bed, and endeavoured to sleep; his spirits, however, were in so great a tumult, that to sleep was impossible, and to attempt it only increased the irritability of his mind. Fatigue, great as he had undergone, could not lull his senses into temporary forgetfulness. The images of Glenmorris, of Medora, and of the beloved wife and mother they lamented, fleeted before his eyes, and merely fatigued by the endeavour to sleep, he started up, and once more took his way to the apartments of Glenmorris.

Medora was sitting with her father, more languid, as Delmont thought, and more affected by their sudden meeting, than she had been at the immediate moment. Glenmorris appeared to him exactly what he had been described; a person above the common height, and giving the idea at once of personal strength and mental dignity. Though his eyes were blue, and remarkably soft, there was at times something so stern in his countenance as inspired awe; and his voice deep, yet musical, was one of those which could not be heard without pleasure, nor, when it was his purpose to persuade, without conviction. His eloquence however was rather natural than acquired. He spoke rather from the feelings of his heart than the acquisition of his understanding, and when animated and interested by his subject, he arose to exercise this native oratory, he appeared rather like an hero, such as Homer or Virgil describes, than a mere mortal of the present day. Glenmorris, who was hardly twenty when he married, was now only in his thirty-eighth year; but a scar across his forehead and nose, which he had received when he became a prisoner to the pirates, and his originally fair complection being very much changed by climate, he appeared two or three years older. Delmont admired the justness of the description he had received from the people of whom he had inquired, in the persuasion that it was Sir Harry Richmond; "that the gentleman was a very *grand* sort of man;" the idea of grandeur being what strikes persons in that rank of life, from a tall, large, and martial looking figure.

The likeness that Medora bore to her father was rendered more remarkable by the dejection which abated much of the fire and vivacity of his countenance. He could not now speak of his wife without betraying by his faltering voice, and by the tears in which his eyes swam, how cruelly he felt her unaccountable absence; yet he evidently endeavoured to stifle these expressions of his concern for Medora's sake, who watched every turn of his countenance with distressing solicitude, and seemed unable to support the complicated pain of reflecting on the anguish of one of her parents, inflicted by the loss of the other.

Glenmorris, who saw that Delmont would be restless and uneasy till he had heard Medora's little history, and anxious himself to go out, though he knew not whither, in search of his Laura, took occasion, after they had drank tea, to leave them together, as he imagined his daughter would be under less restraint when he was absent, and was on reflection sensible of the propriety of what Delmont had said, that she should never be left without the protection of either her father or her lover; Glenmorris therefore, committing his lately recovered treasure to the care of Delmont, set out in search of the other. All that once gave pleasure or pain to him in the great metropolis, which he thus revisited after an absence of above fifteen years, had entirely lost its influence; he now wondered how he ever could have beheld these scenes with such different eyes.

The charm he had formerly found or imagined in society, such as is to be met with in a great city, had vanished; his friends were gone; some were dead, others disappeared from poverty or from weariness; and a few were become what are called statesmen, and had put on the golden fetters, which they fancied were worn for the benefit of their country. It was not these that Glenmorris envied; he envied indeed no one, but rather beheld with wonder the toil and fatigue which were incurred to make a splendid appearance at such an immense expence as would have supported in America fifty families in more real comfort and plenty. He saw men labouring in places like dungeons the greater and better part of their days in the hope of some future satisfaction which great riches were to bestow; but the means were seldom acquired till the end was lost, and till the power of enjoyment existed no longer. He saw the continual and often successful effort of knaves to take advantage of fools, and beheld a spirit of quackery prevail from the state charlatan, exhausting and enfeebling the public constitution, to the advertising puffer of some poisonous nostrum; and hardly as he contemplated the humiliating scene of almost universal imposition and deception, knew whether most to despise or to pity those who acted and those who suffered.

Far from repenting that he had withdrawn himself to America, Glenmorris regretted only that he had, in attempting to obtain gilding for the invaluable jewels, whose intrinsic value nothing could increase, lost perhaps one, and so narrowly escaped being deprived of the other; he now felt from conviction, what indeed he had never doubted, that great fortune had no power to add to that domestic felicity, which alone is worth the wish of a rational being, and he had no hesitation in determining, that when his Laura was restored to him, he would not be detained a moment by those projects of obtaining her fortune, which had been the cause of their cruel separation, but that he would return directly to his farm, and, if it were possible, engage Delmont, with whose appearance and manners he was highly satisfied, to accompany them, and become an inhabitant of the new world.

To cultivate the earth of another continent, to carry the arts of civil life, without its misery and its vices, to the wild regions of the globe, had in it a degree of sublimity, which, in Glenmorris's opinion, sunk the petty politics and false views so eagerly pursued in Europe, into something more despicable than childish imbecility, in proportion as such schemes are injurious to the general happiness of the society where they are exercised. When he reflected on the degradation to which those must submit, who would make what is called a figure in this country; that they must sacrifice their independence, their time, their taste, their liberty, to etiquette, to forms and falsehoods, which would to him be insupportable, he rejoiced that he had made his election where human life was in progressive improvement, and where he had not occasion to turn with disgust, from the exercise of abject meanness to obtain the advantages of affluence, or with pity from fruitless efforts to escape from the humiliations of poverty.

CHAP. IX.

That noble grace, that dash'd brute violence
With sudden adoration and chaste awe.[81]

Alone with Medora, whom he had so lately considered as lost, seeing her restored to him such as she was when he had first given her his whole heart, or even raised to a superior degree of excellence in his opinion, by the courage and propriety of conduct she had shewn, Delmont was unable to repress or conceal the variety of emotions and affections which now crowded on his heart; he took her hands, and as he kissed them, the tears that fell from his eyes seemed to relieve the oppression he had so long laboured under. "Medora," cried he, "my own, my beloved Medora, have you spirits to relate the strange series of circumstances that have torn you from me? that have separated your mother from us both, at the very moment when I hoped we were to be united for ever? But do not, my angel, make any exertion that may be painful to you; I will repress my curiosity, and seeing you safe, will await for a calmer hour before I desire you to recal these painful scenes; yet it seems to me, my love, as if your description alone could afford us some clue, by which we may discover why and where your dear mother is concealed."

"That consideration, Delmont, would alone be enough," answered Medora, "but your wish is with me of force enough to conquer whatever reluctance I may have. I will, however, be as brief as I can.

"You know that a few days after you were gone, letters from that odious Mr. Petrify, and some other circumstances, compelled my mother to go to London. As she hoped to return in a few days, she would not take Susanne with her, for you know I love to do any little services about her, and she was unwilling to increase expence. Once, indeed, she even thought of going to Mrs. Grinsted, merely as less expensive than an hotel, but at my entreaty she determined on the latter. As soon then as we got there, my mother, whose active and intelligent spirit seldom sinks under difficulties, set about the business which had been the occasion of our journey; she would not take me with her, but left me employment in copying letters and papers on business, and I was well content to be in this way at least of some use to her, without going among people who seem to me to be the most disagreeable sort of animals I had ever yet seen—for once, and but once, I found myself among four or five of them, and I knew not why, but they inspired me at once with disgust and abhorrence."

"What were they, Medora?" said Delmont. "Can you describe them, my love?"

"Oh! yes, for they made a most disagreeable impression on my memory. There was that strange awkward old man, whom they call Loadsworth—about his face there is something that conveys ideas of lunacy subdued by self consequence, as if his pride and malignity had made him mad, and his consciousness of self importance prevented his being just as much so, as to lose the little provincial business he has left. His two little fierce grey eyes, his carrotty wig, and his undescribable way of articulating, even when he is not insolently peevish (which he is at all times to every body who are forced to bear it) would render him a most offensive wretch, even if he had not the character of being capable of any roguery, and of having art enough to bear himself through it; and if he were not known to be one of the most malicious and unmanly of a crew, who have in general but very little feeling, and, in being lawyers, forget all that is good as men."

"Indeed, Medora, you do not spare them," said Delmont.

"Of myself, you know, I could not be informed of all this—I could only tell you the impression made by the personal appearance of each of these men; but my mother, who is no bad judge, and who, you know, can draw a tolerable likeness, filled up in some of our conversations the outline my own observation made. Another man, who seemed to me equally worthless, was that Brownjohn, one of the most dauntless and ignorant coxcombs I ever beheld. The disagreeable vulgar fellow prates of people he never saw as if they were his nearest relations; tells of lords, and knights, and esquires, whom he does not know even by sight, and supports an appearance above what his iniquitous practice gives him, by dint of falsehood, fraud, and impudence.—You would not think any thing that can be said of him too harsh, if I had time to relate the anecdotes I have heard of his daring iniquity; and when you know that the extraordinary and disagreeable circumstances I have been involved in were of his contrivance, you will not, I think, imagine I speak of him too severely."

"Of his contrivance!" exclaimed Delmont. "But I will be patient, Medora; proceed."

"I will not give you any more then of these ugly likenesses, but go on to tell you, that every day, on my mother's return from her conferences with these men, she became more and more dejected; her usual courage and just confidence on her own powers deserted her, and for almost the first time in my life I heard her complain, and repent that in coming to England she had sacrificed substantial happiness to the pursuit of a chimera, which, even if it could be attained, was not worth one year, nay, not one month, of the tranquil happiness and domestic comfort we had known in America, before these ambitious projects had been listened to. I once more, for I had often done it before, most earnestly exhorted her to pursue them no farther, but that she would determine, as soon as you returned, which might be expected every day, to go back to America. If, said I, Delmont loves me, he will accompany us—(forgive me Delmont, for the doubts these *if*'s implied;) if he does *not*, the sooner I find shelter with you, my mother and my father, against a conviction that will, I own, give me pain, the sooner I shall be restored to tranquillity, and to the uninterrupted performance of those duties which will always be enough for my heart, while I have such a father and such a mother to love me, and to love."

Delmont, fondly pressing her hand to his lips, sighed, and said, "Medora, you are the only person who could have raised these doubts; but I will not interrupt you."

"My mother," continued she, "for what reason I knew not, always escaped from this sort of discourse, and, I thought, wished, contrary to her usual method in regard to me, to conceal something from me; that something then must be uneasy, for the whole study of her life had been to save me from pain, and to give me pleasure. She had however taught me never to appear inquisitive, never to seek to know more than she thought proper to tell me. I therefore concealed my uneasiness, and endeavoured, when after these disagreeable conferences she returned to me, to receive her with cheerfulness. It happened that in the hope of ending this irksome business a little sooner, she had one day consented to dine with Brownjohn, on a sudden invitation, and as she thought I should be uneasy at her prolonged absence, she wrote a note with a pencil, accounting for it, which was brought to me by one of Brownjohn's clerks. Two days afterwards, my mother being again out, another note was brought to me by the same person, who waited in a coach for an answer. I opened it; but here it is, my dear friend; though almost effaced, you will see how artfully it was copied after the other pencil note written in my mother's hand, and how easy it was for me to be deceived."

Medora then gave Delmont a piece of paper, in which was written with a pencil, in an hand not distinguishable from that of Mrs. Glenmorris, the following words:

My dearest girl, I am unexpectedly detained again, and induced, by the hope of bringing our business sooner to a close, to accept the invitation of Mr. Brownjohn to his house near Barnet, where some of the parties will be, whose advice is the most material to me; and if we are together, we may perhaps be enabled to decide at once; come, therefore, my Medora, with the gentleman who delivers this, to your most affectionate

L. G.

I am now, to save time, setting out in a post-chaise with Mr. Brownjohn; he sends his coach and a confidential person for you.

Not only the hand, but the style of Mrs. Glenmorris were so well imitated in this letter, that Delmont owned he should himself have been deceived. Indignation, however, at so base an artifice was for a moment predominant. Medora proceeded.

"In consequence of this note then I made some very slight alteration in my dress, and got into the coach, taking with me my night linen, as I understood, from the decent looking oldish man in the coach, whom I spoke to before I entered it, that we were to remain one night at the villa of Mr. Brownjohn; and I went the more cheerfully, as I imagined my mother meant that this conference, which I knew to be utterly disagreeable to herself, should be final. I hoped therefore that at its close would be decided either our return to Upwood or to America, or at least that nothing depending on these lawyers would afterwards delay either one or the other.

"In this expectation I got into the coach. The man I saw there was, I thought, between forty and fifty. There was nothing remarkable about him. He was such a man as one every where sees; a round faced man in a light coloured wig; and he put on a sort of cringing complaisance, such as is frequent from people who fancy that servility is politeness. He talked to me as we went along towards Barnet, and called me now and then *Miss*, and *dear Miss*. I could have dispensed with his conversation and his dear Misses; and in fact I found it above all things impossible to give him my attention, for as soon as we got a little out of the immediate neighbourhood of the city, I seemed once more to be in my element; I saw heaths, and fields, and trees. Finchley Common (I did not then know its name) was delightful, and I long'd to wander over its turf; but beyond it the country seemed almost enchanting. I had, you will remember, been shut up more than a week in a dirty hotel, in a close part of London, in the month of August, and to breathe the free air of the country even though there had still a suburbian look about it, was delicious.

"I began, however, to remark to my fellow traveller, that we were a long while on the way. The man answered, that Mr. Brownjohn's horses were fat pampered creatures, his coachman very fond of them, and that the coach was heavy; all which might be very true, and we continued our way for sometime without any farther marks of impatience on my part.

"At length I saw that the sun had sunk below the horizon. I had passed mile stones, which said, from Barnet two, from Barnet one, yet still we went on through a town that I fancied was Barnet, still, still we went on, more and more slowly however, for the horses, though not the sleek pampered steeds of Mr. Attorney Brownjohn, were certainly very tired.

"I now again began to express my uneasiness, and the man again attempted to appease my impatience. He said that Mr. Brownjohn's villa was a little out of the road; a sort of hunting box at the edge of Mr. Somebody's park; and that we should presently turn out of the great north road and arrive at it.

"Turn out of the great north road we certainly did; and went for I think about half a mile up a lane, which seemed but very little frequented. When between two small woods, and in a place where no passengers were likely to pass, the coach stopped.

"I looked out; the fine summer evening was fading into night. I saw no house, and turning to my conductor, whose countenance I thought assumed a very singular look, I asked, but I felt my voice tremble, where was the house of Mr. Brownjohn?

"He looked white; for even a *lawyer* may *sometimes*, I understand, feel compunction. I thought he trembled, but I knew not what he answered, for I heard at that moment the rattle of wheels. An hack postchaise and four drew up to the coach door, and I saw in it a man, whose name I did not remember. He had once been with my mother about business; but I should have forgotten, perhaps, that I had ever seen him at all, if there had not been a something in his countenance particularly pert and disagreeable, a something that though it is felt can hardly be described.

"I looked in wonder and in terror towards the chaise; the man in it was *Darnell*, the brother of Brownjohn.

"He got out, opened the door of the coach as well as that of the chaise, and said, 'Miss Glenmorris, you will please to get into this chaise?'

"'I into that chaise, Sir,' said I, 'for why?'

"'Eh! ah! eh! Miss,' cried the odious looking man, 'Your *Mammaa*, your *Mammaa*, Miss, has, has, has, gone farther on, and wishes you to, to, to, to come with me, Miss, to her.'

"I now began to dread I knew not what—my fear, indeed, was for a moment such as deprived me of every power of conjecture. Recovering my recollection, however, I recovered also some portion of courage, and I positively refused to remove into the chaise. Sir, said I to the man, who had, as he pretended, been sent to conduct me from the hotel, you have brought me here on I know not what false pretences; but farther I will not go. In truth I hardly know what I afterwards said; I only recollect that I resisted to the utmost of my power the compulsion used to oblige me to pass from one carriage to another; but my resistance was useless, and I found myself seated by the side of that Darnell, and proceeding with as much speed as four posthorses could exert, I knew not whither.

"The impertinent man had the rudeness to take my hand, muttering something about his love and his admiration, which he hoped would plead in my fair bosom his excuse for the step he had taken. This insolence roused me—I snatched my hand from him, and asked him how he dared address himself in that manner to me?—I then let down the glass, though he tried to prevent me, and called out to the postillions; but the horses were at their utmost speed; the pebbles and gravel of the road were even forced into my face by the violence with which they galloped. The postillions either could not or would not hear me; and though my determined manner prevented the slightest addition to the impertinence that odious Darnell had before presumed to insult me with, I was, in despite of all my remonstrances, carried on to the next stage.

"There I was determined to make a desperate effort to escape from this insolent and ridiculous man, from whose awkward attempts to make love to me I learned, that he had heard from his brother, Brownjohn, that I was the undoubted heiress to near half the fortune of the rich old Dutch merchant my grandfather; but he fancied he had the art to persuade me that my personal charms had made a deep impression on him, and that it was on that account only he had been impelled, from the *irresistible nature of his passion*, to take the only method which seemed to him likely to secure me to himself. Do you doubt that I treated as he deserved this contemptible miscreant? He had imagined, perhaps, that because I was very young, he might terrify me or impose on me; but I assured him in plain terms, that the first attempt at personal rudeness or impertinence should be the last he would have in his power to make; and I as plainly told him he was to me the object of as much abhorrence as was consistent with the most ineffable scorn and contempt; and that as to the love he pretended, I thought of it only as an insult which he would never have dared to have ventured, if instead of naming it in a postchaise, into which he had so infamously trepanned me, he had been in a place where I could have directed a servant to turn him down stairs."

"Charming girl," cried Delmont, passionately kissing her hand, "how are you raised in my opinion by so proper an exertion of spirit."

"And yet," said Medora, "while I was thus sincere with this miserable Darnell, my cowardly little heart seemed to have left its place, and to have taken up its residence in my throat. The man, however, seemed disappointed, but not repulsed. He probably collected together all the proverbs he had ever heard, such as, 'Faint heart never won fair lady;' 'Speak and speed;' and, 'None but the brave deserve the fair;' for he seemed after a little pause to determine to be very brave; so he told me that I might perhaps suppose he had contrived to elope with me on account of my *fortin*, but 'I asshore you, Miss Glanemorris,' quoth he, seeming much elated as he spoke, 'I asshore you, Ma'am, I've very ansom fortin of my own, and midn't be to seek; for parsons of the fust consequence in the city, and tother end the town too, ave vish'd me to make my addresses to their daaters. Hive a wery good estate in Shropshire as come by my grandmother, and my mother's aunt ave a pretty little property too, I'll assure you, in Yorkshire, and money in the funs, which we're sure of!—besides that hive the onor to bere his majesty's commisshon.'

"'What is all this to me, Sir?' said I. 'Do you imagine if you were possessed of the first property in England, that *I* should for a moment think of *you?*'

"'Indeed, Ma'am, I don't see why not? I asshore you, Miss, if it ad not bin that hive a somethink of an unaccountable sort of a attachment for your parson, it is not your fortin as would ave induced me for to ave taken this missure—But come now, dear Miss, most *amabel* Miss Medorer, let me ope that sins ve har eer . . . . .'[82]—The man would again have taken my hand, but I snatched it from him, and summoning all my resolution, said, 'Mr.——whatever your name is, let me tell you once for all, that I never will listen to you; that I will never endure the slightest liberty; and that unless you immediately take me back to my mother, I will most assuredly have you prosecuted, for I know such conduct is as illegal as it is infamous. Sir I never saw you to exchange a single word with you in my life. I cannot, I think, be an object to you as to fortune, and I beg you will consider the risk you incur of punishment for such an action as this. Take me back, Sir—restore me to my mother, and this ridiculous attempt shall be overlooked.'

"The man, who really seemed to me to be half a fool, had however vanity to so absurd an excess, that I could at any other time have laughed at it. He really, I believe, fancied that his merit and his personal perfections were such as no young woman could behold with indifference, especially when he professed what he termed violent love to her; so he went on to exert this irresistible eloquence, while I was silent, and thinking of the best method of making my escape. I heard however that he was the only son of a man who had been brought up to trade, but succeeding to a fortune had married Brownjohn's mother, then, as he related, a fine buxom widow; and so he vas partly edshewcated at Shrewsbury; and then his father vishing to put him to some business, but thinkink a shop not *genteel enouge* for im, vy he vas put prentice to a Vest Ingée marchant, vere he staid a year or two, but not much liking it, and aving no need to be in trade becaus of his pretty fortin, he ad even become a sojer, and got a commisshon to defind his kink and country.

"There was one advantage in my hearing all this jargon, which seemed to be collected from the different lines of life he had been in; it convinced me the man was a fool; and though I have often heard my mother declare, that no animal is so difficult to manage, I thought the species of fool into whose hands I had so strangely fallen had so little real resolution, that he might be made to desist from his purpose. He seemed as if he had never been accustomed to the company of any woman above the condition of a bar-maid at a tavern, and his notion of saying fine things was, I soon perceived, taken from the scraps of plays he had heard at half-price, which he quoted, as the French say, *a tort et a travers*,[83] and sometimes remembered a whole line, some

times only half a one; poor Shakespeare was most cruelly mangled by him. After
asshoring me of his good qualities, he said with great emphasis;

> Speak hoff me has I ham,
> Nothink hextenerate, nor sit down hought in malice.[84]

I assured him, that if he would sit *me* down where he found me, I should do my
utmost endeavours not only to make no report of him in any way, but to dismiss him
from my mind as soon as possible."

"Dearest Medora," exclaimed Delmont, "that at your time of life you could
have such true courage as to make remarks upon this stupid scoundrel, and to smile!"

"Indeed I did, Delmont; but it was not because my heart was a moment at ease;
it was because I saw that by contemptuous treatment, which the poor wretch knew he
deserved, though it was new to him, I really awed him into respect; and I was not
without hope that I should prevail upon him by this means to give up his insolent yet
senseless project, and to carry me back to my mother, whose anguish of heart, which
I for ever represented to myself, was the most bitter of all my fears, though I was not
ignorant how much injury my character might sustain from this excursion, involuntary as it was. You will wonder, perhaps, that I should have command enough over
myself to recal the past or to think of the future, while the present circumstance was
such as might well overwhelm me with terror; but after the first flutter of my heart had
subsided, and I began to comprehend the character of the man in whose power I was,
I remained still, it is true, under considerable terror, but not to such a degree as to
deprive me for a moment of my recollection and presence of mind. My mother, and
what she would suffer, was my most uneasy thought; but I considered that to suffer
myself to be enervated by fear, when only courage and steadiness could restore me to
her, would be doing her the greatest injury she could sustain—for her sake then, for
her whom I love better than any human being——" (Medora remembered that she
knew not whether her mother yet existed, and her voice failed her)—Recovering herself, however, she proceeded.

"For my mother I determined to exert that resolution, which she had often told
me was a virtue as becoming in a woman as in a man. 'It is not firmness, Medora,' she
has often said, 'that gives an unpleasant and unfeminine character to a woman; on the
contrary, the mind which has acquired a certain degree of reliance on itself, which has
learned to look on the good and evil of life, and to appreciate each, is alone capable of
true gentleness and calmness. Sullen indifference or selfish coldness may sometimes
give something of the same appearance to a character, but they are always repulsive,
and women who assume either affected softness or languid apathy are never beloved.
She who has learned to despise the trifling objects that make women who pursue them
appear so contemptible to men; she who without neglecting her person has ornamented her mind, and not merely ornamented, but has discovered that nothing is
good for any human being, whether man or woman, but a conscientious discharge of
their duty; an humble trust that such a conduct will in any future state of existence
secure more felicity than is attainable here; and an adherence to that pure morality,

which says, Do what good you can to all; never wilfully injure any—these are the acquisitions that will give tranquillity to the heart and courage to the actions, and even amidst the heaviest storms of fortune, bestow repose on their possessor—I say repose, my Medora, because we abuse the word happiness; it is meant to convey an idea which is, I fear, never realized.'"

Medora, never able to express what she felt for Mrs. Glenmorris, was again unable to proceed; yet in a few moments again recovering her voice, she said—"Oh! best and dearest of mothers, what comfort, what inexpressible comfort it would now be to know that you, who have deserved every blessing, are now even tranquil; to know that you do not at this moment experience in your own person the sad conviction that there are evils for which fortitude, and sweetness, and goodness like your's administer no consolation."

Delmont, who saw that Medora was now too much affected to proceed, desired her to delay a little the continuation of her narrative.

CHAP. X.

What peril then in savage wood or waste,
Or forest dark, or where the wild waves roar
Incessant on the bleak and desert shore,
Appals the virgin resolutely chaste
From man's base arts escaping?[85]

Medora thus proceeded:

"Nothing but the vigilance with which it was necessary to guard against the least insolence could perhaps have kept me from sinking under the complicated oppressions of fear and fatigue, added to the distracting conjectures on what my mother would think, and what she would do. Arrived at a considerable town, of which I know not the name, between one and two in the morning, Mr. or, as he chuses to style himself, Captain Darnell, who I believe was little accustomed to expose that beloved person of his to any kind of violent exertion, began to discover that he wanted his supper, an article of which I found he thought as being of considerable importance. After a preamble of some length he said, if I would promise him not to make any complaint to the people of the house, which, after all, they would not believe, we would get out, and would rest for some hours. I told him I should make no promise; that on the contrary I would make every possible effort to escape from him; yet as I perceived he then hesitated whether he should go into the house, I thought it more prudent to dissemble a little, or rather to abate somewhat of my apparent indignation. The poor wretch, for indeed he is a very contemptible animal, suffered himself to believe what he wished though I would promise nothing, and I was handed into the inn. As my hope was that I should have an opportunity of interesting the mistress of the house in my favour, I suffered him to believe me more tranquil than I had hitherto appeared; I even took the refreshment he offered me; and he now supposed, that reconciled to his scheme I was gradually becoming milder, and that what reluctance still remained was only pride, not yet determining how to accommodate itself to circumstances.

"As soon as the waiter withdrew, whom to my infinite mortification I saw considered us a young couple going on a matrimonial expedition to Scotland, I repeated to him, commanding myself however as much as I could, that if he would assure me he would the next day return to London, and restore me to my mother, I would most solemnly promise him to forgive his attempt, and would engage that my relations should not take such vengeance against him as he knew would otherwise be in their power. He again began to plead the violence of his uncontrollable passion, which, he said, rendered it impossible for him to commit so great a violence on all his feelings as to part with me. He threw himself at my feet, and repeated sundry scraps of plays in a tone, and with such grimaces as would at any other time have excited my mirth, but now, as he made an attempt to seize my hands, I was not able to endure his insolent folly, and started from him with a resolution to rush into the most frequented part of the house, and throw myself on the protection of the first person who had the appearance of having human feelings; Darnell, however, who would thus have seen all his fine project overturned, was too strong for me; he threw himself between me and the door, and snatching up at the same time his pistol case, which lay in a chair near it, he took out one of them, though I saw his hand shook as he did it, 'Ma-a-dam,' said he, his voice trembling in his throat, 'Ma-a-dam, I-I I-I cannot endure this cru-cru-cruel tre-e-e-t-ment; I vill put an end to my *torturs* unless you instantly vill consent to become my vife.'

"I know not now," continued Medora, "and at this moment am disposed to wonder how it happened that I felt very little terror at the folly of the man—I thought he loved himself too well to hurt himself, and was tolerably sure that if any mischief happened it would be by accident, and not by any design of this frantic lover; yet I own a loaded pistol in hands that had been accustomed to wield only the pen or the sugar board was not a circumstance one could be very quiet under—I should be very sorry to be the occasion of the death of any creature that breathes, and certainly know not how I should have endured the spectacle with which this new Orlando[86] threatened me; but besides that I had a considerable reliance on his extreme affection for himself, I really had, even at the moment which he intended should oppress me with terror and amazement, so much presence of mind as to reflect, that the loss of an insignificant and useless consumer of the fruits of the earth would be no great evil; and that if he was determined either to kill or marry, he should certainly, if I was to decide, make his election for the first of these desperate deeds.

"I left him, therefore, with the pistol grasped in one hand and the lock of the door in the other, and crossing the room, which was a very large one, I applied myself to the *bell*, and repeatedly rang it with as much force as I could exert.

"The waiter was on one side of the door in a moment; the Captain therefore, not to make what had happened public, was compelled to recede from the other, and without waiting while this hero, whose white face was covered with powder, his hair staring wildly, and his gesture such as might well make the man wonder, accounted for the summons. I passed them both, and going along a passage found the bar, and entering it asked for the mistress of the house.

"'There is no mistress, Ma'am,' said an odd and unpleasant looking woman, to whom I applied myself, 'I has the management of this here house—I begs to know your commands?'—I did not, I own, much like the appearance of this person. 'Is the master of the house within?'—'Yes, Ma'am, he is to be sure, but he's ill in bed with the gout.'

"'Well then,' said I, 'I must apply to you, Madam, and I hope you will protect me. The person who has brought me hither by a stratagem, a trick, is a man I knew not before even by sight. He is endeavouring between force and persuasion to compel me to go with him to Scotland, but I will die first. Whoever assists me in escaping from him will be most liberally rewarded; but those who aid his views and help him to detain me will undoubtedly share in his punishment.' I saw by a glance, that Darnell, who had probably made his bargain with the waiter while I was out of the room, had now crept after me, and stood near me, his mouth half-open, and his detestable eyes staring with an expression of fear and rage. I continued to urge the bar-woman, who at length said, 'Lawk Miss, I'm sure it is a great quandary for me to know how to do in sich a case; law, Miss, why did you come with his honnur, if so be as that you was like for to alter your mind. For my part I don't see what I can do I'm sure. You know, Miss, them there sort of things be not the bisness of we at inns. Ladies and gemmen must settle all that there as they pleases; I don't see how we can hinterfere in no shape.'

"'You are quite right, Miss Jane,' cried Darnell, advancing, 'I admire your good sense, 'tis wery much to your credit I'll asshore you. Indeed, upon the onur of a gentleman and an officer, this young lady has only just changed her mind by reason of a sort of a lover's little quarrel, and all will come right again. Come, come, my dear Miss Medora,' and again he would have taken my hand—'Come, come, let us be friends.' I own, my dear Delmont, that at that moment my courage had nearly forsaken me. What will become of me, thought I—Good God, what will become of me among such people as these. I believe all those in the inn were by this time assembled about us, and I looked round to see if there was in the group one face indicating honesty and sense; but the hostlers, the waiters, the postillions, and the female servants, and even two or three persons who seemed not to belong to the house, all appeared to be mightily amused with the scene, and I found I had no chance of procuring my release from them; I felt too at the same time, that the fatigue and harassing anxiety I had now so long been in were likely, in despite of my struggles to sustain myself, soon to overcome me. I was afraid I should have fallen, and was compelled to hold by and lean on the pillar that supported the window of the bar opening into the entrance of the inn. I recovered, however, voice enough to say, if then there is no one here who will prevent such infamous conduct, I demand the security of a room to myself, where I may be sure of being free from molestation during the night.

"'To be sure,' cried Darnell, 'who ever hintimated any design to hinterrupt you?—Never me, I'm shore—I desire to be upon onour, strict onour, and nothink els; come Miss Jane,' went he on, addressing himself to the bar-woman, 'come, let the *cha-am*-bermaid shew Miss to a proper and genteel room.' A servant girl now came curteyseying with a light; and as I did not see that any situation could be less hateful than that I was now in, I followed her to a neat room, where, having made her go with me round it, and assured myself there was no other door than that I could bolt (for there were very strong bolts to it within side) I dismissed her, not however, till I had offered her all the money in my pocket, if she would contrive my escape; but whether the sum (not above thirty shillings) was too small to tempt her, or whether the girl really was stupid, I know not, but she only looked at me with an ideot grin, and shook her head. When she was gone, I again examined the room, and felt all round the paper; there was no door but that I had bolted and locked; I looked out of the windows, but from thence there was no probability of my escape, for besides that they were very high from the ground, the place beneath them was a stable-yard full of men cleaning their horses; and I saw soldiers, postillions, and waggoners continually passing and repassing. I suffered however the sashes to remain open, because I could hear these persons talking, which seemed to be a sort of protection, and the air was refreshing to my wearied and exhausted frame. I sat down near one of them, and contemplated the skies. My spirits were relieved, but I could not shed tears. My mother, my dear deserted mother, was before me the instant I was alone. I thought I beheld her losing all her fortitude under a stroke so strange, so unexpected; I heard her call for her Medora! I heard her wild, her eager inquiries, and at last conjured up such an image of anguish and despair that I could bear it no longer, but was conscious that unless by an effort of resolution I forced my mind from the contemplation of this fearful subject, I should lose in frenzy the power of so acting as might, when I was restored to her, heal the cruel wounds under which my poor mother at this moment suffered.

"The house soon became as quiet as such an house ever is; I thought its inmates, and Darnell among the rest, were gone to their repose, and finding it difficult to support myself any longer, I lay down in my clothes, and obtained some hours of partial forgetfulness. I could never so far divert myself of terror as to sleep quietly, but started at every noise, and recollected with renewed apprehension where I was and what I had to fear. At five o'clock I arose, however, considerably refreshed, and again looked from the windows, and again reconsidered what could be done to escape. My contrivances, however, were very vain; no means were at hand, and between five and six the bar-woman herself tapped at my door, and said, 'The Captain, Ma'am, gives his compliments, and desires me to let you know that he waits breakfast for you.'

"I answered, that I had nothing to do with the Captain, and meant to stay where I was. To the arguments she thought proper to use I gave no answer; but she had at length the insolence to tell me the door must then be broke open, for nobody should shut themselves up so in her master's house. As I thought her not unlikely to execute this or any other piece of brutality she was paid for, I opened the door, rather I own in a transport of indignation than of fear. Darnell, who had heard of the contest, by this time appeared, and again put on his creeping humility, and began to talk of his passion. I told him that my resolution was unalterable, and that unless he resolved to return to London, nothing but direct force should compel me to enter a carriage with him. He endeavoured by half sentences and vague professions to persuade me that my will should be his; and I in turn dissimulated a little, and affected to believe him, for at that moment it occurred to me, that as there were soldiers in the house, there were certainly officers, and if I could see any one of them, I determined to appeal to him for protection against Darnell, who I was sure was personally a coward. I was aware that there was some hazard in doing this, but I had not so contemptible an opinion of mankind as to suppose it probable I should fall into worse or as bad hands as those of this stupid, obstinate, and worthless pretender to the character of a gentleman. The mere chivalric turn of a military man would, I hoped, be in my favour, and at all events my resolution was taken to risk it; but Mr. Darnell, who perhaps foresaw some such attempt on my part, thought he should do wisely not to put it in my power; and as soon as he had himself swallowed an hasty though a very plentiful breakfast, the chaise was announced, and he desired me to get in. It was in vain I made every excuse, and then peremptorily insisted on delay. The bar-woman seemed to have enlisted in the service of the Captain with a zeal which I believe no more worthy cause would have excited; this wretched woman rather encouraged the man than checked him. She had no notion, she said, of such childish airs; the Captain would be very much to blame indeed if he minded them. I had more fear of remaining where this woman could instigate the foolish animal to persist in or to aggravate his atrocity, than of being left to his mercy, which I knew would be tempered according to his fears. I had heard, that when women are thoroughly bad and abandoned, they are more determined and inveterate in wickedness than men; I therefore resolved to entrust myself once more to the noble Captain, and was once more seated in a postchaise by him, most reluctantly I own; but though I had hitherto been so unsuccessful in my attempts to escape, my contempt of him had increased, and I thought I should hardly fail of meeting at another inn a more womanly and humane governess of it than Miss Jane ——. Our conversation, however, as we proceeded, was for some time carried on with increased asperity on both sides. The Captain seemed to hope to frighten me; I was not without the same hope in regard to him. We arrived at a late hour at Skipton; I there, you know, put myself into the protection of the landlady. You have told me, Delmont, that you know great part of what passed the first time of my being there. Darnell most solemnly promised that he would forthwith return to London, and on the strength of that promise, and because in fact I knew not what else to do, I once more consented to travel with him. The horses heads were undoubtedly, this time at least, turned towards London. I saw by the mile-stones on the road that we were actually going southward, and I hoped that Darnell, repenting of an exploit which must be fruitless and dangerous in the extreme, had determined to give it up. I spoke to him, as if I were in this persuasion, with less acrimony than I had ever done since the beginning of the expedition. He was sullen, however, and the natural malignity of his temper began to shew itself. I imputed it to his finding himself completely baffled, and to the gloomy half-stifled resentment of mortified pride. I was mistaken.

"About two miles before we got to the next stage southward from Skipton, on a wide and dreary moor, an old-fashioned postchaise, that seemed an ancient country apothecary's visiting tub,[87] compelled into a somewhat more active service, stood waiting in the road. Darnell gave a signal, which had, I suppose, been agreed upon between

him and the boy who drove us, for he drew up close to this vehicle, and I was desired
to get out of that I was in, and to enter it.

"Again I would have resisted, and again I found that resistance might subject
me to insults, but would finally avail me nothing. I reproached Darnell with the perfidy and infamy of his conduct. He seemed now to have found an unusual degree of
courage, and answered me with a surly sort of triumph. I implored him to tell me
whither he was about to take me? he said, to people quite as good as I was—people of
honour and character. I could give no other answer to his impertinence, than I should
be very much suprised if I found it so, since it would be indeed extraordinary if people
of honour and character were connected with a man, who was acting in absolute
defiance to both. After travelling, as nearly as I could guess, sixteen or eighteen miles,
and stopping once at a very forlorn looking house, which I have since thought belonged to one of Mr. Darnell's tenants, for the people, as if through fear, preserved a
profound silence, the chaise stopped before the old fashioned thick walls of a sort of
court, surrounding, or rather which was before, an old mansion house of gloomy and
gothic appearance. There were two great brick pillars, with heavy stone work over
them, which time had eaten into excavations, and which chance and nature had sown
with wall-flowers, valerian, rag-wort, and antirhinum;[88] within they were mantled
with ivy, or lined with holly. Over the front of the house a vine was trained, which
concealed some of the casements. I refused to get out, for the appearance of the place,
which I did not then, as you may believe, so minutely investigate, frightened me.
Again however I had no choice. I descended, and entered the house up several steps;
and this I found was the place in Yorkshire Darnell had spoken of, and was the residence of his mother, and of an old aunt of her's, to whom the house belonged. I was
shewn into a parlour, which I am persuaded had remained in the state it was now in
for some centuries. The tapestry with which one side was hung represented Judith
with the head of Holophernes[89]—a most terrific subject and most ghastly execution.
The other two parts of the room were painted to imitate cedar. The curtain of an
immense old window seemed once to have been green mixed damask, but it retained
very little of its original hue, and was now of a dingy yellow. The great chimney was all
shining with brass, and there was a worked[90] skreen and worked chairs, which the old
lady's care had not been able to save from the depredations of the moths. You will
wonder how I could have at that moment a mind sufficiently disengaged to attend to
these minute remarks; but I had time enough to make them after my first disquiet
subsided.

"That disquiet was not, you may imagine, inconsiderable, when I found myself
in such a place, of which I had no doubt but that Darnell was absolute master. He left
me as if to give the first impulses of terror time to operate; but it had a contrary effect,
and allowed me a respite, which I used in considering the means of escape, and resolving rather to hazard my life than long to remain in this man's power.

"After about half an hour, a coarse but clean female servant entered the room,
and took from the corner of it an old Japan tea table, on which was arranged the best
tea equipage. A small silver tea kettle and lamp next made their appearance, and in a
few moments Mrs. Darnell, the buxom widow, as she still affected to be, entered, led

by her son, who with wonderful assurance introduced me as the young lady who had done him the honour to have so favourable an opinion of him. She was a fat gentlewoman, almost as broad as she was high, with her hair or wig frizzled and powdered quite white, fine rosy cheeks hanging down on her surprising bust, which was ornamented with beads, and her son's picture suspended to them. She approached me with the sort of air people have who feel the most perfect confidence in their own powers of pleasing, and would have kissed my cheek, but I liked her familiarity almost as little as her son's, and stepped back, 'You are in an error, Madam,' said I, 'that person whom you call your son, but whose name I hardly know, has deceived you, and I call upon you, as you are a woman, and I am willing to suppose a gentlewoman, to influence him that I may be restored to my mother.'

"'Well,' cried the jolly dame, her great face appearing to enlarge as she spoke, 'Well, this does indeed, Miss, surpass all belief. Humph! Very strange surely! but I will nat believe a young person like *you*, Miss, will stand in her own light so much—and besides, let me tell you, that aftar the step you have taken it is doing yourself a great injary, and you cannot sappose you will make your market alsewhere.' The woman then went on to give me a long history of her son's virtues, qualities, property, and expectations; putting great stress on the great *fortin* he would have, and the *genteel* line of life he was in, as well as on her own *genteel* connections, and the great business and conse*quance*, and *gentility* of her son Brownjohn, who she said was *look'd* upon by people of the first *quality*, and dined very *aften* with my Lord ——and Sir Robart——, and once had even passed two days at the *cauntry* house of the Marquis of——; she did not know what I might think, or what *sart* of people I had been used to in America, but *she* could *infarm* me that few English young ladies of ever so great fortin look'd higher than to Captain Darnell. I seized the only occasion she allowed me to tell her, that to some of those who so looked, I begged she would advise him to recommend himself, for that he was utterly disagreeable to me, and if instead of being as he was, he could offer me a diadem, he would still be the object of my abhorrence and detestation. I am sure it was not without considerable efforts that the sturdy widow checked the violent inclination she felt to strike me; for a moment she even lifted up a fist, the apparent prowess of which a butcher might have envied; and I saw that her son, who had probably felt what it was capable of, turned of a more cadaverous hue as she uttered words which I only recollect as being words of reproach and menace. It would be endless were I to relate the whole conversation; I thought, during its progress, I discovered that this woman acted from other motives than those which appeared on the surface; that she was aware her son had hazarded so much, that he must either go through with the undertaking or be liable to a punishment which might cost him a great deal of that fortune she now so proudly boasted of. After a most wearisome and long dialogue, which would with more propriety be called a monologue (for her son seldom was an interlocutor, and I spoke not) she told me, that though such condact as mine might well *disgast* and alarm any young man, and *fright* away love, yet since her poor Dicky had still the weakness to feel an *unfartinate* affiction *far* me, she should *considar harself* as my *mather*. The odd manner in which she put an a almost always in place of an o, and which I found was the dialect of the common people of a great part of Hampshire, where she had been brought up (not far from Portsmouth) had the effect, I hardly know why, of lessening my apprehensions, by rendering her menaces ridiculous. I thought it abject to fear so ignorant and vulgar a woman, not sufficiently considering that such only, and one who had besides a bad heart, would act as she acted; and that it is from ignorance combined with avarice and malevolence that there is always the most to apprehend.

"I believe she was now irritated by discovering how little I feared her; for when she left the room, and told me she would send her housemaid to shew me to mine, she had the countenance and voice of a fury, only that she was too plump for one of those monsters of poetical antiquity.[91] The housemaid came, and I followed her up an oaken staircase of great width, which was kept nicely waxed and rubbed, so that it was like the fine mahogany of an indefatigable housewife, and it might have been skaited upon with great success. The room I was shewn into was in the same style as the rest of the house. My imagination could people it with nothing but ghosts, but of them I had no fear; my apprehensions were much greater of Master Dicky Darnell, against whose intrusion I guarded with as much care as possible. There were two doors in the room where I was left to my contemplations; one from a passage by which I entered, the other I unbolted, and found it led into a closet which was lined with arras,[92] while the room adjoining, where the bed stood, was of dark wainscot in little pannels, and ornamented only with two full length pictures of some former squire and his spouse, possessors of the mansion, he in blue velvet with skirts[93] sticking out and a tie wig, his fair companion in a fine yellow robe, ornamented with jewels, and holding a very full blown red rose to her bosom; they were superb, and probably it was expected they would impress me with veneration; but the only sentiment they inspired was fearful curiosity to know if they did not conceal behind them any door or entrance to the room. I thought, after the best examination I could make, that they were merely what they appeared, monuments of impotent vanity; but in regard to the arras in the closet I was far less easy. It was nailed down so that I could not move it, nor could the wind perform any of those operations upon it which constitute great part of the terror in some novels I had read at Upwood, little imagining then that I should so soon become involved in adventures, and really be in one of those situations which I have sometimes thought, rather ingeniously imagined than really possible.

"After going round and round it repeatedly without being thoroughly satisfied, I was compelled to have recourse to the only security within my reach, which were bolts within the chamber; they fastened both that door and the other apparently very securely. I examined behind and under my bed, and as to the windows I was sure nobody could get in that way, for I had discovered, in the slight survey I made, that it would be extremely difficult to get out; I did not, however, despair of effecting my escape. As through the vine leaves that almost covered the old casement I looked out to the sky and the stars, I recollected my mother's singular story, and particularly the time when she was a prisoner, a sick and suffering prisoner, in the Abbey of Kilbrodie. Her courage, her trust in heaven, did not fail her, said I, in that trying hour, and wherefore should I allow mine to sink under circumstances of less danger? Oh! my dearest, my adored mother, were I but sure you do not at this moment endure great misery on my account, were I but sure your health has not suffered, I should feel myself strengthened and supported so as perhaps sooner to conquer this temporary tyranny from people so despicable that I cannot fear them. I found reflection, and the ardent hope I entertained of escaping composed my spirits. Ah! it is well that we know not the evils that menace us. Had I then known, that after I had twice escaped, after I had been restored to my father and to Delmont, this dear, dear mother would not be with us; that we should still deplore her absence yet be ignorant of her fate, I know not that it would have been possible for me to have made any struggle against the insolent oppression I underwent."

Medora, affected by what she had said, could not for a moment proceed. Recovering herself, however, she continued.

"I thought I might securely go to bed; and indeed I so greatly wanted repose that I know not if any thing but the certainty of being disturbed by the daring intrusion of Darnell could have given me strength to remain without some repose. I knew, however, that my slumber, if I could obtain it, would be such as it had been the preceding night, when the slightest noise was to me an *alerte*, so much were my fears awake; I therefore went to bed, and slept till sun-rise. The earliest rays of light entered my chamber through the vine leaves, and were hailed by an house-sparrow,[94] which had made its nest among them, and with its loud chirping, the monotony of the chaffinch and the robin, and the shrill short shriek of the swallow, announced the approach of day even before the sun was above the horizon. I found myself restored greatly when, after I had done what I could to supply the want of a more comfortable change of clothes, I sat down to consider once more of my situation, and felt the morning air blow sharp and fresh from the hills or wolds; high heathy lands which I saw beyond the house for some miles. My doubts now were whether I should be confined or no? of which I imagined the transactions of the day would be sufficient for me to judge. The scene soon opened by the entrance of Mrs. Darnell, who once more undertook to try her eloquence. She affected the sensible matron who knew the world, and retailed, like many other preachers, an infinite number of very wise and very true saws and sayings, to every one of which her whole life had probably, and certainly her present conduct, formed the most glaring contradiction. I forebore, however, to remark this, and even let her say what she would, contenting myself, when she seemed nearly to have exhausted her logical powers, with asking her, whether she really thought any thing could justify Mr. Darnell's conduct towards me? The woman still affected to believe that I had encouraged him; that I had even consented to elope with him; and I found my absolute and firm denial of it as vain as were the expressions of scorn and abhorrence, which certainly I did not spare, but I was not absolutely confined. The lady bade me walk with her in the garden, and I obeyed, glad of every opportunity to survey the place, from which I was determined to attempt my escape. The garden, however, was surrounded by a wall high and thick enough to have been designed for a defence at the time it was built, which was, I dare say, three centuries ago; it seemed impossible ever to surmount, by any powers I could exert, so formidable a barrier, and I regarded it with that sickness of the soul which is truly said to be the consequence of disappointed hope.

"Mrs. Darnell still took every occasion to exhort me to a due consideration of my own interest, and pleaded her son's passion with at least more warmth, though certainly with as little effect as he did himself. From the sight of the old lady to whom the house belonged I was concealed; but I had an opportunity of seeing her as I passed by the door of her chamber, and beheld a melancholy example of extreme old age;

Of second childishness and mere oblivion;[95]

And I believe she was entirely ignorant of the whole transaction, in which, however, it is probable Mrs. Darnell had a share even from the first.

"Three days had passed, the greatest part of which I had passed in the room where I slept; for at no other time would Mrs. Darnell suffer me to be absent from her sight. They had no reason to flatter themselves that they had made any progress in their design, for my coldness and aversion would have appeared to increase, if to increase were possible; I spoke in the plainest terms of my resolution never to change my mind in regard to Mr. Darnell; and I believe they were very much at a loss how to proceed, yet saw that their retreat was not unattended with danger. In reconnoitring the garden, even attended as I was, I had observed an old green house, which had long since been dedicated to no other purpose than keeping plants hung up for their seeds to dry, pots, mats, garden tools, and lumber, but there was a door opened in the back of it into a lane, as I saw by pushing against it at a moment when Mrs. Darnell was giving some directions to her gardener. I was almost sure that even if it was locked it was so much decayed that I could force it open. The difficulty was how to get into the garden unperceived, and at an hour when I should not be missed, and to accomplish this I bent my whole thoughts, making light of the hazards I might afterwards have to encounter in a country to which I was a stranger, and which appeared to be remarkably wild and desolate.

"The closet within my room, which had on the first night of my arrival been the subject of my dread, now I hoped offered the means of my escape, for I had discovered that the iron bars of the windows were a part of the casement, and not fastened to the stone work, and I believed I could force myself through it, and descend by the help of the vine, which covered also this side of the house, and was so old that the enwreathed branches seemed capable of supporting a greater weight than mine."

Delmont shuddered—"And had you," said he, "my Medora, courage to undertake this perilous experiment?"

"It was not so great an effort of courage, Delmont," replied she. "How often have I heard of greater hazards incurred by girls to fly from their parents; I thought, I hoped, that I was hastening *to* mine, and hastening too," added she, "from a man I detested to one who had all my love, all my confidence, and with whom I was sure of finding happiness."

To put an end to the acknowledgments Delmont began to make for so sweet and voluntary a declaration of her affection, Medora hastened to proceed with her narrative.

"I knew this way was the only one by which my getting out of the house was possible, for I had tried the maid, and had been repulsed; I had learned too that all the doors were locked every night, and the keys carried to Mrs. Darnell; and there was an house dog in the yard, which she assured me would tear to pieces any stranger who should venture about the buildings of a night. This dog was my principal dread; but of my confinement I saw no end, and it was absolutely necessary for me to hazard something; I perceived that the hope of this woman and son was, that in proportion as my absence from my mother and abode with them was procrastinated, I should consider my marriage inevitable, and be induced to consent to it. While I, alas! thought that my mother's not hearing from me might occasion to her illness or death.—On the third day of my most unwilling residence, however, an opportunity offered, which I seized, to write to you. A travelling Scotchman came to the house: Mrs. Darnell, always eager after dress and fashions, ordered him in, and her son insisted on presenting us with muslins and ribbons. I positively refused to accept any thing, but left the room, and snatched up a pen, with which I wrote the few words you have told me you received at Upwood. I did not till then know the house I was in was in Yorkshire, and the name, whether Dartnell or Darnell, I was yet less perfect in, because I always suspected it was not really the name borne by the man, or at least not by his mother, who had had several husbands; but I wrote in such haste and dread that I knew not what were the words I put on the paper, which having with trembling hands sealed and directed, I ran down again to the pedlar, and for almost the first time in my life uttered a sentence meditated to deceive. I told Mrs. Darnell that I should be extremely glad to purchase some linen and a gown, as nothing could be so distressing as my present want of clothes. The foolish woman, with whom the fineries of dress were of the utmost importance, believed me. I chaffered with the man, though by no means well informed of the price I ought to have given; while she, pleased in believing I began to be reconciled to my destiny, beckoned her son out to tell him how he should manage the little gallantry of presenting me with these things. This was beyond my hopes; I hastily gave my letter to the man, entreated him to put it into the post, and assured him, that on applying to my mother, whose address I gave him, he should be handsomely rewarded. I told him I had no money to make any purchases, and would not accept them from the person who lived there; but I begged he would accept for his trouble the half guinea I gave him. The man seemed willing to oblige me; and on the almost instantaneous return of my persecutors, I excused myself as well as I could from my intended bargains, and retired; trusting that the pedlar would not betray me, and knowing my situation could not be materially worse if he did.

"Mrs. Darnell and her son were both in very good humour at supper; they hardly doubted now of their final success, and seemed already to be allied to, and to possess the fortune of the coheiress of M. De Verdon, for so this sapient Mr. Darnell had heard from Brownjohn that your poor Medora certainly was; and it was Brownjohn who, in consequence of that persuasion, had contrived with his brother the honourable exploit he now thought he should most undoubtedly execute so happily.

"It was in the exultation of his heart, enlivened and elevated too by a considerable quantity of strong beer, that during supper he betrayed to me these particulars. I suffered him to prate and parade of his schemes and projects; and as I never checked his impertinence so little, he seemed at last disposed to carry it farther, and began to leer at me in a most disagreeable way, and to recal some of his scraps of plays; but afraid his mother would leave us, I quitted the room so hastily that he had no power to prevent me, and disregarding his entreaties as he followed me half way up stairs, I locked the door of my room, and he was compelled to repeat to 'the silent moon his enamoured lay,' which I heard him do for some time at the stair-case window to my very great annoyance; and still more was I disquieted by his folly when he came to my door, and quoted from I know not what plays an infinite deal of nonsense, in a tone which he probably thought very theatrical. I collected, however, from his murmuring lower and lower, and speaking more and more inarticulately, that the effects of what he had drank would soon prevent his continuing to molest me. His mother, apprehensive that he might lose the ground she imagined he had gained in my favour, came up, and in a whisper persuaded him to retire. The whole house soon became quiet, and I prepared with a beating heart for my evasion.

"The moon, only in its first quarter, was fading away. I ventured to open the closet window. The wind had risen, menacing a storm, and I saw the branches of some great walnut-trees, which were in a close[96] adjoining to the garden, bend and sway with violence before it. This was in my favour; for the rattling of the old doors and windows, and the fluttering of leaves, would prevent any noise I might make from being attended to. I adjusted my clothes as well as I could, put my night linen and cloak into my pockets, and tied my hat under my chin, and then with all the resolution the urgency of the case required, I mounted on the window seat, and began to try to descend, finding a footing on the vine branches, which befriended me more than I had dared to hope. I held by some while I stepped on others; once one of them loosened from the wall, and I had very nearly fallen; but I leaped down, and found myself on my feet on the ground, with no other hurt than some scratches on my arms from the nails and roughness of the wall, which was not so high as my fears had represented it. I lost not a moment now in hastening away, yet trembling so much for fear of the dog that I could hardly move. I heard no noise, however, and hurried, breathless, and looking behind me at every step, towards the old green house. It was immediately before the windows of the back front of the house; yet I trusted that none would at that hour be on the watch. My heart now fluttered least either of the doors of the greenhouse should be fastened; and when I tried the first, the excess of my fear prevented me some time from opening it, but it was not locked; and I entered the greenhouse, which was almost entirely dark. I stopped to recollect on which side was the door opening to the lane that I had perceived the day before. Oh! there is no conveying an idea how my foolish heart beat, when, as I stood in this old gloomy place, I heard the rustling of the dried pot herbs, and at length something move among them, and softly, softly, step among the matting; it was the garden cat; she came closer, purring and caressing me, and I never remember a sensation more welcome than the certainty that my fears had at that moment been excited only by this inoffensive animal. I now acquired composure enough to find the door; it was fastened, and dread again seized me. I felt about for the bolts, and found them, but could draw only one of them. All my efforts were fruitless with the other, though I applied my whole strength, and I then gave myself up for lost—for a moment I was under the necessity of leaning against the wall to recover my breath, and consider to what expedient I could have recourse. I thought a stone or an iron tool might assist me, and began, though in almost perfect darkness, to search for one, and fortunately I found in the window, to which the little light without doors guided me, a piece of broken iron rake. I returned then with better hope to the inexorable bolt, and at length it gave way before my perseverance. The door was open, and I was in the lane.

"I was again compelled to stop to recover my breath. I looked round me, undetermined which way to go; and indeed I had not yet considered whither to bend my steps if I succeeded in escaping from my prison, the prospect of getting out alone filling my whole mind.

"My situation was still most distressing—I was alone, unprotected, and a stranger—I had not the least idea which direction it would be safe to take to lead me *from* my pursuers, and *to* some place from whence I might find a conveyance to London. But it is, perhaps, only those who have felt themselves in the power of people they at once dread and despise, who can judge how much less wretched any situation appeared than it would have been to have remained in the house I had left. I was, I hoped, free from that odious Darnell, and every other evil seemed light.

"Fortunately I took the way, though by mere chance, that led to a common;[97] and in about half an hour I reached a more sandy and beaten tract, which would, I thought, if I followed it, conduct me to a village or a town. I went on near a mile, and approached the entrance of another lane, but I then found it necessary to sit down, for I feared that if I fatigued myself too much, I should be overtaken by the morning light before I could reach any place that might be an asylum against pursuit. It was better to manage my strength, and not to exhaust it all at once.

"I rested myself, therefore, in a sort of hollow way worn by heavy carriages at the entrance of this lane, and listened to the dull night noises, congratulating myself that all was so quiet; for only the bells of a few sheep that fed on the common, and at a great distance the sound of a water mill, and now and then the barking of a village watch dog, came in the pauses of the wind, which had now much abated of its violence; but judge, my dear friend, of my apprehension and astonishment, when all at once I heard, and as I thought immediately near me, the yell of human voices, of men and women, either in riotous frolic or drunken contention; some laughed, some hooted, others sang or swore, and two or three were quarrelling and uttering words of abuse and menace. I cannot describe what I felt at that moment; I cannot recal it without shuddering. The noise seemed, I thought, approaching me. Oh! yes, there was no doubt but that it came nearer and nearer, and now it was so near that I could distinguish oaths, curses, and threats. How my heart sickened at the dread of falling into such hands! What or who could they be? and was it of me they were in pursuit?— Away fled all the fortitude I fancied I had collected and could exert! Terror absolutely deprived me of my breath. These people, for I heard the voices of women among them, were either villagers sent in pursuit of me by Darnell, or they were night ruffians, vagabonds, gipsies, or some such associated marauders; and the very idea of being in the power of such persons was more terrific than that of even Darnell himself, for of him my contempt abated my apprehension.

"I sat still, however, because I had no power to move, and thought that it was impossible I could escape from this party, of whatsoever persons it was composed; but fortunately they took the way above the excavation of sand-rock where I sat, and I crept closer within its crumbling hollows, as I heard them walking immediately above my head. They passed; I listened, and their voices became fainter and fainter, yet I continued to hear them, and I now dared not move from the place where I was, for still at intervals came the voices that so alarmed me; and therefore I fancied I could not move without rushing into perils that my very soul recoiled but to think of.

"In one of the longest intervals of silence I crept up the bank, and looked over it around the heath; then I heard the sounds of terror more distinctly, and looking towards the side where they seemed to come from, I perceived a barn, which I concluded was the rendezvous of some nightly depredators (either robbers or gipsies, or both) for smoke issued from it, as I could now plainly distinguish, and the wind came loaded with loud noises of singing, hallowing, and quarrelling. The morning was just dawning—I dreaded least issuing from their den any of these ruffians should discover me where I was; I dreaded, least on the other hand, the persons who would undoubtedly be employed by Darnell should overtake me as soon as I was missed, whether I staid in or left this place of concealment. The light, however, rapidly advanced. The song of the larks, to which I had so often delighted to listen, now on this wide plain, as it announced the appearance of the sun above our horizon, seemed to tell me only of danger and horror, while the probability of discovery appeared greater than ever. The noise, however, of the men, gradually sunk away, and I hoped that, like other animals of prey, those which had occasioned to me so much terror were retired to their rest for the day.

"Yet how pass the lane into which the road led almost close to the barn? how return, to meet directly those whom I had fled from?—Every moment that I debated, the danger became more pressing. It was absolutely necessary to determine on something. Oh! Delmont, how did my heart then swell with painful recollections of my mother and of you; mingling with self pity as I said, 'Most beloved of mothers, and you, my dear Delmont, how little do you know the desolate, the perilous state of your Medora.' Several ploughed fields, and others of grass, adjoined the common. I was in hopes that farmers servants might appear, to whom I could apply; yet even from them I might dread the ill office of being betrayed to the Darnells. At length I heard a village clock at some distance strike seven. It was an hour at which I knew I should be missed; and even while I hesitated, the persons sent by Darnell might perhaps be approaching. I arose therefore, and perceiving that in the lane was certainly the most beaten tract, I hurried along it, looking fearfully towards the barn, from whence I expected to see some of those ruffians appear, whose discordant and hideous voices had so much alarmed me. I passed for about three hundred yards unmolested; at length, at an abrupt turning of the lane, I rushed immediately on a place where two women were boiling something in a kettle, and under a sort of tent, composed of a piece of rug suspended on two poles, a man, a most terrific figure, and a boy, lay apparently half asleep. One of the women exclaimed on seeing me, (for I was within a few paces of them) 'Hey day! what have we here?'—The other gave a sort of shout, which roused the man, who started up, and rubbing his eyes, asked, in a gruff voice, what was the matter. You may imagine that instinctively I hurried on, though well aware that no speed I could make would relieve me from the consequences of these people's pursuit, if to pursue me was their purpose.

"The boy, who appeared about fifteen, and two other bare-footed children, instantly overtook me, and began to beg. I knew not whether it was safest to stop and satisfy their demands or to proceed. I looked back, the man was hastening after me, and, I could perceive, gave a sign to the boy to detain me, for he held me by my gown, clamorously demanding my charity. Heaven only knows what would have become of me; but at that moment a small tilted[98] cart appeared, coming along rather fast, in the same direction. Disengaging myself, I know not how, from my pursuers, I darted towards it, and shrieking rather than speaking, implored the driver, who sat on a little seat before, to receive and protect me. The gipsy man whom I had so much dreaded, now retreated with evident marks of ferocious disappointment, while the driver, who had stopped his horses, said, in answer to my entreaties—"Why, Miss, I'd take you in with all my heart, but we be but a baddish sort of a party. I've got a sick woman and her children in this here cart. They've become chargeable,[99] and not belonging to our parish, the overseers have got an order to move them to Skipton. They says 'tis a sort of a catching fever; and sure enough the poor souls are desperate ill.' 'Oh never, never mind,' cried I, 'what it is; do but allow me to get into your cart, and I will make it worth your while.' The man was not unwilling to oblige me, and got down to help me in.

"I never had seen poverty and misery till this moment; I never had an idea of the degree of wretchedness which the laws of England permit a set of men called parish officers to inflict upon the poor. I will not shock you, my dear friend, with a description of the wretched state of these poor creatures, a woman and three helpless children—Of their disease I could not know much, but it seemed to me to arise from poverty and want of necessary food. The little assistance I could give them on our melancholy way was but their due; for how dreadful was the peril from which their chancing to pass had saved me!—I arrived once more at Skipton, and returned to the inn, from whence I had gone with the wretch Darnell, on his promise to restore me to my mother."

The entrance of Glenmorris now occasioned an interruption; and Delmont seeing Medora much affected at his melancholy looks (which too truly told that he had heard nothing of her mother) he would not suffer her to continue her narrative till the following day, when Glenmorris again going out on the same anxious enquiry, Delmont listened with eagerness to its continuance.

CHAP. XI.

Speránza mia cára non ti ho perdúto, vedrò il t'uo sembiánte,
   i tuoi ábiti, la tuá ómbra; ti amero, telo dirò a te stesso.
   Quali sono i torménti a cui úna tal felicità non ripári?[100]

"As I was now," said Medora, "in the house of a person who had before shewn every disposition to protect me, and who now was willing to promote my safe return to London by a conveyance she pointed out, I endeavoured to calm my spirits, and to recover the terror and fatigue I had undergone, before I began my journey, which it was determined I should do by a coach, on the driver of which Mrs. Tarbat said she could rely, and which was to set out at eleven o'clock the next night from her house, coming from a more northern town to London; I therefore obtained some repose during that night, and the next day, on the evening of which I was to depart, I employed myself in writing a narrative of what had happened to me since I was cheated into quitting the hotel, and I anticipated the satisfaction it would give to my mother and to you, my dear friend, when you found that I had exerted in some degree, and as I hoped successfully, fortitude which did not discredit her instructions and your confidence.

"In this occupation, which I found tranquillised my mind, I employed myself till towards evening, then having occasion for some more writing materials, and no one answering my bell, I ventured along an open gallery, which was carried round in the inn yard, to call a servant, when casting my eyes towards the bar windows, which were open, and opposite the place where I stood, I saw a gentleman who struck me as being so like you, Delmont, that my astonishment, mingled with doubt, with hope, and fear, hardly left me the power of moving. I looked steadily at the person; his back was towards me; but he moved a few paces, and his air, his walk, were surely your's. At that moment one of the housemaids passed me; I eagerly enquired of her if she knew who that gentleman was?—'Oh! yes Miss,' answered the girl, 'It is one Squire Delmont, as his sarvents have been a telling below; he's come out of Ireland, and is a going up to London. He only stops a bit here.' This was enough for me to hear—I considered no farther—To me there was only one Delmont in the world—I ran down stairs, and exclaiming, Delmont, my dear, dear friend! I took the arm of him whom I believed to be that dear friend with the familiarity my mother's approbation had authorised; with all the trembling earnestness so naturally inspired by the delight of seeing you again, and of knowing with what joy you would afford me that protection which would end my perils and my fears. Ah! judge then how severe was my mortification, and how cruel my disappointment, when I found my mistake; when vainly apologizing for it, I was treated as an abandoned wanton, and pursued with insolent professions, such as I never listened to or heard before, and such as by a gentleman could be offered only to one whom he considered as a prostitute."

Delmont, at this passage of Medora's narrative, started up, traversed the room with hasty step, and seemed to make every effort to conquer at least the appearance of the passionate indignation this account of his brother's behaviour had raised in his bosom. Medora, frightened at his emotion, repented that she had used such strong terms, and resolved to pass over as slightly as she could what remained to be told of Major Delmont; yet it was impossible altogether to disguise, and indeed difficult to palliate the circumstances which had driven her away from the inn, and compelled her to assume a disguise in order to escape from this new pursuer.

"You should recollect," said she, as soon as Delmont became once more calm enough to listen to her, "you should recollect that your brother knew nothing of me, or that if he had ever heard me mentioned, it was probably in a way very much to my disadvantage. In short, my dear Delmont, there are perhaps excuses to be offered for his conduct, which do not, which are not likely indeed to occur to me, and which, among men, may greatly serve to alter that sort of proceeding, which at the moment it occurred impressed me with fear. I own I did hope when I explained, or attempted to explain who I was, that I should have found protection from your brother; but I know not why, unless because he had received some false impressions from Mrs. Crewkherne as to my mother and myself, he seemed to disbelieve, and to turn into ridicule all I said, and in a word, for I hate the subject, I was so much terrified, perhaps more so than the occasion called for, by his manner, that I considered my intention of going to London that night as impossible to be executed, unless at the hazard of subjecting myself to treatment and persecution I was not able to think of without greater terror than any former circumstances had impressed upon me. This indeed, Delmont, I do not wholly impute to your brother; his manner might seem to convey more than he intended. I had never seen a man of the world before, and what shocked me as unwarrantable freedom, might be nothing but airs which such men assume without much meaning."

"Do not attempt to palliate his conduct, Medora," cried Delmont; "there is no palliation, no excuse; it was cruel, it was unmanly; it cannot, no by heavens! it cannot be forgiven."

"You will compel me, however," said Medora, "to falsify or stifle the rest of what I have to say. Your violence my dear friend, so unlike yourself, is almost as painful to me as were your brother's humiliating freedoms."

"Go on, my dearest love, and I will repress my feelings; go on," cried Delmont.

"I was very probably wrong in so rashly determining to fly. Impute it if you will, to ill placed timidity, increased perhaps by the recollection of scenes in the few novels and romances my mother had given me to read, in which men of such a description are represented as carrying off damsels, and involving them in very disagreeable adventures. However that might be, whether my fears were well or ill founded, I felt them to be such as rendered my staying where I was, or attempting to return alone in the stage to London, impossible; I therefore resolved, and perhaps with the usual rashness of fear, to escape from the inn, where I began to have doubts of every body, and particularly of the landlady, whose countenance towards me I thought was greatly changed. To set out as I was, however, in handsome but dirty clothes, would, I thought, subject me to new insults, and I supposed it an admirable expedient to change habiliments with one of the chambermaids. Such a bargain was not difficult to make, the advantage being greatly on her side in point of value, while I was much gratified by having a change of clean though coarser linen; and when I saw myself so equipped, I hoped that I might pass unremarked and unmolested along the road, and by some of those conveyances to which inferior servants, and persons in humble life, have recourse, obtain my passage to London, I thought the very little money I had left might serve as earnest; and that when I got thither I could somehow or other make up the deficiency.

"With this project in my head, and in my new dress, I walked, as soon as it was dark, out of the garden door of the inn, and crossing two or three fields found myself at the extremity of the town on the side which I knew was the road to London. I passed several people who took no notice of me; yet every time I saw any body advancing along the road my heart sunk within me, and it was still worse when I heard horse or foot passengers coming from the town, for then I concluded I was pursued. Where the road was wide enough I crept out of the path, and moved as near the hedge as I could. As night advanced, however, passengers of any kind became less frequent, and soon I seemed almost the only being in the wide extent of country around me, thus wandering without a shelter and without protection.

"The gipsy party from whom I considered myself as having so narrowly escaped before, was now remembered as a chief object of terror. If I should again, at this lone hour, encounter such another troop! Oh! how anxiously did I desire to hear the distant bells of a waggon! I listened; but through the stillness of the night no such welcome notice reached me. I walked till I was so weary I could go no farther, and then perceiving, for the night was fine and clear, a field of wheat, part of which was uncut, I got over the style, and making a sort of bed and pillow of the sheaves, which were dry and warm, while the corn yet standing served, I hoped, as a concealment, I wrapt my scarlet cloak around me, which, as well as a linen shawl, was part of my purchase; and then I laid me down, and recommending myself to the protection of God, fell asleep, and for two or three hours my fears and fatigues were suspended.

"When I awoke the stars were fading before the sun, and I was completely roused by hearing very near me several voices, which I concluded to be those of the harvest people returning to their tasks. Unwilling to be found trespassing, I put a few ears of wheat in my pocket, to supply in a small degree the want of a breakfast, and stealing from my friendly concealment, continued along what I supposed to be the high road to London. I was not, however, unmindful of the hazard I ran of being overtaken by Major Delmont, or even by Darnell; yet the latter, I thought, would hardly know me. My greatest dread was of your brother; and I endeavoured to escape from it, by taking the path through fields that bounded the road, wherever such a one could be found; it was a satisfaction to me to find, that several peasants I met, taking me for what I appeared to be, gave me the simple salutation of the morning: 'Good *doiy*, pretty *moiden*,' said the honest Yorkshire labourer, and passed on. Had they known the sickness of heart, the weariness I felt, I am persuaded, however, that they would have acted like the good Samaritan,[101] and that their cottages would have been open to me. I met many little parties going to their harvest-work, others to glean, where the work was completed. One of these groups, a woman and her two children, were passing the way I was; I felt a sort of protection in their company, and exerted myself to keep up with them. The woman inquired whither I was travelling, and from whence I came? I answered, from a service in the north, back to my mother, in a county on the other side of London. I told my story very ill, I believe; however it was very short, and my casual companion did not detect its falsity. I added, that I was in hopes of getting a conveyance part of the way in a waggon; and she then informed me, that I was out of the high London road (I had probably taken the wrong during my night-walk) but that by crossing a few fields, and a copse, which she offered to shew me, I should get into a road that went to London, only not through the same towns; and that a waggon, driven by a very honest man, passed by at four o'clock every evening. I readily accepted her offer to shew me the way to this road, which she said was considerably nearer than my going back again to that from Skipton, and reached about one o'clock the hill, where my conductress assured me, that if I waited I should certainly see a waggon pass. It had, she told me, the finest ring of bells of any team in all their country, and I could not fail to hear it at a great distance. She left me to continue her way, and I sat me down by the way side.

"But I soon found my seat a great deal too public; an horseman passed, who seemed to be one of those men I had been shewn, called London riders; he stopped, looked earnestly at me, and said something of which I only heard enough to know it was extremely rude. He seemed disposed to get off his horse; but I sprang over a ditch and stile, among brushwood and furze, a little farther on, with such celerity that he lost sight of me, for I plunged instantly into a copse which clothed the steep hill, and I heard him endeavour, but in vain, to force his horse over, but failing, he uttered a few curses, and I heard him ride away. Alas! my dear Delmont, how despondingly did your poor Medora think at that moment of her destiny; she seemed doomed to endure every species of insult, every attack from insolence or inebriety, that could discourage and appal her. Faintness from want of food helped to increase the dejection I felt; when making my way farther down the copse, in order to be more completely concealed, I at last threw myself on the ground, and exclaimed, 'I must then yield to my destiny; I must die here. Oh! my mother, shall I never see you more! is it denied to me to shew my tenderness, my gratitude, to the dearest, the best of parents! and my father is not with you! you have not the consolation of weeping with him for your poor girl!—Delmont, may you help to console her—yet, ah! yes, Delmont will himself want consolation.' Fatigue, hunger, and despair, thus combined to oppress me. The more immediate fears, which before had given energy to my spirits, were suspended, and I thought at this moment that I could die rather than make any farther exertion.

"The day was extremely hot; it could not yet be more than two o'clock, and I thought that if I did find courage to exist till four, when the waggon was to pass over the hill, it must be where the sun had less power than in the lately cut underwood where I had stopped. The hanger below me looked thick and inviting; I descended among the roots and brush wood, and was refreshed even to *hear* the murmuring of water. Going still lower, I came to a clear and rapid brook that wandered through the wood, and sometimes spread itself into a small pool, then filtered away through sedges, alders, and willows, till it gushed out again, and from the higher ground, and fell on a gravelly hollow, where it seemed to invite the thirsty and weary pilgrim to partake of its pellucid water. No human foot seemed to have violated its wild banks; they appeared to be the unmolested abode of innumerable birds. Here then, said I, I may rest, for here is no path, and cruel man has not yet polluted this quiet solitude. To me, who had not swallowed any thing since the preceding evening but a few grains of wheat, the water was most tempting. I had been sketching some trees when I was alone in the London hotel, and the sketch being worth nothing, I had folded the piece of strong drawing paper, and put it into my pocket; with a little contrivance it now made a cup, not very lasting indeed, but serving to convey the water, which was most refreshing, to my parched mouth. I immerged my hands in the current, and not having been educated with those fears of wetting my feet which are so general in England, I bathed them also in this friendly stream, and dried them with my handkerchief. The relief, the refreshment I thus obtained is inconceivable; I felt my strength renewed, my spirits return. I rested yet some time in this delicious nook, and so much are we creatures of accident and of physical sensations, that I was now ashamed of that feebleness of mind which I had but half an hour before yielded to as inevitable. I had regained courage to consider that it would be folly to lose the only opportunity I might have of being carried forward by the waggon the woman had named; I therefore, though reluctantly, was about to leave my friendly shelter and refreshing rivulet, when the distant bells of the horses were borne in the wind. I was now afraid of arriving on the summit of the hill too late; but when I attained it, I looked down the road, and distinguished the waggon, at what I thought, and I believe it was, a mile off, slowly, slowly, dragging its ponderous weight along; yet it seemed a sort of security to me that it was so near—and I sat down as much out of sight as I could to await its arrival.

"The interval was sufficiently long to give me time to reflect on all the hazards I must incur in one of these waggons. Little as I had travelled in England, I had often observed soldiers, sailors, and persons of all descriptions in such vehicles; I might be liable to insult from the waggoner himself; and in short, before the man who drove it came up and spoke to me, I had contrived to render the same thing an object of terror, which had a little before been that of my ardent wishes; however, the man spoke kindly to me; a very decent looking woman was the only passenger, and I consented to get in.

"As we went, this person entered into conversation with me; I told her as much of my history as I thought might interest her in my favour. She advised me by all means go with *her*, boasted much of her place, and told me she was sure I might stay there as long as I pleased, and till I could hear from my friends; that the lady who had hired her was a very good lady, and Sir Harry Richmond, whose family she managed, one of the most *generoustest* gentlemen in all the country. She then endeavoured to represent the danger of travelling in a waggon. Our present conductor, she said, would go no farther than the next market town, and then there would be all sort of folks. In a word, I thought she could have no motive but a real wish to serve me. I considered that I could write from the place whither she invited me to go, and should not fail in a few days to hear from my mother or you; or one of you, perhaps both, might hasten to your long lost Medora, and restore her at once to happiness.

"Flattered with these hopes, and trusting to the good faith of the woman, who could, I thought, have no interest in deceiving me, I consented to go with her. Depressed by excessive fatigue, by want of nourishment, and by the strange situation in which I found myself, I was glad to take the asylum that was offered me immediately on my arrival, in a very neat servant's room, where my conductress soon came to me, brought me some tea, and told me she had mentioned me to Mrs. Crowling, who had sent her to let me know that I should be welcome to stay there as long as I pleased; and that she desired I would take care of myself, ask for any thing I liked to have, and try to get some rest after my fatigue. I had been used to the hospitality of America, where the stranger, of whatever nation or persuasion, is received with the simplicity of patriarchal kindness; and though I had observed nothing that at all resembled it in London (the only place where we had been in England that we did not consider as our home) yet I believed, at so great a distance from the metropolis, might be found such generous welcome as in America I had been accustomed to see. The idea was consoling, but of the transient tranquillity it promised me I could not avail myself till I had written to Upwood, which I did before I lay down to sleep. The letter, however, you never received; undoubtedly it was suppressed.

"Having, as I supposed, dispatched to my mother and to you such information as I believed would bring you immediately to me, and put an end to our mutual solicitude, and imagining myself in a place of safety, I reasoned myself out of that irritable state, which long anxiety, and a succession of dread and of danger had brought me into, and for the first time since the hour of my quitting the hotel, I obtained many hours of undisturbed repose, and awoke to feel once more the delicious illusion of hope. Ah! it was but illusion; but for some few days it amused a mind which would otherwise have sunk under such long protracted sufferings.

"As soon as my supposed friend Sarah informed Mrs. Crowling that I was up and dressed, that fine lady took the trouble to come to me. I never saw a more disgusting affectation of the manners of a gentlewoman than this woman displayed. She had been, I believe, what is called handsome, if two great full black eyes starting out of their sockets, and a shewy but coarse complexion, had in her youth made amends for an unpleasing expression of countenance; she was tall and confident, and had a something of a daring and masculine air both in her walk and manner, which there is no describing. She looked at me while I was speaking to her, as if she was to make a memorandum of my features; and I shrunk from her big round eyes in uneasiness, and even in some degree of terror; yet she spoke soothingly to me, and seemed trying to engage me in an account of my name, and all circumstances that had happened; in fact, by her artful questions she obtained more than I meant to have told her, but my name I resolutely, as I fancied, concealed. She knew, however, that I was not what my appearance, as well as my first account of myself, had indicated, and instead of treating me like a servant, she desired me to consider myself as her visitor, insisted on my accepting other clothes, and so oppressed me with kindness, that nothing but my ignorance of the existence of such characters of her's would have prevented my seeing that she was over-acting her part.

"I declined, however, every thing she offered me from her wardrobe, that might alter my appearance above the upper classes of the rank I had assumed, and in which I wished to continue (only being suffered to remain in my own room) rather than to be dressed and considered as her visiter, which I thought would expose me to remarks and inquiries that I was on every account solicitous to avoid. I was equipped therefore with clean linen, a plain brown cotton gown, and a straw hat tied with brown ribbons, which was the plainest dress I could select among many she offered me for my choice, and which, except that the gown was too big, did tolerably well. I begged of her to give me some work, and allow me to sit in the room I slept in, adding, that it could not be many days before I should hear from my friends, who would, I knew, help me to acknowledge the kindness I thus received. I should do, she said, as I pleased; if it amused me, she would send some muslin, or any other light work I desired; and as to staying in my own room, I was entirely at liberty, only she hoped, as I was quite alone, I would do her the favour of dining with her. This I could not refuse on the second day of my abode (for on the first I did not leave my bed-chamber) and I found her alone, waiting for me to partake of a dinner which I own I was surprised to see in the house of a steward, for it was sent up with a degree of elegance which is not often seen in middling life, and consisted of fish, venison, and poultry, with pastry, a desert, and ices. Mrs. Crowling, while we sat still at table, took occasion to speak of the large fortune and great generosity of Sir Harry Richmond, who was, she said, one of the best men in the world.—'My dear Mr. Crowling,' said she, in a sort of canting tone, which almost tempted me to smile, 'My dear Mr. Crowling is Sir Harry's bosom friend, and they live more like brothers than patron and servant. Oh! he is an excellent man. No man knows better how to enjoy a fine fortune than Sir Harry; and yet he does abundance of good—vastly charitable—all the poor, I assure you, hereabouts are supported by him; and then he is most exceedingly clever; it is delightful to hear him talk, he has so much wit—he makes one ready to die a laughing at his wit. He is vastly approved of, I assure you, by certain great people; they say they never laugh so much as when Sir Harry is of the party—he has such a funny way, and says such a number of comical things; and as he is always chairman at our quarter sessions,[102] he makes fine sport upon the bench, and it is the drollest thing in the world to hear him hoax any of the rest of them that pretend for to be in opposition, and badger the witnesses whenever he can, and put the counsellors themselves quite out of countenance.' I know not how long this description would have lasted, which was, however, far from giving me a sublime idea of the person for whom the eulogium was intended; but I had at that moment the glimpse of some man passing the windows of the room where we sat, and Mrs. Crowling, affecting surprise, said, 'Dear me! if here is not Sir Harry himself. Lord, I declare, I did not know he was returned to Ardley Forest.[103] Dear! oh! here he comes.' The door opened, and Sir Harry appeared. He made a bow that might have passed rather for a familiar nod. 'Servant, servant, Mrs. Crowling; how do you all do?' 'Oh! law, Sir Harry, I did not know you was come home, Sir Harry. Hope you're quite well, Sir Harry.' I cannot repeat the dialogue. Imagine a sort of quaint conde-scension on one part, and the most abject fawning on the other. I saw the man look now and then at me in a very odd manner. I felt very uneasy, and though Mrs. Crowling almost insisted, and Sir Harry took my hand and entreated me to stay, I seized the first moment it was possible to escape to my own room. Alas! this interview had been settled between them, and was intended only to give Sir Harry a sight of your poor Medora. The woman was a wretch he employed for the most infamous purposes. I knew not that there were such women in the world; yet I extremely disliked both her and this Sir Harry, and determined, at whatever risk, to leave the place. I have since learned that the dairy woman, whom I thought so much my friend, was herself a creature employed by Mrs. Crowling; and that her being hired as a servant was a mere pretence, for that she had been sent beyond Newcastle to inveigle away the wife of a miller, whose extraordinary beauty had in one of his northern tours attracted Sir Harry; but he had conducted himself with so little prudence that the miller had given him a severe beating, which, though he dared not complain of it, added another bad passion, that of revenge, to those he had felt before, and Sarah, whom he had long employed as a deputy to Mrs. Crowling, had been dispatched to try some of those artifices which had often succeeded before, but which had now failed completely; so that having met your luckless Medora on the road, and knowing that youth, and a person only not ugly, were always approved of by Sir Harry as long as they had the recommendation of novelty, she had engaged me to go with her."

"I tremble," exclaimed Delmont, "when I think, my dear love, that you were among such people. How was it possible you could by any fortitude, any exertion of your own, escape from them?"

"It would, indeed, have been difficult," replied Medora; "for the moment (which happened the next day after that I have been speaking of) that I understood from Sir Harry's behaviour into what hands I had fallen, I rejected his insolent offers with the scorn and abhorrence they deserved, and resuming my former humble dress, declared plainly my resolution to leave the place, and menaced the wretch and his agent with the vengeance of my family, if they presumed to make the least attempt to detain me. Alas! Delmont, while I thus put on the semblance of courage, my heart sunk within me; and I said to myself, 'Unhappy girl! where are the friends of whose protection you boast? From your father an immense ocean divides you; Delmont is perhaps still in Ireland; Armitage seems to have forgotten the trust he undertook; and for your mother, your dear and tender mother, who knows whether she has not sunk under the troubles she before had to contend with, aggravated by the loss of her daughter!'

"The high tone I assumed seemed to be a matter of amusement to that detestable Sir Harry; it had, however, one very ill effect; I was watched; and though for the four days I staid I was not actually confined, yet Mrs. Crowling assured me in plain terms, that I should be shut up if I made any attempt to escape; and she had the audacity to add, that *she'd* take care of me till I could be returned safe to my friends, for she had no doubt, notwithstanding the prudish airs I chose to give myself, but that I had run away with some young fellow for Scotland, who had left me in the lurch for an artful girl, as she was afraid I should prove; adding, 'how else indeed should pretty Miss, in a fine romantic disguise, and fancying herself like Pamela,[104] I suppose, in the novel, be found rambling alone about our country? A likely story truly, that she came so many miles against her will! Who's dupe enough to believe that, I wonder!'—No my dear friend," continued Medora, "I should not, perhaps, have now told you my sad history, if a good angel had not been sent to interpose for me; this was Miss Richmond, who, I have since believed, had notice of my being in the house from a young woman who lives there, and who, from whatever motive, contrived to let the admirable daughter of Sir Harry know I was an unwilling resident under the roof of Mrs. Crowling. Miss Richmond contrived, and undoubtedly by the assistance of this young person, to have me conducted in the dead of the night to the mansion house; I saw her; I told her all but my name, which for many reasons I thought it better to conceal. Truth, thank God, never loses its power over an ingenuous mind. Miss Richmond believed me, and contrived my escape that very night with such successful rapidity, that on the evening of the next day, attended by an old servant of her's, on whom she could depend, I found myself at the house of Mr. Meyricke, in London; and then having no fear of pursuit, I was contented oh! I was most happy, to be put into the stage, which I knew would set me down the same evening within six miles of Dalebury and Upwood—there only I could enquire for my mother, of whom I could hear nothing in London; and there only I thought myself secure of meeting her and you.

"A few miles from London the coach took up a chance passenger—My head and heart were too full for conversation, which I therefore very unwillingly listened to, when this gentleman spoke; he spoke not long, however, you may imagine, before I threw myself into the arms of that dear father, who, on the first hint of our pecuniary distresses from the protested bills, and my mother's doubts how to act as to the prosecution of our law suit, had hastened across to Halifax, and the packet being that very day on the point of sailing, had, after a very favourable passage, reached England."

CHAP. XII.

*Si l'homme sçavoit rougir de soy, quels crimes non seulement
cachez, mais public et connus, ne séparneroit' il pas?*[105]

From expressions of those mingled emotions, which such a narrative had given rise to in the heart of Delmont, he was diverted by a letter brought to him by Clement, which a servant had just left at his lodgings. He eagerly opened it at Medora's request, who now referred every thing that happened to some information about her mother—
It was to this effect:

Sir,
Accident having lately discovered to me, that you are much interested
in the fate of a very near relation of mine, I avail myself of the very
slight acquaintance I had the honour of making with you, while with
Miss Richmond, and am persuaded your candour will allow for the
apparent singularity of my requesting to see you here, as what I have to

inform you of cannot so well be communicated by letter. I have the honour to be,

Sir, your most obedient servant,

M.G. CARDONNEL.
——Street,
Grosvenor Square, Thursday.

Delmont immediately gave this letter to Medora, who exclaimed, "It is my mother she means! Oh! hasten, Delmont, immediately; I conjure you lose not a moment! If we can but discover her—if she is but restored to us!—Perhaps, my dear friend, at the very instant I was concealing my name from Miss Cardonnel, she might, if I had revealed it, have directed me to this dear mother; and who knows what she has suffered since! what she may endure at this very time.

The impatience of Delmont was equal to that of Medora. A thousand uneasy conjectures as to the fate of Mrs. Glenmorris had tormented him, though he had feared to reveal them all, and he was affectionately attached to her, as well on account of her own merit, as because the happiness of Medora was so closely interwoven with her safety. He now hurried with a palpitating heart to the house of Lady Mary de Verdon, where he understood Miss Cardonnel expected him, entreating Medora not to leave her lodgings till he, or till her father, returned.

He found himself affected so as to repress his emotion with difficulty, and to tremble and hesitate as he made his compliments to Miss Cardonnel, who was alone in the withdrawing room; but the agitation he remarked in her extremely added to his confusion. Miss Cardonnel was now pale, now red; seemed unable to begin the subject, yet more so to speak on any other. The longer this hesitation and embarrassment continued, the more painful it became. Delmont at length found voice to say, "I consider myself greatly honoured, Madam, in being allowed to wait upon you, and have great hopes that your benevolence will restore to a husband and a daughter, who are now extremely wretched, the blessing they have lost."

"An husband, Sir!" asked Miss Cardonnel—"What then is Mr. Glenmorris in England?"—She became still more agitated as she spoke; but while Delmont was answering her enquiry, she appeared to make an effort to recover herself, and in a low voice proceeded.

"If any thing could add to the pain I have suffered from the circumstances that have come to my knowledge relative to Mrs. Glenmorris, it would be the necessity I am under of arraigning the conduct of one whom I venerate and respect. My grandmother, Lady Mary de Verdon . . . . ."

She again paused.

"Has in some way or other," said Delmont eagerly, "been the cause of Mrs. Glenmorris's disappearance."

Miss Cardonnel now saw that what share Lady Mary had in this mysterious transaction might appear more cruel than it really had been; she therefore began, though with evident difficulty, to relate the circumstances that had accidentally thrown

Mrs. Glenmorris into the power of her mother. "I will not," said she, "affect to say, that Lady Mary might not, from her own desire to secure to me a fortune which she thinks necessary to my happiness, (though I assure you I do not) have taken every advantage, and some perhaps that were altogether unjustifiable—yet I believe I may say Lady Mary would not have acted as she has done, unless she had been influenced by persons, who, besides their wishes for *me*, which I could most willingly dispense with, have some pique against the unhappy lady, who has been so severe a sufferer."

"And where is she now, Madam?" cried Delmont, breathless with concern and astonishment, "Can I see her? can I hasten to her? not a moment should be lost. Good God, Mrs. Glenmorris, the mother of my Medora, in a mad house! Confined, ill treated, driven perhaps by despair to the very state which could be originally only a pretence to commit such wicked injustice."

"You cannot be more sensible than I am," said Miss Cardonnel, "of the injury that has been done a person for whom I have the tenderest esteem—You cannot be more distressed to hear than I am to tell, that Mrs. Glenmorris, within these few days, has found means to leave her confinement, and to wander away alone."

"And why not?" cried Delmont. "If she is not mad, and who will assert that she has ever been so? If she is not mad, wherefore should she be a moment subjected to this infamous oppression? I beg your pardon, Miss Cardonnel; I am convinced that you have no participation in this cruel business; that you are incapable of it; let me urge you then to assist me in putting an end to it for ever. Give me the name of the place where this victim of a mother's inhumanity languished. I can trace her from thence, and find her, perhaps, before her husband and her daughter are shocked by intelligence that must so cruelly disappoint all their future hopes."

Miss Cardonnel with a trembling hand wrote the direction; and Delmont, who saw how much all that had passed had affected her, could not forbear saying, "Pardon me, Miss Cardonnel, if I say, that it seems to me incomprehensible that you, who seem to have, nay, who I am sure have so good an heart, should have lent your countenance to the imprisonment, for what else can it be called? of Mrs. Glenmorris."

"Alas! Sir," replied she, "it is a melancholy truth, that at the time that happened, Mrs. Glenmorris was in a state of such mental derangement, that it was impossible for me to oppose the decision made by my grandmother, certainly at the instigation and by the persuasions of Mrs. Grinsted.—Believe me, Mr. Delmont (the tears ran down her cheeks as she spoke), believe me, that had I been permitted I would have attended on that dear unfortunate woman with the assiduity of a daughter; I would not have left her to strangers in that condition, to which, though I now believe it was only temporary, her cruel loss had certainly reduced her; but Lady Mary, far from allowing me personally to alleviate her sufferings, would not permit me to be told where she was; I was even the more readily allowed to go to Ardley Forest, because Mrs. Grinsted observed that I was extremely restless about my aunt, whose confinement she certainly wished, I know not for what reason, to perpetuate. Indeed I do not know that Lady Mary would have thought of such an expedient, if the people about her (and it is by the upper servants you know that persons of her age are oftenest governed) and Mrs.

Grinsted had not persuaded her to adopt it; the latter enforcing on her mind for a certainty, that the action she thus agreed to was doubly meritorious, inasmuch as she would at once take care of her daughter, however unworthy she was of her maternal solicitude, and put an end, and in the most effectual manner, to what Mrs. Grinsted called an unjust and invidious attempt to take from dear Mary Cardonnel her undoubted right. Lady Mary listened with avidity to counsel that so well agreed with her own feelings; and her resolution was confirmed by I know not what lawyers; who were sent for hither, and closetted with Mrs. Grinsted and that most odious of all odious men, Sir Appulby Gorges. My poor grandmother, whose great age may be some excuse for her being so easily misled by these unworthy people, acted, or rather they acted for her in pursuance of what was decided at this conference. As I could not help betraying many symptoms of uneasiness, I was hurried with my grandmother into the country, from whence I was soon dismissed with Miss Richmond, Mrs. Grinsted undertaking to stay with Lady Mary during my absence. The place where Mrs. Glenmorris was confined I knew only lately, and by accident; and I have reason to believe that her real situation has, from the first certainty of her recovery, been concealed from Lady Mary, who so far from believing she was acting with cruelty and injustice, was, from the representations made to her, taught to imagine that she was doing her duty towards her daughter, and saving her from I know not what guilty connection, which Mrs. Grinsted and Mrs. Crewkherne together had persuaded her Mrs. Glenmorris had formed."

"Infamous!" exclaimed Delmont; "most infamous! To this odious falsehood it is owing that Mrs. Glenmorris has been exposed to every distress; that her daughter has been torn from her; and that she has been driven into a madness, and at length perhaps to beggary—her daughter . . . . ."

"As to my cousin," said Miss Cardonnel, who seemed glad to have an opportunity of calling her so; "my grandmother is firmly persuaded that she voluntarily eloped with some man, almost a stranger to her; and though I have now reason to believe this, like the rest, was the cruel misrepresentation, if not absolutely false, contrived by this knot of men, who seem to have derived an unaccountable pleasure from the sufferings of my unhappy relations, yet I fear it will be extremely difficult, if not impossible, to obliterate from the mind of Lady Mary these impressions, which perhaps were too willingly received at first, and have been so long cherished. Age is naturally tenacious of its opinions, and perhaps my grandmother a little more liable to prejudices than most other persons. My reverence for her does not prevent my being sensible that she is of a very unforgiving temper, and has to a great degree that weakness or obstinacy which I have read of as common to persons of her rank, of whom it is alledged, that having once received a prejudice against any one, they never will take the trouble to consider whether it be well or ill founded; and even when it is shewn them to be unjust, persist in it rather than allow they could be in an error, and rather than be fatigued with explanations."

Delmont, charmed with the candour and understanding of Miss Cardonnel, as well as with the affection with which she seemed to consider her relations, could not forbear expressing his admiration of her virtues; adding, "Believe me, Miss Cardonnel, when I assure you, that if ever Mrs. Glenmorris and her daughter should reunited have together the comfort of knowing you, they will feel more real pleasure in having such a friend than any participation of your fortune can bestow; and against you I dare believe they will never appear as opponents." Delmont then, eager to set out in search of Mrs. Glenmorris, took a respectful leave, and Miss Cardonnel saw him depart with sensations, which, if envy could have had any place in so excellent an heart as her's, would have made the poor and almost portionless Medora the object of that passion.

He no sooner got into the street than he began to consider what he ought to do. Medora, who was fully persuaded that the note of Miss Cardonnel alluded to her mother, would be impatient for his return; but how divulge to her what he had heard? how disclose to her, that after having been confined as a lunatic, her mother was become a wanderer, perhaps again distracted by fears and terrors for her, and again exposed to want and insult? how discover all this to Glenmorris; yet how conceal it from either of them? It had always, however, been a rule with him to act openly where it was possible; and after some consideration he determined to relate the truth to Glenmorris, whom he thought he could have an opportunity of consulting without alarming his daughter.

Delmont repaired therefore to the lodgings in Portland Street, and intended to have inquired for the father before he saw the daughter; but Medora was at the window watching his return, and the moment she saw him from it, ran down stairs and met him. "Delmont!" she exclaimed eagerly, "have you seen my father?"

"Your father! No! Is he not returned?"

"Oh no! he has sent hither twice for you, but the man who brought the message would not tell me from whence he came; and he was so strange, so ill-looking a man, that I cannot help thinking something has happened."

"Where can I see the man? How long is it since he has been here?"

"The last time, hardly a moment ago," said Jason, the negro servant. "If your honour pleases I can overtake him."

"Do then, my good fellow," answered Delmont. "No, stay! I'll go with you myself."—He then hastened away with Jason, and was out of sight in a moment, while Medora, fearing she knew not what, breathless, and with a beating heart, listened to every sound, and wearied herself with conjectures.

And some hours this cruel suspense lasted—Glenmorris returned not—Delmont returned not—and all the information Medora could obtain of Jason was, that Mr. Delmont had in Oxford Street overtaken the messenger sent after his master, on speaking to whom he had appeared much confused and *very vexed* (was Jason's expression); that Mr. Delmont had immediately called a coach, into which he got with this man, but Jason knew not whither he ordered it to be driven, for, a stranger in London, he had no recollection of the names of streets. Medora from this account became more uneasy than ever; yet there appeared no remedy for her uneasiness, for she knew not whither to go nor of whom to enquire. Night came on, but still nobody arrived; even late hours approached, but neither her father or her lover appeared. At last, about half past eleven, a loud rap was heard at the door. Medora, too impatient to wait till the message could be brought up stairs, ran half way down. A person entered, but it was neither Glenmorris or Delmont; it was Mr. Armitage.

He met her, and in his usual friendly and paternal way took her hand. "My dear girl," cried he, "why all this eager solicitude? Why do I find you here?"

"My father! my mother! where are they? and Delmont, too? something is surely wrong? and you, my dear Mr. Armitage," added she, when they entered the room where there were candles; "let me observe your countenance. Oh! all is not right. You come to tell me ill news. Tell me at once if you do, for surely I can bear any thing better than suspense."

"Come, come," answered Armitage, affecting to speak cheerfully, "I will not be questioned in this way by a little inquisitor. What is all this?"

Medora then related what had happened the preceding part of the day, and observing narrowly the countenance of Armitage, saw that he struggled to conceal the effect her account had upon him.

"Well, well," said he, "my dear little girl, as we know not whither to go after these truants, your father and Delmont, we must be quiet; they will come to us no doubt by and by; they know where to find you, and I think you need not doubt the solicitude of both to return to you as soon as they can; it will give them more pain than pleasure to find you thus watchful, thus uneasy. Come, give me a glass of wine and water; you shall drink some with me, and then I shall send you to bed. Good girls should not be rakes you know, and you look already tired."

"No indeed," said Medora, "I shall not think of repose till my father returns. Good God! my dear Mr. Armitage, how can you imagine I can sleep, when there is every reason to believe my father is detained by intelligence of my poor mother, and that the intelligence is unpleasant; for were it otherwise, would not he or would not Delmont have returned?"

Armitage, who was a very bad dissembler, contented himself with assuring her she was mistaken, but he had not courage, and she perceived he had not, to undertake deceiving her by any premeditated falsehood, and it was evident he was himself in so much anxiety, that he could not rally her's. They continued therefore together to listen to every coach that approached, and to start various conjectures, though what Armitage either knew or guessed he carefully concealed from Medora, while she, who knowing nothing, imagined much that was distressing, and dwelt chiefly on her mother, became at length so wretched that Armitage thought it almost cruel not to disclose to her the truth as far as he was acquainted with it.

Between one and two o'clock Delmont's voice was heard in the passage. Armitage with difficulty restrained Medora from flying to him, but assuring her upon his honour he would return to let her know in a moment, she consented to remain quiet, while Delmont, who had sent for him down, took him into a parlour, and said, "I rejoice to see you. Our friend is arrested for a debt due before he left England. It is considerable. I have offered bail with a respectable tradesman whom I knew, but the rascals who have taken Glenmorris have refused it, and he having in his turn refused to go to a spunging house,[106] I have been with him to the Fleet prison,[107] where I have just left him. I am convinced there is something more in it than we know of. Brownjohn has been seen with the attorney employed against him, and it was intimated to me by one of the bailiff's followers, that there were people who were determined at all events to keep him in custody."

Armitage appeared greatly shocked at this account. "Ah! my dear Delmont," said he "what complicated evils are at this moment the lot of our unhappy friends; and how shall we reveal to the lovely girl above stairs an event which is, however, less distressing than that which has befallen her admirable mother—poor Mrs. Glenmorris!"

"You have seen her then?"

"Yes, I have seen her, but in what a state! I know not Delmont, if death itself would not be preferable to so sad a condition. I found her wandering about an absolute maniac, raving for her daughter, and execrating the cruelty of Lady Mary. She had been some days in this deplorable state before I found her, and I fear all help may be now too late. What punishment do they deserve who have occasioned this? Execrable villains! infernal sorceresses! my blood turns to gall when I think of them. Oh! my friend Delmont! we can relieve Glenmorris from their accursed machinations; but who can restore to him his wife? who can give back her mother to Medora?"

Delmont, heart struck, and running over in his mind all the distress that at once awaited his Medora, now heard with increased anguish, the particulars, which Armitage thus related: "I left London," said he, "with a resolution to find this dear unhappy woman if she still existed. It seemed certain from all that passed between you and the porter and his wife, at Lady Mary de Verdon's, that something was known of her in that family. With extreme difficulty I traced her to a confinement, where Lady Mary had placed her, twenty miles south of London. I enquired for her at the house. The people who keep it, positively denied that any lady of the name of Glenmorris either was or ever had been there. They disputed my authority to see, and still more to remove her if she was. I was however sure, by the manner of these people, that they were not ignorant for whom I enquired. After many fruitless attempts, I found out the apothecary who attended the house, and from him extorted an avowal of the truth, under the most positive promise of secrecy towards those with whom my revealing what he told me might injure him. He said then that Mrs. Glenmorris had been sent to that house, undoubtedly, in a state which for the moment authorized her confinement. He related, at some length, the progress of her cure, and her frequent conversations with him, in consequence of which, being convinced that her detention was extremely unjust, he had given it repeatedly as his opinion that she ought to be released; but a lady of the name of Grinston or Grimsted, had been there, and on behalf of Lady Mary de Verdon, her mother, had repeated the order for her confinement, alledging that her mother was her only friend and support, that she was parted from her husband, had been engaged in a discreditable connection, which the worthy old lady was very solicitous to prevent from being known; and that her daughter had eloped from her and was married, therefore such a situation as she was now in, was the only one wherein Lady Mary would support her, of course the only eligible one for her. In consequence of this, every precaution was taken to conceal her residence; and though she was not treated as to discipline like a lunatic, she was still assiduously watched. 'For my own part,' said Mr. Seton the apothecary, 'I felt extremely for this poor lady, who is in truth a most interesting woman, and I did what little I could to alleviate her confinement, since to end it was not in my power. But it was owing to an accident, that at last I was the cause of the desperate resolution she took. I found the lady, who was called in the house Mrs. Tichfield, and whose real name I believe nobody knew but myself, was very fond of fruit; I have a remarkable vine in my garden, and having some very fine grapes, I collected a few of the ripest and finest bunches, and my wife packed them in a little basket, with some of the leaves and some newspapers which were in the parlour—a friend of mine sends the papers to me, though I scarce ever have time to read them. But here, sir,' added Mr. Seton, taking a piece of news-paper out of a drawer, 'this is the paragraph. It was marked on the margin with a pen. "The young lady who lately eloped from————'s, hotel with Captain D***ll, will, it is supposed, be entitled to a very great fortune, as coheiress to the late Gabriel de V————n, esquire. This, however, is disputed by her cousin Miss C————l, and is likely to make well for the gentlemen of the long robe,[108] Captain D***ll being determined to support the pretensions of his fair bride, with whom we understand he is returned from his matrimonial trip, and the young couple are gone down to pass the rest of the autumn at Bogner[109] in Sussex." And here, sir,' continued Mr. Seton, giving me a letter which accompanied this paper, 'is what I received from Mrs. Glenmorris before her departure.

> Sir,
> As you are the only person who have testified any humanity towards
> me, I will not leave this place where I have been most fraudulently and
> unjustly confined, without acquainting you of my departure. The
> paragraph I have marked in this news-paper, accidentally sent me,
> relates to my daughter. Of its truth I am determined to be satisfied, not
> being able to endure life in my present cruel suspence;—I have nothing
> to offer you but my thanks for your kindness, and I wish your happiness.
>
> L.G.
>
> Every enquiry from hence will be useless, and every attempt to stop me
> dangerous, as no person has any right whatever over my person or
> conduct.

"This was written," continued Mr. Armitage, "with a feeble and trembling hand, and blotted in many places with tears. I waited no longer than to hear the particulars of Mrs. Glenmorris's disappearance, and what clothes she wore at the time. I found that at an early hour of the morning she had taken advantage of the absence of the gardener, who was wheeling out the grass he had mown to an unfrequented lane; she had walked away, and was not missed till three hours afterwards, when all search for her was in vain. Not doubting but that she was gone to the place in Sussex, where the paper had reported her daughter to be (though how she could get thither without money I could not imagine) I attempted to trace her, but my endeavours were for some time baffled; I crossed to my own house, where, by letters I found there, I first heard of Glenmorris's arrival, but I thought it better not to acquaint him with what I knew, till more satisfactory information could be obtained. I then went to the place where it seemed to me to be almost certain that Mrs. Glenmorris, misled by the paper I had seen, had gone in search of her daughter.

"There I heard of her; she had sold her watch and some other trinkets for her support, but some information she had received, had induced her to leave the place two days before, and she was gone, the people told me to Rottendean,[110] a few miles beyond Brighthelmstone.

"Thither then I followed her, having sent for Susanne to join me as soon as I found it was probable I was right in my pursuit. I learned that a lady, who was supposed to be disordered in her mind, had two days before taken up her abode at a very poor house in the village; that she had wandered about in the evening either on the shore or on the high cliffs, and the people had been much afraid that though gentle and good natured to them, she meant, in their own phrase, to do herself a mischief.

"Not a moment was to be lost. I was shewn by one of the bathers, who had given me this account, to a very humble cottage—I inquired for the lodger—she was gone, they said, for her evening walk. I bade Susanne accompany me; and we were directed by a fisherman to the place where she was.

"It was on an heap of the fallen cliff, and where other fragments beetled fearfully over head, that the poor mourner sat; her eyes were concealed by her hands, her arms resting on her knees. She seemed listening to the burst of waters on the shore, and to be quite regardless of our approach. I kept a little behind, and bade Susanne, whose voice trembled so as to be hardly articulate, speak to her. 'My dear mistress!' said she—Mrs. Glenmorris did not look up, she only moved one of her hands languidly, and uttered, 'Pray, pray, be gone my good woman!' 'Ah! don't you know me?' cried Susanne, taking her hand, and bursting into tears—Mrs. Glenmorris looked at her—never shall I forget the look!

"'Know you?' repeated she, 'yes, I think I knew you once; but you too, Susanne, if that is still your name, have left me—Yes, I am quite deserted by every body since my child has abandoned me—I am poor and wretched, and persecuted, and have no child, no friend!—none to care for me now, and I came hither to die.'

"'My dear friend,' cried I, then stepping forward, 'this must not be indulged. Come, come, Mrs. Glenmorris, you have been cruelly deceived.'

"'I know it,' answered she, in a low solemn voice—'I know it but too well. Yes, I *have* been cruelly deceived, but who would have thought it possible?' A sigh that seemed ready to burst her heart followed. I said, 'you have been deceived, but not by Medora.' I was afraid of saying too much, fearing that if she comprehended me, which from her now vacant and wandering eye she did not at this moment seem to do, the transition from joy to grief[111] would be so violent, as wholly to overset her injured reason, I therefore spoke to her soothingly and confidently, and suddenly she seemed to recollect me, or at least she had not appeared to do it till, starting from her seat, she held out her hand to me, and said—'a thousand thanks to you, my very good friend, for having taken this trouble; but you will not be offended, if I beg of you not to be seen here,—for,' continued she, speaking very quick, 'Lady Mary, you remember, has declared enmity to you on my account. Oh! you know not half she has suffered people to say; cruel, cruel has been her conduct, cruel indeed to me!——But her causing my child to be taken from me—Oh! that it is which has been the deadly blow, and it has made me almost . . . . almost forget all the rest, except (and she put her hand to her head) except that I would not have any more victims—and who knows, after what Lady Mary has said, what may happen? I am easy, quite easy at present, for if Medora is gone, why should I wish to live? I would see Glenmorris however before I died, if I thought I could bear to meet him now that his daughter is lost; but the very dread of it would kill me, before I could get to America.' I endeavoured," continued Armitage, "to impress on her mind, that nothing of all she seemed to apprehend could happen; but I found the incoherence of her conversation greater, the longer I attempted to reason with her; I could not prevail upon her to allow me to escort her to Upwood or to Dalebury farm, still less would she hear of going to Ashley Combe. She had been happy at all those places with Medora; she said she would never see them more! All I could obtain of her was to allow Susanne to stay with her. Though she often fixed her eyes on that faithful creature with looks of anger and resentment, such as almost broke the poor woman's heart, and such as she said her dear mistress had never, in all the years she had lived with her, looked at any creature with, however they had offended her. In this state I left her, rather calmer however, and ordering Susanne never for a moment to lose sight of her, but if possible to break to her Glenmorris's being in England, and the safety of Medora. I began several times this attempt, but she always stopped me by saying, 'I entreat you, Mr. Armitage, not to attempt to deceive me.— I know the worst.—By the contrivance of my mother, my child has been taken from me.—At last her long meditated curse has been fulfilled. God forgive her, poor un-happy woman, God forgive her.—No, no, Mr. Armitage, none of your pious frauds, your friendly deceptions.—I know the worst—and you see I am not dead!—Time, they say, time cures every thing.—Time will cure me.' She shuddered, and sunk into silence, from which nothing could rouse her; and in fact, my dear friend, it is in vain to flatter ourselves; I do believe her intellects irrecoverably gone. Opposition seems so much to inflame her, that I dared not venture to press even her removing to a better lodging, but I have sent two of my own servants over to attend her; I desired a physi-cian, of whom I have a very good opinion, to see her, but to keep the state she is in a profound secret; and having done this, I hastened hither, as well to soften this severe shock to my poor friend, as to consult with him on his going down with his daughter, and trying how the sight of objects so beloved and lamented, might act on the disor-dered mind of his wife."

"And you find him," said Delmont, "in a prison! and prevented by oppression from flying to the wife he has so long sought, from protecting her and his daughter."

"That, however," replied Armitage, "however distressing it is, can be only tem-porary. My whole fortune, if it is necessary, shall be devoted to release him."

"And mine," interrupted Delmont, "he is already to consider as his own." Delmont now however remembered, almost for the first time since he first knew Medora had disappeared, that his fortune was little better than nominal, for so deeply was it engaged to answer the debts of his brother, that whenever the creditors enforced the payment of those debts, he should not have even Upwood his own. This painful recollection however soon subdued, when he reflected that in consequence of the Major's marriage, he was certainly at this moment in a situation to settle all his pecuniary obligations.

As nothing could be done for Glenmorris that night, the doors of his prison having been long since shut, all that remained was to consider how to conceal from Medora the situation of her father and mother, at least for the night, and in such a case, a pious fraud was undoubtedly allowable. They therefore agreed in telling her that Mr. Glenmorris, having had intelligence of her mother, whom he hoped to find in health and safety, had been detained by his expectations, and his return became uncertain.

"I shall take his place my dear Medora," said Armitage "to night, and shall occupy his room, for as our little heroine has been more than once carried away by 'Paynims vile and wicked Sarracen,' it is necessary some trusty knight should guard her, and modern chivalry is, I am sorry to say, so degenerated, that it is no longer the etiquette to entrust this honourable post to the chosen chevalier of the damsel's heart. Delmont therefore shall retire to his lodgings till to-morrow at an early hour, when he will rejoin us here, and we shall perhaps leave you, my dear Medora, for some hours, with no other protection than Jason, who will faithfully enact the enchanted Moor, against any intruders, for the short time of our absence."[112]

This pleasantry, which it cost Armitage no inconsiderable effort to assume, served in some degree to dissipate the apprehensions that assailed Medora. The countenance of Delmont, who was a wretched dissembler, almost counteracted this attempt at cheerfulness on the part of his friend; but Medora, who had early learned never to appear importunate to those who she knew would entrust her with all it was necessary for her to know, now repressed her uneasiness and suspicion, and as soon as Delmont was gone, retired to her room; Mr. Armitage having informed her he should take the opportunity of writing letters that night, that nothing might impede the business he should have the following day.

To those who have not from sad experience learned what man, in a state of polished society, is capable of executing towards his fellow man, when he can pervert the laws, the customs and prejudices of the community, to the purposes of his passions, it would appear almost impossible that a combination of persons, each acting on different motives, should have the power to oppress, to persecute, and ruin a family; yet so it happened in the instance of Glenmorris. This formidable phalanx consisted of Lady Mary, from whom time had taken every thing but her avarice, her pride, and hatred, against the husband of her daughter, and that daughter herself; Sir Appulby Gorges, who joined against Glenmorris not only from dread of his openly avowed political principles, his enmity to all deceit and corruption, and that manly sincerity which never allowed him to conceal how much he despised such a character as Sir Appulby, (though clad in purple and fine linen, and faring sumptuously every day) but because, if Glenmorris's claims on behalf of his daughter should be established, the fortune of Miss Cardonnel, all of which was not more than enough for Sir Appulby's

ambitious projects for his grandson; would be divided, and enrich a man who had the
insolence to assert, that it was better a great many persons should live in comfort than
that a few such men as Sir Appulby Gorges should wallow in swinish luxury and
selfish indulgences. Totally regardless of every thing, but how to gratify the appetites
he had left, and to enrich his grandchildren, the unfeeling and brutal character of this
old attorney (for he was originally nothing more) became harder and more insolent
every day, as a vicious animal grows more offensive by age; and there was nothing Sir
Appulby Gorges could do with impunity that he was not capable of doing, to add only
a few hundreds, or even a few tens, to the sums he had collected, either while he was
in place, or in consequence of the power his having been in place had given him.
Though he had never had any talents, and only a bustling sort of affected consequence, while he imposed upon those who did not know him for industry and application; and though the small stock of acquired intelligence he ever possessed, was
obscured by the fumes of gluttony, and the imbecility of age, so that he could not now
write a common letter without betraying his ignorance or his indolence, yet was Sir
Appulby Gorges a formidable enemy, in the existing circumstances, to Glenmorris;
for he had a number of retainers around him, men who, though for the most part they
were paid only by hope, were as assiduous as they were base, and there was hardly one
of them who did not possess, in some way or other, the means of injuring a defenceless
stranger who had not money or friends, among the same class of men. As soon as it
was understood that Delmont was most warmly solicitous for the family of Glenmorris,
they became more obnoxious to Sir Appulby; he could not well hate any man more
than the latter, unless it-was the former; of whose legacy, left by Lord Castledanes, as
well as of the sums belonging on the same account to the rest of the Delmont family,
Sir Appulby had in fact long since possessed himself, and though he knew that sooner
or later he must pay these, yet he contrived, with the assistance of his friend Cancer,
the attorney he employed, to raise so many difficulties, to imagine such an infinite
number of precautions, and to use so many of the quirks and tricks which have arisen
like poisonous galls on the branches of the boasted widely spreading oak[113] of English
jurisprudence, that he doubted not of being able to keep possession for some years of
this money, for which he made twenty per cent. while he knew the law would not
oblige him to allow to the proprietors more than *three*. To say nothing of old Cancer
of Gray's Inn (who never failed to stick to any unhappy wretch he fastened on till
mortification and death ensued, but who could only be considered as the creature of
Sir Appulby) the third on the list of Glenmorris's persecutors was Loadsworth, a man
who had taken an aversion to him many years before, and now, though he had almost
forgotten the cause, seemed to have a malignant delight in assisting to do him every
possible prejudice in gratification of this lurking hatred. So little conscious, however,
was Glenmorris of his sullen antipathy, that he had directed him to be employed in
the business of recovering Medora's fortune; and Loadsworth, who had been in habits
of doing such things, made no scruple now of availing himself of the confidence of
Glenmorris, and enlisted himself, armed with all the advantages that confidence might
have given him, under the banners of the opposing party. It happened, however, that
the case was so plain as not to admit of a doubt from any man not predetermined to

raise them, and Loadsworth knew that Medora must eventually possess a very considerable share of her grandfather's fortune; a secret which he had from the very beginning communicated to his friend Brownjohn.

This puffing prater, who contrived, with those as shallow as himself, to make positive assertion pass for sound knowledge, and impudent boasting for eloquence, who was an harpy as inexorable as Cancer, only under a rather less repulsive appearance, having been convinced that he should not ultimately make much, either by acting as the friend or enemy of the Glenmorris's, conceived the very honourable project of marrying his brother to the co-heiress of De Verdon; and by that means aggrandizing his family, and getting into his hands the management of so considerable a property. Darnell himself would never have thought of such an exploit, but he had been persuaded, laughed, and teased into it; for Brownjohn, who would most willingly have been the principal in such a coup de main,[114] especially in a case where he thought there was no father or brother to call him to an account, was unluckily obliged to recommend it to another, it being well known that he had a fine-dressing *wulgar* vife of his own, who had exhibited herself among the crowd of the Margate and Brighthelmstone *wastly genteel wisitors*, every year since he had kept a *carridge*. Brownjohn, who with all his daring volubility, was a wonderfully shallow fellow, had, in common with such sort of men, a great contempt for the understandings of women— He had not the least notion that among them either sense or discernment was to be found, and imagined that a red coat, a tolerable fortune, and a little assurance, would induce any of them to go off with the first young fellow that offered. He no more doubted, therefore, of his own consequence and cleverness, than of the success of the plan he had formed.

The malignant and prying spirit of Mrs. Crewkherne, irritated and stimulated by her desire to aggrandize her family by the marriage of Delmont to Miss Goldthorp, and her inveterate prejudices, as well as her paltry passions, had all been called forth and set in battle array, by Mrs. Glenmorris and her daughter, on account of their personal advantages, their dissent from those forms and ceremonies which made the whole business of her life, and above all from their being under the protection of Armitage, towards whom the venerable spinster avowed a degree of hatred quite inconsistent with her Christian profession, but which her ghostly directors tolerated, not to say encouraged; inasmuch as Armitage, though living in a continued course of beneficence and in charity with all the world, was supposed to have notions on some subjects which, however reasonable, were not *correct*. It was in vain that he restrained himself from any attempt to make converts; never wished to disturb the creed, whether political or religious, of others, and requested nothing but that there might be no attempt to force either the one or the other upon him. Mr. Armitage would long ago have been the martyr of his unobtrusive and simple system of ethics, if these modern saints had, with the spirit of Bonner and Gardner,[115] possessed their power. His last conference with Mrs. Crewkherne had inflamed the zeal of that good lady almost to madness, and she tired every body but herself by raving against him. If that, however, had been the extent of her active malice, no great harm might have been the consequence. But she continued, as well by herself as by her agents and deputy gossips, so to represent him and his connection with Mrs. Glenmorris to Lady Mary—she had so many anecdotes of him, "which she knew to be true," and brought so many proofs which could not be contradicted of his artful and unprincipled deportment, that the impressions thus made, contributed as much as any thing to harden the heart of Lady Mary, and to confirm her, instead of the protectrice, the persecutor and oppressor of her daughter and grand-daughter.

To these were added the officious interference of Mrs. Grinsted, who, deriving her present consequence as she had once drawn her actual support, from her connections with people "*of a certain sort*," could not even though she now loved her ease very much, divest herself of a sort of bustling zeal in their service. She had a perfect conviction that her understanding was of so superior a class, that the moral world would go on much better if she was consulted in its government. She really imagined, that if heaven had made her a man, the great compass of her mind, and her vast fluency of speech, on which she particularly piqued herself, would have placed her in a considerable rank among the statesmen of her day and nation. To this masculine, or rather universal propensity to govern, she added one purely feminine—a latent hatred towards Glenmorris because he had not made love to her when he might, but preferred the little baby-faced Laura to her mature and ripened beauties; and she had quite as great a dislike to Mrs. Glenmorris, who, when a romping girl, had laughed at her prim maxims, and monopolized all the men, in despite of all the wise observations she used to make to her on the impropriety of talking to those "*idle boys that only flattered her.*" Since the last interview between them, Mrs. Grinsted had found new cause to nourish this lurking enmity. Mrs. Glenmorris, though no longer in the bloom of youth, was so handsome that her prudent friend hated the sight of her, and was determined to believe all the ill which, the gossips of a country town having begun, had been seized with such avidity, and disseminated with such fatal success by Mrs. Crewkherne.

Chap. XIII.

Against the threats
Of malice or of sorcery, or that power
Which erring men call chance, this I hold firm,
Virtue may be assail'd but never hurt,
Surprised by unjust force but not enthrall'd,
* * * * *
But evil on itself shall back recoil.[116]

Turning from the group which, thus associated, had worked so much woe to the unoffending family of Glenmorris, and so completely succeeded in destroying the tranquillity, if not the philosophy, of Delmont, the victims of this conspiracy naturally present themselves—Glenmorris in his prison, his wife deprived of her senses, and poor Medora, to whom Armitage had as gently as possible disclosed the truth, dis-

tracted between her agonizing fears for both her parents, and hardly more in possession of her reason than the mother she deplored.

And all this was the consequence of a vicious desire to defame a man, whose
opinions differed from those of the common world, and to detract from the modest
merit of a stranger; for without the malice of Mrs. Crewkherne, the more weighty, but
not less hateful motives that directed the conduct of Sir Appulby Gorges and the
lawyers, could never have effected so much mischief; yet Mrs. Crewkherne was a
woman pretending to many virtues, to a sanctity almost monastic, and a zeal so ardent, that the common feelings of humanity were not purified, but consumed in its
blaze. Oh! if those who calling themselves Christians, yet blinded by passion and by
prejudice, could see the unhappy victims who, remote and unknown, suffer and perish from their politics and their pride; the presumption with which weak, yet arrogant
beings send forth "*the arrow that flyeth in darkness, and the pestilence that walketh at
noon day*,"[117] might be softened into mercy; and he who from his closet or his council-
board directs the extirpation of millions, as well as the minor instigator of mischief,
who only causes the ruin of two or three families, might feel what in so many of the
powerful and the prosperous seems entirely extinct and dead, "*that spark of friendship
for human kind, that particle of the dove kneaded into our frame, along with the elements
of the wolf and the serpent.*"[118]

Nothing of this, however, was visible in the persons into whose immediate power
the unfortunate Glenmorris had fallen. His two anxious friends, Armitage and Delmont,
were with him as soon as his prison doors were open, having left his weeping daughter
somewhat tranquillised by the hope of his immediate release. While Armitage staid
with him to assist him in arranging some papers, Delmont went in search of the
attorney employed by the party who had arrested him.

Armitage plunged into the business with an ardour even greater than its necessity dictated, that he might conceal from the prisoner intelligence which would have
rendered his confinement utterly intolerable. He greatly feared least Glenmorris, already indignant at the persecution he thus suffered, almost at the very moment of his
return to his native land, should know that his wife had also, though on a different
pretence, been long confined; that she was now discovered and at liberty, but that her
reason was lost; for Armitage knew that Glenmorris, who had always declared against
the illegality and cruelty of imprisonment for debt, would incur any personal risk to
shake off these unworthy fetters, and fly to the woman he so fondly loved. Again,
therefore, was Armitage compelled to put aside his sincerity, and with friendly deceit
to engage his impetuous friend to be calm till Delmont could take the steps that were
to liberate him in a common way.

And this might soon have been done, if Glenmorris had only been imprisoned
by the ostensible cause. The debt was sworn to be seven thousand pounds and upwards. It had not been incurred even by any of those indiscretions that had marked his
early life; but occasioned by his having advanced for a friend he loved four thousand
pounds to save him and a woman he was passionately attached to from such destruction as poverty alone could not have inflicted on them. The generous purpose of
Glenmorris, however, was not answered; his friend died abroad, and the heirs refused

to repay him; he had therefore sold one of his Scottish estates to satisfy some portion of the debt, and with the income of what remained, had yearly discharged a part of the interest; but still it had grown upon him, and by the chicane of the attorneys, and the complicated law-charges they had contrived, it now amounted to the sum alledged. The man who acted for his pursuer was a friend of Brownjohn's, and that worthy gentleman no sooner heard that Glenmorris was in England, than conscious of all that must follow, and dreading the vengeance of such a man for Darnell's attempt to carry off his daughter, he made it every way worth the while of this brother attorney to proceed against him, and they concerted such measures as would secure Glenmorris's imprisonment till something more could be found against him which Brownjohn, from what he knew of his affairs, was sure would not be difficult.

When Delmont found this attorney, whose name was Evet, and offered him immediate bail in himself and Mr. Armitage, the man answered, that he should not accept it.

"Not accept it?" cried Delmont; "Pray, Mr. Evet, why not?"

"I am not obliged to give my reasons, Sir."

"I shall certainly insist upon them, Sir."

"You *can't* oblige me to give them, Sir; but if out of pure civility I am disposed to do it, suppose we say, Sir, that I don't think either your security or Mr. Armitage's equal to the sum."

"You don't!"

"No, Sir, I don't."

"This is a most unheard of piece of insolence."

"Insolence! Mr. Delmont!—I don't know, Sir, what right you have to talk to me in that manner, Mr. Delmont, but I say, Sir, that I will not accept your bail. In regard to your friend Armitage, his affairs are known well enough; and I know that he cannot justify fairly for the sum; and then, Sir, I mean no offence, Mr. Delmont; but as to your's—"

"What as to mine, Mr. Attorney?"

"I don't mind your fierce looks, Sir, nor your calling me Attorney. Truth's truth, and I'll speak it, let who will look with knock-me-down looks. I *say*, *Sir*, and *you know*, that your money is all gone, and your estate mortgaged for as much as 'tis worth for Major Delmont. You cannot deny it, Sir; for I know the man who managed it all; and so, Sir, your servant; I am a little busy just now, and I hope you will excuse me."

Delmont had never before felt the passions of anger and contempt struggling so violently in his bosom; he was strongly tempted to strike the man, yet scorn rather than philosophy at that moment withheld him; for if he could not consider such a creature as a gentleman, he could hardly class him in the rank of man. Evet was a shrivelled adust being, who seemed to have been smoke-dried in the dark office where he carried on his iniquitous trade till he had almost lost the form, and entirely the feelings, of humanity. It was hardly worth Delmont's while to waste a thought or a moment on such a reptile, and conquering his anger, as an emotion which such a disgrace to the species was unworthy of exciting, he now hurried to his lodgings, and directing Clement to prepare himself to go off express to Southampton, he wrote to his brother, requesting that, as in consequence of his marriage he could undoubtedly repay the sum advanced for him without inconvenience, he would be so good as to send him by Clement such orders or means of obtaining payment as might enable him to receive the whole in the course of two days. Having done this, Delmont repaired with an heavy heart to Medora.

Though struck with the grief and concern expressed on his countenance, Medora refrained from importuning him with questions; yet the pain of her mind was too great for dissimulation, and while she listened to such an account of her father as he hoped would soothe her, and while he flattered her with the prospect of her mother's restoration to health (for Medora knew only that she was ill) as soon as they should all be together at Upwood, which he said would be in a few days, the tears streamed from her eyes, and seemed to fall upon the heart of her lover as he fondly strained her to his bosom.

Fear for her safety, since she must be frequently left unprotected, had mingled itself with his other apprehensions, and he proposed conducting her to Upwood, where, said he, "Louisa, who is on a visit till my return, shall meet you. Surely, my lovely friend, it would be better than your remaining here."

The tears of Medora now flowed faster than before. "Oh! Delmont," said she, "it is in vain you attempt to deceive me. My poor father's detention will be long, or you would never think it necessary that I should precede him in our journey to Upwood; and if I do leave London before him, if such is his pleasure in regard to me, should my steps be directed to the once happy shades of Upwood? should not the sick bed of my mother be my destination? and is it *you*, my friend, who would have me consult my safety and my ease where she is not?—No, never, never from Delmont should I listen to a proposal that he would detest me if I should consent to. The truth is, that my mother . . . . . . " (she could not finish the sentence) "my dear mother is dead or perhaps she is dying, and your tenderness would save me from undergoing the agony of witnessing her situation, even at the expence of my duty and of future repose."

Delmont was now half-distracted; whether to reveal or still conceal the truth he knew not; nor could he assent to what Medora insisted upon, that she might see her father. At length he obtained, though with infinite difficulty, her promise, that she would endeavour to calm her spirits for that day, on his solemn assurance, that if her father was not, as he hoped and believed he would be, released on the next, she should see him; and that either Armitage or Delmont himself should conduct her to her mother, relative to whose situation he laboured, though by no means with complete success, to reassure her. Delmont then went back to the prison, where it was again necessary to use dissimulation to quiet the ardent and impetuous temper of Glenmorris, who, like a lion in his chains, was enraged by the infamous conduct of lawyers, and revolted at the abuse of law, boasting in vain of its clemency, while liberty and life were continually at the mercy of depravity and tyranny.

Alone with Armitage, Delmont related to him the reception he had met with from the attorney. Armitage, almost as little versed in the forms used on these occasions as Delmont himself, found it necessary to inquire whether this insolent refusal could be defended, and in such wretched debates passed the rest of this and a part of the following day, when Clement, who had travelled all night, arrived from Southampton, and delivered to his master the following letter:

> DR GEO.
> Thou art mistaken in supposing I can pay thee at half an hour's notice. Where the devil should I get it? I lightened myself presently of the little ready money which the ceremony I have gone through entitled me to. There was no putting by certain cursed bores any other way; and I assure you, la bellissima donna, *who has made me the happiest of men*, was more fortified with settlements and deeds (which made the cash say *noli me tangere)[119]* than I expected; and then above half is not tangible till she is five-and-twenty, a secret I was not let into when I entered into the holy estate of matrimony. We have of course occasion for other little sums for present use—and in a word, dear Geo. the money I have not; but as soon as I have time to look about me a little, you shall hear further on that subject from
> Your's, &c.
>
> A. DELMONT.
>
> The first little lord, our cousin, is dead, and the other, it is said, will never be reared to man's estate. To this dost thou say amen as heartily as I do? I feel myself already in my place, and the odds are twenty to one in my favour.

George Delmont, well as he knew his brother, was shocked at this letter; he saw there was no hope of his obtaining the sum necessary to liberate Glenmorris immediately, and all the consequences of a long imprisonment pressed with the bitterest apprehensions on his mind. Unwilling, however, to crush the hopes he had given Armitage, that every thing might be arranged that night, and dreading to see Medora till he could certainly assure her of the approaching freedom of her father, he conquered the extreme aversion to the solicitation of favours, and went to every body he could recollect, who were at all likely to afford him a temporary accommodation. His applications were totally fruitless. This man had been, as they assured him under the necessity of borrowing himself; another had unfortunately purchased into the stocks when they were extremely high, and could not sell out in their present depressed state without such a loss as he was sure his friend Delmont would never require of him. Some offered excuses yet more frivolous. One did not hesitate to reproach him for his peculiar manner of life, and his pretensions to singularity—"You forsake your friends," said this dictatorial personage; "you abandon your prospects, and affect to sink your rank, and then expect that the old friends of your family should come forward to repair the consequence of these derelictions of your honour." It need not be added that Delmont from such arrogant impertinence turned with indignant contempt.

Hopeless of succeeding this way, and almost ashamed of having tried it, he passed another day—night came, and his promise to Medora was neither to be evaded or postponed. He went to her, therefore, without having made up his mind how to tell her that the release of her father was not only not completed but as remote as ever, when with mingled expression on her countenance, for which he could not account, Medora met him, and put into his hands the following letter:

> Though we are unfortunately strangers to each other, my dear cousin, my heart acknowledges the relationship, a relationship which to you has been only productive of misfortune. I am not of age, and to do all I wish to do towards repairing the partial disposition of fortune is not yet in my power; but as I have heard that your father is under difficulties, and know that your mother has been a considerable sufferer from Lady Mary's unhappy prejudice against him, I take the liberty of inclosing what is but a very small part of that which your family, as my nearest relations, are entitled to; it is my own, and cannot inconvenience me to part with it; and be assured, that no other way in which it could be disposed of would give me half the pleasure which it will bestow upon me, if I hear that you accept and use it to remove any present embarrassments, and consider it as a trifling testimony of the intention to do you all the justice possible, when more shall be in the power of
> My dear Cousin's
> very affectionate
>
> M. G. CARDONNEL.

The inclosure was five bank notes of a thousand pounds each.

Never had any circumstance merely pecuniary so warmed and elevated the heart of Delmont. He hesitated not to declare that Medora ought to accept of, and use the notes. "Your father," said he, "my best love, will then be liberated this evening; we shall hasten to your mother; we shall once more see her restored to us, and Medora will be mine, irrevocably mine; hardly dare I trust myself with the delightful contemplation of the happiness thus opening upon me. What an admirable creature is this cousin of yours! and yet do we not think so, because for any one to do their duty, and above all when money is in question, is so very rare, that it has more effect than, simply considered, any such action ought to have? Your cousin has discovered that she has unknowingly and involuntarily injured you, and this is the first generous apology of a noble mind. She is however a glorious girl, and none can be more sensible of her worth than I am." Delmont at that moment thought of his brother's conduct; he felt himself humbled and humiliated for faults not his own, and for the first time in his life blushed to repeat the name of Delmont.

His opinion as to accepting and immediately using the notes was decisive with Medora. She persuaded Delmont to allow of her going with him to her father. The meeting between them was so affecting, that Armitage and Delmont found it absolutely necessary to call off the attention of Glenmorris to the business immediately before them. Mr. Evet was, however, reluctantly obliged to accept the bail of Armitage and Delmont for two thousand pounds; the rest was immediately paid, and a discharge obtained, after which the liberated debtor, his daughter, and his friends, returned to his lodgings, where Armitage hoped to prevail upon him to remain, while he himself went to Mrs. Glenmorris, could satisfy himself of the state she was in, and endeavour to remove her to Upwood or Ashley-Combe, where the favourable change that had happened in their affairs might gradually be disclosed to her, and the family so long separated and so cruelly persecuted, be re-united.

But Glenmorris was not disposed to endure the delay of a moment; and Medora as well as Delmont being eager to second him, they set out the same evening for the place where Mrs. Glenmorris, yet labouring under the cruel prepossession, which with so much pains had been taken to impress on her mind, still lingered in a state that might with too much justice be called a degree of melancholy madness.

Glenmorris, leaving his daughter to the care of his two friends, insisted on being allowed to speak to her alone. It was in vain both Delmont and Armitage remonstrated against it; he would not be restrained; he beheld the woman he had so long, so fondly doated on, resting on one of those raised mounds of earth so frequent on the downs, supposed to be memorials of the dead;[120] she rather reclined than sat, and her head was pillowed by her lovely arm, while her eyes seemed to be fixed on the moon as it rose from the sea. Susanne, who had notice of his approach, glided away. He sat down near his wife, and took her other hand, uttering her name in a low voice, "Laura! my own Laura!" The long frozen chords of her heart vibrated to these well known sounds. Mrs. Glenmorris started up, gazed wildly on him a moment, and fell senseless into his arms.

Delmont, Armitage, and Medora, who dreaded some fatal event from this sudden meeting, were soon on the spot, and while Armitage assisted the half frantic Glenmorris to carry his dying Laura to her bed in the poor cottage where she had insisted on continuing, Medora, with the truest courage and feeling, refrained from expressing the despair which was in her heart, and thought only of being useful to her mother, and of consoling her father. The violent revulsion which the sudden appearance of her husband had occasioned was however useful to the long suffering patient; her senses with her recollection slowly returned; for many days she spoke but little, but listened with intelligent eyes to the long explanation that was given her by degrees, and as she was able to bear it, of the cause of Medora's absence, and the heroic exertions by which she had passed safely through so many perils. Mrs. Glenmorris, on whom the most invidious and cruel arts had been used to persuade her that Medora had forsaken her, and who had suffered her mind, enfeebled by misfortune and crushed by pecuniary distress, to dwell on the imaginary miseries thus presented to her, now sunk again under despondence and self-reproach for having a moment yielded to suspicions so unjust, and which such a daughter could so little deserve; but to what strange changes is not the human mind liable, shook as her's was by personal sufferings, with every thing to irritate and perplex her, without a friend to soothe her sorrow, and appearing to herself to be abandoned by all the world. One of the objects who had constituted the happiness of her life, she believed torn from her, while the other, her husband and her protector, was far away, and to him she was denied the alleviation of communication; it seemed indeed probable she might never see him more!

It was some days before the extreme weakness to which Mrs. Glenmorris was reduced made it safe to remove her to Upwood, where Louisa waited to receive them. Her thoughts often wandered, and often partial relapses alarmed the watchful anxious group around her. When their indefatigable tenderness, with time and tranquillity, had in some degree restored her, the first wish she expressed was for the marriage of Delmont and Medora, the second, that they might go to America. "Oh let us not, my dear friend," said she to Glenmorris, "let us not stay in a country to which we have both returned only to suffer; where we know and have experienced that the poor may, in some cases at least, be persecuted and oppressed with impunity; and where Lady Mary may still think it too much to allow me to breath the same air with her. Do not let us attempt any more to recover that fortune which we *will not want*. Already have we been severely punished for the attempt. Ah! think how many years of comparative felicity we passed before that unfortunate project was suggested to us. I fear, I know not why, that the calm and contented state we then enjoyed, we shall never recover. Oh! no! I feel that my mind is hurt, my temper embittered; and here I shall be haunted by the images of lawyers, the dread of persecution; and such women as Mrs. Grinsted and Mrs. Crewkherne will seem for ever to pursue me; while I stay in England I am sure I shall be incapable of happiness." Glenmorris, though he did not quite assent to her reasons, forbore at that time to contradict her; his whole study was to restore her mind to that firmness and cheerfulness which alone were wanting to the happiness of Delmont and Medora, who were united as soon as the mother they equally loved had regained at least apparent serenity. Very unwilling indeed were both Glenmorris and Delmont to pollute the first months of their happiness with the hostile pursuit of those miscreants who had occasioned to them so much calamity; but Glenmorris conceived it due to public justice to expose men, who (by abuse of law) possessing the power, had the disposition to perpetrate so much evil, and in the event Loadsworth and Brownjohn were punished, the former with the loss of his little remaining business, and by accumulated contempt, the latter by being struck off the roll[121] for *frauds*, in which Glenmorris detected him. Darnell, frightened at what he had done, exchanged his commission for one in a corps going to the Cape, and escaped the chastisement that Glenmorris and Delmont meditated—Much of all the transactions in which Lady Mary was concerned was suffered to sink into oblivion on account of her age, and her being the mother of Mrs. Glenmorris, however unnaturally she had renounced that character, and above all, in consideration of the admirable Miss Cardonnel, who, though she had really preferred Delmont to any man she ever saw, commanded herself so much as to promote, by her generous conduct, his marriage with her cousin, having entered voluntarily into such an engagement as, being under age, she could give, to restore to Mrs. George Delmont all that share of her grandfather's fortune, which, on her attaining her majority, any two men of honour would say she was entitled to. Lady Mary soon quite sunk into second childhood, and Miss Cardonnel was at liberty to cultivate the acquaintance of her only relations, the family of

Glenmorris, where she beheld with concern, which only so good an heart could feel, the ravage which some months of mental suffering had made on the still fine form and face of her aunt. While she was at Upwood for a few days, she was first seen by the elder Delmont, whose wishes being at length accomplished by the death of both his infant relations, he came down in triumph to Belton Tower as Earl of Castledanes. He was already heartily tired of his wife, and imagining he might have done so much better, repented of his precipitancy; he saw united in Miss Cardonnel a fortune thrice as large as that he had obtained, with the various advantages of beauty, sweetness, and understanding, in no common degree; he persuaded himself that he might have married her, and his impatience at the yoke he had so hastily put on empoisoned the delight of his newly acquired title and fortune, while Lady Castledanes, though by no means indifferent to her elevation, secretly envied the humble but more fortunate lot of Medora.

George Delmont, who did not recover even the money of which Sir Appulby Gorges had got possession without a law suit, and who, even when Lord Castledanes had paid him, was very far from being rich, was nevertheless a much happier man than Adolphus, though the latter was now in possession of what he used to believe the summit of his wishes. If George had any wish left, it was to reconcile Mr. and Mrs. Glenmorris to England, and to engage them to fix their residence at Upwood. Armitage too, whose pleasures were solely dependent on literary gratifications, and in witnessing the happiness of his friends, endeavoured to persuade Glenmorris to continue in his native island. He was contented to yield to their solicitations for some time, but never relinquished his intention of returning to America. "If I have those I love with me," said he, "is not every part of the globe equally my country? And has not this, which you are pleased to call my native land, thrown me from her bosom when I *might* have served her? Did she leave me any choice between imprisonment and flight? Now, averse from the means by which political power and influence can be obtained, and without a fortune to live but in continual pecuniary difficulties, why should I ask an asylum of this haughty mother country for my declining days? *If such things were done in the green leaf what shall be done in the dry?*"[122]

"Have a care my good friend," said Armitage, when he was once talking in this manner, "Have a care, lest you yield in all this to a false pride, to a pride utterly unworthy of a mind like your's. You feel yourself out of your place in England, because you have not power, or great affluence (which in fact is power); but is not that a sensation a little bordering on the sentiment,

Better to reign in hell than serve in heaven."[123]

"No," replied Glenmorris, "I have no desire to reign any where; but I do not love to be in a country where I am made to pay very dear for advantages which exist not but in idea. I do not love to live where I see a frightful contrast between luxury and wretchedness; where I must daily witness injustice I cannot repress, and misery I cannot relieve. In America, you say, I must abandon society, and starve my understanding. I deny it, however. The great book of nature is open before me, and poor must be his taste who cannot find in it a more noble study than that of sophisticated minds, which we call society here, where at every step we take something appears to shock or disgust us; where all greatness of character seems lost; and where, if we desire to study human nature unadulterated by *inhuman* prejudices, we act nearly as the painter would do, who should turn from the study of the exquisitely simple Grecian statue to debauch his eyes with the spectacle of court figures in hoops and perriwigs. In this country, my dear Armitage, as you know very well, we do not value, '*le vrai beau*,' which, being translated, seems to me to mean, '*the great simple*;' no, we appreciate moral excellence by success, by fortune, which gives fashion, and imputes perfection (a temporary one indeed, but which still answers all their purposes) to the mere puppets of a season. I will not talk to you about politics, because you are among the moderates and quietists; you endure all things, you hope all things, you believe all things. Now I, who do not love enduring much, who have little to hope, and . . . ."[124]

"And who believe nothing," interrupted Armitage.

"Oh! pardon me," rejoined Glenmorris, "I believe a vast deal; but we will not talk of that; not that we should differ in the great principles of our actions, and all the rest is mere verbal wrangling, a difference in terms rather than things. While you can be tolerably happy yourself, my dear friend, in this country, or believe that you can do good to its people, it is very fit you should stay; for me who, sooth to say, am not happy in it myself, and despair of being of any use in promoting, beyond a very narrow circle indeed, the happiness of others, the necessity of my remaining is by no means so evident. You agree with me, that true philanthropy does not consist in loving John, and Thomas, and George, and James, because they are our brothers, our cousins, our neighbours, our countrymen, but in benevolence to the whole human race; if that be true, let me ask you whether I can be thoroughly contented here, where I see that the miseries inflicted by the social compact greatly exceed the happiness derived from it; where I observe an artificial polish, glaring but fallacious on one side, and on the other real and bitter wretchedness; where for a great part of the year my ears are every week shocked by the cries of hawkers, informing who has been dragged to execution; and where, to come directly home, it is at the mercy of any rascal, to whom I have given an opportunity of cheating me of ten pounds, to swear a debt against me, and carry me to the abodes of horror, where the malefactor groans in irons, the debtor languishes in despair. Is or is not this picture true? and if it be, can I love to live in such a country only because I drew my first breath in a remote corner of it? No, dear Armitage, if Delmont will not fail me, if he will let me for a little while at least have my Medora in my adopted country, if, notwithstanding his advantages here, he has, as I believe, manliness enough to say,

All countries that the eye of heaven visits,
Are to a wise man homes and happy havens,[125]

we will once more cross the Atlantic, and I will try to teach him, that wherever a thinking man enjoys the most uninterrupted domestic felicity, and sees his species the most content, *that* is his country."

Mrs. Glenmorris, whose mind long suffered from the shock she had sustained, and who could not hear some names without trembling, was equally anxious to quit England, and Delmont, who had nothing but his local attachment to Upwood as a balance against his desire to gratify the parents of his wife, hesitated not a moment to determine to do as Glenmorris desired. Indeed the pleasure with which from a boy he had cherished that favourite spot of earth was considerably embittered now, by the residence of his brother so near it. The character of Lord Castledanes had acquired room to display itself, and it became every day more essentially different from that of Delmont. The house was altogether unlike what it once was; Lady Castledanes tried to make herself amends, by the splendor and profusion of her establishment, for the want of real happiness, and unwilling to acknowledge to herself that she failed, affected a sort of haughty gaiety, which made her utterly disagreeable to Mrs. Glenmorris and Medora, the former of whom was compelled entirely to decline parties which were too fatiguing to her in her present state of health. Glenmorris could never command his satyrical vein enough to mix with them, and Delmont persisted now, as he had done formerly, in keeping his personal freedom inviolate, and not being compelled to sacrifice half his time to this man, because he was his relation, to another, because he was rich or powerful, and to a third, because he was reckoned a wit—Still his neighbourhood to, and near connection with, such a family as that which inhabited Belton Tower rendered his own house less pleasant to him, and his immediate study was, to make such regulations as should render his ceasing to reside on his estate as little injurious as possible to those who looked up to him for the comforts of their humble situation; but Louisa was at this time addressed by, and soon after married to, a Mr. Sydenham, a man who appeared to her brother as unexceptionable as he could desire for a beloved sister. It was agreed that they should tenant Upwood, and Delmont had no longer any apprehension that his poor neighbours, and more immediate dependants, would be greatly injured by his temporary absence.

Mrs. Crewkherne, though it could not be said that *concealed* malevolence, *like a worm in the bud, preyed on her sallow cheek*[126] (for she failed not to continue her maledictions against her younger nephew and his connections) yet did not long survive his marriage; she died in charity with nobody; and if Mr. Bethune and Caroline had not taken considerable pains to prevent it, would have altered her will, and have left the bulk of her fortune to the brethren, having been much displeased with her favourite niece in as much as she would not renounce her brother George. With Lord Castledanes she was also at variance, and he scorned to take the least pains to conciliate her. Yet, however dissatisfied with this world, the old lady was extremely unwilling to go to another, which, with those who had heard her aspirations, and seen with whom she was surrounded, did no great credit to their enthusiastic professions.

Miss Richmond, on the return of her brother from abroad, prevailed on her father to consent to her marriage with a man to whom she had long been attached. After their marriage, Miss Cardonnel passed great part of her time with them, where she was addressed by a great number of lovers, all of whom however she declined without assigning the true reason, which was, that she wished to remain unmarried till she became of age, when she was determined on a just and amicable division of the disputed part of her inheritance with Medora, now Mrs. Delmont.

That lovely and beloved young woman, with no other alloy to her happiness than what was created by fears for her mother's health, was the delight of all who knew her, as well in America as in England. In the performance of every duty that could render her dear to her family, and in the possession of every accomplishment that sweetens and adorns society, she seemed to have been created as a counterpart to the generous and almost faultless character, while she constituted the almost perfect felicity, of THE YOUNG PHILOSOPHER.

THE END.

Notes to the Novel

The epigraph on the title page is from William Mason, "Elegy II. Written in the Garden of a Friend," lines 81-84.

Volume 1

1. *An Essay on the Art of Ingeniously Tormenting: With Proper Rules for the Exercise of that Pleasant Art* (London: A. Millar, 1753) is actually by Jane Collier. The fable to which Smith refers is annexed to the essay itself, printed on the last pages of the volume (233-34). Smith quotes from memory—and inaccurately. The fable as reported by Collier concerns the discovery of a poem describing "the misery that is endured, from the entrance of teeth and claws into living flesh." The poem—written by a "beast"—is signed with the letter *L* and therefore is assumed to be authored by a lynx, a lion, a leopard, or a lamb. Ultimately, having heard the arguments in favor of lynx, lion, and leopard authorship, a "generous horse" pronounces his conclusion: "'it is impossible . . . that any beast, that has the feeling which our author shews for the tortured wretches, who are torn by savage teeth and claws, should ever make the ravages, which, it is notorious, are daily made by the three fierce competitors before us. The writer of this poem, therefore, . . . must be no other than the lamb. As it is from suffering, and not from inflicting torments, that the true idea of them is gained.'" This essay became a standard reference for female writers commenting on the wrongs of women (see, for example, Frances Burney's *The Wanderer,* in which the heroine's employer is said to be skilled in this art). Although Smith says the work was out of print in 1798, it was reissued in 1804, 1805, and 1806. See also the paperback facsimile, with an introduction by Judith Hawley (Bristol: Thoemmes, 1994).

2. For Charlotte Smith's sufferings, see the introduction to this book, especially pp. xiv-xv.

3. Smith was accused of plagiarism in her translation of *Manon Lescaut* (above, p. xvi). Mary Wollstonecraft died in 1797; her *Posthumous Works,* including *The Wrongs of Woman, or Maria,* was published by her husband, William Godwin, in 1798. In *The Wrongs of Woman,* Maria is incarcerated in a madhouse, but the narratives bear little resemblance beyond that fact and the radical political slant of both. The *Posthumous Works* also contained Godwin's frank memoir of Wollstonecraft—an essay that created a furor and turned much public opinion against her. Smith's endorsement of Wollstonecraft was therefore an act of integrity in the climate of 1798. Cf. Loraine Fletcher, *Charlotte Smith: A Critical Biography* (London: Macmillan, 1998), p. 279.

4. This meditated essay becomes the subject matter addressed by the title character of a later Smith novel—*Letters of a Solitary Wanderer:*

> You despise, as puerile and ridiculous, the fashionable taste, which has filled all our modern books of entertainment with caverns and castles, peopled our theatres with spectres, and, instead of representing life as it is, has created a new school, where any thing rather than probability, or even possibility, is attended to. . . .
>
> It undoubtedly seems easier to collect surprising events, which, in connecting, setting probability aside, neither time, action, or place, the three unities, need be adhered to, and in composing of which we may indulge ourselves in the most daring and improbable fictions; than it is to draw characters such as we know exist, and to find a fable proper to bring them forward. . . .
>
> Yet it has been asserted that strong native genius can alone succeed in that style of writing where the horrible and supernatural predominate, and where the greatest effect is produced by a certain degree of obscurity. And it is undoubtedly true, that the rudest and wildest sketch of Salvator is more precious than the most laboured piece of the correctest Flemish master. [*Letters of a Solitary Wanderer* (1800), *Revolution and Romanticism, 1789-1834,* a series of facsimile reprints chosen and introduced by Jonathan Wordsworth (New York: Woodstock Books, 1995), pp. 21, 25-26]

Apart from this passage and others in *Conversations Introducing Poetry,* Smith did not formally address the topic; or at least, no essay on fiction has survived.

5. See, e.g., Samuel Johnson, *Rambler* 4, 31 March 1750: "these familiar histories may perhaps be made of greater use than the solemnities of professed morality, and convey the knowledge of vice and virtue with more efficacy than axioms and definitions. [C]are ought to be taken that . . . the best examples only should be exhibited."

6. Magicians, sorcerers.

7. *Othello* 1.3.135.

8. Brighton. In his *Tour through the Whole Island of Great Britain,* written in the 1720s, Defoe described Brighton or Bright Helmston, as it was known then, as "a poor fishing town, old built, and on the very edge of the sea." Since that time, however, the town had become one of the most popular of the English seaside resorts.

9. To test their endurance.

10. A curricle, used primarily for short journeys, is a fashionable, yet sturdy, two-wheeled carriage, drawn by two horses side by side, whereas a post-chaise is a closed carriage, seating up to four passengers, hired for traveling or drawn by hired horses. As the following passage suggests, the Winslows own the post-chaise and are traveling with two of their own horses. Mrs. Winslow's notion of "elegance" involves the hiring of an additional pair of post-horses from the inn.

11. "In 1762 Parliament passed the first of a series of statutes establishing seasons in which game could be legally killed. By 1773 these had assumed their now-familiar form: grouse shooting began on the twelfth of August, partridge shooting on the first of September and pheasant shooting on the first of October." P.B. Munsche, *Gentlemen and Poachers: The English Game Laws, 1671-1831* (New York: Cambridge, 1981),

p. 41. The more strenuous field sports that Dr. Winslow could not enjoy would include hunting stags, hares, or foxes.

12. Jerry's speech is the first instance in this novel of Charlotte Smith's use of colloquialisms and spelling to indicate dialect or pronunciation in the direct speech of her characters. Of her rendering of dialect Hilbish says, "no one earlier than Mrs. Smith does so well." Florence May Anna Hilbish, "Charlotte Smith: Poet and Novelist (1749-1806)," Ph.D. diss., Univ. of Pennsylvania, 1941, p. 552.

13. A guinea was one pound and one shilling.

14. Turnpike roads were toll roads with a gate or barrier placed across the road to block travelers until they paid the toll. Travelers of the day risked highwaymen and carriage accidents, yet despite dangers, as Roy Porter notes, "people travelled more and more." *English Society in the Eighteenth Century* (London: Penguin, 1982), p. 31. Guildford and Godalming are towns in Sussex; Walthamstow is near London to the east.

15. Having no "oil-skin on top of them."

16. "Fid fad" is short for "fiddle faddle"; used as here as an adjective, it means frivolous or finicky.

17. See, for example, Andrew Marvell, *Hodges Vision* (1675); Samuel Butler, *Remains* (c. 1680); Dryden, *Spanish Friar* (1681), Act 4, Scene 2; and Tobias Smollett, *Peregrine Pickle* (1751), chap. 57; all of them employ the phrase almost exactly as Smith does. Jean-Jacques Rousseau, *Du Contrat Social* (1762), book 1, chap. 2, also notes: "Sa première loi est de veiller à sa propre conservation."

18. The *OED* quotes a passage from the *Penny Cyclopedia of the Society for the Diffusion of Useful Knowledge,* explaining the term "cottage" as a fashionable word "for small country residences . . . adapted to a moderate scale of living yet with due attention to comfort and refinement."

19. Not identified.

20. Cut short.

21. A marmoset is a small monkey; when applied to a man, the term is one of derision. Sometimes used interchangably with "ingle" or "catamite" (a court favorite; a boy kept for sexual purposes), the term has homosexual connotations.

22. Pantaloons were "a tight fitting kind of trousers fastened with ribbons or buttons below the calf, or, later by straps passing under the boots, which were introduced late in the 18th c., and began to supersede knee-breeches." *OED.* A waistcoat was a sleeveless, buttoned jacket worn by men, designed to be partly visible under coat or jacket. Charlotte Smith's use of these words in this passage are the first illustrative quotations cited by the *OED* under the terms "pantalooned" and "waistcoated."

23. The Church Fathers, the early Christian writers.

24. Positions within the Church of England were awarded by the state; therefore, Dr. Winslow's attention is more to secular matters than to spiritual ones.

25. Through the mid–nineteenth century, a sergeant-at-law was a member of a high order of barristers from which the Common Law judges were chosen. A chancellor is a still higher office.

26. Mark 14:21, slightly altered from the King James Version.

27. Armitage's belief in the efficacy of works to attain salvation marks him as a

Latitudinarian or broad churchman, who emphasizes the reasonableness of Christianity, as opposed to Mrs. Crewkherne, who has clear Methodist leanings and holds the opposite view—that faith alone is sufficient for salvation.

28. Bishop Samuel Horsley uttered this sentiment on 6 November 1795 in a debate over a treason bill and defended it on 13 November 1795: in England where the laws are "liable to no sudden change or perversion—to no partial application from the passion or the humour of the moment . . . the individual subject . . . 'has nothing to do with the laws but to obey them.'" "My Lords," he declaimed, "it is a maxim which I ever will maintain,—I will maintain it to the *death*,—I will maintain it under the *axe of the guillotine;* if, through any insufficiency of the measures which may now be taken, the time should ever come when the prelates and nobles of this land must stoop their necks to that engine of democratic tyranny." *The Speeches in Parliament of Samuel Horsley, LL.D.F.R.S.F.A.S. Late Lord Bishop of St. Asaph,* 2 vols. (Dundee: Robert Stephen Rintoul, 1813), 1:175-76.

29. Bishops wore ceremonial sleeves of lawn (fine, thin cloth of linen or cotton) or lace.

30. James Beattie, *The Minstrel; or, The Progress of Genius,* lines 146-52.

31. Probably a reference to Thomas Gray's "Ode on a Distant Prospect of Eton College," though the phrase does not actually appear in the poem. Lines 29-31 describe "idle Progeny" who "urge the flying Ball."

32. A slang expression for a studious young person; a bookworm. The *OED* cites this sentence from *The Young Philosopher* as its first illustrative quotation of the usage defined.

33. Though George exercises private charity toward these supplicants, eighteenth-century law provided for public funds to be used toward the maintenance of the poor. Yet, more effort seems to have been expended in trying to evade the law than in complying with it. Each parish was required to give succor to its poor, but the law stated that in order to receive aid, one had to live in the place of one's birth. Parish records were often unreliable, so many had no proof of their right to public charity. Hence, the spectacle—seen here and later in this novel—of the wandering poor, wounded, sick, and dying.

34. Thomas Otway, *The Orphan* Act 2, Scene 1, line 254.

35. Hypocrite, so called after the title character of Molière's 1664 comedy *Tartuffe.*

36. The legendary hero of Switzerland, William Tell, refused to salute a tyrannical steward of Albert I, thereby receiving the famous punishment: that he shoot an apple from the head of his own son. Jean-Jacques Rousseau (1712-78), who lived and wrote in Geneva, was the author of several works that contributed to the theoretical justification of the French Revolution, particularly *Discours sur l'origine de l'inégalité parmi les hommes* (1755) and *Du Contrat social* (1762); the Alpine scenery George Delmont longs to view was associated with feelings of sublimity. Cf. Ann Radcliffe's *Romance of the Forest,* vol. 3, chap. 17, and Percy Bysshe Shelley's *Mount Blanc.* Vaud is a state in western Switzerland; Clarens is a town in Switzerland, and Meillerie, a town in France, both on Lake Geneva. Together they invoke the setting of Rousseau's *Julie, ou la Nouvelle Héloïse* (1761), a novel of romantic passion and philosophical observation that seems to have appealed to the imagination of young George Delmont, no doubt because of its attack on social hypocrisy.

37. The trade of the West Indies was an important and lucrative aspect of eighteenth-century British economy. A military presence was necessary to protect British holdings in the Caribbean, especially during times of European conflict, for Spain, Holland, Denmark, Sweden and—most significantly—France maintained a colonial presence there as well.

38. The West Indies, where Europeans often succumbed to diseases unknown to the English climate.

39. Falmouth in Cornwall is a fine natural harbor on the English Channel near the westernmost tip of England. In the eighteenth century it was an important seaport.

40. Francis Bacon, "An Essay on Death," slightly altered.

41. The foot-guards, the house-guards, or the life-guards—the queen's regiments or the household troops of the English army.

42. The elder Delmont means he has nothing to live on but his pay.

43. Not the foot-guards but a lesser class of infantry. Destined for an appointment in the queen's regiments, Adolphus must now settle for a captaincy of the infantry, a post without the glamor of the household troops and with quite a bit more danger.

44. Actually, the age at which a young man left a public school such as Eton for the university varied greatly in the eighteenth century, ranging anywhere from fifteen to twenty. Jonathan Gathorne-Hardy, *The Old School Tie: The Phenomenon of the English Public School* (New York: Viking, 1977), p. 35.

45. Perhaps a reference to Dryden's poem "The Character of a Good Parson, Imitated from Chaucer and Inlarg'd"; certainly the character sketched by Dryden is "a man dedicated in heart and spirit to the edification and instruction of the world."

46. A troublesome or mischievous child; a boisterous young fellow. Perhaps a reference to the title character of Tobias Smollett's *Peregrine Pickle* (1751).

47. General James Wolfe (1727-59) was a brilliant military officer, famous for the capture of the city of Quebec, in which he was mortally wounded and by which French power in Canada yielded to British rule. According to her sister, Catherine Dorset, Charlotte Smith wrote a poem at the age of ten on the death of General Wolfe. Catherine Dorset, "Charlotte Smith," in *Biographical Memoirs,* in volume 8 of *The Prose Works of Sir Walter Scott* (Paris: A. and W. Galignani, 1834), p. 253.

48. The British court is still known as the Court of St. James, from St. James's Palace in Pall Mall.

49. Corrected in the Dublin edition; see variants, below, p. 391.

50. "A few examples may suffice from the histories we are most familiar with—those of France, Spain, and alas! of England.—'The political well-wrought veil,' with which the follies and enormities of the rulers of the earth would willingly be concealed, may surely be torn (even at the present moment) from such monsters as Louis the Eleventh and Charles the Ninth of France, on whom (to say nothing of most of the rest) the holy cruise certainly bestowed its sacred contents very ill. In Spain it is enough to name 'the demon of the South,'—and England, the country of good sense and of manly daring, has seen its best blood manure its fields in the senseless contention between the rival houses of York and Lancaster; endured the brutal tyrant Henry the Eighth; and saw without resistance the fires of Smithfield lighted by the bigot-fury, his execrable daughter; crouched at the feet of Elizabeth, that compound of feminine weakness and masculine ferocity; and in the Solomon of the North (a miser-

able imbecile being, who wrote a treatise on Witchcraft, and was hurried into war to gratify the romantic intriguing spirit of Stenny, a name childishly given by James to his minion the Duke of Buckingham) still venerated the consecrated folly of the Lord's anointed.—It is needless to go on.—What the English people afterwards suffered from the period when Charles the First set up the standard at Nottingham till the *blessed* restoration—the miseries inflicted by the contention between James and our glorious deliverer, from the expulsion of the first-named monarch, till 'the affair of Glencoe;'—and the two rebellions of 1715 and 1745, may be read as antidotes to a change of kings." [CS's note]

51. Lucius Junius Brutus, who avenged the rape of the chaste Lucretia by Sextus Tarquinius, son of the tyrannous king of Rome, Tarquin. Brutus led the victorious fight against the Tarquins, who were expelled in favor of a republican government. Lucretia, however, stabbed herself, and Shakespeare's rendering of the tale in *The Rape of Lucrece* portrays Brutus at the end of the poem bearing her bloody body through the steets of Rome, a spectacle that generated public demand for the expulsion of the Tarquins and the founding of the new government.

52. "Tiberius and Caius Gracchus, grandsons of Scipio Africanus, who, being tribunes, attempted to enact laws for restoring to the Roman people their share of the conquered lands, of which the nobles and the rich had most unjustly deprived the poorer citizens. They both fell in tumults raised against them by the patricians, whose adherents were armed and mustered to destroy these illustrious brothers—and the people ignobly forsook them!" [CS's note]

53. Marcus Brutus (85?-42 B.C.), Roman politician, general, and friend of Julius Caesar, who was persuaded to join the conspiracy against Caesar to prevent "th' abuse of greatness." Shakespeare, *Julius Caesar* 2.1.18.

54. Marcus Porcius Cato the younger (95-46 B.C.) was a Roman statesman and philosopher who committed suicide rather than submit to Caesar. Joseph Addison's tragedy *Cato* (1713), based on these events, was popular throughout the eighteenth century.

55. Ecclesiasticus 38:25.

56. A reference to the secular courts and the ecclesiastical courts, by which justice was apportioned and laws enforced in the eighteenth century. "Themis" was the ancient Greek goddess of law and justice.

57. A street show or peep show.

58. Alexander Pope, "Epistle to a Lady," line 2.

59. William Cowper, "The Winter Nosegay," lines 10-12, slightly altered.

60. For women and botanical study, see the introduction, p. xxviii.

61. Shakespeare, *As You Like It* 4.1.214-15, altered.

62. From the Latin *post obitum,* after decease. This bond promises a sum of money to be repaid on the death of someone from whom the borrower expects a legacy or inheritance.

63. A younger son or brother, who, by the law or custom of primogeniture, is not entitled to inherit the family estate.

64. As a member of the nobility, the Delmonts' uncle, Lord Castledanes, would be prominent in local affairs. Adolphus suggests that he will appoint George as a voting member of the county government if George continues to "keep in his favor."

65. Gnaeus Julius Agricola (A.D. 40-93) was a Roman soldier and politician, a legate of Britain, under whose command the Romans conquered North Wales, Anglesey, and parts of Scotland. His last name means "farmer." He was noted for his provincial sympathies for the country and people of Britain—a sympathy that aided his military conquests.

66. At the top of his voice.

67. See 1 Samuel 28. The Witch of Endor helped Saul establish communication with the deceased Samuel despite the Hebraic prohibition of necromancy. Adolphus seems to employ the phrase, however, as a general insult to Mrs. Crewkherne's appearance.

68. Country bumpkins.

69. A wether is a castrated ram. Adolphus imagines George inquiring as to the rate or price of a score of such rams. The *OED* cites "How a score of Ewes now?" (Shakespeare, *2 Henry IV*) to illustrate this usage.

70. A soft-leaved plant used for wrapping butter.

71. Commoners.

72. Gibraltar had been a British possession since 1704.

73. Proverbs 22:6.

74. Not identified.

75. A "modus" is "a money payment in lieu of a tithe" (*OED*); "composition" in this context has something of the same meaning: "an agreement for the payment . . . of a sum of money in lieu of the discharge of some other obligation" (*OED*); "the exchequer court" is the branch of the judiciary system concerned with matters of revenue. "Tests" and "the last visitation" are less mercenary terms, though Smith is obviously critical of both as tools of coercion and control. "Tests" determined membership in the Church of England: by taking the sacrament, a man became eligible for political rights or offices from which Dissenters were barred. By the 1780s these "civil disabilities" were creating social tension and galvanizing politically radical forces in opposition to such "tests." See Roy Porter, *English Society in the Eighteenth Century*, p. 363. A "visitation" refers to a bishop's visit to a parish, at which time he would preach a sermon—a "dogmatical piece of eloquence" in Smith's view.

76. "A court of limited criminal and civil jurisdiction, and of appeal, held quarterly by the justices of peace in the counties . . . and by the recorders in boroughs." *OED*.

77. Needlework.

78. An actress.

79. That is, lest. Obsolete now, the spelling "least" was common well into the nineteenth century. Occasionally, the first edition of *The Young Philosopher* employs "lest," and the 1798 Dublin edition regularizes many occurences to the (now) more common spelling, but evidence from Smith's letters substantiates the theory that "least" was her preferred spelling; therefore, I retain the spelling as it appeared in the first edition.

80. Not identified. Between ourselves, tell me, has a philosopher ever caused the least trouble in society? Aren't most of them loners? Are they not poor? without protection or support?

81. The *philosophes*, e.g., Diderot, Voltaire, Rousseau, Montesquieu, Holbach, and

D'Alembert—though often at odds with one another—were regarded as the driving ideological force behind the French Revolution.

82. Smithfield was a major site for burnings of "heretics," especially in the reign of Mary I (1547-58), who was known to Protestants as Bloody Mary.

83. A reference to the fact that only communicants of the Church of England could hold political office.

84. "'A t'on jamais entendu parler d'un philosophe, qui avait voulu faire perir vingt millions de peuples par la famine, comme le voulait, dit on un grand ministre, qui n'etoit pas philosophe.'" [CS's note] Translation of quotation in the text: Have you ever seen philosophers bring war into a country, or famine or plague? Bayle, for example, did he ever wish to burst the dikes of Holland, in order to drown the people, as it is said that one great minister wishes, who isn't a philosopher. Translation of the note: Has a philosopher ever been heard of who wished to kill twenty million people by famine, as it is said that one great minister wishes, who isn't a philosopher.

85. See Judges 16:25-30. Samson, released from prison to perform for the Philistines, shook the pillars of the building in which he was to perform, destroying it but killing himself in the process. A "bastille" is a prison, most often associated with the Parisian jail destroyed in 1789 at the beginning of the French Revolution.

86. Not identified. The failings and the insignificance of these characters who resemble many fashionable people made me reflect on the emptiness of society and the advantage of never being obliged to frequent it.

87. Part of Dr. Winslow's official clerical dress. Cf. *OED*, s.v. "apron."

88. See Acts 8:18-19. Simon Magus offered money to the apostles in exchange for the power of conferring the Holy Ghost through the laying on of hands. His offer was declined. After him, buying and selling ecclesiastical offices was called "simony."

89. Fabricated names signifying the plaintiff and defendant in a legal case.

90. Sixteen eighty-eight was the year of the Glorious Revolution, during which the Roman Catholic James II was deposed in favor of the Protestant William and Mary. John Locke (1632-1704) had interpreted the revolution as a triumph of reason and natural law, a response to monarchial abuse of the natural rights of the governed, an interpretation with which George Delmont's grandfather would have concurred. The conservative Dr. Winslow, however, would have disapproved of the Glorious Revolution as a violation of the rights of succession and the legitimacy of monarchial rule.

91. Ecclesiastes 11:1.

92. Corinthian columns, one of the four types in classical architecture, feature a stylized version of the leaves of the acanthus plant.

93. Gentle simmering, or, perhaps, fussing.

94. A tale of woe and distress. From the Old Testament book of the Lamentations of Jeremiah.

95. Asafetida: a resinous, strong-smelling gum from Central Asia used in medicine as an antispasmodic and in cookery as flavoring.

96. Fashionable, modish, stylish.

97. George Delmont's hair is cut short, as we are told in chapter 2, "like that of the farmer or the peasant." Here, however, the the term "cropped" suggests that the fashion adopted by George may have a more overt political significance, for the Irish

rebels of 1798 wore their hair in this fashion to signify sympathy and affiliation with the French Revolution. One who affected such a style was called a "croppy."

98. The *OED*, citing this passage only, defines "mimpetty mimp" as "prim, precise, affected, mim [with lips pursed]."

99. Gilbert West, "An Epistle to a Lady," lines 97-100.

100. One who thinks for himself (or herself) about matters of religious belief, rather than accepting official doctrine or church authority.

101. The famous, defiant speech of Honore-Gabriel Riquetti, Comte de Mirabeau (1749-91)—in which he refused on behalf of the National Assembly to leave the hall as the king had ordered—was delivered at the royal session on 23 June 1789, not the day before at the Tennis Court, as Smith implies.

102. Part of "the Great Fear," referring to rumors of aristocratic revenge against the third estate for their rioting and protests over predicted food shortages and high prices during the summer of 1789.

103. Edmund Burke (1729-97), author of *Reflections on the Revolution in France* (1790) and other works attacking the French Revolution, stirred much controversy in the 1790s. Smith sided with the anti-Burke writers in works such as *The Young Philosopher* and *Desmond* (1792).

104. In Greek mythology, a goddess of the lower world who presides over witchcraft and magic.

105. A mountain-dwelling goddess of holy madness, another aspect of Hecate. Her rites were characterized by orgiastic, masochistic frenzies.

106. The French had "cured themselves" of papism during the revolution by the process of "dechristianization," which severed the link between the Catholic Church and the republic. Elsewhere Smith attacks the notion that the French and the English were "natural enemies." See, for example, *Minor Morals* 2:8-10.

107. Smith compares Burke's fervor against France to that of Peter the Hermit (c. 1050-1115), one of the instigators of the First Crusade, known for his wild and enthusiastic preaching. The *Monthly Magazine* had described Burke, recently dead, as "[p]ossessing a wonderful irritability of nerves, a warm, and almost disordered imagination, his rage against regenerated France was here sublimed nearly to madness. Another *Peter the Hermit*, he preached up a crusade against the modern Saracens, and, like Peter too, his doctrines proved the destruction of his followers." "Some account of the Late Right Hon. Edumund Burke," *Monthly Magazine*, July 1797, p. 44.

108. George Whitfield or Whitefield (1714-70) was a Methodist preacher, famous for his moving sermons, often preached outdoors, once to a crowd of twenty thousand.

109. "A rich gown trimmed with buttons and loops, fashionable in the late seventeenth and eighteenth centuries." *OED*.

110. A wood of trees in the form of bushes from the stems being regularly cut back every few years for use as poles, etc. From meaning a wood without tall trees, "copse" or "coppice" later came to mean any small wood.

111. To enlist.

112. See Acts 8:23. Bitterness and unpleasantness.

113. "Hoe": care, anxiety, trouble. The *OED* cites this passage and William D.

Parish's *A Dictionary of the Sussex Dialect and Collection of Provincialisms in Use in the County of Sussex* (1875) for this regional expression.

114. Not identified.

115. A children's game for five players. Four of the children stand in each corner of a room; the fifth child stands in the middle of the room. As the four corner players move from corner to corner in succession, the fifth player tries to occupy a corner before another reaches it.

116. Strings with which to guide toddlers as they learn to walk. Used figuratively, the phrase refers to a state of dependence.

117. We have already been told that Delmont's hair is "cropped." What Martha Goldthorp seems to be saying is that if he took clerical orders, Delmont would have to don the traditional dress of a clergyman—a black coat—and that he would have to wear a wig instead of his own hair. For that reason, his close-cut hair would then be shaved.

118. John Trott was a generic name used in the eighteenth century for a dull Englishman. In George Etherege's *The Man of Mode* (1676), Sir Fopling Flutter ridicules the name (Act 3, Scene 3, lines 325-29).

119. It sounds as though Winslow intends to make Miss Goldthorp a ward in Chancery, which was done when the custody of heirs was disputed—in the High Court of Justice where the Lord Chancellor, the highest ranking judiciary official in England, presides.

120. Mrs. Delmont's educational theories are derived from Rousseau as set forth in *Émile*. Another of Smith's characters, Mrs. Belmour of *Minor Morals*, describes Rousseau as having "many fanciful and some erroneous strictures on the subject of education" [(London: Minerva Press for A.K. Newman and Co., 1817), 1:40], but Rousseau's emphasis on the development of reason is a principle Smith endorses. Rousseau was not an atheist, but Mrs. Crewkherne probably refers to him or Diderot along with Goethe or Herder in her vituperative slap at the European Enlightenment.

121. Gilbert West, "An Epistle to a Lady," lines 91-92.

122. "Medora" may be Smith's feminization of "Medoro," the young man loved by Angelica in Ariosto's *Orlando Furioso*. The unusual name was later adopted by the nineteenth-century novelist Medora Gordon Byron, who claimed to be a natural daughter of the poet Byron.

123. The age of twenty-one, that is.

124. Approval or sanction.

125. New residential areas of London built in squares, just fashionable enough to be a goal for middle-class people moving up.

126. There are four "Inns of Court" in London, Lincoln's-Inn-Fields being one. The "woolsack," symbolizing wealth based on sheep-rearing, is the red wool seat used by the Lord Chancellor in his role as Speaker of the House of Lords.

127. One cannot do without that very world that one hates and laughs at.

128. According to legend, St. Ursula, a fifth-century British princess, went with eleven thousand virgins on a pilgrimage to Rome. At Cologne, where they were massacred by Huns, their alleged skulls were still shown to tourists in the nineteenth century. Their supposed number is thought to originate in a misunderstanding of the name Undecimilla.

129. Not identified. Diana was popularly seen as the goddess of chastity, and Bridget, like Ursula, was a virgin and a saint.

130. Kinds of expensive fabric: tiffany is a transparent silk or muslin; tinsel, a silk or wool fabric interwoven with gold or silver thread.

131. That is, a week from tomorrow.

132. Roman Censor Marcus Porcius Cato (234-149 B.C.). To call a man a "Cato" is to imply his nature is self-denying, brusque, and blunt.

133. Medora, the child of nature, is one of several such young women in fiction of the 1790s. Sibella Valmont, of Eliza Fenwick's *Secresy,* and Mary Raymond of Mary Hays's *The Victim of Prejudice,* like Medora, are reared on Rousseauesque principles and designed as perfect companions to men brought up in similar fashion.

134. Scottish-American.

135. The War for American Independence, fought during the reign of George III, and the "heaven-born" minister, Lord North, who in 1772 opposed measures designed to foster religious tolerance, a position that would meet with Mrs. Crewkherne's approval.

136. William Cowper, *The Task,* book 3, lines 290-92.

137. A London street that extends from Piccadilly to Vigo Street. In the late eighteenth century, it was the location of residences, offices, and shops, including that of the famous wine merchants Saccone and Speed.

138. Nothing can go wrong in good company.

VOLUME 2

1. "If in the field she walke, then must she have / [him] lead or guide her in the way; / And by a river in the shadie cave / They oft did use to spend the heate of day." Ariosto, *Orlando Furioso,* canto 19, stanza 35. Translated by Sir John Harington (1591) as canto 19, stanza 27.

2. A building in which merchants gather to transact business. The exchange of London is called the Royal Exchange.

3. A variation on Frances Burney's *Cecilia,* in which the title character inherits her wealth only if her husband takes her name.

4. What is now Holland was at that time the United Provinces.

5. Two Italian dramatic works with pastoral themes and settings. The *Aminta* (1573) is by Tasso and *Il Pastor Fido* (1589) is by Guarini.

6. As a scholar at Westminster School, Glenmorris was maintained out of its endowment ("on the foundation"), while other pupils paid fees.

7. An office appropriated to the keeping of accounts and business correspondence.

8. The order of British nobility (after the royal family) descends as follows: (1) duke and duchess, (2) marquess and marchioness, (3) earl and countess, (4) viscount and viscountess, (5) baron and baroness, and (6) baronet and lady. It had long been possible to purchase the conferring of a title that would then descend from eldest son to eldest son. The new Lord Daventry's family will have jumped several ranks.

9. The city of London, i.e., the medieval part, now the financial district.

10. These stanzas were composed for this novel. See Smith, *Poems,* ed. Stuart Curran (Oxford: Oxford Univ. Press, 1993), p. 122n.

11. Mrs. Glenmorris invokes both the pejorative and the affirmative connotations of the word "romantic," which at this time was associated both with wild, extravagant flights of fancy and with freedom of imagination and refusal to slavishly conform to meaningless—even oppressive—convention.

12. Track.

13. The head domestic in a private home such as De Verdon's, similar to a butler.

14. Shakespeare, *Romeo and Juliet* 2.2.82-84.

15. He did not wait until he was fully of age, that is, twenty-one, before becoming a member of Parliament. It seems that Lord Daventry was elected to the House of Commons when he was twenty and served therein until he took his seat in the House of Lords the following year.

16. A town at which relays of post-horses are kept for hire; a town in which there is a post office.

17. "A kind of glass composed of silica, potash, and lime (without lead or iron), made in circular sheets by blowing and whirling." *OED.*

18. A reference.

19. The Wars of the Roses, which began in 1455 and lasted until the Battle of Bosworth in 1485.

20. Shackles for the legs.

21. A glove.

22. Geoffrey of Anjou (1113-51), was known as Geoffrey Plantagenet from his habit of wearing a sprig of the shrub known as broom ("genet" in French) in his cap. His son, Henry II (who married Elinor of Aquitaine), had four sons of whom the Geoffrey Lady de Verdon claims as an ancestor was the third, not the second. Constance was Geoffrey's wife (the bereaved mother in Shakespeare's *King John*). Lady de Verdon claims descent not from her but from Geoffrey's "illegitimate" union with an unnamed noblewoman in the south of France.

23. Lady Mary has seen or heard of relics of England's heroic past. The story of Bevis of Hampton was told in a verse-romance written in the late thirteenth or early fourteenth century. Bevis avenges his father's death with his sword, called "Morglay." Hotspur is the irascible Harry Percy (1364-1403), son of the first Earl of Northumberland, killed by Prince Hal, later Henry V. Shakespeare, *1 Henry IV.* Guy of Warwick was famous for slaying an enraged dun cow. A huge tusk, said to be the rib of that cow, is still displayed at Warwick Castle. It is Guy of Warwick, not Bevis of Hampton, who is one of the Nine (not Seven) Worthies or Champions. The nine include three worthy pagans—Hector of Troy, Alexander the Great, and Julius Caesar; three Old Testament heroes—Joshua, David, and Judas Maccabaeus; and three Christian warriors—King Arthur, Charlemagne, and either Guy of Warwick or Godfrey of Boulogne.

24. Strange or odd.

25. Humphrey, Duke of Gloucester (1390-1447) was the son of Henry IV and the younger brother of Henry V. He founded what later became the Bodleian Library,

whose oldest room bears his name. "To dine with Duke Humphrey" means not to be fed at all, but the origins of the phrase are unclear.

26. Nonsense with which to frighten children. From the children's tale "Jack, the Giant Killer" or "Jack and the Beanstalk."

27. More commonly, Hogen Mogen, "a popular corruption or perversion of the Dutch *Hoogmogendheiden,* 'High Mightiness.'" *OED.* As used here by Malloch, a contemptuous term for a person in power.

28. Latin for "according to art," i.e., to legal practice.

29. Shakespeare, *Romeo and Juliet* 2.2.66-68.

30. Terrace.

31. One who runs or rides before; a herald or messenger.

32. In the *Vindication of the Rights of Woman,* Mary Wollstonecraft notes how governesses, unlike tutors to boys, were made to feel the pain of dependency. This oppression had been canvassed since Jane Collier's *Art of Tormenting* (above, Preface, n. 1).

33. Charlotte Smith herself had been suffering from arthritis for quite some time, since 1794 at least. She, like Mrs. Margyson, took opiates—laudanum in particular, as she noted to Sarah Rose in a letter dated July 30, 1804: "I . . have lived on 'Brandy, Aether, and Laudanum' now for some years" (quoted by Rufus Paul Turner, "Charlotte Smith (1749-1806): New Light on Her Life and Literary Career," Ph.D. diss., Univ. of Southern California, 1966, p. 84). In a 1797 letter, Smith mentions the use of "Soporiphics" (quoted by Putney, p. 81). Hilbish deduced from *Celestina* (1791) that Smith was quite familiar with the effects of laudanum. "Charlotte Smith," pp. 181-82.

34. Fenced.

35. The armor of the Lancastrians.

36. A place for hanging buckets filled with sand to be employed in case of a fire. In plate 6 of William Hogarth's *Marriage a la Mode,* fire buckets line the hall outside the apartment of Lady Squanderfield's miserly father.

37. Prayers.

38. Hill.

39. Smith's *The Old Manor House* also features an encounter between young lovers and a smuggler. Monimia and Orlando surprise smuggler Jonas Wilkins, who uses the cellars of Rayland Hall to store contraband. Coastal areas of Great Britain were particularly conducive to smuggling.

40. The River Ribble runs through the Yorkshire Dales and Lancashire to the Irish Sea. Charley (i.e., Chorley) is a town in Lancashire, northwest of Manchester.

41. Roads not going through London.

42. Minors, who could not marry in England without their parents' consent, could do so in Scotland simply by avowing in front of two witnesses their desire to wed.

43. Not identified.

44. The North Sea.

45. Samuel Johnson describes the "Highland Hut" as an edifice "with some tendency to circularity." He further notes: "The wall of a common hut is always built without mortar, by a skilful adaptation of loose stones. Sometimes perhaps a double

wall of stones is raised, and the intermediate space filled with earth. The air is thus completely excluded. Some walls are, I think, formed of turfs, held together by a wattle, or texture of twigs. Of the meanest huts, the first room is lighted by the entrance, and the second by the smoke-hole. The fire is usually made in the middle." *A Journey to the Western Islands of Scotland,* published with James Boswell's *The Journal of a Tour to the Hebrides,* ed. R.W. Chapman (Oxford: Oxford Univ. Press, 1924), pp. 28, 91.

46. In the Aegean Sea, between Greece and Asia Minor.

47. This power was considerable, as Johnson attests: "The Laird has all those in his power that live upon his farms. . . . The Laird at pleasure can feed or starve, can give bread, or withold it. This inherent power was yet strengthened by the kindness of consanguinity, and the reverence of patriarchal authority. The Laird was the father of the Clan, and his tenants commonly bore his name. And to these principles of original command was added, for many ages, an exclusive right of legal jurisdiction. . . . Every duty, moral or political, was absorbed in affection and adherence to the Chief." *Journey,* p. 77.

48. Smith is probably thinking here of the poems purportedly written by "Ossian" and translated by James MacPherson: *Fingal* (1762) and *Temora* (1763). In composing his "epics," MacPherson drew on the rich tradition of heroic poetry in Gaelic, though he also undoubtedly shaped the material to enhance analogies with Homer and Milton.

49. The Highlanders used peat for their fires. Johnson notes, "At Nairn we may fix the verge of the Highlands; for here I first saw peat fires, and first heard the *Erse* language." *Journey,* p. 22.

50. Mention.

51. "The celebrated pirate Paul Jones landed in this way more than once on the coast of Scotland, during the American war." [CS's note] Called a pirate by Smith, the Scottish-born John Paul Jones (1747-92) was actually an American naval officer famous for his rather piratical exploits in the American Revolution.

52. Corpse.

53. "The highlanders imagine, that when any person is to die, it is announced by a shadow appearing in his or her likeness, which flits before the spectator, shrieking and lamenting, towards the place of interment." [CS's note] This spectre is known in Gaelic lore as the banshee.

54. Not identified.

55. The Ladie or Lady of Kilbrodie was a Jacobite, one who supported the right to the English throne of the Roman Catholic James II (deposed in 1688 during the Glorious Revolution) and his heirs, the Old Pretender, James Francis Edward Stuart (1688-1766) and the Young Pretender, Charles Edward Stuart (1720-88). The Stuarts' "unhappiness" includes, in addition to the deposing of James II, the execution of Charles I in 1649, during the English Civil War, and the numerous tragedies that beset the Scottish Stuarts from the fourteenth century on.

56. Smith's two sons, William Towers and Nicholas Hankey Smith, were signed on as writers to the East India Company by the age of sixteen and sent to India shortly after. (Both continued to correspond with her.)

57. Cf. Johnson: "Here [in the island of Col] I first mounted a little Highland steed; . . . The horses of the Islands, as of other barren countries, are very low: they are indeed musculous and strong, beyond what their size gives reason for expecting; but a bulky man upon one of their backs makes a very disproportionate appearance." *Journey*, p. 109.

58. St. Cuthbert (d. 687) was the bishop of Lindisfarne, a monk who lived for some time as a hermit on the island of Farne off the English coast. The partially renovated ruins inhabited by Ladie Kilbrodie are the former monastic dwelling of an order of St. Cuthbert.

59. John Knox (1505?-72), leader of the Scottish Reformation, which introduced Calvinism into Scotland. The reformation led to the dissolving of the monasteries and abbeys and the destruction of cathedrals in the countries that rejected Roman Catholicism in favor of various Protestant denominations—in Scotland, Presbyterianism. Cf. Johnson: "[T]hrough the few islands which we visited, we neither saw nor heard of any house of prayer, except in *Sky*, that was not in ruins. The malignant influence of *Calvinism* has blasted ceremony and decency together; and if the remembrance of papal superstition is obliterated, the monuments of papal piety are likewise effaced." *Journey*, p. 58.

60. An echo of Pope's "long-sounding isles, and intermingled graves." *Eloisa to Abelard*, line 164.

61. Perhaps Carn Mor Dearg, in the Grampian Mountains in Western Scotland.

62. "Warlock or witch." [CS's note]

63. "Stuff" refers to woven fabric of any kind. "Rusty" is said of dark clothes that are shabby, worn, or faded.

64. "In certain places the death of people is supposed to be foretold by the cries and shrieks of Benshi [banshee], or the fairies' wife, uttered along the very path where the funeral is to pass; and what in Wales are called corpse candles, are often imagined to appear and foretel mortality. From PENNANT" [CS's note] Her reference is to Pennant's *A Tour in Scotland and Voyage to the Hebrides* (1769).

65. Hobgoblin or ghost.

66. Grannie or granny.

67. "Dr Johnson relates, in his Journey to the Hebrides, that in his passage from one place to another, one of the highland boatmen declared he 'heard the cry of an English ghost.'" [CS's note] See Johnson, *Journey*, p. 67.

68. In Scottish fairy tales, a kelpie is a water spirit that takes the form of a horse and delights in drowning travelers. In its more benign moments, a kelpie has been known to help millers by keeping the mill wheel going throughout the night. William Collins in "An Ode on the Popular Superstitions of the Highlands of Scotland" mentions this "wily monster" (line 100).

69. "Related in Les Causes Celébres." [CS's note] A reference to the work Smith herself translated under the title *The Romance of Real Life*.

70. "Howdie, a midwife." [CS's note]

71. Scottish variant of "moors."

72. "I suspect this to be a line of Miss Sewards." [CS's note] Actually from Erasmus Darwin, *The Botanic Garden, Part II, Containing the Loves of the Plants*, canto 3, line

14. Smith may be right, however. *The Loves of the Plants* had begun as a collaborative project between Seward and Darwin. In the end Darwin wrote the poem, but he silently incorporated some of Seward's verses. See Londa Schiebinger, *Nature's Body: Gender in the Making of Modern Science* (Boston: Beacon Press, 1993), p. 31.

73. When the collies (sheepdogs) go scratching and making croon (howling, whining), dole (suffering, misery) will befall.

74. Erasmus Darwin, *The Botanic Garden,* Part II, *The Loves of the Plants,* canto 3, lines 329-34.

75. "Phillibeg" or filibeg: a kilt. "Bonnet": "A head-dress of men and boys: usually soft and distinguished from the *hat* by want of a brim. In England, superseded in common use (app. 1700) by *cap,* but retained in Scotland; hence sometimes treated as = 'Scotch cap.'" *OED.*

76. Erasmus Darwin, *The Botanic Garden,* part II, *The Loves of the Plants,* canto 1, lines 341-42.

77. Sandpipers.

78. Small castle.

79. Long considered a crime against God, suicide became in the eighteenth century the subject of much discussion. Rousseau's *Julie, ou La Nouvelle Héloise* presents arguments for and against the right to take one's own life in letters 114 and 115. The *Encylopédie* offers a similarly balanced view. Montesquieu (*Lettres persanes,* letter 76) and Hume ("Suicide" in *Five Dissertations*) offer arguments in favor of a lenient, understanding view of such an act. Goethe's *Werther* is the most important of several sentimental novels that treat sympathetically a suicide from lovesickness, melancholy, or despair.

80. "T. Warton." [CS's note] Ode VI, "The Suicide," lines 30-36.

81. "By rendering life insupportable, God orders one to quit it. J.J. ROUSSEAU." [CS's note] From *Julie, ou la Nouvelle Héloise* (1791), letter 114.

82. Tides that attain a minimal rise and fall, observable at or near the first and last quarters of the moon. Smith seems to mistake the term somewhat, because she emphasizes the unusual "reflux" of the ocean rather than the minimal difference between high and low tides, which the term denotes.

83. The language native to the Highlands and the Western Islands of Scotland; also called Gaelic.

84. "Kelpies are spirits haunting the sea and rivers." [CS's note] See above, vol. 2, note 68.

85. A violent storm with wind and rain occurring at the time of the equinox.

86. "Orobus tuberosus, the bulbous roots of which are eaten by the highlanders, and accounted very nourishing." [CS's note]

87. "Or rather, as Dr. Johnson describes them, 'with some tendency to circularity.'" [CS's note] See above, vol. 2, note 45.

88. Old wife.

89. "The name, in Scotland and north of England, of a form in which home-made bread is made; usually unleavened, of large size, round or oval form, and flattish, without being as thin as 'scon' or oat-cake. In Scotland, bannocks are usually of barley- or pease-meal." *OED.*

90. Johnson remarks throughout his *Journey* on the absence of trees in Scotland. However, the Cairngorms (which Johnson did not tour) still contain the last of the great forest of Caledonia (of Scotch pines).

91. Johnson describes these structures, which, he says, are numerous in the High-lands and the Western Islands of Scotland: "These caves . . . are formed . . . by taking advantage of a hollow, where banks or rocks rise on either side. If no such place can be found, the ground must be cut away. The walls are made by piling stones against the earth, on either side. It is then roofed by larger stones laid across the cavern, which therefore cannot be wide. Over the roof, turfs were placed, and grass was suffered to grow; and the mouth was concealed by bushes, or some other cover. . . . I imagine them to have been places only of occasional use, in which the Islander, upon a sudden alarm, hid his utensils, or his cloaths, and perhaps sometimes his wife and children." *Journey,* p. 65.

92. Edmund Spenser, *The Faerie Queene,* book 1, canto 6, stanza 37, lines 325-30, 333. Line 333 is altered slightly: The lesser pangs can beare, who hath endured the chief.

93. "Murmuring or sighing of the wind as it sways the trees." [CS's note]

94. Cf. Thomas Pennant's description of the highland heather beds, which he too extols for their comfort. *A Tour in Scotland and Voyage to the Hebrides* (Chester: John Monk, 1774), p. 329.

95. An inner room.

96. "The holly (ilex-aquifolium). The beautiful plant with which Burns com-posed the chaplet of his Scottish muse." [CS's note] Burns, *The Vision,* lines 49-52.

97. "Rubus preticasus. There is something particularly elegant in the alternate triple leaves and the long weak branches of this plant." [CS's note]

98. "Sempervivum tectorum." [CS's note]

99. "Parietaria officinalis." [CS's note]

100. Meadow grass.

101. "Sedum acre, or wall-pepper." [CS's note]

102. "Geranium sylvaticum." [CS's note]

103. "Lichen scruposus." [CS's note]

104. "Bryum argenteum." [CS's note]

105. "Asplenium tricomanoides, common maiden hair." [CS's note]

106. "Hieracium murorum." [CS's note]

107. In book 5 of *The Odyssey,* the enchantress Calypso's cavern is described as shaded by aspens, alders, and cypresses and ornamented with grape vines around the entrance. Irises and parsley grew amid springs that watered the meadow in which the cave was located.

108. "Rubus chamemorus." [CS's note] Pennant reports being served "*Cloudber-ries,* that grow on the adjacent mountains" for dessert at Dundonnel. *A Tour in Scot-land,* p. 328. A cloudberry is of the same family as the raspberry. It is a large, flavorful, orange-colored fruit.

109. The Scottish wild cat (the same size as a domestic cat but genetically other) and the pine marten (of the weasel family and valued for its fur) are completely differ-ent animals.

110. "Cranberries, mossberries, or moorberries, Vaccinium Oxycocoos." [CS's note]

111. Boswell describes the dress of a "Highland gentleman," Malcolm Macleod: "He wore a pair of brogues,—Tartan hose which came up only near to his knees, and left them bare,—a purple camblet kilt,—a black waistcoat,—a short green cloth coat bound with gold cord,—a yellowish bushy wig,—a large blue bonnet with a gold thread button." *Journal,* p. 264.

112. Since Laura Glenmorris has earlier suggested that Donald and Jeannie cannot write (see p. 129), it is worth noting that the poor were often taught reading but not penmanship if their trade did not demand the keeping of accounts. A fisherman or a herdsman, Laura notes in the earlier passage, would have no need for the skill of writing.

113. "Who so shall set on Cupids snares his foote / Must seeke to draw it backe least it be caught, / And madnes meere in love to overshoot / The foole hath felt, the wise hath ever taught." Ludovico Ariosto, *Orlando Furioso,* trans. Sir John Harington, canto 24, stanza 1.

114. Though not twice as long, the Scottish mile (1980 yards) was longer than the standard English mile (1760 yards).

115. Established in their careers.

116. A day-boarder; one who remains at school for dinner (served in the late eighteenth century around 3:00 or 4:00 P.M.) but goes home at night.

117. Or pendant: A match, a companion piece, a counterpart. Churchill's poem was published in 1763. Its frontispiece depicts the figure of Famine, which the poem describes as follows:

Her hollow cheeks were each a deep-sunk cell,

. . . .

All shrivell'd was her skin, and here and there,
Making their way by force, her bones lay bare: [*The Works of C. Churchill in Four Volumes,* vol. 1, 5th ed. (London: John Churchill, 1774), p. 117]

See figure 1, opposite

118. "'Had Young ever travelled towards the north, I should not have wondered at his becoming enamoured of the moon.'—'The heavens also, of a clear softened blue, throw her forward, and the evening star appears a lesser moon to the naked eye.'"—— ——Letters written from Norway, Sweden, and Denmark, by Mary Wolstoncroft. [CS's note] Both quotations are from Wollstonecraft, *Letters Written during a Short Residence in Sweden, Norway, and Denmark* (1796), letter 5. She refers to Edward Young's *Night Thoughts,* book 3, in which he calls upon the moon for inspiration.

119. Edmund Spenser, *The Faerie Queene,* book 1, canto 3, stanza 27, lines 235-36, 240-42, altered.

And weeping said, 'Ah my long lackèd Lord,
Where have ye bene thus long out of my sight?

. . . .

For since mine eye your joyous sight did mis,
My chearefull day is turnd to chearlesse night,
And eke my night of death the shadow is.

120. Perhaps an echo of *Macbeth* 3.4.61, "the air drawn dagger."

Figure 1. Famine. (Courtesy of Hargrett Rare Book & Manuscript Library/University of Georgia Libraries)

121. Pennant refers to ruins near Tongue and Loch-Eribol distinguished by the name "Dune of Dornadilla." He quotes a correspondent to the *Edinburgh Magazine* who translates the phrase to mean the *"roundstone place of the worship of God." A Tour in Scotland,* pp. 340-41n. If Smith recalls the discussion, she does so in only the vaguest sense, without reference to the ruins or their druidical significance.

122. *Othello* 2.1.183-85.

123. A seaport on the northern coast of France near Brest.

124. John Hampden (1594-1643), a leader of the parliamentary opposition to Charles I, was killed in the Civil War in a battle near Oxford. Algernon Sidney (1622-83) also opposed Charles I and continued to oppose the Stuarts after the Restoration, for which he was condemned to death.

125. A Scotsman. The Scottish were generally sympathetic to the Stuarts because the House of Stuart originated in Scotland. Glenmorris, however, espouses democratic principles, which he sees as informing both the Parliamentarian cause in the English Civil War of the 1640s and the American fight for independence that took place more than a century later.

126. Pope, "Eloisa to Abelard," line 238: "I stretch my empty arms; it glides away."

127. Islands off the southwest coast of England, at the entrance to the English Channel.

128. Carrickfergus is on the eastern coast of Northern Ireland, across the Northern Channel from Portpatrick, Scotland.

129. City of western Switzerland on the North shore of Lake Geneva.

130. Robert Burns, *The Cotter's Saturday Night,* lines 77-81, slightly altered.

131. Catkins: drooping clusters of tiny flowerets.

132. A packet is a boat that carries mail, in this case sailing from Halifax, Nova Scotia.

133. *Paradise Lost* Book V, line 13.

134. Tree trunks.

135. Pollards are made by cutting the top branches of a tree back to its trunk so that a dense growth of new shoots is produced.

136. "Oxalis." [CS's note]

137. From "Columbia," poetical name for America.

138. In debt.

VOLUME 3

1. Not identified.

2. The bills referred to here would be bills of exchange, written orders addressed to a firm to pay a specified sum to a specified individual, in this case Mrs. Glenmorris.

3. The *London Gazette,* published biweekly from 1666 on, lists pensions, promotions, bankruptcies, etc.

4. Revolutionary France declared war on England in 1793; the "bad turn of affairs in Holland" refers to the fact that in 1795 the Netherlands and Dutch provinces were defeated by France and incorporated into the Batavian Republic.

5. St. George's Fields is a burial ground in what is now Albion Street near Marble Arch.

6. Earlier, Petrify and Company refused further advances (see above, p. 153).

7. "These are the notions, not of the hero who is accused of being tainted with modern philosophy, but of a man of the world, ready to acquiesce in all that world dictates." [CS's note]

8. A word that originated in the 1780s among the English as a nickname for any inhabitant of America. Partridge, *Dictionary of Slang.*

9. Slang for cardshark or cheat (c. sixteenth-nineteenth centuries). Partridge, *Dictionary of Slang.*

10. "An old she-cat; *contemptuously* applied to a jealous or imperious old woman." *OED.*

11. Of course, Glenmorris has done no such thing, but Smith had written of such a profligate husband in *Desmond*—Lord Verney, who arranges for the sale of his wife to a degenerate French aristocrat.

12. Commissions in the army were regularly bought and sold in the eighteenth century. Roy Porter reports that "[i]n mid-century an ensigncy cost about £400, a lieutenant-colonelcy about £3,500." *English Society in the Eighteenth Century,* p. 152. A major ranks above an ensign (the lowest officer in the army) and just below a lieutenant colonel. In January of 1804, Smith and her son Lionel's father-in-law bought Lionel a majoralty for £950.

13. The Sabines were an ancient Italian population, conquered by the Romans around 290 B.C.

14. Days of great heat; a reference to the month of July, which marked the end of the London social season.

15. The *OED* cites Smith's use of "lop-eared" as a substitute for the more usual "crop-eared"—a term describing the hairstyle favored by the Puritans, close cut, exposing the ears.

16. Not identified. Medora, my idol, mine among these branches, amidst these new-grown grasses and these flowers, hear how a light wind whispers, sweetly jesting, that takes flight from the fragrant plants, raises the most beautiful spirits and in its vague wanderings forms from a thousand odors a single aroma.

17. One who is at home anywhere. A phrase dating back at least to Cicero (*De Legibus,* Book 1, Sect. 23), it had particular currency in the Enlightenment, Oliver Goldsmith's 1760 satire "Chinese Letters," republished in 1762 under the title *The Citizen of the World,* being perhaps the most prominent use of the expression.

18. "The American Farmer, page 46." [CS's note] St. Jean de Crèvecoeur's *Letters from an American Farmer* (1782) celebrate life in America—its potential prosperity and its rejection of class hierarchy. See "Letter III," "What is an American?"

19. The range of musical notes, extending from G on the bottom line of the bass staff to E on the top line of the treble staff.

20. Nymphs are minor nature goddesses in Greek mythology who represent the spirits of the woods, groves, springs, streams, rivers, etc.

21. Perhaps a reference to Johann Kasper Lavater (1741-1801), Swiss theologian, philosopher, and founder of the study of physiognomy. His *Physiognomische Fragmente*

were widely read and translated, and Smith refers to the study of physiognomy in *Marchmont,* describing her heroine Althea as a "disciple of Lavater" (2:174).

22. Arcadia is a mountainous region of Greece. In the pastoral tradition, it is the domain of rural simplicity, inhabited by shepherds and characterized by happy innocence.

23. Cowper calls London "the great Babel," from the tower whose builders God punished with confusion of unintelligible languages. *The Task,* Book 4, "The Winter Evening," 1:90; Genesis 11.

24. "Flora" is a descriptive catalog of the plants of a region, a country, or a geological period. Medora and Laura Glenmorris's laughingly projected "catalogue" would depict the plants of Delmont's estate, Upwood.

25. Composed of marl, or clay mixed with lime; fertilized.

26. Woods on the side of a steep hill or a bank.

27. "Sterne." [CS's note] In *A Sentimental Journey,* volume 2, Yorick distracts himself from worries over his missing passport by reading *Much Ado About Nothing.* Again, Smith seems to be quoting from memory or adapting the passage.

28. "If any thing disturbs me, I go to my harpsichord, play one of the lively airs I have danced to, and all is forgotten! Goethe in Werter." [CS's note] Charlotte says this to Werter early in book 1 as they talk of the pleasures of reading and dancing.

29. "I give no translation, because those who are interested in such an anecdote will probably understand it as it is, and some others, who are not, may think that it already has taken up too great a space.

"I may however add, that some drawings of plants, done many years ago by a very near relation of mine in a favourite residence, recal to my mind at this moment the scenery of the place, the spots where they grew, and the very sensations that the air, the sunshine, and landscape then gave me." [CS's note] Rousseau, *Confessions,* translated thus by J.M. Cohen for the Penguin edition (1953):

> As she walked she saw something blue in the hedge, and said to me: "Look! There are some periwinkle still in flower." I had never seen a periwinkle, I did not stoop to examine it, and I am too short-sighted to distinguish plants on the ground without doing so. I merely gave it a passing glance, and nearly thirty years elapsed before I saw any periwinkle again, or at least before I noticed any. In 1764, when I was at Cressier with my friend M. du Peyrou, we were climbing a hill, on the top of which he has built a pretty little look-out which he rightly calls Belle Vue. I was then beginning to botanize a little and, as I climbed and looked among the bushes, I gave a shout of joy: "Look, there are some periwinkle!" . . . The reader can judge by the effect on me of something so small, the degree to which I have been moved by everything which relates to that stage in my life. [216]

30. A "chaplet" is a garland or wreath. Here "Flora" refers to the goddess of flowers rather than the botanical catalog signified earlier. See vol. 3, note 24, above.

31. "Pretence to" here signifies practice of, without any implication of deception.

32. "'Bubbling runnels join'd the sound.'" Collins. [CS's note] From "The Passions: An Ode for Music," line 63.

33. Composed for this novel. See Smith, *Poems,* ed. Curran, p. 73.

34. A "special pleader" is a derisive term for an advocate in a lawsuit. The "Inns of Court" in London include Gray's Inn, Lincoln's Inn, and the Inner and Middle Temple. These four sets of buildings house the legal societies that train lawyers and admit them to the bar.

35. Neither to wonder at anything, nor yet to admire anything. Horace, *Epistles* Book I, poem vi, line 1.

36. Perhaps a reference to the Colossus of Rhodes, a bronze statue of a the giant form of Apollo that stood across the entrance of the Rhodian harbor. Here used with negative connotations, as by Peter Pindar (John Wolcot [1738-1819]), who referred to the Colossus as "the Rhodian Bully" in *The Louisiad* (1785-95), canto 2, line 288.

37. "For ev'rie other sowre that gets a place / To seate it selfe amid this pleasant sweet / Doth helpe in th'end to give a greater grace / And makes loves joy more gratful when they meet." Ariosto, *Orlando Furioso,* canto 31, stanza 2, trans. Sir John Harington (1591).

38. In South Wales; one of the largest natural harbors in Britain.

39. Composed by Smith for this novel; see *Poems.* ed. Curran, p. 74.

40. From *The History of the Life and Death of Thomas Lord Cromwell* (anon., 1602).

41. Latin for felon of oneself, that is, a suicide.

42. Michaelmas Day is 29 September: the church festival of St. Michael the archangel. Old Michaelmas Day "is the day that would have been called 29 Sept. if the Old Style had been retained without correction." *OED.* Though Catholic Europe had adopted the Gregorian calendar in the sixteenth century, the "Old Style" calendar had been retained in England until 1752. Reform involved regarding the beginning of the year as 1 January instead of 25 March and dropping eleven days between 2 and 14 September. Thus, Old Michaelmas Day, in 1798, would have been 10 October.

43. Took no notice.

44. "These stanzas were given me by a gentleman, now gone to another quarter of the world. They were composed for a work he meditated, but gave up soon after beginning it, and they have, I believe, no reference to any circumstance of real life. A few words are altered from what they originally were. Some part of them appeared, by the officious indiscretion of an acquaintance, in one of the daily prints some years ago." [CS's note] I have not identified the gentleman, and Smith includes the verses in her *Elegiac Sonnets,* suggesting that her contribution to their authorship was rather more substantial than she here claims.

45. *Tristram Shandy,* vol. 7, chap. 2. Tristram, who is on a ship and feeling seasick, is anxious for the winds to subside.

46. Joseph Addison, *Cato,* Act 1, Scene 1, lines 104-5.

47. James I instituted the order of Baronets in 1611 to raise money for the colonization of Ulster by the fees paid for the title. The senior baronets are thus those whose titles date from 1611. The "bloody hand" is the heraldic device of Ulster and so signifies the rank of baronet. Leadenhall Street was the address of the East India House and other businesses.

48. Burke, *Reflections on the Revolution in France,* speaks in favor of prejudice: "Prejudice renders a man's virtue his habit; and not a series of unconnected acts. Through just prejudice, his duty becomes a part of his nature." Everyman edition, ed. Ernest Rhys (London: J.M. Dent, 1910), p. 84.

49. Paid companions, that is. Cf. Betty Rizzo, *Companions without Vows: Relationships among Eighteenth-Century British Women* (Athens: Univ. of Georgia Press, 1994).

50. Soame Jenyns, "The Modern Fine Lady," line 18-19. Jenyns reads "softer charms."

51. The shield on which a coat of arms is depicted; "a blot on the escutcheon" is a figurative expression meaning a stain on a person's reputation.

52. "Bluestockings" refers to the informal groups held by women in the latter half of the eighteenth century for the purpose of intellectual and literary conversation. Although the company was mixed—and in fact the word originated from the blue stockings worn by Benjamin Stillingfleet to such gatherings—the term refers to the women who held and frequented the meetings. Hostesses and members of such groups included Elizabeth Vesey, Elizabeth Montagu, Elizabeth Carter, Hester Chapone, Frances Boscawen, Mary Delany, and Hannah More. It is not clear whether Mrs. Grinsted is meant to be a satiric portrait of a specific individual or simply to ridicule the pretentiousness of some who attended bluestocking colloquia. In a 26 July 1800 letter to Mary Hays, Smith relates her own experience with the bluestockings: "I was heretofore admitted being then a mere novice & much in favor, to the celebrated conversations at Mrs. Montagues, & I found that the greatest difficulty I had was to resist a violent inclination to yawn, tho I suppose every body talkd their very best. Since I have been at other assemblies of literati, when I own I have been equally disappointed tho not quite in the same way." Misc. MS. 2152. The Carl H. Pforzheimer Collection of Shelley and His Circle, New York Public Library, Astor, Lenox and Tilden Foundations.

53. "Conglomeration," reconciliation;, "approximated," related; "eximious," eminent.

54. From Horace's *sesquipedalia verba,* words a foot and a half long. Richard Brinsley Sheridan's Mrs. Malaprop in *The Rivals* (1775), the most famous of the eighteenth century's many satiric portraits of learned women, shares Mrs. Grinsted's linguistic affectation, though not her semantic accuracy.

55. "Quondam," Latin for "former."

56. *Hamlet* 3.3.58: "Offense's gilded hand may shove by justice."

57. Thoughtlessness, negligence.

58. Way out, evasion.

59. To watch diligently.

60. "Amortise," cancel; "interdictory prohibition," ban; "effervescence," zeal; "fulminated," proclaimed.

61. Obscured.

62. Paid.

63. Horace, *Odes* Book 3, poem 2, line 17: "Virtue, to those that may not die, / Opes the strait doors of heav'n on high, / And with her wings in stretch for that sublime, / Scorns the unletter'd mob, and sordid earth, and time." Christopher Smart, *Verse Translation of Horace's Odes,* ed. Arthur Sherbo, English Literary Studies (Victoria, B.C.: Univ. of Victoria Press, 1979), p. 119.

64. She means exempt or extricate.

65. Smith seems to have forgotten that Mrs. Glenmorris has a *morning* appointment—an inconsistency that may speak to the haste of composition and to the ab-

sence of Hayley's proofreading skills. Hayley quit reviewing the manuscript of *The Young Philosopher* somewhere in volume 3 (perhaps here?), because of his son's illness.

66. A public house, an inn or hostelry, providing accommodation for travelers or members of the general public.

67. Smith's class prejudice is apparent here. By 1798 the term "gentleman" was being appropriated by those she clearly felt had no right to use it: men of trade, from the "dark lanes and narrow alleys in the city," who by attaining a certain amount of wealth affected the habits of their superiors by birth. "Esquire," which had once been a title reserved for those of landed property, was later extended as a courtesy title to men of rank and status in society, including those who had acquired such status through trade. The vulgarity of this company is reminiscent of the coarse behavior and speech of the Branghtons in Frances Burney's *Evelina*.

68. Workhorses.

69. A draught on Aldgate Pump is a worthless check or bill.

70. Out of work.

71. "A sort of jobber in horses, who still calls himself a gentleman." [CS's note]

72. A small house for occupation during the hunting season.

73. Subdivision of shire, here meaning the environs of London.

74. A kind of wild duck supposed to be very stupid, hence a fool.

75. Smith echoes Burke *Reflections on the Revolution in France:* "Along with its natural protectors and guardians, learning will be cast into the mire, and trodden down under the hoofs of a swinish multitude" (76).

76. The plebeians and the lowest multitude. Cicero, "Speech for Milo," line 95.

77. *Romeo and Juliet* 5.1.28-29, slightly misquoted.

78. "A lawyer who prepares documents for the conveyance of property, and investigates titles to property." *OED.*

79. A street in the city of London leading from Bishopsgate to the Bank of England.

80. A fashionable race meeting held, from 1711, in early June on Ascot Heath, Berkshire.

81. In mythology, Trophonius, a Boetian oracle, was approached in his cave dwelling through a narrow passage, entered only at night. One exited by the same passage, walking backwards, appearing melancholy and dejected. To emerge from Trophonius's cave connotes low spirits and gloom.

82. To the convent, young women.

83. *As You Like It*. Oliver, the elder brother, keeps Orlando "rustically at home" (1.1.7), denies him an education, allows him to eat with the farmhands, excludes him from his limited rights as a younger brother, and finally plots to kill him.

84. "Sir William Petty, Parnell, Orrery, Swift, Goldsmith, Burke, Sheridan." [CS's note]

85. "Meeting-house" was the term used for a place of worship frequented by nonconformists, including Presbyterians, who were noted for their solemnity of manner and dress. Meetinghouses, and dissenters in general, were associated in the public mind of the late eighteenth century with the French Revolution. Burke had seized upon the sermon of a dissenting minister, Richard Price, as the occasion for his own

Reflections on the Revolution in France, objecting in the opening pages of that essay to Price's prorevolutionary sentiments and his equation of English liberty and French political action.

86. Grocer.

87. Derisive echoes of the language of the Revolutionary Society and others sympathetic with the French Revolution, including Thomas Paine, whose *Rights of Man* (1791) was written in response to Burke's *Reflections on the Revolution in France.*

88. Seller of small items of clothing.

89. Coarse cloth.

90. Frequented largely by city families and apprentices, Islington, near London, was known for its tea gardens and taverns such as White's Conduit House.

91. A formation of around forty thousand columns made of volcanic rock projecting into the sea about eight miles off the northern coast of Ireland. It is fabled to be the beginning of a road constructed by giants across the channel from Ireland to Scotland.

92. To age the wine, casks of madeira (a dessert wine from the North Atlantic island of the same name) were often shipped as ballast on long sea journeys.

93. Short for hackney coach, a vehicle let out for hire.

94. Another inconsistency. It has appeared up to now that Mrs. Glenmorris never received the money promised her by Mrs. Grinsted.

95. "The name originally given to a coach with glass windows as distinguished from those which were unglazed: esp. applied to a 'private coach' let out for hire, as distinguished from those on public stands." *OED.*

96. A fashionable district in the West End of London, north of Piccadilly, south of Oxford Street, and between Park Lane and Berkeley Square.

97. Shakespeare, *The Life and Death of King John:* "He talks to me that never had a son" (3.4.91).

98. One who prepares and sells medicine; from 1700 through the remainder of the eighteenth century, an apothecary was called upon as a general medical practitioner, one who performed a role as physician and druggist.

99. Used ironically. "Gentry" denotes the class just below the nobility; "quality" would signify both nobility and gentry.

100. The fruit of the colocynth plant is used as a laxative.

101. Northumberland, the northernmost county of England.

102. Mrs. Grinsted has coined a word here, it seems. The *OED* cites this passage from *The Young Philosopher* as the only instance of this adjectival form of predilection. It means showing a predisposition toward the action or attitude specified, in this case, "imprudency" or imprudence.

103. Modern France.

104. Jeremiah 31:29 and Ezekiel 18:2.

105. More of Mrs. Grinsted's affected speech, as is "illuminosity" later in the sentence. This term means guardianship by a woman; "illuminosity" is Mrs. Grinsted's own word for light.

106. *King Lear* 2.4.208-10.

107. Published at the request of a person or group of people who had the social prominence and the money to subsidize the publication.

108. The talk yields to play, that is—card games involving several hands or rubbers, played for a pool of money to which all players contribute.

109. Luke 18:11: "God, I thank thee, that I am not as other men are, extortioners, unjust, adulterers, or even as this publican."

110. According to Bartlett's *Dictionary of Familiar Quotations,* "the phrase 'No man is a hero to his valet' has often been attributed to Madame de Sévigné, but on the authority of Madame Aissé . . . it belongs to Madame Cornuel (1614-94)." Obviously, by 1798 the saying was proverbial.

111. This remark is the first directly anti-Semitic remark in *The Young Philosopher.* There will be others, the most shocking perhaps being in chapter 10 of this volume, wherein sympathetic reference to the plight of the slave is accompanied by a cruel reflection on the English Jews that, in effect, denies them participation in the common humanity shared by all other populations in England and the English colonies (see p. 229-30). Anti-Semitism was the rule rather than the exception in eighteenth-century England. Since Jews (like Catholics and others) lacked civil rights and access to qualifications for the professions, and since their religion had never outlawed usury, many worked as moneylenders. The literary stereotype reflected in *The Young Philosopher* is also evident in Richard Brinsley Sheridan's *The School for Scandal* (1777), Frances Burney's *Cecilia* (1782), and Maria Edgeworth's *Castle Rackrent* (1800).

112. The bowels were regarded as the seat of pity and compassion.

113. 1 Timothy 5:8: "But if any provide not for his own, and specially for those of his own house, he hath denied the faith, and is worse than an infidel."

114. Changes brought about in particular by the French Revolution, which began in 1789 with the fall of the Bastille.

115. During the seventeenth and eighteenth centuries, Charing Cross was a center of information where proclamations were read and offenders pilloried. It was the ideal location for a newspaper office.

116. Mrs. Bayley is a lady's companion (see above, vol. 3, note 49). The humiliations of this position are graphically described by Sarah Fielding, *The Adventures of David Simple,* and Jane Collier, *The Art of Tormenting.*

117. Obviously a reference to the card-playing of the women, but an interesting echo, too, of "the last trump," or the Day of Judgment.

118. Nurse-tender.

119. *Paradise Lost* Book 6, lines 462-64.

120. A fever accompanied by delirium.

121. Bethlehem Hospital, a London lunatic asylum from the fifteenth century on. By the eighteenth century, the word "Bedlam" had attained the figurative sense of a scene of madness, confusion, and uproar.

122. Tantrums.

123. Mrs. Deacon is the literary ancestor of Mrs. Gamp, the disreputable, wine-drinking nurse in Charles Dickens's *Martin Chuzzlewit.*

124. "Vulgar corruption of *e'er a, ever a.*" *OED.*

125. Roy Porter explains that during the eighteenth century those suffering from

mental illness were increasingly felt to benefit by "rural surroundings, set apart from hubbub and anxiety." To achieve this benefit, "privately run madhouses were founded for those who could afford it." There was great optimism during the period about the efficacy of treatment in such a retired setting, but the asylums were also "often used as lock-ups for troublesome relatives; confinement of a wife or a child as insane could be the first step to laying hands on a fortune." *English Society in the Eighteenth Century*, p. 304. See also Eliza Haywood, *The Orphan, or Love in a Mad-House* (1726), and Wollstonecraft, *The Wrongs of Woman: or Maria* (1798).

126. Fee, honorarium.

127. Not identified.

128. At this point in the text, what had been Denbury Farm becomes Dalebury, a name perhaps more descriptive of the location.

129. Mignonette, a Mediterranean plant, cultivated for its fragrant, greenish flowers.

130. "then she was afraid of gipseys, beggars, the sailors with wooden legs, who were prowling round the house;—and one of them was a man who, because I answered him in French, cursed and swore and called me FRENCH BITCH with some 'God Damns' and frightening curses." This speech includes a bilingual pun: the man, speaking in English, has said "French Bitch"; Susanne seems to think he's used the word *franc*, feminine *franche*, which in French means loyal or genuine.

131. Encounters.

132. It is impossible that madame or mademoiselle should not be sick; my God! Ah, monsieur, if you would write!

133. Ah, if monsieur would write a little word.

134. A direction, i.e., an address.

135. Delmont's eager looks and intense questioning soon undermined the secrecy that the waiter had been told to keep or maintain.

136. James Thomson, *The Seasons*, "Summer," lines 1019-20, slightly altered. Petrify is an antiabolitionist in the debate that had been active in England since the founding of the Society for Effecting the Abolition of the Slave Trade in 1787.

137. "Cicero is one of the most remarkable examples." [CS's note]

138. "I do not know whether this expression conveys my meaning, which is, that natural strength and rectitude of mind, seldom seen, because it must be strong indeed where it has resisted the early counteraction of what is called education; but which, where it does survive, forms characters capable of every thing that is good and great." [CS's note]

139. Thinking many things and pitying the unjust lot in his mind. *Aeneid* Book 6, line 332.

140. A wide street in London that extends southward from Coventry Street to Pall Mall. It was the site of a hay market from 1664 until 1830 and also the location of inns and houses of entertainment, including Her Majesty's Theatre, Haymarket (the first opera house in London), and the Haymarket Theatre. According to Boswell the street was also a popular haunt of prostitutes.

141. *1 Henry IV* 1.3.52, slightly altered.

142. Judicial decisions made during the reign or time (L. *tempus*) of Queen Elizabeth I. For "modus," see above, vol. 1, n. 75.

143. Bitter tirade, from Demonsthenes' orations against Philip of Macedon.

144. "In many parts of England, on calcareous soils, are found stones shaped exactly like the heads of arrows, sometimes with great part of the shaft. The peasants call them elf-bolts, and used to imagine they were shot by malignant fairies against their cattle. When a child, I have often seen them about the south downs." [CS's note]

145. Gambling clubs.

146. Haggled, bartered.

147. Purple connotes superior social rank. Smith invokes the term derisively, as does Wollstonecraft in *The Vindication,* wherein she refers to aristocracy as the "pestiferous purple which renders the progress of civilization a curse." *Vindication of the Rights of Woman,* ed. Miriam Brody (London: Penguin, 1983), p. 99.

The parable of Dives and Lazarus relates how the latter, a beggar, asks "to be fed with the crumbs which fell from the rich man's table" but is refused, and how after death he rests in Abraham's bosom while the rich man suffers the torments of hell. See Luke 16:19-31.

148. Short-winded or corpulent. The *OED* lists both meanings; either would seem to do for Sir Appulby Gorges.

149. Penelope was the wife of Odysseus. While her husband was missing, presumed dead in the Trojan War, she held off her unwanted suitors for years by promising to marry when she completed a robe that she wove by day and secretly unwove every night.

150. Matthew Prior, Epigram, *Poems on Several Occasions* (London 1718), slightly altered.

151. Terra cotta or brownish orange.

VOLUME 4

1. Not identified. For me, I haven't any system to defend, me, a man simple and true, who am not led by the fury of any party.

2. Various ideological positions associated with revolutionary or Enlightenment thought in that they represent stances that challenge the religious and political orthodoxy of eighteenth-century Europe. As Armitage notes, at least two of the categories are contraindicatory—for example, one cannot be a deist (who believes in a God he can apprehend through the powers of reason, without the benefit of revelation) and an atheist (one who does not believe in the existence of God) at the same time. The illuminati claimed special enlightenment in religious and intellectual matters. "Freethinker" is a general term that could include all of the above. Jacobins were members of a political club established in France in 1789 for the propagation of democracy and equality; the term was applied, by extension, to their English sympathizers. A republican espouses the same values, maintaining that power rests in the people, who should be governed by elected representatives.

3. "Addison, in Cato." [CS's note] Act 5, scene 1, lines 15-18.

4. Matthew 7:12.

5. Alecto, one of the Furies, who were goddesses of vengeance dedicated to the punishment of transgressors, especially those who neglected the duties of kinship.

6. In his *Discourse Concerning the Mechanical Operation of the Spirit* (London, 1710), Jonathan Swift describes the pulpit oratory of the Dissenters as "snuffling": "*conveying the Sound thro' the Nose.*" The meetinghouses of Protestant nonconformists were often referred to as "tabernacles."

7. Justice, prudence, temperance, and fortitude are the cardinal virtues.

8. "In the late 1790s it was commonly believed that international Jacobinism had been masterminded by a secret society called the 'Illuminati'—neatly cognate with 'Enlightenment'—who originated in the mysterious heartland of Europe round the upper Danube. The Abbé Barruel's highly influential *Memoirs of Jacobinism* . . . [which began appearing in 1797] gave currency to this theory in four large volumes and also connected the conspiracy with the Freemasons." William St. Clair, *The Godwins and the Shelleys* (New York: Norton, 1989), p. 213.

9. The Whig and Tory parties became strongly defined political opponents during the reign of Queen Anne (1702-14), the Whigs basically standing behind moneyed interests, big landholders, the middle class, and business, the Tories representing aristocratic values, landed wealth on a smaller scale, and tradition. The literature of this period, the works of the Scriblerians—Jonathan Swift, Alexander Pope, John Gay—elaborate the opposition through the polemics of satire. Midcentury novelists, especially Henry Fielding (who styled himself Scriblerus Secundus) and Tobias Smollett continued to make references to party politics. See Fielding's *Tom Jones* (1749), book 7, chap. 3, and *Amelia* (1751), book 1, chap. 6; and Smollett's *Peregrine Pickle* (1751), vol. 2, chap. 77, and *Sir Launcelot Greaves* (1760), vol. 1, chaps. 9 and 10.

10. The *OED* notes that "aristocrat" is "a popular formation of the French Revolution," which in opposition to "democrat" signifies one who favors an aristocratic form of government. "Democrat" in this context is a synonym for "republican" and also derives from the specific context of the French Revolution. Armitage's distinction between a democrat and a jacobin is tied to the association between jacobinism and radical reform. Jacobins were extreme democrats, committed to the most radical version of democracy, which Armitage renounces in the following speech.

11. A reference to the Reign of Terror. In the following speech, Armitage articulates the English liberal viewpoint—a repudiation of the excesses of the revolution that stops short of rejection of the revolution itself, its ideals, and its vision of liberty, equality, and fraternity.

12. Said of Death in *Paradise Lost* Book 2, line 846.

13. The Litany in the *Book of Common Prayer* includes the prayer to be delivered from envy, hatred, malice, and all uncharitableness.

14. *Hamlet* 5.1.240-42, slightly altered. Laertes speaks to a doctor of divinity of his sister Ophelia at her gravesite. The priest questions Ophelia's right to be buried in sanctified ground because of the suspicion that her drowning was suicide.

15. An ironic invocation of the prophetic language of the Revelation, which includes references to the dragon and the beast, but not the hippopotamus.

16. Not identified. Money does all; its going is a very sure thing / Haste we then, to conclude this point.

17. Before the mid-nineteenth century it was customary for recipients to pay the postage for letters they received.

18. Good breeding.

19. *King John* 3.1.45-46; obviously quoted from memory: "Full of unpleasing blots and sightless stains, / Lame, foolish, crooked, swart, prodigious."

20. "A stopping-place; lodging." *OED*. This sentence from *The Young Philosopher* is quoted as the first illustrative passage.

21. Folio: a book, the sheets of which have been folded once only so the sheet makes two leaves. A book of large size. Duodecimo: a book whose sheets are folded into twelve leaves each—a small book.

22. Catalog grouped by subject, often with annotations.

23. Adolphus is making fun of eighteenth-century publishing conventions. Many novels were published anonymously ("by a young lady"), and poems were often attributed to "Delia," "Sacharissa," "Astrea," etc. "Parnassia" is a feminized form of "Parnassus," the seat of poetry and the muses. A legitimate sonnet is one regular in form, but here, of course, Adolphus intends a double entendre.

24. See above, vol. 2, n. 124. Sidney was beheaded for his participation in the Rye House Plot (1683).

25. Leave; go away.

26. "A knot or bow of ribbon worn on the top of the head by ladies towards the end of the 17th and in the 18th century." *OED*.

27. In Fielding's *Tom Jones,* the complete title of which is *The History of Tom Jones, a Foundling,* Squire Allworthy lectures Jenny Jones about the importance of chastity and reputation in book 1, chap. 7.

28. First attempt.

29. "Splacknuc. Vide Swift's Gulliver's Travels." [CS's note] In Brobdingnag, Gulliver is compared to a "*Splacknuck*"—a diminutive, nonhuman creature. See *Gulliver's Travels,* part 2, chap. 2.

30. Not identified.

31. First printed in this volume. See Smith, *Poems,* ed. Curran, p. 74.

32. Again, first printed in this volume. See Smith, *Poems,* ed. Curran, p. 125. "Vesper" is the evening star.

33. "'The sleeping leaves and folded flowers.' Vide notes on the sensibility and sleep of plants, and on the horologe of Flora, in the Oeconomy of Vegetation," &c. [CS's note] Smith's reference here is to Erasmus Darwin's *The Botanic Garden: A Poem in Two Parts, containing the Economy of Vegetation and the Loves of the Plants.*

34. Legendary Roman hero (c. 500-430 B.C.). After being consul for a time, Cincinnatus retired to his plough, from which he was called to assume the role of dictator. After he conquered the Equians and saved his country from danger, he laid down his office and returned to his plough once more.

35. Characters in Thomas Otway's *The Orphan,* both in love with the heroine, Monimia, who returns Castalio's love. Castalio and Monimia secretly marry. Not knowing of the marriage, Polydore takes his brother's place one night. When the truth

is discovered, all three characters kill themselves. Smith named the heroine of *The Old Manor House* Monimia after the character in this tragedy.

36. Elder brother's right. Adolphus must mean he is going to *waive* his right, not *wave* it, as he threatens to "enact the younger brother."

37. Adolphus makes fun of George by invoking two schools of philosophy—the Cynics, founded by Antisthenes and made famous by Diogenes, and the Stoics, founded by Zeno. The Cynics were contemptuous of ease and luxury; the Stoics held that the appetites should be subdued by virtue.

38. I came, I saw, I conquered. Said by Julius Caesar of his expedition to Britain.

39. Plump and white.

40. *"Sang froid,"* freedom from excitement, calm; *"haut volée,"* high flight. It was commonly thought in eighteenth-century England that the Muslim ("Mahometan") religion held that women had no souls.

41. Outcome, ending; not disaster.

42. *Othello* 1.3.90-94, altered:

I will a round unvarnish'd tale deliver
Of my whole course of love—what drugs, what charms,
What conjuration, and what mighty magic
(For such proceeding I am charg'd withal)
I won his daughter.

43. *Hamlet* 3.1.144-46: "You jig and amble, and you lisp, you nickname God's creatures and make your wantonness your ignorance." Wollstonecraft also invokes this passage in her indictment of the frivolity of women fostered by their education and the fact that marriage is their only means of advancement in the world. *Vindication*, p. 83.

44. "Skipton is a small market-town, containing 2100 inhabitants. The streets rather dirty and narrow; buildings good." From John Housman's *Tour of England,* reprinted in the *Monthly Magazine* 3 (Jan. 1797): 34.

45. Valiant knight.

46. Originally this word meant a ceremonial kiss bestowed with a knighthood; now generally used of some signal of honor but with no implication of a kiss. Adolphus uses the word with its original meaning in mind.

47. The blacksmith at Gretna Green performed marriages because in Scotland it was legal for any person to do so, and he had the house nearest the English border.

48. Chitty-face or baby-face.

49. Pope, *Epistle to Dr. Arbuthnot,* altered: "A clerk, foredoom'd his father's soul to cross, / Who pens a stanza, when he should engross" (lines 17-18).

50. Should be *une belle soirée:* one beautiful evening.

51. A bird that frequents the rice fields in North America, thus another of Adolphus's derisive references to Medora's nationality.

52. Not identified. Alas! where to find the lines and the colors / Powerfully to delineate the excess of his sorrows.

53. "I believe I have made some of my heroines (I know not which) say the same thing, but it is a sensation ever so present to me in my own person that it must be

forgiven if it is here a repetition, or an instance of egotism." [CS's note] Any number of her heroines could have uttered this sentiment, but Geraldine Vesey of *Desmond* is perhaps the character to whom Smith refers. The exact words are not hers, but certainly she receives strength and succor from her retirement in the country away from her abusive husband. The reference to the "equivocal maniac" is obscure, though perhaps it is another allusion to Stere's Maria.

54. A very fine and soft silk material.

55. Increased hope kindles rage. *Aeneid* Book 10, line 263.

56. The Great North Road was the quickest way from England to Scotland and thus frequently traveled by eloping couples.

57. "From the name of the inventor, Colonel Francis Negus (d. 1732), a mixture of wine (esp. port or sherry) and hot water, sweetened with sugar and flavoured." *OED*.

58. A small inner room, not a cupboard.

59. Not identified. I go from suffering to suffering, one following the other; but the last one that comes is always the worst.

60. This scene involving a loquacious servant who tells urgent information in a dilatory fashion was something of a set piece in late-eighteenth-century fiction. See also Horace Walpole's *Castle of Otranto* and Ann Radcliffe's *Romance of the Forest.*

61. "A rough sounding of the letter r; *spec.* the rough uvular trill characteristic of the county of Northumberland, and found elsewhere as an individual peculiarity." *OED*.

62. A part of a road requiring more than ordinary effort to traverse. This passage is the *OED*'s first illustrative quotation for this meaning of "pull."

63. Sir Harry does not entertain formally often, that is; therefore, the servants do not often benefit from the leftovers, the "offal victuals."

64. "Chalet, a dairy house—so called in Switzerland and in the mountains." [CS's note]

65. Chintz: a fairly recent import from India.

66. It was a common misconception that an icehouse made food into ice rather than merely providing refrigeration.

67. The voluptuousness of Sir Harry Richmond's estate is reminiscent of the villa of the Marquis in Radcliffe's *Romance of the Forest,* vol. 2, chap. 11.

68. Bower, from French word meaning "cradle."

69. "The Gryllus, *gryllo talpa,* mole cricket, haunts moist meadows, and frequents the sides of ponds, and backs of streams, performing all its functions in a swampy wet soil. With a pair of fore feet curiously adapted to the purpose, it burrows and works under ground like the mole. White's Selbourne." [CS's note] Gilbert White (1720-93) was the curate of Selbourne in Sussex and a naturalist. His *Natural History and Antiquities of Selbourne* (1788) was valued by Smith for its description of the flora and fauna of the country she held so dear.

70. Scatterbrained.

71. Joseph Addison, *Cato* Act 5, Scene 4, line 78.

72. According to Dr. Todd Cornish of the Southeastern Cooperative Wildlife Disease Study of the University of Georgia's College of Veterinary Medicine, Smith is, as

usual, an accurate natural historian. She is correct about the keen sense of smell possessed by waterfowl.

73. Pietro Trapassi or Metastasio (1698-1782) was one of Smith's favorite Italian poets. She wrote a sonnet based on his thirteenth cantata, "Il Nome." See Smith, *Poems,* ed. Curran, p. 23.

74. A deliberate allusion to Wollstonecraft's posthumously published novel, *The Wrongs of Woman, or Maria,* to which Smith also refers in her preface.

75. In his essay, "Of Love," Francis Bacon observes, "For there was never proud man thought so absurdly well of himself as the lover doth of the person loved; and therefore it was well said, That it is impossible to love and to be wise." *The Essayes or Counsels, Civill and Morall* (London, 1625).

76. In his search for Medora, Delmont traverses London's fashionable district from the Strand to Vauxhall, then six miles out of London into Surrey, back to Charing Cross, to Piccadilly, to the Haymarket, to Swallow Street, to Oxford Street, and finally to Portland Street.

77. A place available inside the coach, that is, as opposed to a seat with the driver of the vehicle, outside the coach.

78. Perhaps a piece of sarcenet, such as the one with which Laura Glenmorris covers her eyes in vol. 4, chap. 4.

79. Smelling salts; ammonia.

80. This term was offensive to the eighteenth-century person of color, as Ignatius Sancho attests in a letter to Laurence Sterne in which he introduces himself as "one of those people whom the vulgar and illiberal call 'Negurs.'" *The Letters of Ignatius Sancho,* ed. Paul Edwards and Polly Rewt (Edinburgh: Edinburgh Univ. Press, 1994), 85.

81. Milton, *Comus,* lines 451-52, altered.

82. Missure = measure; amabel = amiable; let me ope that sins ve har eer = let me hope that since we are here.

83. At random; haphazardly.

84. *Othello* 5.2.342-43: "Speak of me as I am: nothing extenuate, / Nor set down aught in malice."

85. Not identified.

86. In Ariosto's poem *Orlando Furioso,* Orlando goes mad for love of the beautiful Angelica.

87. Short for "tub-gig," "a deep low-hung gig with rounded corners and seats facing inwards." *OED.*

88. *Antirrhinum,* or snapdragon.

89. A reference to the story of Judith, told in the apocryphal book of that name, who cut off the head of Holofernes, the Assyrian general, to save her town from his tyranny. The story was a popular subject for paintings (e.g. Guido Reni, Michelangelo, and Gentileschi) and tapestries.

90. Embroidered.

91. The Furies of classical mythology are the avengers of wrongdoing. They are winged creatures, driven by a thirst for revenge, hence not plump.

92. A tapestry, behind which an intruder could hide.

93. The lower part of a man's robe.

94. "This bird builds at all seasons, except the deadest months of winter." [CS's note]

95. *As You Like It* 2.7.165. This line describes the last age in Jacques's ages of man.

96. An enclosed space or grass patch.

97. Short for "common land"—land that is not enclosed, that belongs to the community.

98. Covered with an awning or tilt.

99. The family, due to their illness, have become liable to be made an expense to the parish—or chargeable. The parish, however, is not responsible (by eighteenth-century law) for those not born within its confines; therefore, the family must remove to the place of the mother's birth.

100. Not identified. My dear Hope, I have not lost you, I'll see your image, your clothing, your shadow; I'll love you, I'll tell you so directly. What are the torments that such happiness cannot repair?

101. Luke 10:30-37 recounts the parable of the charitable Samaritan who rescues an injured traveler.

102. In England, an appeals court held quarterly and presided over by the justices of the peace in the county.

103. At this point in the text, Arnly Forest becomes Ardley Forest.

104. The title character of Samuel Richardson's *Pamela* (1740-41). At one point in the novel, Pamela dresses in the manner of a country girl, though the costume simply makes her more desireable to her predatory master, Mr. B.

105. Not identified. The last phrase of this quotation is so incorrect as to deserve comment: "ne séparneroit' il pas" should read "ne s'épargneroit-il pas." The mistake is probably the printer's and not Smith's. If man knew how to be ashamed of himself for crimes not only hidden, but public and known, would he not refrain from them?

106. Or, a sponging house, a place of preliminary confinement for debtors.

107. A London debtor's prison, located on the Fleet River. It was demolished in 1848.

108. Lawyers.

109. Now Bognor Regis, about sixty miles from London on the coast.

110. Rottingdean is near Brighton, about thirty miles east along the coast from Bognor.

111. Seems to be a mistake; should be "grief to joy."

112. Armitage employs the language of heroic romance, which included "paynims" (pagans), "saracen" (used for various nomadic tribes), and enchantment. The speech strikes a discordant note in the context, as it seems to echo the ending of Charlotte Lennox's *The Female Quixote*, where Arabella is chided for her imaginative indulgence in romance narrative. Medora cannot be justly accused of doing the same.

113. An oak gall is a small, perfectly spherical lump produced on twigs by a parasite.

114. Sudden attack.

115. Catholic Bishop Edmund Bonner (1500?-69), noted for his participation in persecutions of non-Catholics during the reign of Queen (Bloody) Mary. In a 1789

poem entitled *Bishop Bonner's Ghost,* Hannah More had invoked Bishop Bonner to chastise the modern church for its liberalism. Stephen Gardiner (1483?-1555), bishop of Winchester, was responsible for carrying out similar tortures under Henry VIII.

116. Milton, *Comus,* lines 586-90, 593.

117. Slightly altered from Psalm 91:5-6.

118. "Hume's Essays." [CS's note] "Concerning the Principles of Morals."

119. Latin for "touch me not." These were the words Christ spoke to Mary Magdalene after his resurrection (see John 20:17). Adolphus uses the phrase merely to indicate the unavailabity of part of his wife's fortune.

120. An ancient grave mound; a tumulus.

121. The "roll" is the official list of qualified solicitors or attorneys. To be "struck off the rolls" means to be prohibited from practicing law.

122. Luke 23:31, slightly altered: "If they do these things in a green leaf, what shall be done in the dry."

123. Milton, *Paradise Lost* Book 1, line 263; the sentiments of Satan.

124. Cf. I Corinthians 13:7, in which St. Paul says of charity that it "beareth all things, believeth all things, hopeth all things, endureth all things."

125. *Richard II* 1.3.275-76.

126. *Twelfth Night* 2.4.111-12.

VARIANTS

Note: Collation of the first edition of *The Young Philosopher* (London: T. Cadell, Jr., and W. Davies, 1798) with the Dublin edition, published by John Rice in the same year, reveals the following significant variants.

VOLUME 1

23.00	first silent, sullen] first, sullen
25.00	overtake it.] overtake them.
30.00	required] acquired
44.00	overrun Europe] overturn Europe
72.00	the most lovely girl] the most lively girl

VOLUME 2

91.00	door-wise] door-ways
96.00	a sort of salt marsh] a salt marsh
117.00	a last look] a look
131.00	in his voice and countenance] in his countenance
149.00	present state of things] present stage of things
149.00	walked therefore] walked before

VOLUME 3

163.00	no way whatever] no other way whatever
171.00	fly from every subject] fly from every object
172.00	returned above a month] returned a month
181.00	same moment] same time
183.00	save when it opened] save where it opened
190.00	declared to Lady] declared Lady

190.00	would prevent] could prevent
191.00	it particularly *his* duty] it *his* duty
192.00	and had already acquired] and had acquired
200.00	at some presbyterian] of some presbyterian
207.00	such time as] such times as
214.00	and let her own] to let her own
217.00	in the woman's mind] on the woman's mind
220.00	side, the] side, and the
220.00	not been long so] not long been so
220.00	out a town] out of town
220.00	broke in upon] broken in upon
220.00	and to take] and take
222.00	round red face, an] round red face, and
222.00	lord behaved] lord had behaved
225.00	and people about her] and the people about her
226.00	in her motly language] in the motly language
227.00	her letters to Susanne] his letters to Susanne
228.00	sort of preamble] short preamble
230.00	obtained only by] obtained by
235.00	she mentioned] she mentioned it
238.00	keep back] kept back
238.00	acme of] acme to

VOLUME 4

243.00	the subject of his visit] the subject of the visit
244.00	fact of his existence] fact of the existence
244.00	common sense] common senses
254.00	opposite end] other end
256.00	time, have been] time been
257.00	now is called] is now called
259.00	with present misery] with his present misery
261.00	for some days] for a few days
262.00	an abandoned] and abandoned
263.00	in the eternal] to the eternal
264.00	naturally clear] natural clear
267.00	she was hastened] she hastened
273.00	with a beating heart] with a beaten heart
273.00	remote part of the county] remote part of the country
281.00	largest fortunes in the county] largest fortunes in the country
284.00	thy orb] the orb
285.00	apprehensions] apprehension

286.00	his manner easy] his manners easy
289.00	certainly not] certain not
290.00	great house] great road
293.00	to set out] to have set out
294.00	got out] go out
294.00	"cannot say] "I cannot say
307.00	fortitude, and sweetness, and goodness] fortitude, and goodness
312.00	sufficiently disengaged] sufficiently engaged
314.00	know why] knew why
315.00	have made any struggle] have any struggle
319.00	most distressing] more distressing
320.00	of sand-rock] of a sand-rock
320.00	so much alarmed] so alarmed
320.00	on two poles] on poles
324.00	while I was much] which I was much
329.00	about our country] about the country
329.00	have now told] have told
335.00	message could be] messenger could be
342.00	honourable project] humble project
347.00	made me the happiest] made the happiest
348.00-49.00	business immediately before] business before

BIBLIOGRAPHY

EDITIONS OF *THE YOUNG PHILOSOPHER*

The Young Philosopher: A Novel. 4 vols. London: T. Cadell, Jun. and W. Davies, 1798.
The Young Philosopher: A Novel. 2 vols. Dublin: P. Wogan, H. Colbert, W. Porter, J. Moore, H. Fitzpatrick, J. Rice, and N. Kelly, 1798.
The Young Philosopher: A Novel. 4 vols. in 2. Reprint, London, 1798.
Le Jeune Philosophe. French edition, trans. from English. 3 vols. with 3 figs. Paris: Le Normant, 1799.
The Young Philosopher. 4 vols. Facsimile ed. with an introduction by Gina Luria. New York: Garland, 1974.

FURTHER READING

Albrecht, Françoise. "Charlotte Smith et Rousseau: De L'*Emile* au *Jeune Philosophe*." In *Le Continent et le monde anglo-américain aux XVIIe et XVIIIe siècles,* pp. 82-92. Reims: PU de Reims, 1987. Discusses the affinity between Smith and Rousseau, whose thought influences not only *The Young Philosopher* but other of Smith's works as well.

Bray, Matthew. "Removing the Anglo-Saxon Yoke: The Francocentric Vision of Charlotte Smith's Later Works." *Wordsworth Circle* 24 (1993): 155-58. Focused on the poetry, this essay is a useful discussion of Smith's attitude toward France and British nationalism.

Copeland, Edward. *Women Writing about Money: Women's Fiction in England 1790-1820.* Cambridge: Cambridge Univ. Press, 1995. Talks frequently of Smith in discussions of money as an issue in fiction and as an issue for the women who wrote it. Mentions *The Young Philosopher.*

Fletcher, Loraine. *Charlotte Smith: A Critical Biography.* London: Macmillan, 1998. Includes extensive discussions of all the novels.

Fry, Carrol L. *Charlotte Smith.* New York: Twayne, 1996. Provides a survey of Smith's life and work, including a discussion of *The Young Philosopher* as a radical novel.

Graham, John. "Character Description and Meaning in the Romantic Novel," *Studies in Romanticism* 5 (1966): 208-18. Treats Smith briefly and her use of the theories of Lavater, the physiognomist, in *Desmond* and *Marchmont.*

Hilbish, Florence May Anna. "Charlotte Smith: Poet and Novelist (1749-1806)." Ph.D. diss., Univ. of Pennsylvania, 1941. The still standard biography of Charlotte Smith. Includes discussions of all the published works.

Jones, Chris. *Radical Sensibility: Literature and Ideas in the 1790s.* London: Routledge, 1993. Includes a discussion of the influence of Godwin's *Political Justice* on *The Young Philosopher.*

McKillop, Alan Dugald. "Charlotte Smith's Letters," *Huntington Library Quarterly* 15 (1952): 237-55. Discusses the letters in the collection at the Huntington Library.

Mellor, Anne. "A Novel of Their Own: Romantic Women's Fiction, 1790-1830." In *The Columbia History of the British Novel,* ed. John Richetti, pp. 327-51. New York: Columbia Univ. Press, 1994. Includes a discussion of *The Old Manor House* as a critique of masculinity in terms applicable to *The Young Philosopher.*

Pascoe, Judith. "Female Botanists and the Poetry of Charlotte Smith." In *Re-Visioning Romanticism: British Women Writers, 1776-1837,* ed. Carol Shiner Wilson and Joel Haefner, pp. 193-209. Philadelphia: Univ. of Pennsylvania Press, 1994. Considers the influence of Smith's botanical interests on her poetry as both feminist empowerment and appropriation and tacit endorsement of the masculine gaze.

Rogers, Katharine M. "Inhibitions on Eighteenth-Century Women Novelists: Elizabeth Inchbald and Charlotte Smith." *Eighteenth-Century Studies* 11 (1977): 63-78. Discusses the effect the demands for morality had on the novels of Inchbald and Smith.

———. "Romantic Aspirations, Restricted Possibilities: The Novels of Charlotte Smith." In *Re-Visioning Romanticism: British Women Writers, 1776-1837,* ed. Carol Shiner Wilson and Joel Haefner, pp. 72-88. Philadelphia: Univ. of Pennsylvania Press, 1994. Smith's intense love of Nature links her to Blake and Wordsworth, but she stops short of regarding Nature as a means of transcendence or a defining world view.

Shteir, Ann B. *Cultivating Women, Cultivating Science.* Baltimore: Johns Hopkins Univ. Press, 1996. Considers several of Smith's prose works, including *The Young Philosopher,* influenced by her botanical interests. Particularly interested in the way Smith turned botanical knowledge to profit.

Spacks, Patricia Meyer. "Novels of the 1790s: Action and Impasse." In *The Columbia History of the British Novel,* ed. John Richetti, pp. 247-74. New York: Columbia Univ. Press, 1994. Suggests the merging of the personal and the political in the novels of the 1790s, including several of Smith's works.

Spencer, Jane. *The Rise of the Woman Novelist: From Aphra Behn to Jane Austen.* Oxford: Basil Blackwell, 1986. No extended discussion of Smith, but Spencer links *The Young Philosopher* with the feminist "romances" of Ann Radcliffe and Charlotte Lennox.

Stanton, Judith Phillips. "Charlotte Smith's 'Literary Business': Income, Patronage, and Indigence." *The Age of Johnson: A Scholarly Annual,* ed. Paul J. Korshin, 1 (1987): 375-401. A thorough and informative study of the financial aspect of

Charlotte Smith's literary career. Makes ample use of her letters to document her income and her expenses.

Todd, Janet. *The Sign of Angellica: Women, Writing and Fiction, 1660-1800.* London: Virago, 1989. Contains significant discussion of Smith in the context of the final decades of the eighteenth century.

Turner, Rufus Paul. "Charlotte Smith (1749-1806): New Light on her Life and Literary Career." Ph.D. diss., Univ. of Southern California, 1966. Biographical account; contains some material not covered by Hilbish. Includes discussion of all the published works, including *The Young Philosopher*.

Ty, Eleanor. *Unsex'd Revolutionaries: Five Women Novelists of the 1790s.* Toronto: Univ. of Toronto Press, 1993. Includes a chapter on *The Young Philosopher*, which focuses on the relationship between Laura and Medora Glenmorris.

Zimmerman, Sarah. "Charlotte Smith's Letters and the Practice of Self-Presentation." *Princeton University Library Chronicle* 53 (1991): 50-77. Discusses Smith's self-fashioning.